KINFLICKS

KINFLICKS

□

Lisa Alther

1976
CHATTO & WINDUS
LONDON

Published by
Chatto & Windus
40 William IV Street
London W.C.2

*Published in association with
Alfred A. Knopf, Inc., New York*

ISBN 0 7011 2191 2

Printed in Great Britain
by Ebenezer Baylis & Son Limited
The Trinity Press, Worcester, and London

KINFLICKS

Different sections of the community are, to all realities, "nations." . . .
*The clerics, doctors, literary men, nobles, and peasants really could be
called nations; for each has its own customs and casts of thought. To
imagine that they are just the same as you simply because they live in the
same country or speak the same language is a feeling to be examined.*

—SAMARQANDI, IN *Caravan of Dreams*,
BY IDRIES SHAH

So here it is at last, the Distinguished Thing.

—DYING WORDS OF HENRY JAMES

I

The Art of Dying Well

---------------- □ ----------------

My family has always been into death. My father, the Major, used to insist on having an ice pick next to his placemat at meals so that he could perform an emergency tracheotomy when one of us strangled on a piece of meat. Even now, by running my index fingers along my collarbones to the indentation where the bones join, I can locate the optimal site for a trachial puncture with the same deftness as a junky a vein.

The Major wasn't always a virtuoso at disaster prediction, however. When I was very young, he was all brisk efficiency, and made no room whatsoever for the unscheduled or the unexpected. "Ridiculous!" he would bark at Mother as she sat composing drafts of her epitaph. "Do you want to turn the children into a bunch of psychotics like the rest of your crazy family?" Perhaps, like my southern mother, you have to be the heiress to a conquered civilization to take your own vulnerability seriously prior to actually experiencing it. At least if you were born, as was the Major, in 1918 B.B. (Before the Bomb).

Whatever the reason, the Major's Cassandra complex developed late in life. He was a carpetbagger by profession, brought to Hullsport, Tennessee, from Boston to run the chemical plant that is the town's only industry. During the Korean War the plant, with its acres of red brick buildings and forests of billowing smoke stacks, was converted from production of synthetic fabrics to munitions; there were contracts from the federal government and top-secret contacts with the laboratories at Oak Ridge. On summer evenings, the Major used to take us kids out for cones of soft ice cream dipped in chocolate glaze, and then to the firing range where the new shell models were tested. Licking our dripping cones, we would watch proudly as the Major, tall and thin and elegant, listing forward on the balls of his feet, signaled the blasts with upraised arms, like an orchestra conductor cuing cymbal crashes.

Shortly after the conversion of the plant to munitions, the Major experienced his own personal conversion, and in a fashion that even an experienced aficionado of calamity like Mother could never have foreseen: He caught his platinum wedding band on a loose screw on a loaded truck bed at the factory and was dragged along until his ring finger popped out of its socket like a fried chicken wing being dismembered. Then his legs were run over by the rear wheels. There he lay, a fallen industrial cowboy, his boot caught in a stirrup, trampled by his own horse. Truckloads of hams and cakes and casseroles began arriving at the house from bereaved admirers/employees. All the downtown churches offered up hours of prayers for his recovery.

Ira was hurt, in the early days of our marriage, when I wouldn't wear my wedding band. He considered it symbolic of the tepidity of my response to him. Maybe he was right, but Ira had never seen a hand with only the bloody remains of a knuckle socket where the ring finger used to be. He merely assumed, until the day he ran me out of his house in Vermont with a rifle, that I was frigid. Well, he had to find some rational explanation for the failure of our union, because it was impossible for him to entertain the notion that he, Ira Braithwaite Bliss IV, might simply have picked a lemon from the tree of life. But more later of my refusal to share Ira's bed.

When the Major emerged from his casts, a metamorphosis had occurred: He was no longer bold and brash. In fact, the first project he undertook was to renovate the basement family room into a bomb shelter as a surprise for Mother's birthday. *Her* reaction to the atmospheric nuclear tests going on all over the world then was to join a group in Hullsport called Mothers' Organization for Peace. MOP consisted of a dozen housewives, mostly wives of chemical plant executives who'd been exiled to Hullsport for a dreary year as grooming for high managerial posts in Boston. MOP meetings consisted of a handful of women with abrasive Yankee accents who sipped tea and twisted handkerchief corners and insisted bravely that Russian mothers *must* feel the same about strontium 90 in *their* babies' bones.

The Major, sneering at MOP, kept going with his bomb shelter. We kids were delighted. I took my girl friends down there to play house; and we confronted such ethical issues as whether or not to let old Mr. Thornberg next door share our shelter when the bomb dropped, or whether to slam the door in his miserly face, as he did to us on Halloween nights. Later we girls took Clem Cloyd and the acned boys from Magnolia Manor development down there to play Five Minutes in Heaven. While the others counted outside, the designated couple went into the chemical toilet enclosure to execute the painful grinding of braces that left us all with raw and bruised mouths . . . but in love. And in high school I brought dates down for serious sessions of heavy petting. In fact, I broke the heart of Joe Bob Sparks, star tailback of the Hullsport Pirates and body beautiful of Hullsport Regional High School, by forfeiting my maidenhead to Clem Cloyd one night on the altarlike wooden sleeping platform, double-locked behind the foot-thick steel door, while Mother and the Major slept on blissfully unaware upstairs. But more about the many charms of Joe Bob and Clem later.

Soon, no situation was too safe for the Major to be unable to locate its potential for tragedy. Death to him was not the inevitable companion of one's later years, the kindly warden who freed each soul from its earthly prison. Death to him was a sneak and a cheat who was ever vigilant to ambush the unwary, of whom the Major was determined not to be one. In contrast to Mother, who regarded Death as some kind of demon lover. The challenge, as she saw it, was to be ready for the assignation, so that you weren't distracted during consummation by unresolved earthly matters. The trick was in being both willing to die and able to at the same time. Dying properly was like achieving simultaneous orgasm.

Mother had many photographs, matted in eggshell white and framed in narrow black wood, on the fireplace mantel in her bedroom. As I was growing up, she would sit me on her lap and take down these yellowed cracked photos and tell me about the people in them, people who had already experienced, prepared for it or not, this ultimate fuck with Death. Her grandmother, Dixie Lee Hull, in a blouse with a high lace neck, who had cut her finger on a recipe card for spoon bread and had died of septicemia at age twenty-nine. Great-uncle Lester, a druggist in Sow Gap, who became addicted to cough syrup and one night threw himself under the southbound train to Chattanooga. Cousin Louella, who dove into a nest of water moccasins in an abandoned stone quarry at a family reunion in 1932. Another cousin who stuck his head out of a car window to read a historical marker about the Battle of Lookout Mountain and was sideswiped by a Mason-Dixon transport truck. It was always so unsatisfying to rage at her in a tantrum, as children do, "I *hate* you! I hope you *die!*" She'd reply calmly, "Don't worry, I will. And so will you."

At spots in our decor where lesser women would have settled for Audubon prints or college diplomas, Mother hung handsomely framed and matted rubbings of the tombstones of our forebears, done in dark chalk on fine rice paper. The Major always planned family vacations around business conferences so that expenses would be tax deductible and so that he wouldn't have to spend long stretches trapped with his family. Mother used to coordinate his meetings with trips for the rest of us to unvisited gravesites of remote relations. I spent most of my first seventeen summers weeding and edging and planting around obscure ancestral crypts. Mother considered these pilgrimages to burying plots around the nation as didactic exercises for us children, far superior to the overworked landmarks, like the Statue of Liberty, on the American Freedom Trail.

Apparently a trait like fascination with eschatology is hereditary. At any rate, it seems to run in *our* family. Mother's ancestors, however humble their circumstances (and most of them were in very humble circumstances, being dirt farmers and coal miners), invested a great deal of thought and money in their memorials to themselves. In any given cemetery, the most elaborately carved urns and weeping willows and hands pointing confidently to heaven invariably belong to my ancestors. Also the most catchy epitaphs: "Stop and look as you pass by./ As you are now, so once was I./ As I am now, so you will be./ Prepare to die and follow me." Mother considered that one, by a great-great-aunt named Hattie, the pinnacle of our family's achievement. Mother had dozens of trial epitaphs for herself, saved up in a small black loose-leaf notebook. The prime contender when I left home for college in Boston was, "The way that is weary, dark and cold/ May lead to shelter within the fold./ Grieve not for me when I am gone./ The body's dark night: the soul's dawn."

When Mother wasn't working on her epitaph, she was rewriting her funeral ceremony. "Let's see—" she'd say to me as I sat on the floor beside her mahogany Chippendale desk dressing my doll in black crepe for a wake. "Do you think 'A Mighty Fortress Is Our God' should go before or after 'Deus Noster Refugium'?" I'd look up from my doll's funeral. "You won't forget, will you, dear?" she'd inquire sternly. "The agenda for my memorial service will be in my upper right-hand desk drawer."

Or she'd repolish her obituary and worry over whether or not the Knoxville *Sentinel* would accept it for publication. I have since come to understand her agony. When my classmates were taking frantic notes on penile lengths in first term Physiology 110 at Worthley College, I was diligently preparing the wording of my engagement announcement in the margin of my notebook: "Major and Mrs. Wesley Marshall Babcock IV of Hullsport, Tennessee, and Hickory, Virginia, take pleasure in announcing the engagement of their daughter Virginia Hull Babcock to Clemuel Cloyd. . . ." Years later, when the time finally came to dust off this draft and replace the name of Clemuel Cloyd with Ira Bliss, I discovered that the Boston *Globe* wouldn't print it, in spite of the fact that I'd read their damned paper dutifully every Sunday for the two years I'd been in college there. What could bring more posthumous humiliation than to have your obituary rejected by a paper like the Knoxville *Sentinel?*

2

Saturday, June 24

□

Groggy with two in-flight martinis, Ginny huddled by the DC-7's emergency exit. When she'd picked up her ticket for this flight, she'd made a brave joke to the clerk about someone's wanting to hijack a plane bound between Stark's Bog, Vermont, and Hullsport, Tennessee. The clerk had replied without looking up, "Believe me, honey, no one in their right mind would want anything to do with those planes they send to Tennessee." To be aware of death was one thing, she mused; to accept it, another. All her life, awash with shame, she had secretly rejoiced over each plane crash as it was reported in the papers because it meant They'd missed her again.

She grabbed the plastic card from the nubby green seat-back pocket and studied the operation of the plane's emergency exits, deployment procedures for the inflatable slide. It occurred to her that if use of the emergency exits was required, she'd be frozen by panic and trampled by all her frenzied fellow passengers as they tried to get past her and out the escape hatch. It also occurred to her that perhaps the reason every person in the plane didn't struggle to sit by an emergency exit, as she did, was that they knew something she didn't: that the likelihood of needing to clamber out the exit to safety was more than offset by the likelihood of the exit's flying open in mid-flight and sucking those near it into the troposphere.

But she knew that this pattern of blindly seeking out emergency exits was already too set in her to be thwarted with ease. Just as some people's eyes, due to early experience with The Breast, were irresistibly drawn to bosoms throughout their lives, so were hers riveted by neon signs saying EXIT. At the Saturday morning cowboy serials as a child, she had been required by the Major to sit right next to the exit sign in case the theater should catch fire. He told her about a Boston theater fire when he was young in which a crazed man had carved his way with a Bowie knife through the hysterical crowds to an exit. Ever since, she'd been unable to watch a movie or listen to a lecture or ride in a plane without the comforting glow of an exit sign next to her, like a nightlight in a small child's bedroom.

Nevertheless, on this particular flight, she first realized that the emergency exit, the escape lines coiled in the window casings, the yellow oxygen masks being playfully manipulated by the shapely stewardesses, were all totems designed to distract passengers from the fact that if the plane crashed, they'd all had it—splat! As eager as she was to deny the possibility of personal extinction while negotiating the hostile skies of United Air Lines, even Ginny was only faintly comforted by the presence of her seat cushion flotation device. She knew full well that the Blue Ridge Mountains of Virginia were below her should the engines falter and the plane flutter down like a winged bird. The sea was swelling some three hundred miles to the east. She tried to picture herself, stranded in a mountain crevice, afloat on her ritual seat cushion above a sea of gore and gasoline and in-flight martinis.

In the crush of the waiting room prior to boarding, Ginny had inspected with the intensity of the Ancient Mariner the visages of all her fellow passenger-victims: Were these the kind of people she'd want to be adrift with in a life raft? She could never decide how Fate worked it: Did planes stay aloft because of the absence of actively wicked people on board to be disposed of? Or was the opposite the case: Did planes falter and fall because of the absence of people sufficiently worthy to redeem the flight, people who had to be kept alive to perform crucial missions? Whichever was the case, Ginny had closely studied her companions in folly, looking for both damning and redeeming personality types and laying odds on a mid-air collision. With relief, she'd discovered three small babies.

Her fellow travelers had also scrutinized *her* upon boarding this winged silver coffin, Ginny reflected. In fact, one plump woman in a hideous Indian print caftan had studied her so closely that Ginny was

sure the woman *knew* that she was the one who'd broken the macrobi-
otic recipe chain letter earlier that week. Which of the assembled
Vermont housewives, they all must have wondered as they found
their seats, would be the one to demand six thousand books of S & H
Green Stamps and a parachute for a descent into a redemption
center at a Paramus, New Jersey, shopping mall? Whose tote bag
contained the bomb, nestled in a hollowed-out gift wheel of Vermont
cheddar cheese, or submerged in a take-out container of spaghetti
sauce? Ginny had often thought that she should carry such a bomb
aboard her plane flights herself, because the likelihood of there being
two bomb-toting psychopaths on the same flight was so infinitesimal
as to be an impossibility. It was the mentality that fostered the arms
race: Better to be done in by the bomb that she herself, in a last act
of existential freedom, could detonate.

And, Ginny suspected, they were all—if they'd only admit it—
inspecting each other with the care of housewives at a supermarket
meat counter, as possible main courses should their craft be lost atop
a remote peak in the Smokies.

But at least she still rode planes, Ginny reminded herself—unlike
her mother, who in recent years had scarcely left the house at all for
fear of being overtaken by disaster among strangers, insisting that it
was vulgar to die among people one didn't know. How was her
mother feeling about that now, as she lay in a hospital bed in Hullsport hemorrhaging like an overripe tomato? "A clotting disorder,"
their neighbor Mrs. Yancy had called it in her note suggesting that
Ginny come down and keep her mother company while Mrs. Yancy
went on a trip to the Holy Land. "Nothing serious," the note had
assured her. Her mother knew she'd be out of the hospital soon and
hadn't wanted to worry Ginny with the news. But if it wasn't serious,
why was her mother in a place that she would necessarily hate, feeling
as she did about strangers? And why had Mrs. Yancy asked Ginny to
come down, knowing as she must that in recent years Ginny and her
mother had been hitting it off like Moses and the Pharaoh?

Before giving up flying altogether, her mother had gone on business trips regularly with the Major. His condition on her going was
that they take separate planes so that when one of them died during
landing, the other would remain to carry on.

"Doesn't it just double the likelihood of one of your bags going
to Des Moines?" Ginny had demanded of her mother one winter
afternoon when she was in high school and was making her second

trip to the airport, having taken the Major to catch *his* flight to New York that morning. They were in the Major's huge black Mercedes. Her mother had loved that car. Because it looked and drove like a hearse, Ginny suspected. Practice.

"Don't ask me. Ask your father," she replied, closing her eyes in anticipation of a head-on collision as Ginny negotiated a traffic circle. Any time her mother couldn't be bothered with having an opinion on something, she'd say, "Don't ask me. Ask your father." Ever since the Major had died, she must have been somewhat at a loss for words.

"I don't know why I go along with all this," she mused. "I wouldn't even *want* to 'carry on' if your father's plane crashed."

"You'd just throw yourself on his funeral pyre, like a suttee?" Ginny didn't enjoy being sarcastic to the woman who had rinsed her dirty diapers, but it seemed unjust that she should be saddled with these passive-dependent attitudes simply because this woman and she had lived in the same house for eighteen years. After all, what about free will?

"Yes, I think I would. I don't think it's such a bad custom at all."

"You don't," Ginny said flatly, more as a statement than as a question, since she knew her mother didn't. "Does it bother you that you don't?" Ginny asked this blandly to conceal how much it was bothering *her* that the custom appealed so enormously to her too.

"Bother me?" her mother asked with an intense frown, working an imaginary brake with her foot.

"*Please,* Mother, I'm a very safe driver," Ginny snapped. "Bother you. You know. Do you sometimes wish that there were things in life that seemed important to you other than your family?"

"I'm not really all that interested in life. I mean, it's okay, I guess. But I'm not hog wild about it."

"Well, why do you go on with it?" Ginny demanded irritably.

"Why not?"

"But if the only thing you're interested in is your great family reunion in the sky, why don't you get on with it? What keeps you hanging around here?"

Her mother looked at her thoughtfully for a while and then gave a careful and sincere answer: "It's character building. What does it matter what I might prefer?" As Ginny understood the lengthy explanation that ensued, her mother was saying that the human soul was like a green tomato that had to be ripened by the sun of earthly suffering before the gods would deign to pluck it for use at their cosmic clambake. It hadn't made sense to an impatient sixteen-year-old.

But that incident was why Ginny was so surprised several years later when her mother said, with great intensity, "Ginny, you must promise me that you will put me out of my misery if I'm ever sick and dying a lingering death."

Startled, Ginny had looked at her closely. She had crow's feet at the corners of her eyes and frown lines; and her neat cap of auburn hair was graying here and there. But she was agile and erect. With the insensitivity of the young to the concerns of their elders, Ginny laughed nervously and protested, "But *Mother!* Your hair is hardly even gray or anything. I'd say you've got a few years left!"

She gave Ginny a sharp look of betrayal and said sourly, "Believe me, after age thirty it's all downhill. Everything starts giving out and falling apart."

Her mother hadn't been hog wild about living eleven years ago. Ginny wondered how she was feeling about it now that her bluff was being called. But *was* it being called? "Not serious," Mrs. Yancy had said. And yet Ginny couldn't seem to prevent herself from leaping to all kinds of dire conclusions. Why was her mother in the hospital if it wasn't serious? How sick *was* she?

These questions, swarming through her head like fruit flies, temporarily distracted Ginny from the fact that she had survival problems of her own—both immediate, in that she was trapped aboard this airborne sarcophagus, and long-range with regard to the fact that she couldn't figure out what she wanted to be when she grew up. If indeed she did one day grow up, which was looking increasingly unlikely as she approached early middle age, with her twenty-seventh birthday recently behind her. The incidents in her life to date resembled the Stations of the Cross more than anything else. If this was adulthood, the only improvement she could detect in her situation was that now she could eat dessert without eating her vegetables.

Another problem was that the stewardesses were bullying the passengers that day. They kept parading past selling pennants and souvenirs, and requiring that everyone acknowledge their obvious talents with their lip brushes. Ginny finally concluded that the only way to get rid of them would be to throw up in the air-sickness bag and then try to find one of them to dispose of it.

And then there was the problem of the blond two-year-old in the next seat, imprisoned between her own mother and Ginny. The child kept popping up and down, unfastening and refastening her seat belt, lowering her seat-back tray and then replacing it, scattering the literature in the pocket all over the floor, putting the air-sickness bag over her head and then looking around for applause, removing her shoes and putting them back on the wrong feet, snapping the metal lid to the ashtray. It seemed a shame for all that energy to be going to waste, dissipating throughout the plane. Ginny suddenly understood the rationale behind child labor. Hooked up to a generator, this child's ceaseless contortions could have been fueling the plane.

She found herself unable not to watch the child, as irritating as all her relentless activities were. Ginny was experiencing the Phantom Limb Syndrome familiar to all recent amputees: She felt, unmistakably, Wendy's presence next to her. When she looked over and discovered that this presence was merely an unfamiliar child of the same age, she was flooded with an overwhelming misery that caused her to shut her eyes tightly with pain. Wendy was in Vermont now with her father, the bastard Ira Bliss, living a life that excluded her wicked, adulterous mother.

Ginny reflected glumly that that racy view of her behavior credited her with much more sexual savoir-faire than she actually possessed. Although in principle she was promiscuous, feeling that the wealth should be shared, in practice she had always been morbidly monogamous, even before her marriage to Ira. In fact, until the appearance of Will Hawk that afternoon, nude in her swimming pool in Vermont, she had always been doglike in her devotion to one partner. Even with Hawk, her unfaithfulness to Ira was spiritual only, not physical—although Ira had found that impossible to believe the night he had discovered Ginny and Hawk in his family graveyard in poses that the unenlightened could only identify as postcoital.

Ginny tried to decide if her transports of fidelity were innate—an earthly translation of a transcendent intuition of oneness, a kind of sexual monotheism. Or whether she'd simply been brainwashed by a mother who would have liked nothing better than to throw herself on her husband's funeral pyre. Or whether it was unadulterated practicality, a question of knowing which side her bed was buttered on, her bod was bettered on—a very sensible refusal to bite the hand that feels her. In such a culture as this, perhaps the only prayer most women had was to find a patron and cling to him for all he was worth. People knew a man by the company he kept, but they generally knew a woman by the man who kept her. Or by the woman who kept her, in the case of Ginny and Edna.

At one point the child's mother, noticing Ginny's self-punishing absorption with the little girl, leaned forward and asked with a smile, "Do you have children?"

"Yes," Ginny replied with a pained smile. "One. Just this age."

"Oh, well!" the mother said briskly. "Then you'll want this." She took two index cards from her alligator pocketbook and began copying from one onto the other. When she finished, she reread what she'd written and handed it to Ginny with pride. It read: "Homemade Play Doh: mix 2 1/4 cups flour with 1 cup salt; add 1 cup water mixed with 2 T vegetable oil; add food color to water before mixing."

"Neat," Ginny said, stuffing it quickly into the pocket of her patchwork peasant dress. "Thanks." She decided not to wreck this moment of sharing by mentioning that her child's father had kicked her out and that she might never see Wendy again, much less mix Play Doh for her.

"Be sure to use all the salt. Otherwise they eat it."

"I'll remember," Ginny assured her, wondering if Ira really could prevent her from ever seeing Wendy again, as he had vowed he would. In spite of her apparent moral turpitude, Ginny was still Wendy's natural mother. Didn't that count for something in the eyes of the law?

The child had ripped the arm off her doll and was hitting her mother over the head with it. It occurred to Ginny, as the plane's engines were cut and she grabbed the handle of the emergency door preparing to wrench it open, that someone should invent a God doll —wind Him up and He delivers us from evil. Mattel could make a fortune.

Rather than spiraling down into fiery death, the plane began its normal descent into the Crockett River valley. As it emerged from the fluffy white clouds, Ginny could see the Crockett, forking all along its length into hundreds of tiny capillarylike tributaries that interpenetrated the forested foothills and flashed silver in the sun. The treed bluffs on either side of the river were crimped like a pie crust of green Play Doh.

Soon Hullsport itself was beneath them, its defunct docks crumbling into the Crockett. They were low enough now so that the river, having had its moment of poetry from higher up, looked more like its old self—a dark muddy yellow frothed with chemical wastes from the Major's factory. The river valley containing the town was ringed by red clay foothills, which were gashed with deep red gullies from indiscriminate clearing for housing developments. From eight thousand feet Ginny's home town looked like a case of terminal acne.

She could see the factory now, a veritable city of red brick buildings, their hundreds of windows reflecting the yellow-brown of the river. Dozens of huge white waste tanks, crisscrossed with catwalks of ladders like the stitching on softballs, lined the river bank. Behind the tanks bubbled and swirled murky aeration ponds. Vast groves of tall red tile stacks were exhaling the harmless-looking puffy white smoke that had settled in over the valley like the mists of Nepal, and had given Hullsport the distinction of harboring the vilest air for human lungs of any town its size in a nation of notoriously vile air.

The factory was having its revenge on Hullsport. It had never really been included in the town plan. Everyone knew that it was essential to the economy, in this region that relied mostly on dirt farming and coal mining. But aesthetically the factory had offended; and so it had been stuck out in the low flat flood plain of the Crockett, like an outhouse screened from view behind a mansion. But, like any suppressed or ignored or despised human function, the scorned factory had come to dominate life in Hullsport anyway through its riot of noxious exudations.

On the opposite side of the river from the factory, connected to it by a railroad bridge, a foot bridge, and an auto bridge, was the town of Hullsport itself—the Model City, it had been nicknamed by its founder, Ginny's grandfather, her mother's father, Zedediah Hull, or Mr. Zed as everyone had referred to him. Faced with a lifetime in the coal mines of southwest Virginia, he had packed it in to come to this area of Tennessee. Then he had gone north and, in spite of his doubtful accent, had persuaded Westwood Chemical Company of Boston to open a plant in his as-yet-unbuilt model town and to back his project financially. At that time the rural South was regarded by northern businesses as prime ground for colonization, with all the attractions of any underdeveloped country—cheap land, grateful and obedient labor, low taxes, plentiful raw materials, little likelihood of intervention from local government. Mr. Zed then hired a world-famous town planner to draw up plans for Shangri-La South.

From the plane window, Ginny could see the scattered remnants of this original plan. Five large red brick churches—all various shades of Protestantism, all with white steeples of different design—surrounded a central green. From the church green ran Hull Street, which was lined with furniture stores, department stores, clothing stores, movie theaters, newsstands, finance companies, banks. At the far end of the street, facing the church circle and bordering on the river, was the red brick train station for the Crockett Railroad. The train station and the church circle were the two poles, worldly and otherworldly, that had been yoked together to pattern and energize the surrounding town. Out from this central axis radiated four main streets. Side streets joined these main streets in a pattern of concentric hexagons. Private houses lined the side streets. Squinting so as to see just the original pattern, and not what had been done to it since, Ginny decided that it looked almost like a spider web.

Alas, the master builders of the Model City in 1919 hadn't foreseen the domination of Hullsport life by the motor car. No parking space to speak of had been planned for the church circle or the shopping street, and it was now almost impossible to work your way to Hull Street and back out again during the day. Consequently, half a dozen large shopping plazas and a bustling interstate highway now circled the original hexagon. The farmers, who had come into Hullsport every Saturday of Ginny's childhood in their rusting Ford pickups to sell a few vegetables and buy supplies and swap gossip down by the train station while squirting brown streams of tobacco juice through crooked teeth, were no longer in evidence. The railroad and the river shipping business had gone bankrupt, victims of competition with long-distance trucking. The red brick train station, with its garish late Victorian gingerbread, was deserted and vandalized, with obscene drawings and slogans painted all over the interior walls by the initiates of the Hullsport Regional High School fraternities. The station served now as a hangout for the town derelicts and delinquents and runaways, who congregated there at night to drink liquid shoe polish.

Nor had the town fathers, specifically Ginny's grandfather, anticipated the Dutch elm disease, which had killed off most of the big old trees within the hexagon proper and had left Hullsport looking like a raw new frontier town, baked under the relentless southern sun. Nor had he imagined that six times as many people as he had planned for would one day want to leave the farms and mines and crowd into Hullsport, and that clumps of houses for them would ring the hexagon in chaotic, eczema-like patches.

Hullsport, Tennessee, the Model City, Pearl of the Crockett River valley, birthplace of such notables as Mrs. Melody Dawn Bledsoe, winner of the 1957 National Pillsbury Bake-Off, as a banner draped across Hull Street had reminded everyone ever since. Spawning ground of Joe Bob Sparks, All-South running back for the University of Northeastern Tennessee Renegades—and prince charming for a couple of years to Virginia Hull Babcock, Persimmon Plains Burly Tobacco Festival Queen of 1962. Ginny was prepared to acknowledge that time spent as Persimmon Plains Burly Tobacco Festival Queen sounded trivial in the face of personal and global extinction; but it was as tobacco queen that she had first understood why people were leaving their tobacco farms to crowd into Hullsport and work at the Major's munitions plant, why there were no longer clutches of farmers around the train station on Saturday mornings.

The plane was making its approach now to the pockmarked landing strip that Hullsport called its airport. Ginny could see the shadow of the plane passing over her childhood hermitage below—a huge white neo-Georgian thing with pillars and a portico across the front, a circular drive, a grove of towering magnolia trees out front which at that very moment would be laden with intoxicating cream-colored blossoms. It looked from a thousand feet up like the real thing—an authentic antebellum mansion. But it was a fraud. Her grandfather, apparently suffering the bends from a too-rapid ascent from the mines, had built it in 1921 on five hundred acres of farmland. It was copied from a plantation house in the delta near Memphis. The design clearly wasn't intended for the hills of east Tennessee. Hullsport had expanded to meet the house, which was now surrounded on three sides by housing developments. But behind the house stretched the farm —a tobacco and dairying operation run now by none other than Clem Cloyd, Ginny's first lover, whose father before him had run the farm for Ginny's grandfather and father. The Cloyds' small maroon-shingled house was diagonally across the five hundred acres from Ginny's house. And at the opposite end, in a cleared bowl ringed by wooded foothills, across the invisible Virginia state line, was the restored log cabin that Ginny's grandfather had withdrawn to toward the end of his life, in disgust with the progressive degradation of the Model City.

As she swooped down from the clouds to take the pulse of her ailing mother, Ginny felt a distinct kinship with the angel of death. "I couldn't ask the boys to come," Mrs. Yancy's note had said. "They've got their own lives. Sons aren't like daughters." "Indeed,"

Ginny said to herself in imitation of Miss Head, her mentor at Worthley College, who used to warble the word with a pained grimace on similar occasions.

As they taxied up to the wind-socked cow shed that masqueraded as a terminal, Ginny was reminded of the many times she'd landed there in the past. Her mother had always been addicted to home movie-making and had choreographed the upbringing of Ginny and her brothers through the eyepiece of a camera, eternally poised to capture on Celluloid those golden moments—the first smile, the first step, the first tooth in, the first tooth out, the first day of school, the first dance, year after tedious year. Mother's Kinflicks, Ginny and her brothers had called them. A preview of the Kinflicks of Ginny's arrivals at and departures from this airport would have shown her descending or ascending the steps of neglected DC-7's in a dizzying succession of disguises—a black cardigan buttoned up the back and a too-tight straight skirt and Clem Cloyd's red silk Korean windbreaker when she left home for college in Boston; a smart tweed suit and horn-rim Ben Franklin glasses and a severe bun after a year at Worthley; wheat jeans and a black turtleneck and Goliath sandals after she became Eddie Holzer's lover and dropped out of Worthley; a red Stark's Bog Volunteer Fire Department Women's Auxiliary blazer after her marriage to Ira Bliss. In a restaurant after ordering, she always ended up hoping that the kitchen would be out of her original selection so that she could switch to what her neighbor had. That was the kind of person she was. Panhandlers asking for bus fare to visit dying mothers, bald saffron-robed Hare Krishna devotees with finger cymbals, Jesus freaks carrying signs reading "Come to the Rock and You Won't Have to Get Stoned Anymore"—all these people had invariably sought her out on the crowded Common when she had lived in Boston with Eddie. She had to admit that she was an easy lay, spiritually speaking. Apparently she looked lost and in need, anxious and dazed and vulnerable, a ready convert. And in this case, appearances weren't deceiving. It was quite true. Normally she was prepared to believe in anything. At least for a while.

Ginny remembered, upon each descent to this airport, spotting her mother and the Major from the plane window—each time unchanged, braced to see what form their protean daughter would have assumed for *this* trip home. When Ginny thought of them, it was as a unit, invincible and invulnerable, halves of a whole, silhouettes, shape and bulk only, with features blurred. She decided it was a holdover from early infancy, when they probably hung over her crib and doted, as parents tended to do before they really got to know their offspring. But this trip home there was no one standing by the fence to film her arrival—in a patchwork peasant dress and combat boots and a frizzy Anglo-Afro hairdo, with a knapsack on her back and a Peruvian llama wool poncho over the pack so that she looked like a hunched crone, the thirteenth witch at Sleeping Beauty's christening. Her mother was lying in a hospital bed; and the Major had "gone beyond," as the undertaker with the waxen yellow hands had optimistically put it a year ago.

Apparently she was on her own now.

Her homecoming was less than festive. There were no drill teams in the driveway, no family retainers doing Virginia reels on the front lawn as she got out of the airport limousine. She struggled up the quartz gravel driveway, almost losing her balance because her knapsack straps were forcing her to stand up straighter than usual. She noticed that the lawn was overgrown and that tufts of coarse crabgrass were beginning to poke up among the gravel. She looked with pleasure at the graceful leaded-glass fanlight above the front door. Her home may have been a fraud, but at least it was a tasteful fraud. With a seizure of anxiety, she inspected the Southland Realty FOR SALE sign planted in front of the magnolia thicket.

"You're not *really* selling the house?" she'd demanded of the Major when she'd been in Hullsport shortly before his death a year ago.

"Sure," he replied blandly, holding his pipe to his lips and lighting it with a match held in his left hand, with its alarming missing finger. "Why not?"

"Why *not?* Well, because it's our *home,* that's why not."

"Not *mine,* it isn't. Do you and Ira want to move down and live in it?"

"Well, no, but . . . ."

"Well?"

The last thing in the world she wanted to do was to move back to Hullsport. But it was reassuring to have something stable to reject.

Ginny jiggled the front door handle. It was locked. Setting down her pack, she knocked loudly several times with the huge brass knocker, which was badly tarnished. She had no idea whom she expected to respond, with her mother in the hospital—her childhood

self maybe. She decided to look under the doormat for the key, since
that was the traditional hiding place in movies and novels. Sure
enough, there it was. Which raised the interesting question of why
someone had bothered to lock the door in the first place, since the
entire American criminal population would instantly look under a
doormat for a key.

As the huge door swung inward, a gust of musty air enveloped
her. Hefting her pack, she walked in and cautiously looked around.
Nothing had changed. The damn place was like a time capsule. Her
mother had always refused to repair or redecorate, saying that she
preferred to remember things as they were when her children were
little. Consequently, the green wall-to-wall carpeting through the hall
and up the spiral staircase was almost worn through in spots. The
mahogany banister was still listing outward from when Karl, Ginny's
older brother, had slid down it carrying the dog. The green and white
stenciled wallpaper had smudges all over it alongside the stairs where
sticky hands had steadied small careening bodies. Her mother's
mahogany Chippendale desk, which had had nails hammered by Karl
through its claw feet and which contained her mother's epitaphs and
memorial service plan, still lacked the two handles that her younger
brother Jim had wrenched off after being hogtied to them by Ginny.
Over the desk hung the rubbing from Great-great-aunt Hattie's tombstone: "Stop and look as you pass by./ As you are now, so once was
I./ As I am now, so you will be./ Prepare to die and follow me."

And on the desk itself sat her mother's most treasured possession
—a small walnut clock about a foot and a half high with a peaked top
to its casing like a house roof. A green etched-glass door covered the
face and the clockworks. Fluted pilasters ran up the sides of the casing,
and the hands were of filigreed wrought iron. The numbers on the
face were faded Roman numerals. The clock had belonged to Ginny's
Grandmother Hull, and to her mother before her, and so on. God
only knew where it had come from originally. It had sat for decades
collecting coal dust on shelves and tables in small crumbling company
houses in southwest Virginia mining towns, until Grandma Hull had
brought it, like the household gods in ancient Rome, to Hullsport. As
a child, Ginny had loved to wind it with its large metal key—eight
turns each week and no more—as had her mother before her, and
Grandma Hull before her.

A huge oaken Dutch kas stood against the wall opposite her
mother's desk. One of its paneled doors still hung askew, as it had

ever since Ginny had hidden there among the tablecloths during an inspired game of hide-and-seek. The kas was another heirloom. The wooden pegs that held it together could be removed so that the giant cupboard could be transported in pieces—which had occurred any number of times prior to its being beached here in this pseudo-antebellum mansion.

The Palladian window flooded the hallway at the top of the stairs with sunlight in which legions of motes drifted languidly. Karl and Jim and Ginny used to lie there and watch the motes, blowing up at them to make them dance crazily. Karl was an army captain stationed in Germany now, with a wife and four children. Jim was making Viet-cong sandals from cast-off tires in Palo Alto, California. Ginny had seen them for a brief several hours at the Major's funeral. They had found surprisingly little to say to each other.

The house was utterly silent. Ginny had the feeling she often had when alone and quiet there that a band of sound was present just beyond the range her ears could hear—a dog could probably have heard it. This band, the audio accompaniment to her mother's Kin-flicks, was a replay of all the shouts and laughter and arguments and brawls that had filled this house ever since it was first built. She turned her head this way and that way, teasing herself with the notion that if she could achieve the appropriate angle with her defective hearing apparatus, she could tune into this frequency. It was the same feeling she'd had ever since learning in Botany 104 that in a young forest, the some 124,000 saplings in one acre would eventually be reduced to about 120 mature trees: If she could only have heard the struggle, the din would have been deafening. It was creepy. She decided to stay at the cabin instead.

"Is there anything I should know about Mother?" Ginny asked as she drove Mrs. Yancy to the airport later that afternoon. Mrs. Yancy wore a flowered hat and white gloves and a linen coatdress. She was meeting members of the National Baptist Women's Union in New York for their charter flight to the Holy Land.

"Yes. She has idiopathic thrombocytopenic purpura," she answered carefully.

"I beg your pardon?"

"Idiopathic thrombocytopenic purpura."

"The clotting disorder?"

"Yes."

"You said she was taking steroids. Are they . . . like, working?"

"Have you seen the new fishburger franchise?" Mrs. Yancy asked, pointing out the window at a red and silver building with a sign out front featuring in neon a one-legged pirate tangoing with a laughing swordfish, and the name "Long John Silver's Fishburger."

"No, I haven't," Ginny replied, relieved at not having her question answered definitively. "Have you tried it?"

"Yes, it's very good. You must be *sure* to go while you're here."

"I will," Ginny promised her. "But what about taking care of Mother? What do I do?" What she wanted to ask was how sick her mother really was, but she didn't know how. It would be like asking about her mother's sex life.

"The doctors and nurses have everything under control," Mrs. Yancy assured her. "But she gets lonely. Just visit her some every day. But, Ginny honey, I should warn you so you won't act startled when you see her: She looks just awful. She's covered with big bruises, and her nose is stuffed with cotton to keep it from bleeding. But she'll be all right. It's happened before, a couple of times in the past year."

"But why didn't she *tell* me?"

"Well, because she felt there was no *need* to tell you, honey. It didn't seem important enough to worry you with. She took a few pills and it cleared right up. You know, modern medicine is really remarkable."

"Then why am I being told *this* time, if it wasn't important enough to tell me about last time?"

"Well, honey, it just worked out this way," Mrs. Yancy explained reasonably. "With me going over at the Holy Land and all. I thought it was a shame to leave her all alone. You know how your mama feels about strange places."

"I was glad to come," Ginny assured her hastily. "Is she in pain?"

"Not much. They can control that with all these wonderful new drugs nowadays. Isn't it amazing what they can do?"

Waving as Mrs. Yancy boarded her plane, Ginny reflected that the last time she'd seen somebody off here had been about a year and three months ago, when she'd brought the Major out for a flight to Boston. It turned out to be the last time she saw him alive. It was just at the end of her conciliatory visit undertaken to display Ira and Wendy to her mother and the Major. She had picked the Major up at his office late one afternoon after working her way through gates and past guards by flashing his identification at them like an FBI agent in a raid.

"Tell Ira that there are twenty-two bullets in the drawer by the fireplace," he said casually as they drove toward the airport, just as though he were informing her there were eggs and milk in the refrigerator to be used up.

Startled, having forgotten that this was the same man who had given her a .38 special and a lifetime supply of bullets when she left home for college, Ginny asked, "What for?"

"If anyone bothers you, don't hesitate to blast him one." Ginny knew he meant it, too. Never mind if they *claimed* to be Bible salesmen or trick-or-treaters or heart-fund volunteers. When in doubt, blast them.

"You know something, Dad? You're getting as paranoid as *she* is."

"You call it paranoia, I call it reality."

"*I* think if you spend all your time dwelling on potential disasters, you attract them to yourself," Ginny snapped.

"You know," he said thoughtfully, "sending you to college in Boston was the worst investment I ever made. You used to be such an agreeable, respectful child."

Ginny shot him a look of outraged disbelief. She could recall nothing but conflict with him in the years preceding her departure.

"Well, *you're* the one who wanted me to go."

"*Me?* I assure you, Virginia, that I couldn't have cared less where you went to college. Or whether you went at all, for that matter." Ginny looked at him with astonishment. Was he lying, or had she lived part of her life fulfilling parental wishes that had existed only in her imagination? "I've *never* tried to influence the way you've lived your life."

Ginny gasped at him in fury and concentrated on the road, gripping the steering wheel so tightly that her knuckles turned white.

They rode in hostile silence for a while. Then he said gruffly, "If I don't see you again, Ginny, I want you to know that you've been a very satisfactory daughter, on the whole."

"Father, for *Christ's* sake!" Ginny shrieked, almost running head-on into a concrete abutment.

"Yes, but it's a distinct possibility when you fly as much as I have to. You don't seem to be aware of your own mortality."

Ginny glanced at him helplessly as he sat looking debonair in his three-piece pin-striped suit. "How could I *not* be? What else have I ever heard from you two all my life?"

By now they had reached the airport. Ginny parked the Jeep. "Come in and have a cup of coffee with me," the Major suggested as he hefted his bag out of the back. After checking in, he took Ginny's elbow and directed her to the gray metal flight insurance box in the waiting room, where he filled out a twenty-five-cent policy naming her beneficiary to $7,500 in the event of a fatal crash.

"Thanks," Ginny said absently, folding the policy and stuffing it in the pocket of her Women's Auxiliary blazer.

His hand still on her elbow, he directed her to the luncheonette. They sat at a small Formica table and ordered coffee. When the waitress brought it, they began the undeclared waiting game to see which of them would take the first sip, confirming for the other, like a canary in a coal mine, that the coffee wasn't poisoned, or the cream a host to ptomaine. It was a battle of nerves: Whose desire to drink still-warm coffee would first overcome his embarrassment at death in a public place?

Ginny lifted her cup and slurped, pretending to sip. The Major wasn't fooled. He shifted his lanky frame in the chair and stirred some cream into his coffee. To buy time, Ginny dumped a spoonful of sugar into her heavy white cup and asked, "What does Mother think about the house's being on the market?" Ginny knew what her mother thought, even though they hadn't talked about it: Her mother thought that the Major knew best—in all things.

"She agrees with me that the cabin is big enough for the two of us. We just rattle around in that white elephant. And it doesn't look as though you or the boys are going to want it."

In a diversionary maneuver, the Major removed a bottle from his suit jacket, unscrewed the lid, and took out two small white pills. These he popped into his mouth and downed with half a glass of water.

Watching him, Ginny unthinkingly took a sip of her coffee. Realizing too late what she'd done, she held the liquid in her mouth, trying to decide whether or not to return it unswallowed to the cup. Overcome finally by curiosity, she swallowed. As they both waited for her collapse, she asked, "What were those?"

"Coumadin," he answered blandly.

"Coumadin?"

"Coumadin."

"What *is* Coumadin?"

"An anticoagulant," he mumbled, averting his eyes.

"For your *heart?*" He nodded yes, glumly. "What's wrong with your heart?"

"Nothing. Just a little heart attack."

"*Heart* attack?" she shouted. "When?"

"Last month."

"Why wasn't I *told?*"

"It was nothing. I was just working too hard. I was in bed less than a week." He took a big drink of his coffee. A look of annoyance crossed his face because it was cool by now.

Ginny felt a great upsurge of anxiety. Sweat broke out on her forehead. She had difficulty breathing. So—the coffee was poisoned after all, and she was to meet her long-expected end here on the linoleum floor of this airport luncheonette. Her mother had always warned her to wear her best underwear when leaving the house, since one never knew when one might end up in the emergency room. But had Ginny listened? Of course not. And now here she was facing Eternity with safety pins holding up her bra straps.

"What's wrong?" the Major asked uneasily.

"Nothing," she replied bravely. And soon her symptoms abated, and her seizure assumed the proportions of a normal bout of separation anxiety, a malady she was intimately acquainted with. The house up for sale and the Major on the brink of a heart attack. Yes, those were valid grounds for a seizure.

"How long will you be gone?" she asked faintly.

"Two weeks," he replied with a wide smile. He went on business trips to Boston like a sailor going on shore leave after months of deprivation on the high seas.

"Business?"

"Mostly. I don't know if I told you—we're thinking of moving to Boston."

Scandalized, Ginny looked at him quickly. "How could you? This is our *home*."

"Not mine it isn't. I've always hated this town. You know that. I intended to stay here just a year, as part of my training for a job in Boston. But then I met your mother, who couldn't bear the thought of leaving Hullsport. Though God only knows why."

"But how could you just forfeit thirty-five years of memories?" Ginny wailed, knowing the incredible difficulty she experienced in letting go of anything out of her past, however objectionable.

"Easily. Very easily," he said with a laugh. He threw down the rest of his coffee, stood up, kissed Ginny on the forehead, and raced for his plane, like the candidate for cardiac arrest that he was. Though how a heart of stone could be subject to malfunctions escaped Ginny at the time.

Two and a half months later he was dead, of a heart attack.

After watching Mrs. Yancy's plane take off, Ginny wandered home via the perplexing network of new superhighways and shopping malls. She felt as though another bout of separation anxiety was imminent. It was all too much: her mother sick in the hospital, the Major dead, her childhood home on the auction block, Hullsport being strangled by a kind of cancer. Everything familiar to her in this place seemed to be slipping away. And since Ira had kicked her out, she had no other home, no other family.

She drove by Hullsport Regional High School, a massive red brick construction with white trim. Next to the building was a vast practice field. She was intimately acquainted with every tussock and pothole in that field because she had marched up and down it endlessly, trying to bend her legs at the knees in perfect right angles, almost every afternoon for two years as flag swinger for the Hullsport Pirates. This honor entitled her to strut in front of the marching band at football games, wearing gray twill short shorts and a braided maroon uniform jacket with silver epaulets and white tasseled go-go boots and a high white-plastic visored helmet with a maroon ostrich feather anchored in its band. She carried a maroon and gray flag with the school crest in the middle—a torch of knowledge. And above the crest was the school motto, "To strive, to seek, to find, and not to yield." The flagstaff had a bulb handle which enabled her to twirl and snap the flag around her as she marched, in a variety of dazzling patterns to accompany the fight songs being struggled through by the band. The prestige!

Ginny was driving very slowly past the practice field, savoring crumbs of glory from her past and pondering the fact that it was possible to condition a person to take pride in doing almost anything if his environment labeled that activity desirable.

She knew that cinder track and practice field in another way than just marching over it, though. After she had dropped out of flag swinging, Clem Cloyd and she, if there were no coaches around, would roar out onto the track and race around it on Clem's Harley. The flying wheels would throw cinders up into the red straining faces of the dripping track team, Joe Bob Sparks among them, who would be yelling, "Get that goddam cycle off our track!"

Then Ginny noticed that some boys were in fact running the cinder track now, their bare chests, with their newly sprouting fleeces of hair, slick with sweat under the hot midsummer sun.

Suddenly she jammed on the Jeep brakes and stared at one of the figures. Swerving into the curb, she sat there short of breath. She'd have known that sweaty back anywhere! The muscular ridges that rose up on either side of the backbone were rippling rhythmically as their owner ran. How many times had she danced holding onto those ridges with her hands and wishing fervently that that hard-muscled body were moving up and down on top of hers? Dear God, it was Joe Bob Sparks himself!

3

Walking the Knife's Edge, or Blue Balls in Bibleland

———————————— □ ————————————

The first time I ever saw "the Sparkplug of the Hullsport Pirates," as the sportscaster of WHPT referred to Joe Bob Sparks, he came flying through a paper portrait of a snarling pirate who had a black patch over one eye and a knife between his teeth and a bandanna around his head. Joe Bob led with one cleated foot, his elbows extended and his shoulder pads hunched up around his maroon helmet. Number thirty-eight he was, halfback and captain. I had of course heard of him. He was an area legend by this time. But I had never seen him close up, only on distant athletic fields, because he lived in a housing development on the opposite side of town and we had gone to different elementary schools.

The cheerleaders were leading the packed stands in a frantic yell: "Sparky! Sparky! He's our may-un! If he cain't do hit, Dole cay-un!" (It seemed unlikely to me then, from the fierce good looks of Joe Bob, that there was *anything* he couldn't do. Being all palpitating pudenda, I hadn't yet realized that the ability to think did have its occasional uses.) Then Doyle charged through the deflowered paper hoop. The cheerleaders in their white and brown saddle shoes spun wildly, their full maroon and gray skirts swirling up around their waists to reveal maroon body suits. I spun, too, twirling my flag.

I could see Joe Bob in the middle of the field as I did so. He was prancing in place like a horse in the starting line at the Derby. Once the team had all established that they could leap through the hoop, Head Coach Bicknell appeared, surrounded by his assistants like a Mafioso by his bodyguards. All the players removed their helmets and tucked them under their left arms. The cheerleaders and I stood at attention, me with my flag shouldered like a rifle. The band blared through its unrecognizable rendering of "The Star-Spangled Banner," and I watched with approval as Joe Bob placed his huge right hand over his breast and stared reverently at Old Glory, while most of his teammates fidgeted and flexed. Then the team formed a tight circle, their eyes closed, and Joe Bob's closed most intently of all. Coach Bicknell led them in a prayer for good sportsmanship and teamwork, and, as an afterthought, victory.

Then the cheerleaders led our packed stands in welcoming the Sow Gap Lynxes: "Our game is rough,/ Our boys are rowdy./ But we send Sow Gap/ A great big howdy!"

The Kinflicks of that first heady game, which Mother was shooting from the front row of the bleachers, show me in a variety of prescribed poses: I remove my plumed helmet and do cartwheels as though the rotation of the earth depended on it; I grab up the cheerleaders' megaphone and shriek fervently toward the bleachers, "Y'all yell, ya hee-yah?"; I fall to my knees and raise my eyes to the heavens, pleading for a touchdown; after our first touchdown, I skip through an allemande left with the seven cheerleaders while the band blasts out its unique drum-dominated version of the school song to the tune of "Stars and Stripes Forever." And in one sequence I prophetically savor each letter as, after his first touchdown, we spell out "Sparky." (People around school called Joe Bob "Sparky," though I always preferred the more dignified "Joe Bob.") "Gimme an Ess!" "Ess!" "Gimme a P!" "P!" And so on. "Whaddaya got?" "SPARKY!"

We watched the clock on the scoreboard and counted down the last thirty seconds in a roar. Joe Bob had scored three touchdowns and had led the Pirates to a crashing victory over the Lynxes. He was carried from the field on the shoulders of fans who spilled from the stands. The entire town attended all the high school athletic matches.

Meets with neighboring towns brought out all the latent intertown hostilities. It was as though each town were a warring city-state, and the high school teams were the town heavies.

A victory dance was held in the school gym, which was decorated with maroon and gray streamers and fierce pirates on poster paper. I stood in my short shorts and go-go boots with a couple of the cheerleaders and watched my classmates milling around. Occasionally, I'd flash a smile at a familiar face, a smile too enthusiastic for credibility, and would offer the ritual Hullsport High greeting: "Say hey!"

I was distracted by the presence a few feet away of Joe Bob Sparks himself, changed into a neat plaid sports shirt and slacks, his light brown crew cut still damp from the shower. People kept clapping him on the back and saying, "Great game, Sparky!" Joe Bob would smile his moronic smile and look at the floor with a modest shrug.

Then, as though in response to my yearnings from the sidelines, he sauntered up to me, fans falling away from him on every side like from Christ on Palm Sunday, and introduced himself. Or rather, he presented himself, since he correctly assumed that everyone already knew who *he* was.

"Say hey!" he said with his dopey smile, which smile I tried to overlook the whole time I dated him. It was a smile in excess of any possible stimulus. In fact, now that I think about it, Joe Bob's smile was usually unrelated to external stimuli and generally appeared at the most unlikely or inappropriate times. This smile (I dwell on it so obsessively because, like Mona Lisa's, it embodied his very essence) contorted his entire face. Most people smile from their noses downward. But not Joe Bob. His smile narrowed his eyes to slits, raised his cheekbones to temple level, wrinkled his forehead, and lifted his crew cut. And in spite of the exaggerated width of the smile, his lips never parted, probably because of his omnipresent wad of Juicy Fruit gum, which he minced daintily with his front teeth. In short, Joe Bob's smile was demented. But I managed to overlook this fact almost until the day I left him because I wasn't remotely interested in the state of his mind.

It was his remarkable body that occupied virtually all my thoughts. I loved the way he had no visible neck, his head being permanently stove into his shoulders from leading with it in blocking and tackling. I worshiped his chipped front teeth and mangled upper lip from the time he'd dropped the barbell on his face while trying to press 275 pounds. I adored the Kirk Douglas cleft that made his chin look like an upside-down heart, which cleft was actually a crater from an opponent's cleat. I admired the way his left eye had only half an eyebrow from once when he had hit the linesman's stake after being tackled. Joe Bob was evidently indestructible—a quality of incalculable appeal for someone like me, who was braced for disaster around every corner. But most of all, I loved that sunken valley down the middle of his spine, with the rugged ranges of muscle upon muscle rising up on either side. I loved to hold them, one hand on each ridge, as we danced.

Joe Bob didn't talk much. He preferred to be known by his actions. But when he did talk, his voice was soft and babyish; he would grin and open his mouth much wider than necessary and make flapping sounds. In retrospect, I realize that he had a speech defect, but at the time at Hullsport High a soft baby talk in imitation of Big Sparky was all the rage. His favorite expression, and hence the favorite expression of the entire school, was "Do whut?" He said "Do whut?" punctuated by his demented grin every time he didn't understand what someone had said to him, which was often. It was an all-purpose question, the equivalent of "I beg your pardon?"

For example, after saying "Say hey!" to me at the victory dance, he next asked, "Why haven't ah seed you around before?" As though it were his personal prerogative to approve each student at Hullsport High.

"I'm a sophomore," I explained faintly, dazzled to be the sole focus of his attention. The music was so loud that it drowned me out.

Joe Bob grinned and tilted his head down and said, "Do whut?"

"A sophomore!" I yelled. "I'm a sophomore!"

He nodded, still grinning. "Wanna dance?"

And so we performed those mating rituals called the boogaloo and the chicken scratch. We circled each other slowly with carefully calculated flailings of arms and legs, with coyly disguised thrusts of hips and profferings of breasts. Joe Bob's movements lagged behind by about half a beat due to the five-pound canvas-covered wrist and ankle weights he was wearing, shacklelike, to build up his arms and legs. As though they needed any more building.

Occasionally, unable to tolerate the mounting tension, one of us would whirl off and, back to the other, writhe in narcissistic isolation, eventually spinning back around, restored, to face the other and resume our invocation of the muse of adolescent lust.

And then the reward: a slow song. "Why does my heart go on beating?/ Why do these eyes of mine cry?/ Don't they know it's the end of the world?/ It ended when you said good-by." The heartbreak of the song merely increased Joe Bob's and my delight at having found each other in a world in which, so Skeeter Davis assured us, the only certainty was loss. Joe Bob wrapped his muscled arms around me as though enfolding a football for a line drive, his wrist weights clanking together behind my back. I shyly put my arms around his waist and first discovered those two delightful ranges of rippling muscle down his back.

We didn't really dance. In fact, we scarcely moved, swaying in time to the adenoidal wailings with only enough friction between us to give him an erection, which prodded my lower abdomen. Not knowing then what an erection was, I assumed that this strange protuberance was the result of yet another football injury, a hernia or something. I politely pretended not to notice, as I'd pretended not to notice his moronic smile, though I did wonder at the reason for his chagrined glances down at me.

I must confess at this point that, in spite of having been flag swinger for Hullsport High and girl friend of Joe Bob Sparks and Persimmon Plains Burly Tobacco Festival Queen, I hadn't always been beautiful and gifted. There was a time, when I was thirteen, when I wanted nothing but to be a defensive left tackle for the Oakland Raiders. That was before I learned the bitter lesson that women led their lives through men. In short, that was before I became a flag swinger on the sidelines of Joe Bob's triumphs. I must have suspected what was cooking, deep in the test kitchens of my unconscious, because my football playing had the desperation of the doomed to it. My tackles were performed with the fervor of a soldier making love on the eve of a lost battle. My blocks were positioned with the loving precision lavished on daily routines by terminal cancer patients. Something in me knew that I would never be an Oakland Raider, that I would never even be a Hullsport Pirate, that I would have to pull myself up by my training bra straps into some strange new arena of combat at some unspecified point in the near future.

That point turned out to be the messy morning my first menstrual period began. My family may have been into death in a big way, but they definitely weren't into sex. So unprepared was I for this deluge that I assumed I had dislodged some vital organ during football practice the previous afternoon and was hemorrhaging to death. Blushing and stammering, averting her eyes to Great-great-aunt Hattie's epitaph on the wall, Mother assured me that what was happening was indeed horrible—but quite normal. That bleeding like a stuck pig every month was the price exacted for being allowed to scrub some man's toilet bowl every week.

"That's life," she concluded. She concluded many of her conversations with the phrase, like a fundamentalist preacher's "Praise the Lord." When she said it, though, the implication was not that one should accept the various indignities of corporeal existence with grace, but rather that one should shift one's focus to the dignities of the dead.

"No more football," she added offhandedly. "You're a young woman now." I knew at that moment what Beethoven must have felt when informed that his ears would never hear music again. No more football? She might just as well have told Arthur Murray never to dance again. How was I to exist without the sweet smack of my shoulder pads against some halfback's hips, without the delicious feel of my cleats piercing the turf? I went upstairs, and as I exchanged my shoulder pads for a sanitary pad and elastic belt, I knew that menstruation might just as well have been a gastrointestinal hemorrhage in terms of its repercussions on my life.

But before long, I learned that the same body that could butt a blocking machine down a football field could be used in ways more subtle but just as effective. For example, it could be made to twist and twirl and prance. Its hips could swing and slither with the same skill required to elude enclosing tacklers. Its budding breasts, heretofore regarded as a humiliating defect that distorted the number on my jersey, could be played up to advantage with a Never-Tell padded bra. In short, I was transformed from a left tackle into a flag swinger, into the new girl friend of Joe Bob Sparks. *I* got to be the one to bear his abuse for giving him blue balls, and eventually *I* got to be the one to give him hand jobs at the Family Drive-In.

But I'm getting ahead of myself. We started out together on a more modest scale. Joe Bob picked me up before school the Monday following the victory dance. He roared up our white quartz driveway in a white Ford convertible, which had "Sparkplug" painted in red on the rear fender. His horn blared. As Mother stood looking with horror through the green velvet curtains in the dining room, I slipped out the door and minced my way to the car, completely concealing the fact that, until recently, I could have vied with Joe Bob himself on line drives. I was wearing cordovan loafers with leather tassels and a madras shirtwaist with a Peter Pan collar. Its skirt came to the middle of my kneecaps. Joe Bob looked at me with his insane smile and said softly, "Say hey, Ginny!"

I smiled a smile of infinite promise and climbed in, arranging my skirt to cover my kneecaps, which were padded with scar tissue from being tackled in cinders in the end zone on touchdowns. Joe Bob wore tan chinos and a plaid Gant shirt and penny loafers. We each nodded to ourselves in satisfaction that the other, when not disguised as flag swinger or tailback, looked clean and pressed and identical to every other member of the Hullsport High student body—with the exception of the hoods like Clem Cloyd, in their unspeakable tight studded blue jeans with pegged legs, and black ankle boots and dark T-shirts and windbreakers.

On Friday night we cruised Hull Street in Sparkplug with its top down, along with all the other students worthy of note from Hullsport High. We started at the church circle and drove slowly up Hull Street through three intersections to the train station, Sparkplug's engine idling with noisy impatience. At the train station we circled around and headed back down Hull Street to the church circle, with Joe Bob playfully revving the engine in competition with whoever was stopped next to us at the lights. Then we repeated the circuit.

The other cars accompanying us in this rite contained either established couples from school, or a bunch of unclaimed boys on the prowl, or a bunch of unclaimed girls trying to feign lack of interest. Occasionally, at a stop light, as though compelled by cosmic signals, half the unclaimed girls in one car would leap out and exchange places with half the unclaimed boys in another car in an adolescent version of fruit-basket-upside-down; it was as though each car were an atom exchanging electrons with another atom so as to neutralize their charges. From the air it would have looked like an intricate square-dance figure. It was the modern American adaptation of the old Spanish custom in which the single young people stroll around the town plaza eying each other with scarcely concealed desperation and desire, in full view of placid but watchful adults. In this case the chaperones were the highway patrolmen, not long ago students at Hullsport High themselves, but gone over now to the enemy. Taking their revenge on us for their no longer being young and unfettered by families, they liked nothing better than to ticket someone for driving in the wrong direction around the church circle. Their formerly athletic bodies gone to flab under their khaki shirts, they now cruised for a living and delighted in breaking up back-seat tussles on dark dirt roads. As I soon learned—which was why I finally "went all the way," as the teen jargon discreetly put it, only when locked securely in the bomb shelter in my basement. But I'm getting ahead of myself again.

After half a dozen trips up and down Hull Street, Joe Bob pulled into a parking spot. We got out and sauntered along the sidewalk and looked in the shop windows at the latest in teen fashions, each subtly instructing the other on what outfits to buy next. We lingered long in front of the display windows of Sparks Shoe Store, owned by Joe Bob's father. We both agreed that it had the nicest selection of shoes in town. I noted with approval that, each time we came to a Dixie cup or a candy wrapper wantonly discarded, Joe Bob would pick it up, wrist weights clanking on the sidewalk, and deposit it in a trash can saying "Keep Hullsport Beautiful."

"You can hardly walk down the street anymore without tripping over somebody's garbage," I said appreciatively.

"Do whut?" he asked with a grin, chomping on his Juicy Fruit with his front teeth.

"Garbage. People throw it all over the place."

He nodded serenely, munching.

We got back into Sparkplug and did another half dozen circuits of Hull Street. After which we pulled into the parking lot of the most popular drive-in restaurant, the Dew Drop Inn. The Dew Drop had asphalt ridges in its parking lot to discourage its inclusion in our cruising route. Joe Bob went over the bumps reverently, careful not to scrape his chrome tail pipes. But the following year Clem and I raced over them on his cycle, leaning from side to side, like Eddie Holzer negotiating moguls on cross-country skis on the slopes of Vermont.

Through the microphone next to the car, Joe Bob ordered six half-pints of milk in waxed cardboard containers for himself and a small Seven-Up laced with cherry syrup for me. When the car hop brought them, Joe Bob said, "Thank you, ma'am," in his soft babyish voice with his mad contorted smile, all the time eying her ample chest out the window. Then he removed his wad of Juicy Fruit and stuck it on the dashboard. One after another, he opened the cartons and tossed down the milk, scarcely pausing for breath. He winked at me and smiled dementedly and said, "Trainin."

I had just begun to sip my cherry Seven-Up by the time he had drained all six of his milk containers. He stuck his Juicy Fruit back in his mouth and turned to watch me drink. The be-bosomed carhop whipped by, and Joe Bob's eyes followed her chest. Finally he said, "One time I was here with this cousin of mine. Jim, he's got him this Fairlane 500 with push-button windows. Well, that girl over yonder —I *think* it was that ole girl—anyhow, she brung him this pack of Pall Malls. The window was partway down, and ole Jim, he reached over to roll the window the rest of the way down. Well, he wasn't watchin what he was doin. He was lookin at his change to see if he'd have to break a bill to pay her." I nodded frantic encouragement. I'd never before heard him say so many words at one time. He took a deep breath and continued in his scarcely audible voice. "Well—it turns out he's not rollin the window *down,* he's rollin it *up!*" His grin was pushing his crew cut up. I hadn't caught the joke yet. I smiled uncertainly, hoping for a punch line.

After waiting for an appropriate amount of time, I said hesitantly, "I'm not sure I get it."

He blushed. "Well, she was standin right up against the window of the Fairlane, see? The window rolled *up* without him knowin it, and he like to chopped off her—you know." I flinched reflexlike, imagining the pain of having a push-button window close on my breasts; then I too blushed at this open reference to crucial female anatomy, even though it was obviously the cornerstone of our impending relationship; then I grinned idiotically as the tale began to appeal to me; then I smiled sweetly at Joe Bob for his delicacy in referring to tits as "you know."

Joe Bob pushed back his left wrist weight and glanced at his watch. He sat up straight, hurriedly flashed his headlights, and started up the motor with a roar. The carhop, blessed with chest, sauntered out to retrieve the tray. As Joe Bob threw the car into gear and backed out, he said anxiously, "I like to forgot trainin. Lord, Coach'll kill me!" We roared down Hull Street in the direction of my house.

"What do you mean?" I demanded, injured.

"Got to be in bed by ten," he notified me grimly, weaving Sparkplug in and out of the frivolous cruising traffic.

"You're *kidding!*" My heart sank. A ten o'clock curfew definitely dampened the possibilities for lingering exchanges of sweet nothings. He dumped me at the foot of our driveway and left me to find my own way through the magnolia thicket to the house.

Our courtship was like a silent movie. In those days before the raising of the public's seat-belt consciousness, the progress of a couple's relationship could be gauged by the distance between them as they drove down the street. Who knows how many budding romances have been nipped by the surge in popularity of bucket seats? I started out that first night of cruising crammed next to the door with my hand on the handle so that I could leap out if Joe Bob were transformed into a rape-strangler. But he didn't so much as shake my hand for weeks, first to my relief, and eventually to my distress. Gradually, I began scooting over slightly on the seat after he let me in and before he got back around to his side. In a month's time I had worked my way over almost to his side, under the guise of constantly tuning the radio.

And then it happened! We were at the city-wide Preaching Mission, being held in the cavernous gymnasium of the Civic Auditorium, which, on less sacred occasions, hosted roller derbies and wrestling matches. Joe Bob and I sat on bleachers along one wall with the rest of the student population. The adults sat in rows of folding chairs set up across the floor. It was a Friday night, the climax of the week-long mission. The speaker tonight was Brother Buck Basket from Birmingham, Alabama, come all the way to Hullsport just to spread the good news to his Tennessee brothers and sisters that Death had lost its sting. Joe Bob was all ears. Brother Buck was his idol. He had been a famous All-American guard from the University of Alabama a decade earlier. And then a Baltimore Colt, until he had run into a goal post and suffered a head injury which had left him unconscious for days and then bound up in gauze for a month or more, with every football fan in the country in a frenzy of anxiety. Upon returning to the land of the living, however, Brother Buck had renounced his gridiron glory and dedicated his life to Christ.

His massive, dedicated frame dwarfed the podium. He wore a tan western-cut suit and a string tie and cowboy boots. I knew that soon Joe Bob would own a tan western suit and a string tie.

"Death! Where is your sting? Grave, where is your victory?" Brother Buck thundered. The steel I beams that held up the roof seemed to tremble. He was holding up one fist in a gesture of defiance and was gazing intently at a spot near the rear ceiling. All of us automatically turned in that direction, expecting to see at least the Four Horsemen of the Apocalypse, if not the Four Horsemen of Notre Dame.

"Ah know what you think," he assured us quietly, returning his fist to the podium and his fervid blue gaze to the audience. "You think: It don't matter none *what* kind of a life ah live. Ah can read these here pornographic books, and look at nasty pictures, and defile my body with all manner of vile corruption. Ah can stay up all night drinkin, and ah can run around with fallen women and sleep through church on Sundays. It don't matter none. That's what you think, don't you, now? Admit it right here tonight to ole Brother Buck. You think, ah'd better just live it up today cause tomorrow ah may lie dyin in a pool of black gore, with mah bones smashed and pokin up through mah flesh; with mah guts trailin out and tangled round mah twisted car; with mah brains dribbled acrost the highway like cornmeal mush . . ."

I glanced wearily at Joe Bob. I'd had enough of this from my Cassandran parents to last me a lifetime, which lifetime was apparently predestined to brevity and a bloody ending. But Joe Bob was grinning insanely and was mincing his Juicy Fruit, thrilled at this proximity to his hero.

". . . and tomorrow that there bomb ah'm always hearin about will go off and blow us all sky high in little red pieces, like chaff before the whirlwind. Tomorrow mah plane flight will smash into the side of some mountain, and there'll be jagged bloody chunks of mah body strewn all acrost the forest floor for the wild animals to feast on. Tomorrow some madman with a telescopic sight will use mah eyes for target practice. So ah'd better live it up now while ah can. Ah'd best titillate mah flesh ever which way, cause this breath ah'm takin"—he paused to take a deep illustrative breath—"may be mah last.

"Oh, Brother Buck *knows* how most of you folks live, friends." The suspicion that this might be true, that Brother Buck really *did* know all about my feminine napkins and my padded bra, filled me with the same outraged sense of exposure I used to feel as a child at the line in "Santa Claus Is Coming to Town" that goes, "He sees you when you are sleeping./ He knows if you're awake."

"*How* does Brother Buck know? He knows because he's been there hissef. He knows because he's thought corrupt thoughts. Because he's broken heavenly trainin and lived a pre-verse life hissef, friends, usin ever chanct he got to provoke tinglin sensations in his mortal flesh. Yes, Brother Buck has lived a lustful life full of sin!

"When he played pro ball, he went to all the fancy places where wicked women sold theirselves up to vile corruption. The temptations were many and wondrous to behold for a country boy from Alabama, and Brother Buck failed the test, friends. Yes, he did. He tried em all." I looked over at Joe Bob and discovered that a thin line of saliva was drooling out the corner of his mouth as he munched his Juicy Fruit. His eyes were gleaming.

"But do you *know* what happened to Brother Buck with his wretched ways, friends? He ran into the goal post one night on a football field in Baltimore, Maryland. Yes, he did. And he landed up in a Baltimore hospital. Yes, friends, ah lay with mah entire head wrapped up in bandages for one solid month, alone there in mah private darkness, unable to speak, unable to see. And that solitude, brothers and sisters, that lonely month there in the dark on mah back in bed all alone, was the turning point in mah preverse and sinful life!

"Ah want to tell you what happened to me as ah lay there, not knowin if ah'd ever see again, much less play ball." We were all hanging on the edges of our bleachers waiting for the punch line. "*Jesus* came to me! Yes, he did! He come to me and He says, 'Brother Buck, don't you fret none, son. We're gonna clean out the temple of your soul, buddy, that body of yours whose pleasures you set so much store by. The *devil* has been lyin in wait for you, brother, behind them rhinestone pasties. But ah got plans for you on *mah* team, fella!'

"And that's why ah'm here tonight, friends, Brother Buck right here in—ah—here with all you fine people tonight in—uh—this lovely town of—uh—." He turned around quickly to the clerical-collared men on the stage behind him. Then he turned back around and said casually, "Here in Hullsport, Tennessee. Yes, ah'm here to let you all in on a li'l ole secret."

Joe Bob and I strained forward in our seats, since all the world loves a secret. As we did so, our thighs rubbed together. I hastily moved my legs to one side—and bumped into the thighs of the strange boy next to me. I appeared to have no choice but to allow my left thigh to nestle up against Joe Bob's muscled right one. We sat rigid, pretending not to notice, as Brother Buck told us his secret in a voice that boomed to the rafters: "*You don't have to die, friends!*"

He paused until the echo faded, then continued in a shout: "That body you're abusin, buddy, with your liquor and your lusts, that *body*," he roared, then instantly dropped his voice almost to a whisper so that the audience strained forward as one to hear him, "is the sanctuary of your soul." He stopped, sweat glistening on his forehead beneath his light brown crew cut. "*Your soul!*" he shouted again, so that everyone sat back startled. "The Bible says, 'Know ye not that your body is the temple of the Holy Ghost which is in you, which ye have of God? Ye are not your own.' "

By now Joe Bob's and my thighs were pressed together tightly and were generating hot secrets within our respective soul sanctuaries.

Suddenly Brother Buck burst into the feverish pitch of revival preaching. It was like a thunderstorm finally breaking after hours of black clouds amassing. "Ah came here to save *souls!* Ah came here to share with you mah joy in the *Lord!* Yes, Jesus!" Brother Buck could have been quoting stock prices now and none of us would have noticed.

" 'The Lord is mah *Shepherd!* Ah shall not want!' Yes! The Lord says, He says in that last awful day of reckonin, brothers, on that day when your lungs fill up with blood, yes, and you can't call out to no one to come hep you! Yes! On that day, friends, when the film of death draws acrost your eyes and you can't *see* the loved ones around you! Yes! On that *day,* friends, when your ears are roarin with the sound of your own organs collapsin inside you! Yes! On that *day,* oh dear God that *day,* when your teeth won't stop chatterin from fear, and your bones turn to jelly and your legs collapse underneath you! Oh, *friends!* That day when your precious body is crumblin into dust and swirlin away! Yes! 'Behold!' Isaiah says. 'Behold the Lord maketh the earth empty.' Yes! 'And wastes it, and turns it upside down, and scatters abroad the inhabitants thereof!' Oh *yes,* sweet Jesus! 'The land shall be utterly *spoiled,*' Isaiah says, 'for the earth is *defiled* under the inhabitants thereof!' Yes, praise God!"

The emotional climate in the auditorium was rising now, particularly in the immediate vicinity of Joe Bob and me. Our thighs were positively aglow. People in the audience were starting to shout back at Brother Buck: "Yes, Jesus!" "Praise God!"

"Think about it," he invited us, suddenly quiet. He was playing us as though we were hooked fish, giving us emotional slack now in order to reel us in more quickly later. "You've broken trainin all your life. Your body's a stinkin sewer of ever vile corruption you can name. Your team has lost the game because you're all just reekin with sin. You're slouchin toward the dressin room thinkin bout the hot shower that's gonna feel so great on your bruised body. But as you walk into the locker room, friends, you hear your teammates weepin and howlin with anguish.

"What's waitin for you there in your dressin room, friends? Do you know? Let's listen to the Bible and see," he suggested, holding up a black book as though fading back to pass it into the audience. Flipping through it nonchalantly, he stopped and read slowly, " 'Behold,' Isaiah says, 'the Lord will come with fire, and his chariots like a whirlwind, to render his anger with fury, and his rebuke with flames of fire.' "

His tempo and pitch were picking up again. " 'The people shall be as the burnins of lime, as thorns cut up shall they be burnt in the fire,' says Isaiah. Oh dear God! 'Ah will tread them in mine anger!' Yes! 'Ah will trample them in mah fury!' Yes! 'Their blood shall be sprinkled upon mah garments, and ah will stain all my raiment!' Oh sweet Jesus! 'They shall go forth, friends, yes, and they shall look upon the carcasses of the men that have transgressed against me,' says the Lord. 'Their *worm* shall not die, neither shall their *fire* be quenched!' No! 'And they shall be an *abhorrin* unto all flesh!' Oh woe! *Woe!* Listen to this from Corinthians, brothers and sisters, ah beg of you! 'Be not deceived: neither fornicators, no, nor idolaters, nor adulterers, nor effeminate, nor abusers of themselves, shall inherit the kingdom of God! *The body is not for fornication but for the Lord!*' Yes, praise Jesus! *'Know ye not* that your bodies are the members of Christ?' *Know ye* not? 'Shall I then take the members of Christ and make them the members of an harlot? *God forbid,*' says Corinthians! Rather, 'Flee fornication!' "

Joe Bob and I were unable to sit still. Blood was throbbing in my thigh along the area where it contacted Joe Bob's. The entire audience was squirming. If Brother Buck had told us all to go burn down the Major's munitions factory, we probably would have.

Sweat was dripping from Brother Buck's face as though he had been standing under a shower. "On that horrible last day, friends, when the losin team is howlin in the locker room, what about the winnin team? What happens to them, do you think? 'We need not fear,' says the Psalm, 'though the earth be moved, and though the hills be carried into the midst of the sea; though the waters thereof rage and swell,' friends; 'though the mountains shake at the tempest. We need not fear.' *We need not fear!*' he announced, his face expressing delighted astonishment through its layer of sweat. " 'Be not afraid of them that kill the body and after that have no more that they can do!'

"And so Brother Buck pleads with you tonight, folks: Turn your back on the corruption of this vile and hateful world, and purify yoursef to be worthy of the next. Yes! It's not too late to swap teams if you start followin trainin tonight. 'Flesh and blood cannot inherit the Kingdom, neither doth corruption inherit incorruption. But when the corruptible shall have put on incorruption, the mortal shall have put on immortality.'

"Do it tonight, friends. Brother Buck begs you. He pleads with you from the depths of his heart. Put on incorruption. Put it on tonight. 'Cause then only shall be brought to pass the sayin that is written, 'Death is swallowed up in victory. *O death, where is thy sting? O grave, where is thy victory?'* "

In an exhausted voice, Brother Buck invited everyone who intended to lead a new life as a teammate of Christ to come forward. "Do it tonight, brothers and sisters," he intoned as Joe Bob and I walked automatonlike toward the stage. "Give up your wicked ways and inherit eternity. Shed dishonor and put on glow-ry." If he had invited us to come sip his bathwater, as medieval messianic figures did, Joe Bob and I would have gone forward as obediently. We joined about two hundred people at the foot of the stage.

"Take the hand of the person on either side of you, brothers and sisters," he panted, loosening his string tie as though it were a noose. Joe and I obediently clutched hands, and at that point the dove descended. We stood there, Joe Bob and I, our clasped hands sweating and trembling.

"Let us pray," Brother Buck instructed. "Father, our Coach, hep us, Father, to run Thy plays as Thou wouldst have them run. Knowing, Lord, that Christ Jesus Thy quarterback is there beside us with ever yard we gain, callin those plays and runnin that interference. Hep us, Lord, to understand that winnin ball games depends on followin trainin. Hep us not to abuse our minds and bodies with those worldly temptations that are off-limits to the teammates of Christ . . ." Joe Bob was stroking my palm with his finger tips. Shivering sensations were running up my arm like an electric current and were grounding out somewhere below the navy stretch straw belt of my Villager shirtwaist.

". . . and hep us, Celestial Coach, to understand that the water boys of life are ever bit as precious in Thy sight as the All-American guards. And when that final gun goes off, Lord, mayst Thou welcome us to the locker room of the home team with a slap on the back and a hearty, 'Well done, my good and faithful tailback.' "

"A-man," Brother Buck added as an afterthought.

"A-man," echoed the rest of us.

"All right, you can drop hands now," Brother Buck said sotto voce to the group up front. Regretfully, Joe Bob and I peeled apart our sticky palms. "Now what ah hope," Brother Buck said into the microphone, "is that some of the young people in this group down front here—and any of the rest of you kids in the audience who didn't bother to come down because you've already received the Lord as your Savior—these fine kids, ah hope, will form the nucleus of a Brother Buck Teen Team for Jesus, right here in—ah—Hullsport, Tennessee. There are groups all *over* the South, and ah think you'll find that they're the comin thing in our high schools. Soo . . . that's all for tonight, friends. And God love you!" He waved to the audience, who stood up with much rumbling of folding chairs.

Several dozen of us remained down front—Hullsport's saving remnant. Most were Joe Bob's fellow football players and their girl friends. Joe Bob squared his massive shoulders and walked boldly over to Brother Buck, who was squatting on the edge of the stage talking to prospective Teen Team members.

Joe Bob introduced himself and pointed to me saying, "And this here's my friend Virginia. I'm—uh—the captain of the Hullsport Pirates." He looked at the floor with modesty and minced his Juicy Fruit with his front teeth.

Brother Buck said thoughtfully, "Just a minute now. Joe Bob Sparks, you said? Why, yes, ah do believe ah've heard of you, son." Joe Bob glowed. "You've had a good season so far, as I recall."

"Six and 0," Joe Bob confirmed.

By the time I dragged him away, he had signed us both up for the Teen Team for Jesus, Hullsport branch.

The next night at the Family Drive-In Joe Bob and I were watching a movie called *Girls in Chains*, to which no one under eighteen was supposed to have been admitted. It involved a gang of female motorcyclists who roared around cutting the safety chains off the cycles of their male counterparts and then hiding the cycles in clever places, like in the trunk of a police cruiser.

Joe Bob took his right hand off the steering wheel, which he'd been gripping tightly. Without taking his eyes off the screen, he reached down and groped for my hand, which lay panting, palm up, on the seat next to him. After all, Brother Buck himself had told us to join hands. We knitted our fingers together, both studying the screen intently and trying to pretend that nothing out of the ordinary was happening. His huge hand with its stove-in knuckles enfolded my small skilled flag-twirling hand like a pod around a pea.

This was my first experience with the concept that I have now, after extensive experimentation, formulated into a postulate: It is possible to generate an orgasm at any spot on the human body. Our hands, thus interlocked, took on lives of their own. They trembled and shuddered for the rest of the movie, as Joe Bob and I, though pretending to watch the antics of the girls and their safety chains, made our captive hands the focus of our entire existence.

The movie over, neither of us knew how to disengage ourselves in a nonrejecting fashion, although by now both palms were slimy with stale sweat. Joe Bob shifted into reverse, using our clasped hands as a unit. On the way home I asked, "Do you ever think about stuff like what Brother Buck was saying last night?"

"Naw, never do," Joe Bob replied proudly, mincing his Juicy Fruit daintily. "You know, I liked Brother Buck real good last night, but he's sure a morbid kind of guy, in'nt he? All that 'lungs fillin with blood' junk."

That evening, of course, opened the floodgates of groping. During the next several months, we groped all over each other—from putting our arms around each other timidly, to prim kisses with tightly closed lips, to wet messy gasping kisses with tongues intertwined and teeth clashing like rival bulls' horns. I ran my tongue over his chipped front teeth and nibbled the scar tissue of his mangled upper lip and probed the cleat crater that clefted his heart-shaped chin.

He finally got around to touching my breasts, such as they were, one night after a game against the Davy Crockett Pioneers of Roaring Fork, Kentucky. By now we had hurtled along into basketball season. Joe Bob had scored the tie-breaking basket in the final five seconds of play and was carried from the floor on his teammates' envious shoulders. I had also enjoyed a triumph of sorts, performing solo in center court at half time a routine that involved winding the flagstaff over and under my legs in an intricate pattern. An error would have left me sprawling deflowered in the center circle. But I had performed the difficult number flawlessly and was rewarded with wild cheering. We had both imbibed enough ego tonic to last us until next week's game.

We were at a favorite parking spot high up on one of the red clay hills that ringed Hullsport. Below us, the lights of town were spread out. We were clutching each other in a panting embrace, me running one hand back and forth over his flat top, which could have served as a scrub brush by lopping off the top of his head. My other arm circled his waist, and my fingers clung to the delicious crevices of his spine as though they were toe holds on a mountain wall. Joe Bob with his left hand poked tentatively at my right breast, or rather poked the mound of my maroon uniform jacket, poked the padding of my Never-Tell bra. As I kept up my patting and rubbing on him, which required the concentration and coordination of rubbing my own head while patting my stomach, Joe Bob began prodding and kneading my breast as though he were a gynecologist performing a breast check. His hand trembled from the strain of holding up his wrist weight.

By the time baseball season arrived, anything above the waist was fair ball, so to speak. The evenings were so abbreviated, what with Joe Bob's having to be in bed by ten, alone, that we didn't waste any time. We would drive directly to our parking spot, which by now had been appropriated by the rest of the Hullsport High football, basketball, and baseball teams and was littered with used condoms and empty beer cans. We would take up where we had left off the previous evening, which by this time involved some hasty and perfunctory kissing and squeezing and nibbling. Then Joe Bob would dutifully knead my breasts through my uniform jacket and padded bra, as though he were a housewife poking plums to determine their ripeness. Then he would efficiently unstrap his wrist weights and lay them side by side on his dashboard. Next, he would unbutton and remove my jacket, and, amid much stroking and sighing, manage adroitly to unhook my Never-Tell and remove it.

There we would sit in Sparkplug, me undressed to my waist, but with my lap covered and my hands folded neatly and my back straight and my knees primly together, like a patient awaiting a pelvic exam. Joe Bob would suck away at my nipples while I tried to decide what to do with my hands to indicate my continuing involvement in the project. Sometimes I would run one hand over his lowered scrub brush head or caress his stove-in neck, while running the other hand up and down the muscular ridges of his back. Other times, I'd grab one of his thighs midway up and squeeze it, to transmit restrained passion without signaling any willingness to yield further favors. After all, we were only dating. It wasn't as though we were steadies. I had my reputation to think of.

One particular night during baseball season, Joe Bob had just hit a home run—in the last of the ninth with the bases filled and two men out, naturally—to snatch victory from the jaws of defeat. I had ascended to new heights in the realm of flag swinging, having successfully executed the nearly impossible feat of tossing the flag high into the air in end-over-end swirls and then catching it, without the flag's becoming wrapped around its staff. No other Hullsport High flag swinger, to my knowledge, had ever before performed this routine for public consumption.

When we reached our parking spot, Joe Bob turned to me in the dark and said softly, "Ginny, will you wear my class ring?"

Would I wear his ring? Would Elizabeth Taylor wear the Hope diamond? "Oh yes, Joe Bob, *yes!*"

He handed it to me. It was huge—gilded shanks and setting, with a black onyx in the middle. Inside, etched in the shank, were his initials—J.B.S. I put the ring on my thumb, but there was still room for another finger or two. Joe Bob took out his Juicy Fruit and stuck it on the dashboard, and enfolded me in his bulging arms. Hullsport High tradition required that each new material commitment between a couple signal a new array of carnal privileges. We both knew, by the instinct that tells birds when to migrate and where, that the unexplored territories below the waist were now up for grabs. In the dim light of the quarter moon, I could see a tear squeezing out from under one of Joe Bob's closed eyelids.

"I'm so happy, Joe Bob," I whispered.

"Do whut?"

"Happy," I repeated loudly. "I'm happy."

"Oh, yeah, me too."

That out of the way, he whipped off his button-down-collar Gant shirt. There they were—the furry deltoids of the body beautiful of Hullsport High. And they were *mine* now, to do with as I willed. He unstrapped his wrist weights and laid them on the dashboard alongside his Juicy Fruit. Then he unbuttoned the twelve gold embossed buttons of my jacket and helped me out of it, unhooked my bra, and tossed them both into the back. We embraced and, for the first time, felt the delicious warmth of our bare chests joined, his bulging pectoral muscles dwarfing my breasts into obscurity without the assistance of my Never-Tell. A feathery arrow of pubic hair ran down his firm stomach to his navel and disappeared tantalizingly behind his belt. We leaned apart so that my stiffening nipples just touched his chest, and then we moved sideways in opposite directions, playfully, so that my nipples brushed his chest and got tangled up in his mat of blond hair.

Then slowly, cautiously, expecting to be stopped, he slid his famous catching hand up under the leg of my gray twill shorts, while his equally fabled pitching hand pulled me tightly to him. His fingers sallied forth into the mysterious folds of the dampening nylon crotch of my panties and dallied there with feigned casualness. Then, in one of the lightning-quick plays he was so renowned for on the athletic fields, one of his fingers skirted the elastic and buried itself in me like Jack Horner's thumb in a Christmas pudding.

We both sat immobile, startled by the success of his venture and uncertain of the next way station in our journey together toward the Golgotha of sexual intercourse. We looked at each other, perplexed. With my middle finger, I twirled Joe Bob's ring, the token of my continued respectability, on my thumb.

We sat motionless for a couple of minutes, uncertain of how to disentangle ourselves and proceed, just as we had sat with interminably interlocked hands that first night at the Family Drive-In. He couldn't remove his finger because he didn't want to yield any yardage gained. On the other hand, he didn't know exactly what to do with the finger now that it had achieved its much vaunted destination. He wiggled it tentatively. I smiled fondly at him, as much in the dark as he. He finally leaned his head over and simultaneously sucked a nipple and ground his finger around in me for a while.

Nor did I know where to position my hands for maximum effect. Displaying a woeful lack of imagination, I tried putting one on his hand in my crotch. With my other hand I caressed his bristly head. Without looking up, he took my hand, the one on his, and placed it on the lump of his fly, which lump I had by now astutely concluded was not a hernia after all, but was rather something infinitely more integral to our undertaking.

He stopped sucking long enough to gasp, "Rub it!" Delighted to have an apparently meaningful task to perform, I devoted all my heretofore unchanneled enthusiasm to rubbing the lump, like Aladdin his lamp. By now our various limbs were tangled up like the Laocoön in my Latin II textbook; but rather than being frozen in stone for all eternity, the frieze composed of Joe Bob and me sprawled panting across the front seat of Sparkplug was heaving and trembling and shuddering.

Suddenly Joe Bob sat bolt upright, his finger popping out of me like a cork out of a champagne bottle; the elastic of my pants leg snapped with nearly enough force to sever my femoral artery. The hard lump under my hand was going all soft and squishy.

"What's *wrong?*" I asked in horror. "Have I done something wrong?"

"Trainin!" Joe Bob moaned, looking at his watch. "Coach'll kill me! It's almost eleven!" I pictured him turning into a medicine ball at the stroke of eleven.

"How would Coach know?" I asked, starting to feel faintly resentful.

"He cruises our houses to see if our cars are in and our bedroom lights off," he gasped, pulling on his shirt and strapping on his wrist weights.

"What will he do to you?"

"He might take me off the startin line-up for the next game," he said grimly, throwing Sparkplug into reverse and scratching out backwards as I scrambled into my Never-Tell.

"He *couldn't.* You're the star."

He shifted into first, and we tore down the dirt road in a cloud of condoms and clattering beer cans, like newlyweds making their honeymoon getaway. "*Especially* me. To prove that even Joe Bob Sparks can't get away with violatin trainin."

On the drive to my house, he calmed down somewhat; and by the time he let me out in front of the magnolia thicket, he was sniffing his middle finger wistfully and had an agonized look on his face.

"What's wrong?" I asked.

"Blue balls," he moaned.

"Do *what?*" He roared off.

I walked up the driveway, Joe Bob's ring dangling from my thumb and my cunt tingling from all the unaccustomed attention. Blue balls?

Having turned out the lights, I went upstairs. On the way up, I glanced into the hall mirror and noted with satisfaction that my uniform jacket was misbuttoned and that my lipstick was smeared around my mouth in a large O like a circus clown, that wisps of hair had freed themselves from my pony tail and hung lasciviously in my eyes and that my eye shadow was smeared raccoon-fashion.

The Major was sitting on the end of my bed in his gold terry cloth bathrobe. As I skulked in, he studied my disheveled appearance with interest. "You're late," he pointed out pleasantly.

"Yes," I agreed, thinking fast. "We went to the Dew Drop after the game, but it was so crowded that it took us *hours* to get Joe Bob his milk."

"Uh-huh." Then, in the bland understatement that was the Major's specialty, he asked, "Have you been letting Joe Bob kiss you?"

I blushed and said with noncommittal reproof, "Oh, *Father!*" Then I held up Joe Bob's ring as a diversionary tactic and said brightly, "We're going steady."

"What the hell does *that* mean?"

"Well, it means, uh, that we like each other a lot. And, uh, that we aren't dating anyone else."

He stood up and stalked toward the door. "Well, if you want to spend your life married to a shoe salesman, that's your business. After all, maybe the girl's a foot fetishist," he muttered under his breath.

"Who said anything about marriage?"

"Well, from the looks of you tonight, my dear child, you'd better file marriage away in the back of your mind as a potential necessity."

I scowled at him. The idea! Reducing the romance of the decade, between the Hullsport Pirate Little All-American running back and the Hullsport High flag swinger, to the level of mere physical function! "Besides, he isn't going to *be* a shoe salesman. He's going to be a coach. And what's *wrong* with being a shoe salesman? It sure beats making bombs, or whatever you do at that filthy place of yours."

Aha! A hit! "Those 'bombs,' as you call them, my dear young lady, *happen* to be what's keeping you in your unending supply of Villager blouses. Or out of them, as it appears at the moment."

Even then I suspected that more was at stake here than my passion for the ever-muscular Joe Bob Sparks. The Major and I were enacting the ancient sexual drama in which a daughter makes the break with her father, her true love since infancy, by taking a man her own age. The script had been written centuries ago, and we were merely stepping into the parts required of us. Women typically married men very much like their fathers. So said the Psychology 101 text at Worthley, at any rate. If a woman chose someone *unlike* her father, it was a rejection of him, consciously or not. Well, there could be no one *less* like the suave haughty Major than Joe Bob Sparks. Unless it was Clem Cloyd, who entered the picture later as a potential son-in-law for the poor beleaguered Major. No youthful romance was ever as pure and innocent as it seemed. The choice of partners was always a commentary on one or both parents on each side.

"I didn't *ask* to be born!" I informed the Major, in response to his pomposity about paying me my clothing allowance.

"Oh, go ahead and wreck your life!" He stomped from the room. Reconsidering, he paused at the door and explained wearily, "You've *got* to get away from Hullsport, Ginny. You're going to college in the North if I have to hogtie you and ship you up there. You're *not* one of these people, and you can return only when you've learned that."

"What *am* I then?" I shrieked. "*You're* not one of them maybe. But *I am!* This is *my* home!"

He shook his head, perplexed, and closed the door behind him. Then he opened it and said, "I don't want to alarm you unnecessarily, Virginia. But you *are* aware, I trust, that lovers' lanes attract psychopaths of all kinds."

The news that Joe Bob and I were going steady spread around school like the plague. Friends kept coming up the next day to look at the black onyx ring. I'd dripped almost an entire candle behind the stone to make the ring fit. It stuck out an inch and weighted my arm down as I walked, just as Joe Bob's wrist weights did his. If I had slugged someone with that fist, my unfortunate victim would have had the crest of Hullsport Regional High School embossed on his jaw for life, like the Phantom's victims in the funny pages.

At lunchtime as all we students lounged in the fold-out seats in the gym idly watching intramural basketball games, Joe Bob's and my friends cheered in unison, "Hi, Ginny! Yay, Sparks! Hi yay! Ginny, Sparks!" All the girls cheered shrilly. The boys whistled with their fingers and stomped their feet and hooted knowingly and yelled to Joe Bob, "Gettin much, Sparky?" Joe Bob smiled an enigmatic smile and raised our clasped hands high into the air in a victory salute like a prizefighter and the referee. We were now one of the officially established couples at Hullsport High.

That afternoon in study hall, as I sat distractedly sketching breasts in the margin of my Latin notebook, the boy behind me dropped a note in my lap. It was in Joe Bob's childlike printing: "Meet me in the darkroom at 2:25."

At 2:22, I went to the study hall teacher's desk and requested a bathroom pass. The teacher this period happened to be Coach Bicknell, a huge muscled man in his forties with a gunboat gray crew cut and squinty eyes, and the inevitable non-neck. His massive chest and shoulders narrowed to a slim waist and hips, so that his silhouette would have looked like an ice cream cone with arms, and with a cherry on top of the scoop for a head.

"Ah want you back here in *five* minutes," he growled, narrowing his eyes to ominous slits. "Ah don't want any smokin in there."

"But I don't smoke."

"That's what you *all* say."

"But I *don't.*" Admittedly and inevitably, I *had* smoked, sneaking here and there for those stolen puffs, made doubly delicious by being prohibited by every adult in sight. But with Joe Bob in training, it seemed simpler just to go along with his perverted notions of bodily well-being.

"Don't get smart with *me.*" I looked at him in amazement. He'd never liked me. In fact, he'd never been that crazy about *any* of the girls at school, and especially not the ones who dated his athletes. But he'd never before unleashed unveiled hostility on me, the daughter of Major Babcock.

Playing it safe, I said briskly, "Yes, *sir.*" And took my pass and walked out.

The darkroom belonged to the Camera Club but was in constant use for assignations of all sorts. It was double-locked, but there were some two dozen copies of the keys floating around school. I knocked softly. The door opened slightly. Joe Bob reached out and pulled me into the dark.

It was so unutterably black that I couldn't even see his Juicy Fruit-stained teeth as he talked.

"What's up?" I asked, as he pinned me against the door. His erection poked at me through his chinos as he covered my face with wet kisses.

"It's *awful,*" he wailed.

"*What* is?"

"Coach has grounded me for bein out after curfew last night. I'm not startin in next week's game. And he says I shouldn't see you any more until after track season."

"You're *kidding!*"

"I wish I were." We held each other tightly, engulfed in waves of self-pity.

"Oh, Joe Bob, what can we *do?*" I moaned with a grimace copied from Vivien Leigh in *Gone With the Wind.*

"He says you're ruinin me. He says he doesn't understand what I see in you."

"Oh *yeah?*" I snarled, with a sneer copied from Elvis Presley in *Bikini Beach Party.*

"He says you're out to sap my strength."

"He *does,* does he? Are you going to take that from him?"

"But what if he's right? You *know* that if I don't play well this year, I won't get no scholarship offers next year. And if I don't go to college, I can't coach."

I pondered life as the wife of an unhappy Hullsport shoe salesman and balked. "We're no good for each other, Joe Bob. Coach and the Major are right."

"Your *father?* What does *he* have to do with it?"

"He was waiting up when I got in last night. He said I was wasting my time on you."

"Oh *yeah?* Are you going to *take* that from him?"

"But what if he's right?" I asked miserably, thinking of the attractions of a college career in Boston.

"Look, ain't no coach tellin Joe Bob Sparks how to run his life. Not your father neither. Borrow your father's car tonight. Tell him you're going to the library or somethin. Pick me up at the end of my block at seven."

"Okay," I purred. We held each other with the devotion of the thwarted. Then, to be sure that the ground he had gained last night was still his, he reached down and ran his hand up my skirt. This time, for variety, he pulled down the top of my panties and placed his pitching hand over my pubes and dipped his finger in and out of me, like testing bath water prior to plunging in. His wrist weight was cold against my pubic bone.

"I've got to get back," I informed him regretfully. "Coach has it in for me today. Now I understand why."

"Do whut?" Joe Bob muttered distractedly.

"Coach. He told me to be back in five minutes. I have a bathroom pass."

" Oh. Well, see you tonight," he whispered as he let me out the door, his crazy grin taking a lascivious turn.

That night, ensconced in the Major's black Mercedes with his gilded initials on each front door, I pulled over to the curb at the corner of Joe Bob's block in the Sewanee Acres development. He was crouched behind some boxwood, glancing around furtively. He hopped in quickly.

"Where to?" I asked, as Joe Bob lay down on the front seat so that he couldn't be seen. "Our spot?"

"No," he whispered. "Out the river road. I'll tell you where to turn."

We rode in silence, parallel to the murky river, the Major's poison factory flashing past on the opposite bank. I kept glancing in the rear-view mirror to see if we were being tailed by Coach. "Where do your parents think you are?" I asked.

"I said I was meetin Dole down at the Dew Drop."

"Did you warn Doyle to cover for you?"

"Yeah."

"Can you trust him? Do you think he might turn you in to Coach?" Doyle, Joe Bob's best friend, was the other halfback, the other forward, and the shortstop for the various Hullsport Pirate teams. Their friendship was heavily tainted with competition.

"Do *whut?* Dole? Well, I just *got* to trust him. It's the only way I can see to do it." He rose up carefully until his eyes were at the level of the car window ledge. "Second left," he whispered.

As we headed down an unfamiliar dirt road, Joe Bob sat up and straightened out his maroon and gray letter jacket and sighed with relief. The road was rutted, but the Major's expensive car floated along oblivious.

"Left here," Joe Bob said in his normal voice, the hushed mumble a doctor would use to discuss the prognosis of a terminal patient with the patient's family. The road dwindled to a muddy turn-around, which was littered liberally with the inevitable used condoms and empty beer cans. I shut off the lights and the motor. As I looked up from the dashboard, I saw the Crockett River before me, framed by low-hanging trees.

"This is *beautiful*," I informed him, connoisseur of parking spots that I had become in recent months. I had to hand it to Joe Bob: He knew how to pick scenic settings for our indiscretions. "Why haven't you brought me here before?"

"Do whut?"

"How do you know about this place?" I was picturing other girls than me sprawled half-dressed, or worse, across the front seat of Sparkplug.

He shrugged and grinned and chomped furiously on his Juicy Fruit. "Well, I like the other one better. Since you and me found it together. This one here gets pretty crowded later on at night." He unsnapped his letter jacket slowly, slipped it off and dropped it into the back floor. "Let's get in back," he suggested. "Don't have to wrap yoursef around the gear shift." He grinned at me dementedly.

To make a long story short, in time, we were both completely undressed, our modish outfits lying in a heap on the back floor. Inspired by the excess space the Mercedes back seat offered over the front seat of Sparkplug, I was lying spread-eagle on the leather seat. Joe Bob was kneeling between my legs; his miraculous erection, finally freed, pointed at my nose as he rifled his chino pockets with desperation.

Finally, in triumph, he dropped his chinos and held up a small foil packet. I had seen the packet, or an identical one, before when I had taken money from his wallet to pay for his milk one night at the Dew Drop while he was in the men's room. But I was only just now beginning to grasp its significance: Its contents would be the only thing standing between me and early motherhood. I chewed my lower lip nervously. Joe Bob tore off one end of the packet and began pulling the balloonlike object onto himself, like a housewife donning rubber gloves prior to washing the dishes. Something slimy dripped onto my stomach.

When it came right down to it, I wasn't absolutely certain that this was what I'd had in mind all these months. French kissing—yes. Heavy petting—certainly. Finger fucking—by all means. But the actual Act itself—*that* was perhaps carrying things too far. These being the days when one screw tended to commit you for life, college in Boston was suddenly seeming like a lot to sacrifice, even to as true a love as Joe Bob's and mine so obviously was. After all, girls dropped out of Hullsport High every day to go off and give birth to illegitimate babies. And what about respect? Would Joe Bob still respect me if I went all the way with him, I asked myself as I raised my head and looked up at him where he knelt between my legs struggling with his rubber. Would I become like my old grade-school chum, Maxine Pruitt, who hung out with Clem Cloyd and his ratty crew at the Bloody Bucket, and whom Joe Bob and his friends referred to with snickers as "Do-It" Pruitt? And what about training? What had Brother Buck said about fornication? Flee fornication, he had instructed the Teen Team for Jesus, of which Joe Bob was president. I had hoped and expected to be swept away at a time like this beyond all possible rational objections. It wasn't happening. My brain was churning out objections at an incredible clip.

Resolutely, I propped myself up on my elbows and said, "Joe Bob, wait a minute. Let's discuss this."

"Do *whut?*" he gasped. "I never took you for a cock tease, Ginny."

A car pulled up behind us. "Oh no," I groaned. This was it. The lovers' lane psychopath the Major had warned me about had arrived. Almost more upsetting than the prospect of my impending rape and mutilation was the necessity of acknowledging that, once again, the Major had been right.

A whirling light bathed the trees and the swift river in eerie flashes of red.

"Oh God," Joe Bob moaned, gallantly snatching up his jacket from the floor and tossing it to me as I scrambled to a sitting position. Joe Bob grabbed for himself the first thing he came to in our tangled pile of clothes, which was my navy blue wraparound skirt. He threw it around his waist just as two flashlight beams swept through the car. His sheathed erection, though wilting fast, still poked my skirt out like a suspended pup tent. He opened the door and climbed out bravely.

One of the patrolmen shone his flashlight into Joe Bob's anguished face. "Well, well, if it in'nt ole Joe Bob Sparks hissef! Sorry to interrupt your ball game there, feller!" He guffawed. The other trooper guffawed too.

"Don't you guys have somethin better to do?" Joe Bob asked.

The other patrolman flashed his light down Joe Bob's massive trunk and lingered in the area of my skirt. "That looks real sweet, Sparks," he said with a grin.

"Thanks. Look, give a fella a break, will ya?"

"Major Babcock's daughter!" the first one gloated, apparently recognizing the initialed car, since I was huddled cravenly out of sight in the corner of the back seat, my knees drawn up to my chest and Joe Bob's jacket snapped around the whole package.

"Parkin's not against the law."

"Here it happens to be," the second one countered. "Hit's private property. And look at the mess you punks has made of it." He waved his flashlighted arm at the layer of debris.

"Look," said the first one, "we're just issuin you a warnin this time. Get yoursef dressed and go find someplace that ain't private property for this stuff. But as a piece of personal advice, Sparks, do like Coach tells you.''

Joe Bob's head snapped to attention. "Do *whut?* Did *he* send you? How did he know?" Joe Bob's babyish voice was dripping with fear.

"Naw, he didn't send us," the first patrolman assured him. "But hell, son. You're livin in a goddam fishbowl. Everbody in town knows you've done been grounded. We've got us a stake in you boys. The whole town's ridin on you. Coach wins games. If Coach says be in bed by ten, boy, and don't mess around with the women, you damn well better do it.''

"Yeah, okay.''

The patrolmen got back in their cruiser and crept off on their mission of crippling young sex lives. Joe Bob climbed in and sat back, his feet planted well apart and his legs spread so that the wrap-around skirt fell open across his lap. His cock was all shriveled and the condom hung on it loosely. I sat silent in my corner, encased in the letter jacket. After a couple of minutes, Joe Bob started groaning.

"What's wrong?''

"Blue balls," he whimpered.

"Do *what?*''

"Blue balls.''

"What *are* blue balls?''

"It's when you get all worked up but don't come," he explained through gritted teeth. I realize now that Joe Bob was missing his calling by pursuing coaching rather than the acting profession.

"Do what? Isn't there anything you can do about it?''

He looked up with a sly expression.

"The cops said to get dressed and move on," I reminded him quickly.

"We will," he assured me, rolling off the rubber and tossing it out the window. He scooted across the seat and took my arm. My hand was lost up the giant sleeve of his jacket. He rolled up the sleeve until my hand appeared. He took it and placed it on his penis. "Rub it, please," he begged.

I toyed with it half-heartedly, fighting the instinctive aversion that made me wonder during Psychology 101 at Worthley about the validity of penis envy. But God knows, I didn't want to be responsible for blue balls, whatever they might be. All my repressed Florence Nightingale tendencies flooded me with an aching concern for poor suffering Joe Bob, tormented because of his love for me. In addition,

I didn't want it to get around school that I was a "cock tease"—any more than I relished the prospect of the nickname "Do-It" Babcock. What was I to do, other than to stay home alone on Saturday nights while all the other girls in town administered hand jobs at the drive-in? As I grappled with this moral dilemma, wonder of wonders, the bundle of tissue in my hand began swelling. I knew instantly that I'd made a bad mistake.

Joe Bob reached up under his jacket and inserted a finger between my legs. With his free hand, he instructed mine in how to move back and forth on him. It was similar to milking a cow, which Clem Cloyd had taught me to do years before. There we sat, me engulfed in his letter jacket, my chin resting on my knees; and him, sprawled next to me in my wrap-around skirt, his huge furry chest bare, his head against the seat back, and his eyes closed. Our hands moved with the coordination of clockworks. I suppressed a yawn and pondered the topic of whether I even *wanted* to go to college, much less in Boston. After all, I could probably get a majorette scholarship to UT. . . .

Joe Bob was twitching and gasping. He collapsed in a limp heap next to me, his finger slipping slowly out out of me. I looked down at him with concern. Was he a closet epileptic or what? "Are you okay?" He lay there panting, without answering. I put my hand on his chest. His heart was beating frenziedly. This was just what I needed—to have Joe Bob Sparks have a heart attack, nude, in the back seat of the Major's Mercedes on a remote dirt road. I decided, if he *had* had a heart attack, just to throw myself into the Crockett and be done with it.

Gingerly I reached over and lifted one of his eyelids, and found myself staring at his eyeball. "What are you doin?" he inquired languidly.

"Are you all right?"

"Do whut?"

Eventually we sat up and sorted out our clothes. When he handed me my skirt, I discovered a damp stain down one side.

"Sperm," he said with his idiotic smile.

"Aargh!" I held the skirt away from myself between two fingers. My prior knowledge of sperm was based on an animated Walt Disney film shown in Physical Education class in eighth grade, in which wicked Sammy Sperm had tried to corner luscious Ellie Ovum, the sweet farm girl newly arrived in the Big Womb. I dropped my skirt onto the seat and began beating the spot with my fists. "Kill them!"

Joe Bob grinned dementedly, thinking I was trying to be funny. The truth was, I feared sperm almost as much as I feared Communists.

"You look good in my jacket," he said thoughtfully. "Will you wear it?" Unexpected delight at this, my reward for performing the unappetizing task of jerking him off, swept over me. The wearing of one's steady's letter jacket at Hullsport High was the ultimate in commitment, far more binding than a simple exchange of rings. Naturally, Joe Bob's jacket was the most remarkable one in the entire school, covered as it was with patches in the shape of basketballs and winged feet and crossed baseball bats and footballs, in addition to several large H's. It looked like the rear window of a Winnebago, with stickers from every state.

I threw the floppy jacket arms around his neck and hugged him. Seeing an opening, he charged into it, like the skilled tailback that he was, pinning me under him on the seat and reaching up under the jacket to twist one of my nipples as though tuning a radio.

"Training," I whispered in his ear. He sat up quickly and started pulling on clothes.

The next evening after supper, the Major pulled me aside and said in a voice choked with anger, "Listen to me, Virginia. I will *not* have *my* daughter slinking around town like a cur bitch in heat. Do you understand me?"

"I don't know what you mean." With a father like the Major, who needed Big Brother? His information networks would have put the CIA to shame.

"The hell you don't! I'd think you'd at *least* have the sense not to go out for your whoring in the only black Mercedes in town."

"I wasn't—whoring." I wondered if, like doctors, highway patrolmen didn't have a set of professional ethics to prevent their discussing their clients with the public at large. "Joe Bob and I were—uh—talking."

"Like hell you were! Look, you give that idiot back that ridiculous bowling ball of a ring! And that jacket, too!" I had scarcely removed the letter jacket since Joe Bob had given it to me. The sleeves were a foot too long and I'd rolled them up. It hung almost to my knees. "You look like a goddam dwarf in it anyway. And if I *ever* catch you two together . . ."

"You'll *what?*"

"If you were lucky enough to have inherited your mother's brains and your father's survival instinct, you won't wait around to find out!"

I whirled around with a contemptuous toss of my pony tail. But, after all, it was the Major who was keeping me in tampons. So the next day I returned the jacket and the ring to Joe Bob in the darkroom. I clung to him, bathing us both in tears.

The next thing I knew, I was holding his stiff cock in one hand as he lurched back and forth in front of me. I felt as though I were an animal trainer trying to lead a recalcitrant baby elephant by the trunk. But at least Doyle and Joe Bob's other friends weren't snickering and calling me a cock tease—or a Do-It Pruitt—behind my back. The knife's edge of respectability made precarious walking.

"Joe Bob," I wailed, as he collapsed against the wall gasping, "I can't give you up. What can we *do?*"

And at that point, a romance which would soon have lost momentum, left to its own motive power, gained a dizzying impetus from the interference provided by Coach and the Major. In the gym at lunchtime I sat with my girl friends, who swooned with pity for Joe Bob and me. Joe Bob sat with his male friends on the opposite side of the basketball court, and he and I gazed torridly at each other throughout the remainder of the school year. And of course there were the five-minute grapplings in the darkroom three afternoons a week. I would get a bathroom pass, race to the darkroom, signal my arrival by a secret knock. Joe Bob would turn on the photography club timer to four minutes so that I wouldn't be late in getting back. Then I'd roll up my sleeves, unzip Joe Bob's chinos, and, like an efficient housewife, jerk him off in the sink. Then we'd exchange half a dozen muffled endearments until the timer went off, at which time I'd race gasping back to my seat in study hall as Coach eyed me with generalized disaffection.

With the arrival of summer, the darkroom was no longer accessible. Cruising Hull Street every night, Joe Bob and I would pass each other going in opposite directions, me with my friends and Joe Bob with his. The drivers of our respective cars would slow down reverently while we panted at each other. One night Joe Bob leaned halfway out the window of the car in which he was riding to hand me a crumpled note. He gazed fervently into my eyes and squeezed my hand as he did so.

It read: "Be on the corner of Hull and Broad tomorrow night at nine and watch for Doyle's Dodge."

The next night on the appointed street corner I waved as cars full of cruising classmates drifted by. Shortly I saw Doyle's maroon Dodge

—his mobile mattress he called it. Doyle was at the wheel and Doreen, his girl friend, was draped over him like a fox boa. No sign of Joe Bob.

Doyle pulled over to the curb. Doreen, her fluffy bouffant overpowering her small painted face, waved cheerfully. Doyle hopped out and walked around to the trunk. Leaning on it with one hand, he watched the passing cars.

"What's happening, Doyle? Where's Joe Bob?" He didn't answer and started whistling casually through his front teeth. A large black DeSoto crept by, and Doyle waved wildly with a big smile. It was Coach, scowling. His car slowed to a crawl as he passed us. Doyle leaned over at the waist so as to look in the window, and he waved again with just his fingers.

The window rolled down and a voice boomed out, "One hour and forty-eight minutes to summer curfew, Roller!"

"Right, Coach!"

When the DeSoto was well out of sight, Doyle glanced around furtively and opened the trunk lid. "Get in," he ordered out of the side of his mouth.

"Do *what?*"

"*Get in!*"

"I'll suffocate," I pointed out.

"No, you won't. Trust me, Ginny. I'm Joe Bob's best friend, ain't I? Get in. Quick."

So I climbed in and found myself lying next to Joe Bob as Doyle slammed shut the lid. "Well! What do you think of my plan?" Joe Bob demanded proudly.

"Not much," I assured him sourly, as I rearranged my limbs trying to get comfortable. He scooted over, his chest to my back, and wrapped his wrist-weighted arms around me, a hand molding each of my breasts.

"Is this any better?" He buried his mouth in my neck and nibbled my flesh. I decided to reserve comment.

The car was moving fast now. "Where are we going?"

"You'll see," he answered mysteriously. I felt as though I'd been shanghaied into white slavery, which would undoubtedly require that I spend my days jerking off unending lines of horny young men. I could feel Joe Bob's inevitable hard-on prodding my kidney like a gangster's revolver.

"Oh, all *right!*" I reached behind me, unzipped his chinos, and went to work with a backhand stroke. In the ensuing months, I mastered backhand, forehand, overhand, underhand, according to our positions in the cramped enclosure. Anything to postpone the issue of intercourse, which loomed over me as had dust clouds from the approaching Huns over Rome in its last days.

After a while, we heard a car door slam. The lid of the trunk opened and Doyle hissed, "Quick, Sparks. Get out." We scrambled out, and Joe Bob dragged me around to the car door and onto the floor of the back seat while Doyle glanced around frantically. Inside the car, a speaker was blaring, and I realized that we were at the drive-in. We scooted cautiously up onto the seat, slouching so that our heads were below the window sills.

Doreen in the front seat swiveled her bouffant around and offered, "You want me to turn down this seat so's you can see?"

"Yeah, great," Joe Bob said. As she leaned over from the passenger side, I noticed that she was already stripped down to her bra on top. "Hey, thanks for this, Doreen," Joe Bob added. "I know it's not so great doublin to the drive-in."

"Oh Lord, Sparky, we're just real *thrilled* to hep you all out. Shoot, you'd do the same for Dole and me."

Doyle let himself in the passenger-side door. The movie was *The Ten Commandments*. Mixed with the dialogue were various sighs and gasps and sucking sounds from the front seat, and blasts from car horns throughout the parking area as, in keeping with Hullsport High tradition, couples signaled that they'd gone all the way.

At a point in the movie at which a slave woman was about to be crushed on the pyramid construction site by a ten-ton block of stone, the front seat back slammed up abruptly. Joe Bob and I sat up straight so as to be able to see the fate of the unfortunate slave woman. It became apparent that a well-timed miracle would save her; the camera cut to a scene at the foot of a mountain, where the frenzied Israelites were dancing around the golden calf. We glanced down into the front seat and discovered Doyle and Doreen prostrate on it. Doyle's bare hips were pounding up and down, flashing white in the light from the screen.

Joe Bob and I looked quickly out the window, pretending not to notice anything out of the ordinary. Simultaneously, we hit the floor like soldiers throwing themselves into trenches during an enemy shelling. By the flickering light from the screen, where the Israelites were still busy with their revelry, we had seen the profile of Coach, a hand bringing popcorn from a cardboard carton to his mouth. He sat in his big black DeSoto two cars away.

Waiting discreetly until the thrashing in the front seat had ceased, and until Doyle had tooted the horn with his foot to indicate to his teammates that he had scored, Joe Bob whispered urgently through the space between the seat backs, "Dole! Dole! It's Coach! Two cars down!"

"Do whut? Oh Christ! He's everwhere. And it's eleven o'clock." Clothes swirled like autumn leaves, front seat and back.

Doyle, on his knees in front, leaned over and said, "I don't think we can get you back in the trunk with Coach there. You'll have to lie on the floor and pray." Doyle spread a blanket over us, tucking it in. It smelled of stale semen, an odor I was by now thoroughly acquainted with.

This arrangement continued into the next school year. Joe Bob and I would see each other up close three times a week for five minutes in the darkroom, and a couple of hours every other week in the trunk of Doyle's Dodge. Otherwise, we pined for each other across vast acres of bleachers in the gym at lunch-time, and from neighboring cars at night.

Sometimes as Teen Team for Jesus officers we were slated to read devotions together over the public address system, the microphone for which was located in a small soundproofed studio. It opened off the principal's office and was locked from inside when announcements were in progress.

" 'For this is the will of God, even your sanctification, that ye should abstain from fornication,' " Joe Bob would read from the devotion sheet mailed out by the Teen Team Headquarters in Birmingham, undressing me with his eyes.

" 'That every one of you should know how to possess his vessel in sanctification and honor, not in the lust of concupiscence,' " I would respond, watching his cock stirring against his chino leg.

" 'For God hath not called us unto uncleanness, but unto holiness,' " Joe Bob would continue through the microphone. " 'But I say unto you that every one that looketh on a woman to lust after her hath committed adultery with her already.' "

" 'Fornication and all uncleanness, or covetousness, let it not be once named among you, as becometh saints,' " I would instruct over the airways of Hullsport High as Joe Bob grabbed my breasts with his huge mittlike hands and buried his face in my neck. " 'For this ye know, that no whoremonger, nor unclean person hath any inheritance in the kingdom of Christ and of God . . .' " I would feel his erection prodding my back as the Bible trembled in my hopelessly sin-stained hands. " '. . .because of these things cometh the wrath of God upon the children of disobedience,' " I would conclude with a gasp, as his hands fought their way into the secret folds of my soul's sanctuary.

And of course Joe Bob and I would catch glimpses of each other at ball games—me in my gray twill shorts and maroon uniform jacket, twirling my flag; and Joe Bob in his various Hullsport Pirate uniforms. I would watch with helpless fury as Coach patted Joe Bob on his ass when sending him into games, as he threw his arm around Joe Bob's shoulders when he called him out, as he personally took the towel from the water boy and gently dabbed the sweat from Joe Bob's upper lip and temples.

My considerable spare time I spent collecting bottle caps from Nehi soft drinks at area vending machines. The local radio station was sponsoring a contest to determine the most popular high school athlete within its listening range. Each bottle cap from a Nehi grape or orange drink counted as one vote. I had collected 41,212 bottle caps for Joe Bob. Doreen had submitted 35,080 for Doyle, when she reminded me of how generous she and Doyle had been to Joe Bob and me over the past months. So I stopped collecting bottle caps and allowed Doyle to steal the title of most popular athlete, with 42,683 votes. Although the entire school knew that it was a lie, that Joe Bob Sparks, not Doyle Roller, was in fact most popular, that back-seat politics alone had swung the election.

The Major was getting suspicious. "Why don't you ever go out on dates anymore?"

"No one asks me."

"Why not?"

"I guess they don't want to."

"Or maybe they don't want to horn in on Joe Bob?" he suggested unpleasantly.

"I gave back his ring and his jacket as I was instructed," I shot back haughtily. But I knew I had to come up with some dates to throw the Major off the scent. For the time being, he had only his suspicions, but knowing how he operated, he would doubtless turn up some concrete proof before long unless I diverted him. Admittedly, I had an ulterior motive for selecting my former dear friend Clem Cloyd, son of the Major's tenant farmer, for my escort in deceit: I intended to illustrate to the Major that, out of the male material available to me, Joe Bob wasn't such a disaster after all. Joe Bob was delighted with the plan because Clem seemed such flimsy competition as not even to merit the title. Never did it occur to any of us that I might actually come to prefer Clem Cloyd, crippled hood-about-town, to Joe Bob Sparks.

4

Saturday, June 24

□

As Ginny sat in the Jeep overlooking the athletic fields of Hullsport High, Joe Bob Sparks trotted toward her from the track. His once-firm belly was somewhat flabby. He waved wildly. She waved back. Her time sense, shaky and unreliable in the best of times, was temporarily stunned. Past had inundated present. She felt she should be dressed in her by now moth-riddled flag swinger outfit. She looked down, perplexed, at her patchwork peasant dress and combat boots.

She was annoyed with her body. Ten years had intervened since she'd last seen Joe Bob, but even so, given license, it would have raced over and flung itself down on the ground in front of him. She realized with dismay that the patterns of activity set up the first time you did anything could recur to plague you for the rest of your life. Like the many times she had found herself saying automatically to Wendy, "Don't talk with your mouth full." And not because she particularly cared, but because that was what her own mother had told her time and again. The phrase was wired into her circuits. She had held and kissed Clem and Eddie and Ira in substantially the same way that Joe Bob had taught her to hold and kiss him. And many of her subsequent failures at lovemaking were directly traceable to her unfortunate formative experiences with Joe Bob and with Clem.

"Say hey!" Joe Bob said, his face contorted by his crazy grin, his front teeth munching Juicy Fruit, possibly the same wad from ten years ago. "Knew it couldn't be your mother sittin up here watchin us for so long."

"Nope, it's not," Ginny agreed, suddenly as tongue-tied as a schoolgirl.

"How ya doin?" He placed both wrist-weighted hands on the roof-frame bar as though he were about to push the Jeep over on its side and looked down at her through his arms. He wore a stop watch around his neck; it hung spiraling in the air between his furry chest and Ginny's face.

"Okay." She decided not to itemize for the time being the various ways in which she wasn't okay. "How about you?"

"Great. Just great. You know I'm the coach here now?"

"I heard. You're doing well, I also heard."

"Yeah, not bad."

Their conversation, scant even at the peak of their romance, was about to exhaust itself. Ginny searched her mind for topics. The weather?

"You wanna watch that blond fella," Joe Bob said proudly, pointing toward the track at a large handsome boy with long blond hair tamed with a headband.

"He looks good."

"You'll be hearin his name—Billy Barnes. He's the finest athlete I've coached."

Ginny watched Billy Barnes with interest as he jogged along, chest out and arms high.

"Hey!" Joe Bob said with sudden inspiration. "You know you even *sound* like a Yankee now?"

"Do I?" Ginny asked with horror. "I'm sorry."

"Do whut?"

"Well, it's not necessarily something I'd have chosen to have happen to me." She was looking up at him but kept having to glance away because the dangling stop watch was exercising a hypnotic effect. Feeling her eyelids growing heavy, she blinked several times.

"It's not so bad."

"Good."

"I read in the paper you got married up north a while back. On a pond in the middle of winter or somethin?"

"Yeah, my husband sells snow machines. You know what snow machines are? Yeah. So when we decided to get married, he wanted to have the ceremony on a beaver pond in the woods. To promote sales. *You* know."

Joe Bob was smiling politely. "You live up north now?"

Ginny pondered the question. Ira had kicked her out. Her mother was in the hospital and her childhood home was up for sale. Where could she be said to live? "Yeah. In Vermont," she replied, sidestepping.

"Vermont. Is that on the ocean?"

"No. It's on a big lake, though. There are lots of mountains. It looks like around here, only there's snow half the year. It's nice."

"Well, I'm real glad for you."

"Thanks."

"Did you know I married Doreen?" he inquired gingerly, Doreen being the first girl he'd taken up with after Ginny.

"Yes, I think I did hear that. That's great." Ginny was interested to note her nonreaction—no regret, no pleasure at the knowledge that Joe Bob was happily married. Nothing.

"Are you home for long?"

"I don't know. A couple of weeks, I guess."

"Why don't you stop over sometime? Doreen would just love to see you."

"Maybe I will."

"Good. Do that. We're over at Plantation Estates. Do you know where that's at?" Ginny nodded, recognizing the name of one of the new developments on the foothills across from the factory, and very near the parking spot Joe Bob and she had discovered early in their days together. "Well, got to get back to my boys. Nice to see you."

"Nice to see *you*. And see you later maybe." She watched the muscles rippling down his spine as he jogged off in his white gym shorts. It was a relief to discover that he apparently bore no lifelong scars or grudges from the shoddy way she'd handled the termination of their romance.

Holding his stop watch with his thumb on the trigger, Joe Bob yelled, "All right, you fellas! Haul ass! Let's *move* it!" He snapped the watch with an exaggerated downward movement. Instantaneously, the jouncing boys tensed up and shot off around the track as though pursued by hungry wolves. Billy Barnes, his long blond hair flowing out behind him, streaked along well in the lead like Joe Bob himself in his racing days.

Although you couldn't go home again, you couldn't really get away either. Without hesitation her fingers spun the radio dial to 1490, WHPT. The number was indelibly imprinted on her brain. As the radio blared country music, the Jeep shuddered and bucked up the dirt road that formed a boundary of her family's farm. Below her she could see the land, chopped into neat blocks as though some giant had whacked the valley with a huge butcher's cubing hammer. In an intriguing Mondrian pattern, some of the blocks were blue-green with alfalfa; others were dark brown bottom land newly planted to corn; some were pale green with tobacco seedlings; yet others were gullied red clay planted with dark green kudzu.

After a mile, she came to the Cloyds' tenant house, which was shingled in maroon asphalt tiles and clashed hideously with the orange-red clay of the front yard. Behind and below the house were the dark brown barns and white silos and spotless gray-cinderblock milking parlor. Lined up patiently outside the milking parlor were the Holsteins. She decided not to find Clem and announce her arrival. She'd stop later, when he wouldn't be too busy to chat.

What would Clem be like now that he had to be up at four A.M. for milking and could no longer prowl the streets on his Harley until early morning? Ginny had seen him at the Major's funeral—looking intensely uncomfortable in a dark suit and starched shirt. But she had only exchanged greetings with him and received his condolences. The Major had praised Clem's running of the farm. Some sort of metamorphosis must have occurred. The Clem Ginny had known could never have endured such a purposeful life.

On the radio the Piny Flats Gospel Quartet was just completing the jingle for White Rose Petroleum Jelly. Ginny smiled faintly recalling one of Clem's pranks which involved mixing sand into the White Rose in his brother Floyd's glove compartment.

She tooted the horn gently in the old tattoo her family had always used to indicate to the Cloyds that it was Babcocks going past to the cabin, not vandals and thieves. She drove on for another mile down the ever-narrowing dirt track through a woods of oak and sycamore and sassafras, redbud, poplar, and dogwood—a woods so different in composition from that behind Ira's house in Vermont, with its birch and ash and sugar maples, its dozen varieties of evergreen.

Stopping in front of the aluminum gate, she got out and unlocked the chain and drove the Jeep through. She descended the hill into the kudzu-lined bowl which housed the cabin and the pond. The cabin, built of chinked logs and covered by a dull green tin roof, had a patchwork history of occupation. It had been built around 1800 by the original settler of the farm—one of the motley breed of horse thieves and adventurers and deserters who had crossed the Blue Ridge Mountains, fleeing the civilized coastal regions of Virginia and North Carolina for the mountainous backwoods of Kentucky and Tennessee and southwest Virginia. By the time her grandfather, Mr. Zed, eluded his destiny as a coal miner and bought the farm, the cabin had been deserted for decades. Mr. Zed rebuilt the cabin and lived there with his wife and his small daughter, Ginny's mother, while his pseudo-antebellum mansion was under construction. When Ginny's mother and father were first married, they had lived in the cabin. Ginny herself had been born there. Shortly after Jim's birth, her grandparents had traded her parents the mansion for the cabin. After her grandmother's death, Mr. Zed had spent the rest of his life in virtual seclusion at the cabin, trying to figure out how to undo what he had spent his lifetime doing—founding Hullsport and establishing the factory.

Hence the kudzu. The kudzu vines served a double purpose: First, they held up the red clay sides of the bowl, which were always threatening to collapse into the pond; and secondly, they were an experiment with far-reaching implications in the deranged mind of the aging Mr. Zed. Kudzu was being highly touted at the time by the agricultural extension agents as the wonder vine of the century. Not only did its tenacious roots fix nitrogen in depleted soils; not only did the high-protein foliage make nutritious cattle fodder, *but* the plant spread so voraciously that only a few starter plants were required to take over an entire hillside.

It was to explore this promise that Ginny's grandfather, his scramble of long white hair whipping in the breeze, had carefully placed plants all around the bowl. In no time at all, every object in sight had been swallowed up—bushes, rocks, trees, fences, an old tobacco shed, rusted equipment parts. The vines were six feet deep in spots. Her grandfather had spent most of his twilight years, when his peers were engaged in shuffleboard tournaments at Sun City, Arizona, hacking away with a machete as the kudzu threatened to engulf his front lawn. But he hacked without malice, because he saw kudzu as his secret weapon. He would plant it, under cover of night, at selected spots around the factory and the town. The vines would silently take hold and begin their stealthy spread. Before Hullsporters were even aware of their existence, the grasping tendrils would choke out all life in the Model City. The site would be returned to Nature.

Word got around town to humor the old man as he crept around furtively planting, and scowling at the smokestacks and holding tanks, and shaking his fist at the encroaching superhighways and shopping malls and housing developments. "Senile," they would say, shaking their heads sadly. "Mr. Zed's done gone mental."

To Ginny, when she would walk up to visit him, he would shake his wild crop of tangled hair and say plaintively, "I never should of left Sow Gap, honey. I was a miner's son. I had no bidness tryin to be nothin else. Lord God, I done made a mess. Virginia, honey, don't you never try to be what you ain't."

"But what *am* I?" she'd ask him, reviewing her history of being born in a farm cabin in Virginia with a rural southern mother and an industrialist father from Boston, and with refugees from the coal mines for grandparents; growing up in a fake antebellum mansion in a factory town in the New South with a dairy farm out her back door; being christened "Virginia" by her mother in a burst of geographic chauvinism, and "Babcock" by her father, which name emblazoned the walls of a hall at Harvard. Being a human melting pot, to what one god—social or economic or geographic—was she to direct her scattered allegiances? How she had envied her friends at public meetings who could stand up and belt out a belligerent version of "Dixie"; on such occasions Ginny herself had sometimes remained seated, sometimes stood but not sung, sometimes sung halfheartedly.

Ginny had decided to put the issue of scattered allegiances behind her and start out fresh when she left Hullsport for Boston. And what had she done since? She'd married a Yankee businessman whose parents were Vermont farmers; she'd taken a hippy army deserter as a lover, if that was the right term for Hawk's relationship to her; she'd been living a suburban life in a small town in Vermont. Given her chance at transcendence, she'd merely re-created the muddle of loyalties she'd left Hullsport to escape.

She got out of the Jeep, lugging her pack and some groceries, and stumbled over dark green kudzu vines all the way to the cabin. The vines had taken over the stone steps and were partway up the log sides of the cabin. Someone hadn't been performing Mr. Zed's former duties with the machete. Stepping firmly on the vines that covered the steps, Ginny wrenched open the front door, walked in, and began opening shutters.

There were veils of cobwebs in the corners and a layer of dust over all horizontal surfaces. Otherwise, the place was relatively neat and inhabitable. She threw the switch on the fuse box, and the various motors in the cabin—the pump, the refrigerator, the hot water heater —-started humming on cue. After putting away the groceries in the small kitchen, cheery with its red gingham curtains and hooked rugs, she took a mop and knocked down the spiderwebs and dusted the dark wide-plank floors.

The last time she'd been here, a few months before her grandfather's death, her cousin Raymond had arrived for a visit. Raymond was tall and painfully thin with black bags under his eyes and hollows under his cheekbones. His coloring was almost albino, like a crayfish from an underground stream. He talked very little, mostly sat hunched over wheezing. Black lung from the mines, her grandfather explained later.

"I tell you the truth, Raymond," Mr. Zed said, shaking his bushy white head angrily, "I declare, I rue the day I left Sow Gap!"

"You're plumb crazy iffen you do," Raymond gasped. "Sow Gap like to have killed me. Can't do nothin no more cept sit around tryin to breathe."

"Hullsport is worse than them mines ever was," Mr. Zed insisted. "The air's ever bit as foul, and you can't fish the Crockett no more."

"Hit beats the hell out of them slag heaps up at Sow Gap. I bet you done forgot what hit's like in the pits, Zed. When the pumps don't work and you're stoopin over in a four-foot crawl space with water to your knees hot-wirin a 440 cable with maskin tape?"

"You know what that damn fool Yankee son-in-law of mine is makin at that factory, Raymond? Bombs, that's what. Roof falls is nothin compared to that. It's these Yankee Episcopalians—hell, they're gonna kill us all."

Ginny had returned to Miss Head in Boston the next week more intent than ever on a career as a scholar, so that she need have nothing more to do with either slag heaps or holding tanks. But then she had met Eddie Holzer.

Ginny took her grandfather's machete from over the huge stone fireplace. She went outside and hacked away at the kudzu, tearing it one vine at a time off the cabin and severing it at ground level with a rhythmic sweep of her arm, like Ira's practice golf swings. Gradually she chopped a no-man's land of several feet around the cabin. She was imagining as she swung what it would feel like to live in a rain forest in the Amazon Basin: If your perseverance flagged even briefly, you would disappear in the encroaching undergrowth. Soon she was splattered with pale green kudzu blood. The summer sun was hot; it hung midway between its noon position and the rim of the red clay bowl on the far side of the pond. It would set that evening behind the very spot on the ridge where Mr. Zed was buried, his headstone now swallowed up by the kudzu. Ginny walked down to the pond, stepping carefully through the tangled vines, whose relatives she had just executed. A layer of chartreuse scum covered at least a third of the pond surface. She threw off her peasant dress, unlaced her boots, and walked into the water, sinking up to her ankles in the squish on the pond bottom. Farther out, scum clinging to her pubic hair, she lowered herself into the water and began a stately breast stroke, sweeping scum out of her path as she went.

Crockett Valley Community Hospital was a boxy, unadorned three-story building of the same omnipresent red brick as the rest of the structures in Hullsport. The bricks themselves were made from the red clay of the surrounding countryside.

"It's very sensible," the Major used to assure Ginny during the Cold War when she would complain about the drab uniformity of the red brick factory. "If enemy bombers fly over, we'll be camouflaged. They won't be able to pick us out from the landscape."

"But why would anyone want to bomb *us*?" she'd demand indignantly.

The hospital lobby was jammed with people in various states of decay and collapse, most of them acutely anxious and suffering. It looked like the waiting room for extreme unction.

The volunteer receptionist, dressed in a pink and white striped pinafore, eyed uneasily Ginny's peasant dress and combat boots. "I'm Mrs. Babcock's daughter," Ginny said reassuringly. "Really I am."

"Room 307," the woman finally disclosed.

As Ginny clomped down the septic vinyl-floored hallway, several patients rushed to the doors of their rooms to inspect her. It occurred to her that she was probably the most interesting arrival since their postbreakfast enemas.

The door of room 307 was tightly closed. Pausing outside it to brace herself for this meeting with her mother, she heard a male voice coming from the room next door. It was droning the same thing over and over again, like a stuck record: "Can you do that for me? I need me three new men out there right now. Can you do that for me? What did you say? Can you do that or not? Can you send me three new men out there right now? Or not?"

Out of the doorway across the hall shuffled a large old woman in a pink dressing gown. Her gray hair was oily and hung in her eyes. Drool dribbled out of one corner of her mouth. She took Ginny's arm and shook it.

"Hi," Ginny said with an uncertain smile, inching away. The old woman pointed at the floor, grunting. Ginny looked down. The woman was wearing new red slippers, the kind that made people's feet look twice as big as they really were. "Beautiful," Ginny assured her. "They're just great." The woman nodded with satisfaction and shuffled slowly back to her room. As she did so, Ginny realized who she was—Mrs. Cabel, her primary class Sunday school teacher, the woman who had taught Ginny right from wrong, the woman who had repeatedly assured her that Jesus loved all the little children of the world.

Ginny gritted her teeth and knocked softly on the door of room 307. The last time she had seen her mother had been a little more than a year ago, at the Major's funeral, prior to any suspicion that Mrs. Babcock was seriously ill herself. Her powerful mother vulnerable after all? The idea was so new that she simply didn't know how to deal with it.

There was no answer to her knock, so she slowly pushed the door open. The room was pale green, with windows all along one wall. Fresh flowers stood in several vases on the window sills—summer flowers of white and yellow. The other walls were stark. A TV, two imitation Danish modern armchairs, a couple of matching dressers cluttered with the paraphernalia of sick rooms, and two beds, one with a woman asleep in it. For a moment, Ginny thought she was in the wrong room. This sleeping woman wasn't her mother. But as she tiptoed closer, she decided that it was her mother after all. The formerly auburn hair had gone almost completely gray and was beginning to thin on top. All the familiar lines in the face—the frown lines between the eyes and the laugh lines around the mouth—had deepened into permanent crevices. The entire face with its sharp attractive features and prominent cheekbones had altered subtly: It had a yellowish tinge and was fuller and puffy, almost rounded. The nostrils were packed with cotton, and she was breathing raspily through the mouth. The arms, which lay outside the bedcovers, were covered with large bruises of different colors—black and blue, or red, yellow, and green. They looked like the smeared palette of an insane painter, of a Van Gogh. This woman, who for years had served Ginny sometimes as honored exemplar, sometimes as loathed and resented antagonist, was now lying here, asleep and helpless, giving off a stale, musty odor from her bruised flesh.

Stunned, Ginny sat down at the foot of the bed, relieved to have this opportunity to accustom herself to her mother's appearance unobserved by her mother, who always seemed able to interpret Ginny's every thought—by the way her mouth twitched, or by the angle at which she held her head. And right now the shock and distaste she was feeling were probably showing quite openly on her face. Could her mother be looking much worse than she really was? Christ, the poor woman looked like the descriptions of plague victims from the Middle Ages. It was incredible that anyone could look so awful and live to tell about it.

A crisp nurse in a pert cap like a blanched potato chip whirled through the door like a dervish and started briskly rearranging the things on the bedside table.

When she finally noticed Ginny, she reprimanded her in a loud whisper. "Mrs. Babcock is *not* supposed to be sleeping now. It's time for her craft program."

"*Craft* program?" Her mother was definitely not the craft program type. Or hadn't been.

"Craft program."

"What do they do?"

"Mrs. Babcock is embroidering a sampler."

"I didn't even know she could embroider," Ginny said, wondering at how little she really knew about this woman with whom she'd spent eighteen years. The nurse handed her an embroidery frame from the foot of her mother's bed. Apparently her mother *couldn't* embroider. The frame was a mess—colors and stitches all scrambled together in no apparent pattern. Unless it was a new folk art form.

"Who's the man next door?" Ginny asked in a whisper.

The nurse looked at her suspiciously. "Bicknell," she replied out of the corner of her mouth, with a nervous glance around the room to see if she'd been overhead. "He was Coach over at the high school before Coach Sparks." Ginny's heart leapt with terror at the nearness of her old enemy. "He had a stroke."

"That's too bad," Ginny said with scarcely contained pleasure. "I used to know him."

"Won two hundred and three football games and lost eight. Can't beat that, can you? He was a great athlete and an outstanding coach."

But a lousy son of a bitch, Ginny thought as she nodded solemnly —and then, suddenly, felt uncharitable. The poor man was a demented vegetable now—no threat to her any longer, if he ever really had been. Why should she corrode her heart by harboring an enduring hatred for him? And yet . . . if she gave up her grudge, wouldn't that be admitting that *all* the burning loves and hatreds of her life were nothing but fleeting whims in the face of ultimate mortal frailty?

As the nurse whisked out the door, a whirlwind of white-starched competence, Ginny could hear Coach's disembodied commands still floating up and down the hall: "Now, you listen to me right now: I need me three men out there on that field right now. No more, and no less. Can you get me those men? I need three men. . . ." The door sucked shut and all was quiet.

Ginny stood up and walked over to her mother's bedside table. It was littered with magazines. Volume 22 of the family's encyclopedia lay on top of the magazines, a marker at the two-thirds point. Her remarkable mother had read the whole set straight through in the past nine years and was now a storehouse of all kinds of fascinating, if useless, crumbs of knowledge. Also on the table was a large syringe, poised for action, which the nurse had just left.

Carefully, Ginny opened the table drawer, thinking of her promise to her mother years ago to put her out of her misery and hoping to find huge bottles crammed with pain-killing tablets and capsules of all kinds that she could slip to her mother if that was what the situation required. But there were no bottles, only a worn Bible and an Anglican prayer book. The central commissary was elsewhere. Ginny tried picturing the alternatives—smuggling a pistol in under her poncho, concealing a razor blade in her Afro. She could see the spotless sheets and septic walls splattered with her mother's blood. . . .

But why such morbid thoughts? Her mother had a clotting disorder, that was all. She'd had it before, Mrs. Yancy had said. She'd probably have it again. It hadn't even merited a phone call to Vermont the last time. Yes, she *looked* grotesque, but basically she wasn't that sick. Mrs. Yancy had said so. And anyway, it was impossible for a woman her mother's age to be mortally ill.

The nurse streaked back in. Unobtrusively, Ginny tried to close the drawer.

"*Excuse* me," the nurse said irritably, shoving Ginny away. She picked up the syringe, reached under the covers with a cotton swab, and injected whatever it was into Mrs. Babcock's hip. Mrs. Babcock didn't so much as flinch.

"You may as well go home and come back in the morning. Mrs. Babcock will be out for the night."

"But I just *got* here," Ginny protested. "I haven't even said hello to her."

"I can't help *that.*"

"What exactly *is* idiopathic thrombo—whatever it is?"

The nurse glared at her. "Have you talked with the doctor yet?"

"Dr. Tyler?" Ginny asked, invoking the sacred name of the general practitioner who had for decades performed every medical service the family had required. He had, for instance, delivered Ginny.

"Tyler's retired."

Dr. Tyler retired? How was that possible? How could he desert her family just when they needed him? It was unthinkable. "Who *is* her doctor then?"

"Vogel," snapped the nurse. "The new hematologist. You ask *him* about Mrs. Babcock's condition. I'm not permitted to discuss it."

"Why not?" Ginny asked, staring with anxiety at her mother's round yellow moonlike face and cotton-packed nostrils. The nurse stared with obvious displeasure at Ginny's peasant dress and combat boots and then raced out of the room on stiff legs, like an angry marathon walker.

Hearing her door open, Mrs. Babcock lay still and breathed as evenly and as quietly as she could with cotton wadded in her nostrils. She hoped to fool Miss Sturgill into letting her "sleep" through the infernal craft program. Although she'd gotten much better in recent years about saying no to things she really didn't want to do, she was having a difficult time saying no to the craft program. It was run by young high school girls; and Mrs. Babcock, well trained in the art of nurturing young egos, couldn't bring herself to tell them that she'd rather be left alone to lick her wounds in solitude, like a cat. The girls assumed that the patients were bored and loved the invigorating company of young people. They were wrong; but no mother would ever dream of disillusioning them in their first fumbling attempts at philanthropy. Dressed in pink striped pinafores, fresh and scrubbed, they were always so pathetically eager to sympathize with complaints, to chatter mindlessly about themselves and their activities at school. In sum, they were so unlike Ginny at sixteen. That was what was appealing about them; that was why Mrs. Babcock twice a week embroidered a sampler she wasn't remotely interested in. The sessions furnished her with the companionship of young girls that Ginny had deprived her of by being so resolutely secretive. Of course, a great deal of Ginny's conduct had merited secrecy. Mrs. Babcock would sit in the activity room, fumbling with her embroidery frame and studying these lively charming chattering female creatures, and would wonder where she had gone wrong with Ginny. Or did these girls become sullen and defiant the minute they set foot in their own houses?

Well, Ginny had always been a difficult child. A sharp word or an unpleasant look had triggered a flood of penitent tears in Karl and Jim as small children. But Ginny had merely turned around and glared, making Mrs. Babcock think of Lizzie Borden and her ax. The boys were reliable, predictable in their very different ways. Karl, after West Point, had been sent to Germany and had recently been promoted to captain. As his father had been, Karl was matter-of-fact and disciplined and efficient. Jim was probably more like herself, Mrs. Babcock thought—laboring under a disinclination to become involved in the real world. His meager living at sandal making had to be supplemented by the dividend checks from his trust fund.

But Ginny, born between the two boys, was the difficult one— difficult because she was neither a Karl nor a Jim. She fluctuated between the two personality types at such a rate that one never knew how to approach her, never knew which role she was "into" at any given moment. Although Jim professed to hate everything his "bourgeois" parents stood for, at least they always knew where they stood with him. With Ginny they were never sure. You never knew from one week to the next whether you were a heinous criminal perpetrating crimes on humanity, or whether you were eligible for sainthood and an exemplar of all virtue.

The one thing the three children did share, though, was the requirement that their parents not change. Children could change, could wear different kinds of clothes, try out new hairdos, espouse new ideologies—but parents were not allowed to change because it would confuse the children, who needed something stable and consistent to butt heads with. It was most irritating if you yourself, as a parent, didn't happen to consider your development a closed book. "But, *Mother,*" they would shriek when she would toss out an idea that they'd never expected from her, "you're not being *consistent!*" Never mind that none of them had ever been consistent for longer than two minutes at any point in their lives.

Mrs. Babcock hadn't heard the door reopen. Apparently Miss Sturgill hadn't yet given up on her as a candidate for the craft program and was still lurking somewhere in the room waiting to pounce on her should she open an eye. This was so childish! It was like playing possum as a child, when she hadn't wanted to get up on a summer morning. She had to get out of this place before she regressed to infancy.

Mrs. Babcock could sense the presence of another person at the foot of her bed. Cautiously, she opened one eye just enough to see through her eyelashes. It clearly wasn't Miss Sturgill. For one thing, Miss Sturgill would never stand still for that long. Besides, the form, a silhouette against the bright light through the window, wasn't dressed in dazzling white. It looked like Ginny, of all people. Was she dreaming without realizing it? Or hallucinating due to having been thinking about Ginny?

Mrs. Babcock strained her faintly opened eye. Yes, it was definitely Ginny, this wan unhappy-looking creature, dressed in a colorful patchwork dress with puffy sleeves and a low neck and a laced bodice. Who was she this time—Heidi? She wore a leather thong of some sort on one wrist. And her hair—dear God, what had she done to her hair? It was cut short. Its natural curl had made it lie in soft damp ringlets around her flushed face during her sleep when she was a toddler. Ginny had spent probably three whole years of her life sporting giant pink curlers that resembled cardboard toilet paper cylinders in order to eliminate this curl. Wesley used to enrage her by telling her that the rollers made her look as though she had holes in her head. This same natural curl, unleashed, now made Ginny's hair stick out frizzily, as though she were holding a bared electric wire. The Unkempt Look, it was probably called in the fashion magazines. It looked awful, of course, but no worse than the hairdos she'd come up with half a dozen times in the last twelve years—the ridiculous pony tail she'd insisted on when she was a flag swinger; the puffy bouffant when she'd been hanging around with the horrid Cloyd boy, which had made her head look twice its normal size and had required half an hour of back-combing; the severe bun she'd returned from Worthley with; the plaited braid the time she'd brought home that unfortunate Holzer girl and had picketed Wesley's factory. Honestly, when would Ginny listen to her mother and accept the fact that her hair would look most becoming simply cut short and allowed to wave softly, as it had when she was a little girl?

So annoyed was she with Ginny's obstinacy that Mrs. Babcock almost gave herself away by sitting up to suggest that Ginny try wetting her hair down to see if she couldn't do something more attractive with it than this current fright wig. Then she realized that the crucial issue for the moment was not Ginny's hair but rather the fact of her presence. Why was she here, standing at the foot of the bed? Mrs. Babcock pondered the topic for a while and finally concluded that she was dreaming. How ridiculous! Of course she was dreaming. Ginny was in Vermont and rarely came to Hullsport anymore if she could avoid it. It must be the drugs they'd been giving her.

Just then the door burst open. Miss Sturgill this time, come to shanghai her to the activity room. Mrs. Babcock stubbornly closed her eye—confused, because if she was dreaming, then why would she have to pretend to be asleep to outwit Miss Sturgill? Or was Miss Sturgill part of the dream too? She heard the two of them whispering, and was lulled off into authentic sleep.

The next morning Mrs. Childress came in to wake her. It was unclear to Mrs. Babcock why she had to wake up at 6:30 each morning when she had very little to do all day except to lie in bed and try to nap. Nevertheless, that was the rule, and she was in no position to challenge it, trapped as she was in this unfamiliar place at the mercy of unending streams of strangers dressed in starched white.

Mrs. Childress was taking her pulse, studying the large round face of her sturdy man's wrist watch. Mrs. Babcock found this pulse ritual profoundly reassuring. The rest of her system might be breaking down, but her faithful heart was still pumping away, albeit faster than usual because of her blood loss. More than 89,000 times each day it expanded and contracted to circulate some 72,000 quarts of defective blood through her tired bruised body. Two and a half billion times it would beat, if God granted her a normal life. (All of these things she knew from the encyclopedia.) Such dependability was gratifying wherever you found it. But why did Mrs. Childress have to check it every morning at 6:30? What was she expecting to discover?

"Why do you do this every morning?"

Mrs. Childress shut her eyes, calculating Mrs. Babcock's pulse rate. "Standard procedure," she grumbled as she pulled up the sleeve of Mrs. Babcock's nightgown and wrapped the blood pressure cuff around her upper arm. This was how they had first confirmed that she was having another bout with idiopathic thrombocytopenic purpura, that afternoon when she had appeared in the emergency room with a nose that wouldn't stop bleeding—with a blood pressure cuff. A tourniquet test, it was called, to determine capillary fragility. Dr. Vogel had arrived, blond and breathless and red-faced. He had taken her blood pressure, pausing for five minutes midway between diastolic and systolic. With a pen he had drawn a circle five centimeters in diameter on her forearm. Fifteen minutes later he had counted the tiny bruises that had formed. There were dozens, when five or so would have been normal. It seemed such a quaint technique, in these days of heart-lung machines and organ transplants. Since that unfortunate afternoon, the tiny bruises—petechiae, as Dr. Vogel insisted on referring to them—had appeared all over her body. They had proceeded to grow and merge with each other to form large bruises—ecchymoses, he called them, for reasons known only to the medical profession.

As Mrs. Childress squeezed the bulb to tighten the cuff, the colorful yellow and green and black and purple bruises on Mrs. Babcock's arm began their dull ache, an ache that would eventually spread throughout her body. Mrs. Babcock grimaced. Another day of dull pain was beginning.

"Sorry, honey," Mrs. Childress said, watching the jerking dial. Mrs. Childress was a good person. It was always a relief to find herself awakened by Mrs. Childress rather than by the efficient Miss Sturgill. Mrs. Childress was older and more patient. In addition, her husband worked at the chemical plant. Mrs. Childress was honored to be packing the bloody nose of Major Babcock's wife. Mrs. Childress suffered periodically from sciatica; her pain had mellowed her. But Miss Sturgill had promise. Let her give birth to a few babies or undergo a head-on collision or something, and she would mellow too.

Mrs. Childress made notations on a chart. Then she picked up a spring lancet with a pointed razor blade on the end. Mrs. Babcock flinched reflexively, like one of Pavlov's dogs.

"Yes," Mrs. Childress said firmly. "I'm afraid we have to do a bleeding test today."

"But you just *did* one yesterday."

"The last one was three days ago," Mrs. Childress assured her, taking her left ear lobe in one hand and pricking it quickly.

Mrs. Babcock reflected that she was getting to be like a junky: They were running out of sites for their tests. Could it be possible that the last one had been three days ago? Mrs. Childress dabbed at her bleeding lobe with a round disk of filter paper. The management of this place may have been utterly wrapped up in their variety of ways for measuring time—pulses and blood pressures and bleeding times. But for the patients, the only demarcations during the day were the various routines—the nurses' rounds with medication and tests, meals, visitors. Otherwise, Mrs. Babcock had floated through her two weeks here suspended in time, with no awareness of its passage.

Even when she had been well and at home, her time sense had been fuzzy. She knew the date only by counting backward to some significant date in the recent past—a birthday or a holiday, some milepost on the calendar. This was in glaring contrast to Wesley, who had known at all times not only the exact day, month, and year, but the precise hour and minute as well. Even without his habit of constantly glancing at his calendar watch as he talked. He had regarded time as a precious natural resource, to be parceled out to other people stingily and with reluctance. He had been robbed. His heart had stopped beating before completing its allotted 2.5 billion contractions.

But here in the hospital there was nothing to look back on, to count forward from, with pleasure. There were no photos around to remind her of the children as babies, or of Wesley as a handsome young army officer, or of her wild white-haired father, or of any of the dozens of people that popped into her mind associatively at home. At home she could spend hours doing nothing but strolling through the rooms recalling incidents from the past. Here in this gleaming hospital, here in this anonymous green room, she had no past.

Likewise, there was nothing here to look forward to. Either she would die here or she would leave as soon as she was well. In either case, the hospital itself was merely a way station, a purgatory of the present.

But it was morbid to be thinking like this. Of course she wouldn't die here, couldn't even if she wanted to, which she had often enough in recent years. She was no longer young, but she wasn't old yet either. She hadn't paid her dues, done her time on earth. She wouldn't be allowed to close out her accounts this soon, she was sure of it. She would recover from this attack just as she had from the two previous ones; she would survive, no doubt to sustain yet another attack of this disease before long. Or of another disease. So it went.

Mrs. Childress was dabbing her ear lobe faithfully every fifteen seconds. Mrs. Childress' filter paper disks were usually masterpieces. She blotted the cuts in spirals, the large stains on the outer rim growing progressively smaller as they swirled toward the center, eventually disappearing altogether when the blood finally clotted. Dr. Vogel had only to glance at a disk done by Mrs. Childress to read how long clotting had taken, how copiously the blood had flowed. Miss Sturgill tended to be too impatient when she did the test; her blots would smear or merge, or she would dislodge the newly forming clot and upset the reading.

Mrs. Childress sighed sadly. Apparently her blood was failing the test once again. "Twelve minutes," Mrs. Childress muttered to herself, shaking her head. "What we gonna do wid you, honey?"

"The drugs aren't working then?"

"Well, I don't know about *that*. You'll have to ask the doctor, honey." Then in a whisper she added, "But if you want my opinion, dear, they ain't no tellin what would happen without em. So you just keep takin em like the doctor says." She handed Mrs. Babcock her prednisone, and Mrs. Babcock raised her hand to her mouth and placed the white pills on her tongue, like a communicant the wafer. Mrs. Childress held a cup of water to her lips. All that was needed was for Mrs. Childress to recite, "The Blood of our Lord Jesus Christ, which was shed for thee, preserve thy body and soul unto everlasting life."

Mrs. Childress held an enamel pan under Mrs. Babcock's nose. With tweezers she began pulling out the bloody cotton wads. They were saturated and had been on the verge of leaking. Mrs. Babcock held the pan and watched blood dribble from her nostrils onto the soaked cotton. Then she laid her head against her pillows while Mrs. Childress blotted her nose and mouth with tissue and started packing her nostrils with fresh cotton. Blood was oozing down her throat. She had to keep swallowing in order not to choke on it. Standing and walking increased the bleeding. But she still tried to get around as much as she could. For instance, she walked to the sun porch for meals. She figured that if she gave in to the temptation of lying around in bed all day, she never would get out of this place and back to her own house where the silver had to be polished, and the closets straightened, and a hundred different things she resolutely tried to look forward to.

"Do you have to go into the bathroom?" Mrs. Childress' approach to this topic was an advance on that of Miss Sturgill, who would bark like an army sergeant, "How about a B.M. for us, Mrs. Babcock?"

"No thanks," Mrs. Babcock said, sitting up and swinging her legs slowly over the side. Mrs. Childress put the fur-lined suede slippers on Mrs. Babcock's feet, inspecting with a sympathetic grimace the giant moist purple bruise that covered most of Mrs. Babcock's left foot and ankle. It was throbbing dully as blood rushed to it. Mrs. Childress held out her arm, like a gentleman to a lady at a dance. Mrs. Babcock clasped it and stood up, her limbs aching as her faulty arterial system revved up.

And so she and Mrs. Childress began their thrice daily stroll down the dim hallway with its spotless white plaster walls and green marble-ized tile floor. Mrs. Babcock negotiated the fifty feet to the sun porch by shuffling her feet forward a few inches at a time.

"I had the strangest dream last night," she told Mrs. Childress companionably. "I dreamed that Miss Sturgill and my daughter, Ginny, the one in Vermont, were whispering at the foot of my bed. I wonder what that means. Funny how real dreams can seem."

"Weren't no dream, honey. I seen her mysef."

Mrs. Babcock stopped. "You mean Ginny's *here?*" Mrs. Childress nodded. "But *why?*"

"Mrs. Yancy explained it to you. Don't you remember?"

"She did?"

"How she had to go over at Europe, and how your daughter was comin down to keep you company?"

"Yes?" Mrs. Babcock honestly couldn't remember. Was it the drugs, or was it senility? "But I don't *need* someone here with me every day. You'd think I were dying or something!" She chuckled. When Mrs. Childress didn't laugh, she looked at her face questioningly, like a prisoner studying her jailer for some clue as to when she'd be paroled. Mrs. Childress' face was masklike, but it was always mask-like when her sciatica was bothering her.

The others were already at their places at the table—Mr. Solomon, Sister Theresa, and Mrs. Cabel. The four of them were the only ones on the corridor who were ambulatory. The other dozen or so ate in their rooms and were seldom seen, either because they couldn't make it to the sun porch or because they chose not to try. Mrs. Babcock nodded and took her seat between Mr. Solomon and Mrs. Cabel. Mr. Solomon was a wizened little man with a band of frizzy gray hair encircling his bald dome. His glasses lenses were probably half an inch thick and magnified his eyes to the size of dinner plates. Behind these lenses his eyes were clouded over with the gray film of inoperable cataracts.

"Nice day," he said with a wide smile.

"Yes," Mrs. Babcock agreed coolly. She had known Mr. Solomon slightly for many years. He had been head of the jewelry department at one of the downtown department stores, and Wesley had always taken him their clocks and watches for repair. Wesley had also bought Ginny's high school graduation present from Mr. Solomon—a twenty-one-jewel white gold Lady Bulova wrist watch, which Ginny had since worn only sporadically. Nevertheless, Mrs. Babcock preferred to keep her distance. After all, just because they were stuck in this hospital together was no reason for instant friendship, when twenty-five years of acquaintanceship hadn't produced it. Anyhow, why invest the emotional energy necessary to initiate a friendship when it would be terminated very soon by her leaving. And perhaps by his leaving as well. She couldn't be sure. He had emphysema and sounded awful, but she was no doctor.

Mrs. Babcock glanced out the window to check on the "nice day" Mr. Solomon had mentioned. The morning sun had just cleared one of the red clay foothills behind Wesley's factory. The face of the foothill was etched with interconnected gullies which fed run-off water into the Crockett River below. Because of the nature of her illness, Mrs. Babcock knew that she was bound to see the gully pattern as an arterial system, the huge gullies at the top branching down the face of the slope into dozens of lesser gullies, which branched in their turn into an intricate lacy design and eventually tapered off into nothingness.

Mrs. Cabel was grunting insistently. Mrs. Babcock looked in her direction, determined to be pleasant, no matter how upsetting she might find Mrs. Cabel's greasy hair and crossed eyes and sputtering efforts to make words. They had gone to the Episcopal church together for years; Mrs. Cabel had taught Mrs. Babcock's children in Sunday school. It certainly wasn't Mrs. Cabel's fault that she had had a stroke. But on the other hand, it wasn't Mrs. Babcock's fault either; and she didn't understand why, when she herself was sick, she should be required to function as a social chairman when she just wanted to be left alone. Of course, she could remain in her room for meals, and thus never have to see these people, but that wasn't the point. She needed to be up and around. If she could only be at home, she could do that without encountering at every corner fellow townspeople who were even sicker than she and who served merely to depress her. Why did Dr. Vogel insist that she be here? It wasn't as though she were dying.

Miss Sturgill came in pushing the food trays. Mrs. Babcock couldn't figure out why she looked forward to mealtimes when the food was invariably bland and unattractive. Perhaps it was because mealtime was one of the few activities in her day, and about the only activity she could anticipate with pleasure, the others being shots and tests and so on. She lifted the metal warming pan and confronted an ice cream scoop of Cream of Wheat, powdered scrambled eggs, limp greasy bacon, Mother's Glory white toast and strawberry jam.

Sister Theresa reverently crossed herself and folded her hands at chest level and bowed her head. Mr. Solomon and Mrs. Babcock froze guiltily in mid-bite, though Mrs. Cabel went on eating noisily. Sister was a large beefy woman with a red face and with gray hair pinned into a severe bun. She had taught for many years at the Catholic grammar school in town. She wore the hospital-issue gown and robe of green wash-and-wear material; around her neck hung a gold-plated medallion featuring praying hands and the phrase, "Not My Will But Thine." Sister had cancer, had had one breast removed. Secondary tumors had popped up since in her lungs, and there was a chance that the other breast would have to go, too.

They ate in silence. Partway through her reconstituted eggs, Mrs. Babcock heard the theme from "Love Story" wafting up from the Southern Baptist church on the circle in downtown Hullsport.

"I installed those chimes," Mr. Solomon informed them with a modest blush.

"They're lovely," Mrs. Babcock assured him.

"Vell, at least you can rely on them for a change." They were gonging out the hour—six, seven.

"What do you mean?" Mrs. Babcock asked.

"Vell, they're electric. The hand chimes only got rung if somebody vas there and felt like ringing them. But these go off every fifteen minutes vithout fail, rain or shine, day in and day out. And you get a different song every hour."

"Hmmm, yes," Mrs. Babcock said doubtfully, remembering ringing the carillon bells herself as a member of the Southern Baptist
youth group—prior to marriage and to Wesley's insistence that she
convert to the more dignified Episcopal church. Ringing the chimes
had been considered a rare honor then. People scheduled themselves
months in advance. She and two others would climb the steep narrow
steps into the white wooden bell tower. From there you could see
across the Crockett to her father's factory, with the then-forested
foothills behind it. You could see the white mansion where she lived,
and the farm stretching out behind it, until the ridge on which the
Cloyds' maroon house sat intervened. You could look down at the
much lower steeples of the four other churches around the circle. The
barn swallows who lived in the bell tower would be darting around
at eye level. You could look past them down Hull Street to the train
station, where a train might be arriving in great puffs of black smoke,
pulling cars mounded high with gleaming chunks of black coal from
southwest Virginia.

When the clock on the face of the train station read 4:55 they
would begin the hymns, pulling carefully on their assigned ropes.
Sometimes someone pulled the wrong one, or two discordant notes
were sounded in unison, or the beat faltered. But usually it went
pretty well, and "The Old Rugged Cross" or "Rock of Ages" or
"What a Friend We Have in Jesus" would peal out across the town
and countryside, bouncing back and forth among the surrounding
foothills. Townspeople, wherever they were and whatever they were
doing, would stop everything to listen to the concert. And when the
hands on the train station clock read approximately 5:00, the hymns
would end and the hour would toll.

If it was winter and the sun was due to set soon, she and the others
would sometimes stay up in the tower and watch for it, their chatter
falling silent as the orange ball slid behind the jagged pines on a
foothill that bordered her family's farm. As the bats in the tower
began stirring in the dusk, the young people would descend to their
families and their suppers. Somehow, this ritual gave them a comforting sense of control over the passing time of their lives.

But now, thanks to Mr. Solomon and modern technology, the
chimes tolled every fifteen minutes, a different show tune every hour.
People could confidently set their Accutron watches by the chimes.
And no one had to go to the "bother" of clambering up that rickety
bell tower every afternoon. There was progress for you!

Clutching the chrome bar on the tile wall next to the tub, Mrs. Babcock slowly lowered herself into the cool water. She would have preferred a good hot steaming bath, but Dr. Vogel forbade it, insisting that it would cause her blood to flow even more copiously. Settled in the tub with water to her chin, she regarded her submerged body. There was a dark blue cast to the water. At all the points where bone rubbed flesh—in other words, almost everywhere but on her inner thighs, her buttocks and her breasts—were huge bruises of variegated colors, according to their age. A bruise would start out black and blue, then mellow to purple, then green, then yellow, like a fruit ripening. Once it had faded completely, it would be replaced by a fresh new bruise, as the regenerated capillaries reruptured. Her flesh was a veritable rainbow. She could have provided a perfect instructional exercise for young children in the ways colors blend together to form new colors. . . .

As Dr. Vogel explained it, everyone's capillaries were ripped open all the time by the ordinary activities of living. Normally, platelets would mass at the site of these rips and mend them. In her case, however, there were very few platelets, and rips didn't get mended. Her blood oozed from the rips and into her tissues to form the bruises. She'd read in the encyclopedia that the gorgeous fall leaf colors that everyone gasped at resulted from essentially the same process. The membranes around each cell in a leaf became leaky and no longer functioned as a semipermeable wall, so that the cell fluids began seeping into the surrounding spaces, rendering the leaf translucent. Wesley, on the other hand, had had an abundance of platelets that were overly eager to amass; they had formed the clots that had caused his heart attacks. If only the two of them could somehow have merged their blood supplies, as they had their minds and their bodies and their lives in almost every other way. . . .

Hunching up into a sitting position, she inspected herself more closely. Her pale breasts, drooping and etched with silver stretch marks from childbearing, stood out in sharp contrast to their colorful backdrop. She looked like the Japanese Irezumi men she'd read about in the encyclopedia who were tattooed all over with stylized dragons and sumaris in shades of black and blue and red and purple. That anyone would actually choose this condition for his body was beyond her comprehension. Her pubic hair, sodden and matted, surrounded by hues of blue, perched like a rain-soaked bird's nest. Her whole body was puffing up like a weather balloon from the steroids. She had already gained ten pounds, and her flesh was spongy to the touch. Her hair was coming out in clumps. . . .

All in all, she was just as glad that Wesley wasn't around to witness what had happened to her body since his death. Their life together had been predicated upon this body—his attraction to it, and its own greed to replicate itself. The children found it difficult to believe that she and their father could have a sex life. She smiled remembering the embarrassed scandalized looks on their faces whenever, as young children and especially as adolescents, they had walked in on their parents' embraces and caresses. One weekend afternoon when Ginny was at the high school practicing her ridiculous flag swinging, she and Wesley had begun by kissing and had ended up in bed together. This happened only rarely by this time because Wesley was always exhausted after work during the week, and because the children were always around with their friends the rest of the time. But the interest and the capacity were still there, and flowered on these rare and prized occasions. This particular time, however, Ginny had come bursting back into the house shortly after leaving. She and Wesley froze in the act, as guilty as two teen-agers whose parents have come home unexpectedly. Ginny started calling for Wesley. They heard her footsteps on the stairs and stared at each other in consternation. Finally, swearing under his breath, Wesley rolled out of bed and threw on a robe and went out to confront her, his face scarlet from embarrassment and exertion.

"I need the Jeep, Pop. I'm going up to see Grandpa."

"So *take* it."

"I can't find the keys."

"I left them in it."

"Where's Mother? I need to ask her something."

"Uh, yes, well your mother and I are—uh, taking a nap right now."

"A *nap?* At twelve thirty in the—oh. Yeah. Well, uh. See you, Pop." She careened down the steps.

Why could children not accept the fact that their parents had had their days in the sun, too? Ginny appeared to believe that she had sprung full grown into existence through a sort of spontaneous regeneration. She liked to think that her generation had discovered the pleasures of the flesh. Whereas in fact, this despised body of her mother's, and her father's attraction to it, and nothing to do with the inherent desirability of Ginny herself, accounted for Ginny's existence. Because of this body (she now knew, though at the time she would have vehemently denied it), Wesley and she had married and had one day found themselves with three children to raise. Because of it, Wesley had spent three decades in a town he didn't much like. And now that body, which had largely determined the shape of his life and of hers, was a puffed-up mass of overlapping hematomas that ached to the touch. It was another example of the elaborate scheme of malicious practical jokes that Wesley had always insisted constituted the phenomenon known as Life. In any case, malicious or not in intent, what was happening now definitely made one wonder about the point of all the attention she and Wesley had showered on this body over the years. Yes, Wesley was fortunate to have been spared this punch line in the anecdote that was their life together.

Mrs. Babcock grabbed the chrome bar and hauled herself out of the water. When she returned to her room in a fresh yellow gown, she discovered with satisfaction that her bed was already done, fresh sheets replacing the old ones, which had had dribbles of dried blood here and there. She paused and gently touched the shocking pink peonies in a vase on the window sill. She almost allowed herself tears of frustration. She couldn't smell with her nose packed, and peonies were her favorite. She made do with looking at them and touching them. Then she turned on the television and hoisted herself into bed. Rarely had she watched television, except for the evening news. But her eyes could endure only so much reading; they strained very easily these days. A church service was on.

Bored, Mrs. Babcock picked up her embroidery hoop and started stitching compulsively. What had Ginny's get-up yesterday signified? The last time she'd been home, for Wesley's funeral, she'd been wearing a pantsuit, and her hair was long and neat and tied back with a scarf. What did a Heidi dress mean? With irritation she threw down the hoop. Why was Ginny here anyhow? As a silent reprimand after their years of failing to get through to each other?

She picked up volume 22 of the encyclopedia and opened it at "Varicose Veins." After nine years, she was finally reaching the end of this ill-conceived project. One more volume and she'd be finished.

For whatever good that would do her. She had started reading them when Ginny left for Boston for several reasons: to have something to do with herself; to round out her liberal arts education, which had been abruptly terminated by marriage and by the relentless arrival of babies. But mostly she'd been looking for some pegs to hang her philosophical hat on. She'd grown up terrorized by the prospect of hell-fire and damnation from sermons every Sunday at the Southern Baptist church. The austere Anglican Book of Common Prayer had been balm to her cowering spirit. The Episcopal approach was really more her style: "We acknowledge and bewail our manifold sins and wickedness, which we, from time to time, most grievously have committed, by thought, word, and deed, against thy Divine Majesty, provoking most justly thy wrath and indignation against us. We do earnestly repent, and are heartily sorry for these our misdoings; the remembrance of them is grievous unto us; the burden of them is intolerable. . . ."

But she regarded the Book of Common Prayer as uplifting literature, the Episcopal services as soothing ritual, a ceremonial link to the past. Her faith had always resided elsewhere, in the form of a mute confidence in the scheme of things. However much she might question some of its manifestations, she had maintained a silent conviction that there was a point to life, and to having lived. She had begun reading the encyclopedia in search of labels. What was this kind of religious belief called? Who were the people who saw things as she did? As she approached the last volume, though, she had no more idea than when she had started. What she *did* have was a miraculous backlog of little-known facts that would have allowed her to clean up on any television quiz show. Ever since volume 12 or so, she'd been reading on strictly to satisfy her neurotic compulsion to finish things begun, like cleaning up your plate at a meal.

The real problem now was that her simple nameless faith had really been put to the test the past couple of years. It definitely needed bolstering of some kind. The form this faith had taken in the past had been a dedication to what she had seen as her duty—the care of three young lives, the nurturing of her relationship with Wesley. But now Wesley was dead, and the children were gone. Not only were the children gone, they were more or less a flop. She had devoted her life to them, and she couldn't see that they'd turned out very impressively. Karl was responsible; he did his job, looked after his family. But he lacked imagination; he led an unexamined life. She hated to admit it, but she found her own son—her heir, the product of years of her selfless devotion—a bore, a drudge. Jim, in California making sandals, was dear, but a mess. He had dropped out of college, had been dishonorably discharged from the army, had taken up and cast off a dozen kinds of work, a dozen serious girl friends. Apparently he now lived primarily to take drugs. He couldn't seem to stay with anything else that might give him long-term satisfaction. After many trying years, Ginny appeared to be coming around, had a charming child and a devoted young husband. But who knew how long it would last? She had about as much staying power as a spring snowstorm.

When she really faced up to it, Mrs. Babcock couldn't place herself in the vanguard of her profession of parenthood. She had been committed to endowing the world with three decent, imaginative, hardworking citizens. But she had to say now that she'd failed. There was nothing much wrong with her offspring, but they clearly weren't the superior beings she'd envisioned. It wasn't easy to admit that perhaps your life had been wasted. Having done so was possibly why she had found herself hemorrhaging in the emergency room on the first anniversary of her husband's death. In any case, it was definitely the reason why she was scouring these last two volumes of the encyclopedia so greedily. If assuring the continuation of the species wasn't what she was on earth for, what was?

There was a soft knock at her door. Normally the staff didn't bother knocking, and visiting hours were in the afternoon. Who could it be? The door swung inward. A stream of words came from the next room: ". . .I don't want to hear no excuses. You git out there and you do like I tell you, boy. You run till you drop, and then you pick yoursef up and you run some more. Do you understand? Do you understand? No excuses. Do you understand me or not? . . ."

A young woman stood in the doorway. She was dressed in stained white overalls such as housepainters wore and a faded navy blue T-shirt that had writing of some sort on it—"Sisterhood Is Powerful," whatever that meant.

"Hello," Ginny said. Her mother looked up from her encyclopedia, then looked back down with indifference. Ginny couldn't detect any hint of recognition. She was hurt. She hadn't come all the way from Vermont to be not recognized by her own mother, for Christ's sake.

"How are you feeling today?" Ginny asked.

Mrs. Babcock looked up again and studied the friendly young woman. What did she want anyhow? Who was she—a young nursing trainee from the lab? That might explain the unbecoming white work pants. Mrs. Babcock was an intriguing case to the staff. Strangers were forever popping in to poke at her bruises and take blood samples, but rarely were they so insistently sociable. "Which one are *you?*" Mrs. Babcock asked in a hoarse, tired voice.

Ginny stared at her. Was it the drugs? "I'm *Ginny,* Mother." Her mother looked at her as though sorting through a stack of names and faces of other daughters.

"Oh yes, of course, Ginny." But she was taken aback. She had seen Ginny yesterday, had accustomed herself to the notion of Ginny's presence, had been expecting her to appear today. But what she had been expecting was the Austrian mountain girl from *The Sound of Music,* not this housepainter's apprentice. Who, pray, was Ginny today?

Ginny was waiting to be told how nice it was of her to come all the way from Vermont. "From Vermont," she added pointedly.

"I'm aware of that." Why was it that when someone was flat on her back, everyone immediately started patronizing her?

Ginny walked to her mother's bed, leaned down and kissed her lined forehead. She felt her mother studying her quizzically, critically. Backing over to a chair, she plopped down in it and braced herself for complaints about her appearance, her posture, her failure to write once a week. A beam of sunlight through the window fell across her mother's blanket at knee level.

"Pretty day," Ginny suggested. When in doubt discuss the weather, she had learned at Tupperware parties in Stark's Bog.

"Is it?" Mrs. Babcock rarely noticed the weather here in her hospital room, rarely glanced out the window. Doing so, she discovered that the leaves of an elm tree outside her window were a bright yellow-green. A red squirrel perched chattering on a branch.

"It's still June?" Mrs. Babcock asked. Ginny nodded yes, startled. "How's your infant and your charming husband?"

Ginny grimaced. She longed to come clean right from the start and admit that Ira had kicked her out for cuckolding him—although in fact it hadn't been like that all. But she and her mother had never been noted for candor. "They're fine, thank you."

Miss Sturgill came leaping in like a Cossack dancer and said brightly, "Good morning, Mrs. Babcock. How are we today?" She nodded briskly to Ginny and then said to her mother, "All ready to go?"

Closing her eyes, Mrs. Babcock asked wearily, "Where is it you're taking me *now?*" If only they'd all go away and leave her alone with her bruised body. Here she was, supposed to be resting and recovering; and yet she was having to function like the hostess of a television talk show, humoring Mrs. Childress with her sciatica and the candy-striped volunteers with their tedious craft program, trying to figure out how to engage Miss Sturgill and Ginny in a conversation. It was exhausting.

"To the porch. For lunch." Miss Sturgill folded back Mrs. Babcock's bedcovers, helped her sit up.

The sun porch struck Ginny as a cheerful place, with windows on three sides and views of pine trees holding squirrels and bird feeders. In the distance was the Major's factory with its billowing smokestacks, the ocher Crockett oozing in front of it. And beyond the factory were the scarred foothills blotched with housing developments, one of them Plantation Estates, where Joe Bob and Doreen were living.

Three other patients—two women and a man—were already seated around the Formica table. She and Mr. Solomon recognized each other at the same time. "Why, hello, Virginia!"

"Hello, Mr. Solomon." She had always known him. He sold class rings to the Hullsport High students, had sold Joe Bob the huge ring that the Major had made her return. He'd also sold the Major the watch he'd given her for high school graduation. The tan plastic-covered matchbox of a couch trembled as Ginny plopped down on it. How come Mr. Solomon could recognize her when her own mother couldn't?

"Home for a visit?" he asked. Ginny nodded. "Vhere is it you live?"

"Vermont." Ginny was amazed at the ease with which this lie rolled off her tongue. She no longer lived in Vermont, but Vermont would have to serve as her official place of residence until she could figure out someplace else

"Vermont. Vehrr-mon. Green Mountain. Lovely state, Vermont."

"You've been there?"

"I've ridden through on a bus. My boat from Germany after the var vent down the St. Lawrence and docked at Montreal. I've never been so happy to see any place in my life. I rode a bus to my uncle's in New York. It vas vinter. In Vermont the snow vas piled up along the road six feet high. I thought to myself, good God, vhat kind of people could live in a place like this. So now I know—Tennesseans." Everyone laughed.

"Luckily, it's only under snow half the year," said Ginny.

"Good, good. You're married?"

"Well, yes," Ginny said with a quick glance at her mother.

"Children?"

"One. A little girl." With this admission came a sharp pang of desolation. By the time Ginny left, the interior of Ira's house had looked like a flood plain after a flood. Toys, dishes, books, clothes, were strewn everywhere by little toddling Wendy. Like a tornado, she left a wake of destruction in her path. Ginny had finally stopped even trying to keep walkways cleared through the rubble. But actually the debris that Ira was always ranting about wasn't debris at all. It played a vital role in their family ecosystem. Wendy was a cheery little spider in that cave of a house who spent her days spinning shimmering webs of fantasy out of whatever material was at hand. Watching her at play among the cabinets and drawers and bookshelves had ushered Ginny back into the musty chambers of her own childhood. Through Wendy she had been able to hack out new toe holds in the slippery face of her past. She felt a tremendous debt to the little girl, a debt she was defaulting on by having left her. Where was Wendy today? What was she doing? Was she happy? Ginny began chewing her nails.

"Ah, children!" Mr. Solomon exclaimed. "Take my advice and have a houseful."

"Well, I don't know . . ." Ginny said. Why was it that this piece of advice always came from people past menopause? She wanted to ask him how he felt, what was wrong with him, why he was here. "Still selling class rings?" she asked instead.

"Ach, these kids today! They don't buy rings like you did. In their ears. That's how they vear rings today, girls *and* boys. Not on their fingers."

"So you're selling lots of class earrings now?"

He chuckled. "I did sell earrings. I sold lots of earrings before I came here." He fell silent.

The electric chimes on the Southern Baptist church began playing "Some Very Special Someone." Ginny looked up with horror. "*What is that?*"

"The electric chimes *Mr. Solomon* installed at the Baptist church," Mrs. Babcock informed her hastily. "Aren't they lovely?" Ginny nodded with a tentative smile. After six of the twelve bongs to announce noon, the chimes were totally blotted out by the harsh protracted noontime whistle from the Major's factory. No one anywhere in Hullsport could fail to know that it was now emphatically noon.

"This is Sister Theresa, Ginny," her mother said. "Sister used to teach at St. Anthony's." Sister Theresa blushed and studied her plate intently. "And you remember Mrs. Cabel?" Ginny nodded with a polite smile at the drooling Mrs. Cabel, remembering her swaying on a rickety piano stool as she pumped the organ with both feet and pounded out "Jesus Loves the Little Children of the World," while singing loudly in an off-key soprano. Now Mrs. Cabel was completely absorbed in trying to raise a forkful of rice to her mouth, guided by her crossed eyes. She kept spilling grains on her lap and stabbing her chin with the tines.

After lunch Ginny held her mother's arm as they walked slowly back to her room. Her mother sat on the bed. Leaning against Ginny's arm, she swung her legs up. Ginny found this proximity to her mother's body very difficult to take and averted her eyes from the yellow gown that stretched tightly across her mother's breasts. Here it was—the Forbidden Flesh, the Taboo Torso. And it was black and blue, and puffy and in pain. Ginny shut her eyes tightly with grief as she pulled the covers up around her mother's chest.

All these bodies that she wasn't permitted to lust after. First her mother's and the Major's, her brothers'. Then Wendy's. But there was no denying that the bond between Wendy and herself was intensely physical. The most severe physical pain she could remember had been during Wendy's birth. The most intense joy had been during her conception, or perhaps during breast feeding. Of the pain she couldn't remember, undoubtedly battering her way out of her mother's birth canal had been the most severe; and being suckled and bathed and cuddled and cooed at must have been the most intense joy. Both Wendy and her mother she thought of largely in association with certain sounds, smells, caresses. And yet her interest in them both was expected to be platonic. It would be so much simpler and cheaper than a lifetime in psychoanalysis if the entire family—her mother, the Major, Karl and Jim, Ira and Wendy— had just gone to bed together in one writhing mass some night and acted out all their repressed desires. This technique, applied on a nationwide scale, would force one analyst after another into bankruptcy. Western civilization would collapse once and for all, which would probably be an incredible relief.

As an infant, Wendy would wake in the night crying. Ginny would change her and wrap her in a flannel blanket and carry her, as cuddly as a baby kitten, into Ira's and her bed. Outside, icy branches would etch lacy designs on the frosted windowpanes, and the spring snows would drift soft and deep. Wendy would nurse noisily, kneading Ginny's bursting breast with her chubby fingers as Ginny's other nipple burned and spurted and demanded equal time. In the moonlight through the window Ginny and Wendy would gaze at each other with mutual contentment. Ira would stir in his sleep and wrap his arms around them, and the three of them would fall asleep there until morning.

Had her own mother felt these things about her? Ginny glanced questioningly at her mother's round yellow face. Surely not. Her mother was loath to admit that Ginny even *had* a body, had blushed and stammered every time the topic of sex had come up around the house.

As Wendy grew older, a routine developed. Her ears pricked like a fawn's for early morning noises, Wendy would call out when she heard her parents stirring, "Mommy, come *find* me!" Ginny would go into her room and search the drawers, the hamper, the bookcases. The more unlikely the places, the more it delighted Wendy. Finally Ginny would pounce on the giggling wiggly little mound and carry her off to Ira's and her bed, where the three of them would make a tent with the covers and snuggle together with Wendy in the middle.

Often Wendy would grab one of Ginny's nipples and lisp, "Wha dis?"

"My nipple."

"Me drank milk there, right?" She found this unlikely story hard to grasp and kept going over it to be sure she had it straight.

"Right," Ginny would say firmly, determined not to pervert Wendy's nascent sex life by acting embarrassed, as her own mother always had on similar occasions. Ira would laugh silently, and she would blush as her nipple became stiff in Wendy's fingers.

Wendy would touch her own tiny nipples and say, "*My* nipples. For *my* babies."

"How many babies are you going to have?" Ira would ask. She would hold up stubby fingers, one at a time. Seven, eight, nine. "*Nine?*" He would laugh. "You're going to be very busy feeding them all."

"Mommy can help me," she'd say solemnly. . . .

Shit. Why was she torturing them all like this? Why not just go back to Ira and have another baby, damn it? He was a kind man, a devoted father, a reliable wage earner. She knew he would welcome her back if she went about it the right way. . . .

Her eyes still shut with pain, Mrs. Babcock said with forced heartiness, "Well, thank goodness I'm not as bad off as Mr. Solomon and Sister Theresa."

"What's wrong with them?" Ginny asked dully.

"Mr. Solomon has emphysema, and Sister Theresa has cancer. But they're just keeping me here for a while to be sure I don't have anything serious. Then I can go home."

She sounded to Ginny like a small child trying to talk herself into believing that there were no monsters under her bed. "What do they say you have?" Ginny asked, interested to hear what her mother's version would be.

"Dr. Vogel says I have idiopathic thrombocytopenic purpura."

"But what does *that* mean?"

"Clotting disorders, that's all."

"Caused by what?"

"Cause unknown. Idiopathic. 'Not preceded or caused by any known condition.' "

"So how do they know how to treat it if they don't know what causes it?"

"They don't know what causes cancer either, but they treat it, don't they?" She looked up at Ginny pleadingly. "When can I go home?"

Ginny looked back with dismay. The tables had turned; her mother was looking at her as though she were the one in control of the situation. "I don't know, Mother. I just got here. You know more about it than I do. I haven't even seen Dr. Vogel. Who *is* Dr. Vogel, anyway? Where's Dr. Tyler?" Ginny was accustomed, when being around her mother, to sinking into a stupor of passivity as her mother took charge of everything, organizing, arranging, planning, scheduling. The ball having been tossed to her, Ginny's inclination was to toss it back as quickly as possible.

"He's retired," Mrs. Babcock replied glumly.

"How can he be retired? You don't just stop seeing people you've cared for all your life."

"I don't know. Ask Dr. Tyler. I guess he had to quit sometime."

"What does this Vogel say about when you can go home?"

"I haven't asked," she confessed miserably.

"*I'll* ask." It was like playing dress-up as a child—putting on her mother's lipstick and spike heels and pretending that *she* was in charge. It was so ludicrous that Ginny almost laughed out loud.

Just then, as though summoned by their conversation, a beefy face crowned by a blond flat top appeared around the door. The face was attached to a tall broad frame that looked like that of a defensive left tackle for the Minnesota Vikings. "How are we today?" he asked cheerfully, glancing at a chart in his hand. Not waiting for an answer, he inquired of the air-conditioned room at large, "Hot enough for ya today?" And then the head disappeared as abruptly as it had appeared.

"Was that Vogel?" Ginny asked. Her mother nodded yes, her eyes closed again. Ginny raced out into the hall, catching sight of a massive white back turning a corner.

She sprinted down the hall, her clogs clattering like the hoofs of a runaway horse. Her wide painter's overall legs swirling like dust mops gone berserk, she skidded around the corner and almost ran into a huge white wall. Dr. Vogel turned around at the clattering and looked at Ginny with alarm.

"Excuse me, Doctor. I'm Mrs. Babcock's daughter, Virginia. May I ask you a few questions about my mother?"

"Well, I'm pretty busy, Miss Babcock."

"Then I'll just take a couple of minutes. What's her prognosis?"

"She has idiopathic thrombocytopenic purpura."

"So I hear. But what does that mean?"

"Platelet insufficiency of unknown origin. Perhaps an autoimmune response. Perhaps a malfunction of the spleen, or a megakaryocytic disorder. Characterized by multiple petechiae and ecchymoses."

"The bruises?"

"Hmmm, yes. Hemorrhagic bullae of the buccal mucosa are a common feature. . . ."

"I see," said Ginny, dazed. "Is she—like, you know—badly sick or anything?"

"Please don't worry about your mother, Miss Babcock," he said with a winning smile. "We're performing batteries of tests. There's quite an arsenal of treatments. If one doesn't work, we'll try another." He patted her shoulder paternally.

Ginny felt a great sense of relief. This white giant of a man had the situation firmly in hand, backed by legions of modern medicine men in starched white lab coats who carried racks of test tubes bubbling with newly synthesized wonder drugs. There was nothing for Virginia Babcock, college dropout, to worry her empty little head about.

But if everything was "under control," why was her mother in the hospital, at $70 a day? "When can she go home?"

"When we get her bleeding under control." He waved good-by with the fingers of one hand, whirled, and strode off down the hall like a Norse deity.

Her mother was asleep, so Ginny decided to go calling.

Driving through town, she followed the exact route Joe Bob and she used to take to their parking spot overlooking Hullsport. As she started up the hill, she passed through an entrance marked on each side by a free-standing white Corinthian column. A plaster cast of a liveried darkie held out a sign which said in Olde English script "Plantation Estates." Bouncing up the gravel road in the Jeep, she passed on either side identical single-level ranch houses with flat roofs which stuck out in front to form porticoes and which were supported by four skinny four-by-fours apiece. It looked as though the whole thing would start flapping in a strong breeze.

Ginny pulled into Joe Bob's driveway. Black letters above the garage door spelled out "Thirty-eight," Joe Bob's old football jersey number. As Ginny was walking toward the front door, Doreen came bursting out and hurled her arms around her, overcompensating for the fact that ten years ago she had seduced Joe Bob. "Why I declare!" she said petulantly, thrusting out her lower lip and stepping back to eye Ginny's Afro and her Sisterhood Is Powerful T-shirt. "I wouldn't of knowed you, Ginny Babcock!" That was her tactful way of expressing distaste.

"Well, Doreen, I would have known *you* anywhere. You haven't changed a *bit* since high school!" Doreen preened with pleasure. And in fact she *hadn't* changed a bit. She looked exactly as she had when Joe Bob and Ginny double-dated with her and Doyle at the Family Drive-In. Except for her chest, which had increased by probably ten inches. She was playing her new-found bounty to the hilt, too, displaying her tight cleavage in a ruffled blouse with a nursing neckline. Ginny's eyes were transfixed. If Doreen had lowered her chin ever so slightly, she could have rested it on these billowing piles of flesh.

Joe Bob stood behind Doreen, beaming with pride. Ginny would have known Joe Bob anywhere, too, even if she hadn't run into him yesterday. In fact, a bulletin mailed out after their Hullsport High homecoming last year had included a note about Joe Bob's being the new coach: "Those of you who were classmates of Joe Bob Sparks will be relieved to hear that ole Sparky hasn't changed one bit since high school days!" Ginny hadn't been relieved; she'd been appalled. It took an extraordinary mentality to be *relieved* to find that old friends hadn't changed since you'd known them—a mentality based on insecurity, as if change always had to be equated to deterioration. On her better days, the notion of change seemed profoundly liberating: She wouldn't have to be a flag swinger through all eternity! Not that her current role as the Madame Bovary of Stark's Bog was anything to boast about. But at least it was different, and there was a modicum of comfort in variety.

"Only those who continue to change remain my kin," Nietzsche had said in a Philosophy 240 text at Worthley. Miss Head had hated Nietzsche, though. And now that Ginny thought about it, who'd want to be kin to *him?*

Doreen took Ginny's hand and led her into the plantation estate itself. It was furnished with new pecan furniture—tables, chairs, and sideboard in the dining nook, sofa and armchairs and coffee table in the living room. "The Heirloom I-talian Mediterranean Ensemble," Doreen informed her. And spreading across one entire eggshell white wall in the living room was a vast piece that looked like a king-sized coffin. It was embossed with the inevitable factory-hacked filigree. This piece, occupying the spot that an altar would in a church, with all seats turned to face it in worship, was the pecan Italian Mediterranean solid state TV-stereo color console. The rugs and curtains of the living room and dining nook were in tones of harvest gold and antique yellow.

"What do you think?" Doreen asked, gesturing expansively around the living room.

"You've done quite a job," Ginny said.

"Doreen's a real little homemaker," Joe Bob said, hugging her from behind.

"I can see that she is."

With one of his wrist-weighted arms, he reached down and patted Doreen's stomach proprietarily. "Got me an Oakland Raider cookin in here."

Doreen poked him playfully with an elbow and said, "Sparky, honey, you *know* we're not tellin people yet."

"Ginny's not *people*, sweetie. Ginny's a *friend*. Anyhow, if we don't tell her now, she won't never know. She's going back up at Vermont in a few days."

Finally realizing what they were telling her, Ginny said, "Oh! A *baby*. How nice. But what if it's a girl?"

"Well," Joe Bob said thoughtfully, distractedly scratching his crotch, "if it's a girl, I reckon we just keep on tryin till I get me mah boy."

Ginny knew that if he could, Joe Bob would have the fetus growing in a decanter on his coffee table so that he could oversee its development—flushing it down the toilet and starting over if it was a girl. But if it was a boy—*if it was a boy!* He would pipe fight songs through the amniotic fluid and exercise its tiny embryonic limbs with electric currents. He would prop his stop watch next to the bottle so that the fetus could accustom itself to the challenging sweep of the second hand.

"Doreen, honey, get me a Pabst, will you?" he asked, looking at a huge Swiss clock on the wall. He opened the doors of his color console and turned it on. He also turned on a small black-and-white portable set on top of the console. Then he dragged an armchair to within five feet of the two sets, which featured two different baseball games. "I'll let you girls talk about woman things," he said with a coy grin as he sank into the chair, like a flight engineer at Mission Control in Houston. Without taking his eyes from the screens, he extended his hand for the beer that Doreen brought him. With his other hand, he fingered the stop watch around his neck.

"*Beer?*" Ginny asked.

He grinned. "Shoot, I'm *done* with my trainin. Let my boys suffer now."

"Let me show you the rest of the house," Doreen insisted, dragging Ginny into her all-electric harvest gold kitchen. They inspected each of her appliances with care—from the twin-door side-by-side refrigerator/freezer, right through to the eleven-speed multi-attachment mixer/grinder/blender. All the accessories—note pads and pencils, dish towels, toothpicks—were in complementary shades of yellow and gold. Doreen pointed to eighteen king-sized cans of corned beef hash and said proudly, "On sale at the Super Mart for seventy-three cents a can."

"Well, I swear," Ginny said.

"I *wish* there were something new to do with hash."

Ginny forced herself not to suggest that she try smoking it. "I know what you mean."

"The bedroom next," Doreen promised, leading Ginny down a short dark hallway. Opening a door, Doreen revealed a room that was all bed. It was king-sized and stretched from one wall across to the opposite wall. The headboard was pecan Italian Mediterranean. The spread was quilted harvest-gold flowers. "Sparky calls it Sparks Field," Doreen giggled. "Ball park. Get it?"

"Oh *ho!* Yes!" Ginny laughed weakly. She squelched the urge to say, "Oh, you mean he's finally getting it up?"

Doreen gasped with horror. "Oh Ginny, *honey*! Forgive me!" She poked Ginny's arm apologetically with two outstretched fingers. "I forgot about you and Sparky. . . . This is real insensitive of me to be talkin like this."

"It's okay. That was *years* ago."

"Oh, I'm just mortified!"

"Don't be. It doesn't matter. Really it doesn't." And the interesting thing was that it didn't. In fact, Ginny at the moment was awash with relief, thinking, "This could have been me, my house, my life." On the other hand, there was a certain appeal to it all. She had to own up to it. Part of her secretly longed to be immersed in such issues as, "Are the dishes in the dishwasher clean or dirty?" But mostly she continued to be transfixed by Doreen's remarkable bosom. She couldn't take her eyes off those breasts, kept studying them with quick sideward glances.

"Go ahead," Doreen said, noticing Ginny's fascination and moving closer. "Poke one."

Ginny was startled. Doreen was bisexual? Too bad, because Ginny thought that on the whole she herself wasn't anymore. Or at least not with Doreen. "Oh no, Doreen. I wasn't—"

"Go *on. Poke* one." Obligingly, Ginny poked one. She wasn't sure what she was supposed to be noting about it. It felt pliably firm and smooth, like your normal run-of-the-mill tit. She looked at Doreen questioningly. Was there a tumor she was supposed to be feeling? "Feels like the real thing, don't it?"

"It isn't?"

"I had me a boob job," she whispered. "It was my Christmas present to Sparky last year."

"They're magnificent. Joe Bob must love them," said Ginny, not without personal knowledge of his tastes in female anatomy. She remembered his initial disappointment when he discovered that her Never-Tell padded bra had contributed a fraudulent fullness to her minimal chest. If bras, like shoes, had come in quadruple A cups, that would have been her size then. Things were better now, though.

"Oh, he's crazy about them. He just can't get enough of them," she confided, as Joe Bob in the next room shouted at the TV, "*Nail* the bastard, you idiot!" "Why, if I let him, he'd spend all night just—" Throwing her hands to her face, she squealed, "Oh, *shit!* I've done it *again!* Ginny honey, you'll *never* forgive me!"

"It's *okay*," Ginny insisted, as Doreen threw open the closet doors to reveal silver lamé jump suits, suede pantsuits, sheer midriff tops, high-waisted Loretta Young hostess pants, filmy flowing harem pants, lacy body shirts, turbans, boas, Grecian halters, long skirts, mini-skirts, maxi-skirts, diaphanous dressing gowns, hot pants, high-neck gowns, low-neck gowns, no-back gowns, saris, dozens of pairs of boots and clogs and sandals, each with matching handbag. Ginny stifled a yawn. "Joe Bob's closet?"

Doreen giggled. "Still that same old sense of humor, Ginny. Law, I like to *died* those nights at the Family Drive-In listenin to you explainin to Sparky why you couldn't screw him. Dole and I lay up there in the front seat just howlin at some of the things you come up with."

Ginny repressed her reaction of outrage at knowing that she'd been eavesdropped on. To change the subject she nodded at Sparks Field and said cooperatively, "To spend so much time undressed, you sure have a lot of nice clothes." Then, suddenly, she felt very tired of all this. "Look," she said in a subdued voice, "my mother's sick in the hospital, and I've got to get back to her."

"Oh, that's *terrible!* Nothing serious, I hope?"

"I don't exactly know. I don't think so. It's a clotting disorder. She's had it before."

"Sparky darling," Doreen called, leading Ginny away from Sparks Field and toward Mission Control. "Ginny's mother's in the *hospital*, honey."

Eyes glued to the color console, Joe Bob said with annoyance, "Do whut, Doreen?"

"The *hospital*, honey."

"It's too *soon* to go to the hospital, baby love. You're just three months, peaches."

"No. Ginny's mother, sweetie. She's in the hospital."

"Well, I swear," he said, finally looking up. "I hate to hear that, Ginny. Is she real sick?"

"I don't know exactly. But I've got to get back over there." Actually, she was going back to the cabin. But she'd had enough here.

"Well, I hoped you'd set a spell and have a Pabst. But I can see you've got to go."

"Wait!" screeched Doreen. "You haven't seen the *bathroom!*" She pushed Ginny in front of her through another doorway and threw on a light switch. They were both reflected in a huge mirror that covered half of one wall. The light was harsh. Ginny felt as though she were in a police line-up. Squinting, she glanced hastily at herself in the mirror. Horrified, she looked away. The tile was harvest gold, and the towels and soap and toilet paper were yellow. Doreen threw open the cabinet doors so that Ginny could view her Isotoner Chin Strap and her Sauna girdle, her hair wax and deep cleanser and turtle oil moisturizer, several pairs of wash 'n' wear eyelashes, mud pack mix, six economy boxes of raspberry douche mix, depilatory cream, eyelash dye, every kind of hair roller, sixteen shades of nail polish, a Water Pik, tweezers, endless tubes and vials and bottles.

With renewed fascination, Ginny studied Doreen in the mirror. For an afternoon around the house, she had on blusher, eye liner, eye shadow, eyebrow pencil, mascara, lip gloss, and powder. Her pierced ear lobes sagged under gold filigree. She reeked of deodorant and perfume, and undoubtedly of raspberry douche if Ginny were to sniff up close. Her blond hair was impeccably dyed and teased and waxed and curled; pink nail polish, flawlessly unchipped; calves and armpits, satiny; chin, firm. She wore bright green contact lenses. Her E-cup breasts were artificially inflated, and an embryonic Oakland Raider inhabited her womb. What part of her body could she call her own?

Ginny's thoughts flashed briefly to her mother's black and blue swollen body. What was the point of Doreen's machinations? If she herself were in Doreen's rhinestone wedgies, as she might very well have been but for Clem Cloyd, would Ginny have gone this route, too? Or would she have vanished from Plantation Estates one dark November night and have turned up the next morning, corroded to death in the fetid Crockett River? Would she have hijacked a plane to Esalen? What *would* she have done? She didn't know. In any case, she wouldn't have been what she was now. Which probably would have been a considerable relief to everyone.

Doreen was studying Ginny in the mirror, too. She reached over and started yanking out Ginny's gray hairs as though plucking a dead hen. "It's *such* a shame," she murmured, "when there are so many nice shades of brown on the market." Ginny shot her a resentful look. Doreen was sounding alarmingly like Ginny's own mother. "*Well!* But if you don't start dyein pretty soon, everone's goin to *know* when you *do*."

"Do you think so?" Ginny asked wearily. She was thinking about what a truly terrible thing it was to have hair too limp for an Afro, but too wavy to be worn long and straight and parted in the middle. She had to concede that her mother's unspoken criticism was right; she looked like the Before picture in a cream rinse ad. Not that she would ever have admitted it to her mother.

"Let me walk you to your car," Joe Bob suggested gallantly as Ginny was leaving. Just then the doors on the Swiss clock opened. A man in lederhosen ducked in and out alternately with a fräulein in a dirndl, while "Edelweiss" played. It seemed out of keeping with an Italian Mediterranean ensemble.

"I'll leave you two alone," Doreen said coyly, fading into her kitchen, a domestic scientist retiring to her laboratory to discover something new to do with hash. Her harvest-gold hairdo blended right into the surroundings. Ginny wondered if she was supposed to pull Joe Bob down on top of her on the living room rug to fulfill Doreen's fantasies. Doreen was okay, though. There was nothing wrong with her that a vasectomy of the vocal cords wouldn't fix.

"Good luck with the baby," Ginny called. And as she walked with Joe Bob toward the Jeep, she said, "Guess who's in the room next to Mother at the hospital?"

"Who?"

"Coach."

Joe Bob's face sagged with grief. "I know. In'nt it pathetic? I been up to see him a time or two, and he didn't anymore know who I *was!* Law, it like to broke my heart. He's a great athlete and a fine human being, Coach is." Could they be talking about the same coach? Ginny nodded reverently and climbed into the Jeep.

"Listen, Ginny," Joe Bob said urgently. She looked at him. His face was tense with effort. "There's somethin I been wantin to say to you all these years. I've felt real bad about standin you up in the darkroom that day."

"Which day?"

"That day we was supposed to meet and decide whether or not to—you know, run off and get married. And stuff."

Ginny looked at him in amazement. That wasn't how she recalled things. "What do you mean *you* stood *me* up?"

"Well, to tell you the truth, I just couldn't face you. I took up with Doreen the day before we was supposed to meet. I don't know how it happened. Somethin just clicked an we got carried away, and—well, you see what's come of it." He gestured to his house. "But I've felt real awful about the way I let you down that day, not even showin up to explain or nothin. I've always felt like it was my fault you took up with that Cloyd creep and let him almost kill you on his cycle, to try to get over me."

"Please, Joe Bob," Ginny said, nurturing male ego as she had been trained to do since infancy, "don't apologize. Sometimes I feel *I* let *you* down that day." But basically she was outraged. The bastard had stood her up! And she hadn't even known it because she'd stood him up too.

"I'm glad we can still be friends, in spite of it all," Joe Bob said, tears filling his eyes.

"Me too," she said, extending her hand for him to shake, knowing she'd probably never see him again.

Ginny continued up Joe Bob's road until it deadended. Then she took a right across the ridge, intending to check out their old parking spot. What had been a Jeep track then was now a well-maintained gravel road. It ended abruptly where it always had. Dead ahead was a discreet sign saying "Valley View Slumberland." The vacant field their spot had overlooked was now filled with sunken brass plaques and plastic flowers and miniature American and Confederate flags. Below in the smoky valley was Hullsport. Ginny was startled to see how the town, in her time away from this spot, had crept up all the surrounding foothills.

She turned the Jeep around. As she drove slowly down the hill past Joe Bob's house, she reflected that the demise of their relationship had been utterly foreseeable to those not blinded by lust: The requirements of romantic love are difficult to satisfy in the trunk of a Dodge Dart.

5

Harleys, Hoodlums, and Home-Brew

---- □ ----

I had always known Clem. We were inseparable throughout childhood, riding our ponies all over the farm and swimming in the pond
and building forts in the woods. There was an old springhouse on a
hill above his house; it was a weathered board construction that shel-
tered the spring, which bubbled out of the hillside, and flowed across
the stone floor in a wide channel, exiting into a pipe leading to the
Cloyd kitchen. It had formerly served as a refrigerating area for the
farm's milk until the truck came to get it. It was deliciously cool and
damp there during the endless sticky Tennessee summers, and Clem's
parents let him have the ramshackle shed for a playhouse. He had
built crude furniture from scrap lumber—a table and benches and
shelves. He had installed a lock and a knocker on the door, and he
kept all his most cherished possessions there on the shelves—his Swiss
army knife, a hatchet, his marbles and comic books and magic stones.
I was the only other person allowed inside. Because, in a secret pact
in which we pricked our index fingers and mingled our blood, we
were married. I gathered pieces of bark for dishes and twigs for
silverware. He made me a broom with his knife by peeling and tying

a small witch hazel limb. I cooked ghastly concoctions from berries and nuts and mud, and cleaned more zealously than I've ever cleaned a real house since; and Clem stalked the woods pursuing manly activities, returning for our mock meals and for bedtime, in keeping with our abbreviated time scheme in which six play days might very well pass during one real day.

Clem as a little boy was short and slight, with a tangled mat of black hair that hung in his dark serious eyes. He was an ideal subject for a Save the Children ad. His family was part Melungeon, members of a mysterious, graceful, dark-complexioned people whose ancestors were found already inhabiting the east Tennessee hills by the first white settlers. Admirers of the Melungeons claimed for them descent from shipwrecked Portuguese sailors, from deserters from DeSoto's exploring party, from the survivors of the Lost Colony of Roanoke Island. Detractors protrayed them as half-breeds, riffraff from the mating activities of runaway slaves and renegade Indians. The truth was anyone's guess. And in any case, the Cloyds themselves couldn't have been less interested. Their forebears having endured various minor persecutions due to being labeled "free persons of color," the present-day Cloyd family longed to forget all about their obscure origins and get on with the business of living. All that remained to mark them as Melungeon was their gypsylike good looks.

Clem's older brother, Floyd Cloyd, even as a child was tall and slim and elegant—and mean as hell. He was Clem's and my sworn enemy, forever devising ways of wrecking our games and destroying our property. His specialty was known as the Floyd Raid. It required that both Clem and I race into the springhouse, gathering up scattered comic books and other treasures lying outside. Once inside, we barred the door and quaked in the corner until it became clear whether or not the raid was a false alarm. Floyd, like the wolf in the "Three Little Pigs," used a variety of tricks to get us to let down our guard. Once he caught us and tied us to trees and tickled us mercilessly for half an hour, until he lost interest and took Clem's keys and left to ransack the springhouse and steal our favorite Scrooge comic books.

The farmers in the area several times a summer organized wagon trains. Their families, in horse-drawn wagons or on horseback, would travel in huge groups over dirt roads and logging trails for several days at a time, covering a hundred miles or more. They camped out along the trail at night, cooking over campfires and then gathering around one huge fire to tell stories and sing and play instruments and barn dance. I often went with Clem's family, and Clem and I shared a double sleeping bag. Until we hit the age of nine or so and found this inexplicably prohibited.

Once, about this same time, we stripped to our underwear in the springhouse, which involved removing shorts in my case and baggy bib overalls in his, since we wore nothing else during those sweltering summers. We inspected each other uncertainly in our respective white cotton briefs. Then we hastily started whooping an Indian chant and danced around each other with writhing hops.

When the dance was over, we painted each other's back and chest with paint made from squishing pokeberries. Clem said as he was painting purple concentric circles around my nipples, "I betcha won't go around without a shirt when you're seventeen!"

"*Ha!* I will *too!*"

"Wanna bet on hit?" he asked, holding out his purple hand.

"Yeah," I sneered, seizing his hand.

"Five dollars?"

"It's a deal."

By the time we were ten, Clem wasn't available so often in the summers. His father had started putting him to work. I tailed woefully along for a while, helping where I could. We were riding on the tractor cutting hay one afternoon when we felt the mowing attachment lurch and heave. Looking back as the machine continued laying down alfalfa in neat swaths, we saw a doe bounding toward the woods on the far side of the field. At the edge of the woods, she stood still for a few moments, looking back and snorting asthmatically with fear. Then she leapt neatly over the barbed-wire fence and disappeared behind the mountain laurel.

Clem and I noticed some thrashing in the piled grass. Clem cut the motor, and we hopped down and ran back to it. About fifteen feet behind us, to one side of our path on the tractor, the cut grass was matted down and splattered with blood. A small fawn, still spotted white, lay on its side, its head raised. It froze when it saw us, its eyes wide and rolled back. Looking around with frantic dismay, Clem bent down and picked up a sticklike object which was dribbling long threads of black gore. It was the better part of one of the fawn's legs. There was a tiny dainty pointed hoof on one end.

Clem and I stood paralyzed with horror, Clem clutching the tiny leg. Clem's father, who was working on the fence in another part of the field, saw us and came sauntering over.

"What a shame. Poor li'l fella," he muttered. He drew his hunting knife from the leather sheath on his belt.

"Wait!" Clem ordered. "Me and Ginny, we want to keep hit, Pa. We'll fix it up and take care of hit good, Pa. Ain't that right, Ginny?" I nodded.

"Nope. Got to put hit out of hits misery. Just die slowlike anyhow. Can't function no more like the good Lord meant." And with a deft stroke of his sharp knife, he slit the fawn's quivering throat. The small animal jerked and twitched, and its eyes clouded over. It shuddered spasmodically and then lay still.

Clem and I glared at his horrible father and dragged the fawn, in a trail of blood, over to the woods. We scooped out a grave in the leaf mold and buried the fawn and its severed leg, muttering imprecations against Mr. Cloyd.

One day when Clem and I were playing in the woods near the springhouse, we came upon a black snake lying among the leaves devouring a large frog. The unfortunate frog was half in the snake's mouth and half out, and was kicking its legs crazily. It seemed impossible that the struggling amphibian could fit down the snake's throat. But as we watched, the snake drew the thrashing frog, a fraction of an inch at a time, farther into its mouth. Finally, unable to stand it any longer, Clem raced to the springhouse, came back with his army knife, and plunged the blade repeatedly into the long black snake while it thrashed and twitched. When the snake finally lay still, Clem wrenched open its jaws and pulled out the kicking frog. With horror we discovered that the frog was already dead. It lay twitching mindlessly next to the dead snake on the forest floor, its head and neck lacerated from the snake's fangs. Clem and I looked at each other with despair and ran as fast as we could to the springhouse and locked ourselves in.

I filled the playmate vacuum by seeking out some of the girls in the nearby development, Magnolia Manor. We played house in our bomb shelter. One afternoon we girls decided to have a party. Each of us five picked one boy to invite. For lack of anyone else, I named Clem while the other girls groaned with distaste.

Two afternoons later, when our five chosen knights arrived, we descended to the family room/bomb shelter with a pitcher of Kool-Aid and an economy pack of Oreos, and a stack of records with names like "The Twelfth of Never."

Clem and I were the only ones who didn't live in split-level ranch houses in Magnolia Manor. That put us at the bottom of the pecking order. Besides, the others were obviously old hands at boy-girl parties. So much so that they quickly became bored with eating Oreos and listening to records and watching the girls dance with each other. Someone suggested Spin the Bottle, and everyone groaned. "That's so *corny*," one Magnolia Manor sophisticate moaned. "How about Five Minutes in Heaven?"

In the face of unanimous enthusiasm, Clem and I nodded our consent, though neither of us had any idea what it would entail. What it *did* entail was that each couple vanished into the chemical toilet cubicle while the others sat outside and timed the tryst (and, in my case, wondered what the couple inside could possibly be finding to do with each other for five minutes in a dark closet). Clem's and my turn came last. They shut us in, our faces burning with embarrassment. I sat down on the lid of the toilet, while Clem leaned up against the wall with an effort at world-weary nonchalance.

"Nice party."

"Yeah," I agreed, vowing never again to participate in a party of any sort.

"Got the third cut of hay in on the south forty yesterday."

"Did you? How many bales?"

"Same as last cut."

"Great." We lapsed into strained silence. One of the boys outside hooted, "Hurry up and finish, you two. Your time's almost up."

We glanced at each other with dismay. Finish? We hadn't even begun, had no idea what we were supposed to be in the middle *of*. Clem leaned over and ground a kiss onto my tightly closed lips, holding my shoulders intently. "There!" he said proudly, wiping his mouth with the sleeve of his work shirt. I looked at him in horror. "Well, in'nt that what we're *supposed* to be doin in here?" he demanded.

Just then the door burst open. "*Caught* you!" everybody screamed.

"You did *not*," I said sourly, standing up and walking out.

From then on, Clem Cloyd was my arch enemy. Both he and I began playing football with the boys in Magnolia Manor. We always tried to be on opposite teams so that we could smear each other into the dirt. Clem was often the quarterback since he was so small and fast. There was nothing I savored more than dodging my blockers and racing into the backfield and hitting Clem's hips and bringing him crashing to the ground under me. Or being opposite him in the line and locking shoulders with him when the ball was snapped, both of us gritting our teeth ferociously and grunting with exertion. Or straight-arming him as he closed in on me during an end run. Sometimes after he had tackled me, he would lie on top of me longer than necessary, his chin resting on my stomach and his dark eyes looking slyly up at me over my shoulder pads. At such times I would wrap a leg around his hips and gouge him with my cleats until he rolled off me in pain.

This went on until his accident, at which time he supposedly ceased to be a factor in my existence. He was disking a new field on a hillside when the tractor tire hit a buried boulder and reared up like a startled horse. The tractor rolled over on him, crushing one of his legs.

I visited him once in the hospital. He lay swathed in white linens, his injured leg suspended from a pulley arrangement and encased in a full cast. We had nothing to say to each other. My life was all football now, and Clem would never play football again.

From then on Clem Cloyd was very much on the periphery of my life. He limped around school in his orthopedic motorcycle boots which had a four-inch sole for his injured leg; his dark greasy hair hung in his scowling face. He wore tight blue jeans, which had pegged legs and were studded down the leg seams and around the rear pockets with bronze upholstery tacks; and a faded dark green T-shirt; and a red silk windbreaker Floyd had brought him from Korea. The windbreaker had the island of Korea embroidered in garish yellows and greens on one breast, and an Oriental dragon all across the back. It was a masterpiece of tackiness.

To compensate for his injured leg, which was now somewhat shriveled with its foot twisted inward, his entire body alignment had altered. He dragged the injured leg, and the shoulder on that same side hunched down and forward. Because of this deformed gait, he preferred, whenever possible, to roar around on his dark green Harley motorcycle, which he'd bought with the prize money he'd won in the state fair with his show steers. The Harley had jeweled mud flaps and two huge chrome tail pipes. The seat was covered in imitation leopard skin, and a racoon tail hung from the antenna. When he was riding, he sometimes wore a molded plastic helmet of metallic green (the color of the cycle), which was decorated with a large Confederate flag decal. Other times he wore only yellow-tinted goggles and no head covering, so that his pomaded pompadour quivered in the breeze. Unfortunately, his thug image was undercut by the fact that he reeked of manure. From his barn chores, his body and all his possessions were permeated with the acrid odor, and the less kind students at Hullsport High, to be funny, sometimes held their noses after he had walked past.

Before long, I was flag swinger for Hullsport High and Clem was the town hoodlum. Sometimes I nodded coolly to him as he lurched along the hall. He never acknowledged me.

In the morning before school, when the popular students like Joe Bob and me and all our friends and fans were sitting in the gym, Clem sat outside in his leopard-skin cycle saddle with one or two lesser hoods. They smoked Lucky Strikes and stomped out the butts with their boots on school property. One morning after Joe Bob and I had decided that I had to dredge up some dates in order to throw Coach and my father off the scent of our trunk-bound liaison, I went up to Clem where he slouched in his saddle smoking.

"Say hey!" I said with my brightest flag-swinger smile.

He glared at me glumly and spat into the scruffy grass in the parkway that was struggling to grow up among the cigarette butts. "Can I speak to you?" I asked, undaunted.

"Why?"

"It's important," I assured him, as though he might imagine that anything I involved myself with could possibly be unimportant. He glanced over at me, his dark eyes unhappy and unfriendly—surly, in fact. Then he got off his cycle with exaggerated effort and limped over to me.

"Whaddaya want from me?"

"Would you do me a favor, Clem? For old time's sake?" I asked with a winning smile.

"Screw that. But whaddaya want?"

"Will you ask me out?"

He looked at me with suspicious amazement. "*Ask* you *out?*" His eyes narrowed. "You tryin to put the screws on what's his name—that fairy you run around with? Or what?"

"It would be a favor to Joe Bob, too," I assured him, certain that pleasing Joe Bob Sparks would appeal to Clem. Then I explained the situation.

Clem took a big drag on his Lucky Strike and let the smoke drift out his nostrils and waft around in front of his face. "If I *do* take you out—and I ain't sayin yet that I will—hit won't be as no favor to that fairy creep of yours. Hit'll be cause I happen to *want* to. Got that straight?''

"Okay." I was prepared to accept almost any terms in order to accomplish the deceit.

"Okay, then. I'll pick you up some time Friday night. You can wear my helmet so's you don't get blown around none or nothin.''

Joe Bob was delighted when I told him of Clem's cooperation as I jerked him off in the darkroom that afternoon. "Maybe he's not such a bad guy after all," Joe Bob gasped hopefully as he spurted into the sink.

Friday night when Clem's cycle came roaring up the driveway, the Major sat scowling behind his newspaper. I had been waiting by the window for Clem for about two hours. Occasionally during my vigil, the Major had interjected a remark about brain damage and amputation and the various other occupational hazards of motorcycle riding.

"He has a helmet for me."

"For your entire body?" he'd asked.

"Look! If I didn't do anything that might hurt me, I'd sit in this house in a rocking chair all day. Maybe not even that—a rocker might break, or the ceiling might fall in."

"Yes, but you don't have to court disaster," my mother had said.

I ran out and slammed the door on her as she called, "You can't be too careful!"

Clem sat there revving his motor with one gloved hand, on the wrist of which hung a silver-plated identification bracelet. He didn't greet me or look at me. He merely inclined his head toward the rear seat and handed me the Confederate flag-decaled helmet. I put it on and climbed on behind and experimentally put my hands on his narrow hips. I inhaled deeply of his manure scent, hoping soon to become oblivious to it through proximity.

Over his shoulder, he said, "All right. Where to?"

I was speechless. I was accustomed to being taken places by my dates, not to deciding where myself. "I don't care," I said meekly. "You decide."

Spraying a shower of white quartz pebbles onto the front porch, he threw the Harley into gear and scratched out. We cruised Hull Street a few times. Once at a stop light we were next to Doyle's Dodge. I looked over and saw Joe Bob staring at me wanly, his nose pressed against the window. I smiled bravely over my shoulder as the

Harley roared off, leaving the Dodge behind as though it were standing still. The skirt of my madras shirtwaist billowed like a sail.

On another circuit of Hull Street, I glimpsed Coach in his black DeSoto. I waved gaily. He scowled back.

Then we turned in at the Dew Drop, where Clem roared over the asphalt ridges, leaning from side to side as the cycle careened madly under us. I wrapped my arms tightly around his waist and clung in terror. He pulled up in front of a microphone and said over his shoulder, "What'll ya have?"

"A cherry Seven-Up, please."

"Two cherry Seven-Ups," he said scornfully into the speaker.

When the drinks came, he tossed his down in one gulp; I sipped mine demurely, trying not to notice the heads of classmates in nearby cars, all turned to stare in disbelief at Ginny Babcock perched on the back of Clem Cloyd's Harley. After I had finished my Seven-Up, we drove home slowly. He stopped in front of the porch to let me off. "Did everyone who was supposed to see us together see us?"

"I think so."

"Good."

"Well, thanks a lot," I said brightly. "I'd love to do it again if you feel like it sometime." This seemed a painless enough fashion in which to sidetrack the opponents of Joe Bob's and my passion. I turned to walk toward the house.

"*Wait* a minute," he said sinisterly. He threw down his kickstand and got off the cycle. I froze in my tracks as he limped over to me.

"What?" I asked nervously, turning to face him. I wondered if he was now going to require me to reimburse him for the evening with physical favors. I felt queasy at the thought. We stood facing each other, me in the visored helmet and him in his yellow-tinted goggles, like a space-age Adam and Eve.

"The helmet. You forgot to give hit back," he pointed out with a grin.

"Oh, how silly of me!" I gasped with relief, throwing it off and handing it to him.

"*You* let *me* know if you want to play your little game again sometime," he suggested over his shoulder, as he limped back to the cycle. He leapt on and started it up with a lunge of his good foot.

In the darkroom the next day, Joe Bob inquired miserably, "Well, how did it go?"

"*Awful.* He's such a creep. I hate him really."

"You're a saint to go through all this for us," he said, unhooking my Never-Tell. He pulled my shirt up around my neck and pinned me against the wall and devoted himself to chewing on my nipples as though they were wads of Juicy Fruit.

That afternoon as I walked out of the building, I just happened to pass the section of the parking area where all the hoods parked their cycles. Clem was lounging in his saddle, inhaling deeply on a Lucky Strike. I strolled over and said sheepishly, "Say hey, Clem." He didn't answer or look at me. I stood shifting my books uneasily from arm to arm. "How about this Friday?" I finally blurted out. Without looking at me, he nodded assent and took another deep drag on his Lucky Strike. Then he snapped his hideous red silk windbreaker and removed his goggles from the handle bars and fitted them so that the elastic band didn't disturb his unguentary pompadour. I halfway expected him to offer me a ride home and was planning my haughty refusal, but he started up the cycle with a lunge of his foot, revved the motor with his hand, and then roared off without a backward glance.

"Don't expect your mother or me to empty your bedpan when you're a paraplegic," the Major called as I ran out the door that Friday night. I had been waiting for Clem two and a half hours.

I put on the green metallic helmet, which I was coming to regard as "mine"; and I clambered on behind him, putting my hands firmly around his skinny waist.

"Last time we done hit *your* way," he shouted over his shoulder. "Tonight we do hit *mine*."

Titillated, I pondered the topic of what "his way" would involve. We sped out the Crockett River road, the warm night wind whipping my London Fog like a flag in a hurricane, and whistling up under the skirt of my shirtwaist. I realized that there were practical reasons for Clem's outrageous wardrobe—his tight pegged jeans and windbreaker. I knew that I'd have to acquire some new outfits if our relationship was to continue. Looking down, I studied the tacky dragon embroidered on the back of his windbreaker. It evinced the inscrutable Oriental talent for busywork.

We pulled off the river road onto a dirt road. With alarm, I recognized it as leading to the parking spot along the river where Joe Bob and I had been discovered *flagrante delicto* by the highway patrolmen. But instead of turning left, we turned right onto two muddy tire tracks.

With almost any other Hullsport hoodlum, I would have been paralyzed with fear by now. But I knew that Clem couldn't be planning to rape and strangle me because his family's livelihood depended on the Major's continuing good will. Power, however obscene, did have its uses. Also, I knew, and knew that Clem knew, that Joe Bob would rip him limb from deformed limb should he in any way whatsoever displease me. It was like having a body guard *in absentia.*

But the main reason I wasn't petrified to be whipping down a dirt track through a lonely stretch of woods with the most notorious thug in town was that I had a pretty good idea where we were going. Although I'd never been to the Bloody Bucket, it hovered like Gomorrah in my imagination, as in the imaginations of all the respectable townspeople. The Bloody Bucket was a country nightclub run by Clem's brother, Floyd Cloyd. By day Floyd was the industrious janitor at the state school for the blind and deaf in Knoxville, in the basement of which he reputedly ran the largest still in the eastern part of a still-strewn state. By night he crept around town in a black hearse with a false floor, delivering his bootlegged liquor to all the upstanding citizens of the dry town of Hullsport. The Major, for instance, bought all his Chivas Regal through Floyd. On the nights when he wasn't making deliveries, Floyd opened up his nightclub, dubbed the Bloody Bucket ever since a knife fight there in which the loser had had his head jammed into a metal pail. At the Bloody Bucket, Floyd sold his famous home-brew by the drink to those who ventured in.

The nature of the goings-on at the Bloody Bucket had long since assumed epic proportions in the town mythology. According to the popular imagination, the Bloody Bucket was the scene of poker games with stakes of many hundreds of dollars, of knife fights, of lascivious floor shows and wanton prostitution, of racial integration and every other vice known to modern man. The clientele of the Bloody Bucket, in the eyes of the rest of us, inhabited a sort of shadow world, the seedy flip side to Bingo games at the Moose Club and preaching missions at the civic auditorium. Because it was so irresistibly appealing, we, the uninitiated, naturally reacted publicly to its presence on the outskirts of our town with scandalized outrage. Preachers at the church circle on Sundays were forever deploring its existence. And men running for sheriff each term pledged to "Shut Down That Sewer of Vice and Corruption." But no law enforcement agency had ever been able to surprise Floyd Cloyd with liquor in his possession.

Soon Clem was pulling the Harley up beside half a dozen cars in front of a small sagging building covered with tar paper. Clem climbed down and limped to the door. "Comin?" he asked as he discovered me still sitting hesitantly in the cycle saddle.

"Am *I* invited too?"

"Oh come off hit! Don't hand me none of that grand lady shit, Ginny. Whaddaya want from me—to spread my jacket on the ground for you to climb down on? Git your ass over here if you're comin."

I scrambled off the cycle and glided over to him with injured dignity. "Who do you think you *are*, talking to me like that?" He opened the sagging door and walked in, in front of me, ignoring me.

The cigarette smoke was so thick that it burned my eyes and veiled the contents of the dim room. Floyd appeared in front of us, elegant in a white shirt and brocade vest. I scarcely recognized him. I was accustomed to seeing him come to visit his parents in the dark green work clothes he wore to the school for the blind and deaf. His long dark hair kept falling into his eyes, and he kept throwing it off his face with sharp indolent tosses of his head.

"Well, well, if it ain't the li'l lame prince hissef," he said, putting a hand on Clem's shoulder. "And who's this princess he's got with him? Why, I do believe it's none other than the good Major's lovely daughter." He smiled and bowed with exaggerated politeness. Then he dragged Clem away by gouging a thumb under his collarbone. They stood to one side, Clem wincing as Floyd gouged his shoulder, locked in a fierce but quiet argument—over my presence, apparently, because I kept hearing phrases like "that Babcock bastard" and "lookin for an excuse to shut me down."

Certain that I was the object of scrutiny for everyone in the room, I finally summoned the courage to glance around boldly. And discovered that no one was remotely interested in me. In the dim orange light of the room, I could see that it was starkly unadorned—bare floor, bare walls, a couple of dozen straight-back chairs and several square wooden tables. To my overwhelming disappointment, it looked just like someone's tool shed. My vision of plush carpets and flocked wallpaper and red velvet curtains faded. Along the far wall was a row of windows which looked out on the fetid Crockett. In a far corner was a raised platform, on which sat two men, one playing a guitar and the other a banjo. Standing in front of a microphone singing, dressed in a tight black straight skirt and a low-necked rayon jersey and ballet slippers, was Maxine "Do-It" Pruitt, my best friend from the first to the fifth grades. In the sixth grade we had gone our separate ways, me to become a left tackle and then a flag swinger, and Maxine to become "Sausage: Everyman's meat," as a moralistic girlhood book had warned us.

Maxine's hair, which had been a dirty blond in the fifth grade, was now strawberry blond and was teased into cascades of ringlets that made it look as though her neck would inevitably snap under the excess bulk. She had also been transformed from a stringy lanky kid into a warm soft voluptuous young woman with huge breasts that were molded by her bra into bulletlike projectiles. I had to hand it to Maxine: She was a professional, something I would never be if I didn't settle down and devote myself exclusively to some one trade, rather than flopping back and forth between football and flag swinging, or their equivalents. She was singing a popular country song, "Don't Come Home A'Drinkin' with Lovin' on Your Mind." She extended her hands, pleading, and threw her magnificent Marie Antoinette headpiece back and wailed in nasal agony, "You never take me anywhere/ Because you're always gone./ Many a night I've laid alone/ And cried here all night long. . . ."

Half a dozen rough-looking men in green work clothes, and a couple of excessively made-up and bouffanted women, one of them black, sat around the tables with Dixie cups full of ice and a clear liquid. At one table men were playing cards in tense silence.

Floyd had apparently decided to let me stay, in spite of my father. Clem lurched across the room to the cluster of people. Several looked up and greeted him with familiarity. He turned around and gestured impatiently for me. I walked over, feeling out of place in my London Fog and tasseled Weejuns and madras shirtwaist. I sat down stiffly in one of the straight chairs, carefully choosing one with its back to the wall, as I had done habitually ever since reading as a child of Wild Bill Hickok's being shot unawares due to his sitting with his back to a doorway. If I was going to be murdered in the Bloody Bucket, at least I wanted to be able to see who was doing it.

I smiled uneasily, although no one was acknowledging my existence. Floyd came over and put cups full of ice and the clear liquid in front of Clem and me. Clem took a gingerly sip. I stared at my cup unhappily. The most I'd ever had to drink had been a can of 3.2 beer at the Family Drive-In with Joe Bob when he had been between basketball and baseball seasons; he had felt he could celebrate by breaking training and trying to get me drunk so that he could lay me.

"Try it," Clem ordered.

Obediently, I picked up the sweating cup and raised it to my mouth. I made the mistake of sniffing deeply and was almost anesthetized by the vapors. "Drink," Clem said menacingly. So I drank. The liquid burned my mouth, and I could have sworn I felt it corroding my esophagus inch by inch as it descended into my poor unwitting stomach. The vapors ascended into my sinuses and foamed and fizzed like Drano in a drain.

"Well?"

"Delicious!" I gasped, desperately eager to please him for reasons that were unclear to me at the time.

"Good. She likes it," he called to Floyd at the next table. I smiled bravely at Floyd, who grinned back.

A few minutes later, taking a break, Maxine came over to our table. She stood with a hand with grotesquely long orange nails propped on one cocked hip. "I'm not believin it's Ginny Babcock!"

"Say hey, Maxine. I didn't know you sang. You're very good."

"Thanks," she said with indifference. "Clem, honey, what you doin bringin this poor girl here? You oughta be shamed of yourself."

"Hit's a free country."

"That's what they say," she said with a mocking laugh. "Don't you drink too much of that there poison," she said maternally to me. "Hit'll rot your gut good." And she went over and sat down next to Floyd, who put his hand under her skirt halfway up her thigh.

"You come here much?" I asked Clem in order to have something to say.

"Ever night."

"Don't your parents make you study?"

"Don't *nobody* tell Clem Cloyd what to do." If that was true, then his relationship with his father had altered dramatically since our childhood. I remembered Mr. Cloyd's beating hell out of him all the time as his way of "telling" him what to do.

Maxine got up and sang first "When My Pain Turns to Shame" and then "How Can I Miss You When You Won't Go Away." I had drunk about a third of my home-brew and was feeling giddy. Clem had downed all of his. He stood up abruptly and said, "Let's go." I trailed along after him to the cycle, its metallic green glowing like a June bug in the light from over the door of the building. I disappeared into the cavernous helmet. I was very conscious, as I tucked the skirt of my shirtwaist under my thighs, of the way my legs spread around Clem's hips. On the trip home, I was fixated by the way my thighs tightened around him and clung as we whipped around the curves of the river road. I felt genuine disappointment as he pulled into the driveway and waited for me to dismount, revving the motor impatiently with his leather-gloved hand. I sat still, savoring the feel of my knees on his upper thighs, and my hands around his skinny waist.

"Clem?"

"Yeah?"

"You know what?"

"What?"

"Whatever happened to the springhouse?"

"Hit's still there. Why?" He sounded hostile.

"I'd love to see it again sometime. We used to have fun there."

"No."

"No what?" I asked, hurt at the idea that he hadn't had fun there.

"No, you can't see hit sometime. Hit's *my* place."

"Oh," I said, feeling as though he'd kicked me in the stomach. It used to be *our* place. After all, hadn't we pricked index fingers and mingled our blood in a secret lifetime pact? But of course it was true that I hadn't shown the least interest in it in four years, so perhaps I'd forfeited my rights.

"Come on, get off, will ya?" I scrambled down and handed him my helmet. What was wrong with Clem? I was prepared to allow him to kiss me, even to feel me up. I had as much as asked him to take me to the springhouse. But he didn't appear remotely interested. Was he a queer, maybe, the puny stunted little runt? But then why was he bothering with me at all? To get at Joe Bob, the big handsome hunk? The mere thought of someone's moving in on Joe Bob and me made me furious!

"Next Friday?" Clem inquired with indifference.

"Yes!" He roared off without a backward glance.

In the trunk of Doyle's Dodge the next night, Joe Bob was reciting a list of the couples at school who were screwing. "And Ida Tolliver and Stan Strickler, and—"

"*No*. Not *Ida*."

"*Yes*. Stan swears they do it all the time."

"*Stan* says so," I said, trying to ignore Joe Bob's hard-on, which was punching me in the buttocks with each bump we went over. "And I bet *Stan* is telling *Ida* that *you* say that you and I are screwing." We had come quite a way in conversational candor from our first date when Joe Bob had referred to tits as "you know."

"I've *never* said that to *anyone*."

"I bet," I said, gradually being convinced by Joe Bob's long list that maybe in fact it was the thing to do. The other persuasive factor was that Joe Bob's hand was in my panties pummeling something that he referred to as my clitoris. As I had climbed into the trunk, I had noticed by the streetlight that his face was red and swollen. Settling into the curve of his body, I observed that he didn't wrap himself around me as usual. And he wouldn't talk. He was clearly sulking. Finally, one hand job later, I wheedled it out of him: "Why didn't you *tell* me about clitorises?" he demanded sullenly.

"Do *what?*"

"You been makin a damn fool of me, Ginny. Lettin me think I'm gettin you all worked up."

"What are you *talking* about?" I demanded with annoyance. In reply, he slipped his hand into my panties. Soon the notion of a college education in Boston seemed very distant indeed, and life as the wife of a Hullsport shoe salesman not at all unattractive. In short, as hot waves of desire licked through my body, a decision seemed imminent.

"Ginny," he announced, "the time has come for you to prove your love for me."

I gasped unintelligibly as he speeded up his kneading and resumed his list of our classmates who had fallen by the wayside in the ranks of Brother Buck's Teen Team for Jesus. "Look," I panted, "it doesn't matter who's screwing who. Whom. Even if I were to let you, we don't have anywhere we could do it."

"How bout tonight in Doyle's back seat?" he suggested eagerly, his fondling now sending icy shivers of craving through my body. I considered the possibility, with all the soundness of judgment of a junky in need of a fix.

"I couldn't," I concluded, in despair. "Not with Doyle and Doreen in the front seat. Not our first time."

"Maybe they'll get in the trunk for a while," Joe Bob speculated, chomping his Juicy Fruit with wild abandon. "I'll ask em."

"Did you bring a rubber?"

"Of course." Of course?

Just then the car stopped for Doyle to buy tickets. We waited patiently, having no other choice, Joe Bob's hand generating shuddering currents of lust up and down my limbs.

The trunk lid suddenly flew open. Doyle was standing over us looking mortified. Next to him was the irate box office manager. Joe

Bob hastily withdrew his hand. The manager shrieked, "I've *had* it with you goddam high school jerk-offs! Sneakin in here and robbin me of ever penny I make! If I ever catch any of you all here agin, I'll turn you over to the highway patrol *so* fast you won't know what hit you! I don't kear if you *are* big football heroes! I'm trying to make my fuckin livin! Now, get the hell out of my drive-in!"

As Joe Bob and I clambered out of the trunk, the headlights of the car behind us switched to high beam. I felt as though we were refugees being picked up by a searchlight during an attempted border crossing. My skin prickled with fear.

Out from the car behind us stepped Coach, his 250 pounds of flesh quivering with rage. "What the *shit* are you two tryin to pull, Sparks?" He grabbed Doyle and Joe Bob by the backs of their necks and dragged them off to one side. Swear words kept drifting over to Doreen and me as we stood trembling under the black gaze of the manager. Doreen was weeping and wailing, "I ain't never been in no trouble before. What'll *Daddy* say?"

And from the vicinity of Coach and Joe Bob and Doyle floated: "goddam mother-fuckin son of a bitch," "bust your goddam balls," etc. Apart from its being close to curfew for both Joe Bob and Doyle, Coach considered it essential that his athletes be moral paragons in the community. They had clearly blown it.

Doyle and Joe Bob skulked to the car, ashen in the high beams of Coach's DeSoto. We all climbed into the Dodge in silence, and Doyle turned around and drove me directly home.

"We're both benched at the next two games," Joe Bob mumbled, close to tears. I put my hand over his, intending for us to lock fingers in mutual support. Joe Bob didn't respond.

The next morning at breakfast, the Major said, "Well, congratulations, Ginny. You've done it. You're wrecking Joe Bob's coaching career." I glared at him over my poached egg, already consumed with guilt over the fact that I alone would be responsible for Joe Bob's future as a shoe salesman.

"How did you hear?" I asked sullenly. I had expected him to hear, but not so quickly.

He laughed hollowly. "Do you really think that anything goes on in this town that I don't hear about?" He slashed savagely at his country ham with his knife. "For example, do you really think that I don't know you were at the Bloody Bucket with Clem Cloyd the other night?"

I looked at him, startled. In fact, I really *had* expected to get away with that one. I hadn't figured that the Major's sources, whoever they might be, would include the clientele of the Bloody Bucket. But I had once again underestimated the efficiency of the Hullsport grapevine.

He sighed wearily, smoothing his dark graying hair. "I've tried warning you calmly, Ginny. I've tried forbidding you to see Joe Bob. Neither approach has worked. I'm washing my hands of the whole thing. Forget college. Forget Boston. Spend the rest of your life in Hullsport as some goon's slave if you want to. I really don't care anymore."

"But I'm *dating* other people."

"Oh yes. Clem Cloyd. What superb taste you have, my dear. Joe Bob Sparks and Clem Cloyd. Jesus!" He stood up abruptly and stalked from the room.

"Who would *you* suggest?" I called after him.

"*Whom*," Mother called from her desk, where she was shuffling epitaphs. She added, "Dear, I've heard that moonshine can blind people. And don't those men at the Bloody Bucket carry knives?"

"I haven't seen any," I assured her absently as I too stalked from the dining room.

Pushed by the Major into the muscled arms of Joe Bob, I made my long-awaited decision: We would screw. Oh God, would we screw! I couldn't wait. Not only would we screw, we would drive across the border into Virginia and get married. And we would live happily ever after in Hullsport with Joe Bob supporting us, when the Major disinherited me, on a shoe salesman's salary.

In the darkroom the next day as we rubbed our hips together, side to side in opposite directions, I said softly, "Joe Bob, we can't go on like this."

"I been thinkin the same thing. I guess we got to break up."

I stopped shifting my hips. "That *wasn't* what I meant."

"What did you have in mind?"

"I *meant* that we have to tell them all off—Coach, my father, everyone. Joe Bob, we're in *love*. They're jealous, that's what. Cause they're not young and in love. That's why they're trying to wreck it for us. But I *want* you, Joe Bob. I want you to—screw me. And then I want us to go to Virginia and get married." I ground my hips into his for emphasis. His cock was getting big and hard.

"Oh God!" he gasped. "But what about my scholarship?" The timer went off.

"Think about it. We can meet here on Monday to plan it." I slipped out the door for my sprint back to study hall.

Friday night as Clem and I pulled in my driveway after several hours and two cups of moonshine each at the Bloody Bucket, Clem said, "I've decided somethin."

"What?" I asked with inebriated interest. It was almost the first time since we'd been dating that he had directed an ostensibly pleasant comment to me of his own accord.

"You can see the springhouse again if I can see your bomb shelter." I looked at him with surprise. I couldn't imagine why he'd be interested. "You've never asked me into your house since that party when we was thirteen." I was touched that he should remember the party where he had kissed me for the first and last time. Could he possibly have a sentimental interest in seeing the chemical toilet enclosure where we had undergone this ordeal?

"Sure. Come on in." I hung my helmet on his handle bars, and he hung his goggles next to it. We stumbled inside. I put my finger to my lips and stood still in the downstairs hall, listening to see if the Major was lurking around. But from upstairs came the reassuring roar of his snoring. I opened the cellar door and turned on the lights, and Clem followed me down.

It wasn't unattractive, considering its function, though we never used it as a family room anymore. There were comfortable chairs and tables—in addition to the stockpile of canned food and first aid supplies, the plastic containers of water, the bedding and clothing and splints and rifles and boxes of bullets stacked along the walls.

Clem was inspecting the foot-thick metal door. "Does this thing close?"

"Sure," I said, closing and bolting it to demonstrate.

"Good," he said, rubbing his gloved hands. He drew off his black leather driving gloves and unsnapped his hideous red windbreaker. As he removed the windbreaker, I realized that I'd never seen him without it since we'd been dating. His chest under his dark green T-shirt was painfully scrawny, but perhaps only in contrast to Joe Bob's massive deltoids. On his forearm was a skull and crossbones tattoo, done by gouging out the design with a knife and filling the wound with ink; it looked self-administered, probably during an especially tedious history class. Tossing the windbreaker onto a chair, Clem sauntered over to the stack of weaponry and picked up a .22 with a telescopic sight. He sighted through it at the far corner of the

room, and then swept the gun around in a semicircle, as though
drawing a bead on a scurrying cockroach. He carefully replaced it.

Then he unbuckled his wide leather belt with its huge brass buckle
and whipped it out of its loops. Folding it in quarters, he slapped it
thoughtfully against one palm. I flinched, thinking he was about to
beat me. He smiled pleasantly instead and tossed it into the chair.
Then he limped over to me and clasped a breast in each hand and
pulled me to him. He kissed me, his tongue darting in and out of my
mouth like a snake's. "That's more like hit than last time, huh?" he
asked, stepping back from me. I smiled uncertainly, feeling woozy
from the moonshine.

He untied the sash of my wraparound skirt. Pulling one end, he
gave my shoulder a sharp push, so that I twirled out of my skirt like
a tango dancer. Then he methodically unbuttoned my Peter Pan-
collared shirt and held it while I slipped out of it. He shook his head
with mock disapproval and clucked his tongue as he unhooked my bra
and discovered the inch of padding.

"By the way," he said as he inspected my bare breasts, whose
nipples he had encircled with pokeberry paint eight years earlier,
"you owe me five bucks." I looked at him uncomprehendingly.
"You're seventeen now, and you're wearin shirts." I remembered our
childhood bet and blushed. "But," he assured me magnanimously,
taking me by the upper arm and directing me to the wooden sleeping
platform, "I'll settle for this instead." He removed my panties with
one deft movement and settled me on my back. The ceiling, as I stared
at it, began to spin. I opened and shut my eyes several times and tried
focusing on Clem. He was taking a jar of White Rose Petroleum Jelly
from his windbreaker pocket. Then he turned out the overhead light,
throwing the room into blackness.

I heard the sound of a zipper being unzipped nearby. Then I heard
a tearing sound, followed by a snapping sound. My eyes wide open
in the blackness, I saw something coming at me. It was the size and
shape of a small salami, lime green and glowing fluorescently. Small
green prongs, like on a space satellite, protruded from the rounded
end. As I watched with the absorption of St. Theresa viewing the
stigmata, this phosphorescent vision descended until it was hovering
over my abdomen. Then, as I watched, the object plunged itself
between my legs. I felt it enter me with a searing pain. Then I heard
Clem saying, "Oh *Christ!* You mean to tell me that you and that Sparks
fairy have just been jerkin off all this time?"

I nodded yes in the dark. After all, this was it. This was the experience that people down through the ages had sacrificed life and limb to achieve. Wars had been fought, kingdoms had fallen over the issue of who got to perform this act with whom. I wished Clem would get on with it. We didn't have much time left before Joe Bob would rip us both limb from limb; we might as well enjoy it to the hilt, so to speak.

Get on with it Clem did, thrusting himself into me savagely time after time, like a murderer stabbing a still stirring victim. This went on for quite a while. Finally, as I was mentally drumming my fingers on the platform, Clem stopped abruptly. The lime salami reemerged and floated in the air for a few moments, looking as though it were about to ascend into the heavens, whence it had come. Then there was a snapping noise and it vanished.

I found it hard to believe that this was what Joe Bob and I had spent almost two years building up to. "You mean that's *it?*" I asked with dismay. It hadn't been unpleasant, except for the first pain, but I couldn't exactly view it as the culmination of my womanhood. Frankly, the rupturing of my maidenhead had been just about as meaningful as the breaking of a paper Saniband on a motel toilet.

"Don't ask so many questions," he hissed. By the time he turned on the light, he was fully dressed, as though the incident of the glowing salami had never occurred. I looked at him, through my drunken haze, perplexed.

"Friday night," he said, not looking at me, as he heaved open the steel door and left me lying there in a small puddle of blood. Poor Mother, she had failed to capture yet another of my golden firsts with her Kodak M24 Instamatic.

I didn't keep my appointment with Joe Bob the following Monday to learn of his choice between marriage with me and his coaching career. I had made the choice for both of us. Or so I thought. Joe Bob and I avoided each other assiduously until he went away to college the following fall. I dropped out of Brother Buck's Teen Team for Jesus so that I wouldn't have to read the morning devotions with him. I put away my flag and uniform under the prodding of Clem's scorn, and I didn't even appear at the last few baseball games and track meets of the year. Joe Bob's and my eyes no longer sought each other out across the bleachers in the gym at lunch, or from neighboring cars cruising Hull Street at night. In an insultingly short time, Doreen appeared around school in Joe Bob's letter jacket, hefting his wax-filled class ring on her left hand. I could tell by the way they stood together—with her cooing and fondling the collars of his plaid Gant shirts, and with Joe Bob's patting her ass possessively—that they were screwing their heads off. It hurt. I cried unexpectedly over trivial things. My stomach churned when I saw them together. I didn't want Joe Bob anymore, but I sure as hell didn't want anyone *else* to have him. The only solution appeared to be homicide. But it had been my choice. And I was trying to do some compensatory screwing of my own.

Clem and I, children of the soil, would have done our rolling in the hay, one would have thought. But anyone thinking that has clearly never taken a roll on baled hay. Clem and I had to make do with the sleeping platform in the bomb shelter—and with the damp stone floor in his springhouse, which was where our second attempt at moving the earth occurred. Leaving his Harley by the road, we sneaked through the woods, along the overgrown paths of our childhood, arriving at the springhouse without passing his house and alerting his parents. He took out a key ring and unlocked an intricate series of bolts and chains and padlocks.

It was dark inside. Clem struck a match and lit a kerosene lantern. Then he locked another series of bolts and padlocks from within. Basically, the place looked much as it had when we were younger, though naturally it seemed smaller than my memories of it, since I was bigger now. The spring still bubbled up on one side and gurgled all the way across the stone floor in its channel. But taped around the walls, luridly resplendent in the flickering light of the lantern, were posters featuring every conceivable combination of man, woman, child, and animal, putting every possible body part into every available orifice. I stared.

Clem stood with his legs planted well apart and his arms folded, his hard-on prodding at his tight jeans. "Do much for you, woe-man?" He had started addressing me, out of the side of his mouth, as "woman" ever since our session in the bomb shelter.

"Well, it isn't how I remember the place," I admitted, wondering what I'd gotten myself into and how to get out of it. I was perhaps in over my head with Clem—his tastes were a little too exotic for me. I no longer had Joe Bob as a body guard, but at least the Major still retained power of the purse over Clem's family.

"We can take em down if they bother you," he offered.

Thrown off guard by his cooperative attitude, I replied with equal amiability, "Oh no, let's leave them up and see how it goes." I was trying to sound blasé and experienced, for whose benefit I didn't know since Clem was, by now, well aware of my woeful inexperience.

Our second attempt wasn't much more impressive than the first. By the lantern light he donned an orange neon condom whose foil wrapper read "Fiesta Brand." "Where do you get those?" I asked nonchalantly. Joe Bob's Dixie Delite condoms had been a utilitarian tan. Perhaps that was why I had never let him screw me. Could condoms, like Holy Communion, be an outward and visible sign of one's inward and spiritual grace?

"Floyd gets em somewhere. He says that French tickler like I used last time like to drives Maxine Pruitt wild."

"Oh yeah?" What was wrong with me that I hadn't been driven wild too? If I was to be driven wild at some point in the future, would I *know* that I was being driven wild?

Part way through our second assay, Clem leaned back on his knees and snarled, "Shit, woe-man, this is dumb." I couldn't have agreed more. I reviewed the undertaking and tried to figure out what I was doing wrong. We both sat up. Clem crawled in his studded blue jeans, which he hadn't removed for the occasion—never removed so long as I was with him in fact, since he didn't want me to see his shriveled leg—over to the shelves where he had once displayed his marbles and magic stones and bird nests. The shelves were now filled with paperback books. He scanned their spines and pulled one out and brought it over. Then he started reading:

". . . and so with a mighty heave on the crowbar, the heavy lid lifted. There she was, the only woman he had ever loved. Her flesh had dried up and fallen as dust to the floor of the coffin. All that remained of the warm mounds of flesh that he had stroked and nibbled were the underpinnings—bare bleached bones. The candle he was holding guttered in a damp draft of musty air. He leaned over and kissed her bare cheekbones. As he did so, strands of her brittle hair intertwined with his. . . ."

Noting that Clem's erection was miraculously reviving, I resolutely focused my attention on one of the posters. A voluptuous nude woman, built not unlike Do-It Pruitt herself, was kneeling on a low table, her pert ass in the air. A great brute of a man, masked and dressed all in black leather, stood behind her, his erection protruding from his black leather fly and partly inserted into her. He was pulling her toward himself with a chain wrapped tightly around her hips.

Starved rats on the table gnawed the woman's pendulous breasts, which were dripping blood. The expression on her face was of unreserved ecstasy.

"Uh, Clem . . ." The man in his story had just climbed into the coffin to embrace his loved one's skeleton, and the lid had slammed shut on him. "I've got to be going now."

"What's the rush, woe-man," he asked menacingly, in a tone I didn't recognize as his. My armpits were clammy. Then I remembered with relief that the Major could destroy Clem's family.

"Where did you get all the wild pictures?" I asked brightly, pulling up my underpants. As he stared at me, his face, cold and cruel, underwent a Jekyll-Hyde transformation, and he became "himself" again.

"In the mail. I ordered em up at New York."

"Aren't you worried that your father will find them?" I inquired with interest, having Big Brother for a father myself.

"This is *my* place. They leave me alone here. Always have. Anyhow, I got me eight locks on the place."

"I noticed," I said uneasily, eying them all. "Well! Guess I'd better be getting home. My *father* will be wondering where I am."

"Sure." He hopped up and discarded the orange neon condom and did up his fly.

One night that summer we rode on the Harley down to the dump, me with Clem's .22 rifle in my lap. Clem cut the motor a hundred yards away and rolled the cycle to the edge of the debris. He took the rifle and loaded it and held it experimentally to his shoulder, sighting. Then he gave me a handful of bullets.

"Get ready, woe-man," he whispered.

At his signal, I flipped on the cycle headlight. Poking through the layers of dirt down to the piles of decaying food were hundreds of rats. Clem aimed and fired. One of the rats was tossed into the air. Clem rapidly unloaded and reloaded, me handing him a bullet. The rat population was suddenly in a frenzy, scurrying around in frantic desperation, looking for hiding places. Clem had managed to pick off several rats by the time they had all vanished. The corpses lay twitching on heaps of dirt.

Clem turned off the headlight and led me back into the woods. "We'll wait until they come back out and try again," he promised.

We sat on a fallen tree trunk while Clem smoked a Lucky Strike.

I was having doubts about the validity of this pogrom as a pleasant way to spend an evening with the one you loved. But I had to admit that it beat the hell out of sex.

"Uh, Clem."

"What's the matter, woe-man? You don't like it?"

"Not much."

"Goddam vermin, that's all they are."

"Yes, but why bother?" He didn't answer. He took deep drags on his Lucky Strike, the tip flaring in the dark. "I mean, they aren't hurting you, are they?"

Finally he answered, seeming to wander from the point. "That day the tractor flipped on me—do you remember? Well, hit reared right up in the air. And while hit was turnin, I just kept thinkin, 'Naw, she'll straighten up. This ain't happenin to *me,* Clem Cloyd.' Well, when she *didn't* straighten up, I thought, 'Clem boy, this is hit. You've had hit, buddy.' And I got so mad I started shakin. Why me? I kept askin. I'd been a good boy. I'd hepped my daddy with chores. I'd been polite at school. I'd kept myself washed and done my lessons. Why was this thing happenin to *me?*

"Well, I know this sounds crazy like, that I could be thinkin all these things in the time hit took that tractor to flip. But I *did.* Hit seemed like hit took hours. I'd never been much on religion, but while that tractor was flippin, and the dirt and sky were tiltin under me, I made this here bargain with the Lord. I promised Him I'd go to church ever week with Ma if He'd just straighten up that damn tractor. Well, we just kept on a turnin, that tractor and me. And then I got real sad thinkin about all the chores Ma and Pa had asked me to do that I *hadn't* done, all the times Pa had had to whup me, thinkin of my lousy report cards, and like that. Thinkin maybe there *was* a hell, like Ma had always said, and I was goin straight to hit to roast on a spit forever.

"Then I started missin people—Ma and Pa, Floyd . . . you. The farm, my springhouse. Never mind *hell,* I was imaginin what hit would be like if there weren't *nothin* at all—cepting black and cold and loneliness. I think I screamed then. Pa said he heard me scream.

"But the funny thing was, by the time I hit the dirt, in fact while I was lyin there watchin that big red machine comin down on top of me, and knowin hit was gonna squash me like I weren't nothin but a corn borer, I didn't care no more. About nothin. I wasn't afraid, I wasn't lonely, I wasn't happy, I wasn't nothin. And when the tractor finally landed on me, hit didn't even hurt, Ginny. Everythin was— heat and light sort of. Dyin is no big deal. To tell you the truth, I was kinda disappointed to come to and find mysef still alive."

"So you're doing the rats a favor by shooting them?"

"I *knew* you wouldn't understand. I don't know why I tried to tell you." We sat silent, me penitent for having missed his point and having squelched one of his few attempts to confide in me.

"*You* should try goin through life crippled," he suddenly snarled, his face contorted with misery. "Why *me?* Why not *you?* What did I ever do to end up with a shriveled leg? How come you rich people get all the breaks and us poor people get crapped on all the time? *Tell me, damn it!*" He was screaming by this time.

"Shut up!" I screamed back. "How the hell am *I* supposed to know? I can't help it if you were dumb enough to turn a tractor over on yourself!"

His expression darkened. "I tell you what, woe-man. I done paid my dues. Ain't nothin nobody can do to ole Clem no more. They can't *touch* me. I'm runnin the show now. *I* decide who gets hurt and when and how. I been dead, and I done come back *alive,* woe-man. So don't mess around with ole Clem." We stared at each other with hatred for at least a minute in the semidark of the quarter moon.

On the way home, Clem hit an open stretch of road and gunned the Harley. Little by little, we picked up speed until we were tearing along through the night with the speedometer reading 90 mph. I clutched Clem tightly around the waist and buried my face in his back, gagging on the stench of manure.

Clem began screaming into the roaring wind, "Go ahead! Kill us, you bastard! I dare you to!" Gradually Clem's hysteria spread itself to me, and I was barely able to prevent myself from joining in screaming and jeering at the gods. I was far too caught up in the thrill of the fatal high speed, and the wind howling in my ears, and my bouffant hairdo lashing my face, to worry about the likelihood of being smeared all across the highway like peanut butter on bread. Or to question the mental make-up of the boy to whom I was entrusting my precious and precarious life.

Later that night in the bomb shelter, I sat fully clothed on the sleeping platform waiting to see what would happen next. I wasn't really up for screwing—there was a question in my mind as to whether our couplings to date had been worth the effort. With a shrug, Clem removed his windbreaker and tossed it into the corner. The hollow eyes of his ugly blue skull tattoo stared at me from across the room. He limped over, the scrawniness of his chest painfully apparent in his T-shirt. He stood directly in front of me and unzipped the fly of his tight studded jeans. His swollen purple organ swatted my nose.

"Eat me, woe-man," Clem suggested pleasantly.

"I beg your pardon?" I said, equally pleasantly.

"Don't ask questions, woe-man. Just *do* it."

"Do *what?*"

"*Eat me,*" he said, seizing my head with his hands and fitting my mouth around his cock and moving my head back and forth.

"You're *kidding?*" I mumbled.

"Do it, damn it, woe-man!" Obediently, my legs crossed and my hands folded in my lap, I licked and nibbled at the thing as best I could. After all, this was love.

After a couple of minutes, bored, I leaned my head back and looked up at Clem's attractive face with its fine dark Melungeon features. His teeth were clenched and his mouth was set in a mean grimace. His eyes were tightly shut, as though he were steeling himself for something. "Well!" I said efficiently. "I really need my beauty sleep. I guess I'd better be going."

His black eyes flew open, and he looked down at me in disbelief. Then, with his hand open, he swatted me hard across the face. The sharp sound echoed hollowly. I could feel the pain assuming the shape of a handprint. My tooth had punctured my upper lip, and I could taste blood. His hand was in the air, ready to hit me again.

"I'll scream," I announced with a calm of unknown origin. "My father will kill you and run your family out of town." We froze, glaring at each other with hatred.

Then, Clem turned away muttering, "You goddam mother fuckin li'l cock tease."

By the time his jeans were zipped and his windbreaker snapped, his face had relaxed into a pleasant smile, as though he had never so much as thought of hitting me. "How about the Bloody Bucket tomorrow night, woe-man?"

I hesitated. My instinct for self-preservation told me not to see him again. My instinct for self-preservation, however, wasn't in the ascendancy. "Sure."

"Oh," he added as we were leaving the shelter, "will you wear this?" He unhooked and thrust at me his name bracelet. On its plaque was engraved in block letters CLEM; the plaque was attached to a chain of large thick silver-plated links. It was a massive thing, and it clanked like a slave's wrist iron as I proudly put it on.

Maxine and I were becoming friends again, now that I had dropped flag swinging. I had begun imitating her mode of dress—a long-sleeved cardigan sweater buttoned up the back, with a bra that had pointed cups like party hats; a small gold cross on a fine gold chain, lodged between my breasts; a too-tight straight skirt that hugged my ass so closely as to make me look as though I were sitting down when I was still standing; black ballet slippers, which I shuffled as I walked. I had donated my madras shirtwaists and wraparound skirts and Villager blouses and tasseled Weejuns and London Fog raincoat to a Teen Team for Jesus rummage sale as my parting gesture. They were trying to raise money for Brother Buck to go spread the word to his European brothers and sisters that Death had lost its sting.

One night that fall after Maxine had finished singing "Spoon with Me, Darlin', 'Cause You Dish It Out So Good," she shuffled over and sat down next to me. Clem was in the far corner threatening someone with his Swiss army knife.

"Nice song."

"Glad you liked it." I offered her my cup of moonshine, and she took a hefty gulp.

"Hey, you know you're strange?" she said.

"Who, me?"

"Yeah. I can't figure you out no more."

"You can't?"

"You remember that first night you come in here?" I nodded. How could I forget? "I tell you, that was the shock of my life to look up and see Ginny Babcock standin in the doorway of the Bloody Bucket."

"It was the shock of *my* life too."

"What I *really* thought was that you'd come to make fun of us."

"You *did?*"

"Well, you know, there you was in your fancy raincoat and all, kinda smirkin."

"I was embarrassed. I didn't know how to act. I'm sorry if I looked as though I were smirking. I really wasn't."

"How come you to stop that flag swingin stuff over at the school?"

"I don't know. I got tired of it. It's kind of dumb, don't you think?"

"Shit, if I could be flag swinger, do you think I'd hang around this dump?" Her green eyes flashed. I looked at her with surprise. "And how come you to take up with ole Clem here when you had that Joe Bob Sparks hunk?"

"Clem's not so bad."

"Clem's not so bad, but he's no Joe Bob Sparks."

"Yes, but Joe Bob Sparks isn't Joe Bob Sparks either." She looked at me oddly. "Joe Bob's not *that* great." I was feeling pangs of regret. I had thought I was stepping *up* in the scheme of things when I renounced flag swinging and Joe Bob. I had thought that Maxine and the Bloody Bucket clientele were sublimely indifferent to the standards of the flag-swinging set. Could Maxine be merely a frustrated flag swinger?

A middle-aged man sauntered over. He was dressed in green work clothes and needed a shave. A gaunt face, slicked down hair, a lanky but wiry frame. It was a configuration typical of the mountain men who had moved from the coal fields to work in the Major's munitions plant.

"How ya doin, Harry?" Maxine asked, pushing out a chair.

"Not bad. Who's yer friend here, Maxine?"

"Ginny Babcock. Her daddy's Major Babcock." The man's eyes got wide and he sat up straighter in his chair. I restrained myself from kicking Maxine.

"Well, I declare!" he said with delight, sticking his hand, permanently stained with grease, across the table. I shook it gingerly. "We think your daddy's pretty special around these parts. I work up at his plant. Building maintenance division. Yes sir, he's a great man, your daddy is—a patriot and a gentleman."

"I'm sure he'd be pleased . . ." I mumbled.

Harry said dreamily, almost to himself, "Yes sir, truly a fine man. Lord, you shoulda seen how we lived when I worked them mines up near Harlan. Wouldn't no *dog* live that way. Roof falls and float dust. Shoot, you couldn't *pay* me to go back there." He looked up as though seeing me for the first time. "What you doin in a place like this?"

"I like it here," I said with resentment.

Harry looked at me sadly and shook his head. "You *like* the

Bloody Bucket. Does Daddy know where his li'l gal is at tonight?"

"Uh, no. I mean, yes. Well, I mean he knows I've been here before. I don't know if he knows I'm here tonight or not."

Harry sighed wearily. "I got me two daughters, and if either of em *ever* showed up here, why, I'd . . ."

"If you've got daughters and stuff, then what are *you* doing here?" I inquired victoriously.

A guilty look crept across his face. "Well, I was jest leavin," he assured me, starting for the door. "I'm real pleased to have met you, Miss Babcock. Listen, you tell that daddy of yours that Harry over at Building Maintenance sends him a great big howdy." He added with a cringing grin, "But maybe you might say we met downtown or somethin?"

One night at the Bloody Bucket a trap door in the plank floor was removed to reveal a cock-fighting pit. Chairs ringed the pit, their backs facing inward to form a wall between the spectators and the cocks. Eight or ten men straddled the chairs, and others stood behind them. Wads of money lay on one of the tables.

Two tough-looking men in khaki work clothes took cocks from burlap feed sacks. One was red with a black tail and wing feathers. The other was gray and white striped. As soon as they saw each other, their neck feathers flared out like Elizabethan collars, and they started struggling to get at each other. Steel spurs were fitted onto their yellow legs. Bending over the pit from either side, the men released the cocks, who met each other spurs first in mid-air. The men backed away quickly and moved the chairs in to close off the circle.

Soon blood and feathers were flying everywhere. Shouting was filling the room: "Shit! Kill that red bastard! Rip him to pieces, you mother fucker!" Feet were stomping and fists were waving. Clem, sitting in the chair in front of me, didn't even notice when I removed my hands from his bony shoulders and walked away. His eyes were glittering and were fixed on the pit, where the interlocked pair of mangled roosters kept bobbing up and down in a flurry of spattering gore.

I stood by the windows, looking through the low-hanging willows at the moonlight glinting off the river. I liked this view at night. You couldn't see how the Major's factory had turned the river yellow and fringed it with white foam.

Floyd sauntered over. "What's the matter, baby?" he asked,

throwing his dark hair out of his eyes with an indolent toss of his handsome head. "You don't like to watch things die?"

"I guess not."

"Ain't you runnin around with the wrong boy friend, then?"

"Probably."

"Then find another," he suggested, putting his arm around me and pulling me up against his chest so that my nose rested on his elegant gold brocade vest. All I could think of was Floyd as a boy trying to steal all of Clem's Scrooge comic books.

"Dry up, Floyd." He let go of me and laughed.

"Sure, baby. But when you work up to a *real* man, kid, you let Floyd know."

"Drop dead."

"Them French ticklers do much for you? Or in'nt our li'l Clem gettin it up for you these days?"

"Go to *hell,* you miserable creep!" Floyd laughed and strolled off.

Not only was my nonresponse to French ticklers none of his business, he'd touched on a sore topic—Clem's and my sex life, which was definitely not a source of bliss for either of us. Clem in recent weeks had tried binding my wrists and ankles with rawhide thongs to the platform in the bomb shelter. One night in the springhouse, he asked me to wear one of my stockings over my face like a burglar's mask. Another night he drove the Harley to the lonely stretch of dirt road between his house and Grandpa's cabin. Pantieless, I straddled him as he sat in the leopard-skin saddle and revved the engine with his gloved hand. But nothing seemed to work for him. We had never even approached the topic of what might work for me, what the goal was with regard to my physiology. The basic problem was that Clem was convinced that if he should discharge, he would be dead. This concept of the Ultimate Orgasm fascinated him at the same time that it terrified him. And the models on the posters in his springhouse made it all look so easy.

I watched now as the two men fished their mangled birds out of the pit. Both were still breathing, even though their feathers had been ripped out in clumps and flaps of jagged flesh were dripping blood. I didn't know or care which had won, but everyone else seemed to.

Floyd looked at his watch and yelled, "Okay, folks. It's time now."

It was as though a switch had been thrown. Everyone but me raced around doing things. The lid was replaced over the pit. The chairs were returned to the tables. Floyd came over to where I was standing and lifted open another trap door. Two men carrying a wooden keg emptied its contents into the opening. I could hear the moonshine splashing into the river below. Clem lurched over and dropped half a dozen papers cups through the trap door.

Someone knocked on the door into the other room. Shortly Maxine and a black woman I hadn't seen before came out, followed by two men who were buttoning their trousers. The guitar player sat on the raised platform with his legs crossed, tuning his instrument. Clem brought out a cross-shaped sign with the words "Gospel Tabernacle" printed on it, and leaned it against the platform. Maxine and the black woman mounted the platform, and everyone else closed in around its base. Floyd appeared, hastily draping a fringed black silk ministerial stole around his neck and carrying a large Bible. He joined Maxine and the black woman.

Clem called, "Quick! Get over here, Ginny!"

"Hit it," Floyd said calmly. The guitar player started strumming softly. Maxine and the black woman searched around for their notes, and then swung into a rhythmic version in close harmony of "Oh Happy Day," clapping in time. Everyone else joined in softly. Floyd cleared his throat.

Red lights flashed through the windows, and sirens whooped, and tires screeched. The door burst open as Floyd declaimed in a sonorous voice, "And thus sayeth the Lord . . ." In charged several troopers, brandishing pistols. They scurried into the other room, sniffing, like bloodhounds after a bitch in heat.

By this time Floyd was reading loudly and solemnly from the Bible, " 'Let every person be subject to the governing authorities. For there is no authority except from God, and those that exist have been instituted by God. . . . He who resists the authorities resists God. . . .' " And Maxine and the black woman and their clapping chorus were softly wailing in the background, "Oh happy day/ Oh happy happy day/ When Jesus walked/ Yes, when He walked/ When Jesus walked/ And showed the way."

Floyd looked up from his Bible, feigning surprise, and said, "Good evening, sheriff. Always delighted to have you and your boys here. You know that."

"Damn you, Cloyd," the sheriff snarled. "You done it again. But we gonna git you one day, buddy." He and his men turned around and stomped out, and the cruisers disappeared.

The next evening at supper the Major said, "Don't come to *me* for bail." I scowled at him. "I don't know exactly what you think you're doing," he said pleasantly, "but I hope to God that you get it done before you get into bad trouble."

I didn't know what I was doing either, but I was damned if I'd admit it to him. In some obscure way, I think I was hoping to be commanded never to see Clem or the Bloody Bucket again.

"Your mother and I have discussed it," he continued amiably. "We could of course confine you to the house and install locks on your door and so on. Or we could throw you out altogether and be done with it. Or"—here he paused significantly, for effect—"I could fire Clem's father, and he'd probably have to leave town to find work." I looked at him quickly with hatred as he played his trump card—guilt. Would I sit by and see Clem's family ruined for the sake of my own personal pleasures, or hang-ups?

"But of course I won't do that," the Major continued. "Cloyd can't help it if he's raised an idiot son, any more than I can help having raised an idiot daughter. And so your mother and I are washing our hands of the matter, having offered our more mature perspective in every way that we know how. It would be time now, if you were planning to go to college in the North, to be doing something about it. Since you're not, I assume that settles the matter." He took a bite of steak, thus concluding his dissertation on my character.

I was looking down at my plate, half-obscured as it was by my tits, which protruded in my Do-It Pruitt bra like two upended ice cream cones. At this point, I was the only child left at home and had the great good fortune of being the sole focus for their parental-anxiety syndrome. They had profited by their experience with me: Karl was happily ensconced at West Point, and Jim was sullenly detained at a military academy in Chattanooga. Only I had escaped the rigors of military discipline, and I was really rubbing it in.

I mumbled, "I never really *wanted* to go up north for college. That was *your* plan. I like it here in Hullsport. If I *go* to college, I'll go to State or Tech."

"Very well," the Major (BA Harvard '39) said calmly. I was impressed by his self-control. I knew I was killing him, unaccustomed as he was to being disobeyed.

Mother quickly reviewed the various threats to which I was exposing myself through my continued association with Clem—being splattered all over the highway; being rounded up in a police raid ("How would a police record look on your college application, dear?''); blinding myself from improperly distilled liquor; being stabbed in a knife fight; being raped and dismembered on a lovers' lane. Tellingly, she didn't breathe a word about the most likely afflictions—pregnancy and venereal disease. Apparently the bomb shelter and the spring-house weren't bugged by the Major after all?

"But it's not *like* that," I lied. "To hear you two talk, you'd think I was out *looking* for a way to get hurt, or something." The conversation ended with their giving me sorrowful looks, as though I were in a leaking boat and they were pushing me off, expecting the waves to swallow me.

Which is what nearly happened. Because I had been the Persimmon Plains Burly Tobacco Festival Queen the previous year, I felt a certain obligation to appear at this year's festival to crown my successor. Being Tobacco Festival Queen had fit my flag-swinger image, but it definitely *didn't* fit my current image as gun moll to Clem Cloyd.

Nevertheless, the morning of the festival I dutifully donned my yellow chiffon gown, and my carbine belt of a ribbon reading "Persimmon Plains Queen," and my cardboard crown spangled with glitter. The Major drove me to Persimmon Plains because he was on the organizing committee for the festival. He wanted to handle his neighbors' tobacco and to watch part of the auction to see what the crop from our farm would bring. Mother came along for the ride, toting her Instamatic.

Persimmon Plains was a small town whose only distinction was its central location to the farming regions of east Tennessee. The auction barn was a huge wooden warehouse, its red stain weathered and fading. The whole building looked as though it might collapse in a strong breeze. The inside was dingy and dark, and the plank floor was covered with shallow baskets of cured tobacco leaves and with throngs of buyers from the large tobacco companies and sellers from area farms. The sharp tingling odor of tobacco filled the cavernous room.

Blessedly for my bouffant hairdo, which was sagging under the weight of my crown, the crowning of the new queen was the first event. I dutifully plunked the cardboard crown on the head of this year's sucker, a cheerleader from Hullsport High, and kissed her cheek and smiled into the cameras. The Major hopped up on the platform. The Kinflick of that morning shows us in various poses conveying strained affection, alternately growling and smiling as flash-bulbs go off on all sides. Then the wife of the farmer whose crop had won first prize climbed up to pose with the new queen and me. She wasn't much older than I and was dressed in faded bib overalls and flannel shirt. Her hair was dull and frizzy, especially in contrast to the glossy bouffanted manes of the new queen and me. Her wide smile revealed several missing teeth. She seized one handle of a basket containing some of her husband's prize leaves, and I took the other handle. My free arm I draped across her shoulder for the cameras. Her free arm was amputated at the elbow. She said she'd driven a metal point through her hand while stringing tobacco stalks on wooden stakes for curing. She'd wrapped a greasy rag around the wound and had gone on working. Then she'd forgotten about it. The wound had become badly infected, but she continued to ignore it. Gangrene had set in.

After Mother and the photographers were finished with us, I told her how much I admired her way of life, how real it seemed to me, how I was planning to marry a farmer and live her kind of life, "in touch with nature." Clem and I had been discussing elopement proceedings the night before, after I had described how impossible it was becoming to live with my neurotically worried parents.

The girl looked at me with disbelief, and for the first time I noticed that her eyes were crossed. "Lord *God*, honey," she gasped, "don't you *never* marry no farmer. Hit's a durn sight better to be rich and healthy and happy."

I looked at her with surprise. Then I quickly gathered up my layers of yellow chiffon skirting to go in search of Clem, who was lurching around sniffing and feeling the dried leaves in the various baskets like the connoisseur he in fact was. He looked up at me with a sneer from where he squatted.

"I *had* to do it. After all, I *was* the queen last year."

"Shit, woe-man, you love this queen crap." He stood up and took my hand, and grazed and nibbled about my bare shoulders and throat with his soulful black eyes. My face flushed, and I could feel the red spreading across my upper chest, which was left uncovered by my strapless gown. "Let's go fuck, queenie," Clem suggested. This was intended as a joke, a sad joke, but nevertheless a joke.

"*Please,* Clem." I glanced around nervously.

The Major was involved with setting up the auctioning procedures and Mother was filming him, so I decided to leave without bothering them.

Outside, Clem gave me his red windbreaker to wear over my

gown, since he was wearing a heavy sweater. I put on the green metallic helmet and climbed onto the Harley. Then I gathered my chiffon skirts and tucked them under my thighs in big clumps.

It had rained the night before, and the roads were still damp. But the sun was bright, and the fields and the bare trees sparkled with moisture. The road between Persimmon Plains and Hullsport was narrow and wound up and down, over and around the foothills. In spots there were almost no shoulders, and sharp drops down cliffs just beyond the road's edge. The road signs read "65 mph—Speed Checked by Radar." But only Clem went more than forty on that road. It was, in fact, Clem's very favorite road, and he tore along it that day in his best form, leaning out and speeding up on the curves. His body and the cycle were one, satyrlike. The only problem was me, clinging to him from behind in my yellow chiffon gown. My arms were wrapped around him at hip level, and I could feel his cock stirring as he hit sixty-five on a curve.

He started shouting into the wind, "Do hit! Do hit to me, you mother fucker! Go ahead! Kill me if you can!"

I peeked over his shoulder, the wind whipping wildly past my helmet, and watched with fascination as the quivering needle on the speedometer mounted slowly. "Sixty-five miles an hour!" I yelled gleefully in his ear. "Seventy!"

"Kill us, you fuckin bastard!" he howled into the wind, hunching over to decrease his wind resistance. "I *dare* you!"

"Seventy-five!" I screamed. It seemed likely that we might hurtle out of the time-distance grid altogether. "Eighty!"

Just then my yellow skirts, which the wind had been tugging at, flapped loose. The chiffon material seemed to float on the wind. It swept and swirled playfully, and eventually wrapped itself around Clem's head.

"Christ, woe-man! What the *fuck* are you *doin?*" Clem screamed, starting to lose control on a curve. I let go of Clem's hips, and with both hands tried to haul in my skirts like sails in a typhoon. As I was doing this, I lost my balance. I grabbed for Clem, but missed.

The next thing I knew, my helmeted head was bouncing down the road like a plastic basketball. My skirts, caught in the rear wheel, tore as my body fell clear of the machine.

An experience that, objectively speaking, took perhaps ten seconds seemed to stretch out into at least two decades as I slid on my side across the asphalt and off the road and down the rocky cliff. I waited for the heat and light that Clem had described from his tractor incident. After all, this was it—the Ultimate Orgasm. I knew I was as good as dead. I waited to feel pain as I bounced down the rocks. I felt nothing. Except a faint twinge of annoyance, as I floated through the air with my skirts billowing like a parachute, that once again my parents had been right.

6

Monday, June 26

☐

Ginny woke up to bright sunlight streaming through the cabin shutters and onto the huge spool bedstead in which she had been born twenty-seven years before. From the musty smell of the mattress, she judged it not to have been aired out since. She lay still, watching motes dance like fools. The housewife in her wondered if the number of motes in any given patch of sunlight was proportional to the cleanliness of the house in which they occurred. If that theory was correct, Ira's house would have been crammed wall-to-wall with motes by the time she had left it, with Ira's gun in her back.

Ginny became aware of a screeching noise coming from behind the closed door leading into the living room. The grating screech would last for half a minute or so, then cease abruptly for about the same amount of time, then start up again.

Warily, she climbed out of bed and tiptoed to the door and opened it, expecting a flush of crazed bats to assault her. But all was quiet.

She tiptoed into the living room. In mid-step the screech began again. Startled, Ginny raced to the front door and hurled it open to allow more light into the shadowy room. She could detect nothing unusual—the same old sofa and armchairs covered in gold gingham material, end tables, the wall lined with guns and machetes and fishing poles and hunting knives, the stone fireplace and the old wooden mantel.

She traced the sporadic noise to the fireplace, but by the time she got over to it the noise had stopped. She tried to pinpoint the quality of the noise—it was a cross between the whirring of locusts and the cawing of several hoarse crows and the rattling of a rattlesnake. Apparently, the creature was insect, bird, or reptile. Unless it was mammal or amphibian.

The noise started up again. Ginny grabbed a knife from a sheath on the wall. Then she removed the spark guard from the fireplace. The noise stopped abruptly. Squatting by the fireplace, waiting for the noise to resume, she realized that she was naked. Not that it mattered. Who was around to be appalled by the way her sleek flag swinger's figure was being obscured by a layer of matronly flab?

When the noise started up again, Ginny was right there, but she couldn't actually see any creature to account for it. Gritting her teeth against an attack by a snake curled in the ashes, she patted her hands gingerly over the stone wall inside the fireplace, blackening them with soot in the process.

Finally she felt something furry. Boldly, she pulled it off the wall, halfway expecting to lose a finger in the process. It was a tiny baby bird, egg-sized. She held it up to her face, and she and the bird gazed at each other with fear and curiosity. But as she did so, she realized that, although her bird was quiet, the noise continued.

Going into the kitchen, she tore some rags into strips and put them into a bowl, and then put the baby bird on the rags. It was a tiny gray creature, covered with gray-black fluff, with a yellow beak and serious black eyes. With the help of a flashlight, she pried four more baby birds out of the crevices between the stones. Using a piece of cloth to disguise the odor of her meddling human hands, she placed them in the nest of rags. Shining the flashlight into the ashes, she discovered the remains of their nest, which apparently had fallen loose from the inside of the chimney. Which probably meant they were chimney swifts. Lying beside the torn nest was the corpse of yet another baby bird, coated with a soft powdering of ashes.

The five remaining birds were screeching madly in their bowl. They were frightened. They were hungry. They wanted their parents. They didn't want Ginny any more than she wanted them. This whole misfortune had nothing to do with her. She had to get rid of them as quickly as possible.

In a burst of inspiration, she climbed the stairs. Opening a bedroom window, she scrambled out onto the dull green tin roof. Carrying the bowl without spilling the birds was possible only because she had the reflexes of the mother of a two-year-old. Balancing herself against the chimney, she placed the bowl on the roof against the chimney. The baby birds started their frantic chorus, craning their heads back and thrusting their quivering pink throats upward.

Ginny peered around like a lookout in a ship's crow's-nest. From this vantage point, she could see over the lip of the kudzu-lined bowl, all the way through fields and pastures to Clem's maroon house. If Clem had been interested, he could have looked through binoculars from his attic window and seen her balancing nude on her tin roof gazing in his direction.

Looking straight up, Ginny saw a bright blue sky. And perched on the top of the chimney, looking down, an adult chimney swift. Hastily, she crawled back into the house to leave the scene open for a joyous reunion.

Still nude, the original Liberated Housewife, Ginny fixed herself some toast and tea, cleaned up, and made her bed. She dusted and swept and rearranged. Then she took the machete and went outside and hacked at the kudzu. She could have sworn that what she had chopped the previous evening had regenerated itself during the night.

Before long, the sun was moving toward noon and was blazing hot. Her body was clammy with sweat. She walked to the pond and swam her regal breast stroke through the scum. Then she returned to the house and got out a straw mat to lie on.

She knew that she ought to be at the hospital by now. But she couldn't face it just yet. Her mother and she had had very little to say to each other even when they had lived together full time. Her mother had always insisted, "I am your parent, not your pal." But Ginny had always envied friends who had had the pal-type mothers, mothers you could speak to frankly without disappointing or horrifying them, Ann Landers-type mothers you could burden with your problems. Instead, her own mother had erected an impenetrable barrier of propriety between them. She was forever declaiming principles like "Sex outside of marriage is vulgar." The only way Ginny had been able to approach her principled mother in those years when she had most wanted to was under the guise of pretense—pretending she wasn't giving Joe Bob hand jobs in the trunk of Doyle's Dodge and so forth. Until the time had finally come when she had simply stopped trying to approach her at all. And what was there to say now, when they had seen each other only four times in the last nine years?

Anything she could tell her mother about herself—that Ira had run her out with a rifle for screwing an army deserter in his family grave-yard—would be bound to trigger a relapse. What was Mrs. Yancy thinking of when she asked Ginny to keep her mother company? Did you invite snakes to keep company with toads?

But pal or not, her mother had left her mark, Ginny reflected. She had a recurring daydream: Her mother was dressed in a hard hat and work clothes and wielded a jackhammer, with which she was drilling neural channels through the gray matter of Ginny's brain. Ginny knew that almost everything she had done to date had been either in emulation of, or in reaction against, this powerful nonpal of a woman, or her equally influential husband. The house of Ira, for instance, the man she had "chosen" for her husband, had a shape and room layout identical to that of the white mansion in which she'd grown up. "Men are sometimes free to do what they wish," Hobbes said in a Philosophy 108 text at Worthley, "but they are never free in their wishes." Ginny had no idea how her parents might better have occupied themselves in life, but there had to be other ways for adults to amuse themselves than by irreparably molding the young minds placed in their charge. By leaving Wendy was Ginny setting her free from this? Or was it too late, had Ginny already wired her circuits in their years together? Or was it inescapable, would a new electrician merely take up where Ginny had left off?

But the main reason Ginny couldn't get up off her straw mat to head for the hospital was that she was profoundly upset at seeing her mother covered with black and blue bruises, her attractive face round and yellow from drugs. She preferred to think of her mother, *needed* to think of her, as strong and healthy and invulnerable—a shield between Ginny and mortality.

Ginny was calculating how few visits she could get away with in all decency when she remembered the baby birds on the roof. She decided to check to be sure their parents had rescued them, or were at least feeding them. And to postpone even further the dreaded trip to the hospital. She went upstairs and looked out the bedroom window. Nestled by the chimney was the rag-filled bowl, but it was empty. With relief, Ginny climbed out to retrieve it.

There, to one side of the bowl, were two stiff baby bird corpses, wings spread and heads thrown back. They had fried to a crisp on the hot tin roof. Given a plate and a lettuce leaf, they could have passed for the scrawny game birds Ira was always bagging on hunting trips and insisting on Ginny's rendering edible. A great wave of guilt and grief washed over her. She had placed birds that were accustomed to the cool damp of an unused stone chimney in a blast furnace.

But at least three had been saved. She put the two rigid birds reverently in the dish. Then she turned to climb back in the window —and discovered, clinging to the house in a small patch of shifting shade, the three remaining birds. Their small bright yellow beaks were opening and shutting convulsively but noiselessly.

As she stood there, in imminent danger of falling to her death on the stone steps below, studying with horror her three surviving charges, an adult swift swooped down and glided across the roof and disappeared over its peak.

"You goddam *bastard!*" Ginny screamed. "Come help your *babies!*" She stood trembling with rage.

Drained by her outburst, Ginny began reasoning: There was probably no way the parents could get the baby birds back into the chimney unless the babies were on the verge of flight, which they didn't appear to be. And the tin roof was too hot for them. Therefore, the thing to do next was to place the surviving babies in a tree, where the parents could come to feed them and eventually teach them to fly. Resolutely, she took a piece of rag to pick up the three living birds. They hung vertically like bats, their tiny talons dug deeply into the crumbling chinking between two logs. Detaching them was like removing burrs from a dog's coat. They clung so frantically that she was afraid of tearing off their little claws.

In the side yard, swamped by kudzu, was a sturdy pine tree. The lower branches spread out almost horizontally. Ginny placed the bowl on a platform of pine needles formed by two branches. She removed the two dead birds and tossed them into the kudzu, saying a silent eulogy. She had thought Nature took care of Her own. It hadn't occurred to her that She would need Ginny Babcock Bliss's fumbling assistance.

As she turned away, she looked up toward the chimney and thought she caught a glimpse of a bird's head peering down over the edge. "They're all yours," she called up cheerily.

When Mrs. Childress clomped in at 6:30 to wake her, Mrs. Babcock was furious. Not over being awakened so early, though that in itself was reason enough. She was just generally enraged, as she couldn't remember being since once, when she was a small child, when her pony had thrown her on purpose into a rose bush. If she hadn't been so weak, she suspected she might have been on her feet smashing windows and hurling that hideous fake Danish modern furniture against the walls.

Instead, she snatched the thermometer out of her mouth and threw it on the floor. Both she and Mrs. Childress watched as tiny silver balls of mercury skittered around the tiles like minute insects. Then Mrs. Childress looked at her in startled reprimand.

"I'm—sorry," Mrs. Babcock fumbled, startled herself at the force of her outburst. "It was—ah—an accident." So well-trained was she in the notion that one didn't even feel hostile emotions, much less give expression to them, for a moment she genuinely believed that it had been an accident, that her hand had simply slipped.

But then a wave of fury swept over her again. No! It *hadn't* been an accident, and she was perfectly justified in having done it! Why was someone always coming in here and waking her up to shove things in her mouth or her nose, to slice her with razors, to jab her with needles? What right had they? Whose body was it?

Mrs. Childress handed her her prednisone. "No," Mrs. Babcock announced, not taking the pills. Mrs. Childress looked at her with surprise and held out the pills again. "I said *no.*"

"Honey, you got to take your medicine to get better," Mrs. Childress explained patiently, as though to a small child.

"I'm not taking it. It isn't working, and I'm sick of gaining all this weight."

"How do *you* know it ain't workin, Mrs. Babcock honey? You don't know how you'd be widout it, do you now?"

"*Obviously* it's not working," Mrs. Babcock snapped, holding out her swollen bruised arms.

"You got to give it *time,* honey."

"I'm not taking it," Mrs. Babcock repeated, amazed with herself.

"Ain't no telling what'll happen." Mrs. Childress looked at her once-amiable patient with amazement.

"Let it. It couldn't be worse than this."

"We'll see what the doctor says," Mrs. Childress said primly, putting the pills on the table, clearly appalled that anyone could question treatment prescribed by a doctor.

"And I'm skipping breakfast this morning."

Mrs. Childress looked at her with a perplexed frown. "Honey, you *got* to *eat.*"

"*Why* do I?"

"So's you'll get well. You're anemic, you know, from losin so much blood."

"I don't see that the garbage we're fed here is going to contribute much to my health." She felt ill at the thought of the inevitable powdered eggs and canned orange juice and Cream of Wheat. And the prunes for her anemia.

"Mrs. Carter, our dietitian, knows what our patients need," Mrs. Childress replied righteously as she exited.

A bath was what she wanted, a hot steamy bath that would bake away her aches. She sat up slowly and swung her legs to the floor. She closed her eyes as the blood rushed down her bruised legs, causing them to throb dully. She shuffled into the bathroom and turned on the hot water.

Settled with warm water to her chin, she felt her rage subside somewhat. She closed her eyes and allowed her battered limbs to float. The ache was relieved when, like this, her circulatory system wasn't having to battle gravity along with everything else.

She lay suspended for a while—how long she had no idea—devoid of thoughts and feelings. But gradually thoughts began seeping in, like waste water in a leach field, uncharitable thoughts that triggered a return of the anger. So Wesley had failed her again. He wasn't here when *she* needed *him*. It was so typical. Regularly he had come home from work with migraines and had taken to bed, whimpering. Illness, he felt, was beyond any mortal's control; therefore, it was all right for him to collapse with headaches. She was sure that he had sat around his office yearning for migraines, so that he could lie in a darkened room and have her bring him meals on trays and bathe his throbbing forehead with cloths dampened in vinegar and make the children tiptoe and whisper. But let *her* come down with something and want to go to bed and be waited on and have the children tended, and he'd be nowhere in sight—hiding out in his office. Goodness knows at how many Boy Scout banquets, Little League games, father/son car washes she'd had to stand in for him.

He had always behaved as though he hated Hullsport, as though it were his cross to bear for the sake of his poor wife, who couldn't face leaving the South for someplace where he might have been happier. The truth was that a position in Boston had never been offered him. He had been sent to Hullsport fresh out of Harvard. Normally trainees stayed in Hullsport only a couple of years. After a couple of years, however, Wesley had gone into the army and been sent overseas. When he was mustered out, he had lost his place in the corporate scramble and was sent back to Hullsport and had never been recalled to Boston. Whether it was bad timing or a reflection on his capabilities, the fact remained that it wasn't her fault that he had spent his adult years in Hullsport. And yet in order to spare his ego, everyone, herself included, until the afternoon he had died on his office floor, had gone through this charade of pretending that Major Babcock remained in Hullsport to humor his wife.

It seemed to Mrs. Babcock suddenly that she had spent her entire life pampering other people's egos. Ginny's, for instance. She had a real nerve, showing up here in those dingy white overalls and a T-shirt without a bra. She had always done her best to chagrin her parents, and her performance yesterday was in keeping with that tradition. Yet Mrs. Babcock had endured it all silently, not daring to ask her to wear a nice dress or suit next time for fear of hurting her feelings, or making her self-conscious about her appearance, or causing her to rebel and come up with something even more outlandish.

But the real question was why Ginny was here at all. She was like some kind of vulture: She couldn't be bothered to pay regular visits to her parents like normal children; it required a major catastrophe to coerce her into behaving as she should have all along. Probably the only reason she was here this time was to go through the furniture and claim what she wanted for her house in Vermont before Karl and Jim had a chance at it. She had always been so secretive about her activities and her motives, but a mother could see through them anyway.

Stepping back from herself for a moment, Mrs. Babcock was appalled. These unpleasant sentiments about the people she loved were a new experience for her. She had spent her entire life in mediation. Wesley and the children had brawled throughout the width and breadth of the big house. She had trailed along behind, wiping away the tears of the combatants, explaining Wesley to the children and the children to Wesley. Never had she given vent to her own opinions, so that she rarely even knew what her own opinions were. Until today, when they were flooding in on her with a vengeance. But were they what she "really" thought?

Lifting her head, she glanced into the blue-black water—and discovered a weblike pattern of blood quivering near her upper thighs. Startled, she sat up and grabbed the overhead bar and hauled herself out. As she dried herself, she realized that blood was oozing from her vagina, which was theoretically impossible since she'd reached menopause several years ago.

As she stood there perplexed, there was a knock at the door. "Who is it?"

"Dr. Vogel. May I come in?"

"I'm not dressed. I'll be out in a moment." She drew on her gown and robe and stuffed some toilet paper between her legs.

The young blond Dr. Vogel was half-sitting on her bed. When she emerged, he rushed over and took one of her arms.

She jerked the arm away and snapped, "Take your hands off me, young man! I'm perfectly capable of walking by myself."

When she was settled in bed, acutely conscious of the leakage between her legs, Dr. Vogel said, "Now, Mrs. Babcock, what's this I hear about your not wanting to take your medicine?"

Instantly she felt apologetic; it would hurt this earnest young man's feeling if she questioned the treatment he was prescribing for her. And if anything had been drummed into her in her years of motherhood, it was that you mustn't squelch the young. It might stunt their precious development. Never mind about your own development. That was no longer important once you were a parent; you had been superseded as an evolving being. Her development hadn't mattered since she was a junior at Bryn Mawr, when she had dropped out to marry Wesley, who was about to go off to war. And where was Wesley now?

"That's right. I'm not taking it anymore."

"But, Mrs. Babcock, this isn't *like* you."

"How do *you* know what I'm like?"

"*Why* won't you take it?" he asked, humoring her.

Why was it, she wondered, that because she was ill, everyone insisted on treating her like a babbling idiot? "It isn't working, Dr. Vogel. You might as well face it. I have more bruises every day. My nose is gushing. And I've gained ten pounds."

"You have to give it *time*, Mrs. Babcock."

"I've given it over two weeks. The way things are going, I may not have much time left to give it."

"Now, now. What *morbid* thoughts we're having," he said with a nervous laugh.

"The last two times the medication had a noticeable effect in ten days."

He nodded, admitting the justice of her analysis. "All right!" he said briskly, standing up. "I can't force you to take the pills. I could give you an injection. But I won't against your wishes. But please reconsider, Mrs. Babcock. I can't take responsibility for what might happen to you if you continue to refuse your medication."

"I'm not asking you to," she informed him coolly, restraining a smile of satisfaction. "Uh, Dr. Vogel," she asked as his broad white back moved toward the door, "is it possible for a woman to resume her menstrual periods after reaching menopause?"

He turned quickly to look at her. "You're having a vaginal discharge?" She nodded. He sighed and suppressed a frown. "I'll have the nurse bring you some pads. But *please* reconsider your position on the medication, Mrs. Babcock. I'll examine you after I finish my rounds, but I suspect . . ." He whisked from the room.

He suspects what? Mrs. Babcock wondered. He suspects that the bleeding from my vagina is an extension of the bleeding in my nose? If so, isn't that proof that the drugs aren't working?

The door swung open and in walked Ginny in her low-cut Heidi dress. She was singed to the unattractive bright pink of a cooked shrimp.

"Hello, Mother," she mumbled, her shifty eyes lowered to the floor.

"Oh, it's you."

"I saw Vogel in the hall. He says you won't take your medicine."

"That's right. And don't *you* patronize me too. I'm not dead yet."

Ginny looked at this unknown woman with amazement. She remembered her mother as either mild and forbearing, or silent and disapproving. Maybe it was the drugs?

As Ginny walked slowly to the sun porch with her mother on her arm, she could hear Coach talking loudly in his room: "Yes, but I *happen* to be the coach around here. You tell him I said so. I don't care *what* he said. Just tell him I said to tell him *I'm* coach around here. When *he's* coach, he can run things his way. Ha, ha, ha, ha. . . ."

"Does that bother you?" Ginny asked.

"Bother me? Of *course* it bothers me. Wouldn't it bother *you* to have to listen all day to a lunatic?"

"Yes, I guess it would."

"You'd better believe it would!"

Mr. Solomon and Sister Theresa nodded at Ginny and her mother. Ginny sat down and watched in silence as the others ate.

Part way through the meal, Ginny suggested, "Mother, you'd better eat your beets."

"I don't *like* beets."

"Eat them anyway. They're good for your anemia." Ginny realized with a start that she was stepping into the dietitian's role her mother had performed for her for so many years. It occurred to her that parents spent years urging their children to eat, and that those children, grown, spent the rest of their lives trying to stop eating.

"*Good* for me? *Good* for me? Since when have *you* ever cared what's good for me?"

"Now, Mother," Ginny said with an embarrassed chuckle. She looked to Mr. Solomon and Sister Theresa for support against this irrational harpy who was inhabiting her meek mother's body. But they went on eating quietly without looking up. "Don't get all upset, Mother. Just eat your beets, that's all."

" 'Eat your beets,' she says. You just want me to choke down this garbage so that I'll go take a nap and you can get out of this place." She had scored a direct hit. Ginny looked down at her hands with a guilty blush. "Well?" Mrs. Babcock inquired triumphantly. "Isn't that right?"

Ginny said nothing. She couldn't figure out how to behave. Everything she could think of to say, her mother in this mood would be able to twist around and quarrel with. She had never seen her like this. It seemed best to say nothing at all.

Finally her mother said more quietly, "But at least you come to see me. That's more than I can say for my sons."

"But—" Ginny started to point out that they were in California and Germany, but then thought better of saying anything in support of her rival siblings.

"I asked them *never* to give me squash," Mr. Solomon sighed, "and here it is again."

Mrs. Babcock—whom Ginny had never seen do anything more insurrectionary than prop open an occasional pay-toilet door—suggested under her breath, "Dump it on the floor and pretend you spilled it."

"*Mother!*" Ginny said with mock horror, intending to turn it into a joke.

Mrs. Babcock looked at her, her eyes flashing, and said, "Don't you 'Mother' me. I don't even know you."

Ginny turned the laced leather thong on her wrist around and around as she tried to decide whether her mother's statement was intended to be factual or figurative: The drugs had affected her so that she literally didn't know who Ginny was; or she could identify Ginny as her daughter but didn't know what she was really like?

Ginny helped her mother back to her room and into bed. "Shall I do your hair?" she offered lamely, trying to think of something noncontroversial to occupy them. "You know, comb it out and stuff?"

"What's wrong with it the way it is?"

"Nothing. It looks fine. I just thought maybe—"

Miss Sturgill burst in, saying like a disconnected operator, "Hello, hello, hello!"

She started cranking up Mrs. Babcock's bed to a sitting position. Mrs. Babcock said sharply, "If I wanted my chin resting on my knees, I'd do sit-ups, Miss Sturgill."

Miss Sturgill stopped cranking and stuck a thermometer in Mrs. Babcock's mouth, which Mrs. Babcock suffered to remain there. After reading the thermometer and shaking it down, the nurse departed in a cloud of starch to perform other errands of mercy.

Ginny turned on the television to the afternoon soap opera, "Hidden Heartbeats," and settled into the easy chair. In the first place, she and her mother could stare at the program and thus have a socially acceptable excuse for not talking. In the second place, Ginny had a secret passion for "Hidden Heartbeats." She had watched it faithfully every afternoon as she was nursing Wendy. What sort of bizarre influences had she unleashed on her baby by requiring her to imbibe "Hidden Heartbeats" with her afternoon quota of mother's milk? There she had lain, as Wendy's little tummy had swelled with milk, contrasting her own bliss with the misery of most of the characters on "Hidden Heartbeats." She wanted to take them all fondly by the hand and counsel them to have babies. It was clearly the only route to true contentment. She had slipped her nipple out of the sleeping baby's mouth and had whiled away the rest of the program by working Wendy's joints. The toes and fingers, the knees and ankles and elbows, all bent where they were supposed to! The fine brown eyelashes resting on the chubby pink cheeks, the moist pink lips still pursed for sucking. It was a miracle! How had two such flawed mortals as Ira and she managed to create this perfection in miniature. . . .

But she was tormenting herself again. She focused resolutely on the TV screen, where Sheila was on the phone with Ella. It was like meeting Joe Bob yesterday and discovering that he hadn't changed.

A year later Mark still hadn't confessed to Sheila that the daughter being raised by her sister Linda had been fathered by their mother's uncle.

"I can't believe it," Ginny said out loud to herself.

"What?" her mother asked. "You mean that Sheila still doesn't know about Susie's father?" Ginny glanced at her quickly, suppressing a grin. So her own mother shared her vice, sneaked in afternoons when no one was around and turned on "Hidden Heartbeats"?

"Right. How could Sheila *not* know? In the first place, Susie doesn't look a bit like Frank. Frank is very blond, but Susie has red hair, for Christ's sake."

"Yes, but Linda's hair is auburn. Besides, genes are very curious things."

"True," Ginny agreed, grateful that they were finally having a civil conversation. "But don't you think Mark *owes* it to Sheila to let her know why Uncle Clarence cut her out of the will?"

"I'm not sure," her mother said, biting her lower lip as she considered the ethics of the situation. "After all, there's no telling *how* Sheila would react to Linda if she knew the truth, and they've got enough problems as it is, those two."

"Oh, *I* don't think Sheila would be upset at *all*. Do you really?"

"Well, look at the way she reacted to being told about Regina's unwed pregnancy. Knowing Sheila, I wouldn't be surprised at anything she did."

"Hmm, I guess you're right."

Sheila was having a bridge party. She stayed in the store picking out tallies for the last twenty minutes of the half-hour program. Soap operas were unsurpassable as social realism. Most fictional forms pruned and highlighted and rearranged, whereas soap operas were almost as tedious as real life itself. What got accomplished during half an hour in a soap opera closely approximated what was accomplished in half an hour of real life—i.e., next to nothing. The only thing that had occurred in the year since Ginny had last watched was that Frank had lost his job at the commercial art studio for doing pornographic photography on company time. Linda was suing for divorce, this being the last straw in a whole hayloft of previous offenses. Sheila was still unable to have children because of her distended cervix from a hatchet abortion when she was a teen-ager; and Mark, his ever-sensible and forbearing self, was still trying to talk her into adoption.

When "Hidden Heartbeats" was over, Ginny looked around to

ask her mother which show she'd like to watch next. She was curious to discover if her mother's addiction to the soaps involved a whole string of them, or just "Hidden Heartbeats." But her mother was asleep.

Clomping down the hall in her combat boots, Ginny asked a volunteer at the nurses' desk where she could find Dr. Vogel.

"Try the lab. First floor."

When she asked for Vogel at the lab door, the secretary said, "I'm sorry, but he's tied up right now."

Just then, he came racing out, his white lab coat flying behind him.

"Dr. Vogel, can I speak to you a minute please?"

"I'm very busy," he explained as he handed some papers to the secretary.

"I'll just take a minute." She was unaccustomed to this new twist in the art of healing. Dr. Tyler had appeared to spend most of his time talking to patients and their families, explaining what was going on, what treatments he was prescribing. "These drugs my mother won't take—Mrs. Babcock in 307—what are they supposed to do?"

"There's some evidence to support the concept that steroids— prednisone, cortisone—increase the clotting tendencies of the blood by reducing capillary fragility."

"Do you think they're helping in her case?"

He raised his blue eyes to the ceiling, struggling to be patient. "Obviously we do, or we wouldn't be giving them to her, would we, Miss Babcock?"

"How do they work?"

"Uh—yes, well. We don't know exactly." Ginny could tell that, like her parents, he admitted to not knowing something with great difficulty.

"What can you do if she continues to refuse the steroids?"

"We intended to transfuse anyway. She's anemic, her blood volume is down, she needs donor platelets." He was alternately smiling sympathetically and twitching irritably in his impatience to resume his lab work. He clearly wasn't accustomed to revealing his proposed treatments or to having them questioned by a layman.

Back at the cabin, Ginny went directly to the pine tree. She was delighted not to see baby birds in the wooden bowl or on the ground below. They were fairly old; it was possible that the parents had been able to give them quick flying lessons. As she strolled with relief back toward the house, the forlorn screeching started up. She whirled around and spotted them. They had climbed out of the dish and were hanging vertically from twigs. Presumably they had hung on the chimney wall and preferred it to sitting. All right. Let them hang.

Ginny went into the cabin and watched out the window to see if the parents were arriving with food and comfort. But nothing happened, no beaks full of worms arrived. Finally she went into the kitchen and made a tuna sandwich. When she returned to her lookout, she discovered a wild tabby cat crouching expectantly under the tree, paw poised and eyes gleaming. As she raced out the door, the cat leapt away. Upon closer observation, it looked likely that the birds' claws would slip right off the twigs and that they'd crash to the ground. So she returned them to their dish.

As she was finishing this operation, an adult swift swooped down and perched on the chimney. Another wave of rage swept over her, and she shrieked, "Goddam it! You get your ass down here right now! Your babies need you!" She was so furious that she couldn't move. Gradually, she contained herself by speculating on the absurdity of attributing human motives and powers of comprehension to birds. But goddam it, did they or didn't they fly thousands of miles in the autumn unaided by a compass?

Penitent, Ginny went in and phoned Dr. Tyler. She wanted to pick his brain on the topic of steroids, but there was no answer.

To delay her return to the hospital, she drove the long way around, past Hullsport High. Neither Joe Bob nor his "boys" were on the track. Ginny crept past the practice field in the Jeep. By the gym door were three young girls. They were marching, and yes, they were twirling flags. She stopped and watched, remembering, the past as usual threatening to swamp the present. The maroon and gray flags swirled and snapped hypnotically in the familiar patterns.

"Can I hep you?" a young man's voice asked.

"What?" Ginny asked, startled. Looking up, she saw a teen-age boy, his long blond hair damp and slicked back. He wore bell bottom jeans and a T-shirt. She recognized him as Billy Barnes, the prize stud in Joe Bob's stable.

"You look, like, lost. I wondered if you needed, like, directions or somethin."

"Oh, thanks. Actually, I was just watching the flag swingers."

"Yeah? Good, aren't they?"

"Not bad. I used to be the flag swinger here." For some unknown reason, she said this with pride.

"No kiddin," he said with a pleasant, even, white-toothed grin. Ginny felt he was studying her lined forehead and graying Afro with disbelief; she suppressed a need to assure him that it was true, that she had once been as slim and fresh and graceful as the three young girls they were both watching with admiration.

"Yes, ten years ago."

"Yeah?"

"Yeah. It doesn't look as though the routines have changed much."

"No?" He was now obviously humoring her. She was feeling more middle-aged all the time.

"Well, I've got to be going. Thanks anyway for the offer of directions." She revved up the Jeep. "Say, do you need a ride somewhere?"

He hesitated and blushed. "Sure," he said nervously, climbing in. "Where to?"

He stuttered. Ginny knew his problem. He didn't know how to take her: Was she offering him a ride, or was she offering more? Joe Bob had often mentioned with relish the women who tried to pick him up—the Yummy Mummies, he and Doyle called them. They were former cheerleaders or former girl friends of football stars who, closing in on middle age, panicked and began yearning for past glory. These women, once dazzlingly good-looking but now dowdy from years of housework and children, descended on the current crop of sports giants, offering themselves up in hopes of recapturing a taste of that fleeting glory. Was Ginny offering this handsome muscular young man a ride home, or was she now a Yummy Mummy, offering him herself? She wasn't sure. She was merely waiting to see what would happen.

"Yeah, well . . ." he said uneasily, blushing and running his hand through his long hair. "Say, you live here now?"

"No. I live in Vermont." His eyes brightened. A quickie maybe, with no strings attached?

"Vermont, huh? That's a weird place to live."

"Yeah. My mother lives here, though."

"Come back for a visit, huh?" He clasped his hands and hung them between his knees and shifted his muscled shoulders awkwardly.

"Right." It was interesting, this maneuvering between them as to who was going to suggest a tryst first. Ginny revved up the Jeep again and pulled out, heading for Hull Street. From Hull Street, who knew what might develop? She was getting more interested in Yummy Mummyhood all the time. She hadn't had any really fervent sex for —God, for years and years, if ever at all. Sex for her had always been complicated and confused and permeated with every emotion and motive imaginable. Maybe a mindless tussle with a hot horny youth would be just the thing—an act of pure present, performed without distorting influences from her past, and without expectations for the future. A quickie, in other words. After all, if Ira was going to banish her for adultery, she might as well commit some. Whatever she and Hawk had thought they were doing that night, it wasn't adultery.

"What sports do you play?" she asked, glancing at his hard young body appraisingly. With a paper bag over his blond head he could have passed for Joe Bob at age seventeen any day—he possessed the identical bulging nonchalance.

"All of em."

"Yeah? Which do you like best?"

"Oh, football, I guess. I want to get me a football scholarship next year. Maybe to Ole Miss. And then I want to coach."

Ginny rounded the church circle and turned down Hull Street, joining the stream of cruising cars that had already assembled in the early evening sunlight. "We used to do the same thing," Ginny said, with pain. "Spend all night driving up and down' this street."

"Yeah?" he said with his tolerant grin.

"Do people still go to the Dew Drop?"

"Oh sure. A lot go out on the Sow Gap Highway, though. There's a chain of new places—a McDonald's and stuff."

The only difference that Ginny could see, as she crept under the banner welcoming Mrs. Melody Dawn Bledsoe home as 1957 Pillsbury Bake-Off Champion, was that the clusters of boys sitting on their cars watching the passing traffic now had long hair instead of crew cuts, and patchy mustaches; and they wore bell bottoms and T-shirts instead of chinos and sports shirts.

At a stop light, a Chevy pulled up beside the Jeep. A bunch of boys, friends of Billy's apparently, made suggestive faces; Billy blushed and tried not to grin with pleasure at his friends' knowing that he was about to get laid by an older woman. He shifted his muscled shoulders so as to turn his back on their obscenities.

This was getting ridiculous. Ginny realized in a flash that she wasn't a Yummy Mummy, that flag swinging and Joe Bob Sparks were dead for her, and that even this gorgeous young hunk of horny male flesh couldn't flog any more sentiment from this segment of her past. She decided to put a swift end to it. "You want to coach, huh? You know, I used to date your coach when I was in high school here."

The boy snapped to attention, knees together, hands by his sides, and eyes straight ahead. "Coach Sparks?" he asked in a small nervous voice.

"Yes. For almost two years." Billy was immobilized at the mere mention of the name. Joe Bob had apparently done an admirable job of replacing the feared Coach Bicknell. She could just picture Joe Bob now, prowling through the Family Drive-In in search of curfew violators. "Where do you live?" she asked the terrified boy gently. He mentioned one of the developments in a weak voice, and she drove him directly there. She watched with regret as he lumbered up his sidewalk.

By the time Ginny got to the hospital, Mrs. Babcock was just finishing her dinner of canned ham and boiled potatoes and creamed spinach and applesauce. Unacknowledged, Ginny sat down on the sofa in silence.

Finally, wondering who or what would answer her, Ginny said, "Hello, Mother."

"I wondered if you'd deign to visit me."

Ginny suppressed irritation and reminded her mother, "But I was here this afternoon. Have you forgotten? We watched 'Hidden Heartbeats.'"

"No, of course I haven't forgotten. What do you think I am, senile or something?"

Through a major effort of will, Ginny managed not to reply unpleasantly. She looked out the window resolutely. It was her favorite time of day in the South—early evening when the sun was low, but not yet setting. The landscape—the factory and the foothills and the church circle and the train station—was bathed in an indirect golden glow; and all God's creatures, her peevish mother included, seemed to pause for a moment and reflect, suspended between the frantic flurry of daytime activity and the long night of rest and oblivion. Ginny took a deep breath and sighed.

"Bored?" her mother inquired. "Just remember that *I* didn't ask you to come down from Vermont."

"No, Mother, I'm not bored, I'm relaxed," Ginny assured her, surprised at her unexpected reserves of patience.

Back in her mother's room, Ginny turned on the television again in desperation. There were only cartoons and a cowboy show on now. Ginny left the cowboy show on. The blond beefy crew-cut head of Dr. Vogel appeared around the door, like a decoy on a target shooting game. "And how are we tonight?"

"How do you *think* I am?" Mrs. Babcock shot back. She'd absolutely had it. She felt she was going to scream if anyone asked her one more polite question that he didn't really want answered.

"Good. Fine," Dr. Vogel chuckled uncertainly.

"*Doctor!*" He looked at her anxiously, then looked at the floor. "Am I dying?"

There was total silence for about ten seconds. Taking a deep breath, Dr. Vogel said, "What black thoughts we're having on this lovely summer evening, Mrs. Babcock." His eyes darted nervously around the room, avoiding Mrs. Babcock's. "We've done regular platelet counts, Ivy bleeding times, a one-stage prothrombin time, a fibrinogen level"—he was ticking these off doggedly on his meaty red fingers—"MacPherson and Hardisty's modification of the Hicks-Pitney thromboplastin screening test, the euglobulin clot lysis time, clot retraction time, bone marrow studies. We should know any day now whether your disorder is associated with megakaryocytic hyperplasia of the bone marrow, or consumption coagulopathy, extravascular sequestration, or an autoimmune mechanism. Please count on us, Mrs. Babcock. I assure you that we are using every tool modern medicine has available. But it *would* help if you would cooperate." He hesitated, then turned around quickly and left.

What kind of an answer was that to a simple question, Ginny wondered as she sat with her head propped on her hand staring blankly at the cowboy show. Was it a yes or a no? Ginny glanced at her mother, who was looking dazed. A pile of mangled bodies dominated the foreground of the television screen. The main characters— two cowboy brothers—sat off to one side drinking and laughing. Mrs. Babcock pointed at the screen. "Look at that! Look at that! Every idiot in America thinks you kill somebody and they just pop right back up. They should all try dying sometime themselves and see how much fun it is!"

"They will."

"And you!" she cried. "Why are *you* still alive? *You* should be the one in this bed instead of me. You've done nothing but ask for it your entire life—racing around on motorcycles and drinking moonshine and going on peace marches. You've done *nothing* with your life but pursue your selfish personal pleasures. Me—I've *always* done my duty. I waited on you and your father and your brothers hand and foot for years. For the first time in my life, I had no one to account to but myself. I was going to travel, go back to college, teach. And now *this. Why me?*"

"What do you *mean*, 'why you'?" Ginny raged back, suddenly out of control. "Why *not* you, Mother? Millions of people die every day. You've been preparing for this ever since I can remember, with your goddam tombstone rubbings and your fucking epitaphs. That's all I ever *heard* from you and the Major. Why are you so offended now that your bluff is being called?"

"Don't use your gutter language on *me*, Virginia Babcock Bliss!"

"And as for your waiting on us hand and foot, as you say, we never *asked* you to. You did it so that you'd have something to do with yourself. It was for *you*, Mother, not for us. And if all I've ever done is chase after my personal pleasures, then how come I'm not having any fun?" She collapsed into her chair. Beads of sweat stood out on her mother's round yellow face. They sat exhausted, glaring at each other. After a while, Ginny closed her eyes in remorse.

Mrs. Babcock felt incapable of a rebuttal. She had detected some truth in Ginny's outburst. Somewhere along the line she, Mrs. Babcock, had gone wrong. It was true. She had pandered to the needs of those ingrates she called her family for so long that her chief need had come to be that of being needed by them. What else could account for the depressions that had plagued her ever since the last of the children had left home? She had pinned the blame on a lot of external factors, but what it was, she knew, was that she was no longer needed, had no function, had to create a new function for herself—or die.

Where had she gone wrong in the first place, though? At what one point could she have said no to the demands other people were placing on her? When she had dropped out of Bryn Mawr to marry Wesley had been such a point. She could have insisted on postponing the marriage to get her degree so that she could have taught history, which was what had interested her. But *could* she have, with Wesley's marching off to war and conceivably to his death? During those chaotic years all sorts of disastrous marriages occurred; people were having babies left and right, as though in response to unconscious urgings to replace all those who were being killed, just as a barren fruit tree will fruit when its trunk is girdled by a knife (according to the encyclopedia). And so she had married Wesley and had given birth to Karl ten months later. She and Karl followed Wesley to army bases around the country in an old Ford at 35 mph. And a year later Ginny was born in Hullsport during Wesley's leave prior to his being shipped overseas. He left for France when Ginny was two months old. After that, Ginny woke up every night at 3 A.M. and screamed inconsolably. Only holding her while standing upright and singing lullabies would calm her. She clung like a little monkey, and whenever Mrs. Babcock tried to sit or lie down, Ginny would jerk awake and start screaming again. Then Karl would wake up and the two fatherless babies would wail together until dawn.

Exhausted from lack of sleep and buffeted daily between hope and despair by the battle reports and by the arrival or nonarrival of letters from Wesley, Mrs. Babcock soon became a numb automaton. What she personally might or might not want became irrelevant. Here were these two pathetic children to bolster, who seemed somehow tuned in to the chaos loose in the world. And so she acted cheerful and sang and danced and rolled with them on the floor of the cabin, when she really wanted to be alone weeping or rereading Wesley's love letters. And before long she no longer wanted to be alone weeping.

And so Ginny was correct. Mrs. Babcock knew that she was a martyr. The children's needs in those confused and unhappy war years had swamped her own needs, had *become* her own needs. And when the war years had passed, her needs were no longer in evidence; her awareness of them had been trained out of her, except for one brief flare-up during the time she now referred to, in her middle-aged mellowness, as the Tired Years, that seemingly endless chunk of her life when the three children were little. It had been all she could do then to drag herself from one hamper of dirty diapers to the next. She had been too worn out for sex most of the time, and she and Wesley were quarreling over a lot of secondary issues. Finding herself one day on the verge of busting open Karl's head with a paperweight for sliding down the stair rail carrying the dog, she seized on the idea of just packing up and leaving the whole mess. She went to see her mother in the cabin and spelled out her despair in great detail. Her mother had looked at her coolly and had said, "You must do your duty, dear." So she had.

And now here she was—falling apart in a hospital bed after years of satisfying other people's needs, without ever having had a chance to figure out what *she* might need. It wasn't Wesley's or the children's fault, but she couldn't help feeling that it wasn't her own fault either.

Ginny seemed to think that how many children to have and when to have them, how to rear them, were rational decisions based on personal preference. She would insist righteously on the integrity of the individual, the inviolability of human reason. She was probably incapable of seeing humanity as colonies of microbes, shunted here and there in response to force fields and chemical secretions. Becoming an adult was a process of becoming aware of one's limitations, and therefore of one's possibilities. Children couldn't really appreciate a good ballet dancer, for example. They took the ability to leap gracefully five feet in the air for granted. It was only when you became conscious of all the massed forces a dancer was overcoming with his skill that you could begin to savor his achievement. Ginny had a lot to learn, even though she thought she already knew everything.

Ginny sat with her eyes closed, unable to apologize but unable to resume the attack, paralyzed by her mother's most deadly weapon—guilt. Because every word her mother had spoken had been true. She *had* slaved for Ginny and her father and brothers, thanklessly, for years. But the pound of flesh her mother extracted for this selfless devotion was that its recipients adorn her self-concept. Ginny had failed to do this. She didn't know exactly what her mother would have liked her to be—but it was clearly nothing that she had been so far. All attempted roles to date had been disasters in her mother's eyes, Ginny knew. Wife to Ira, mother to Wendy—this her mother approved of. But it was all over. Guilt.

Ginny's last Hullsport Christmas was the year before she left for Boston. Karl and Jim were home from their schools. Their mother had rushed around merrily performing all the preparation rituals singlehandedly—the wreaths, the cookies, the tree, the presents. On Christmas Eve they had had their standard feast—roast goose and fixings and plum pudding. The Major was upstairs in bed with a migraine. After dinner they retired to the living room and sang carols in front of the fire, as they had done every Christmas Eve of recorded history. That year, though, each of the three children had dates later on, to midnight services at various churches. As a family choir, they'd always been agonizingly off key, but they'd scarcely noticed it before. That particular Christmas Eve, however, Jim's newly changed voice was cracking as he sang. Ginny was preoccupied with the prospect of some heavy petting with Clem after the midnight service. Karl, bored, was singing dutifully. Here they were, new and different people, grubs sprung from the cocoons of childhood into resplendent pubescence, still struggling to perform the scorned rituals of their despised grubhood.

Suddenly all the children stopped singing and started laughing. It was an example of laughter at its most pure: a release of the nervous tension that stemmed from the superimposition of two contradictory concepts. They laughed and laughed. There wasn't enough laughter in all of Hullsport to relieve the strain of this absurdity—grown-up young people, for so they regarded themselves, engaged in a tired replay of meaningless myths and rituals. Their mother began to weep quietly. Gradually as one after another noticed her, their mirth died. Finally, the three of them skulked from the room to their private pursuits, each in various stages of resentment and remorse, leaving their mother there shaking with mute sobs. She didn't know how to let go gracefully, and they didn't know how to take their leave with tact. Independence was rarely given, Ginny knew; it was taken. But to take it would be to deprive her mother of her function in life. Guilt.

"But Vogel didn't *say* you were dying, Mother," Ginny mumbled.

Mrs. Babcock shook her head no.

"Shall I leave?"

Her mother shook her head no again. Then she reached over to her bedside table and picked up the white pills from that morning and downed them with a sip of water. "What time is it?"

"About seven, I think."

"I keep losing track of the time here."

"I'll bring you a clock."

A little later Ginny told her about the baby birds. "What do you think I should do with them?"

Mrs. Babcock was startled to be asked for an opinion. She'd been looked after for so long in this hospital that it was hard for her to believe that someone actually cared what she thought about anything. "Well, I don't know really. Things like that always used to kill me when you children were little. I'd put them up in trees, and the cats would get them, and you could never understand why nature was set up that way. And of course I never knew what to tell you because I didn't understand either.

"Remember our yellow cat Molly? We had her when you were six or so. One time you went out in the back yard and found her under the mulberry tree with a tiny bird head in front of her. You started screaming and throwing sticks at her, I remember. I raced out and you were standing there sobbing. 'But it's not *fair*, Mommy,' you kept saying. Without thinking, I said, 'But *life's* not fair, sweetie.' You wouldn't speak to me for days. The parent birds don't appear to be feeding them?''

"I don't think so."

"You mean they're just sitting on the chimney watching them starve?"

"It looks like it." Ginny could tell that their unparently behavior was annoying her mother as much as it had her.

"They should be shot."

"I agree. But I don't know what to do. After all, they're birds, not people. I guess you can't bind them to our codes."

"There's that bird book in the bookcase by the fireplace. Maybe you can find something in there."

Ginny and her mother went on chatting as though their outburst had never happened, until Miss Sturgill arrived with a sleeping pill.

It was late twilight as Ginny passed the Cloyd house. She tooted. Through the fuzzy gloom that made everything look out of focus, she saw a figure down the hill waving its hand. She stopped and backed up and got out. It was Clem, walking toward her, smiling.

"Heard you was comin'," he said. "Otherwise, I wouldn't of knowed it was you." He nodded at her peasant dress. He was in a dirty sweat-stained T-shirt and jeans and manure-caked high-top work shoes. He looked hot and tired.

"Just finished chores?"

"Yup. Little late tonight. My hired man's sick."

"I hear you're doing good things with the farm."

"Highest production per head in the state. Got me $18,000's worth of prize sperm in the freezer," he said with a proud smile, wiping beads of sweat from his upper lip with the back of his hand.

"That's great. Did you hear my mother is in the hospital?"

"Yeah, I did. I'm real sorry. She's done had a bad year, ain't she? Pray God she'll be out soon. Is she bad sick this time?"

Ginny looked at him quickly. Pray God? Was this *the* Clem Cloyd, star of Hullsport low life? "Uh, well, I don't know exactly. She's had this before and has snapped right out of it. I don't see why she shouldn't this time. She looks terrible, but she's up and around, more or less."

"Why don't you come in for a while and say hi to Maxine?"

"Okay. For a minute. If you have to milk in the morning, you'll be wanting to eat and get to bed."

The bright light in the kitchen blinded Ginny long enough for Maxine to bustle over and enclose her between her arms and her soft massive mammaries. When Ginny could see again, she discovered that Maxine looked much as she had during Bloody Bucket days, only more so. Her huge breasts, no longer shaped to points, hung nearly to her waist; her golden cross was still lodged firmly between them. There were women who looked merely dumpy when they got fat, and there were women whose appearance increased in warmth and voluptuosity as the pounds added up. Maxine was in the latter category. She dwarfed Clem, who was still slight, though wiry and toughened by all his physical labor. His face, on the other hand, usually tense and sneering and unhappy in high school, had softened and relaxed. With a start, Ginny put her finger on the big change in Clem: He no longer limped. She had known him so well that she had become almost unaware of his crippled gait, but it was definitely gone altogether now. Unobtrusively she glanced at the floor and noted that his left work shoe had a normal sole and his right foot no longer turned inward. He'd had surgery or something?

Supper sat steaming on the table. Three small dark children with Clem's Melungeon features squirmed shyly at their places. This didn't seem the time to be asking about Clem's leg.

"Eat with us," Maxine insisted.

"Thanks, but I've eaten. Anyhow, I've got to get back to the cabin to check on some things. But I'll be back."

"Make it soon," Maxine instructed.

7

Worthley Material

———————— □ ————————

When I regained consciousness after my plunge from Clem's speeding
Harley—a princess restored to life by a watchful genie—I found
myself swathed in gauze and plaster, with various limbs suspended
from pulleys. Out the window the sun was shining, and the trees were
tufted with the fluffy chartreuse of leafing buds. Several weeks had
passed without my knowledge.

Clem wasn't allowed to visit me during my convalescence. It was
just as well. I was extremely busy filling out college applications,
under duress applied in my weakened condition by the Major. They
were all to women's colleges in New England. "Why do you wish to
attend Worthley?" Answer: "I don't really wish to attend Worthley.
I'm being held prisoner in a hospital bed. Please send help."

I got a letter back from the Worthley board of admissions inviting
me for an interview, based on my "most intriguing and original
application." The Major intercepted the letter before I had a chance
to chew it up and swallow it. Hardly was I up off my skin-grafted back
than I was whisked away for my interview, by the Major himself, who
had to go to Boston on business.

In a last-ditch gesture of defiance, I wore a black, too-tight straight
skirt; a black cardigan buttoned up the back with a Do-It Pruitt
pointed bra underneath; Clem's red dragon windbreaker, the tatters
of which I had carefully stitched together upon finding them among

Mother's cleaning cloths; black ballet slippers; and Clem's huge clanking identification bracelet.

When Miss Head saw me in her doorway, she eyed me uneasily, as though expecting to be mugged among her eighteenth-century antiques. She had wavy gray hair pulled back in a severe bun. The stubborn crimp of her hair made her head look like the plastic model of the human cerebrum that sat in the Hullsport High biology lab. Her coloring was ashen. She wore Ben Franklin horn-rim glasses with a chain attached to either earpiece; they bounced precariously on her nose as she talked. Her beige nylon blouse was high-necked and firmly secured at the throat by a rose-tinted cameo brooch; the brooch featured chaste maidens in diaphanous gowns who were wafting around a tumbled Grecian pillar. On the jacket of her burnt orange tweed suit, over her left breast, hung a small round watch, suspended from a tiny bow fashioned of gold.

As we talked, the corners of her mouth soon began twitching. She was trying not to smile at my answers. In short, she liked me. I was appalled. I had been doing my Hullsport best to wreck my chances of ever obtaining a spot on the Worthley roster. Her office was furnished in Sheraton pieces and Oriental carpets and elaborately engraved copper trays. One wall was of hand-hewn stone. I had found this place only after wandering lost through miles of twisting stone corridors. Everywhere I went, medieval gargoyles and portraits of Renaissance ladies in gilded frames stared down at me, judging. Was I Worthley material, they seemed to demand of each other. I sincerely hoped not. The odor was of moldy stone and desiccated woodwork. The din of pealing carillon bells, echoing and reechoing through the hollow deserted stone hallways, filled my ears as I walked faster and faster, and finally ran—a Rapunzel from Hullsport, held captive in this castle keep of academe.

"There seems to be some kind of mistake," I was explaining to this nice lady, Miss Head. "As you can probably see from my transcript, I don't *begin* to have the grades or test scores to come to Worthley. I'd be lost here. It would be *such* a waste when there are so many well-prepared girls in Westchester who'd love to come."

"Oh well, grades. What are a few—" Leaning her head back on her neck and looking down through her half-lenses at my transcript, she blanched. "Indeed," she said, sobered.

"So you see," I continued eagerly, "it would probably be just as well if I withdrew my application right now, and saved you the trouble of having to mail me a rejection letter." I lunged for my application, which Miss Head deftly whisked out of my reach. I looked up at her from where I lay sprawled across her antique desk top.

"Yes, but you see, we've never had a girl here from, ah— Hullsport, as it were."

"Yes, I can appreciate that," I said reasonably, plopping back into my comb-back Windsor chair.

"And you see, this year, ah—perhaps I shouldn't be telling you this, as it were. But just between the two of us, this year at Worthley we *do have* a geographical quota to fill, ah, in order to qualify, as it were, for a sizable bequest from an alumna. And we *do* have to have" —she was beaming and pointing at me with her index finger—"one more Tennessean. And I'm sure you can appreciate the fact, Miss Babcock, that Tennesseans aren't exactly beating down our doors here at Worthley. So I'm afraid, young lady, that it has to be you." She was like an obstetrician notifying me that I was premaritally pregnant. She lifted the small clock hanging over her breast and glanced at it. "So could you just run and call in that nice father of yours, so that we can share with him your exciting news?"

"He's not out there," I said glumly.

"Indeed," she intoned with evident displeasure, accustomed to having anxious parents hovering in her foyer awaiting her pleasure. "Well, then, we'll just sit and get acquainted until he comes, shall we?" She whisked out of the office.

If I could somehow get out of this stone fortress, I could get a message to Clem and we could flee somewhere together. . . . I hunted through my pocketbook and discovered twenty-three cents, not even enough for a phone call to Clem. I leapt up and felt along the cold damp stone wall in hopes of finding a secret doorway into another world.

Miss Head returned, carrying a silver tray with a silver tea service and cups and saucers on it. She looked at me strangely as I stood propped against her wall.

"Just admiring your lovely stone wall," I explained feebly, patting one of the boulders with affection.

"It *is* lovely, isn't it? But there are *lots* of stone walls around campus. Oh, I'm sure you'll come to love Worthley just as we all do."

I smiled weakly and returned to my chair. Although I didn't know it at the time, the ritual I was watching was to be the one skill I salvaged from my Worthley experience. Miss Head performed it slowly, repeating for me to watch the especially intricate steps, like a master craftswoman coaching her apprentice. She picked up a flowered bone china saucer and gently but firmly placed a matching cup on it. Holding the saucer rim between thumb and forefinger, with the remaining fingers of that hand stretched out gracefully, she moved the cup below and in front of the ornate silver tea pot, which was encrusted with stylized vines and leaves. I expected her to pick up the tea pot with her free hand. But no! Instead she deftly tilted the trick pot on its hinged base. Just so, so that a steady, but not gushing, stream of reddish brown tea poured into the cup, the cup being held close enough to the spout so as not to splash out the tea, but far enough away so as not to look too easy. When the cup was half full, she returned the pot to its base. Then she moved the cup underneath the tap on the other silver urn, turned the handle forty-five degrees and no more, and finished filling the cup with water until it was three-quarters of an inch from the top. Looking up with the confident smile of experts who know they're good, she inquired, "Milk or lemon?"

"Both, please."

She frowned slightly, so that I knew I'd done something gauche. But she could afford to be generous, from her perch at the pinnacle of world tea service, so she laughed merrily, her glasses bouncing on her nose and said, "But of *course!* One teaspoon of sugar or two?"

"Three?"

Grimacing, she ladled three spoonfuls of sugar into my tea, added the optimum amount of milk, and placed a thin lemon slice on my saucer. Then, with a flourish, she handed me the chef-d'oeuvre.

Miss Head clutched the edge of her desk and leaned forward aggressively, staring at me over the top of her glasses, and said through clenched teeth, "And now *tell* me about yourself, Miss Babcock. Now that that nasty business of my having to pass judgment on you no longer stands between us. Who *is* Virginia Babcock from Hullsport, Tennessee? What books does she read? What *kinds* of activities are most meaningful to her self-concept?"

"*Which* self-concept? I've had several." I speculated as to whether or not I could admit that my reading list over the past year had mostly consisted of such old favorites from Clem Cloyd's bookshelves as *Hard Bargain* and *Tongue Power*, with their blacked-out cover illustrations and their vast vocabulary of words never tested for on the SAT exams.

"Oh ho ho. That's what attracted me to your application, Miss

Babcock. Among other things. I can be quite honest with you now. 'Being held prisoner in a hospital bed,' indeed!"

"But I *was*."

"A delicious wit you displayed, Miss Babcock, in your handling of the questions. Most refreshing. I'm sure you can appreciate how tedious it becomes for those of us who have to read these endless applications. 'I desire to attain a Worthley education in order more fully to appreciate the world around me.' But *your* answers, Miss Babcock, well, they betrayed you as being *true* Worthley material, as it were. What field do you plan to pursue?" She consulted her watch quickly.

"Well, to tell you the truth, Miss Head, I hadn't planned to pursue much of anything. I hadn't expected to be accepted. I guess I'll have to get busy and think of something." I was becoming somewhat reconciled to the concept of spending four years of my life at this place. Miss Head wasn't a bad sort—for a jailer.

Miss Head, staring at me through her half-lenses, asked, "What *had* you planned to do, dear?"

"Get married, I guess. Mess around." If I had denounced football to Joe Bob Sparks, my remark couldn't have been more poorly received. Miss Head sat back in her chair and closed her eyes and massaged her temples with her finger tips.

"Do you teach, too?" I asked, to shift her attention from her horrible realization that she'd just admitted the village idiot of Hullsport, Tennessee, to Worthley College, alma mater of vast battalions of female overachievers.

"Yes. Yes, I do indeed. Philosophy. The Descartes seminar."

"Oh. Well, I guess I probably won't be seeing you in the class-room then." I had in mind a physical education major.

Miss Head sat up straight in her chair, a potential convert before her. "Whatever you do," she pleaded, *"don't* write off philosophy without even trying it. It could be the mistake of your *life*, Miss Babcock!"

I thought it over and concluded that I really might as well take philosophy as physical education or domestic science. I didn't much care. I told Miss Head I'd take introductory philosophy. She was thrilled. Clem Cloyd suddenly seemed very far away from Kant and Hegel and all the other Teutonic-sounding names Miss Head was reeling off as subjects of my freshman scrutiny.

When I got back to Hullsport, I sneaked up through the woods late one afternoon to the springhouse. I was limping slightly from the accident, due to an improperly healed break. But the plan was to rebreak and reset the bone that summer so as to eliminate the limp before I left for Boston in the fall. Had I not been going to Boston, I'm sure I'd still be limping today as punishment from the Major. Clem and I were officially prohibited by both sets of parents from ever seeing each other again. Needless to say, that prohibition exercised about as much influence over me as did a papal bull over a medieval monk.

I knocked, not really expecting Clem to be there. But he was. He stepped back in surprise when he saw me, saying nothing. I limped past him. The crude furniture was still there, but the pornographic pictures were down off the walls, and the paperbacks were gone from the shelves. Lying on the table was an open Bible. And a crucifix hung where the poster of the rats gnawing the woman's breasts had been.

Clem stared at me, cringing almost, as though afraid I was going to hit him.

"Hi," I said at last.

"Hi."

"You took the pictures down," I improvised.

"Yeah, I ain't got no use for em now."

"There must be other girls," I suggested bravely.

"I ain't interested in stuff like that no more."

"Really? No?"

"Sold the Harley too."

"You're kidding? That's *awful*. Did your parents make you?"

"Didn't have to. I done hit mysef. Listen, Ginny, I'm so sorry. Dear *God*, I'm sorry." His dark face was twisted with remorse.

"It wasn't your fault that I fell off the Harley."

"Hit was my fault that we was going so fast when you did. I don't know what I can say to you, Ginny—just that I'm sorry. I like to killed you. And you're the only person, ceptin Ma and Pa, I've ever cared about."

"Please. It's all right. It wasn't your fault." I was getting embarrassed.

"I done thought about you a lot, Ginny. I tried all sorts of ways to get in to see you. I put on an orderly uniform and got as far as the nurses' desk on your floor." I smiled. He was starting to sound more like himself.

"I've thought about you, too. Did you know I've been in Boston?"

"Pa mentioned hit."

"I'm going to college there in the fall." I was gratified that his face, which I was watching closely, fell. "I didn't want to at first. My father made me go up for the interview. But it's not such a bad place. If you like tea."

Clem limped over and sat down on the bench he'd made when we were eight and had mingled our blood. I limped over and sat down beside him, on the table next to the Bible.

"Maybe you could come up and see me there?"

His glum face brightened, then darkened again. "We're not even allowed to see each other here. Hit ain't likely that I could come a thousand miles without nobody knowin hit."

"Maybe they'll change their minds. It might work out. Wait and see."

"You'd better go. I got to hep with milkin. Is there any way for us to get together again?"

I explained that I'd be in the hospital for a while with my leg, and that I'd be doing make-up work to prepare for my courses all summer. "Maybe we could set a time to meet here every week. Like we used to for our Floyd drills. Do you remember? We'd gather up all our stuff and lock ourselves in here for practice? Then whichever of us could get away would come here, and if the other wasn't here, could go on back home until the next week."

"If we get caught, we're dead."

I was surprised. I'd never heard Clem worry about getting caught on anything, ever. "Then maybe we'd better just forget about it." My sense of loss was getting less acute all the time. Maybe a fast clean break would be kindest to us both.

"No, let's at least try hit. I'll have keys made for you the next time you come. Let's make hit Fridays at two."

Clem and I managed to meet half a dozen times before I left for Boston. I was amazed that our plan worked. Never before had Clem been within an hour of being on time anyplace. But he was invariably at the springhouse Fridays at two. Mostly we chatted companionably about the farm. Clem was working full time for his father, having graduated from Hullsport High with our class. (I was given special dispensation, considering "who I was," and finished up my senior year during that summer.) We gossiped about friends—the people at the Bloody Bucket whom I never saw anymore. Maxine's name came up a lot. I wondered with sharp pangs of jealousy if he was dating her. He never said, and I was too envious to ask.

We never touched each other. It was no great sacrifice. Our efforts along that line hadn't been too inspiring.

Two days before I was to leave for Boston, we met and agreed that I would come home at Thanksgiving. Perhaps by then, if we proved ourselves mature and cooperative in our newly responsible circumstances, our parents would relent and permit us to meet out in the open as consenting adults. I walked up the path behind the springhouse which led to my house. In our childhood it had been a muddy rut worn a foot below the level of the ground from overuse. Now it was nearly undetectable, snarled with wild raspberry canes and wild grape vines. I turned around at the top of the hill. The farmland spread out below me, the fields starting to yellow into fall. The Holsteins were lined up at the milking parlor, waiting for Clem to relieve them. Clem, however, was standing, dark and slight and twisted, in the doorway of his sagging springhouse looking at me. He raised a hand slowly. I raised my hand in reply. Then I turned around and limped home.

My room at Worthley was high atop a crenelated stone neo-Gothic dormitory that looked like a stage set for a Walt Disney filming of *Sleeping Beauty*. I picked my particular room because it was located next to a fire escape. I overlooked a flagstone courtyard, which opened onto a small lake on which the college Brünnhildes rowed in their galleys at six every morning. In the middle of the courtyard on a sandstone stand sat a huge bronze sundial decorated with scrolled metal leaves. At the far end of the courtyard, overlooking the lake, was a bronze cast of Artemis, virgin huntress. The bathroom for my hall was located opposite my room. My first intimation of an order in the universe was when I made the discovery that bathrooms in multi-storied buildings are located directly above each other on every floor.

My room made up in charm for what it lacked in size. It had dormer windows and a window seat. It was an authentic garret. I spent most of my first couple of months in there and in the library. I had no social life and wanted none. I'd had my fill in high school. Besides, every available nerve impulse at my disposal was required for my course work, which was going poorly in spite of my devotion to my summer reading list. My history professor called me a "bigoted materialist," and my English professor returned my autobiography marked in red "trite." The problem wasn't primarily the many books I hadn't read, the course work I hadn't had at Hullsport High; it was my mental habits, or lack of them. In short, I was incapable of sustained thought. After all, I'd never had to practice it before. Suddenly, after an adolescence characterized by relative competence, I was a bumbling idiot.

I wrote Clem lots of lonely letters. He wrote me lots of identical lonely letters. We could have saved enough money in postage to have financed an elopement by writing lonely letters to ourselves. Their essence was that we wanted to be married and living happily ever after, rather than each struggling away in chaste isolation. When Thanksgiving came, I was definitely ready to go home for some southern solace. I phoned the Major to announce my plans.

"Not on your life!" he informed me. "It's too soon. You just left. Anyway, I know from Clem's father that he's been getting letters from you."

"So what's wrong with that?"

"Nothing, but you sure as hell aren't coming home." We hung up on each other, me thinking that he'd better not come to *my* doorstep when he was old and sick and impoverished. I wrote Clem an airmail letter asking him to come to Boston over Thanksgiving and enclosing a check for his fare. He wrote to thank me anyway and notify me that the check had bounced, the Major having stopped payment, he being a director of the bank in Hullsport where my account was.

With hatred in my heart, I ate my Thanksgiving turkey in the company of solitary derelicts at Waldorf's Cafeteria in Harvard Square. Then I encouraged an acned bespectacled Harvard sophomore from Birmingham, Alabama, to pick me up. He was as miserable as I was to be alone in a strange land on Thanksgiving. He took me back to his rooms (in Babcock Hall, which gave me malicious satisfaction), plied me with Southern Comfort, and led me to his unmade come-stained bed, where he screwed me halfheartedly and without finesse among the stacks of notes for his term paper on Kierkegaard's *The Sickness unto Death.*

"What's the 'sickness unto death'?" I asked him gently, as we lay awkwardly intertwined in the dim light of late afternoon.

"Despair," he said, his eyes tightly shut and his teeth clenched.

As I disentangled my limbs and hunted through the rubble on his floor for my Do-It Pruitt bra and my black cardigan, he politely asked for my name and phone number, like the southern gentleman that he was. Southern lady that I was, I said my name was Lora Lee Calhoun, knowing that he'd never phone to catch me in my deceit.

On the MTA back to Worthley, I decided to forget about sex altogether, my awakening brain being by now in the ascendance over my body.

Several days later, as I was beginning to look forward to Christmas vacation in Hullsport, I had a letter from Clem saying that he and Maxine were engaged. He was sorry. He hoped I wasn't hurt. Obviously we could never have a life together. But after all that we'd shared over so many years, obviously our lives could never be totally separate either, and he hoped we could remain close friends.

It was a very kind and tactful letter. Objectively speaking, I admired the wording and doubted if I could have done as well. I wasn't particularly surprised or hurt by its contents. After all, it was months since I'd had any genuine claims on, or romantic feelings for, Clem. And I was the one who had gone away. But try telling my emotions that. As far as they were concerned, it couldn't be true that Clem had thrown me over! The lousy bastard, first trying to kill me, and then deserting me, alone and unloved in this dark cold city full of hostile strangers. I would get him back somehow; I would fly directly from Logan Airport and into my own true love's arms, never more to part. I would fight that sneaky whore Maxine for him, sliding my pointed nail file into her jugular vein.

When I had finished emoting, I admitted myself to the infirmary, ignoring final papers and exams. There I developed a raging fever and raw throat, all of which eventually cooperated by turning into pneumonia. Miss Head brought course books over so that I could study for exams, but I turned my face to the wall and decided to die, unloved, unwanted, and unneeded as I so clearly was.

Miss Head arrived in my infirmary room on Christmas Eve. The staff psychologist had just been there trying to persuade me to "talk things out." I had resolutely pretended to be asleep, as I was doing now with Miss Head.

"I have a new Descartes for you, Miss Babcock." Prior to my decision to die, I'd been doing surprisingly well in her course, mainly because I liked her and wanted to do well for her, in contrast to my other professors. I especially liked Descartes, largely because he was Miss Head's specialty. "But I'm not leaving it. You have to turn over and take it from me." I was tempted, especially since I had some very painful bed sores on that side, due to my determination to turn my face to the wall and await my death.

"Well, I have to get home now to baste my turkey," she announced regretfully. "And to mash my potatoes and bake my rolls and so on."

Against my better judgment, my mouth watering, I began turning, Lazarus rising from the dead. Miss Head was standing there in a green loden coat, her sallow cheeks flushed from the cold. She extended a wrapped present saying, "Merry Christmas, Miss Babcock."

I started crying in great wracking sobs. "But I don't have anything for *you!*" I wailed.

Miss Head turned away, looking embarrassed. "Yes, you do."

"What?" I asked suspiciously. Who was this woman who could manipulate me so shamelessly—getting me to Worthley in the first place, and now trying to interfere with my death plans?

"Get up and get dressed and come have Christmas dinner with me."

"I couldn't possibly. I have pneumonia."

"Not anymore you don't, Miss Babcock. I asked your doctor. She said it was a good idea for you to get up and around, as it were."

"How would *she* know? *She's* not the one who's sick."

"And *you're* not either," Miss Head insisted, looking out over the rims of her glasses. She was suppressing a faint amused smile.

The thing was, I'd come to like the infirmary in my weeks there. I lay silently all day in a bed, with metal bars enclosing me like the sides of a casket. My meals were brought to me, when I deigned to eat. I was bathed without my having to move. My back was rubbed. Bedpans appeared and disappeared. Nothing was expected of me, least of all that I think. It was as close to being dead without actually being in the ground as I could hope for. It would be tough to give up this way of life. Damn Miss Head anyway.

"You'd been working too hard. Why don't you come over to my apartment and have a relaxing evening? Just the two of us. You'd be doing me a favor. After all, I persuaded the admissions board to accept you. I do have a professional stake in your well-being, as it were. Apart from any personal stake I might have. Come along, Miss Babcock."

Obediently, I swung my legs out of the bed. My feet hit the floor for the first time in three weeks. I fancied that my circulatory system was thrown out of kilter by this unexpected development, after weeks of lying supine, and that all the blood was rushing to my toes. I would have thrown myself back under the covers in a blind panic except that Miss Head was holding my hand and leading me over to the chair where my clothes lay. Shakily, I dressed, while she went discreetly into the bathroom and patted her crimped gray bun in front of the mirror.

I walked into the bathroom and glanced around her into the mirror. "Oh, Christ!" I moaned. My hair was so oily and dirty from three weeks of neglect that it was plastered to my skull. And my face was gaunt from eating as little as was consonant with staying conscious so that I could savor my suffering.

"You can wash your hair at my apartment if you want to." I looked at her, startled. My dealings with Miss Head in the past had been of such an ethereal nature that it had never occurred to me that she knew about normal bodily functions like the washing of hair.

I threw Clem's red dragon windbreaker on over my straight black skirt and black cardigan. Miss Head glanced at me doubtfully but said nothing.

I hobbled down the hall next to her, my legs rubbery from disuse. My left leg was aching badly at the site of its break and rebreak.

Miss Head's apartment was in a wing of my dormitory, down a hall lined with inspirational portraits of stern alumnae who had managed to accomplish significant things in the world. One of these portraits had two right hands, a fact that Miss Head had never noticed until I pointed it out to her that night.

Miss Head's door was of oak with wrought-iron strap hinges and hardware. It was located in a dark stone alcove, reached by ducking through an archway lined with stone gargoyles. Above this archway, carved into the stone, was the phrase, "In the quiet and still air of delightful studies."

The apartment consisted of a living room, bathroom, kitchen, and bedroom, and was furnished with Orientals and with prim-looking Victorian settees and fragile chairs whose seats were covered with needlepoint. Turkey odors wafted through the living room as Miss Head hung up her loden coat and my windbreaker.

"Just make yourself comfortable while I tend to a few things in the kitchen, as it were." I perched tentatively on the edge of a needlepoint chair whose back consisted of carved wooden rosettes and dedicated myself to the considerable task of making myself comfortable in it.

Miss Head, turning around just before entering the kitchen, grimaced and said quickly, "Not *that* chair, I'm afraid. It's just to look at." I jumped up and backed away and placed myself on the overly bespringed horsehair sofa, which had claws for feet and was as challenging as the rickety chair, comfort-wise. Miss Head offered me some sherry, which I eagerly accepted. She handed me a small crystal goblet only a third full. "We don't want it to go to your head, as it were." I decided this wasn't the time to mention the raw moonshine at the Bloody Bucket.

I placed my glass on a coaster on a marble-top table and set about opening my gift. My heart leapt when I saw it—*Discourse on the Method of Rightly Conducting the Reason* by René Descartes! Inside the front cover was an inscription: "To Virginia Babcock from Helena Head, Christmas 1963."

Eagerly I opened the book and read with delight: "In our search for the direct road towards the truth we should busy ourselves with no object about which we cannot attain a certainty equal to that of the demonstrations of arithmetic and geometry."

As I sat absorbed in Descartes's instructions for the attainment of certainty, Miss Head poured herself some sherry and sat down opposite me on a small settee covered in gold. "Now! What's this all about?"

"What?"

"This business of your lying in bed and missing your exams?"

I sighed weakly and looked at Miss Head for a long time, trying to think how to unburden myself. Finally I blurted out, "My boy friend from high school married someone else."

She waited. When I didn't continue, she said with disbelief, "You mean that's *all?*"

"That's not enough?"

"Well, it hardly seems worth sacrificing your college career to." At the time, it never occurred to me that I was in the process of being brainwashed.

"Now that you put it that way," I replied, cooperative convert that I've always been, "it *does* seem kind of dumb."

"Well, not *dumb* exactly, but illogical certainly." I nodded in agreement, noting that the worst condemnation Miss Head could heap on any action was to label it "illogical."

"You see," Miss Head explained, "the human organism has only so much energy at its disposal. If you divert a great deal of it into any one channel, you can expect the others to collapse or atrophy. If you squander your vital energies on your emotional life, as you have been doing, plan to be physically and mentally bankrupt, as it were." I didn't know what she was talking about. It sounded suspiciously mystical for someone devoted to rationality in all its manifestations.

"Do you think I'll be allowed to make up the papers and exams?"

"Well, you *were* in the infirmary with pneumonia, apart from the fact that you were there twice as long as was medically indicated, as it were. But I should think that if you went to your professors individually and apologized and explained the circumstances—the physical illness, not the rest of it—that each would be willing to make special arrangements. I, for one, certainly will."

"Oh, thank you, Miss Head. What shall I do to complete your course?"

"I'd like a twenty-page paper by the end of next month on a topic of your choosing. Perhaps something dealing with Descartes? And for your own edification and enjoyment, I should think you would want to finish the reading list. Of course, you've missed quite a number of lectures. But I'll be delighted to talk with you any time about questions you may have." The mind's equivalent of the body's adrenaline was surging through my system. I wanted nothing more than to race to my garret and tear into unexpurgated Spinoza.

"But relax this evening and have a nice dinner with me. You may call your parents on my phone to wish them a Merry Christmas if you like." I shot her a look of betrayal. She'd been consorting with the enemy? "Well, obviously they've been worried." I glared at her with distrust. If you couldn't trust your philosophy professor, whom *could* you trust? "All right, I've been in touch with your parents a time or two," she confessed. "Is that so terrible?" If my infirmary bed had been there, I would have climbed into it immediately and turned my face to the wall. Miss Head was faithless and treacherous after all. She shrugged and went into the kitchen.

After several phone calls from Hullsport, which I had refused to answer, the Major had one day appeared in my infirmary room. I had declined to acknowledge his existence. After all, but for him, I might at that very moment have been Mrs. Clem Cloyd. All my current problems would have been nonexistent. Finally he had roared, "Ginny, this is ridiculous! Get up out of that bed this instant! I'm taking you *home!*"

I had looked at him disdainfully and said, "I don't know what you're talking about, I'm sure. I *have* no home." A couple of doctors had appeared and had lured him into the hall, where a heated discussion had ensued, the result of which was that I had remained where I was.

As I sat fuming, Miss Head called me to the table—a mahogany-veneer pedestal-type table. The spread was dazzling to someone accustomed to hospital trays—Limoges china, Waterford crystal, encrusted antique silverware, Brussels lace place mats and napkins. A small golden turkey; silver dishes of pale mashed potatoes, orange butternut squash, dark brown gravy, dark red cranberry sauce, bright green peas. All my weeks of self-denial came to a head, and I almost did a half-gainer into the gravy boat. Miss Head smiled at my exuberance and nodded for me to sit down.

As I did so, a new aspect of the situation presented itself to me: Here was this gorgeous Christmas feast prepared by Miss Head—for me? What if I had refused to come? Miss Head would be sitting here eating all this alone? My heart ached for her, as she looked over the tops of her half-lenses to carve the turkey. Tears filled my eyes. This competent, self-contained woman—could it be that she was ever actually lonely, the way I had been lonely as I lay week after week pretending I wanted to die? Did she have a secret lover, or some good friend whom she had evicted tonight so that she could save my soul? I sincerely hoped so.

"Where did you get all this beautiful china and stuff?" I asked.

"It was my mother's. I was their only child, so I inherited it all. Although I have very little use for twelve place settings, since there's just me." I was studying her face intently, trying to decide whether or not that bothered her—the way it was bothering me, being, for all practical purposes, parentless and loverless and friendless. Was it possible for life to go on under these circumstances?

After dinner we returned to our respective settees for coffee and mints. Then she went into her bedroom and returned with a gleaming reddish cello. She sat on the edge of a kindling-like needlepoint chair. Balancing the point of the cello on the Oriental prayer rug, she spread her knees and positioned the instrument between them. She inspected the bow, turning it over and sighting down it like an archer with an arrow. Then she reached over and took the lid off a metronome and set it going.

Nodding in time to it, she abruptly reached up the neck and began fingering with one hand, while she drew and pushed the bow with the other. She played the cello part to various songs from *The Messiah* in an irrepressible fashion, the chair swaying alarmingly under her. Like the bluegrass banjo at the Bloody Bucket, which technique had developed in response to the dreary life in Appalachian mining towns, Miss Head's baroque cello refused to yield a beat to the massed forces of despair and dispersal. Her glasses bounced precariously.

At the conclusion of the Hallelujah Chorus, she leaned her head against the neck and closed her eyes. After a minute or two, she opened her eyes, set her cello against the wall, and turned over the watch on her breast. She stood up, saying quietly, "It's ten thirty. You must be tired, Miss Babcock, on your first night out. I'll drive you back to the infirmary."

"I guess I'll go up to my room here in the dorm."

She looked at me with a tired smile and patted my shoulder and said, "Indeed. Yes. Good."

I heaved open her massive oaken door and found myself alone in the echoing alcove, the glaring portraits lying in wait for me in the hall beyond. Squaring my shoulders, I walked bravely into their collective stare. I had failed them so far. I had squandered my personal resources, yearning only to be loved and protected and defined by a man. I would not fail them in the future, however. I strode confidently up the hall under their gaze, past the antique high-backed wooden bishops' chairs that lined the dim corridor.

The topic I chose for my paper for Miss Head was the following: "Who made the world and why?" I sat down that night and wrote until four o'clock on Christmas morning. I had finished fourteen pages and had dealt with the first half of the topic. Using the Cartesian method, I had constructed an elegant proof of the existence of God, based on the postulate that it was impossible to conceive of something unless it existed in the first place. I read what I had written, and I saw that it was good, and I went to bed as well pleased as God Himself must have been after that sixth day on which *He* had conjured man into existence.

On Christmas morning I leapt out of bed and threw on a bathrobe and sat down at my desk and set to work finishing it. But the "why" had me stumped. Every string of interlaced theorems I unveiled collapsed like a house of cards. Finally I chopped the "why" off the topic and submitted a fourteen-page paper.

A couple of days later, Miss Head returned it to me with a big red

C and a note saying that she was giving me a break because I'd missed so many classes. I had posed my topic incorrectly. My argument suffered from circularity. The wording of the topic implied its answer. "Who" presupposed an anthropomorphic creator of some sort. Likewise, "made" implied a specific process of bringing the "world" into being, whereas it may in fact have come to be what it is through a number of other processes. As for my use of the word "world," well, no one could possibly take my question, thus stated, seriously enough to attempt an answer. "World" contained an ambiguity that rendered the question untenable. By "world" did I intend to indicate the total complex of entities and occurrences that have existed in the past and will exist in the future and are existing in the present? Because if so, such a "world" includes all beings who have ever made anything and all things ever made, and therefore could not be the subject of the erroneously used verb "to make" anyway. Or did I intend to indicate some fragmentary portion of the above-mentioned totality; and if so, what portion? In spite of my false start, I had handled my proof of the existence of God skillfully. My grasp of the mind-body dichotomy was sound. My improvement over the semester had been striking and would continue to be, she was certain. I must not be discouraged by my C. I was clinging to sentimental assumptions, conditioned into me by my upbringing. She had marked the points at which these assumptions had surfaced with a red pencil. I should work at rooting out such subjective emotional reactions.

I was very discouraged, not the least by the fact that I couldn't fathom the meaning of her remarks. She might just as well have been talking in Urdu. I sulked around and thought about reenrolling in the infirmary.

Instead I went out and bought Clem and Maxine a wedding gift —a salt shaker in the shape of a bull's head and a pepper shaker in the shape of a cow's head. These I mailed with a friendly note apologizing for my tardiness and wishing them many years of great happiness. In the package I included Clem's patched windbreaker and his bracelet.

Then I went to a beauty parlor and had my hair done. I was letting it grow out so as to wear it in a bun. In the meantime, I wanted it as flat and unobtrusive as possible. After a year and a half of hefting around a lacquered bouffant, like a plastic space helmet, a close-fitting coif was a considerable relief.

I also bought half a dozen wool suits and some high-necked nylon blouses, an antique cameo brooch, and some low-heeled simple shoes. I now wore a size smaller than upon entering the infirmary with my broken heart. It was good to have less of me to keep track of.

Dressed in a new outfit, I descended to Miss Head's chambers. The Christmas vacation was ending the next day, and the other students would begin returning in early evening. I wanted to gobble up Miss Head's undivided attention while I could.

She opened her huge door, looked me up and down, and exclaimed, "Why, Miss Babcock! I scarcely recognized you. You have a new suit. It's perfectly lovely." She invited me in, and I perched on the overstuffed horsehair loveseat. "I was just making myself some tea. Would you like some?"

I was by now well hooked on tea. I required it, fixlike, every afternoon. "Thank you. Yes." Miss Head performed the intricate tea rite in exactly the same way as the day of my interview. Only this time, wiser, I said, "With lemon, please. But no sugar."

Nodding with satisfaction at my acquired finesse, she handed me my cup. Then she looked at me questioningly. "I wondered," I explained, "if you could help me with my schedule for next term. I have no idea what to take."

She looked at me, perplexed. "Well, what are you interested in, Miss Babcock?"

"That's just it. I don't know. I didn't have enough of any one thing in high school to *know* what I'm interested in." Other than kinky sex and motorcycles and flag swinging and moonshine, which I knew I *wasn't* interested in any longer. "There's so much I should take that I don't know where to start. My education is one big gap."

"Well!" she said briskly, her Galatea sitting ready to be molded in front of her. "To start with, you'll certainly want to take the last half of my philosophy course."

"Of course."

"More Descartes and Spinoza. Some Locke and Berkeley, Hume and Hegel. It should be a *most* exciting spring!"

"Hmmm."

"And you're required to finish English 102. So that leaves just three courses. Science or humanities?" I shrugged, indicating that I was putty in her hands.

"All right. I'd suggest beginning chemistry and physiology, maybe some introductory physics, to balance out the English and philosophy. Then next year perhaps you'll have the basis for a choice between science and humanities."

"Great," I said, rapidly filling out my form and handing it to her to sign, as my adviser and current exemplar.

"Now! What else?" She peered at me through her lenses with her head resting back on her neck.

"That's all. Thank you." I set down my cup and prepared to leave.

"Don't rush off," she said, glancing at her watch. "I was just working on my book. But I'm in no great hurry to get back to it."

"What's your book?"

"I haven't named it yet. It's a comparison of the methods of the eighteenth-century empiricist philosophers to Newtonian mechanics."

"Oh," I said in a daze. "Sounds interesting."

"Oh, quite. I've been working on it for seven years."

I gulped. "And it's almost done?"

"Oh, another two years ought to do it," she said with satisfaction, thrusting forward her lower jaw in a friendly smile. "And now tell me what *you've* been engaged in, Miss Babcock?"

"I've been catching up on my reading. And I've written a make-up paper for History 103 on the use of the astrolabe in fifteenth-century Portuguese exploration in the southern hemisphere."

"Indeed."

"I'm sorry, by the way, about my Descartes paper. I did try on it."

She waved her hand grandly. "Never mind. You'll catch on. You display a remarkable ability, Miss Babcock, to adapt yourself to your surroundings—a sort of protective coloration, as it were. I'm certain, Miss Babcock, that you'll pick up the philosophic method in no time if you decide to."

"Do you really think so?" It seemed unlikely. I could dress like Miss Head, but thinking like her was another matter altogether.

"I'm sure of it. Have you called your parents?" I scowled. She laughed. "Oh, come now, Miss Babcock. Must you be so insistently melodramatic?"

"Yes, I called them."

"And are you on speaking terms with them now?"

"I suppose so."

"Good." She sighed and poured herself another cup of tea. I handed her my cup for a refill. "I remember the battles I used to have with *my* parents," she said with a smile, removing her glasses so that they dangled from their chain and knocked against her chest. She had blue eyes, weak and watery. "It seemed so crucial at the time. But now they're dead."

My indomitable parents dead? Never! They would rust or corrode, but they would never expire. "What did you and your parents fight about?"

Miss Head was staring absently out the window, where the winter sun was burning cryptic patterns into the snow. Huge gleaming icicles hung halfway down her windows. She hadn't heard my question. I repeated it.

She looked up, startled. "Oh yes, ah, let me see." She shifted her position and settled back in her fragile chair. I took the opportunity to shift in my unfamiliar suit to a spot where there wasn't a spring poking insistently into my buttock.

"Well, Miss Babcock, like you I grew up in a small town—Morgan, Oklahoma."

"You're kidding? Where's your Okie accent?"

"You forget that I've been away from Oklahoma for many years. Anyway, my father drilled wells for people—water wells, not oil wells, alas. I went to school there—twelve grades in four rooms. And I lived a normal stifling small-town life. But for some reason, I don't know why, I always harbored a secret ambition to go to an Ivy League women's college. Well, even *college* for a girl was a difficult concept for my parents. They didn't have much money, certainly not enough to send me to college. It was during the Depression. Nevertheless, for years I wrote off for catalogues to all the fanciest schools. I hid them in my closet and sometimes locked myself in with a flashlight and fantasized over my future as a student at one of those places.

"Well, when the time came, I somehow managed to wrest a scholarship offer out of Vassar. After all, I'd been in correspondence with them for years. And then their geographical quota had a lot to do with it, no doubt." She said this with a wry glance at me.

"But my parents wouldn't hear of my going so far away. Why couldn't I marry some nice Oklahoma boy and settle down and raise a family like a normal Oklahoma girl? Why did I have to go around puttin on airs?" Remarkably, as she talked, her cultivated eastern accent started slipping, and the nasal Oklahoma twang appeared ever so faintly around the edges of her discourse.

"So we fought and we fought and I eventually allowed them to win. I renounced my scholarship. But secretly I had applied to Emory in Atlanta, which was just barely near enough to defuse their distance argument. Emory came through with a scholarship, and I took it.

"And then they didn't want me to go for my Ph.D., and they didn't want me to go to New York to do it. And so it was one continuous struggle with them. Until, as I say, they died."

"But how could they possibly object to your getting a Ph.D.?"

She shrugged and sipped her tea. "I dare say they wanted a son-in-law and lots of grandchildren. There was a man I was—involved with about that time. A graduate student in chemistry. He was going overseas to fight. He wanted me to marry him and to start on a baby before he was shipped out. But I had just begun my Ph.D. program at Columbia and had all these other things I wanted to do. So I turned him down. It was viewed as a very unpatriotic thing to do at the time, heartless. And especially by my parents, who had met him and were crazy about him. Well, he was killed. In Belgium. But that's beside the point."

I looked at her questioningly. If the fact of her lover's being killed in Belgium was beside the point, what *was* the point?

"All parents—the exceptions should be enshrined—view their offspring as reincarnations of themselves," she continued. "If those children veer too sharply in either direction from the path staked out by their parents, the parents feel rejected, become offended. But what is one to do?" She smiled tolerantly. "What are *they* to do? What are *any* of us to do? We're all trapped. However, one dies."

I sipped my tea thoughtfully, fondling these new insights into the character formation of my mentor. "But if your parents were impoverished, where did all that beautiful china and stuff they left you come from?"

"It had been in my mother's family—relics of better times. My mother doted over it. My father didn't know the difference between Waterford crystal and Welch's grape jelly glasses. Or care. I remember he used to sit in the kitchen in his dirty T-shirt, with the wind blowing dust through the cracks around the door; and he'd tease my mother by picking up one of those goblets in a huge grimy hand and pretending that he was going to tighten his grip and crumble it to powder. She'd sit there weeping and pleading with him to put it down, and she'd call him an ignorant clod and a crude dolt and anything else she could think of to hurt him. And it did hurt him. He was very aware of the fact that Mother had married beneath herself, as it were. Finally, as she kept needling him about what a great hulking hick he was, he'd set the goblet down and leap to his feet with his eyes bulging and his face purple; and he'd stomp over to her and slap her. She'd scream, and he'd hit her some more and start yelling things like, 'Just remember, Maude, why you married a stupid ox like me! None of them fancy fellers you used to run with could put it to you like I done, and thas a fact.' And she'd hiss at him, 'The child, Raymond! The child!' I'd usually be cowering behind a chair somewhere. And eventually, after he'd slapped her around some more, and she'd pounded him on his huge chest, and they'd both called each other horrible names and had tears streaming down their faces, he'd drag her off to the bedroom and lock the door. They'd reemerge several hours later—she prim and regal, and he humble and gentle.''

I stared at Miss Head with fascination. It was as though she'd just done a psychological strip tease for me. Her Oklahoma accent was as heavy as my Tennessee one by now.

"So you see," Miss Head concluded briskly, "I made it. I got away from all that nonsense. And so can you. It's simply a matter of choosing how to parcel out your energies, as it were." Suddenly I understood Miss Head's interest in me: She identified with me. I was the daughter she'd never have. She wanted to mold me into her image every bit as much as her parents had wanted to mold her into theirs. I couldn't decide whether I felt flattered or threatened. The key question was whether or not I wanted to be a professor at an Ivy League women's college and spend nine years writing one book. At least it was decent of her to level with me about her intentions—if she was aware she'd done so.

"Yes, but there's a difference," I insisted. "You wanted a college in the East, and I didn't. I had to be dragged here by my father. Though I *do* like it now." The other difference, which I decided not to mention, was the fact that the Major was filthy rich, and that presumably I would be too one day if I outlived him. I didn't have the Dust Bowl in the Depression to escape from. Nor were my parents' sadomasochistic tendencies quite so overt as those of her parents.

"Sometimes converts make the most ardent adherents," she said quietly, looking into her cup as though reading my future in her tea leaves.

Following this exchange, I devoted myself with ardor to my studies. My typical day began at seven with a breakfast of boiled eggs and orange juice and coffee at the dorm cafeteria. I had classes all morning. I returned to the cafeteria for lunch. And then I studied all afternoon at the library. Two afternoons a week I had physiology and chemistry labs. After supper, I went to my room and studied until midnight, and then I went to bed. On most weekends I allowed myself to sleep until nine, but then studied until bedtime, with time out only for dinner. I was like a nun. This was my novitiate.

I was very strict, allowing myself few recreational lapses. One I did allow, however, was trips around Boston with Miss Head to various cultural activities. I could rationalize taking time out for this because they were didactic exercises.

Once we went to the Museum of Fine Arts. Identical in our green loden coats and wool suits, we stood in one of the echoing marble hallways reverently inspecting some paintings.

"Why'd that guy paint so many pictures of the exact same haystack?" I asked indignantly.

Miss Head looked at me with reproof, to indicate that I was once again displaying my hillbilly origins. "You must try not to look at them as 'haystacks.' Regard them as studies in the relationship between form and light, as it were."

I nodded and studied the paintings again. I squinted and turned my head back and forth, but try as I might, I still saw them as haystacks.

"What a wild jug!" I laughed, pointing to a glass case that contained an earthenware pitcher with intertwined serpents for handles —"606 B.C., " the tag said.

Miss Head sighed wearily. "My dear Miss Babcock," she intoned, looking out at me over her glasses with her eyebrows raised in disbelief, "*try* not to think of it as a 'jug.' Regard it as symbolic of a lost civilization. Think of it as—ah—a Rosetta stone to the soul of a vanished race, as it were. Read its form and lines as a template, so to speak, to the minds of an alien species."

I shook my head doubtfully. "Shall we have a bite to eat?" Miss Head suggested in an exhausted voice.

"Sure. I saw a hamburg place one block over—Steer Haven or something."

She lowered her head and looked at me over the top of her glasses again and shook her head sadly. "Steer Haven *indeed.*"

"No?" What did people in Boston eat then?

There was room for only eight Formica tables inside the Acropolis Grill. We took the last empty one.

"Good evening, Demetrius," Miss Head said, nodding her gray-bunned head to the corpulent waiter who handed us our menus. I scanned mine, looking for the hamburger and hot dog section.

"Shall I order for you?" Miss Head offered. I nodded numbly.

Without enthusiasm, I scooped up mashed eggplant and chick peas on unleavened bread. I gritted my teeth and dug into sautéed squid, washing it down with a strong wine that smelled and tasted like the creosote Clem used on fence posts.

"Delicious," Miss Head notified me.

"Yes." In fact, it was pretty good, but when your heart is set on French fries, carp roe salad won't do.

We wound up this gastronomic exploration, undertaken for my edification (because surely Miss Head didn't eat here because she actually *enjoyed* it?), with a licorice liqueur.

Another time Miss Head took me to hear the Boston Symphony play Beethoven's Second. I settled back for a relaxing evening with this middle-aged woman, my teacher and my friend—even if she did persist in calling me Miss Babcock. My *only* friend at Worthley, in fact, since I'd been too busy studying to make more than passing acquaintance with anyone my own age.

The director strode out and we all applauded, for reasons that were unclear to me since he hadn't done anything applause-worthy yet. He raised his arms, and I snuggled down in my seat. Miss Head gouged me with her elbow and whispered sternly, "Concentrate, Miss Babcock. Notice how Beethoven will transform and reintroduce themes throughout the first movement in a standard sonata form."

I sat straight up and stared at the orchestra, my ears straining like an awakened housewife listening for burglars. I wasn't sure that I'd caught the themes, that I'd know a theme if it were served to me on a platter. Aha! There was one. I was sure of it. No. That tune? Yes! No? The orchestra hurtled along, unsympathetic. I glanced at Miss Head in agony. She was nodding in time, serenely, and was shifting her focus from one part of the orchestra to another.

As the expansive second movement swept in, I settled back with a sigh of relief. Miss Head leaned over and hissed, "Be alert, Miss Babcock! Notice the devices Beethoven employs to achieve this illusion of peace, hedged in by the intricate construction of the first movement and the lively pace of the third."

I shot back up in my seat and concentrated on the concept of repose, how one achieved it in melodic form without violating the rules of symphonic construction.

I was exhausted by the time the scherzo lurched in, but its lively rhythm soon had me perched on the edge of my seat. I leaned over and said to Miss Head, "Kind of makes you want to leap up there and dance, doesn't it?" She looked at me with a frown, to indicate that nothing could have been further from her mind.

By the end of the fourth movement, the armpits of my high-necked blouse were drenched with sweat.

As we drove in Miss Head's Opel sedan back to Worthley, I said, "Well, thanks, Miss Head. That was neat."

"*Neat?*"

"Uh, interesting. Elevating?" I hadn't yet mastered the adjectives of academe. "I particularly savored the mellifluous second movement," I tried tentatively. She looked at me strangely. "I mean, I found it very sonorous." I decided to forget it.

She took me back to her apartment and poured me my nightly fix of tea and played on her cello the themes and some of the variations. She illustrated the features of a good theme and the transformations one underwent in symphonic treatment.

At some point, she must have looked up to discover me sunk deep in a sleep of intellectual exhaustion on her horsehair loveseat.

The next day in her class, she called on me to discuss the ways in which Descartes's "necessarily true propositions" were used in the construction of his proofs. I parroted what she'd told me the night before about the qualities of symphonic themes—their clarity and simplicity and intrinsic necessity, the ways in which they were and were not susceptible to modification and adaptation. She nodded with satisfaction. Apparently I was progressing well as her mouthpiece. The thought left me vaguely uneasy. I was gaining Worthley, but was I losing Hullsport in the bargain?

Marion, a girl on my hall whom I vaguely knew, was concerned about my lack of social life and invited me to go to Princeton with her for a weekend. She was meeting her boy friend Jerry, and he had a roommate who needed a date. Please would I go?

My immediate gut reaction, which I should have honored, was to refuse. I had an important physiology paper due the next week, and

I hadn't even picked a topic. Out of curiosity to see firsthand the famous Princeton, I agreed to go (strictly as a didactic experience, of course).

The two boys met us at the bus station Friday night. Marion's man was tall and dark and debonair. Mine was short and acned. He was also surly when he discovered that he'd been paired with a pituitary giant for the weekend. We smiled sickly at each other, having both lost out at the potluck supper of weekend blind dates.

Their neo-Gothic stone dormitory looked very similar to our own neo-Gothic stone dormitory except that it was filled to the rafters with male sexual psychopaths rather than female ones. Their entry was having a party—thirty of us were crammed into a small dark third-floor room. Everyone but Marion and me was already drunk, and we were well on our way, guzzling gin and orange juice. The din from the records and the shouting was deafening—blessedly so, because it meant that my date, Ron, and I didn't have to try to converse civilly. Clutching my paper cup of gin and juice, I stood crushed against Ron in the packed room, swaying back and forth in time to the music. Ron's head came to my chest level. If we had been so inclined, he could have chewed my nipples without moving a muscle. As things were, though, we merely swayed to the music.

After a couple of hours, people started disappearing, and enough space developed for some heavy breathing. Someone put on the Beach Boys singing "Surfin' Safari." I hadn't danced in years. It had been out of the question with Clem because of his leg. And Joe Bob and I had had too many other things to attend to. But at one time I had loved it. Under the influence of that forgotten love, and of the dozen or so cups of gin and juice I'd tossed down, I leapt up from the sofa on which we were sprawled, grabbing the stunted young Ron by the hand. We stood facing each other like David and Goliath. We worked our way into the beat, and soon we could have joined any burlesque show in the country, with our obscene thrustings and gyratings and shudderings. My befogged Miss Head-trained brain tried briefly to explore the thematic material of "Surfin' Safari" and the ways in which those themes were being developed. But soon, these efforts were swamped by the hungers of my neglected flesh.

Ron and I were not alone on the dance floor. The music, the people, the time of night, the gin and juice—everything was converging to trigger an orgy. We were all writhing in the grip of the Beach Boys. A dateless boy was standing on the couch exposing himself.

He supervised the scene with satisfaction, a Priapus at a garden party.

"Surfin' Safari" ended with a crash. We dancers slumped like puppets whose strings had been cut, breathing fast and sweating. When "The Little Old Lady from Pasadena" began, Marion stumbled over and slurred, "You and Ron wanna come downa Jerry's room and relax?"

Jerry locked his door from inside. The furnishings consisted of two beds. Jerry and Marion sat on one, Ron and I on the other.

"Some party," I suggested brightly. No one answered. They were all breathing heavily.

"Yup, I can see that you Princeton men are real hellers," I said amiably to Ron, who had been at great pains to convince me of that earlier in the evening. Again, no one replied.

Jerry fell back. He reached up and pulled Marion down beside him. Kissing her ravenously, he began working his knee between her legs. He reached over and turned out the light.

I sat in the dark, trying not to eavesdrop on the gasps and slurping sounds coming from the other bed. This scene was strangely familiar to me. Before I had a chance to put my finger on exactly why it should be, I felt myself being dragged down onto my back. Before I could say Tom Thumb, nimble Ron had ripped the cameo brooch from my throat and laid my nylon blouse open to the navel. Now he was trying to reach around me to unhook my bra. Recalling reflexively my football skills, I straight-armed him, and he fell off the bed with a crash.

However, I underestimated his perseverance and cunning. The next thing I knew, he was crawling between my legs, forcing my tweed skirt up to my waist. I heard a zipper unzip and then felt him plunge into me.

Unfortunately for him, I was wearing a girdle. He shot out of me as though on a trampoline. I felt like a cow with a gnat buzzing around my tail.

Suddenly I found myself pinned spread-eagle under his small frame; his hand was groping for the top of my girdle.

I'd had enough. In fact, I'd had more than enough. Miss Head was right. One had to make a choice as to how to expend one's limited energies. I chose to expend mine at Princeton's Spring Fling no longer. I brought one of my pinned knees up sharply between Ron's legs. With a scream he rolled off me and crashed to the floor.

Snatching up my brooch, I sprinted for the door. Finding it locked, I raced for the light and threw it on.

"May I have the key please?" I asked Jerry. By the time my eyes were used to the light, I had figured out that Jerry was no longer on the bed. Nor was Marion. But I heard her voice, emanating from somewhere in that room. She was gasping, "Dear God, I'm dying!"

I looked around frantically. What was happening to her? What was her Princeton sex deviant doing? I knelt down between the beds and looked under them. Marion shrieked, "Yes! Mother of Jesus, yes!" Under the bed I saw a disembodied limb twitching through the folds of the bedspread. Good grief, I had to help her!

I scrambled to my feet and tore around to the far side of the bed. There on the floor, in the space between the bed and the wall, were Jerry and Marion, locked in furious anal intercourse. With a sigh of relief that Marion's sodomization was evidently voluntary, I picked up Jerry's impeccably creased and pressed blue jeans, extracted the key and left them—Ron in one whimpering heap, and Marion and Jerry in a second one.

By the time I got back to Worthley, I had settled on a topic for my physiology paper: "Venous Congestion and Edema as a Determining Factor in the Intensity of Human Orgasm." I spent the remainder of the Princeton Spring Fling in the library researching and writing it.

The thrust of the paper, as it were, was that blood was the key factor in sexual response in humans. Blood, many ounces of it, surged into the areas involved. Or as one of my sources put it with regard to the female, "The bulbous vestibule, plexus pudendalis, plexus uterovaginalis, and, questionably, the plexus vesicalis and plexus hemorrhoidalis externus are all involved in a fulminating vasocongestive reaction." The tissues, engorged with blood, pinched the veins so that none of the blood being pumped in along the arteries could drain away. Being a corpuscle in such a situation was equivalent to being an MTA passenger on a platform during rush hour with no trains appearing; more corpuscles kept arriving but none could depart. This state of affairs continued until the distention reached its outer limits and triggered a reflex stretch mechanism in the neighboring muscles. These muscles then contracted in spasms, which expelled the blood along the pinched veins in spurts. The collective experience of the muscular spasms and the blood expulsion was referred to as "orgasm." The tissues and muscles involved in this female orgasm had their precise counterparts in the male.

In other words, the back-seat blue balls of high school days had been caused by the failure, for different sociocultural reasons, to trigger reflexive contractions of the bilateral bulbocavernosi, the transverse perineals, the external anal sphincter, the rectus abdominus, the levator ani, and the irschiocavernosi, which would have drained the congested venous erectile bodies of the corpora cavernosi of the penile shaft and the sinuslike cavities of the penile bulb, the glans, and the corpus spongiosum of the blood that had engorged them. This blood lingered on in oxygen-starved puddles. (Oh, Joe Bob, where are you now? I asked of the shelf of thirty-pound anatomy texts I was consulting.)

But why? What was the point of eternally filling those mysterious interconnected venous chambers with blood, and then pulling the plug and draining them—only to start filling them all over again almost immediately? It seemed like the task of Sisyphus. Luckily, I had learned from my philosophy paper about who made the world never to tack a "why" on to the end of my topics. I now limited myself to the "how."

But this much I *did* know: Although my pudenda personally hadn't experienced much in the way of fulminating vasocongestion of the venous plexus, I had no intention of spending my life functioning as a hydraulic engineer. Miss Head apparently did without fulminating vasocongestion, and so could I. It was simply a question of channeling my energies in a more rarefied direction. I was delighted that I was at last having the great good sense to forswear the whole ridiculous enterprise.

I tacked onto the paper a few arresting statistics about the relation of different coital positions to the degree of vasocongestion, and therefore the intensity of orgasm. Then I turned it in. It came back marked A. I had known that the scientific detachment I'd inherited from the Major would come in handy one day.

Miss Head invited me to a production of *Aïda* in Boston, being given by the Metropolitan Opera Company on tour.

We were practically in Aïda's lap when she sang her death aria while sealed in the tomb by the Nile. Being sealed in a tomb by a high priest and suffocating was one hazard Mother hadn't thought to warn me about. By this time, I had become quite attached to both Aïda and Rhadames, and was appalled by their approaching deaths, by their hostile environment, by the perfidy of Princess Amneris, by Rhadames's moral dilemma over whether or not to reveal military secrets to his would-be father-in-law.

They pulled out all the stops for their final duet. Although I knew it was just a story, I found myself very moved. Tears, of all things, spilled from my eyes and ran down my cheeks, as the oxygen inside the tomb ran out.

Her eyes on the stage, Miss Head leaned over and said softly, "Notice how Verdi increases the atmosphere of doom and poignancy with the sharp drops in the soprano melody line, and by his insistent refusal to return to the tonic."

Blotting my tears with a Kleenex, I did as I was instructed, and let Aïda herself go hang.

After the performance, I suggested we go eat at a pizza parlor. "Well, pizza *is* Italian, isn't it?" I protested, as Miss Head dragged me toward a Pakistani restaurant. Haltingly, I was absorbing this strange new set of tastes and standards. I had figured out that anything American—hamburgers, fried chicken, steaks—wasn't *comme il faut*. Colonel Sanders and Bonanza Beef were out. Small crowded foreign restaurants were in, preferably those featuring foods of an underdeveloped nation. So be it. But what was wrong with pizza?

"How did you like the opera?" Miss Head asked, as we ate murgh musallam and sanzi seeni and bushels of rice.

"It was wild!"

"*Wild?*" she asked, closing her eyes and raising her eyebrows. "Indeed."

"Neat. *You* know."

"Yes, of course. Neat, as it were. In other words, you found the performance satisfying?"

"Right. Sure. Did you?" Suddenly I was hesitant about my enthusiasm. After all, I'd never seen an opera before. How was I to know whether or not this one had been neat? I had nothing to compare it to.

"I don't know. I thought the baritone left a lot to be desired. And the staging was overdone, as it tends to be for *Aïda*. Otherwise, it was adequate."

"Of course." Adequate. That was like getting a C on a paper. When would I develop the ability to distinguish, as Miss Head did with such ease, between the merely adequate and the excellent?

"The soprano was very good, though. Did you notice how she was able to change the emotional coloration of a line simply by varying the harmonics of her voice?"

I nodded yes, lying shamelessly.

"Excellent, she was. Superb."

The reason I couldn't distinguish between excellence and mere adequacy, I concluded as I lay in my bed the next morning waiting for my alarm to go off so that I could officially wake up, was that I had allowed my emotions to swamp my intellect. I had permitted myself the indulgence of becoming personally involved in Aïda's and Rhadames's deaths in a neurotic process of identification. I had failed Miss Head.

In propitiation, I went that afternoon to biology lab and scraped some cells from inside my cheek, smeared them on a slide, and dripped some water on them. Under high magnification, I zeroed in on one cell. Then I watched. Gradually the tiny inclusions in the cell body began bobbing around. Then the cytoplasm itself began puffing up as it imbibed water from outside the cell. The nucleus ruptured next and released its material into the cytoplasm. Although I couldn't actually see it happening, I knew from my reading that now the ionic equilibrium was collapsing and that sodium ions were rushing into the cell and upsetting the potassium balance.

The entire process I'd been witnessing was the death of the cell. The final act of dying was merely a formality: It occurred when the cell wall burst open with a sickening gasp of bubbles and the cytoplasm with its dancing inclusions streamed out. What remained on my slide now, of the formerly living and functioning cell from my own body, was nothing but an undifferentiated mass of denatured proteins with small amounts of degraded nucleic acids mixed in. I knew that if I stood over this eyepiece watching for long enough, the material would eventually curl up and crumble into its molecular components.

This cell of mine was an intermediate step between two worlds. On the atomic level, protons were busy swapping electrons, like kids trading marbles; in the process, they would transform the proteins into their constituent amino acids, and the amino acids into their component elements—hydrogen, oxygen, nitrogen. If the amino acids were the letters of the alphabet that combined to form word proteins, proteins in turn formed sentences—cells like this one. The paragraphs in the book of life and death were multicelled organisms. Cells were dying continuously in this same fashion in Aïda's body, in my body, in Miss Head's body.

When cell death got out of hand, though, and the forces of chaos won out over those of elaboration and order, what happened? Those cells synthesizing the most protein burst first—the adrenals, the testes, the pancreas, the gastrointestinal tract; then the liver, kidneys, endocrine glands. The more inert substances like skin and muscle and bone and cartilage held up for a comparatively long time—so that a body could look normal from without, but inside consist solely of a bubbling soup of collapsing cytoplasm.

I washed the slide and put away my equipment. Miss Head was working on her book when I reached her apartment, it being precisely 4:40, according to my Lady Bulova. Reluctantly, she put it aside to play Aïda's death aria on her cello, at my insistence. I listened with detachment, without the faintest twinge of fear or sorrow. I had spent my afternoon productively. I had seen Death, and it was no big deal. Only the unfamiliar had the power to stir neurotic emotions. So I reasoned.

The next day in class Miss Head called on me to summarize Spinoza's attitude toward the human passions.

"Spinoza feels," I stated confidently, "that in order to achieve virtue, a man must detach himself from the transitory passions that he suffers, so as to gain an understanding, through reason, of the nature and origin of those passions. Only by struggling to develop his intellect so as to attain this knowledge can he make himself free."

"Free?" she prompted, with a pleased smile.

"Free from his passions, which are simply a form of misunderstanding. Because to view the world as a whole, with all its interconnected necessities, is to extinguish such fleeting personal whims. Free, in the sense of choosing to accept the inevitable."

Miss Head nodded, her face glazed with surprised pride.

On my way back to the dorm for lunch, a green VW pulled over next to me. A pleasant male voice asked, "Can you please tell me how to get to Castle? I've never come in this entrance before and I seem to be lost."

Castle was my dorm. "I'm going there now. If you'll give me a ride, I'll direct you." I climbed in and inspected the driver. He was tall, thin, pleasant-looking, had brown hair and eyes that squinted in amusement as he talked.

"Who are you looking for?" I asked.

"Marion Marshall." I regarded Marion with new respect. This man clearly wasn't her Jerry. She had admirers all across the Northeast?

"She's on my hall."

"She's my sister."

"Oh."

He parked the VW, and we walked through the vaulted stone porte-cochere and into the dorm. In the waiting room, I buzzed Marion on the PA system. There was no answer.

"Was she expecting you?"

"Not really. I'm at Harvard. I just thought it was too pretty a day to study so I decided to drive out and get her to give me some lunch and take me around your lake. But I guess I've struck out."

I hesitated. I had a biology lab that afternoon, and a paper to write for the end of the week. But it seemed only civil to offer him lunch until Marion appeared. After all, she was more or less a friend of mine —as close to being my friend as anyone at Worthley, except for Miss Head. Also, until her brother mentioned it, I hadn't been aware of what kind of day it was. But since he'd brought it up, I had to acknowledge that there was a gorgeous sunny spring afternoon outside, the kind of overpoweringly sunny day that I hadn't seen since last September. The grass was greening up, some early flowers were blooming, foolhardy robins were trickling back in from the South.

"You could have lunch with me. Marion's bound to be back soon."

"Oh, no, I don't want to bother you."

"It's no bother. I was going to eat anyway."

We ate asparagus tips on toast with Hollandaise sauce. He chatted amiably about himself, about being from Michigan and liking to sail and fly planes. He was studying architecture and described his projects and some of the interesting new buildings in Cambridge.

"Come in sometime. I'll take you around to see them," he offered, in response to my very genuine interest.

After lunch Marion still hadn't appeared. Her brother and I strolled around the lake. Birds were warbling in the trees as they built their nests. Tree branches were covered with swelling buds. Gusty breezes blew patterns of ripples across the lake surface and rustled last fall's dried rushes. I talked about Hullsport and Miss Head and my various academic difficulties.

"I know," he said with a laugh. "It's a whole different vocabulary these professors have. They're like a subspecies of the human race. The trick to getting along with them is to become schizophrenic: Talk their jargon when you're with them, be yourself when you're not."

I looked at him closely. He said that with such deceptive ease: Be yourself when you're not. Did anyone really know that effortlessly what his real self *was?* I was almost convinced by now that my "real self" was in fact that aspect of me that most resembled Miss Head. But I was willing to listen to arguments from the opposition.

By the time we had completed our circuit of the lake, he was no longer concerned about finding Marion, and I was no longer concerned about my biology lab. We lay in the grass by the edge of the lake and exchanged memories dredged up from early childhood. The spring sun beat down on our pallid faces and baked our winter-weary bodies. I felt as though a huge chunk of ice located inside my abdomen were thawing. Fluffy clouds drifted overhead, assuming all sorts of fabulous shapes. On a hill across the lake were half a dozen small children. Two flew colorful kites out over the lake. The others tumbled around in the new grass and rolled down the face of the hill like small puppies. I sighed with contentment. As I did so, I found my hand being held. Delicious sensations of warmth began creeping up my arm, and my fingers trembled in his.

"Why don't we go into Cambridge a little later?" he suggested. "I could show you those buildings I was telling you about. And then we could have dinner somewhere. I know a great Spanish restaurant near the Square."

It required every fiber of self-restraint that I possessed to prevent my body from rolling over and snuggling companionably up against him. Thoughts of my unwritten paper were as distant and as uncompelling as memories of last winter's ice storms.

Just as I was about to accept, I jerked my hand away and scrambled to my feet, like Cinderella at the ball at midnight. "I'm sorry but I have a biology lab," I mumbled. "It's been a nice afternoon. I hope you find Marion." I whirled around and raced off.

"Wait!" he yelled. "What's your name?" I didn't answer.

I was gasping for breath by the time I sprinted into the biology lab. Professor Aitken looked at me with displeasure. I mumbled apologies as I slipped on my lab coat. Half a dozen other girls were already working silently at their microscopes.

I prepared my slides, using specimens from a Petri dish teeming with protozoa. I took them to a microscope and adjusted the eyepiece. Looking into it, I focused in on an ever-smaller segment of the slide. Finally, I had a good picture of two protozoa, surrounded by dozens more. I could see the outer membranes that enclosed their cytoplasm; and in the cytoplasm, the mitochondria where they produced energy, the nuclei which contained their genetic material.

As I watched, waiting for nothing in particular, the two protozoa began approaching each other by extending their comical pseudopods, the tiny bulges of protoplasm that functioned for them almost like feet. When they were within a certain distance of each other, they appeared to perform some sort of dance: They moved toward each other; then they backed away; they circled each other; they rotated in place. Finally, after many tedious minutes of this coy microscopic Virginia reel, they drew up side by side. Gradually, out of the side of one of the protozoa there extended a tiny point of protoplasm. This point grew and grew. Eventually it bridged the gap to the other protozoa. I ceased to be able to see exactly what was happening, but the end result was that the bridge of protoplasm penetrated the other protozoa and merged with it, so that the interiors of the two cells were now continuous.

"Professor Aitken!" I shrieked. He came rushing over, his white coat flying behind him. "Something strange is going on with my protozoa!"

He peered through my microscope. "Oh yes," he said, disappointed that I hadn't uncovered some Nobel Prize material. "They're exchanging genic material."

"What does that mean?"

"It's equivalent to what happens in human conception. Each receives a portion of the other's genes so that when each cell divides, the four daughter cells will be combinations of the two parent cells. It's an elaboration on simple cell division."

"But *why?*" I asked, forgetting for the moment my resolution only to ask "how," never "why."

"So that evolution of the species can occur. If each cell merely reproduced itself, changes—improvements or otherwise—couldn't take place, except randomly through trauma-induced mutation."

"How come these two picked each other to swap genes with?"

" 'Picked'? Please, Miss Babcock, try not to be so insistently anthropomorphic. We think it's simply a question of electrical charges on the cell membranes. But of course the same thing is going on all through the Petri dish."

By the time I returned to my high-magnification peep show, the one protozoa was retracting its protoplasmic protuberance, and the other was swimming languidly away into the surrounding soup.

That night at supper I saw Marion. "I met your brother this afternoon. Did he ever find you?"

"Yes. He said he met someone from Tennessee. I figured it had to be you. He really liked you. But he said you ran off when he asked you out."

"I had a biology lab."

"I think he thought you were rejecting him."

I didn't say anything.

"Should I tell him you weren't?"

Finally I said, "I'm really pretty busy this term. I don't have time to go out."

She shook her head sadly. "Okay. Suit yourself."

I was very irritated by her solicitous attitude. Just because she spent most of her spare time on her back with her legs spread, she wanted everyone else to as well. Well, my destiny did not lie in some man's unmade bed.

I shut myself away in a library carrel that night and wrote a paper for my biology course. It was based on the concept that human emotions were a repertoire of behavioral patterns bred into an organism, just as anatomical features were bred into it. The patterns characteristic of any given organism, love in humans for instance, were those that had exhibited survival value for the species as a whole. But it was quite possible that what was beneficial to the species might *not* be beneficial to the individual organism. And in such a case, the interests of the individual were ruthlessly forfeited to those of the species. For example, the vivid feathering of some birds enhanced their mating prowess but also enhanced their vulnerability to predators. Individual survival was assigned a secondary place to species propagation by the Management.

I, however, was a daughter of Spinoza. My talent lay in detaching myself from this scheme. I had studied sentic cycles; I knew that each person's finger presses a sensitized key in an identical wave pattern when that person is imagining situations that elicit a given emotion. I also knew that people could be trained to reproduce the wave pattern characteristic of any given emotion without reference to internal or external stimuli. I would not serve, under the guise of sublime emotion, as a vessel for chromosome interchange with Marion's brother or with anyone else, be it for the well-being of my species or not. In short, I decided not to go out on any more dates. Not that my phone was ringing off the wall.

I went home to Hullsport for the summer, having been dateless for two months and without sex for much longer.

I worked at the Major's factory as a file clerk. The Major often took time out from his duties to diagram for me the chemical composition of the explosives being synthesized there, and I admired the elegance of the formulas. All summer the Major and I were each other's biggest admirer.

The testing procedures at the factory had gained considerably in sophistication since the evenings of my childhood when the Major had bought us kids ice cream cones and had taken us to view his performances at the test firing range. By now all the testing for detonation speeds was done in a blast chamber and was monitored by a huge pie-shaped camera that used special lenses and whirling mirrors to snap photographs at three-microsecond intervals.

One afternoon, the Major invited me to a meeting of himself and the technicians who conducted these tests. They had the photo series from a test for a new explosive to be used in large shells consigned to a place people were just beginning to hear of—Vietnam. There were eight pictures in this series, which from start to finish took about twenty-four microseconds. I was impressed. The fastest speed on Miss Head's metronome was four beats per second. Joe Bob in his track meets had striven against a stopwatch that was divided into hundredths of seconds. Clem, even on the morning when he had nearly killed me, had been traveling only about 117 feet per second. But here in these photos, we were witnessing a blast whose waves could travel twenty thousand feet per second, a blast that was completed before Joe Bob's stop watch could even start.

I studied the photos with fascination as the blast pictured in them grew and grew, preceded by white shock waves. Halfway through the sequence, the explosion began puffing into fantastic shapes, like the cumulus clouds Marion's brother and I had watched and labeled on that warm spring afternoon at Worthley. The last frame in the photo series was mostly gray and black, with gases and debris enshrouding the eye of the explosion.

"What do you think, Major?" asked a technician in a white lab coat.

The Major cleared his throat and held the series up to the light in his deformed left hand with its missing finger. "Yes, well, I think it's what we've been looking for, don't you, Hal?" Hal nodded. "I mean the shattering effect is ideal, it seems to me. Look at the size of those shock waves!" We all stared at the white shock waves greedily, as though they were the billowing breasts of a *Playboy* centerfold.

"Gorgeous!" Hal said.

I saw Clem only once that summer. I stopped by after work one afternoon and found him in the barnyard standing on the running board of a tractor. He was wearing green work pants and a grease-smeared T-shirt. His dark hair hung in his eyes. He was using a large screwdriver to pry something out of the tractor engine. His face was drenched with sweat, and his T-shirt clung to his scrawny back in dark patches.

He smiled when he saw me. I rested my elbows on the hood and looked down into the engine. Drawing on my knowledge of the internal combustion engine from Physics 140, and my knowledge of the human body from Physiology 110, I described to Clem the similarities between the two: The lungs functioned as a sort of carburetor to mix with oxygen the fuel transported from the stomach via the bloodstream, just as fuel traveling down the gas line from the gas tank mixed with oxygen in the carburetor of an engine; muscle cells, drawing energy from the combustion of simple sugars, expanded and contracted like the pistons of an engine in order to drive the limbs. . . .

Clem frowned at me, his screwdriver at rest and his face smeared with dirt and grease. He said with concern, "Shoot, Ginny, you done gone plumb crazy up at Boston."

Fortunately, I no longer cared what Clem thought. I had studied Hegel. I knew that Clem had merely played the antithesis to Joe Bob's thesis, and that Miss Head was the pure and elevated synthesis. That Miss Head herself might be the thesis for a yet higher synthesis, as Hegel would have insisted, was unthinkable.

Immediately upon my return to Worthley in the fall, I went to Miss Head's apartment to get her to sign my course selection. When she opened her door, she looked just as she had the spring day I had left her to go home for the summer—in a tweed suit and nylon blouse, her Greek cameo at her throat and her Swiss watch hanging above her heart.

She stared out at me over the top of her horn-rim half glasses and smiled. I felt an impulse to embrace her. My arms rose slightly from my sides. I hastily suppressed the impulse, feeling that Miss Head would be startled and displeased by an expression of physical intimacy from me. Instead, we stood looking at each other awkwardly, beaming with repressed pleasure.

"Come in, come in," she finally said, stepping aside.

She had obviously been working on her Descartes book. Papers were stacked all over her mahogany dining table.

"I hope I didn't interrupt you?" I knew how she loathed having her schedules upset.

She consulted her watch and said, "No, indeed. It's six thirty-five. Time for me to stop anyway. So you're back, are you?"

"Did you think I wouldn't be?"

"One never knows. Summer vacations are quite a test. I remember reluctantly going back to Oklahoma every summer. For several months I'd listen to my parents' propaganda about how delightful it would be if I'd forget about my fancy education and settle down with some nice man and give them some grandchildren. By the end of the summer, with another grueling academic year ahead of me, they'd have me nearly won over. I'd walk out to the edge of town, where I was usually working as a waitress or a chambermaid or something. I'd watch the tumbleweed swirl by and the dust clouds sift down over everything, and I'd struggle with myself over how I wanted to spend my life. Finally, I just stopped going home. I couldn't take it."

"It never occurred to me not to come back," I confessed, distressed by my lack of soul.

"Good! I'm delighted to see you. You look marvelous. You must have had a pleasant summer."

"I did. I worked at my father's factory. It was fascinating. I've never properly appreciated him before."

"What kind of factory is it?"

"Munitions," I replied offhandedly.

She lowered her gray head and looked at me over the top of her glasses and said in a deep noncommittal voice, "Indeed."

"You should see the neat photo series they do of explosions in the blast chamber to check detonation speeds."

"What are these explosives *for*, as it were?"

"Bombs and shells and stuff."

"Indeed." She looked at me strangely.

"Well, he just *makes* them. He's presented with a chemical problem: how to maximize shock waves within a given number of microseconds. It's not *his* fault if his solutions are sometimes misused." Miss Head said nothing. "Well, *is* it?"

"I wouldn't know, I'm sure. I'm strictly apolitical, Miss Babcock. I happen to agree with Descartes when he says that his maxim is 'to try always to conquer [h .nself] rather than fortune, and to alter [his] desires rather than change the order of the world, and generally accustom [himself] to believe that there is nothing entirely within [his] power but [his] own thoughts.' I've always felt that a person's intelligence is directly reflected by the number of conflicting points of view he can entertain simultaneously on the same topic."

I thought about it. I wasn't absolutely positive that I agreed with Descartes in this case. But if Miss Head agreed, I was sure I'd come to in time.

"Well, anyhow, I need your signature."

"Let me see," she said, taking my schedule.

I was pleased with myself for having decided what to take without her advice—astronomy, physics, nineteenth-century philosophy, psychology. She blanched. What was wrong with it?

"I had thought," she said, sounding somewhat miffed, "that you might want to do some independent study under me on Descartes or Spinoza."

"Well, I did think about it. And then I decided that I'd better cover some more ground in a rather superficial fashion before I zero in on any one specialty."

"That's probably an excellent idea. But how about eighteenth-century music, say, or the early English novel?"

"Well, I don't know, I mean, I'd like to take them, but I can't take *everything,* can I?"

"No, but I really don't think you'll be happy with the nineteenth-century philosophers, Miss Babcock. They're quite different from Descartes and Spinoza, you know. Schopenhauer and Nietzsche and Kierkegaard, indeed!" She snorted so forcefully that her glasses popped off and dangled on their chain. "And in combination with your other choices—no, I think you're making a mistake, Miss Babcock. As your adviser, I feel I must warn you."

"But *why*, Miss Head? I don't *understand*." I was truly perplexed.
I had expected her to be pleased that I had made up my own mind
this time.

"It's too much at once," she explained mysteriously.

"*I'm* the one who has to take these courses, Miss Head, and these
are the ones I want to take. I can switch at mid-term if they're not what
I want. And I definitely plan to take your Descartes seminar in January."

She looked at me, at a loss. Never having been a mother, she was
new to the battles of will that went on constantly between parent and
child. Finally, she signed the form and handed it to me.

"Thank you, Miss Head," I said, standing up.

"You're welcome, I'm sure, Miss Babcock," she replied coolly.

Panic seized me. I longed to rip up my schedule and fill out a new
one entirely in keeping with her wishes. If I didn't please this woman,
she would withdraw her affection and support. On the other hand, if
I didn't please myself, I might end up like my mother, sacrificed to
others' whims for so long that I'd no longer know what I wanted. And
what other message had I been deciphering from Miss Head's example all these months: I wasn't doomed to repeat my mother's patterns
of behavior. There were alternatives.

Struggling in the grip of this paradox, I managed to say to Miss
Head with equal iciness, "It's very nice seeing you again."

She nodded her gray-bunned head slightly and offered me a
pained smile. Again I wanted to embrace her, to reassure myself of
her continuing affection in spite of it all. Again I stopped myself. I had
to steady myself against the wall with one hand as I passed through
her alcove and into the hall.

I had the same room I'd had the previous year—a small garret on
the fifth floor with a window seat overlooking the courtyard. It
smelled musty. I threw open the casement windows and looked toward the lake, past the bronze cast of Artemis on whose outstretched
finger someone had hung a yo-yo.

There was a crash and a clatter, and I heard a voice in the next
room shout, "Oh fuck!"

A tin can was falling through the air. Turning slowly, end over
end, it spewed a red liquid onto the gray flagstones and the Flemish
sundial in the courtyard below.

There was another clatter next door, and the same coarse voice yelled, "Goddam it to hell!" The can landed with a hollow crunch. As it lay there, the red liquid oozed from the holes in its top. The stones all around it and the bronze sundial were splattered with rusty red dribbles, as though some wild animal had been dismembering its prey on that very spot.

"Shit, shit, shit!" the voice roared.

Interested to meet my articulate new neighbor, I knocked tentatively at her door.

"Yeah?"

I looked in. "Are you okay?"

The girl was wearing wheat jeans and a black turtleneck jersey, which fitted snugly around her large breasts. She was tall, big, statuesque. Her thick brown hair was plaited in a single braid down her back. Her features were coarse—a wide forehead, a large nose, prominent cheekbones. They had a plasticity that gave her face a startling expressiveness. In the few seconds between my opening her door and speaking to her, a phenomenal range of emotions had flitted across her face—surprise, embarrassment, irritation, curiosity.

"Are you okay?"

"I didn't know anyone but me was on the hall yet."

"I just got here. I guess we're neighbors. I'm Ginny Babcock."

"Edna Holzer. Eddie."

I recognized the name. She was a junior, an editor on the campus newspaper. I glanced around her room. It looked remarkably lived in to have been occupied for only a day or two. There were playbills and a Bob Dylan poster plastered across one wall, a Mexican blanket on another, a guitar propped in a corner, some small clay sculptures sitting on the college-issue desk and on the window seat.

"What happened—the crashing and the yelling?"

"I knocked over a can of tomato juice. I keep stuff for breakfast on my outside window ledge. For the mornings when I oversleep and miss breakfast. Which is often."

"Oh. I see. Well, nice to meet you. See you later, I imagine," I said, withdrawing from her room. "Glad you're all right. That tomato juice splattering all over everything looked like blood."

She looked at me with interest. "Did you think so?" I felt as though I'd just unwittingly handed her the key to my character. "Where are you from, Ginny?"

"Tennessee."

The look of disgust that seemed the most natural expression in her vast repertoire, held in abeyance until now, came over her face. "Christ, you southerners make me sick."

"Why?" I asked in amazement at this unprovoked assault.

"Have you been reading the papers? Those civil rights workers getting murdered and buried in the levees? Jesus, are there really such morons down there?"

"We're not much different from people up here. We just *sound* different. Well, see you around, Eddie. I've got to get back to my unpacking." I stomped from her room, amazed to find myself suddenly functioning as an ambassador from the South.

The next morning I met my neighbor on the other side—a freshman from Iowa named Bev Martin. She was tall and bony and awkward, with wide panicked eyes that shifted like a frightened rabbit's. She spoke in a near whisper. High strung, I labeled her. She and Eddie and I made good neighbors: We left each other strictly alone. Bev and I studied continuously, either in the library or in our rooms. And Eddie was always working on editorials for the newspaper—proposing trade embargoes on South Africa, demanding that the college sell its defense industry stocks, insisting that birth control pills be dispensed by the desiccated spinsters at the college infirmary. Or sculpting in a studio at the arts center. I also learned that she was on a scholarship and earned her spending money by playing her guitar in a coffee house in Cambridge. When she had time to do things like reading assignments and papers, I never found out. Perhaps she *didn't* do them, and persuaded me to drop out of Worthley with her at the end of that year merely because she was going to be thrown out anyway. But I'm getting ahead of myself.

One night I was lying on my bed reading in my physics text that, due to tidal friction, the rotation of the earth was slowing down by ten to fifteen microseconds a day. On a scratch pad I was trying to estimate how long it would take for the rotation of the earth to cease altogether, for the oceans on the sun side to reach the boiling point, when my door crashed open and in strolled Eddie Holzer in her wheat jeans and turtleneck.

"You might at least *knock*," I said sourly, irritated at being interrupted in my calculation of the apocalypse.

"Oh, excuse me, were you masturbating?" I flushed scarlet. "You *do* masturbate, don't you? No? You really should try it. I recommend it highly. It relieves all *sorts* of tensions. Or do you have a regular man?"

I pulled myself together and notified her primly, "I'm not interested in that sort of thing."

"You're *not*? What *are* you interested in?" she asked, flopping down familiarly on the foot of my bed.

"Knowledge, truth, stuff like that."

"You say that as though it's something you can go out and buy in a package."

"Well, you can, in a way. You can buy books that contain it."

"So that it's just a question of transferring information from the pages of a book into your head?"

"More or less."

"How quaint!"

"I don't see what's quaint about it. It's just a question of being able to find enough *uninterrupted* time to be able to absorb it all."

"Yeah. All right. I get you," she snapped, standing up. "I just wanted to ask if you'd take part in a Fast for Freedom tomorrow night. For each student who skips supper, Worthley will give fifty cents to the fund to bus black children out of Roxbury to white schools."

"Do I have any choice?"

"Of course you have a choice. You either go to dinner or you don't. I'm just asking you not to."

"Actually, I think I'll go to dinner. You see, I'm apolitical. I agree with Descartes when he says his maxim is 'to try always to conquer [himself] rather than fortune, and to alter [his] desires rather than change the order of the world, and generally accustom [himself] to believe that there is nothing entirely within [his] power but [his] own thoughts.' " I had memorized word for word the quote first presented to me by Miss Head.

"*Descartes!* Do you think I give a *shit* what Descartes says? If my eyes were rotting in my skull from disuse, I wouldn't read Descartes. That fascist son of a bitch!"

"Politics is nothing but personal opinion," I replied disdainfully. "For every person who agrees with your editorials about busing children out of Roxbury, you'll find an equal number who disagree. And for equally logical reasons. Maybe not here at Worthley, where it's high fashion to be liberal, but certainly in the outside world."

"I never said the world isn't full of fascists. That's why those of us who aren't have to speak out."

"What makes you so sure *your* opinions are correct? That's why

I'm apolitical. I'm not interested in opinions. I'm interested in *Truth!*"

"*Truth!* Truth! Ginny, you're priceless, just priceless. Really you are. And Descartes is Truth?"

"Descartes at least has the intellectual humility to limit his pronouncements to areas in which he can discern the truth, rather than mouthing off irresponsible opinions about every topic under the sun."

"That I-think-therefore-I-am crap?"

"I don't see that it's 'crap,' as you so inelegantly call it. It happens to be as verifiable as a mathematical proof."

"Have you read any Nietzsche yet?"

"I'm reading him this term."

"Read what Nietzsche has to say about your precious Descartes. You've been hanging out with that Head chick, haven't you?" She shook her braided head sadly.

"Miss Head is a friend of mine. What of it?"

Eddie sighed with pity. "You're hopeless. I bet you even go for that Hegelian thesis-antithesis garbage in a big way? You southerners are so predictably reactionary."

"Who asked *you?*" I shot back as she vanished out my door.

Never did I enjoy a Worthley meal more than supper the next night—me and Miss Head and half a dozen insistently apolitical others, all alone in the vast echoing dining hall under the gaze of the medieval gargoyles that ringed the pillars. At one point Eddie appeared in the doorway and rapidly jotted down all our names.

However, after dinner, I did hesitantly look up in *Beyond Good and Evil* what Nietzsche had to say about Descartes:

There are still harmless self-observers who believe that there are "immediate certainties"; for instance, "I think." . . . They all pose as though their real opinions had been discovered and attained through the self-evolving of a cold, pure, divinely indifferent dialectic . . . whereas, in fact, a prejudiced proposition, idea, or "suggestion," which is generally their heart's desire abstracted and refined, is defended by them with arguments sought out after the event. . . . When I analyze the process that is experienced "I think," I find a whole series of daring assertions, the argumentative proof of which would be difficult, perhaps impossible: for instance, that it is I who think, that there must necessarily be something that thinks, that thinking is an activity and operation on the part of a being who is thought of as a cause, that there is an "ego," and finally, that it is already determined what is to be designated by thinking—that I *know* what thinking is. For if I had not already decided within myself what it is, by what standard could I determine whether that which is just happening is not perhaps "willing" or "feeling"?

I leapt up enraged at (although unable to refute) this attack on the noble Descartes. I threw open my door and stalked to Eddie's and hurled it open with a crash. Peter, Paul and Mary's "Blowing in the Wind" blared out from her record player. She looked up from her desk with alarm, then smiled when she saw me and said in a fair imitation of a southern drawl, "Way-ell, if hit in'nt mah li'l southren buddy!" When I didn't smile, and when my face remained contorted with rage, she added with concern, "Is something wrong?"

"Yes! Something very definitely *is* wrong. I just read what that bastard Nietzsche has to say about Descartes."

She grinned knowingly. "What do you think about it?"

Deciding that creeps like Eddie had to be dealt with on their own terms, I snarled, "I think it sucks."

Eddie positively beamed. "It sucks, huh? Do you know what that means—'to suck'?"

I glared at her. "I don't know why you're always so goddam patronizing to me. You seem to think I'm some kind of naïve belle or something. Yes, I know what 'to suck' means." Presumably, that was what I had failed to do to Clem the night he beat me up in the bomb shelter.

"What do you think of it?"

"Of what?"

"Of sucking."

"What does that have to do with Descartes?"

"Absolutely nothing!" she declared triumphantly. "That's my whole point. I suck, therefore I am. What do you think?"

"Man *happens* to be more than—"

"Man—*shit!* I don't even *talk* to people who try to tell me what 'man' is or isn't. If you want to talk about some one particular action of one particular person, okay. But don't hand me any of this pompous 'Mankind is this or that' garbage because I'm not interested. Go see your Miss Head." She turned back to her desk. I skulked to my room and brooded on into the night. The citadels constructed by Miss Head were clearly under attack.

Miss Head left a note in my mailbox inviting me to a production of Wagner's *Das Rheingold*. I hadn't seen her very much since the term began because I wasn't taking one of her courses, and because we were both so busy otherwise. So I accepted with delight.

We met in the downstairs hall. She looked almost pretty, despite her gray bun and her shapeless loden coat. In my pleasure at seeing her, I reached out and hugged her with one arm. She stiffened and drew back, blushing and searching for her watch underneath her coat. "My car's outside. We're late. We'd better rush."

Even being late didn't prevent my inspecting the back floor of her car for hidden murderers, as the Major had always advised. On the way to the opera, we took a wrong turn. As we wound through strange streets, the neighborhood got more and more seedy. Trash filled the gutters, and the shop fronts needed painting. The MTA rumbled past on grimy overhead tracks, and the people on the streets were mostly black. I realized that we were in Roxbury. The fast that Eddie had organized had been for the purpose of busing schoolchildren out of here.

"I don't know," I said hesitantly. "Maybe we should have fasted that night. This is a pretty grim setting for children, don't you think?"

Miss Head glanced at me impatiently. "Please spare me your sentimentalizing, Miss Babcock. You've clearly been reading too many editorials by that Holzer girl."

"Well, but don't you find it a little depressing?" We were driving down a block of crumbling row houses, where a group of black children were poking with sticks at candy wrappers and newspapers that floated sluggishly in the murky water around a clogged gutter drain.

"You can't generalize. Squalid circumstances can sometimes produce outstanding achievers."

She was clearly referring to herself and her Dust Bowl origins. "Well, you got *out* of Morgan. But what about those who didn't?"

"My childhood friends aren't unhappy with their lives. Or not any more so than anyone else. After all, they have nothing to compare Morgan *with*."

"But isn't that in itself a shame? That they were never exposed to any other possibilities for themselves?"

"What makes you so sure that Worthley beats Morgan?" she asked with a faint ironic smile. "It is so *condescending* of you, Miss Babcock. It shows a basic lack of respect for the dignity of people different from yourself. That's what irritates me so much about Miss Holzer's half-baked editorials. It never occurs to her that there might be anything in Roxbury for the children of value equivalent to a white middle-class education."

"But *I* haven't said that Worthley beats Morgan. *Or* Hullsport. If you'll recall, *I* didn't even want to leave Hullsport. I had to be dragged up here by my father. But *you*, Miss Head, *have* said that Worthley beats Morgan."

"For me, as I am now, it does," she said patiently. "But if I had stayed in Morgan, I'd have been a different person than I am now, and Morgan would suit me better."

"A *better* person than you are now?"

"I didn't say better or worse, I said different. Really, Miss Babcock, you must work on your objectivity. It's nonsense using words like 'good' and 'bad.' What happens happens. That's not *your* concern."

"You mean no one course of action is any better or worse than another?" I demanded, scandalized to see where Miss Head's line of thought—and mine insofar as I had taken her as my mentor—was leading.

"Courses of action aren't your concern, Miss Babcock. Your concern is to understand, to locate the Truth in a situation. Which is done, as Spinoza told you last year if you were paying attention, by stilling your emotions, your passions, and functioning as an instrument of pure thought. Detachment is *everything*, Miss Babcock, believe me. Evil is always with us, Spinoza says. 'Things are not more or less perfect, according as they delight or offend human senses, or according as they are serviceable or repugnant to mankind. . . . Matter was not lacking to God for the creation of every degree of perfection from highest to lowest. The laws of His nature are so vast as to suffice for the production of everything conceivable by an infinite intelligence.' "

"But Miss Head, I don't know if I *agree* with that. I mean, look what Nietzsche says about the possibility of there even *being* such a thing as detachment or 'pure thought.' "

She blanched in the dim street light through the car window. "Well, of course, if you're going to fall under the spell of that miserable neurotic mystic, there's not a great deal that Descartes can do for you, Miss Babcock. Do you know that Mussolini adored Nietzsche? No, of course you don't. I'd look into Nietzsche's pedigree before enrolling myself under his banner if I were you, Miss Babcock."

I reflected that for someone who had supposedly scaled the heights of detachment, Miss Head was sounding suspiciously angry.

During the opera, I developed a special sympathy for the poor dwarfs who were being whipped to shreds by the wicked Alberich. They were so small that his demands—that they mine minerals for him with their minuscule picks—were impossible to fulfill. Yet they struggled on faithfully and industriously. My heart went out to them. I imagined that Eddie, had she been there, would have leapt onto the stage and started unionizing them. Beads of sweat were popping out on my upper lip as I strained with them in their agony.

Miss Head leaned over and whispered, "Notice the incessant recurrence of the dwarfs' leitmotif, the ways in which its tonal structure hints at the futility of their attempts."

I gritted my teeth and whirled toward her. Miss Head was serenely watching the stage over the tops of her lenses, and was nodding slightly to the rhythm of the leitmotif.

When I went into Eddie's room the next night, she was sitting on her window seat, in a spot cleared out among stacks of newspapers, playing her guitar and singing "Mr. Tambourine Man." She saw me and nodded pleasantly but kept on singing, determined to finish out the song. She had a very appealing husky alto singing voice.

I glanced around the room. There was a new reddish clay model of something or other sitting on her bookcase. I walked over to it. Two nude women were lying on their sides facing each other. Their arms were wrapped around each other, and their legs were entwined. On both faces were expressions of ecstasy.

Finishing the song with a loud self-mocking strum, Eddie laid the guitar on the stacks of paper and stood up and stretched her statuesque body languidly like a cat. "Do you like it?" she asked me, nodding toward the model. "I just finished it."

"Uh, yes. The pattern of the lines is fascinating."

"Yes, I know. It's brilliant technically. But what I *asked* is whether you like it."

"Sure. Yeah. It's very nice."

"How do you feel about the subject matter?"

Detaching myself in my best Spinozan fashion from the fleeting sense of panic I'd felt upon first seeing it, I said calmly, "I feel it's a valid form of sexual expression. After all, Freud says that man is essentially bisexual and is channeled in one direction or the other by his conditioning."

"Screw Freud and screw that 'man is' crap. What emotions does this particular clay model elicit from you, Ginny Babcock?"

I drew a deep breath. "Well, frankly, Eddie, I'm not very interested in sexuality in any of its forms."

"I see."

"I had too much inept sex at too early an age, and I'm fed up with it, that's all. I have more important things to think about."

"Indeed," Eddie said gravely, tucking in her chin and looking out over imaginary glasses in a good imitation of Miss Head. "By the way," she asked brightly, "would you be interested in signing my petition to President Johnson demanding that he end our military involvement in southeast Asia?"

"Why do you bother asking me when you know what I'll say?"

"Just trying to give you a chance to save your soul."

"Thanks, but no thanks."

"Why not? Don't you *want* to save your soul?"

"You say it's a civil war and we shouldn't interfere. My father says it's the vanguard of the world-wide Communist take-over and has to be nipped in the bud. You feel sorry for the innocent people who are being maimed and killed by American troops. He feels sorry for the innocent people who are getting other people's theories crammed into their brains, and who are being maimed and killed by Communist troops. How do I know which of you is right?"

"Which do you *feel* is right?"

"Neither. I feel nothing. I'm not interested. I'm interested in fact, not opinion. I happen to feel that the degree of a person's intelligence is directly reflected by the number of conflicting attitudes she can bring to bear on the same topic," I announced, resolutely parroting Miss Head.

"Intelligence, *garbage*! You're talking about *paralysis*, moral paralysis! The way you live your life is a political act, whether you like it or not. You're taking a stand by the very fact of refusing to take a stand."

For several moments, we glared at each other with ideological contempt. "But to what elevated purpose do I owe the honor of your presence in my humble garret?" Eddie asked.

"Well, actually, I came in to ask how the Roxbury busing is going."

She glanced at me quickly. "What's it to you, fascist?"

"I went through Roxbury last night on the way to the opera with

Miss Head, and I sort of saw your point." I was appearing to yield now in order to gain more yardage later.

"Big of you. It's going quite well, no thanks to you and your Miss Head."

"But I do have a question," I said innocently. Eddie raised her hands, palms up, and bowed her head to indicate that her ears were at my service. "Don't you think it's patronizing of you to assume that our way of life is so superior to theirs, that they should be given the opportunity to ape us?" I was hoping against hope that Eddie wouldn't have an answer for this argument of Miss Head's.

Eddie shrugged impatiently. "It's patronizing to want to give someone the skills and attitudes necessary to earn enough money so that his children won't have to be gnawed by rats when they go to sleep at night?"

"But don't you think that the cream will rise to the top anyway?"

"Perhaps. But a lot of perfectly adequate whole milk goes sour in the meantime."

"How do you know that the people in Roxbury aren't just as content with their lives as people anywhere else?"

"I'll tell you how I know," she said, turning on me with fervor. "I know because I grew up in a slum in Boston. Do you *know* who my father was?"

I hesitated, feeling as though I *should* know. So many people here had diplomats, famous academicians, important businessmen for fathers. Holzer. Holzer. Who was Eddie's father, and why on earth would he have raised her in a Boston slum? "No, I don't."

"Well, we're even. I don't either. He was a rapist. He dragged my mother into a cellar hole and stuffed a rag in her mouth and tied her wrists with his belt and beat her black and blue and then raped her."

I stared at her with horror. "I'm—sorry."

"Oh, *I'm* not," Eddie said harshly. "I mean, if it hadn't happened, I wouldn't be here, would I? Or at least not in my current configuration. But your cream rising bit is crap. Cream *doesn't* rise under constant agitation, or when the fucking bottle is smashed to bits."

"But it *does*," I insisted, holding out my hand illustratively. "*Look* at you."

"You know why I'm at Worthley? I'm here because one lousy teacher at that hellhole where I went to school took a special interest in me and loaded me down with books and devoted herself to my progress. But there weren't enough of her to go around. In fact, I was the only one in my whole class who benefited like that." She looked at me defiantly, waiting to see what sort of half-baked notions I would come up with next for her to refute from her position of superior experience.

"Well! I guess that only proves my point—that rational people stay clear of politics. I mean, you can't understand a situation and know how to approach it until all the facts are in—and how many situations are like that in life?"

"Rubbish!" Eddie shrieked. "Reactionary rubbish! Your head is just packed full of *shit* by that Head bitch, Ginny! Go ahead, model yourself after her! Spend your life with a clock tacked to your boob —everything safe and neat and orderly. No risks, therefore no mistakes. No mate, no children, no animals to interfere with her precious schedules. Her cello to wrap her legs around when she's lonely, and her magnum opus on Descartes to occupy her busy little brain. Ideal, you would say. So go ahead!"

"It's not such a bad life she has. It beats the hell out of careening from one disaster to the next, as I did before I came to Worthley."

"It's not so bad if you don't mind a living death."

"You're so goddam self-righteous!" I gasped. "What makes you think your approach to life is superior to hers?"

"I don't *think*, I *know*. I *know* that plunging into involvements with other people, and risking rejection and ridicule in a good cause is better than self-embalmment. The only passion Miss Head has ever experienced in her life is her passion for certainty à la Descartes and Spinoza."

"Well, I happen not to know what constitutes a 'good cause,' Eddie, and that's why I'm apolitical. Look at all the atrocities that have been committed in the name of good causes. I'll stick, along with Miss Head, to areas in which I *do* 'know.' "

She shook her head, her braid lashing in disgust. "But you *don't* know. You only *think* you know. You think, therefore you know. Ha!"

"Even if I were to admit to being convinced by Nietzsche's remarks, which I'm not doing, there *are* other areas of knowledge that *are* unquestionable facts."

Eddie snickered. "Like *what*, for example?"

"Like the fact that a second is 1/31,556,925.9747's of the orbital year that began at noon on January 1, 1900. And the fact that you can take this fact, and with it construct other *facts* called minutes, hours, days, years. Like the fact that an atom is constructed of positive charges called protons and negative charges called electrons, and that if they are combined in a designated manner, you will *always* get a certain element.''

Eddie shook her head and said, "And so you don't have to be involved with other people because you're so busy tracking down these important truths? Well, if you say so. But do you know that there's a culture in India that happens to use as its basic time unit the period required to boil a pot of rice? And they seem to get along all right.''

I turned around and stormed out, slamming her door. I charged down the hall, got into the rickety elevator, and descended to the first floor. I ran through the reception hall and past the rows of imposing portraits and under the vaulted stone archway. I pounded on Miss Head's massive door.

She opened it, holding her cello in one hand. "Oh, Miss Babcock, it's only you. Good heavens, I thought it was at least a fire warning. Come in, come in.''

I marched in and sank down on the horsehair loveseat.

"Whatever *is* the matter?'' I breathed deeply, trying to relax. "Would you like some tea? I just made some.''

"Yes, thank you. With lemon, please.'' What Eddie had said about Miss Head simply wasn't true. She *had* involved herself with other people—with me, for instance. Never mind that she had ulterior motives.

Miss Head leaned her cello against a chair and sat down at her Queen Anne tea table and poured from her encrusted silver urn. "Now! What brings you here so late at night?''

"Did I disturb you? I'm sorry.''

"No, no, it's perfectly all right. I was just playing some Vivaldi.''

"Is it too late to change out of nineteenth-century philosophy and into your advanced Descartes seminar for this term?''

"Hmmm,'' she said, glancing at me shrewdly, forcing herself not to say "I told you so.'' "Well, it *is* a little late. I mean the term's half over, isn't it? But let me think about it. It helps that I happen to be your class dean, your adviser, *and* the professor of the seminar you want to get into, doesn't it? But it *is* a highly irregular request. Most unusual indeed. . . .''

"I'd really appreciate it, Miss Head. I think Nietzsche's getting me down.'' To say nothing of his disciple Eddie Holzer.

"Indeed," she said. "Indeed. Yes, I know exactly what you mean. Well, I'll give you my decision in a few days. You can count on it."

She set down her teacup and unleashed her metronome at a dizzying rate. Then she picked up her cello, fitted it between her knees, and filled her chambers with a driving rendition of sections of "The Four Seasons." I followed the straightforward themes and variations with ease and was soon feeling much better. The polished red cello gleamed mellowly in the dim light from a converted oil lamp. Outside her windows, blue icicles hung from the gutter like stalactites.

"Thank you, Miss Head," I said, as I was setting down my cup and preparing to leave. "I needed that." I felt as serene now as a harried housewife after her morning dose of Librium.

"You're quite welcome, Miss Babcock. Any time. Within reason."

That Wednesday as I sat in the dining hall eating chop suey, Eddie sauntered up with her lunch tray and began unloading her dishes next to mine. I acknowledged her with a cold nod. I, in my neat tweed suit, found Eddie's studied sloppiness—her wheat jeans and turtleneck and Goliath sandals, her messy braid with strands of straggly hair escaping —objectionable, aesthetically offensive.

"Well, and how's the grande dame of Castle Court?"

"Are you referring to me?" I inquired with dignity.

"Yup, to you, sweetheart. How ya doin?"

"Fine, until your arrival, thank you."

"Oh, come on, Ginny. We have many more tedious months next door to each other. Let's be civil, okay?"

"It's all right with me. If you'll recall, *you* were the one who started us off on this note just now when you referred to me as a grande dame."

"All right. Yes. You're right. I apologize. Look, I need your help."

"What?" I asked, surprised at the notion that she could need anything from me.

"Some friends of mine are doing an experiment for Psychology 302. They need some more subjects. Will you volunteer? It'll just take half an hour in one of the labs."

"Well, I don't know. . . . I have a paper due and—"

"*Please.*"

"All right," I said, delighted to have the notorious Eddie Holzer begging me for something.

After lunch, we walked through the courtyard en route to the psychology labs. Eddie stopped and studied the bronze sundial with its ornate leaves and vines and reclining gods and goddesses. Its scrolled gnomon cast a shadow at 2:15.

"My God!" I exclaimed. "*Two fifteen?* I have an appointment with Miss Head at two thirty." She was going to give me the word on her Descartes seminar.

Eddie laughed. "Don't panic, kid. It's not two fifteen. This fucking thing is Flemish. It's set for the latitude of Flanders."

When we got to the lab, Eddie's friends were already there— several juniors and seniors, all members of the very small artsy set on campus, who wrote and directed and acted in the plays, who wrote and edited the paper and the literary magazine. They all looked identical to Eddie in their wheat jeans and turtlenecks and sandals, with long straight hair or braids. I felt instantly intimidated in my Helena Head tweed suit and bun.

"We're all here now," said a tall, dark hunched senior who had a painting exhibit in the arts center at that very moment. The psychology project was apparently hers. Eddie and I and two others sat side by side; the senior and another girl stood in front of us. A third girl sat in the corner taking notes.

The senior explained the rules. She herself would hold up a constant control card made of cardboard. The other girl up front would hold up a succession of cards of different lengths. One at a time, we four subjects were to say whether the second card was longer than, shorter than, or the same length as the control card. It seemed simple enough. In fact, it seemed downright simple-minded. I couldn't believe that these hypercreative upperclassmen couldn't come up with more intriguing ways to spend their time.

After several practice runs, the experiment began in earnest. I was sitting on the far end and was always the last to express my judgment, but it really didn't matter because we all agreed anyway. Yes, yes, that card was shorter than the control. And that one was longer. And so on. I was becoming very impatient and irritable. After all, I *did* have a paper to write.

During the sixth round the atmosphere of bored agreement suddenly shifted, and I found the three others blandly agreeing that a card was shorter, which to me was obviously longer.

And again. "Longer," said the first girl.

"Longer," agreed the second.

"Longer," said Eddie with a yawn.

"The *same*," I insisted staunchly.

And yet again. I kept glancing around furtively as the others perjured with indifference the testimony of their senses. Or at least of *my* senses.

"The same," said the first girl.

"The same."

"The same," agreed Eddie.

"*Longer*," I mumbled belligerently. Damn! How could they call it the same, when it was so obviously longer?

"Shorter," said the first girl.

"Shorter," said the second.

"Shorter," said Eddie, stretching luxuriously.

"The same?" I suggested uncertainly. It *couldn't* be shorter. Could it? The others glanced at me with surprise.

"Longer," said the first girl, about a card that to me was clearly shorter.

"Longer," confirmed the second girl.

"Longer," agreed Eddie.

Unable to endure the social isolation any longer, I intentionally belied the verdict of my eyes and said casually, "Longer." It felt marvelous to be in step with the others. I breathed a deep sigh of relief.

"The same," said the first girl.

"The same."

"The same."

"Shorter," I wailed pitifully. Was something wrong with my eyes? I squinted and then opened them as wide as possible, trying to rectify my apparently faulty vision. Then I stared so intently at the control card that my vision blanked out altogether and I couldn't see anything for a few seconds. Eddie and the first girl looked at me, then glanced at each other and shrugged.

After two dozen of these runs, in which they agreed and I differed, or in which they agreed and I pretended to agree, interspersed with runs in which we all genuinely *did* agree, I could no longer tell what was shorter or longer than what. I would see a card as shorter. The others would call it longer, and before my very eyes the card would quiver and expand until it did in fact look longer. Or it would waver playfully back and forth between long and short.

Soon I was feeling nauseated, and my eyes were burning.

"The same," said the first girl, about a card that had originally looked longer to me.

"The same," said the second.

"The same," said Eddie.

I widened and narrowed my eyes several times, as the size of the card fluctuated. Then I fell out of my chair and collapsed on the floor, sobbing.

Eddie knelt down and helped me up, saying, "Now, now Ginny. It's just an experiment. Where's your Spinozan detachment?"

I collapsed on her shoulder and wept while she patted my back consolingly. The senior running the test came up and said, "You really did quite well, Ginny. You stood up to the others sixty-five percent of the time. The average so far is forty-three percent."

"*What* average?" I asked between sobs, looking up.

"The average number of correct responses the subject gives in contradiction to the pretend subjects."

"*Pretend* subjects? You mean this whole thing was staged?" I turned on Eddie in a rage.

"We thought you'd figured it out by now," the senior said. "You mean you hadn't?"

I raised a fist to slug Eddie. She put an arm around me affectionately. I pulled away.

"I'm sorry, Ginny, but it had to be done," Eddie said.

"*Why* did it? You could have at least told me."

"If I'd told you, it wouldn't have worked, would it? And you *are* in search of Truth, aren't you? Or doesn't that extend to the truth about yourself?"

I stomped out of the lab, my vision so strained and blurred that I bumped into the door casing. Back on my hall, I went to the bathroom and threw up. Then I went to my room and drew the curtains and climbed in bed and pulled the covers over my head. I stayed there until the following day, missing my appointment with Miss Head and several classes as well.

Christmas vacation came and went. Mid-winter faded into early spring. The snow cover melted and ran off the flagstones in rivulets. Still I hadn't spoken to Eddie. She had humiliated me in front of her artsy friends. I knew they were snickering behind their hands about the weakness of my character as I passed them en route to the library or to classes. I had decided never to speak to Eddie again. When I encountered her in the dining hall or as we entered our rooms, I turned my head away. She respected my pique and didn't make any effort to approach me. Sometimes I heard her in her room singing Bob Dylan songs. Occasionally I would deign to read one of her ridiculous editorials in the campus paper demanding that the college government abolish curfew, that the trustees run a camp for ghetto children on the campus in the summer. A couple of times when I was sure she was out, I crept through her sloppy room and out her casement window to a flat roof where I could sunbathe nude and undisturbed in the late April sun.

Mostly, though, I studied. I had no friends except Miss Head, saw no one except in classes and at meals. I was too busy pursuing Truth to have a social life. Under Miss Head's tutelage I was exploring the topic of free will versus determinism as handled by the eighteenth-century rationalist philosophers. Determinism was winning out hands down. I was pleased. I was making mincemeat of Eddie's principles of social action.

Otherwise, however, my courses were not going well. Schopenhauer in Philosophy 240 was saying distressing things like, "No truth therefore is more certain, more independent of all others, and less in need of proof than this, that all that exists for knowledge, and therefore for this whole world, is only object in relation to subject, perception of a perceiver, in a word, idea. This is obviously true of the past and the future, as well as of the present, of what is farthest off, as of what is near; for it is true of time and space themselves, in which alone these distinctions arise. All that in any way belongs or can belong to the world is inevitably thus conditioned through the subject, and exists only for the subject. The world is idea."

In astronomy I was going to the observatory every night and watching a galaxy group called the Hydra cluster; the light I was viewing had left there two billion years earlier. In short, I was looking at the past. The concept unnerved me. With outrage I studied the red shift of its spectrum, which indicated that the galaxy was moving away from me at the rate of 38,000 miles per second.

And in physics I was studying the subatomic particles—mesons and neutrinos—whose existence was proved only by the wakes of tiny bubbles they left as they shot through liquid hydrogen. Some were too short-lived to do even that, with life spans of ten millionths of a billionth of a billionth of a second.

I brooded over the vast range of electromagnetic radiations on either side of the tiny band that could be discerned by human sense organs. They made me absolutely furious.

But the last straw was Einstein's theory of relativity. It scandalized me that even time could not be counted on, that its perceived duration shifted in relation to the orientation in space and motion of the perceiver. Suddenly I was surrounded by modern science with forces and particles I couldn't see or hear or taste or feel. I felt bombarded—by a hundred different kinds of electromagnetic waves and subatomic particles, by fractions of time too minute to measure, by light rays that had left their source before life even existed on earth. All these things were showering down on me. Yet Lord Kelvin had promised me certainty in return for studying physics. "When you can measure what you are speaking about and express it in numbers, you know something about it," he had said in introductory physics last year. I felt betrayed.

In the depths of my despair, who should arrive at my door but Bev Martin, my next-door neighbor, the freshman from Iowa. I had scarcely seen her the entire year—a few times when I had been up at dawn to finish a paper, I had caught a glimpse of her down by the lake shore in a navy sweat suit jogging through the snow, bathed in the purple sunrise. I at least saw Miss Head occasionally. Bev saw no one.

Which was why I was startled when she appeared in my room for a chat that evening as I was agonizing over a chart on the age of the universe, the Milky Way galaxy, our sun, the earth: according to it, mankind was too recent an arrival even to merit mention. I was sick with indignation. I looked up impatiently, waiting to find out what Bev wanted from *me*, a miserable mote stirred up by Eternity's spring cleaning.

"I wondered if you'd like to go into town with me for supper tonight." She was blushing and looking at the floor, and chewing her chapped lower lip. Her eyes were wide and terrified. It was obviously difficult for her to ask me.

But I said promptly, through gritted teeth, "I'm sorry, Bev, but I *just don't have time*. I have a Descartes paper due tomorrow and I haven't finished it."

"Oh. Okay."

"But thanks. Some other time maybe."

"Sure." She scuttled out.

That night as I was preparing to go to bed, I walked across the hall to the bathroom. Inside, I glanced under the stall doors, to be sure there were no concealed rapists, as Mother had taught me to do at an early age. The door of the bathtub enclosure caught my eye. Behind it an arm hung almost to the floor. I pushed open the door. Slumped in a chair beside the tub was Bev. She smiled up at me weakly, her hyperthyroidal eyes glazed over. A Miltown bottle lay on the floor next to her. I picked it up. It was empty.

I looked back and forth between Bev and the bottle. I considered the topic of suicide. Suicide: On the one hand, it could be regarded as a plea for help. After all, why had Bev done this here rather than in her room where no one would have found her for weeks? A person attempting suicide, in the view of many specialists, didn't really want to die, but was rather adopting this desperate tactic as the only remaining means of exerting an impact on an unresponsive environment. It was only a passing aberration. Thwarted, the person would in many cases go on to live a long and productive life.

Bev slumped lower in the chair. Her eyes were half shut.

On the other hand, a person's life belonged to her alone, and she had the right to end it if she so chose. Robbing someone of this right, stifling this expression of a person's desire for greater autonomy, might very well deprive that person of the self-respect essential to the conduct of an existentially meaningful existence. Interfering in someone's suicide while claiming to be concerned for that person's well-being might actually be undertaken solely to spare the rescuer from having to confront doubts about the value of his own existence. . . .

Bev fell onto the floor.

And of course there was an entire school of psychiatry that felt. . . . Eddie walked in in her bathrobe. She bent over the sink to brush her teeth. But then she stood back up and stared at me in the doorway of the tub stall.

Walking over, she took in the situation in one quick glance—Bev slumped on the floor, the empty bottle in my hand. Looking at me for a moment in disbelief, she raced from the bathroom. When she returned, she pushed me aside and knelt beside Bev. She slapped her face hard several times and soon had her sitting up and drinking glass after glass of warm salt water. Before long, the entire floor of the stall, and Eddie and Bev as well, were splattered with vomit.

A couple of doctors arrived and whisked Bev off to the infirmary. I went to bed and pulled the covers over my head. I dreamed that night of the seashore. Miss Head in a tweed suit was sitting on the sand in a carved Victorian chair with a needlepoint seat. The metronome sat ticking at her feet, and she nodded her gray bun in time. She played Handel's "Water Music" on her cello. As she played, the waves broke rhythmically and washed up around her feet. Her chair, her cello, and she herself were sinking into the sand. The breaking waves consisted of dilute blood. Occasionally, along with seaweed and shells and fluorescent blue Portuguese men-of-war, the waves would toss up a mangled human limb or a staring eyeball. Miss Head observed these without interest and never missed a beat.

The next morning in nineteenth-century philosophy we studied Schopenhauer's remarks from *The World as Will and Idea:* "We must, without reserve, regard all presented objects, even our own bodies, merely as ideas, and call them merely ideas." In physics the next period we busied ourselves with the concept that all objects, organic and inorganic, were merely empty space with trillions of particles chasing each other through the void, and that even these "particles," taken a step further, were nothing more than energy waves and probability functions.

I decided to skip lunch. I had lost my appetite, possibly forever. As I walked to the biology lab, where I hadn't been since the previous year, I re-created in my mind the picture of Bev slumped over in her chair with me watching her, paralyzed. I tried regarding the scene as merely an idea originating in my own isolated brain, as Schopenhauer suggested. Then I tried dissecting it into energy waves and probability functions. Neither exercise worked. I continued to tremble with guilt and horror—at not making time for Bev when she asked me to, and at my subsequent paralysis in the face of her despair.

No one was in the lab. I put on a white coat. I took a bacteria smear from a Petri dish and dyed a small portion of it. Then I slipped the slide under a microscope. I watched as the stained bacteria fluttered and shuddered trying to assimilate the poison dye.

After a valiant struggle, one by one the contaminated cells released the contents of their vacuoles, the enzymes they used to digest foreign cells, thereby destroying themselves.

I shifted the slide to inspect the unstained bacteria. They were quivering and were edging away from their dying fellows. None of them, in spite of their exterior membranes, would go unaffected—all had channels that led from the soup deep into their own interiors. And under an electron microscope, I knew that those seemingly impermeable exterior membranes themselves would dissolve into a series of perforations.

I knew, too, that radioactive tracers applied on a tree stump shortly turned up inside all the neighboring trees. Bev's action was not a self-contained incident; its reverberations would affect us all.

I washed the slides and hung up my coat. As I walked back to the dorm, I plucked a leaf off a forsythia bush and stared at it as though I had never seen a leaf before. Its atoms and subatomic particles were identical to those making up my fingers. Those atoms combined to form molecules that were identical—in the leaf and in my fingers. The molecules formed amino acids—identical. The acids formed proteins and enzymes and hormones—similar in the leaf and in my fingers. The enzymes in grasses closely resembled those in an elephant. The sap flowing through the forsythia bush, in composition almost identical to blood, which in turn was identical to dilute sea water—from which all life came, to which it would return. And in that sap substances similar to those distinguishing human blood as type A or type B. Our earth was a burned-out hunk of mineral ash, but we—this leaf and Eddie and Bev and I—we were star stuff. Our bodies were almost entirely made up of light volatile elements. We had origins far grander than the cinder we inhabited would indicate. What affected one segment affected us all. I shuddered as the vision of Bev and me in the bathtub stall passed before my eyes.

I left my books in my room and grabbed a notebook and a quilt. After listening at Eddie's door and concluding that she was out, I opened it and crossed her room, tiptoeing over full ashtrays and stacks of magazines and newspapers. There was a new sculpture on her window seat since the last time I'd sneaked through—a polished mahogany carving of a woman's torso, from neck to upper thighs. The body was voluptuous, solid and firm, not flabby. Eddie herself might have been the model for it. Bev's body floated through my head in contrast—long, lean, gawky, angular.

Trying to dispel this persistent mental picture of Bev slumped over dying while I debated the topic of suicide prevention, I opened the window and climbed out on the roof. It had walls on two sides, and so was partially protected from breezes. A third side was a low wall that overlooked the courtyard and the lake. I stood behind this wall and looked down, down, five floors down to the stone courtyard below. A rehearsal was underway there for the May Court, to be held the next day. The May Court was a Worthley ritual involving various rites of spring and dances around the statue of Artemis, virgin huntress. A May Court Mistress and attendants were elected from the student body each spring. In keeping with Worthley's liberal tradition, the queen was usually handicapped in some way—an amputee or a member of a racial minority. This year's queen had had a radical mastectomy and wasn't expected to survive the summer.

I spread the quilt and removed my clothes and lay down on my stomach. I read at random through my notes, marking here and there with a pen, trying to get an idea for a term paper for my nineteenth-century philosophy course.

Soon I realized that I'd been reading and rereading two passages. I'd underlined each with my felt pen a couple of dozen times, until the underlinings had overlapped to form a big wet blue blotch that was soaking through the page. The sun was high and hot, but I felt as though dark clouds had moved in front of it. My body was clammy, and my teeth started chattering. I dropped the notebook and rolled over on my back and wrapped the quilt around me and lay still, my eyes closed, unable to move. I felt my lips turning blue. My stomach was a knot of panic. I kept taking deep breaths to still the fear.

I heard a noise. I couldn't open my eyes to trace its origin. I heard a voice, Eddie's, saying, "Christ, Ginny, you look awful. Are you all right?" I couldn't move my lips to answer her.

"Ginny?" she said with alarm in her voice.

She was somewhere near my head. I heard my notebook rustling. She was reading to herself the quotes I had underlined from Nietzsche and Kierkegaard: " 'Do we not now wander through an endless Nothingness?' 'Philosophy has tried anything and everything in the effort to help the individual to transcend himself objectively, which is a wholly impossible feat; existence exercises its restraining influence, and if philosophers nowadays had not become mere scribblers in the service of a fantastic thinking and its preoccupation, they would long ago have perceived that suicide was the only tolerable practical interpretation of its striving.' "

"Jesus," she said quietly. I was shivering spasmodically under my quilt. I breathed in deep irregular gasps. I was perfectly aware of doing these things, but I seemed incapable of stopping them or of doing anything else.

"But Ginny," she pointed out, as though I were sitting up conversing with her, "you didn't underline the rest of that Kierkegaard

quote. Did you read it? Shall I read it to you?" Undaunted by the
absence of an answer, she read it: " 'The scribbling modern philosophy holds passion in contempt; and yet passion is the culmination of
existence for an existing individual—and we are all of us existing
individuals. In passion the existing subject is rendered infinite in the
eternity of the imaginative representative, and yet he is at the same
time most definitely himself.' "

She stopped reading. I heard some movements to one side. Then
she asked matter-of-factly, "Ginny, could you please put some of this
baby oil on my back? I was out yesterday, and I'm getting burned."

Wonder of wonders, I tossed off my quilt, sat up obediently, took
the lotion from her, and began rubbing it into her smooth reddish
brown back.

Then I lay back down on my stomach and wrapped up in the quilt
and resumed my shivering.

"Shall I put some on you? You're looking pink, too."

When I didn't answer, she crawled over and removed the quilt
and started anointing my back. She covered my arms and shoulders
and hips and legs with the oil as well. It was as though she were
rubbing life back into me. Where her hands had been, my flesh
glowed with warmth. She pushed me, and I rolled over cooperatively.
She rubbed the baby oil into my chest and breasts and abdomen and
legs. My shivering subsided. The lump in my stomach began breaking
up under her hands like a frozen pond in the spring. She crawled
down to my feet and massaged them. Then she crawled up to my
shoulder level and patted oil on my cheeks and forehead and across
my upper lip. Then she lay down next to me and cradled me in her
arms, my head on her chest right over her heart.

I don't know how long we'd been lying like that, me listening to
her pounding heart and timing my breathing to it. It might have been
minutes or hours. In any case, at some point, we heard a rapid flapping
sound. And soon our bodies were being swept by great swirling
eddies of air.

Above us hovered a helicopter from the nearby air force base. A
shaven male head leaned out and shouted through cupped hands at
the top of his voice, "You goddam Worthley dykes!" Then a hand
reached out with a can of some sort, and soon Eddie and I were
splattered with showers of Coca Cola.

Eddie leapt up in all her nude magnificence and raised both arms high above her head and shook her middle fingers. "Pigs!" she screamed. "Goddam fucking fascist pigs!"

The copter swept off on its other missions of national defense. The rehearsal in the courtyard was a shambles as the May Court stood staring skyward at Eddie's gorgeous body, poised on the roof five floors above them. "Don't jump!" someone screamed, and the courtyard erupted in a flurry of activity, people racing for the doors to take the elevator to the roof to restrain Eddie.

"Well!" Eddie said with a grin, "shall we be licking the Coke off each other when they arrive?"

We crawled rapidly to her window and scrambled through it. As we raced, hand in sticky hand, to the bathroom, we heard the whir of ascending elevators.

I hesitated at the bathroom door. "It's been cleaned up," Eddie assured me grimly. I walked in with all the enthusiasm of a plane crash survivor boarding a new plane. I sniffed and thought I could smell sour vomit. I began shivering as I looked in the tub enclosure.

Eddie pulled me into the shower stall. She lathered me with soap. Then I lathered her. Then we held each other and kissed in the spray. We stayed there until we'd used up all the hot water in the dorm; the pipes began clanking furiously.

We spent that night in Eddie's narrow lumpy institutional bed, sleeping in each other's arms until after lunch. I woke up delighted finally to know who put what where in physical love between women.

When I got up and had dressed in my tweed suit, I descended in the elevator to the first floor. It was 3:25. I knew Miss Head would be just finishing her afternoon cello practice and settling down to work on her book.

I paused outside her door, under the stern gaze of the Worthley hall of fame, and tried to decide exactly why I was there. Unsuccessful, I knocked on the thick door. Miss Head opened it and inspected me with a mixture of pleasure and irritation at having her careful afternoon schedule interrupted, and by someone who knew how important it was to her.

"Come in," she invited reluctantly. I marched in and stood awkwardly in her living room shifting from one low-heeled pump to the other. "Sit down," she suggested, looking at me curiously. "Tea?"

"Yes, thanks."

"Well! What can I do for you, Miss Babcock?" she asked as she handed me a cup and saucer.

I braced myself and waited for my words to flow. I even opened my mouth. But nothing came out. The speech centers of my brain were betraying me. "Nothing much. Just passing by."

"How nice," she said, with a forced smile. I knew how it upset her to have her routine disturbed because I had experienced the same irritation two nights ago when Bev had asked me to drop everything and have supper with her.

"Excuse me," she said, after a long wait to see what I wanted, "but I was just finishing up work on some Schubert lieder. Let me run through one to be sure I've got it." She set the metronome to ticking at a slow pace. Then she picked up her bow and positioned her cello. After one measure, she stopped and said, "Be sure to notice the exquisite coloratura, Miss Babcock. A young man is singing. It's spring and the flowers are blooming and the birds are singing and building their nests. But he is distraught, and unable to participate in this sense of renewal because his true love has died during the winter. I suggest you observe the ways in which Schubert manipulates his melodies so as to set up this tension between the living and the dead." She nodded at me sternly.

I gritted my teeth, but she didn't notice my anger. Nodding to pick up the beat from the metronome, she began again, swaying on her antique chair. The song alternated between a sweeping soulful line in the lower registers, and a high, light dancing line that suggested flickering sunlight and fluttering leaves and warbling birds. Miss Head started singing the German words softly. She closed her eyes and rested her head against the neck of the cello as she fingered the strings with a trembling pressure. As I watched, her knees tightened their grip on the curved cello sides, and a flush rose into her pallid face.

I jumped up and stalked over and stood in front of her trembling.

"Miss Head, I—I—" I was trying to tell her that I loved her, or something equally ill-thought-out. I yearned to grab away her infernal red cello and enfold the dear misguided woman in my strong, alive flesh. Because of my tutelage under Eddie last night, I felt it my mission to save Miss Head from her own plodding brain.

Her eyes flew open, and she stared at me with alarm as I stood quivering with repressed fervor before her.

"Why, Miss Babcock, whatever *is* the matter?" she demanded, letting her bow drop to the floor. The metronome ticked on slowly. The hot spring sun beat down through her leaded glass windows and onto her Oriental rugs.

"It's not possible," I insisted in a low anguished voice. "What you want. It isn't possible. You have to plunge in and make messes and risk rejection—and stuff." My sermonette wasn't coming off as I'd intended.

She sat up stiffly in her chair and inquired coolly, "What *are* you talking about, Miss Babcock? You're not making sense."

I looked at her helplessly as the metronome ticked slower and slower; either it was running down, or time was telescoping. "I—I— I'm not going to finish out my independent study with you this term!"

"Nonsense. Of course you are, Miss Babcock."

"But I'm *not.*"

"Don't be ridiculous."

"I *can't.*"

"Of course you can."

"I *won't!*"

"You will!"

"Miss Head, I'm a lesbian," I announced defiantly.

She sat perfectly still and said nothing.

I cleared my throat. "I spent all last night making love with Eddie Holzer, and it was wonderful."

Eventually Miss Head looked up. "Indeed," she said. "And would you like some more tea?"

I grabbed the metronome and wrenched off the pendulum and hurled it to the floor. "Will you stop this goddam thing and *listen* to me?"

"My dear Miss Babcock," she replied evenly, looking at her wrecked metronome, "I am *not* your mother. Don't come to me for approval."

"I *haven't* come to you for approval! I don't give a *shit* what you think!"

"Then why are you here?"

She had me there. I thought about it for a few moments. "I'm here, Miss Head, to try to save you from yourself before it's too late. Don't you *see* where you're heading? You're so goddam detached that you're morally paralyzed! You're so busy with your fucking ideas that you never have time for *people!* This is a living *death!*" I gestured expansively around her apartment.

"I'm afraid I shall have to ask you to leave, Miss Babcock."

Aha! I *knew* it! I *knew* she would reject me if I failed to conform to her way of life. I stalked triumphantly to the door.

At the door I faltered. I turned around, and Miss Head and I gazed at each other with pain. I retained enough tattered objectivity to recognize what I had just said as a lie. I was projecting shamelessly, pinning my own failings with regard to Bev onto Miss Head. Miss Head, to the contrary, *had* involved herself—with me. She loved me almost as though I were her daughter, and I knew it. But she had served her purpose. She had been the thesis to Eddie's antithesis. The show had to go on—however ruthlessly.

I looked at her helplessly. She seemed numb—gray and tired there in the spring sun. Did she understand what was taking place—that it was necessary to my development that I reject her by manipulating her into rejecting me? (I hadn't taken Psychology 101 for nothing.) I almost ran back over to her to apologize, to explain this Hegelian phenomenon to which I was apparently a puppet. But *she* was the professor. And Eddie was waiting.

My face contorted with anguish, I spun around and strode out.

Eddie sat on her window seat in the sun. She had her carving of the female torso in her lap and was lovingly rubbing linseed oil into it. I watched as she ran her hands up and down it, smoothing the oil over the breasts and down the thighs and into the crotch. My breathing quickened. Smiling with mixed delight and embarrassment at my new state of affairs, I curled up with Heidegger's *Being and Time* on the foot of Eddie's bed.

At some point I realized that I had been reading the same paragraph over and over again for several minutes without understanding any of it. I frowned. Finally I screamed, "Jesus! This doesn't make any *sense!*"

Eddie looked up from her mahogany torso. "*What* doesn't?"

"*Listen* to this! 'The running-ahead reveals to Being-there the lostness into Oneself and brings it before the possibility . . . of Being itself—itself, however, in the passionate *freedom for death* which has rid itself of the illusion of the One, become factual, certain of itself, and full of anxiety. The of-what of anxiety is Being-in-the-world as such. That that which is threatening is *nowhere*, is characteristic of the of-what of anxiety. Dying shows that death is constituted ontologically by always-mineness and existence. It is in the Being *(Sein)* of the things-that-are that the nihilation of Nothing *(das Nichten des Nichte)* recurs!' "

I was shivering by the time I finished, and I could hardly read the last sentence for the chattering of my teeth. A billowing black curtain was being drawn across my mind. Logic, pushed to its extreme, was about to short-circuit my brain.

Eddie wiped the linseed oil off her hands and onto her jeans. She took the book from me and threw it across the room and sat down and took my head in her lap and stroked my face and hair. Slowly, as though waiting for me to stop her, she pulled my hairpins out and undid my tight Helena Head bun. She ran her hands through my hair and covered my face with it playfully. Then she divided it into three clumps and began plaiting it into one large braid down my back. "We've got to get out of this place," she said quietly, as the May Court danced around Artemis in the courtyard. "It's a goddam madhouse."

8

Tuesday, June 27

—————————— □ ——————————

Mrs. Babcock could see nothing. It was pitch black and quiet as a tomb. Where was she? Her body was chilled. She was shivering, and her teeth were chattering. She couldn't think where she was. She felt around her with her hands. She was clearly in a bed, on a mattress. She began enumerating the various beds in her life—the narrow cot at the farm cabin when she was a small child, the king-sized bed she had shared with Wesley. . . . This bed was too wide to be the cot, too narrow to be the king-sized bed. Where *was* she?

She felt something clammy and sticky on the sheets. Panic flared up in her. Oh God, it was so cold and dark! Was she alone here, wherever she was? She listened intensely, but heard nothing. She could taste blood as she swallowed. She thrashed out in terror, and in doing so found the light switch against her headboard.

Light flooded her hospital room. She sighed with relief. Until she looked down and discovered that her pillow and sheets were soaked with dark blood. She studied the blood with detachment, as though it had nothing to do with her. It looked like anyone else's blood. It looked exactly as her own blood had always looked. What then was wrong with it, that it was gushing out like this? She rubbed an index finger in a congealing splotch and brought it to her tongue. The blood tasted as salty as usual. She joined her thumb and index finger, and then pulled them gently apart. It seemed as sticky as ever. *Why* was it failing her like this?

She pressed her call button. Soon she heard steps. In bustled Miss Sturgill, who froze halfway across the room, staring with concealed horror at Mrs. Babcock's bedding. "Oh dear!" she said. "Oh my!"

"I'm sorry. I'm afraid I've made a mess."

"Oh goodness."

Miss Sturgill helped Mrs. Babcock to the bathroom and handed her a sanitary pad. "Wait a minute. Let me get you some tampons too."

When Mrs. Babcock emerged, Miss Sturgill had changed the bed. The stained sheets lay in a heap. Miss Sturgill helped her back into bed and then pulled the saturated cotton from her nose and into a pan. Mrs. Babcock lay back exhausted, with blood trickling down her throat, while Miss Sturgill repacked her nostrils and scrubbed the caked blood off her cheeks and chin and thighs with a sponge.

"There!" Miss Sturgill said briskly, as though to a child. "Doesn't it feel nice having fresh clean sheets?"

"*Not* in the middle of the night." She'd intended the remark to sound wry and witty. Instead it came out whiny and pathetic. "Thank you, Miss Sturgill," she added, trying to redeem herself.

Miss Sturgill rushed out to call Dr. Vogel. She rushed back in and gave Mrs. Babcock half a sleeping pill. "He wants you to sleep until he comes in to do his rounds in a couple of hours."

Dr. Vogel dragged her from her drug-induced slumber by inquiring with forced cheer, "And how are we this morning, Mrs. Babcock?"

Mrs. Babcock explored her body mentally and decided that "we" felt pretty well, all in all, considering that she'd nearly bled to death in the night. Dr. Vogel examined her chart and poked at the cotton in her nostrils and inspected the pad between her legs and took her pulse and blood pressure and temperature. Occasionally he muttered, "Hmmm, yes, hmmm."

"I must remind you, Mrs. Babcock," he finally said, "that I *did* warn you of possible repercussions from failure to take your medication."

Mrs. Babcock pointed mutely to the empty spot on her table, formerly occupied by the spurned steroids. Dr. Vogel flushed and said, "Hmmm, yes, hmmm."

"Well!" he said. "Hot enough for you?"

"I haven't been outside for weeks."

"Yup, a scorcher today. A real scorcher." He folded his stethoscope and stuck it in the jacket of his lab coat and sidled toward the door.

"Dr. Vogel?"

His blond head swiveled toward her with reluctance; his hand was on the door handle.

"I don't understand what's happening to me, Dr. Vogel. Would you be good enough to explain it, in simple words?"

He blushed to the roots of his blond hair. "Well, I *do* have to complete my rounds. . . ."

"After your rounds, then."

"Yes, certainly, Mrs. Babcock."

Mrs. Babcock settled back to await the arrival of a nurse to walk her to breakfast. She punched impatiently at her embroidery hoop with the needle. Pamela, the high school girl who was helping her with it, would be crushed this afternoon at how little she'd accomplished in a week. She glanced out the window at the red squirrels, which were dashing up and down the trunk of the elm and flicking their tails and chattering busily.

She tried to calculate when Ginny would be arriving. It was difficult without a clock. If only Ginny would think to bring her one. But Ginny had never been noted for her thoughtfulness. . . . Judging from the sun, it was about six. Knowing Ginny, she wouldn't be out of bed before ten. Today Mrs. Babcock proposed to suggest that she return to Vermont. After all, these weren't ideal conditions for a pleasant mother/daughter visit. Ginny could return to Tennessee when Mrs. Babcock had recovered. Their relationship had been difficult in the best of times: Ginny's repertoire of responses to her parents had been twofold—sulking and joking, both equally irritating. But the relationship which even normally was trying for them both seemed impossible under these circumstances. The blow-up yesterday had been absurd. If inevitable: Ginny had her household in Vermont to worry about, and Mrs. Babcock her blood. They couldn't help each other, and it was ridiculous to try. It was best that Ginny leave. Her child and her husband needed her.

After a breakfast of tea and toast, Ginny went to the pine to check her birds. They were hanging from twigs, their eyes closed and their mouths open—screaming silently. No sign of their parents.

Ginny searched the bookcases, finally locating the bird book her mother had mentioned. It was bulky and authoritative-looking and had been written by the famous ornithologist Wilbur J. Birdsall, living proof of the axiom that name is destiny. Under a section entitled "Fledglings," Mr. Birdsall said, "Only ten to thirty percent of all baby birds survive to maturity. The others die of starvation, exposure or disease. Parents do not feed congenitally deformed offspring. Some disaster may befall the parent birds, on whom the infants are totally dependent for food. Often baby birds fall from the nest, either by accident or when learning to fly, where they either starve or are eaten by animals. The young of some species can be raised successfully by humans. Others, the swift family for example, feed on partially digested regurgitated food from the parent birds and cannot be hand fed in captivity. It is best to kill such birds should they be found, to avoid prolonging their suffering."

Feeling ill, Ginny shut the book and sat for a long time. Then she went in the kitchen and got a glass of water. Outside she dipped her index finger in the water and shook a drop into the open mouth of a baby bird. Its eyes opened wide, and it trembled—and finally its pink throat contorted and the water disappeared. She repeated this several times for all three birds. It occurred to her that she could just as well pick them up one at a time and submerge them in the glass until they stopped struggling.

Instead, she sat on the stone steps and brooded. It seemed unlikely that she could throw up at will to provide them with food. And anyway, human digestive juices would probably corrode a bird's gastric tract. Staring distractedly at the stone steps, another image assembled itself: She was holding a baby bird on a step in one hand. In the other hand, she held a big stone, like the decorative piece of white quartz next to the doorway. One well-aimed stroke would do it. . . .

Seizing a machete off the wall, she went out front and hacked away at the kudzu in the hot sun, trying to postpone the decision. But as she was hacking, she had another vision: a baby bird on the chopping block by the side of the cabin; one deft slice with the machete. . . .

She marched to the pine tree. As she unhooked one bird from his perch, he opened his dark round eyes and screeched at her, as though beseeching her to deal with him mercifully. The water had apparently revived him? She made the decision not to decide. She would give the horrid parents one more chance. She definitely didn't relish being God.

She put on a fresh Boone's Farm Apple Wine T-shirt and some bib overalls. Then she sat down and tried to decide whether even to go to the hospital. She and her mother had wound up yesterday yelling at each other. That certainly couldn't be very good for her mother. And she *knew* it wasn't good for herself. She had woken up that morning with a horrible headache and overwhelming seizures of remorse. Maybe she should think of an excuse for rushing back to Vermont? And then go somewhere else instead. If only she had somewhere else, anywhere else, to go. And if only she could learn how serious this disease was.

She went to the phone and dialed Dr. Tyler. No answer again.

On the way to the hospital, she stopped at the big house and gathered up the photos of relatives from her mother's bedroom mantel. She would take them as a peace offering. Taking down the photo of her Great-grandmother Hull, her mother's grandmother, Ginny scrutinized it. Her mother had always said that Ginny looked so much like her. She was Ginny's age in this photo, in her late twenties. She wore a high-necked lace blouse with a pin of some sort at the throat. Her hair was mostly pinned up, but wisps escaped here and there.

Ginny moved in front of the ornate gilded mirror above the mantel and studied herself. As always, it was a shock. She rarely recognized her own reflection. Her estimation of her looks varied with her mood; today she rated herself well below average. She held up the picture of her great-grandmother so that she could see the two of them side by side. Squinting her eyes and then opening them wide, she still couldn't see the physical similarities that everyone had always insisted existed—other than the fact that they each had a nose and two eyes and so forth.

She stared hard at this great-grandmother whom she'd never met. Dixie Lee Hull. She had been a legendary cook, right up until the day she had cut her finger on the recipe card for spoon bread and had died of blood poisoning. Nine children she left behind her. One of her daughters, Ginny's grandmother, had loathed housework and cooking and had spent her adulthood going to club meetings. One child had been more than enough for Ginny's grandmother—Ginny's mother, who had devoted herself completely to her family and her home. And so it went, alternating generations, each new scion implicitly criticizing its parents by rejecting their way of life. Ginny knew that even before she was born, she had been fated to neglect her child and her housework, to be driven from her home at gunpoint. Just as poor Wendy was now fated to pick up the gauntlet thrown down by her grandmother, Ginny's mother, and to keep a spotless house packed to the rafters with babies. It was exhausting, this process, and in contradiction to Hegel, no progress appeared to be resulting from this recurring juxtaposition of thesis and antithesis.

But the most remarkable thing, Ginny reflected, was that she contained within each of her cells the tiniest fraction of a germ of nucleic acid from the very body of the woman in this cracked yellow photo, delivered to her via the intercession of her mother and grandmother. Traced back twenty generations, or six hundred years, Ginny calculated that she would find herself directly related to some 1,048,576 people—probably the entire population of northern Europe at that time, which was where her forebears had come from. It gave her a creepy sense of continuity, as though she were onstage now muffing her lines, with ghostly ranks of ancestors backstage hissing and booing.

If you cared to carry it back through the centuries, every person in existence had identical submicroscopic specks of genetic material from the original man and woman. Forget Adam and Eve—each person had the tiniest imaginable flecks from the original cell, fertilized into existence by a lightning bolt.

It was stifling really. No wonder humankind was insane, with so much inbreeding through the eons. This speck of genetic material from her great-grandmother exercised such a pervasive influence as to make Ginny look almost identical to her—or so everyone said, although Ginny herself still couldn't see it. This speck accounted for the fact that, although they had never met, Ginny could see that their smiles were exact duplicates: They both smiled mostly with their eyes rather than with their mouths.

Ginny wondered what one picture her descendants would seize on to remember her by. This was probably one of the only pictures ever taken of Dixie Lee Hull. To have it done, she would have had to take a day out from her spoon bread baking, put on what was probably her only fancy outfit, and travel to Big Stone Forge by wagon. It must have been a big deal. Whereas Ginny had appeared in hundreds of photos by now, in various poses and moods and modes of dress, to

say nothing of the thousands of feet of Kinflicks that featured her.
How would her descendants be able to settle on one shot as representative? Which one would Ginny herself select?

Then she remembered that this question was strictly academic. At
the rate she was going, her descendants would hasten to prune her
from the family tree. Ira was doing his best to make Wendy forget her,
and Ginny couldn't imagine that she'd ever marry again or have
another child. The line of Hull women had perhaps gasped its last.

Inordinately distressed by this thought, Ginny rushed downstairs
and rifled her mother's desk. She removed some pictures from an
album—a shot of Ginny as a baby in a white dress being held by her
own mother, and another of Wendy as a baby being held by Ginny.
She stuffed these in an envelope and addressed it to Wendy in Vermont. Surely Ira wouldn't dare to confiscate Wendy's mail?

Drained, she picked up the cherished Hull family clock with its
steepled roof and etched glass door. She dusted it carefully with the
tail of her shirt. Then she wound it—eight turns and no more. She and
Karl and Jim had waged horrible battles over whose turn it was to
wind the clock each week. Even as a supposed adult, Ginny enjoyed
the crunching sound as she wound. As she was wrapping the clock in
a sheet, she heard a scratching sound at the door. In burst a middle-
aged woman in a blond wig. Close behind her came a middle-aged
couple, both dressed in fashionable summer suits. The woman was
shrieking in a thick New Jersey accent, "Oh *Harry!* Don't you just
love it? The children would be so *thrilled* to live in a *real* southern
mansion!"

Harry grumbled, "Well, it needs a lot of *work*, dear. . . ."

The woman in the wig drawled encouragingly, "Well, honey, you
can't get much more authentic than this in Hullsport. It was *built* by
Mr. Zed Hull hissef. Lord, if you *knew* the people that would love to
live in this house! Why, it's a gem, purely a gem!" She looked up,
startled to find Ginny suspended midway through wrapping a clock
in a sheet.

"Well, howdy, honey," said the woman in the wig. "I bet you're
the cleaning girl?"

"No, I'm a burglar," Ginny said, staring insolently at the three
housebreakers. "Actually, I'm Virginia Babcock. Who are *you?*"

"Why, I declare!" the woman cried. "Ginny, honey, it's been so
long since I've seen you that I like to not knowed you! Why, you must
have grown *two feet!*"

"No, I've always had two feet," Ginny replied, glaring at her. Who was this babbling idiot?

"Thelma Buford, honey, from up at Southland Realty," the wigged woman reminded her, sounding hurt.

"Oh. Yes, of course. Mrs. Buford. How are you?" Ginny had been at Hullsport High with her daughter. The daughter had talked too much, too.

"Fine, thank you. And yoursef?"

"Fine, thank you."

"These here people are the Hotchkisses. They're moving down from up at New Jersey. Mr. Hotchkiss is with your daddy's plant. They're just real interested in your house here."

"We think it's just elegant," Mrs. Hotchkiss assured Ginny.

Thinking fast, Ginny said "Oh, you mean my father cleared up that mess about the title before he died?"

"*What* mess?" Mrs. Buford snapped. "The title is clear as a bell." She smiled reassuringly at the Hotchkisses.

"Oh, that's *right!*" Ginny gasped. She threw her hand to her mouth. "I wasn't supposed to mention it, was I?"

Mr. and Mrs. Hotchkiss were glancing at each other uneasily. "What *are* you talking about, Ginny?" Mrs. Buford demanded.

"'Oh nothing!" Ginny said brightly, with a knowing glance at Mrs. Buford to indicate her infinite cooperation in deception. "Nothing at all."

The Hotchkisses fidgeted nervously. "Well! What else do you have to show us, Mrs. Buford?" Mr. Hotchkiss finally asked.

Her mother was at breakfast when Ginny arrived in her room. Hurriedly she unwrapped the clock and placed it on the bedside table. Then she took out some gummed picture hangers and positioned them on the wall bedside the bed. When they had dried, she hung the photos—Dixie Lee Hull, Great-uncle Lester, Cousin Louella, Grandpa Zed with his wild white hair. Nothing got things accomplished quite so efficiently as guilt, Ginny reflected.

Then she sat down and listened with pleasure to the steady tick-tock. Soon her pulse was throbbing in cadence with the ancestral clock.

As Ginny sat concentrating on this unlikely biological feat, her mother shuffled in on the arm of Mrs. Childress. Mrs. Babcock glanced around the room, startled. As she saw the clock and the photos, her tired yellow face burst into a smile, and she said with surprise, "Why, thank you, dear."

Ginny smiled back, her guilt temporarily allayed. It was really so easy to please her mother. She didn't require much. Why then had she, Ginny, spent most of her life trying to make her miserable? "How are you feeling today?"

"Fine, thank you. Better." Mrs. Babcock settled herself in bed and gazed with affection at the faces in the photographs while the clock ticked away.

Soon Dr. Vogel appeared. He sat in an armchair and crossed his legs, prepared to stay a while for once. "All right, Mrs. Babcock, I'll give it to you straight, since you've asked me to." They settled back, bracing themselves for their respective tasks in this interchange.

"Now. How does blood clot? All right. In grossly oversimplified terms, there are some twelve compounds referred to as clotting factors. These factors interact in various ways to produce an enzyme called prothrombinase. Prothrombin in the presence of prothrombinase and calcium yields thrombin. And fibrinogen in the presence of thrombin yields fibrin. Platelets under the influence of thrombin break down so as to liberate ADP, which causes other platelets to clump at the site of tissue injury. The clumping platelets, interspersed along fibrin, form the clot."

Ginny looked at him with disgust. Was this the best he could do for the unfortunate layman? Mrs. Babcock looked dazed.

"Hmmm, yes, hmmm," he continued. "So you see, a disorder at any point in this chain can inhibit clotting—the absence of any of the twelve factors in appropriate amounts, a malfunction of any of the chemical reactions. Hemophilia, for example, results from a factor deficiency. However, because of your platelet count, one can conclude that factor deficiency doesn't apply in your case. You see, those with factor deficiencies don't exhibit low platelet counts as well. Hmmm, yes. So—you are not factor deficient, you are platelet deficient. You have only $16,000/mm^3$ compared to a normal count of over $150,000/mm^3$, using the Coulter Counter Model F.

"Hmmm, yes, hmmm. Now. How do platelets come to be deficient? Hmmm, yes, hmmm. Well, platelets can be deficient if an insufficient number is being produced. Yes? Or if they've gone into hiding somewhere. Hmmm, yes. Or if they're being destroyed. The reason people have been extracting all the blood from you, Mrs. Babcock, is that we've been doing tests to try to narrow down the reason in your particular case. Hmmm, yes. Now cells in the bone marrow called megakaryocytes exude the small bodies of protoplasm that we call platelets. If platelet production were low, one would expect the megakaryocyte count in the bone marrow to be depressed. However, we've done a bone marrow aspiration and your megakaryocytic count appears to be normal. This is nice because it means that you aren't in the early stages of leukemia, which sometimes exhibits symptoms similar to yours."

Mrs. Babcock felt stricken. She might have been dying of leukemia unawares because nobody had bothered to consult the subject of all these amazing tests?

"Hmmm, yes. So—this would indicate that your platelets are hiding, Mrs. Babcock. Or that they're being destroyed. Now. How are platelets destroyed?"

Ginny felt as though she were being hypnotized by the ticking of the clock and the simultaneous pulsing of her blood, which blood was apparently healthy only through some fluke of nature. How could *anyone's* blood be healthy with all these things to go wrong?

"The spleen functions as a filter," Dr. Vogel was saying. "It sequesters and destroys worn out or diseased blood components. It's possible that your body has formed an antibody to your own platelets and your spleen is destroying them. We're still trying to narrow this down and should have an answer for you in the next few days. Well! Any questions?"

Ginny and Mrs. Babcock sat as mute as college students during a discussion period. "How does the spleen destroy platelets?" Ginny asked finally.

"Hmmm, yes, hmmm. Ah, actually we don't exactly know."

"Who is this 'we' you keep referring to?" Mrs. Babcock asked.

"Hmmm, yes. 'We.' Modern medicine, I suppose." He blushed and shifted in his chair.

"So you gave me steroids to spur platelet production even though you already knew from my bone marrow aspiration that I was producing enough?" Mrs. Babcock asked casually.

"Hmmm, yes. Well, no, not exactly. Well, you see, we don't know exactly how steroids work. We just know that often they *do* work."

"But not this time," Mrs. Babcock reminded him.

"Well, no."

"So what happens next?" Ginny asked

"Hmmm, yes. Well, next we try a transfusion. We'll give you two units of whole blood, Mrs. Babcock, with the idea that your bloodstream can use the foreign platelets to stem your bleeding, until they die off. Plus it will alleviate your anemia and low blood pressure for a time. By then we expect to have pinned down your difficulty so that we can treat it directly. It's also possible, though not medically proven, that these foreign platelets could exercise some sort of 'priming' effect on your own bloodstream. I've seen it happen."

"What you're saying is that you really don't know what you're doing?" Ginny asked.

Dr. Vogel stood up. "My dear young lady, I assure you that we in the medical profession know a good bit more about what we're doing than a layman."

Ginny didn't reply. She had learned from observing Eddie Holzer, who had done it all the time, that it was impossible to discuss issues civilly with a person who insisted on referring to himself as "we."

"Granted it's trial and error, to an extent, but it's *educated* trial, *trained* error."

Ginny stared at him evenly.

"And so we'll begin the transfusions as soon as we can find a donor. We need fresh blood, not more than an hour old, because the platelets in stored blood are often injured or dead. But you have an uncommon blood type, Mrs. Babcock. Did you know that? You could get forty-five dollars a pint for it on the Bowery in New York City." He laughed weakly. "But we're typing the staff for a donor right now."

"What type is it?" Ginny asked.

"B negative."

"That's my type. I could maybe be her donor."

"Why didn't I think of you? Let me type you." He raced from the room in search of a syringe.

Only then did Ginny and Mrs. Babcock realize simultaneously that they still hadn't gotten any definitive answer about the ultimate severity of Mrs. Babcock's condition.

"What did he say?" Mrs. Babcock asked, her yellow face haggard.

"I don't know," Ginny confessed. "But I think it sounds pretty good, don't you? I mean, they're certainly going all out with these tests and things." She knew that her efforts to feign cheerfulness weren't convincing. "Where's Dr. Tyler these days?" she asked, intent upon tracking him down so that she could question him.

"He goes to his cabin at Spruce Pine near Asheville in the summer now."

Ginny turned on the television. "The Price Is Right" was on. She and her mother stared at it vacantly. Ginny was well-acquainted with the show. It had formed the backdrop for much of her morning housework in Vermont. Most of the things being won—a lifetime supply of Alpo dog food, a ceiling-to-floor bookcase complete with a leather-bound set of the outer covers of the world classics, a year's subscription to New York's most prestigious wake-up service, a ship-to-shore short-wave radio—neither of them needed, which was nice because it meant that they didn't have to squander their vital energies being envious of the shrieking winners.

But eventually a three-week tour of Ireland was up for grabs. Mrs. Babcock had always longed to go to Ireland, Scotland, England in search of the towns her forebears had come from. Wesley had always refused to take her. He had no business to do over there. The trip wouldn't be tax-deductible. It was out of the question. What about the IRA? she had suggested. Don't they make bombs? It had never occurred to her to go alone. The household would collapse in her absence.

"Let's go on a trip to Ireland when I get out of here," Mrs. Babcock suggested.

Ginny glanced at her doubtfully—doubtful about her mother's getting out in the first place, doubtful about her stamina for a trip if she did, doubtful about the two of them even going to downtown Hullsport in a friendly fashion, and especially doubtful about the strained cheerfulness of her mother's voice. "Sure. That would be fun," Ginny said brightly. The thing was, she'd love to go to Ireland, all those places. From her mother's stories, she felt a definite bond with her ancestors. They had been German Lutherans from the Catholic part of Germany, Puritans and Pilgrims from Anglican England, Anglicans in the Catholic south of Ireland, Scotch Irish Presbyterians in the Catholic sector of Scotland after the '45. Misfits, all of them, with loyalties every bit as confused and fragmented as Ginny's had always been. Was this proclivity for propelling oneself into circumstances in which one was bound to feel set apart from the surrounding community hereditary, a result of those minute flecks of nucleic acid in each cell? Or was the proclivity absorbed from one's parents, in the same way that kittens learned to drink milk by watching their mother?

". . . and I consider it a *privilege* to be deemed worthy of suffering like this," Sister Theresa was saying fervently, when Ginny and Mrs. Babcock arrived at the sun porch for lunch.

"A *privilege!*" Mr. Solomon snorted, his thick lenses magnifying his eyes to the size of platters. "A *privilege!* You think you've been singled out for special favors, eh, Sister? I like that vun. God says, 'There's Sister Theresa. I think so highly of her that I'd like to give her cancer.'"

Sister Theresa crossed herself. "A *privilege,*" she confirmed, fingering the medal around her neck with the praying hands and the slogan "Not My Will But Thine." "The Lord gives no one more than he can endure. The cross and the strength to bear it."

"Big of Him. So the number of misfortunes you experience is a token of the cosmic judgment on the well-being of your soul?"

"When I was a little girl at school, Mr. Solomon," Sister Theresa explained earnestly, "sometimes I would come home crying because the bigger boys had teased me. And my mother would say, 'But they wouldn't tease you if they didn't like you, child.' That's how I see my present situation, Mr. Solomon."

"Vell! At last ve have something to agree on, Sister. God—your God and my God—God is a bully!"

Sister Theresa crossed herself again. "I didn't say that, Mr. Solomon," she said, her eyes lowered and her beefy face turning red. "I *said* that it is a pleasure for me to bear whatever burden the Lord chooses to place on me. I am strong and the burdens make me stronger."

"Vell, if that vere how it vorked, Sister, I would now be a Charles Atlas of the soul!"

Sister Theresa looked at him questioningly.

"My vife and my three little children vere herded into box cars, Sister. I suppose they died. I *hope* they died. It vould have been a blessing compared to life in the camps."

That's not fair, Ginny thought. Jewish people always won out in the one-upmanship of suffering.

"I'm sorry, Mr. Solomon." After a delicate pause, she added, "There has always been evil in the world, since the Fall. Evil will flourish until all men in their hearts and minds accept Christ our Lord as their savior. God does not perform or condone evil. However, He can turn it to His own ends sometimes. Look what a bright and sensitive race yours is for its suffering, Mr. Solomon."

Mr. Solomon cleared his throat, aware that he was being drowned in honey. "Thank you, Sister. But I still say it's vun hell of a lousy vay to run a vorld. If I had run my jewelry department the vay your God runs this vorld, do you think I'd have lasted a veek? No, I'd have been out valking the streets looking for vork."

The electric chimes on the Southern Baptist church were now playing "Call Me Unreliable." Mrs. Babcock was struggling with an overcooked piece of meat that might have been beef or veal or pork or lamb.

"How can you call it 'lousy,' Mr. Solomon, when you can look out the window on a beautiful sunny day and see a bird singing?" Sister Theresa pointed to the bird feeder in the pine tree on which sat a mocking bird.

Mr. Solomon's fist hit the table hard. The dishes jumped, and the silverware clattered. Mrs. Cabel looked up from her meal in alarm for the first time during the entire discussion; she had food smeared across her face. "I call it lousy for that very reason! God put me on this earth and made me love vat I found here. Little by little, He's taken it all avay from me. First my parents, then my vife and babies, then my house and country, and now my occupation and means of livelihood." He pointed at his cloudy eyes. "I can't fix clocks anymore. I can hardly even *see* the bird you're talking about, Sister. And soon He vill take avay my breath, and vith it my life." He was very upset and was breathing with difficulty. "You know vat I call your God, Sister? I call Him a sadist."

"No, Mr. Solomon, *no.* This life is only a pale hint of the next. Death is the beginning, not the end. You lose *nothing*, you gain *everything.* Everything precious that's been taken from you here, you retrieve with interest on the other side. I'm *sure* of it, Mr. Solomon. Your wife, your children, everything."

"Yes, I know vat your people say, Sister Theresa. And so you must. You have a product to sell, like all the rest of us. But it vas *your* man Pascal, Sister, who said, 'The eternal silence of these infinite spaces frightens me.' But tell me, Sister, ven did you go into the convent?"

This question seemed beside the point to Ginny. She glanced at her mother, who had been watching the exchange intently, like a tennis match. "I was sixteen, Mr. Solomon. Why do you ask?"

"Forgive me for saying this, Sister. I'm obviously upset and out of control. But vat do you know of losing a mate and three children to psychopathic maniacs?"

Sister Theresa flushed and said nothing. The conversation appeared to be at an end. The four ate in silence, Ginny looking on from the sofa.

That afternoon Ginny lay on the spare bed in her mother's room, a needle in her right arm. Her blood was spurting down a tube and into a plastic bag that was strapped to the side of the bed.

She and her mother had just watched "Hidden Heartbeats." Sheila's bridge party had gone poorly. Ella, the wife of Mark's boss, had not appeared, leaving Sheila one player short. As they limped along with their game, the other women kept whispering behind their cards, as Sheila struggled to maintain a stiff upper lip, about why Ella had snubbed Sheila and wrecked her card party. At the end of the half-hour show, the phone rang. Was it Ella calling to explain her absence? They wouldn't know until the next day. The tallies, however, which Sheila had spent yesterday's program picking out in the five-and-ten, had been a great success. All the ladies at the party asked how in the *world* she'd managed to find such clever ones. "And on Mark's salary, too," a lady added behind her cards to the others.

"Do you think it's Ella on the phone?" Mrs. Babcock asked Ginny.

"I doubt it. Really I think it's Mark. He's probably had a run-in at work with Ted, and Ted told Ella not to go to the party."

"Oh, Ella's not *that* spineless."

"Don't you think so?"

"Heavens no. She'd have *called* at least, if she weren't going. Something must have happened to her."

"Well, maybe you're right."

Now "Westview General" was on, which Ginny also remembered from her breast-feeding days.

Dr. Marsh was talking to Sam, whose wife had been his patient. "Sam, we've been friends for a long time, Sam."

"Yes, Doc, and that's the truth, too."

"So, Sam, when I say I hate to—"

"Doc, you don't mean—"

"Sam, buddy, you know I wouldn't want to lead a friend on—"

"Doc, you're not sayin—"

"Sam, you have to be strong—"

"You mean—"

"I've always leveled with you, haven't I, Sam?"

"Is it—"

"I've done the very best I can for you, Sam fella."

Sam finally broke down in manly sobs.

Dr. Marsh put his arm around Sam's heaving shoulders and handed him a bill. "Now, Sam, Blue Cross will pay most of it. And you *do* have your dear wife well and back home again, don't you now?"

Ginny lay watching her blood flow out of her arm and down the tube. Her blood. She knew a great many things about it from physiology at Worthley. For instance, she knew that only 1.5 percent of Americans had her mother's and her blood type, B negative. Type B was much more common in Central Asia. How it had found its way to southwest Virginia was a mystery. She also knew that platelets died in three to four days. And she knew that her own healthy bone marrow was turning out five hundred billion of them each day. In other words, Ginny was not returning to Vermont, or to anywhere else, for the present. Her mother needed *her*. The shoe was on the other foot for a change. It was a novel sensation.

She lay still listening to the ticking of the Hull clock, "Westview General" providing the background. She concentrated on her heart, zeroing in on a single red cell. She traced its pathway out of her heart and through her lungs and down her arteries and capillaries to her big toe, where it released its oxygen. Then it raced back up the capillaries to her veins, and from there back to her heart. If she had been timing this circuit correctly, it should have taken about twenty-five seconds. She looked at the filigreed second hand on the steepled clock and confirmed with satisfaction that it had.

Never mind why people died. Why was anyone *alive?* How could any one body possibly coordinate all that it had to coordinate? It was mind-boggling. Red cells, white cells, platelets, antibodies, the twelve clotting factors. The surprising thing was not that the production and delivery system sometimes broke down. The surprise was that it ever functioned flawlessly at all, much less in most of the people one met.

When her bag was full of dark red blood, Dr. Vogel removed the needle and told her to hold her arm over her head for a while. Then he put a tourniquet on Mrs. Babcock's upper arm and began prodding with a sterile needle for a vein. He appeared to be having difficulty. He made several trial punctures and had to withdraw the needle each time.

"Young man, must you do your internship on *me?*" Mrs. Babcock meant it as a joke, but it came out peevish. Ginny laughed heartily, trying to carry it off. Finally Dr. Vogel found a cooperative vein and settled the needle in it. Ginny's blood flowed down the tube from the plastic bag and into Mrs. Babcock's body.

Ginny, as she rested, considered the justice of this arrangement: Her mother shared her blood with Ginny via the placenta when Ginny had needed it. Now Ginny was simply returning the favor via rubber tubing. There was undeniable satisfaction in the concept that her mother's blood might "learn" about platelet management from Ginny's blood. After all, the flow of instruction between them had generally run in the opposite direction. Ginny savored the idea of a reciprocal arrangement. However, if they shared blood type and had shared actual blood at some remote point, did that mean that, genes being what they were, Ginny's own healthy blood was programmed to break down at some point? And Wendy's?

At least this had gotten her out of the craft program, Mrs. Babcock reflected as she watched Ginny's blood flow into her arm. She remembered from the encyclopedia how the audience at Roman gladiator fights would leap from the stands and vie to drink the blood of especially skilled and courageous gladiators as they died in the dirt, the idea being to imbibe via their blood their nerve and vigor.

"He took the cup; and when he had given thanks, he gave it to them, saying, Drink ye all of this; for this is my Blood of the New Covenant, which is shed for you, and for many, for the remission of sins." Mrs. Babcock suspected that the wine/blood ritual in Holy Communion had its origin in fact as much as in symbolism. Scientists could take a worm trained to perform some simple activity, chop it in bits, and feed it to an untrained worm; the untrained worm would suddenly be found to possess the skill of the worm that had made up its meal. Genes, RNA, DNA, chromosomes . . . the accumulated experience of the species, passed on in encoded form down through the ages. Just so this transfusion. Her own defective blood could "learn" about platelet husbandry from Ginny's healthy blood.

There was something altogether alarming about this. About her being ill enough to *need* a transfusion, certainly. But more than that. She didn't like having Ginny as her donor. In the first place, it meant that she couldn't suggest that Ginny go back to Vermont. Surely the tension between them couldn't be good for either of them, particularly for Mrs. Babcock herself when she needed thorough rest to aid in her recovery.

But there was another factor in all this that she was persistently refusing to face, she knew. A subtle shift in the balance of power between Ginny and herself had occurred, and she didn't like it at all. The pattern had always been Mrs. Babcock's bleeding herself dry, as it were, for the children. Nothing had ever been too much for them to demand of her. "I live but to serve," she had quipped gaily when they had come bursting in demanding three dozen chocolate chip cookies for a class Christmas party, or tuna sandwiches for eighteen for a club picnic. But there had been truth in this quip, she now knew. Ceasing to serve, she had collapsed, mentally and physically. And now here Ginny was, serving *her*—lying on the spare bed with an expression of smug satisfaction at doing so. Mrs. Babcock was profoundly uncomfortable with this reversal of roles.

That she should feel so uneasy about this suggested to her an unflattering possibility—that she had dominated the children through weakness; she had smothered them with her martyrdom. By always doing everything for them, usually in advance of their requesting it, had she undermined their drive and self-confidence? That was perhaps why Jim and Ginny had such difficulty ever sticking with anything, why Karl clung so fanatically to his routines? But here she was lapsing into self-reproach. Perhaps if she had turned some of this reproach on them in their early years, rather than always in on herself, she wouldn't be here in this hospital bed today. The truth was that she had done the best she knew how, being an amateur at parenting. Now that she was a professional, having turned out three finished products, her skills were no longer in demand, and it was too late to rectify mistakes committed during her apprenticeship.

When Ginny got back to the cabin, the sun was about to plunge behind the kudzu-faced bowl. She went out to the pine tree. Two baby birds hung from twigs, their heads back, their eyes closed, and their yellow beaks open to reveal their delicate pink throats. Suffering, Wilbur J. Birdsall said they were; and she was allowing them to, requiring them to. She glanced around for the third baby, searching the dish and all the nearby branches. She found it on the ground— a stiff corpse, wings outstretched and rigid and mouth gaping for food. Feeling nauseated, Ginny heaved the graceful little body into the kudzu.

Then she sat on the stone steps. Her options were clear. She could flush them down the toilet. They would go down with the same ease as a Tampax. She could smash their skulls on the stone steps. She could guillotine them with the machete. If she chose not to sully herself by performing their execution in person, she could move them to the ground, so that the wild cats could find them more easily. Or she could leave them to starve.

No, damn it! She wouldn't buckle under to the verdict of Wilbur J. Birdsall, world renowned authority or not. These baby birds normally fed on their parents' vomit. But at some point their tiny gastrointestinal systems *had* to make the conversion to self-digestion. It seemed distinctly possible to Ginny that under extremely stressful conditions such as these, the babies' systems could develop and convert more rapidly than usual. It was worth a try anyway.

She got a glass of water and fed a drop to each bird. At first she wasn't sure they were still alive. They didn't move at all. But they were warm, and there were faint hints on their fluff-covered breasts of beating hearts. After a minute or so, each bird swallowed his droplet. And then one drop after another.

Ginny mixed raw hamburger and tuna and whole wheat flour into a disgusting paste. Taking a minute bit, she formed a tiny ball. Holding it between thumb and forefinger, she carefully dropped it into the mouth of one of the babies. She waited. Nothing happened. But then, slowly, the bird's beak began to twitch. And then the membrane of its pink throat began to expand and contract convulsively, and the tiny ball disappeared, like an insect enfolded by a Venus's-flytrap.

Cheered, Ginny fed each bird several balls. In the cabin, she found a small deep basket with a lid. They could cling to its sides, and it would be dark and cool like their lost chimney. She put them in, no longer worrying about sullying them with her odor, since the parents had copped out anyway. Wouldn't Wendy love to be helping her with this project? Ginny could almost see her mushing her chubby little fingers in the meat paste, trying with an intense frown to form a tiny ball like Mommy's. She would clutch a bird in a sticky hand and giggle gleefully as it screeched in her face. If only there were some way to prevent her from ripping the birds to pieces in her enthusiasm. She'd pry their beaks open and poke at their eyes with sticks and dismember their wings in her exuberant curiosity. An idea popped into Ginny's head with the force and clarity of true inspiration: There was no need to sell the big house! She and Wendy would live there together; her mother could live in the cabin. Three generations of Hull women, all in a row!

Cheered by this thought, she went to the phone and got Dr. Tyler's number in Spruce Pine.

"Why, Ginny, what a pleasure," he said. "I haven't seen you in years."

"I haven't been home much lately."

"What a shame. You know, I feel a special attachment to the people I've delivered."

"It's mutual. In fact, I'm sitting on the bed you delivered me in."

"Is that a fact? I declare. Law, I member that night so well. Your mother was having really strong contractions, and what do you think happened? Half a dozen swifts flew down the chimney! Why, I never saw anything like it in my life! Those birds fluttered through that cabin in an absolute panic, getting soot all over everything, the ceiling, the walls, the upholstery. Your mother had just cleaned that day so's everything would be nice and straight while she was laid up with you. Why, she hopped up out of that bed, and she grabbed a broom, and she chased those damn swifts all through the cabin, swatting at em. And every now and then, she'd have a contraction and collapse on the floor. But after it was over, she'd hop right back up and chase after em with tears just *pouring* down her face. And of course your daddy and I were chasing right behind her, trying to get her back to bed and she kept whacking *us* with her broom, too!" They were both laughing. "Oh my, it was something to behold!"

"What happened to them?"

"I think your daddy finally managed to get them out the front door."

"Why did they fly down in the first place?"

"Oh, I don't know. They do that sometimes. Nothing but trouble, swifts. Rats with feathers, I call em. But I don't imagine you're calling to discuss birds. What can I do for you, honey?"

"Mother's in the hospital."

"Is she? I hadn't heard. What's wrong?" Ginny had expected him to don his professional manner and take charge of everything at once. She was alarmed when he sounded merely interested, concerned but detached.

"Idiopathic thrombocytopenic purpura."

"Hmmm. How's she doing?"

"I don't know. That's why I'm calling you. To find out."

"Who's her doctor?"

"Vogel."

"*Vogel.* Fine young man. Excellent doctor. Just excellent. She couldn't be in better hands."

"He's been giving her steroids. And today she had a transfusion."

"Standard."

"Yes, but Mother felt the steroids weren't helping."

"Ginny, honey, in the old days before steroids, do you know what we used to do when someone came in with undiagnosable bleeding? We'd transfuse, and maybe we'd excise the spleen. Sometimes it worked, sometimes not. If it didn't, we had to just sit there helplessly and watch more and more hemorrhages develop until the brain hemorrhaged and the patient blessedly died. They're invaluable, steroids are. And antibiotics, used right. They've revolutionized the practice of medicine. Why, if you came down with pneumonia when I was first practicing in Hullsport, you spent all winter in bed. *If* you were lucky. Lots died. Now they're up and around in days."

"Well, today, Dr. Tyler, with the steroids and stuff, is idiopathic thrombocytopenic purpura, you know, like, serious?"

"I can't tell you, Ginny. Your mother's not my patient. In general, it's usually not that serious in children. It tends to clear right up. In adults, it can be more serious. As I said, there's this danger of cerebral hemorrhage. But it happens rarely these days."

"She couldn't, like, die or anything, could she?"

"You know, Ginny, the trouble with patients is that they expect their doctors to be shamans or seers or something. I don't know. I doubt if Vogel knows. Modern medicine has come a long way, but there are many, many things we still simply *don't know.* Idiopathic. Cause unknown. There are hundreds of thousands of things that can go wrong with the human body. We've catalogued several thousand. One of my teachers in medical school in Richmond once told me, 'As you practice medicine, you'll find your hat will fit your head better. You will realize that there are many things you *don't* know.' Has your mother been unhappy?"

"Unhappy?" It had never occurred to Ginny to consider the topic before. Except for the outburst the other day, her mother had invariably been briskly cheerful for as far back as Ginny could remember.

"She *has* been the past few years, you know."

"No, I didn't know," Ginny insisted.

"Well, then, I clearly shouldn't be mentioning it. I'm an old man and my sense of professional ethics is slipping."

"Unhappy about *what?*"

"Whatever people find to be unhappy about when they're in a depressed state—everything, in short."

"But what was she depressed about?"

"Well—maybe you should ask her that."

"Who, *me?*"

"Well, child, you *are* her daughter."

"But what does depression have to do with her physical health?"

"A great deal, I assure you."

"Then why hasn't Vogel mentioned it?"

"It's a notion that is—out of favor among the medical profession at present. We have our fads and fashions like every other field, you know. Tonsillectomies are out now, phenobarbital for infants who convulse is in. And so on. But when you've been at it as long as I have, when you've treated people under all sorts of circumstances, when you've treated their parents and their children, you begin to see patterns. Illness doesn't strike randomly, like a thief in the night. Certain types of people at certain points in their lives will come down with certain kinds of ailments. You can almost predict it after a while. A disease can serve the same function for an alert doctor as a Rorschach inkblot for a psychologist; it's a form of existential self-expression for a patient, if you like. I know this may sound a little farfetched, my dear, but disease is not arbitrary, and it does not 'attack.' But goodness, you're not interested in an old man's pet theories. . . ."

Ginny politely said nothing. Tyler was apparently freaking out in his retirement.

"But I can assure you, Ginny," he added, "that you couldn't do better than Vogel. I know that he's doing everything that can be done."

Ginny had secretly been fantasizing that Dr. Tyler would come out of retirement and take over her mother's case himself. "Do you think I should tell Mother that there's this chance of cerebral hemorrhage?"

There was a long pause. "Well, honey, that's something you have to decide for yourself. You and your brothers. You see, my dear, I'm a very old man now, and I have to be thinking about my own death, not other people's."

Unnerved, Ginny said, "Yes, well, it's been nice talking with you, Dr. Tyler. Thanks for your help."

"Not at all, my dear. Any time. Give your mother my love, and tell her I'll be over to see her when I'm back home at the end of the summer."

"Yes, I will. Good-by."

She hung up and sat motionless. The phrase "cerebral hemorrhage" kept drifting through her brain. If she were in her mother's place, she concluded that she'd want Wendy to tell her. On the other hand, could the specter of cerebral hemorrhage help to trigger one by placing the patient under tension?

Once again she decided not to decide. She preferred being compelled into her decisions. She would see how her mother responded to the transfusion.

She found a pen and some letter paper and began a letter. "Dear Miss Head: I am writing you from a need to acknowledge past debts. I know that when I was at Worthley you were trying to teach me to regard issues critically and with detachment, and to organize them into orderly patterns. To the extent that I absorbed these skills, they have proved invaluable. Your philosophy courses and the trips into Boston and the visits in your apartment were bright spots in what was otherwise a difficult and unhappy time for me, and I thank you for them from the bottom of my heart. I have thought about you with pleasure and affection ever since, and I only wish that the circumstances under which I left Worthley could have been more mature and more graceful. But you must know that they couldn't have been, given what I was like at that time. I'm sorry I disappointed you so terribly. It's one of the things in my life I'm least proud of. I hope you are well, and are busy on your book, or on another one. With warm regards, Ginny Babcock Bliss."

She took it to the mailbox at the bottom of Cloyds' hill before she could reconsider and tear it up. The kitchen lights were still on at Clem and Maxine's. She decided to stop.

"How's your mother today?" Clem asked, as Ginny sat down at their dinner table, which was strewn with dirty dishes. The three small dark children, replicas of Clem as a child, were coloring on the floor in a corner.

"I don't know really. She had a transfusion this afternoon. The doctor is very hopeful about the effect it will have."

"How about some soup beans and corn bread?" Maxine asked. "There's lots left."

Ginny hadn't eaten all day and had given a pint of blood. "I'd love some if you've got it. I'm starved." Maxine dished her up a plate. Ginny poured ketchup on the gooey brown beans and dug in greedily.

"Doesn't that man of yours feed you up at Vermont?" Clem asked with a laugh.

Ginny laughed, too, and decided not to mention that "her man" had run her out. Why wreck a good plate of soup beans? "Clem, tell me to shut up if this is rude," Ginny said between bites, "but what's happened to your leg?"

Clem and Maxine smiled serenely. "Hit's well," he said.

"I noticed. But how come? Did you have an operation or something?"

"No, the Lord has made me whole."

"Oh, brother," Ginny said with a grin.

"But He *has,* Ginny. I pledged my life to Jesus after our wreck, and my leg growed out and straightened hitself."

Ginny stared at him with disbelief. He pulled up his overall leg. Several appalling scars ran the length of his calf. The scars included puncture marks from the stitches, so that they looked like the seams on a football. He had had over a hundred stitches in his calf alone. But otherwise the leg looked sound and normal. The healing episode was apparently true.

"Well, do you belong to one of the churches at the circle, or what?" Ginny sputtered.

"We got our own ministry, me and Maxine. We meet up at the springhouse, a couple dozen of us, ever Friday night."

"What? Right up here you meet?"

"Yeah. We'd love to have you come Friday, wouldn't we, Maxine?" Maxine nodded.

Ginny sat silent, prodding her sticky beans with her fork.

"How about it?" Clem demanded. "You wouldn't have to join in. You could just watch."

"Wouldn't it bother the others?" Ginny asked, trying to manufacture an excuse for not going.

"Not once I told them you was an old friend of mine."

"I don't know. . . ." She blotted up the juice from the beans with her corn bread and ate it.

"Hit could change your life. Like hit done mine," Clem assured her. "But even if hit don't, what have you lost? A couple of hours maybe."

"Do you preach, or what?"

"We don't have no set schedule. We do whatever the good Lord instructs us to."

Realizing how deeply offended Clem would be if she refused, Ginny accepted. "What time?"

"Seven thirty, Friday."

"All right. I'll be there."

"Good," Maxine and Clem said in unison.

"Thanks for supper." She stood up.

Mrs. Babcock woke up on her own the next morning, without having a thermometer crammed in her mouth. She lay still and listened with pleasure to the ticktock of the old clock on her bedside table. That sound had been her constant companion through life. It had filled the cabin when she was a little girl. And when her parents and she had moved to the big house, the clock had sat on the mantel in the living room. Sometimes she had perched on the Empire sofa and just listened for an hour or more to the steady ticking. And the most exciting time of the week had been Sunday morning after church when her mother would bring the clock down and allow her to wind it with its filigreed key—eight turns and no more.

When she and Wesley had married and had begun living in the cabin, her mother had let her take the clock, like the ark in the Old Testament. When Wesley was overseas and Ginny would wake up screaming in the night, Mrs. Babcock would carry her into the living room and walk up and down the length of the room. Holding the tiny baby against her heart, which was beating in time to the clock, she would stroll and would pat Ginny's shuddering back. She could understand the baby's alarm—this understanding was the only thing that prevented her some nights from taking the baby by the feet and swinging her against the wall. Having been rocked in the amniotic fluid for nine months on its mother's heartbeat, a baby was conditioned to that rhythm. Take it away and a baby was lost. It was a need one never got over, Mrs. Babcock had reflected on those dark cold lonely nights as she had strolled endlessly in obedience to the ticking. She had calmed her own self with the conviction that Wesley would be safely home again once the relentless pendulum had ticked off eight more months, or whatever the figure happened to be.

And when Wesley did return—some twenty-one million ticks of the clock later, as she had calculated one night while hiking up and down with the howling baby—the passionate love they had made for many months afterwards was rendered that much more passionate for her because it was accompanied with the ticking of that clock, which served to remind her of the unutterable deprivation of Wesley's absence and possible death.

And when she and Wesley and the children had moved to the big house, the clock came along too, and sat on Mrs. Babcock's desk in the hallway. The children tumbled around on the floor like puppies, fighting over whose turn it was to wind it. During the day, when she paused in the middle of her housework, she could hear the clock. If she woke up in a panic in the middle of the night, as she had often during her depressions in recent years, she could hear it. The clock had ticked just like this for her great-grandmother, for her grandmother, for her mother. Life went on, states of mind shifted with the ticking, her fears would pass. And they did. But only to return again, as the relentless ticking carried her ever closer to old age and death, ever farther away from the crammed years of young motherhood when she had been too busy or too exhausted to consider the inevitability of either.

She opened one eye and glanced at the clock—the familiar yellowed face and script Roman numerals, the filigreed hands. Her friend, her enemy. Some days it was an enemy toward whom she felt a reluctant affection due simply to familiarity. Today, however, the clock was a friend—given how many ticks, would she be out of the hospital and back home? Already she was feeling better. She prodded the wads in her nose and the pad between her legs and found them unstained. The transfusion appeared to be working.

Mrs. Babcock stretched all over luxuriously, like a cat in the sun. Someone who had never been seriously ill, who had never observed her bodily processes stalling and sputtering, couldn't begin to appreciate the overwhelming sense of physical well-being engendered as those processes began righting themselves. Young Dr. Vogel knew what he was about. There was no longer any question in her mind. She felt sheepish about having challenged his judgment on the steroids.

Sliding out of bed, Mrs. Babcock put on her green flannel robe. Her bruises weren't aching, as they usually did when she first stood up in the morning. Looking out the window, she saw the sun coming up—a glowing red ball—over the hill behind the factory. At her eye level in the tree outside were the frantically busy squirrels who leapt from branch to branch in scurrying pursuit of each other.

Mrs. Childress came in with her razor. Mrs. Babcock lay down and, with her eyes closed, felt her stabbed ear lobe throbbing to the ticking of the clock. Mrs. Childress was alternately dabbing the puncture and following the second hand of her watch. Much sooner than usual, she turned away.

"Seven and a half minutes, Mrs. Babcock!" she announced, as though Mrs. Babcock had just broken a track record of long standing.

"Is that normal?"

"Close to it."

"What's normal?"

"You have to ask Dr. Vogel. I'm not permitted to discuss it."

"Why in the world *not?*"

"He's the doctor."

"*You're* the nurse."

"Four minutes is normal," she whispered, glancing around guiltily. "But you're down from twelve, honey. That's real fine!"

9

Divided Loyalties

□

Eddie's and my life after Worthley stood outside of time. Contrary to popular belief, there are really *three* kinds of people in the world: those who wear watches, those who don't wear watches, and those who sometimes do and sometimes don't. Eddie was firmly entrenched in the second category and was compulsively late in everything she did; I am in the third category, but that year I was decidedly watchless.

Our apartment was on Broadway in Cambridge, on the third floor of a decaying tenement that was slated for urban renewal some time in the next decade. The pipe to the gas stove leaked, so that we had to leave the kitchen window cracked, even in the winter as snow drifted in. We were limited to sponge baths because the shower leaked into the apartment below, which was occupied by a frazzled welfare mother of five who had enough problems without her plaster ceiling's collapsing as well. The narrow porch off the living room, which overlooked the busy trash-strewn street, was infested with squatters—pigeons who cooed and shat all day long. The entire place, advertised by its unscrupulous owner as "furnished," was fitted out with the rejects from some furniture store's Fire Damage Sale. The gas oven was so slow in lighting that it threatened to blow up the dreary linoleumed kitchen.

In short, it was squalid. Eddie and I loved it. We were finally living arm in arm, cheek by jowl, with The People. Was it our fault if all The

People in our neighborhood had applications in for the high rises in the redevelopment areas? Could we help it that they moved out as fast as they could, only to be replaced by people like ourselves? Were we to blame that the welfare mother below us scowled and guarded her small children behind her back when we passed on the stairs, muttering under her breath, "Filthy dykes"? I had to keep reminding myself that I was now officially a "lesbian." I felt that, although I now wore wheat jeans and turtlenecks and sandals and a braid like Eddie's, basically *I* hadn't changed. Faces glared as Eddie and I strolled to the Stop & Shop with our arms around each other; necks craned with outrage in movie theaters when we held hands. Public indifference to me had shifted to disapproval since I had left Worthley; but I was still me, whoever that might be.

Our only heat was an aging kerosene space heater in the living room, and the only really cozy spot was our bed with its endless layers of ratty quilts salvaged from trash cans and institutional blankets ripped off from Worthley as our parting gesture. Since we were paying our rent and meager expenses with my dividend checks, we had no appointments to keep. Consequently, we spent most of our time huddled in this bed, not particularly knowing or caring if it was day or night.

Eddie did, however, continue to play her guitar two nights a week at a coffee house in Cambridge, as she had when she was at Worthley. I became her groupie and sat alone at a dark corner table, listening to her protest songs and watching with pride as people admired her husky voice and her earthy good looks, which were amply evident in the black turtleneck and tights and skirt she wore for performances. At her breaks, we would sneak a joint together, hiding it under the table. We would get back to our dingy apartment at 3 A.M. or later and would sleep until late afternoon the next day. One day blended into another, and we lost all sense of the passage of time. I slipped into my majority—and into control of my trust fund—without even knowing it, until papers requiring my signature began arriving from lawyers and brokers.

In the process of looking them over and taking charge of "my" monies, a dilemma started nagging at me over the nature of my investments. Eddie and I, for all our languid lolling in bed, were also on the demonstration circuit. We had bought crash helmets and had put American flag decals on them, upside down. Like horse owners on the racing circuit, or football fans with season passes, we went to

every demonstration, large or small, that we happened to hear about
—peace marches, rent strikes, work slowdowns. Usually we took
picnic lunches, and we had gotten to know many of our fellow career
demonstrators quite well.

One gorgeous October afternoon we went to a war protest in
downtown Boston. The air was crisp, and the sun was hot, and colorful leaves skittered around on the pavement. We were all in high
spirits, even more so when we saw how unalone each of us was, how
packed the spacious courtyard was becoming. To the clerks looking
down from the towering office buildings and dropping shredded government documents as confetti, we must have looked like a palpitating
invasion of locusts.

The speaker, a former official in the attorney general's office who
had lost his position due to his vehement antiwar stand, was eloquent
on the topic of the futility of violence. Earnest young mothers with
sleeping babies in back packs nodded intent agreement. Students led
cheers at appropriate points. Suited businessmen flashed peace signs
to delighted young rabble rousers. It seemed impossible on that brilliant afternoon that peace and good will could *not* prevail among all
the peoples of the world; surely in a matter of days President Johnson
would bow to the will of The People and withdraw American troops
from southeast Asia. The crowds in the square, abasing themselves at
the feet of the gleaming glass and steel government buildings,
throbbed with brotherly love. And not the least Eddie and I, who
hadn't even brought our crash helmets, which at that time we reserved
for use on picket lines at construction sites. As I surveyed the babies
and the dogs and the mothers and the businessmen and the students
and the government workers leaning out their windows, a lump rose
in my throat. It was the same lump that used to rise there when, as
a child, I had recited the Lord's Prayer or sung "America the Beautiful." We could not fail! Eddie and I looked at each other, and then
threw our arms around each other and burst into tears of joy. How
sweet it was to be so right, and in such company!

The glow lasted all the way back to the apartment. The sun was
setting as we wearily climbed our dark dirty staircase, past the battered door behind which several children and their mother were
shouting abuse. Eddie and I gazed at each other expectantly and
walked hand in hand to our bed, trembling with moral and spiritual
uplift from the triumphant afternoon. We enjoyed a round of incredibly passionate sex, culminating in a breathtaking series of multiple

orgasms, triggered by the insertion of greased little fingers into each other's anus.

From Physiology 110, I knew that our inordinate response to this gimmick was merely a function of the reflex stretch mechanism of our anal sphincters. But I was striving mightily to forget much of what I had learned at Worthley in order to elevate my view of our love to a loftier plane than chemical secretions and genetically induced reflexes. Besides, things were going on between Eddie and me that Physiology 110 hadn't covered. For instance, the way in which our bodies, immersed in smells and sounds and sights and tastes, would suddenly lurch like cars going too slow for the gear they were in, until we were swept up out of the realm of physical sensation. Seconds or minutes or hours passed, we never knew or cared. Exciting stuff for a country girl, but sinister, too, as I lay scarcely breathing afterwards, speculating on its similarities to my plunge down the cliff from Clem's speeding Harley.

But on the whole, I had to admit that lovemaking with Eddie agreed with me, never mind what Mother would say. The goal being so much less apparent than in heterosexual encounters, more imagination was required. And after that evening's display of imagination, I decided that I had to come clean. I felt dread unhinging my joints. How could she ever lick me to orgasm again if she knew the real truth? True, Eddie felt that the wealth should be shared, starting with *my* wealth. But would she still want to share blood money? On the other hand, I knew I couldn't *not* tell her.

"Eddie?"

"Ummm?" she sighed, wrapping her arms around me from behind and burying her mouth in my neck just as Joe Bob had loved to do in the trunk of Doyle's Dodge.

"There's something I have to tell you."

"Ummm?"

"Are you listening, Ed? This is very important."

"Ummm? Can't it wait?" She nibbled my ear lobe.

"No, it can't. I have to tell you now. I can't stand it any longer." I was about to cry.

"Why, what's wrong, Ginny?"

"You know those papers I signed about my trust fund?"

"Ummm."

"Do you know where my money comes from, Eddie?"

"Where?" she asked with a yawn.

"Mostly from my father's factory, that's where." There! It was out. What Eddie did about it was up to her. At least I'd leveled with her.

"So what?" So what? Had I misunderstood Eddie's principles somewhere along the line? "So what?" Maybe there was no moral conflict in paying our expenses to antiwar marches with money generated by supplying explosives to that war? After all, what had Eddie been teaching me if not that logic à la Miss Head was flawed, that commitment and contradiction were the way to Truth? Perhaps the only conflict was in my own overrational brain?

"I didn't even know your father *had* a factory," Eddie murmured. "What does he make?"

Oh oh. So that was it. The truth *wasn't* out after all. "Explosives," I whispered in misery.

"You mean like for digging mines and building highways and stuff?"

"No, I mean like for shells and bombs. I mean like for Vietnam."

No sound or movement came from Eddie for a long time. Eventually I rolled over. Her face was frozen into a grimace.

"If you want to leave me, I can understand why," I said faintly. "I'm sorry, Eddie. I should have told you sooner. But I didn't really get the picture until I saw those papers."

Eddie, still grimacing, said nothing. "Can you ever love me again?" I wailed. "*Can* you?" Still she didn't answer. I looked at her closely. She had fallen asleep.

If that night I dared to hope that that was the end of the matter, the next morning I discovered I was sadly mistaken. When I got up around noon, Eddie was stalking through the living room muttering, "Jesus Christ. Jesus Christ."

She resolutely refused to look at me or speak to me. I mumbled humbly several times, "I'm *sorry*, Eddie."

Finally she demanded coldly, "Have you told anyone else about this?" I nodded no miserably. "You must tell *no one.* Do you understand? *No one.* My reputation could be ruined."

"You can count on me," I assured her gravely, as a pigeon pecked at the chipping putty around a broken storm window.

"Now! As I see it, you have to cash in your stocks and invest the money in a company that makes medical supplies or artificial limbs or something."

"I *can't.*"

"What do you mean you can't? They're yours, aren't they?"

"Yes, but I can't do anything with them until both my parents are dead. It's a tax gimmick. To escape inheritance taxes. Besides, a subsidiary of the same corporation in New Jersey *does* make medical supplies—plasma bottles."

"Well, that's *something,* I suppose," she said thoughtfully. "Oh *Jesus.*" She resumed her trek across the listing living room. "The *corruption* of it all is overwhelming. I'm so appalled that I can hardly bear looking at you, Ginny. I've been living on profits from companies that are fueling the war machine!"

"I'm sorry. I know it must make you feel so dirty. I'd give anything to have been able to spare you this, Eddie. I've hurt the woman I love. I can't bear it!" I burst into tears and collapsed onto the rickety couch, which in turn collapsed onto the floor.

I lay, weeping, on the faded flowered rug. Eddie squatted down like a baseball catcher and caressed my moist face. "There, there. Don't worry. We'll figure something out."

What we figured out was a trip to Tennessee to picket the factory and to confront the Major with his war crimes. If I couldn't divest myself of my stocks, I could at least funnel some stockholder input into the executive level.

As she surveyed the huge white-columned mansion, Eddie grumbled, "Jesus. It's downright feudal!" Maybelle, our cook, came rushing out and whirled me across the lawn in an embrace. I tried to offer her my hand in a gesture of dignified equality instead, having read disapproval in Eddie's face. But finally I gave in and whirled with Maybelle of my own accord.

"Law, yes!" Maybelle said to Eddie in her Power to the People T-shirt, "I done been wid de Babcocks eber since Miss Virginia was two foot tall! Law, I used to set her in mah lap an teach dat po li'l thing how to tie her shoes. . . . Why, Miss Ginny, she don't hardly know *nuthin* ole Maybelle ain't taught her. Why, I declare, iffen . . ." She went on and on, her accent getting thicker and thicker, thicker than I could remember its ever having been. I studied her black face closely and thought I detected malicious pleasure in her eyes. Whether the malice was directed at Eddie or at me, I couldn't be completely certain. Eddie was thoroughly scandalized.

Mother showed us to our rooms. "It's so nice to meet you, Edna. Ginny has written so many interesting things about you."

"Unh," Eddie grunted.

Mother had placed me in my old room, and Eddie across the hall in Jim's old room. Eddie had briefed me on how to handle this situation in a morally upright fashion.

"Mother," I announced, blushing scarlet, "Eddie and I will be sleeping in my room." There! I had done it! I had come out of the closet, and before my own mother!

Mother said gaily, "Fine, dear. Fine. You girls have a slumber party if you want to."

I was content to let the topic drop, but Eddie kicked me with her Goliath sandal. "Ah, Mother, Eddie and I will be—ah—sleeping together in my bed."

"Yes, of course," Mother said brightly. "That's fine, dear. Whatever suits you girls is fine with me."

Eddie shrugged.

The next day Eddie and I made a couple of signs; they read "Workers Unite! All Power to the People!" and "Tennessee Westwood Corp.: Fascist Flunkies to the Imperialist Pigs!" We drove in the Major's Jeep across the river to the plant and stationed ourselves in front of the chain-link fence and began to march back and forth with the signs. A security guard came out, studied the signs, and said, "I'm afraid you girls had better move along." Eddie bristled at being called a "girl."

"It's all right, I'm Major Babcock's daughter."

"Yeah. Sure you are," he said. I flashed a Shell credit card at him like an FBI plainclothesman and he said uncertainly, "Oh. Okay, Miss Babcock. Sorry."

Just then the noon whistle blasted. We dropped our signs to cover our ears, then picked them up just as the night shift streamed out the gates, heading for the parking lots. Several workers in their green twill work clothes studied the signs; most didn't notice them. I recognized faces here and there, people I'd been in high school with, people I just knew from a lifetime in the same town together.

Two young men were studying Eddie's sign. We sauntered over to them. "F—A—S—" one was saying. They blushed when we stopped in front of them, and glanced around nervously to see if anyone was noticing or caring that they were about to be sucked into conversation with two weird young women in Power to the People T-shirts who bore incomprehensible placards.

"Fascist," Eddie said for them.

"Fascist," one repeated with a dopey grin. "Whas that mean, anyhow?"

Eddie looked at him in disbelief. "Fascist? Ah—well, it means, like Hitler."

"Shoot!" one said, spitting on the sidewalk.

"How do you feel about what you're forced to make here?" Eddie asked diplomatically, as though the two men were dwarfs out of *Das Rheingold.* "Explosives for Vietnam."

"Oh, is that what they're for?"

"Yeh, dummy," the other said, laughing and poking him in the side.

"Shoot, I don't care," the first one said. "I jes work here, thas all. They pay me an I do like they says."

"Well, *I* care," the second one said.

Eddie brightened. "Yes?"

"I got me a brother fightin over there, an I aim to keep his guns loaded, I can tell you that!"

"Oh," said Eddie. "Well, do you know anyone who *doesn't* like making stuff for Vietnam?"

The two looked at each other questioningly. "If they is any such a one," the second one said, "*I'd* better not hear about him."

We slunk off, in search of more cooperative prey. We cornered a skinny, meek-looking middle-aged man. He was standing by the chain fence, which had several strands of barbed wire across the top. When he saw us bearing down upon him, he tried to sidle away, but we had him surrounded.

"Look," he whispered nervously, holding up his hands to fend us off, "I don't want no trouble. I got me five kids."

With relief I spotted Harry from Building Maintenance, whom I hadn't seen since the summer I worked in the factory. He recognized me as well, in spite of my current disguise as savior of The People, and waved wildly. "Lor, I guess it's been two year since I seed you! I like to not knowed you." He nodded at my wheat jeans and T-shirt and the braid down the middle of my back, Red Chinese-like.

"Harry, tell me the truth now," I said. "How do you feel about making bombs for the war?"

He sighed wearily. "Well, honey, how I feel is that hit beats the hell out of them coal pits up at Sow Gap."

"But *Harry!*"

"But I ain't *makin* em, honey! I'm jes maintenance. Anyhow, if your daddy says hit's right, then hit's right by me, too."

"*Speak* of the devil," Eddie drawled. The Major in his pin-striped suit came marching toward us at an incredible clip. I automatically flinched.

"What *are* you girls *doing?*" I blushed and shrugged sheepishly. "Virginia! If you and your friend don't dispose of those signs and get out of here immediately . . . I'll cut off your dividend checks!"

"You *can't!* They're in *my* name now!"

"I can do whatever I please. You seem to forget that I run this place."

"Then you can make something else besides bombs?" I asked hopefully, not knowing that I had punched his button.

"What I am doing here *happens* to be essential to national security, my dear child. A strong offense is the best defense. I know that *some* people"—he glanced contemptuously at Eddie—"would like to bring this nation to its knees and hand the keys to its portals over to the Communists, but *I* am not one of them." I decided that this was not the time to point out that he was mixing his metaphors. "I fought too long and too hard against Hitler not to have learned that you can't allow tyranny of any political stripe to get a toe hold. Besides, what's manufactured in this plant isn't my decision. Those decisions are made at headquarters in Boston. So why don't you two hop the next plane back to where you came from with your idiot signs and your half-baked political opinions?"

"Bastard!" Eddie hissed as we slunk over to the Jeep. "Christ, what a bastard!"

Back in Boston, Eddie and I concluded that the best thing for my political development would be to sever all ties with my reactionary family. They were obviously the source of all my neuroses and bourgeois political attitudes. It was best never to get in touch with them again, thereby liberating myself with one deft hack from the net of capitalist hang-ups they had cast over me.

"You can't allow your roots to become ruts," Eddie announced. "Or routs."

I got a Standard & Poor's sheet on Westwood Chemical Corporation and calculated the percentage of profits stemming from the Hullsport plant. Then I deducted that amount from our spending money as the quarterly dividend checks wandered in, and sent donations to free schools and people's clinics and minority liberation groups throughout Boston. Let admirable ends justify nefarious means, we decided. Eddie took further comfort in the fact that we were boycotting one aspect of the corrupt death-dealing male power structure that was perpetrating all the misery in the world by seeking our sexual fulfillment elsewhere.

One April evening Eddie came galloping up the stairs. She stood in the doorway panting, distress spread over her expressive face.

"What's wrong?" I asked nervously from the desk where I sat writing a check to a struggling head shop.

"The coffee house is being torn down to build a bank!" She lowered herself gingerly onto the sagging couch.

"You're kidding? That's awful!"

"But I'm afraid there's more."

"What?"

"This dump we call home has been condemned. We have to get out by next month."

"*What?* Where are we supposed to go?" We sat staring at each other, perplexed. Our cozy world was tumbling down.

When the initial shock had worn off, we huddled over my checkbook and the Apartments for Rent section of the *Globe.* According to our calculations, either we would have to cut off our blood money donations to the Day-Glo poster shops and related enterprises and spend it for rent, or one of us would have to find a job.

We both looked around halfheartedly for work for a couple of weeks. Singers of protest songs weren't in demand by that time, acid rock having taken over. And without a college degree, I could find only a waitress job at Waldorf's Cafeteria in Harvard Square, where I had eaten Thanksgiving dinner my freshman year. Eddie was trying to persuade me that the job was a worthy one, would expose me to contact with The People, would perhaps correct some of the unfortunate petit bourgeois prejudices I'd inherited from my impossible parents, would inestimably enhance my political education. I resisted because I felt incapable any longer of keeping to a schedule. And what had Eddie been teaching me if not to honor my feelings?

With two weeks to go before we would be evicted, we decided to ignore this impasse and visit two friends of Eddie's in Vermont. They had been seniors at Worthley when she was a sophomore and had been editors on the paper when Eddie had been a reporter. Eddie credited them with having "politicized" her. She bore them the same sentimental affection that I did Clem Cloyd for having deflowered me.

Both women, having been social workers in Newark, were now living with some other people on a farm near a town called Stark's Bog.

Mona was tall and emaciated, with wide feverish eyes which she shielded behind purple-tinted goggle lenses that made her eye sockets look bruised. She wore her black hair in a Prince Valiant cut with long bangs. She had a way of hunching her back and tucking in her chin and gazing through her purple lenses that made her look a little like a vulture.

Atheliah was also tall, but was broad and muscled as well, with frizzy red hair that shot out like solar flares during an eclipse. She was jovial, laughing and smiling almost constantly in a way that narrowed her eyes to slits. They both embraced Eddie—Mona gravely and Atheliah boisterously. They lived with five men and one other woman in a crumbling white farmhouse which was attached by a sagging ell to a huge barn. In the barn, when our tour took us there, along with several decades' worth of trampled manure were a couple of Holsteins and some scavenging hens.

The inside of the house looked like Coney Island the day after the Fourth of July. Clothes and bedding and books and papers and dishes and sleeping bodies were strewn everywhere. The damp interior walls were coated with a bright green mold.

It was planting season, and Eddie and I spent most of our first afternoon helping the brothers and sisters plant the seeds in carefree lines across the freshly tilled garden soil. The sun was hot, and clouds of moisture steamed up from the soggy, thawing fields. Sluggish flies buzzed languidly in the grass; and in the distance, treed foothills tinged with the chartreuse of new leaves rose up in layer upon layer.

Dinner was a murky soup, filled with dark sodden clumps that looked like leaves from the bottom of a compost pile and that tasted like decomposing seaweed, and whole grain bread which you needed diamond-tipped teeth to chew. Afterward seven of us lay around on the living room debris passing joints as two mangy barn cats climbed up on the dining table and licked our dishes clean for us.

"What's *happened* to you?" Eddie demanded of Mona and Atheliah. "You two used to be the most socially concerned people I knew. I modeled myself after you. After you left Worthley, I tried to run the paper the same way you had. Articles about world affairs and stuff and not just coming-out-party portraits. And fasts for Roxbury busing and stuff. I don't get this earth trip you're on."

"I got tired," Mona said languidly, holding the last quarter inch of the most recent joint between her thumb and index fingernails and sucking the smoke into her lungs through clenched teeth with a hiss. Holding her breath until her face turned a distressing purple, she squashed the glowing tip on her boot sole and leaned back and closed her alarming dark dilated eyes.

"So it's a cop-out, then? A sort of rural rest home for fucked-over radicals?" Eddie asked.

"No, not at all," Atheliah corrected her, in a brisk voice like Julia Child's on "The French Chef" just after she's dropped a roast on the floor and tossed it back on the platter. "We're trying to live our theories. Do you know who paid my salary when I was organizing in Newark? HEW, that's who! You can't work to overthrow a system, and live off it at the same time. When the host dies, so do its parasites. First earn an honest living side by side with The People. Then talk to me about death-dealing societies and inequity and injustice! Anything else is schizie."

Mona nodded in agreement, letting out her smoke in a great gush of breathlessness. She wove into the kitchen and fumbled around in the freezer and returned with a plastic container of frozen Magic Mushrooms. " 'Teonanactl,' the Aztecs called them," Mona muttered, litanylike, as she passed them. " 'God's flesh,' the key to communion with the Deity."

Hesitantly I took one of the icy chunks and pondered the topic of eating God, turning the mushroom in my fingers and staring at it with distaste.

"What's the matter? Don't you do drugs?" Mona asked incredulously, poised to cross me off their Christmas card list.

"Of course she does," Eddie assured them.

My upbringing won out over my eagerness to please Eddie: I didn't trust pushers; I'd read that Magic Mushrooms were often regular mushrooms dipped in hog tranquilizer. If I ate this thing, I would die a horrible death on the floor of this remote Vermont farmhouse. Feigning a bite, I held it down by my side and offered it to the cats, who sniffed it and then wanted nothing to do with it either.

Eddie was clearly impressed by Atheliah's line of reasoning. She looked thoughtful for the rest of our visit and asked a lot of questions about gardening and animal care and land prices.

"Are Mona and Atheliah, like—simpatico, sexually?" I asked Eddie as we slouched in our bus seats on the way back to Boston. Our knees were propped on the seat backs in front of us. Soggy meadows and evergreen forests and mountain peaks with faint remnants of snow flashed by the bus windows.

"Well, they're not asimpatico, which is all that matters, isn't it?"

"What does *that* mean?"

"They're not lovers, if that's what you're asking. Neither of them is interested in sex with anybody, as far as I can tell. I think that's the bond between them."

"How dull."

"Do you think so? I find it refreshing." We glared at each other with hostility, at having come to need each other physically.

"How did they come to be so blessed?"

"Well, I remember Mona had this—male friend when she was at Worthley. A medical student he was. She used to meet him in the morgue when he was on night duty at some Boston hospital, and they'd make love all night on a stretcher in the office."

"At least they didn't have to worry about getting caught," I said, weak with distaste. A morgue was almost as creepy a site for sex as a bomb shelter.

"Ah, but they *did* get caught! She became pregnant. I remember the day she told me. We were sitting in the newspaper office correcting the proofs of an editorial on the Free Speech Movement, and all of a sudden she collapsed on the table and started weeping. I couldn't believe it. I'd always thought of Mona as this paragon of restraint. Well, it all came out in a great gush of confession. And then she sat up and blew her nose and set about trying to blot the tear-soaked proofs. 'What are you going to do?' I asked. 'Leave school and get married of course,' she said curtly. Well, she disappeared one weekend, and then returned looking all gray and haggard. And she never said another word about it. She was on my hall, and as far as I know, she never went out on a date again—not with her medical student or with anyone else. I never felt at liberty to ask her about it."

"Couldn't you have asked Atheliah?"

"No. I never felt I could. For all I knew, Atheliah didn't even know about it. Anyhow, it wasn't the sort of thing you *asked* Atheliah. She's probably the only twenty-six-year-old virgin I know."

"Has she *told* you she is?"

"No, of course not. I'm just, like, speculating."

Back in Boston we continued our search for jobs, or for an apartment we could afford on my unsupplemented dividend checks. Our search took us one afternoon to an area of Boston I'd never seen before. Even though it was a sunny afternoon, the streets we were walking down were dark and damp, permanently shielded from the sun by towering expressway ramps overhead. Trash cans were overflowing; and the facades of the formerly elegant townhouses, with crumbling plaster cupids in their cornices, were grimy and bleak. A blanket of damp exhaust fumes lay over the section.

Eddie was unusually quiet as we searched for an address listed in the paper as containing a cheap two-room apartment. As we passed a flight of concrete steps that descended into a dark basement, Eddie said grimly, "That was the site of my conception."

"What are you talking about?" I asked, staring with horror at a drunk collapsed in a nearby doorway and trying to picture this as my new neighborhood.

"Down in that cellar. That's where my father, whoever he was, raped my mother."

I asked carefully, "Uh, how do you know?" We stopped and stared down the grungy steps and into the recessed doorway, which was strewn with empty liquor bottles and broken glass.

She laughed bitterly. "How do I *know?* It's the family shrine, that's how. My mother used to bring me here and point it out when I was a teen-ager. As an instructive exercise about the male of the species, in whom I was exhibiting an inordinate interest at the time."

"You mean you *lived* around here?"

"Five blocks east," she said with a defiant look. "Does that appall you, Scarlett?" She'd taken to calling me Scarlett, after Scarlett O'Hara in *Gone With the Wind*, every time I displayed my southern refinement.

"I—I—didn't know."

She sighed with disgust. "Does it *matter* where I grew up? You grew up in a mansion with slaves, and I grew up in a slum. So what?"

Feeling that she was being unusually charitable about my feudal origins, I nodded in eager agreement. We stood frozen to the spot, gazing down the steps, picturing the rape scene with loathing for the male animal in our hearts.

"He held a knife to her throat," Eddie added in a choked voice. "She was fifteen. On her way home from school late one afternoon in early spring. She wanted to be a hairdresser, but she had to drop out of school when she turned out to be pregnant with me."

"Couldn't she have had an abortion?"

"Are you kidding? In 1944? In Massachusetts? With no bread?"

"She's not very old then. Does she still live around here?"
Eddie nodded.

"Maybe we should go see her. I'd like to meet your mother. After all, you've met mine. And it *is* a rather crucial factor in a person's life, as we all know from Psychology 101."

"You *wouldn't* like to meet my mother."

"Oh, but I *would*."

"No," Eddie said abruptly. "I haven't seen her for a year or more. Families are a real bummer."

"*Please.*"

"*No!*" I looked at her with surprise. Her face was twitching with suppressed emotion. "We've got to get out of here," she said, grabbing my hand and dragging me back the way we'd come.

A month later we were living in a rented prefab log cabin on a farm adjacent to Mona's and Atheliah's. The cabin sat on a hill overlooking an eighteen-acre beaver pond. A wide meadow of timothy stretched from the cabin to the thicket of cattails at the pond edge. Out of the pond pointed the dead gray branches of hundreds of drowned trees. And at one end, in an area cleared of the skeletal trees, was the mud lodge where the beavers lived.

The evening of our arrival, with our possessions in a U-Haul truck, Eddie and I sat in rush-seated rocking chairs on the front porch. I was leaning back, my feet propped on a log railing. Eddie sat behind me gravely smoothing and rebraiding my hair. The sun had set in a red smear behind the tree-covered cliffs that formed a backdrop to the pond, and a dense mist was rising up from the pond surface and enveloping the gray trunks.

Eddie and I sighed simultaneously with contentment as she stroked my frizzy hair into orderly plaitable bundles.

"What do you think?" I asked.

"I think we're finally getting our heads straight."

But of course we'd only just arrived. Compared to Broadway in Cambridge, our rutted dirt road in Stark's Bog, Vermont, was the end of the earth. Little did we know that we'd moved onto a battlefield. But the battles came later. Our first month was untainted bliss. We felt we'd come home at last, only now realizing how far astray we'd gone. We had renounced our pasts totally by not leaving a forwarding address at the Cambridge post office (except of course with the West-wood Chemical Corporation, so that they would know where to send the checks).

The cabin stood on the site of an old farmhouse, which had burned down. It had been built only a few years earlier as a summer retreat and winter ski house by a stockbroker in New York City. It was unclear why he was willing to rent such a slice of heaven, though it became clearer as time went on. But the original farmhouse had belonged to several generations of working farmers, so that the barn nearby was in good condition. We rushed out and bought a Guernsey milking cow named Minnie and half a dozen red and black Rhode Island hens and a vicious black and white Barred Rock rooster. All these we ensconced in the huge moldy old barn, the framework of which was massive hand-hewn pine beams. We ordered a beehive and nailed it together and dumped a package of bees from Kentucky into it. We placed the hive in an old apple orchard behind the house; the blossoms had recently fallen off, and tiny green apples were forming. The growing season well under way, we dug and planted a hasty garden, reading instructions from a manual.

We had left behind The Family and The City. The plan now, according to Eddie, our resident theoretician, was to leave behind the American capitalist-imperialist economy altogether. We would grow and make almost all our material requirements—our food, our clothes, our fuel. Inconvenient expenses like taxes we would cover from our maple sugaring operation in early spring, there being a vast sugar bush and a sugar shack filled with all the necessary equipment on a high hill behind the cabin. By saving my dividend checks, we could soon afford a down payment on the farm, which was for sale at a ludicrously low price, for reasons which too soon became apparent to us. And eventually we might even be able to wean ourselves entirely from that corporate enemy of The People, the Westwood Chemical Corporation. We concluded that very soon we would be able authentically to cast our lot with The People.

As far as representatives of The People went in Stark's Bog, we didn't know any. We had been into town several times in the old Ford pickup owned by Mona and Atheliah to buy supplies. As we clattered and jounced down the hill on which our farms sat, we could see Stark's Bog below us. Frame buildings clustered around three sides of the bog that gave the town its name. In most parts of Vermont could be seen houses of brick and stone, built to last for generations. In Stark's

Bog, however, every house was frame, except Ira Bliss's stone one. Apparently none of the early settlers except the Blisses had planned to stay if they could help it.

In the winter, according to Mona and Atheliah, the marsh mud in the bog froze over. In the spring, it became a sea of muck, and animals that strayed into it were trapped and sucked under, like mammoth elephants in prehistoric asphalt pits. Now, however, it was summer, and the marsh grasses rustled. The mud had grown a coat of brilliant green slime. Mosquitoes teemed in fetid pools.

Driving into town we would first pass the Dairy Delite soft ice cream stand. The Stark's Boggers would cluster here after supper to buy root beer floats or butterscotch sundaes. Then they would drive or walk to the bog to watch the struggles of whatever animals were sinking in the goo offshore. Or if it was close to 6:27, they would amble to the train track and wait for the New York–Montreal special to roar through. (It had never stopped there. In fact, passengers tended to pull down their window shades as they passed through, to the disappointment of the frantically waving town children.)

Athough Stark's Bog township actually included the bog and the surrounding hills and farms, the town proper consisted of one road, which came from St. Johnsbury and led to a border crossing into Quebec. Where the road passed through town, it was lined with a feed store, a hardware store, a hotel where hunters stayed in the fall, an IGA grocery store, a gun shop, a taxidermy parlor, a funeral home, a farm equipment franchise, and a snow machine showroom called Sno Cat City. All these were housed in buildings from the early 1800's with colonial cornices and returns and doorways, which were pleasing in their simplicity. Pleasing to everyone but the Stark's Boggers, who were sick to death of them and had done their best to tear them down or cover them over with fluorescent plastic and neon tubing and plate glass and gleaming chrome. Each businessman yearned to raze the clapboard and beam structure on his premises and erect a molded plastic- and aluminum-sided showroom in its place. Sno Cat City, for instance, owned by Ira Bliss IV, had a huge orange mountain lion springing out from its facade; it being summer, row after row of gleaming yellow Honda trail bikes sat out front. Likewise, the goal of each Stark's Bog householder was to knock down or sell the despised frame colonial his family had infested for centuries, and to throw up a prefab ranch house that would be airtight, with everything working properly.

We found all this profoundly disturbing. It indicated a willingness to participate in modern American society. We didn't approve at all, and so we went into Stark's Bog as little as possible. When we did, the Stark's Boggers eyed us—as we strolled from the feed store to the hardware store in our Off the Pigs T-shirts, with our braids swishing behind us in unison—with all the enthusiasm of Incas inspecting newly arrived Spaniards. We learned from Mona that they referred to us all as the Soybean People due to the fact that we bought fifty-pound sacks of soybeans at the feed store for our own consumption, not for our animals. Eddie had decided that it was politically reprehensible of us not to be vegetarians when each fattened steer starved five Third World citizens. "Who *needs* the decaying flesh of festering corpses?" she asked, as she burned all our cookbooks containing meat recipes in the wood stove. "We should be able to make it on our own life force without holding innocent animals in bondage."

It didn't take long for things to start going sour—not more than a couple of blissful sunlit months. One problem was that the regimens of farming didn't fit our lifestyle. One morning Eddie went to the barn to collect some fresh eggs for breakfast, while I put a cast iron skillet on the burner of the wood cookstove and fed the coals from the night before into a modest fire. Intending to scramble the eggs, I cracked one on the rim of a bowl. A foul odor wafted up to me. I opened the shell and dumped its contents into the bowl. It was tinged with brown and stank. "Uh, Ed, I think they're rotten." She stalked over and peered into the bowl and nearly gagged. I broke open a couple more that were the same shade of murky brown.

"Maybe collecting them once a week isn't enough?" I suggested.

"Shit! I'm *damned* if I'm going to spend my whole fucking life collecting eggs!" She collapsed in a captain's chair in front of the stove.

"It wouldn't take more than a few minutes every other day if we took turns," I pointed out.

"Turns! Schedules! Lists! Did anyone ever tell you that you have an accountant mentality, Ginny? I suppose you'd like to mark on a calendar when to have sex, too?"

I hadn't found it easy sharing a bathroom with a member of The Elect all these years, and my accumulated resentments poured out in response to this unwarranted attack. "An *accountant mentality!* Well, it's a goddam good thing that *somebody* in this place does! If I weren't around to pay your bills, Eddie, you'd be out on your ass so fast—"

"There!" Eddie said triumphantly, gesturing toward me with her hand. "It's out at last! I knew it all along! I *knew* that deep down you resented sharing your fucking blood money with me. You grasping bourgeois types are all the same. I can read you like a book!"

"Oh *yeah?*" I screamed, standing over her, a quivering mass of bourgeois rage. "I don't notice *you* making any efforts to earn honest money, Miss Holier Than Thou! You seem perfectly content to let me pay *your* way with *my* despised blood money!"

"*Your* money, *my* money! Who gives a shit about your goddam fucking money? Shove it up your ass, Scarlett." She slouched lower in her chair and glowered.

"Get out! *Get out,* you freeloader! *I'm* paying the rent, this is *my* place. And I don't need you around calling me 'grasping' and 'bourgeois' while you live off me, like the cock-sucking parasite you are!"

I had never before let the phrase "cock-sucking" pass my lips, though I had heard it often enough during my days with Clem. Eddie looked startled, but no more startled than I. We stared at each other in mutual shock.

"So *that's* it," Eddie said, nodding her head knowingly.

"What's it?"

"You know as well as I do from Psychology 101, Ginny, that there's more at stake here than rotten eggs or who pays the rent. And I've just realized what it is."

"What *is* it?"

"You're tired of me, Ginny. You want a man. A cock," she added with distaste.

"No! That's not true!"

"I've been expecting it. You don't need to deny it. It was bound to happen sooner or later. You've just been playing around with me. Basically you're as hetero as they come."

"But you're *wrong,* Eddie. You're all I want. With one functioning lover, what would I want with any more? After all, how much sex can one person endure?" I knelt beside her chair and began massaging her throbbing temples.

"It's no use," Eddie said glumly, pushing my hands away. "What's done is done."

"But nothing's *done,* Eddie," I protested with a laugh. "What do I want with a man? I've *had* men. You're so far superior as a lover, and in every other way, that it's ridiculous even to talk about it." I kissed her on the mouth tenderly. This was followed by an embrace. "You're crazy, Eddie," I whispered fondly in her ear.

"I guess I am."

Lacking eggs, I dished us up bowls of molded soybean salad left over from the night before. There was a great deal left over, almost the entire salad, in fact. We ate in silence at the table, which overlooked the beaver pond. I kept trying not to breathe as I ate so that I wouldn't be able to taste very well.

"Delicious," Eddie said firmly, trying to convince herself.

"Delicious," I echoed faintly. "And *full* of protein."

The summer sun shone down bright and hot on the pond. Shimmering heat waves rose up all around the cabin. Bees bumbled in the weed flowers that were thigh-high in the yard.

"I was wondering, Eddie," I said between hastily swallowed bites, "if we maybe shouldn't rent a power tiller for the garden down at the hardware store." The garden we had so carefully planted was now overrun with weeds. We had to do something quick—either get rid of the weeds, or get used to them in lieu of tomatoes.

"Are you *kidding?* A *power tiller?* Are you out of your mind? You don't actually want to patronize an economy that turns The People into interchangeable cogs in some vast assembly line, do you? You couldn't possibly want to participate in a system of production that makes medical supplies with one hand and bombs with the other. I mean, that's why we're up here, isn't it, to wean ourselves from that sort of hypocrisy, to become honest working-class people? Well, isn't it?"

I said nothing. I wasn't at all sure that that was why I was in Vermont. I reviewed my motives and concluded that I was mostly here because Eddie wanted to be, for reasons of her own, and I wanted to be with Eddie. Once again I was shamelessly allowing myself to be defined by another person. I was afraid it would sound at best hopelessly bougie (Eddie's shorthand for "bourgeois") if I admitted this—and counterrevolutionary at worst. So instead I asked meekly, "Yes, but what about the weeds?"

"We'll pull them by hand," Eddie announced grandly, "like *every* person in the Third World does!"

That afternoon, shirtless, sweat pouring out of our hairy armpits, we pulled weeds in the hot sun for about fifteen minutes, clearing a small corner of the tomato patch. Our bodies clammy with sweat, we lay under an apple tree and smoked a joint.

"If tomatoes can't prevail against the weeds, they don't deserve to live," Eddie concluded. "To pull the weeds would be to weaken the tomatoes and make them dependent on us."

"Maybe it's too late. I think they're already corrupted. They appear to need us."

The apples hanging above us were tinged with pink. Because we had failed to prune the trees or to control the insects, they were tiny and deformed and riddled with worm holes. We turned over on our stomachs so that we wouldn't have to look at yet another tribute to our ineptitude.

"We may not be freeing up our former food supplies for shipment to the Third World," I said, "but we're sure providing one hell of a feast for the area insects."

When Eddie looked at me, I knew that my remark hadn't been amusing, it had been reactionary. "What do you expect?" she demanded. "We're just picking up on all this soil shit. We'll get it together for next summer."

We passed the joint and became less and less glum. We glanced off and on at the beehive under a neighboring tree. At least we would have honey. We had left the bees almost entirely alone, in keeping with our policy of letting things fend for themselves. Only the bees had come through under this regime. They were rushing in and out with loads of nectar and pollen. Talk about accountant mentalities. . . .

"We should do more hives next year," Eddie said, yawning. "That's my kind of project." She rolled over and wrapped her arms around me and nibbled my neck.

Eddie and I went one day to Mona's and Atheliah's for an autumnal equinox party. The plan was that we would all help them harvest their crops, and then we would have a big feed. I took soybean croquettes creole as our contribution. When we arrived at their crumbling farmhouse, a dozen people in various stages of undress were lolling around in the weed patch that was their front lawn. I recognized about half the people as being in Mona's and Atheliah's group. The others were from nearby farms. Marijuana smoke hung around the group like a London pea-soup fog. A woman in a long Indian shirt with hair to her waist was plucking a dulcimer and singing a Kentucky coal mining song with a Brooklyn accent: "I hope when I'm gone and the ages shall roll,/ My body will blacken and turn into coal./ Then I'll look from the door of my heavenly home/ And pity the miner digging my bones/ Where it's dark as a dungeon, damp as the dew,/ Where the danger is double, the pleasures are few,/ Where the rain never falls and the sun never shines/ It's dark as a dungeon way down in the mines." I felt a passing seizure of nostalgia for the mines of Appalachia that I had never known. Genes, no doubt. The collective experience of my forebears encoded within each of my cells.

A shirtless man with a Simon Legree mustache was silk-screening "Power to the People" in white on his dark blue T-shirt. Atheliah was stirring something in a big cast iron pot that sat in the middle of a small fire. A naked boy baby was tottering around with his arms outstretched for his mother, whom he couldn't locate. I handed my earthenware dish to Mona, who lifted the lid and sniffed and said, "Soybeans. Far out."

After a while a few people wandered out to the corn patch, which was almost as full of weeds as our tomato patch. Eddie sat down next to the woman with the dulcimer and started harmonizing. I went out to the corn patch to help pick. We ripped the ears off the stalks, shucked them, and tossed them in a cart. They were mostly four inches long and etched with brown worm tracks.

Halfway through the patch, Laverne, a woman in Mona's house, found a stunted Hubbard squash that was about the size and shape of a small football. Laverne was statuesque. There was no other word for her. Her shapely hips and large breasts strained the seams of her T-shirt and jeans. She had long blond naturally curly hair and blue eyes. In another era she would have been a movie starlet, a model for Rubens. She held up her squash triumphantly.

"A football!" gasped a bearded man with bleary eyes, who looked like Sherman on his march through Georgia. He grabbed the squash, faded back, and passed it to another man, who wore nothing but jeans, which were too large for him and were bunched together and held up with a belt fashioned from a silk rep tie.

"Keep-away," he suggested. "Shirts against the skins." We glanced around. Five of us wore shirts; three men were shirtless.

Laverne threw off her T-shirt with one smooth upward movement. "I'll be a skin!"

Everyone stood transfixed, staring with awe at her magnificent brown breasts, which were very tanned and evidently accustomed to exposure. Trying to pretend that we hadn't been staring, that we all saw bare bosoms this breathtaking every day, that the female chest was no big deal to people as sexually liberated as we, we began a frantic game of keep-away through the corn patch, trampling the juicy green stalks and passing and handing off the squash as we went. Everyone was clandestinely sneaking glimpses of Laverne's breasts, bouncing firmly as she ran and gleaming bronze under the September sun.

The game got progressively rougher, and soon people were tackling each other and grappling in the dirt, over the squash. At one point I lay trying to catch my breath after a savage tackle by General Sherman. As I picked myself up, I saw that the game had moved from the garden and into the high grass. Laverne, her jeans hanging on her hips just above her pubic hair, was dancing in place signaling to the man with the tie belt to throw her the squash. Her arms were raised high over her head, accentuating the narrowness of her waist. Her breasts were shaking in place like Jell-O.

The squash was flying through the air. Laverne leapt up to catch it. As she did, she was hit from three sides by male tacklers. The squash sailed over her head and smashed open, spilling its orange guts on the grass. Laverne herself landed on her back in the dirt with her jeans to her knees.

I watched in amazement as the bearded man threw himself on her and started lunging his hips into hers. I heard her gasping and shrieking. Shortly, he rolled off and another man climbed on, like a cowboy trying to ride a bronco.

I glanced back toward the house. A couple of people watched indifferently. No one seemed concerned. But from where I stood, with my mouth hanging open, it looked for all the world like what Clem used to call a gang bang. They were like a pack of mongrels balling a bitch in heat. Laverne was being raped and no one was helping! I ran closer, speculating that she had perhaps been asking for it.

By the time I was ten yards away, I could see that her legs were sprawled open and her whole luscious body was smeared with dirt and sweat and semen. I could also hear what she was screaming: "Faster! Faster! Don't stop *now*, you mother fucker! Oh mother of Christ! Don't *stop!*" Her body was arcing up off the ground and twitching spasmodically, like a frog's leg hooked into an electric current. Three men lay in panting heaps next to her, like bees after stinging.

I stopped running to her assistance and stood frozen to the spot. As I watched, blood rushed to my face. My nipples began tingling with excitement. I realized I wanted to join the fray, but whether on top of Laverne or underneath the men I was no longer certain. Divided loyalties.

I turned around and walked slowly back toward the house, breathing deeply to quell my beast.

I sat down next to Eddie, who was scowling. ". . . really disgusting," Mona was saying.

"Revolting," Eddie agreed, looking at me. But I said nothing.

Later Eddie and I passed by Atheliah's cast iron pot and got a bowl of soup. "Dr. Dekleine's Victory Soup," Atheliah informed us. "Brewer's yeast, powdered milk, and toasted soy flour. Delicious. And packed with protein."

We sat on the steps, and Eddie said casually, "You liked it, didn't you?"

"Liked what?"

"Laverne's charming number in the corn patch."

"Oh, that."

"I saw you standing there watching and getting off on it."

"I thought they were raping her. I was worried."

"You don't need to worry about Laverne. It's *you* I'm worried about."

"*Me?*"

"Admit it. You loved it. You wanted to be right in there with them. Didn't you?"

"It occurred to me."

"I knew it! You're tired of me!"

"I'm not," I assured her without conviction.

"Can I help it if I don't have a penis?"

"Of course not," I said wearily. "I've told you that it doesn't matter to me. There are all sorts of compensations to being with you instead of a man."

"Compensations? *Compensations?* Go ahead, Scarlett. Go drag one of those young studs on his macho trip out into the woods with you! I dare you to! You'll come crawling back to me in minutes! Go on!"

"Maybe I will." Under Eddie's abuse, I was becoming more interested in the idea all the time.

That night we walked back to our cabin in an icy silence, me with the crusted soybean croquette dish under my arm. We climbed into bed and turned our backs on each other.

Later that night I woke up being caressed by Eddie. Warm tears were dripping from her eyes and onto my bare chest. "Don't leave me, Ginny. Please don't. I couldn't stand it if I knew you were with a man. I get sick just thinking about it. Don't do it to us."

Reflexively, I took her in my arms, and we kissed and held each other. She parted my knees and began stroking me. On the verge of orgasm, I felt something hard and cold slide into me and start moving back and forth. It felt fantastic. Curiosity finally quelling lust, I sat up and said, "What *are* you doing, Eddie?" I turned on the light.

She smiled sheepishly and held up a greased cucumber. I looked at her with horror. "It's all right," she assured me. "It's organically grown."

The incident with Laverne, as unimpressed as people had seemed by it at the time, had repercussions far beyond those on Eddie's and my relationship. For one thing, Mona and Atheliah moved in with us the following week.

"We didn't want to interfere with Laverne's honeymoon," Mona said with distaste as we sat in captain's chairs around our wood stove the night of their arrival. The autumn air was chilly, and we had a small fire going.

"You mean—she's there with all those men just . . . ?" Eddie asked with uncharacteristic delicacy. As Mona nodded with a sardonic smile, Eddie shuddered. "Well, I can certainly understand your leaving. You're welcome to live with us for as long as you like."

"Be fair, Mona," Atheliah said. "It wasn't just Laverne. This has been building up for a long time." Atheliah was sharpening her ax on a whetstone, testing the blade with her callused thumb. Occasionally she'd put it down to smoke a cigarette, which she'd hold between her thumb and index finger, cupping the glowing butt in her huge hand.

Mona nodded in agreement. She was smoking a joint, had inhaled deeply and was holding her breath. Her face was turning dark red, like a child's in a tantrum. Her bruised-looking eyes were beginning to glaze over behind her purple lenses.

"It got to be a total turn-off," Atheliah continued. "They wanted to fart around in the garden all day and come in to find that the womenfolk had hot meals waiting for them."

"*No!*" said Eddie. She picked up her chair and moved it behind mine. Sitting with a knee on either side of my chair, she began unbraiding my hair carefully.

"Yes," Atheliah confirmed. "Or one of them would say, peremptorily, 'Mona?' And would point to his cup to indicate that he wanted more tea. It was totally unreal."

"I can't believe it," Eddie said.

"I know, but it's true," Atheliah insisted. "They're on a real macho trip over there—me Tarzan, you Jane."

"What it comes down to," Mona said in a gush of exhaled smoke, "is that Atheliah and I just need a larger life space to work in. Laverne gets her rocks off on this macho stuff, but it's a total turn-off for us."

"Turn-off isn't the word for it," Eddie said with disgust. She was brushing out my tangled hair with short sharp brush strokes.

"It's not their fault," I suggested, speaking from personal experience. "It's how they were brought up, with their masochistic mothers hovering over them anticipating their every need. They're macho, I'm bougie. We can't help ourselves."

"That's cool," Mona agreed, hunched over with her elbows on her chair arms and her dark hair hanging in her eyes. "But at what point do the obnoxious personality traits that have survived your childhood start being your own responsibility, rather than your parents'?"

We all sat meditating upon this question and listening to the hypnotic grinding whir of Atheliah's ax on the whetstone. Eddie got up and shoved a log into the stove. When she sat back down, she began to smooth my long mass of hair, which crackled with electricity. A window rattled in its frame, and a few flakes of early snow whirled past. The effect of the grinding fell somewhere between a back rub and fingernails skittering across a blackboard.

"Jesus," Mona sighed, sinking lower in her chair and sticking her feet out straight. "I'm really getting off on that grinding. It's enough to totally bliss me out."

After a few more minutes, having finally satisfied herself as to the sharpness of her blade, Atheliah oiled it and sheathed it in a tan leather case, for all the world like a mother bathing and oiling and dressing a well-loved baby.

"Thanks for taking us in," Atheliah said.

"It feels good having you here," Eddie said. "And we could use a couple more backs on the land." I laughed. "What's so funny?" Eddie asked affectionately.

"It's just that I haven't been referred to as a 'back' since my football days. A brain, a cunt, a piece of ass. But never a back. It's refreshing, to say the least."

The next morning Atheliah showed us how to fell trees. There had been a small supply of firewood on the front porch when we arrived, but it had almost all been used for cooking. Now that autumn was upon us, we needed wood for heat. It unsettled both Eddie and me that we hadn't realized this fact until recently—that we had taken heat for granted, as something supplied automatically by one's landlord. Luckily, we now had two extra "backs."

Dressed in a red plaid lumberjack shirt and olive army fatigue pants and green rubber boots, Atheliah flicked the ax blade with her thumb to test it, as though she hadn't spent an hour the previous evening honing it to razor sharpness. She planted her legs firmly and raised her treasured ax in both hands high over one shoulder like a baseball bat. Her frozen breath encircled her Medusa-esque head of red hair like an aura. Then she brought the ax down diagonally on a birch trunk. Working the ax back and forth, she withdrew it from the trunk and swung again. A large triangular chunk of white barked wood flew out. Half a dozen carefully positioned strokes later, the trunk was cut halfway through. Then she shifted to the other side of the tree and whacked out a chunk slightly higher than the original cut. The tree listed slowly. Atheliah threw her shoulder against it, and it came crashing down.

"*Where* did you learn *that?*" Eddie asked in awe.

"I used to be a Curved Bar Girl Scout back in Ohio," Atheliah admitted.

"Far out," Eddie said. Mona took the ax and began deftly trimming off branches. Her chopping technique was less dramatic than Atheliah's, but was equally effective; she chopped with short quick strokes, her back hunched, throwing up a shower of tiny wood chips. When the flurry of chips settled, the log was cut to order.

A pattern developed at the Free Farm, as we had come to call the place. Every morning when we got up, I would cook breakfast. Then as I did the dishes, Eddie and Atheliah and Mona would hitch up the work horses we had bought and would go up the hill to the woodlot. We soon had nearly enough wood for the winter, but the others wanted to fill the wood bin at the sugar shack now so that everything would be ready for sugaring in late February. While they were up the hill, I stayed at the cabin and cleaned. I also spun and dyed wool, and used it to crochet rainbow curtains for our bare windows. I felt like Snow White, the others of course being the dwarfs.

And by the time I heard the clanking of the horses' harnesses coming down the hill, I would have a hearty lunch ready—soybean fritters or sprouted soybean sukiyaki or soy grits pilaf. Each noon we four would sit at our groaning board, as I'd serve up a new culinary delight. Everyone would take a cautious bite, wait for a moment, and then Eddie would say, "Well! This is certainly delicious, Ginny."

"Delicious," the other two would echo.

"And so much roughage," one would add.

One morning as I sat crocheting the violet band of my fifth rainbow curtain, there was a knock at the door. I was startled because I hadn't heard any car or truck arrive. When I opened the door, there was Laverne, a knapsack on her back and a duffel bag in her hand, looking luscious in faded bib overalls and a flannel shirt, with her curly blond hair waving around her fresh face.

"Hi, Ginny."

"What do you want?" I asked, trying to sound disapproving.

"To move in with you all."

"You're kidding? What's wrong? Did your boy friends kick you out?"

"I'm through with men forever! I've *had* it with them!"

I looked at her suspiciously, but stood aside and let her enter. She dumped her gear on the floor and looked around. I was proud of the place, which was a model of cleanliness compared to the disaster area she had just fled from.

"I don't know, Laverne. I don't know if you can stay or not. You'll have to see what the others say. They'll be back for lunch soon."

"I know they don't care for my sexual proclivities." She had a habit of wetting her lower lip with her tongue and then slowly rubbing the lip with her middle finger.

"That's putting it mildly."

"But that's over. I've reformed. I never want another man again as long as I live."

Just then the others entered, clomping across my clean floor in their muddy boots. "Take off your boots!" I shrieked, like a housewife on a daytime TV commercial.

They all bent over to remove their boots, but one by one they became aware of Laverne's presence.

Finally Eddie said, "Well, well. If it isn't the Wife of Bath. To what do we owe the pleasure of your lascivious presence in our chaste abode?"

Laverne giggled nervously.

"She wants to move in," I explained

"*Here?*" the three asked simultaneously.

"I never want to *see* another man."

"He can *do* whatever he wants to with you just so long as you don't have to *see* him?" Eddie inquired.

"Honestly. I'm through with men. They're just one disappointment after another. Their readiness and their stamina are just so unreliable. Believe me, I just want to be left alone with my vibrator."

We all laughed at this, yet another example of job obsolescence, men being replaced by their machines. Then we stopped laughing as we sat down to curried soybean cutlets.

The time had come, we decided, to involve ourselves with The People. We had kept to ourselves for too long, allowing a mythology to spring up among the Stark's Boggers: The Soybean People were Communists, lesbians, draft dodgers, atheists, food stamp recipients. Our seclusion had been necessary to get the Free Farmlet going. But now the sparse stunted produce from our overgrown garden was in jars and trays of sand in the musty dirt cellar. Wood for the cabin and for the sugar shack was cut and split and stacked. It was time to descend into Stark's Bog and mix and mingle with the folk with whom we had cast our lot. It was time to win over their heads and their hearts to The Revolution!

Our first gesture of solidarity was to attend the local blood drawing, which was being held at the grammar school. It was here that I first saw Ira face to face. I'm sure I must have seen him earlier—he being one of the active young businessmen about town, president of the Stark's Bog Volunteer Fire Department, veteran square dancer with the Wheelers 'n' Reelers, and member of the Stark's Bog Cemetery Commission. But it is from the blood drawing that I retain my first clear picture of him.

The five of us walked into the school gym en masse, identical in our plaid wool lumberjack shirts and khaki army fatigue pants and green rubber boots. A hush fell over the large room as we gave our names to the kindly gray-haired lady behind the table. We sat side by side in folding chairs, waiting to be called for medical histories by a white-starched volunteer nurse. Part of the gym was occupied by wooden pallets on wheels with plastic bags strapped to their sides. Tubes led from the bags and into the arms of the supine Stark's Boggers. In one corner was a refreshment area, where the survivors stood chatting and munching doughnuts. I recognized the bag boy from the IGA, the owner of the feed store, a farmer down the road from us, a couple of other familiar faces. It gave me a great feeling of kinship to know that my plastic bag would nestle in the blood bank next to theirs. We were all in this business of life together.

One by one we were called for a conference with the nurse. Eventually, we lay on the tables, donating our life's blood for the well-being of our community—blood that would go into the veins of Vermont farmers who had had tractor accidents, Vermont women hemorrhaging during childbirth, Vermont children cut by their sled runners. We felt very good about the whole thing. Afterwards we mingled with our neighbors, endlessly exchanging such profundities as "Cold enough for you?" and "Looks like snow clouds blowing in from the north." After doughnuts and Coke, we headed for the door.

There, handing out small red plastic hearts, was Ira Bliss IV, Missouri Mutual Insurance agent and owner of Sno Cat City. He looked like Victor Mature in the *The Robe,* with high cheekbones and a firm mouth with full lips and wide dark alarmed eyes with bushy eyebrows that gave him a perpetually startled expression. His dark wavy hair hung so as partially to conceal a high forehead. His forehead and cheeks were ruddy and gleamed with sweat, making him look as though he'd just come up from some enforced rowing in the galley of a Roman ship. He wore a red soft-collared sports shirt, too tight, so that his biceps and chest muscles rippled the shirt when he moved. Three buttons were undone, and shocks of black curly chest hair peeked out. He stood just inside the doorway, his nostrils flaring like a race horse's. In retrospect, I could swear that he and I exchanged lingering stares fraught with meaning. At the time, though, I merely stood still and allowed him to pin the plastic heart to the collar of my lumberjack shirt, like a young man's pinning a corsage on his date.

When he had pinned the hearts on all five of us, he nodded and said, "Thank you, girls, for helping out our boys in Vietnam."

In unison we did a double take. "Is *that* what happens to it?" Eddie asked. "I thought it was for the blood bank that serves *our* area."

"Usually it is," he said with a pleasant smile. "But today is a special drawing for American troops."

Eddie blanched and clutched my arm all the way back to the truck. We rode to the cabin in a politically uncomfortable silence, and not entirely because of Ira's patriarchal *faux pas* in referring to us women as "girls."

The next time I saw Ira was under considerably less friendly circumstances, in our birth control information center on Main Street. Our personal finances had started rankling: We had continued to send checks to underground theater groups and counterculture coffee houses in Boston. But, not being there to survey their operations, Eddie had become uneasy. She insisted that a drug rehabilitation center we were helping was a front for FBI infiltration of radical politics. So we abruptly cut them off. Besides, we wanted to brighten our own immediate corner. Each time we had ventured into town for supplies, we had seen women our own age, grossly overweight with no teeth and greasy hair, being dragged in four directions at once by as many small children. These women were our sisters. They merited our help more than a bunch of storefront rip-offs in Boston.

And so we had rented a vacant shop. We furnished it with castoffs and stocked it with free literature on "family management" from Planned Parenthood. We put a sign out front that euphemistically read "Family Planning Center." One of us was there at all times during working hours, prepared to discuss birth control devices and to refer women to the local doctor to acquire one. We also planned to refer women under the table to sympathetic doctors in Montreal for illegal abortions and to lobby at the statehouse in Montpelier to liberalize the state abortion laws.

All of us did these things except Mona, who explained one night, "Kill yourself first, but don't have an abortion. Not if the father is a man you love, or have loved. It's like ripping off one of your own limbs and stomping on it."

"Sometimes you have to sacrifice a limb for the well-being of the tree," Eddie replied curtly.

After ten days, we had had two clients. The first was a frail young woman with darting eyes. She sneaked through the door, glancing nervously up and down the street to be sure she wasn't being observed by her friends and neighbors.

"May I help you?" I inquired cordially, as she stood squirming in front of the desk.

"I—I want to do it," she stuttered, blushing.

"Yes, certainly," I said, assuming that she was a young virgin about to embark upon the treacherous sea of sexuality, a high school girl perhaps whose illegitimate pregnancy I would prevent. "Won't you have a seat?" She perched tentatively, prepared to flee.

"Now!" I began, searching for tactful terminology. "Your—partner, have you known him long?"

She looked at me strangely. "Well, yes. I mean, we been *married* four years, but nothing happens."

I pondered this revelation carefully. "You mean you—uh—" I broke into a sweat. The girl's eyes whirled in their sockets with stress. "I'm not sure I understand. You've been married four years, you say. But you've never—ah—*done it?*" When in doubt, resort to the client's phraseology.

"Done what?"

"Well, *you* know." I had used the verb "to fuck" for so long that I couldn't remember its socially acceptable synonym. "It."

"It?"

"Well, when you came in, you said you wanted to 'do it.' "

"Yes. Plan my family," she mumbled. "It said on the sign 'Family Planning Center.' Is this the wrong place?"

"No, no," I assured her hastily. "Yes, that's what we do here all right—plan families. Now, all right, yes. Four years you've been married, you say? Yes, so what have you been—using, as it were?"

"Using? Using for what?"

"For family planning."

She stared at me with consternation. "Well, you know, the same as what everyone else uses."

I realized that I wasn't as up on the contraceptive folkways of Vermont as I should have been. "What's that—condoms or a diaphragm or what?"

She looked at me blankly. "I thought you didn't use none of that stuff when you're trying to have a family?"

"No, but I thought you were trying *not* to?"

"I said I come in here because the sign said 'Family Planning Center.' I been trying to have a family for four years now and nothing happens."

I looked at her, horrified. "You mean you *want* to get pregnant?"

"Thank you all the same, ma'am," she whispered, sidling toward the door and bolting out.

Our second client had been handled by Eddie with somewhat more finesse. She was a high school girl, premaritally pregnant. The father of the child was desperate to marry her, according to her. But she wanted nothing to do with him. Eddie made arrangements with a doctor in Montreal and lent her some dividend money. She wrote Eddie the next week saying that the operation had gone well, that she had gotten a work permit and found a waitressing job, that she intended to stay in Montreal, and she was very happy and very grateful.

Soon afterwards, Ira came storming into the clinic, his nostrils flaring and his forehead glistening with sweat. With him was a short stout man in green work clothes who slammed the glass door with a shuddering crash.

I looked up from a pamphlet on breast self-examination, which had just convinced me that I was dying of breast cancer. Recognizing Ira, I smiled. After all, we were fellow volunteers to the cause of alleviating human suffering, never mind if that suffering was self-inflicted in the case of the blood drawing for troops in Vietnam.

"May I help you?"

"Yes, you can!" Ira's fat friend growled. "Get the hell out of this town and take your goddam bull-dyke friends with you!"

I stared at him. "I beg your pardon?"

"I was going to marry that girl!" he informed me, his voice quivering.

"What girl?"

"That girl you and your lesbo friends sent up to Montreal to be butchered!"

"Maybe she didn't want to marry *you*."

"Of course she didn't," he growled. "That's why I knocked her up."

I looked first at Ira and then at his friend in wonderment. "You did it on *purpose?*"

"How else could I get her to marry me?"

"Do you know what it's *like* to be pregnant if you don't want to be?" I asked, implying that I *did*.

"Shut up, cunt!" he shouted, and stormed over to my desk, Ira lingering by the door. "Bunch of goddam Commies! Comin in here tryin to bust up The Home and The Family!"

"You wanted to marry her," I snapped, gaining gumption. "What about what *she* wanted? Don't you care about that? Maybe she didn't *want* a home and a family."

"What *she* wanted was to get knocked up and *have* to have a home and a family. You women are all the same! That's what you *all* want!"

"Garbage!" I screamed, leaping to my feet. "Bullshit! You men—"

The man reached out his stubby hands and wrapped a bumper sticker around my mouth, ending my stream of antimale invective. "And *you* want it, too, baby. Don't kid yourself," he informed me as he stomped out.

Ira looked at me apologetically and said by way of explanation, "Rodney is a broken man. He loved that little girl." He left, climbing into a beige Bronco outside. Rodney sat inside, doubled over, sobbing. Ira threw the Bronco into gear and roared off. A sticker on its rear bumper read "Abortion Is Murder."

On my way home that afternoon I passed the beige Bronco parked at the back side of the hills that bordered our beaver pond. On its roof was tied a huge black bear corpse. Blood dribbled down the back of the Bronco and onto the "Abortion Is Murder" sticker. To each of the front fenders was lashed a small bear cub. I stopped the truck and gazed in horror, my stomach churning with nausea.

Eventually I walked to the edge of the road and looked into the woods. I saw a faint path leading up through our land. I squatted down and let the air out of each tire. For good measure, I grabbed the radio antenna and snapped it off.

The war was on.

The next time I saw Ira he was a distant duck-shooting silhouette.

Earlier that week Atheliah had been slogging around in hip boots in the marsh on the far side of the pond looking for holes in the barbed-wire fence. We had half a dozen heifers by this time, and they kept getting out. They'd appear, milling around in dazed bovine confusion, on the road to town. We'd have to drive down and herd them home.

Atheliah, as reliable and relentless as a St. Bernard in an avalanche, tracked down and repaired the holes. But at the same time, she discovered a sagging gray duck blind. We'd never seen it before because it was largely camouflaged by the gray skeletons of drowned trees. Even after Atheliah pointed it out from the cabin, we could just barely pick it out when the light was right. Other times it blended right into the graveyard of standing tree trunks.

"Just left over from other years," Eddie informed us confidently. "No one would dare to use it now that we're here." Eddie's method of expression—her deep voice and authoritative inflections, the way she stood with her legs planted like the pilings of a pier and with her arms folded serenely across her chest—gave her opinions the force of decrees. That was why I was so startled to be awakened at dawn on the opening day of duck season by rifle blasts.

I lay still trying to remember where I was. Gunshots weren't an unfamiliar sound to me. The Cloyds were forever killing something or other. Each Cloyd had his favorite rifle, and gun racks hung in their house with the frequency of crucifixes in a Catholic church. They were always dragging in bloodied carcasses as special treats for our family. Mother had tried to instill in me forbearance of the folkway: "Country people are just *like* that." And she had exclaimed over the gory corpses like a mother over a small child's first finger painting. Somehow she usually managed to render them edible as well. Remembering Mother and her compulsive kindness sent pangs of remorse through me: I hadn't written or phoned in almost a year; I had thrown her letters unread into the trash in Cambridge; I had departed without leaving a forwarding address, so that her current letters were being returned stamped "Addressee Unknown." She deserved better.

Having finally recognized the rough log wall as belonging to our Vermont cabin, I dragged myself out of bed and across the cold plank floor to the window. There were more shots, and a flock of ducks lifted off the pond in a flurry of feathers. A couple fell lifeless into the water. By straining my eyes in the gray dawn, I could barely pick out two human figures (one of them Ira, as it turned out) peering over the edge of the blind.

Then I saw Eddie marching down the meadow, her braid flicking and lashing behind her like the tail of an enraged lion. Atheliah, Mona, and Laverne, dressed identically in lumberjack shirts and fatigues and boots, trailed in Eddie's outraged wake like dinghies behind an ocean liner.

Atheliah, of course, could never be said to "trail" anywhere. She barreled along like a diesel truck on a down grade, carrying her ax. Laverne came next, stalking lithely through the timothy. If Laverne had fallen from the roof yesterday when she and Atheliah had been up there caulking, she would have managed to twist around in mid-air and land lightly on all fours. Whereas Atheliah would have crashed to the ground and left a crater like a giant meteorite. Atheliah was round-shouldered from years of playing down what she considered merely two absurd mounds of woefully misplaced flesh. But Laverne led with her chest at all times.

Bringing up the rear was Mona. If Laverne exuded an aura of

invitation, Mona exuded one of confrontation. Behind her purple-tinted goggle lenses, her wide eyes periodically became squinty and sinister. She looked like the Gestapo interrogator in spy movies who had lines like, "Ve haff vays off makingk you talk."

Eddie halted abruptly at the pond edge, the others almost colliding with her. She nodded at the dark green rowboat. Atheliah turned it upright with a flick of her wrist and pushed it into the water with her foot. Eddie climbed in, her weight immediately grounding it. The other three finally freed it by pushing in unison and tripping and splashing in the cold slimy water. Then they hopped in too.

Atheliah rowed them through the open water toward the blind, the oars moving in great swooping strokes like the wings of a giant bird. The heads in the blind stared as the boat slipped through the dead gray trees like a skier down a slalom course. Eddie, in a grand gesture, stood on the front seat and placed a rubber-booted foot on the prow, like Washington crossing the Delaware. The little rowboat, sunk already to its gunwales, listed dangerously. I gritted my teeth. Just in time, they arrived at the blind, and Eddie grabbed hold and righted the tilting craft.

She yelled up in her most authoritative voice. The heads yelled back. Atheliah reached over and shook the post nearest her like a puppy shaking a rag in its teeth. The blind trembled and swayed as though it were made of weathered toothpicks. The heads yelled down at her. Eddie turned around and said something to Atheliah. Atheliah lowered an oar, blade first, into the water. Then, holding onto the blind, she climbed into the knee-deep water, leading with one hip-booted leg. Mona handed her the ax. Reverently, Atheliah removed its leather case. Then, taking the handle in both hands, she raised it above her head. The honed blade flashed red in the rising sun. With one powerful swing, she buried it in the post. The little boat quaked and pitched in the tidal wave produced by the lurching of the blind. Atheliah pulled the ax loose and, just as she was poised for another stroke, the two men scrambled down with their rifles into their inflatable canvas boat. They rowed quickly to shore and disappeared into the woods, carrying the boat.

Atheliah's second stroke severed the leg, and the blind listed sharply. She chopped through two of the remaining legs, until the last one snapped of its own accord. The entire structure toppled into the pond with a splash.

Later that day Eddie had us all out stepping off the borders of our property and planting every fifty feet shiny silver signs that read "No hunting, trapping, fishing or snowmobiling." Laverne paced off the sections and tied pieces of yarn to twigs to mark the spot for each post. Eddie and I were nailing signs onto the posts. Mona, in a flurry of chips, was shaping branches into posts. Atheliah, rising to her full six feet with the post maul outstretched over her head, drove the posts with resounding thuds.

During a rest period, I said to Eddie with tentative disapproval, "After all, this *has* been their hunting ground for generations. And besides, I thought you didn't like the idea of private ownership. I thought you believed that the wealth should be shared?"

Eddie, startled to be questioned, replied, "Communal ownership only works if the people involved are highly evolved types. Most Stark's Boggers need rehabilitation before they'd be suited for it. In the meantime, they need guidelines to restrain their savagery. It's not their fault, however: They've been raised in a corrupt, death-dealing society. How could they turn out any other way?"

" 'Highly evolved'? Does that mean anyone who happens to agree with you?" I asked, amazed at my daring. As usual, my loyalties were torn. I had spent too much time with Clem to feel free to pass judgment with confidence about the level of evolution attained by the different social groups.

Eddie glared at me. " 'Highly evolved': attuned to The Revolution. This macho shit—stalking and killing and terrorizing—is about as low as you can go, evolutionarily."

By the end of the day, we had placed eighty-three signs around the hills that formed the circumference of our property. We returned to the cabin and were standing with our backs to the stove in our mud-caked boots with our callused chapped hands behind our backs. Eddie said, "*Well*, that's that!"

Unfortunately, that *wasn't* that. The following week Eddie and I were in the woods checking on the heifers. The colorful fall leaf display had withered and fallen, and crunched under our boots. We had found the six black and white heifers, but Minnie, the milk cow, was missing. Minnie had dried up, leaving us milkless. I had forgotten that we had to have her bred, and let her have a calf, in order to continue to get milk. The Planned Parenthood literature had not reviewed this aspect of female sexuality. We searched the woods for her. Normally she would come to find us if she heard us. But this time she didn't appear.

I was peering nervously into a cave that looked as though it might house bears when I heard Eddie exclaim, "Oh Christ!"

I ran over and saw with horror the target of her blasphemy: A bloodied brown cowhide hung wrapped like a robe around one of our No Trespassing posts. Rammed down on top of the post was Minnie's head, eyes closed. Beside the post on the carpet of vivid leaves were strewn severed cow legs and ropelike guts and globs of white quivering fat.

"The bastards butchered Minnie!" Eddie screamed. I felt distinctly sick and turned away from the gory mess. As I did so, I discovered tire tracks from two trail bikes in a patch of loam.

Gingerly folding Minnie's hide and carrying it between us, we walked back to the cabin, stunned.

Buck season opened the next week. We were eating our dessert of soy date bars by the window that overlooked the pond. The sun had set behind the hill. It was twilight. As we watched, a buck and two does leapt out from the woods, paused and listened and sniffed, and then walked grandly to the pond edge. As they reached out their heads to drink, a rifle fired. The handsome buck shook his magnificent antlers ferociously a couple of times. As his head drooped, the two does looked around frantically. They sprang away from the pond, then stopped and looked back quizzically at the buck, who had sunk to his knees in the shallow water. As the does bounded into the woods, the buck collapsed on his side.

We five sat with our dessert suspended midway to our mouths. When we realized what had happened, we leapt up and raced for the door. Once outside, Eddie screamed in the general direction of the woods, "Goddam fucking murderers!"

We stumbled through the tangled timothy. By the time we reached the shore, the water on which the large tan buck floated was murky with blood. The buck wasn't dead. When he heard us, he gave a snort and a few weak token tosses of his headpiece—which had nine points on it, a huntsman's trophy indeed. This gesture of protest apparently drained him of his last reserves of strength. As we watched, his eyes clouded over; he twitched, sending out ripples, and then he lay still.

"Damn you!" we screamed to the darkening woods, tears gushing.

We each grabbed a leg, and with much grunting and straining, managed to drag the carcass out of the water and onto a patch of timothy. We studied the neat hole in the buck's muscled white chest. That accomplished, we didn't know what else to do. It seemed a waste to bury all that protein; on the other hand, we couldn't have eaten it, and we were damned if we'd let the trespassing hunters have it.

By now the sky was black. The only light anywhere around was the weak glow of a lamp in our kitchen at the top of the meadow. Eventually we left the buck where he was. The next morning he was gone.

The snows began, and late one blustery night we were awakened by a deafening roar from outside. Eddie and I lay still under the army surplus sleeping bag we used as a quilt, listening in terror as the roar circled and recircled our cabin. Finally we got up and walked fearfully to the window. Looking out through the mis-stitches in my crocheted rainbow curtains, we witnessed half a dozen snow machines shooting past, their headlights sweeping eerily across the new snow on the meadow.

Relieved and enraged, Eddie stomped out of the bedroom and over to the door. Atheliah was already standing there in rubber boots, her flannel nightgown hanging out from under her olive air force parka. She was holding her ax and was placidly flicking her callused thumb on the blade. Laverne and Mona were nowhere in sight. Eddie and I put on our boots and parkas over our sweat suits; and the three of us marched onto the porch.

The six snow machines swept past us and continued their circuit around the cabin like marauding Indians around a wagon train, enveloping us in clouds of exhaust. At the controls of each machine knelt a figure of indeterminate sex, encased in a quilted body suit and felted rubber boots and a huge crash helmet with a visor like on a knight's helmet. I was certain that I detected Ira's flaring nostrils behind one of the visors, and the fat face of his friend Rodney behind another.

Eddie yelled in a great booming voice that was inaudible in the roaring of the engines, "Get the hell out of here, or I'll call the cops!"

There were no cops in Stark's Bog, but the expression on her face seemed to make up for what her message lacked in content—because, after one more spin around the cabin, the machines broke away one by one and filed down the meadow toward the pond. In the meadow, they paused long enough to weave some intricate crisscrossing patterns through the snow, their headlights sweeping crazily across the field. And then they disappeared over the hill toward town.

The next morning Eddie marched us out to the meadow. We scraped a patch of ground clear of its shallow snow. The ground hadn't yet frozen, and so we were able to dig a deep hole, working in shifts with two shovels. By the end of the afternoon, the hole was the size of a hefty grave, five feet deep and maybe six feet in diameter. Eddie disappeared into the barn and returned with a dozen stakes with sharp points that looked like the poles the Cloyds used for curing tobacco. When I finally got the picture of what we were doing— setting a trap based on Vietcong guerrilla techniques—I balked.

"Wait a minute, Eddie. We just want to *scare* them, not *kill* them."

"*Who* doesn't?" Eddie asked, looking around for support.

Laverne shrugged.

Mona said gleefully, "I'd just as soon hurt them while we're at it." Atheliah nodded soberly in agreement.

"I don't want any part of it," I announced, turning around and heading for the cabin. My stand wasn't entirely disinterested. I suspected that Ira and his friend Rodney had been among the snowmobilers. Although I hated their macho guts, I didn't want to see them spilled all across our meadow either. The old spike-in-the-pit routine required that your victim be a faceless abstraction. Alas, Ira and Rodney were becoming real people to me.

I peeked out the window through my rainbow curtains as the others sunk the sharp stakes in the pit. Then they laid fir branches across its mouth, and piled snow on the branches. When they had finished packing the snow, the location of the pit was still evident to someone who knew of its existence. But at night, and to the unsuspecting, it would be invisible.

Later that week after a heavy snow the snowmobiles returned in in the middle of the night. Once again we were wrenched from sleep by their roaring. The five of us jumped from our beds and flocked to the window overlooking the meadow. As before, after a couple of dozen circuits of our cabin, the snowmobilers broke away one by one and swept down the meadow. The first three machines were nowhere near the pit. Each time one reached the bottom without mishap, the others groaned with disappointment.

But the driver of the fourth machine was a showoff. He zigzagged down the top part of the meadow, wagging the tail of his machine like a wedeln skier. His fall line passed directly over the pit, but whether or not his swooping antics would cause him to miss it was uncertain. I held my breath, suppressing an inclination to rush out and stop him. He fishtailed whimsically along, kneeling on his seat and leaning back and forth with the careening machine, as Clem used to do with his Harley.

Just when I was sure that he had passed the pit, the ground fell out from under him and his machine was swallowed up. Eddie whooped with delight. The driver himself sailed clear of the machine. He lay half buried in the snow, dazed. Flames suddenly flared out from the pit.

Mona said uneasily, "Jesus." We all watched in terrified awe as flames roared and melted the snow on all sides. The driver was rolling fast down the hill.

"Now what?" I asked Eddie, our field marshal, as I trembled with fear.

"We go out and 'help,'" Eddie said with an insane giggle.

Throwing on parkas and ski boots, we trooped from the cabin and strapped on our cross-country skis. We glided down the meadow along the packed snowmobile tracks. By now, the fire had burned down. The other snowmobiles were flocked close by, and their drivers were standing looking into the fading inferno and shaking their helmeted heads. The fire had fortunately burned away all traces of our stakes and fir branches. Only the blackened gutted carcass of a Sno Cat remained.

"Goodness me, what *happened?*" Eddie inquired.

"I dunno," one driver mumbled. "Jesum Crow, didn't see the goldurn hole."

"Can we *help?*" Mona asked.

"Don't suppose none of us can now," another driver replied dourly.

The driver of the burnt-out machine was still lying in the snow down the hill. A couple of his friends were with him. Eddie and I strolled over.

"Are you okay?" she asked gravely.

The unhappy victim had his helmet off. It was Rodney, his round mean face shaken. Squatting next to him was Ira, his visor raised to display his ruddy high-boned cheeks and his quivering nostrils. He and I smiled slightly in recognition.

"*I'm* all right," Rodney snarled, "but you're gonna have to pay for my machine." I immediately assumed that we had been found out.

Eddie, however, gasped with feigned outrage. "Why, we wouldn't *think* of it!"

"You had no goldurn warning signs up, so you'll have to replace my machine!"

"That beats anything I've ever heard! You trespass on our posted property. You harass us in the middle of the night in our private home by circling around on those—lawn mowers. And now you ask us to buy you *another* one when you're dumb enough to fall in a hole!"

"Jesum Crow, lady!" Rodney yelled. "We've driven our machines on this field and this pond for years! It's the best race track in the county. You can't post it just like that!"

"The hell we *can't!*" Eddie turned around on her skis. Ira and I looked at each other and shrugged. Eddie and I began herringboning back up the meadow, hunched over and pushing with our poles and looking altogether like arthritic flamingos.

"See you in court!" Rodney yelled.

Soon the snows began to fall in earnest. We five were spending quite a bit of time in the cabin. The atmosphere was tense. We were waiting to see what would happen next in our sheepmen/cattlemen feud with the Stark's Boggers, whom we had intended to befriend and instruct in the ways of The Revolution. For another thing, we had run out of things to say to each other. After several weeks of sitting around the stove in the evenings, we had completely exhausted the possibilities for conversation contained in each of our autobiographies. We had heard a limb by limb description of the dismemberment of the fetus in Mona's womb by suction aspiration. Eddie had spoken haltingly, but at great length, about her mother, who turned out to be a prostitute and who had brought her clients home for her couplings. Atheliah told about being called Goliath behind her back in secondary school. She had begun slouching and hunching in order to minimize her size, her spine becoming increasingly bowed under the weight of derision from diminutive pubescent males. Then, once she had successfully slumped down to their size, they began imitating her hunch when she wasn't looking, stooping over and swaying their arms with their hands brushing their kneecaps. They began calling her Atheliah the Ape.

Once we had all established that nothing about us was our own fault, that we were all victims of the exploitative patriarchal society we were now dedicated to overthrowing, that we were in the process of breaking free from the social constraints that had been imprisoning us, and that we were well on our way toward realizing our full goodness and virtue—what was there left to say?

So we took up hobbies. One dark snowy afternoon Laverne had shut herself into her room with her vibrator. Squeals of ecstasy were filling the cabin. The electric lights in the kitchen where Eddie and I sat were dimming and brightening rhythmically, like the lights on death row during an electrocution. Our electric bill had jumped five percent since Laverne had moved in.

I was sitting next to the wood stove crocheting the green section of my ninth rainbow curtain, to be used in Eddie's and my bedroom. Eddie had installed a foot-powered potter's wheel in the kitchen corner and was directing her considerable sculpting talents into more immediately relevant channels by making dishes. That afternoon she was working on soup bowls. Snow was lashing against the windows, and the fire felt good.

Mona and Atheliah were in the living room practicing their Tae Kwon Do, which they were learning via a correspondence course from Boston. Grunts and jarring crashes blended with the gasps and shrieks from Laverne's bedroom to make the cabin sound like a medieval torture chamber.

"What did you and Laverne do all day alone here together when the rest of us used to go up to the woodlot?" Eddie inquired casually, wetting her fingers in a dish of water and pedaling the wheel with her foot.

"Oh, nothing much. I did the usual stuff—cooking and cleaning. And Laverne just wandered around trying to figure out what she should be doing."

"I bet." I let my hands and my crocheting fall into my lap and looked over at her. "Did she use it on you?" she asked, not meeting my eyes.

"Use *what* on me? What are you talking about?"

"That appliance of hers. That plastic phallus."

"What—the vibrator? I've never even seen it. Look, *now* what's bugging you, Eddie?"

"Oh, *I* know you wish you were up there with her right now. Don't think I don't notice the way you look at each other." She smoothed the clay with her fingers.

"Eddie, *no*. You're on the wrong track, sweetheart. If I wanted another lover, it certainly wouldn't be a wo—" It was too late.

"A woman?" Eddie crowed. "I *knew* it: You're going straight! Who do you go to down in Stark's Bog, Ginny? Which one of the village studs is putting it to you? There's no use pretending it doesn't happen. I'm onto your game. I've been at the clinic when you were supposed to be on duty and weren't there."

I blushed and looked away guiltily. She had indeed found me out. I had been unfaithful to her a number of times over the past month or so. On my days at our center, I'd dutifully make myself a sandwich for lunch—soy-olive spread on dense whole wheat bread. But not only had I come to loathe the sight of a soybean, our jars of unsprayed grains and seeds had turned into terrariums, insects of every type hatching and flourishing in them. Consequently, at lunchtime, I'd taken to sneaking over to the IGA. I'd buy a can of Franco-American Spaghetti-O's and wolf it down out back by the garbage cans, one of which would be blessed with the deposit of my untouched soy-olive sandwich. I remained silent, unable to confess this to Eddie.

"Don't think I didn't notice the sly smile you gave that creep whose friend wracked up his snow machine in the meadow!"

I looked at her helplessly and picked up my crocheting and jerked its strands straight with a gesture of disgust. "I've seen him around town," I replied with dignity. "I was just being pleasant."

"Oh *sure*. How does it feel to have the real thing, Ginny, after all these months of makeshift sex with me?"

"That settles it," I said calmly, dropping my crocheting into my lap. "I've had it. I'm leaving."

"Oh *no* you aren't," Eddie informed me. I looked at her. "*I'm* leaving." She stood up.

"*I'm* leaving," I insisted, standing up. "I thought of it first." I began to stalk from the room.

I felt a sharp pain on the side of my head and heard something hit the floor and shatter beside me. I felt dizzy and propped myself against the doorjamb.

"God *damn* you, Ginny!" Eddie yelled through clenched teeth. "Don't you *ever* turn your back when I'm talking to you, you fucking bitch!"

I put my fingers to my forehead and brought them down covered with blood.

In a moment, Eddie was standing next to me in the shattered earthenware, dabbing ineffectually at my forehead and sobbing,

"Christ! I've killed her! Oh God! What have I done? Ginny, you're bleeding!"

The cut turned out to be minor, though the bruise would be more major, to my satisfaction. Later, after it was cleaned up, I said, "Eddie, something scary is happening to you. You've got to get a grip on yourself. This jealousy number just doesn't make sense."

"Maybe it doesn't make *sense*," she said sullenly, slumped over her wheel, "but I *feel* that it's valid. It's *you* something is happening to, not me. And what's happening is that you're going straight. I know it as clearly as if you'd said it."

I sighed and then said calmly, fearful of another outburst, "You've always insisted, Eddie, that two opposite points of view on something could be argued equally convincingly in rational terms by merely switching the underlying assumptions. You said that to find out the truth about a situation, I had to rely on what I *felt* about it. Well, *you* feel I'm losing interest. But *I* feel I'm not. Which of us is right, Eddie?"

"*I'm* right because I know I'm right."

"And I know *I'm* right. So where does that leave us?"

Eddie brooded, while I crocheted. That night at supper she asked, "At what point do people cease to be roommates and begin to be a commune?" We all shrugged indifferently, me holding an ice pack to my swollen eye.

"This set-up is getting to be, like, incestuous," Eddie continued. "It doesn't feel good to me anymore. I think in time we're going to drive each other crazy."

Mona shook her head in emphatic agreement. "You're right, Eddie. It's a totally insular existence."

"It *had* to be," I insisted. "We had to get everything going around here. But lately we've been getting involved—with the clinic and all."

"That isn't the kind of involvement I mean," Eddie said scornfully. "That's small-time stuff. I've been thinking about this all afternoon. See what you think of it: a Third World Women's Commune here at the Free Farm! We buy the land, and we get groups of women from the cities—black women, Puerto Ricans, American Indians—to build houses all over. Not randomly, but planned so that everyone would have both privacy and community. Then we build a community center with potter's wheels and woodworking equipment, all kinds of craft supplies. And a day care area! We work the land together and become financially self-sustaining with cash crops of maple sugar and apple cider. A truck garden. Facilities for radical groups from the cities to come up with their families for vacations in the country. We prove right here in Stark's Bog, Vermont, that it's possible for women of different races and classes to live together in peace and loving cooperation. We establish once and for all that when life is otherwise, it's only because people have been so fucked over by the macho ruling class!"

I prodded my bruised eye, wondering how we were to get along with unknown blacks and Puerto Ricans when we couldn't even get along with each other more than intermittently. But Eddie's words had kindled a fire in the others. By the time she had finished, the hills around us were dotted with owner-built homes; the fields were full of bare-breasted sisters of all colors, sweating shoulder to shoulder. A community center sat by the beaver pond and was packed with talented craftswomen who were cheerfully casting and molding and weaving all the material goods needed by the entire group. The hills rang out with hymns of female solidarity.

"Eddie," I asked hesitantly, afraid of sounding bougie, "where are we going to get the $60,000 to buy the land?"

"You and your fucking accountant mentality!" Eddie said grandly, waving the question aside.

"I have an idea!" Atheliah said with an inspired smile, her frizzy red hair waving around her head like a mad inventor's. "We have, like, a women's festival. A weekend thing with workshops and stuff. The Free Farm Women's Weekend! I can spread the word through friends in Newark and New York. That way we can get women here, they can see the place, we can see them, and maybe some will join us!"

"In other words, we need reinforcements against the Stark's Boggers?" I asked sourly. I was ignored. An accountant mentality had no place in The Revolution.

God only knows how we fitted eighty women into our cabin. The first night their sleeping-bagged bodies covered the floors like casualties waiting to be evacuated from a battlefield. They came from the surrounding towns and woods of Vermont. They also came, women of all sizes and shapes, from Montreal and Boston, from New York and Philadelphia. The grapevine approach had worked. The men in Mona's and Atheliah's former house had agreed to babysit as their contribution to the cause of female freedom and were now saddled, in their moss-lined living room, with twenty-eight frightened and unhappy children in various phases of toilet training.

The next morning, after the frantic line-up in front of our one toilet, and after volunteers had cleared away the remains of some 148 pieces of whole wheat toast and half that many styrofoam cups of rose hip tea, we divided into groups and went into different rooms for our seminars. My job was to supervise volunteers in assembling a lunch out of the food everyone had donated. I had some free time, so I wandered quietly from room to room. Eddie's group, called "Women and Politics," went on a tour of the Free Farm, taking in such inspiring sights as the manure-filled barn, the eggs we had neglected to collect, the unpruned orchard. Eddie considered her workshop the equivalent of a model home showing in a suburban development. She was out to make converts to the simple life, which ours was, to hear her tell it.

But she had a devil's advocate—a tall, attractive, intelligent woman who kept making uncomfortable remarks like, "What you *doin* up here in the woods, man? The world's crashin down around your heads, and you're playin at being peasants! You're on a fuckin earth trip, man!"

Huffily, Eddie replied, "Like, it's not enough to say that you're against war, or you're against the society that's fighting it. What are you *for*, man? It's not enough to be antideath, you got to be prolife. You can't criticize a society and expect to enjoy its fruits at the same time, man. You have to *produce*, not just consume. It's not enough to *believe* certain things, you have to live them as well."

"I *am* living my beliefs," the woman protested, glancing with distaste at the piles of manure. "And *not* in Outer East Judas, Vermont, where no one cares. I teach at Boston University. I'm changing society directly by my influence on the heads of my students, the future leaders of this oppressive society. There's no more radical trip a person can get into than teaching. *You're* the one that's copping out —stuck away in some snowbound corner of the nation playing with yourself!"

Eddie and the woman were locked in a match of revolutionary oneupmanship, both having adopted more-radical-than-thou tones of voice. This might go on all weekend, I speculated as I turned to leave.

"Garbage!" Eddie snorted. "You're ensconced there in that temple of learning where every student in sight already agrees with every word you utter. They come from the exact same background as you, they think the same thoughts, they use the same words. The *real* radical trip is to voluntarily place yourself among The People, who may scorn everything about you. To win *them* over to The Revolution is an achievement. Well, we're working shoulder to shoulder with people like that every day. Making inroads into their heads, winning over their hearts by stealth.''

I turned around and shot Eddie a questioning look. Could she possibly be speaking of *us*—the Commie outcasts of Stark's Bog, who were engaged in weekly skirmishes with The People over our continued corporeal existence? I headed back through the snow toward the cabin.

Laverne's group, "Women and Their Bodies," in Eddie's and my first-floor bedroom, was in a fascinated cluster around Laverne herself. She sat in a chair, her knees drawn up to her shoulders like chicken wings. With the aid of a complex arrangement of an inserted plastic speculum, mirrors, and a flashlight, Laverne was demonstrating to the intrigued gathering how it was possible, if one possessed the flexibility of an Olympic gymnast, to view the inside of one's vagina and the mouth of one's cervix. I stood transfixed, gazing at the moist red hole. But for the life of me, I couldn't grasp why anyone would *want* to view the mouth of her cervix as reflected in a mirror. I felt I couldn't ask Laverne at the risk of sounding bougie.

I kept going. In the living room was Mona's group, the "Women and Rage" set. A woman in a Sisterhood Is Powerful T-shirt was lying on the floor. Tears were gushing from her closed eyes and down her cheeks. She was shaking with sobs. Mona and her group were lined up on either side of her, slowly massaging the entire length and breadth of her shuddering body.

"It's cool," Mona was saying quietly, kneading a thigh. "We're all sisters. Most of us have been in the same space. Go ahead. Lay it on us."

"Well," she gasped, between sobs, "so I told him I was pregnant. I thought he'd be, like, you know, happy or something." She paused to shake with sobs. Someone stationed near her head leaned over and gently licked the tears from her cheeks. It seemed to calm her, although it was driving me wild with revulsion.

She continued shakily, ". . . so he stood up. I thought he was coming over to kiss me or hold me or something. I smiled at him. I was so proud and pleased. You know what he did? He slapped me, as hard as he could. It knocked me out of the chair and onto the floor. He started yelling, calling me a whore and a cunt and a bitch, and accusing me of trying to, like, trap him." She wailed in agony. The group speeded up their massage. Mona crawled around to the top of her head, looked down at her fondly through purple-tinted lenses, and began massaging her temples.

"What did you do?" Mona prompted, tossing her long black hair out of her eyes with a jerk of her head.

"I just lay there. I was so stunned. I couldn't believe it. I lay there trying to get my head straight. Stunned first that he wasn't pleased like I was; and second that he was calling me a whore, because I had really loved him. He knew I had never had sex with anyone before him. And I especially couldn't believe that he had hit me. He'd always been, like, so kind and so gentle. But the next thing I knew, he was kicking me in the stomach. He was wearing combat boots, and he just kept kicking me, hard. He kept yelling that he wasn't going to let himself be tied down by some two-bit whore. And he kept kicking me in the stomach, so that I couldn't get my breath." She started gasping for breath. One of the group began pumping her chest to help her breathe. Everyone's face was set in a grim expression.

"And what happened?" Mona asked, looking more and more vindictive.

"When I was seven months pregnant, he walked out and never came back. It was six in the morning, I remember. I was on my knees scrubbing the kitchen linoleum. He was a real cleanliness freak. I didn't care that much about gleaming linoleum. I was doing it for him, before I left for work. He wasn't working regularly at the time. Some nights he played with a band. I was supporting both of us. Anyhow, that morning I was kneeling over the scrub bucket, surrounded by a floorful of dirty water, and I started crying. I was just so tired, with working all day and being seven months pregnant and getting up early to scrub the floor and iron his shirts. Tears were dripping off my face and into the sudsy water. About that time, he stomped in. He'd been out all night, possibly with another woman. He stared at me with disgust and said, 'Christ! *Look* at you! You're a mess—dirt all over you and your hair in tangles. Is it any wonder I stay away from you as much as I can?' And he threw his stuff in a duffel bag and left. I haven't seen him since."

"Go on. Get angry," Mona whispered. "Give in to it."

The woman's expression changed abruptly from luxurious self-pity to fury. "The bastard!" she screamed. "The goddam mother-fucking son of a bitch! Jesus, I hate that lousy cock-sucking Spic!"

The group rolled her over on her stomach. She began pounding the floor with her fists in a rhythmic tattoo of rage.

"And what would you like to do to him?" Mona whispered.

"I'd like to take a huge sharp carving knife and—"

I walked fast into the kitchen so that I wouldn't have to hear what she was going to do with her knife. Much as I sympathized with her, I found it distinctly embarrassing to have experienced such unearned intimacy with a woman I'd never seen before and would most likely never see again. A quickie of the emotions.

Atheliah was somewhere in the cabin, conducting a session on "Women and Work." I knew that housework and child-rearing were being roundly dumped on, and that I would feel agonizingly bougie once I felt compelled to mention what a trip I found cleaning the shower to be; how I would remove all my clothes and climb in with a sponge and Comet and really get into it.

I sat down and tried not to listen to the poundings and shrieking from the "Women and Rage" workshop, where the woman was in the process of hacking her ex-lover to bits. I was feeling estranged from my sisters, and forlorn about feeling estranged. And I was a little bit scared because I knew that if I sat in on the "Women and Rage" workshop for a few minutes, having lowered this sense of estrangement that I used as a defense, I'd be beating the floor with the best of them.

After lunch came recreation. Some women went sledding and skiing and snowshoeing on the meadow. Several built a great towering female torso from snow outside the living room window. Others sat around smoking dope and drinking Annie Green Springs Country Cherry Wine. A couple were playing guitars and singing.

After dinner Bev Butch and the Four Femmes, a women's rock band from Boston who had come for the weekend, set up their instruments and speakers in the living room. They played loud songs from the early sixties, and we all boogied, either as couples or singly. It was like being at a junior high sock hop before any of the boys had gotten up the courage or coordination to dance.

As the evening progressed, the living room became hot and stuffy from all the exercising bodies, in spite of subzero temperatures outside. Every dancer's face was dripping with sweat, and each Anglo-

Afro hairdo was becoming even frizzier. Country Cherry Wine was being guzzled like lemonade on a summer afternoon. Finally Laverne in a grand gesture threw off her Off the Pigs T-shirt. There it was— her magnificent chest, glistening with sweat. A dozen or more women followed suit, until the entire living room seemed filled with bare breasts swaying and jouncing to the driving beat. I was lying with Eddie against someone's rolled up sleeping bag. We were holding hands and were passing a joint.

"Well, I think it's a success, don't you?" I asked.

"I guess so," she agreed. "But I think most of them are just here for a good time."

"That's okay, isn't it?" I was forgetting Eddie's vision of a multi-hued phalanx of women working the land shoulder to shoulder.

"Sure, if you're running a fucking resort. Besides, there's only one black woman here. No Puerto Ricans, no Indians. How can we have a Third World Collective with no Third World women?"

"I'm part Cherokee Indian," I offered.

She turned on me with astonished delight. "You're *kidding?* How come you never told me? Are you ashamed of it or what?"

"To tell you the truth, I never think about it. Does that make me an Uncle Tom-tom?" I collapsed with laughter at my little joke.

"Repression," she said darkly. "You're repressing your heritage. Society has made you ashamed of your birthright. You think Indians are second-class citizens."

"I don't think so," I said, ever vigilant for my manifestations of bourgeois prejudice. "It just never seemed that significant. My great-great-great-grandmother was a Cherokee squaw. That makes me one thirty-second part Cherokee Indian. Up against all that Anglo-Saxonry. Big deal."

"Big deal? That *happens* to be the missing link in your character! I could never figure out why you weren't altogether impossible with that mansion of yours, and those fascist parents. But you've got soul after all, Ginny." She rolled over and kissed me passionately. I was pleased that my genetic configuration had made her so happy.

"And my grandfather was a coal miner," I offered, wanting to make her another gift. "Lots of my cousins still are. In the Appalachians."

"You're *kidding?*" Eddie said, beaming. "Far *out.* Jesus, Ginny, you've been holding out on me! Let's dance. I want to hold you."

Bev Butch was singing a slow song, "Longer Than Always Is a Long Long Time." Eddie and I wrapped our arms around each other and swayed in place, burying our mouths in each other's neck. Around the room many other couples were embracing in time to the music—in several cases one or both partners were shirtless, and much caressing of breasts was going on. Marijuana smoke hung over the room like industrial smog over Hullsport. Most of the lights were out. Those that were still on were flickering rhythmically to Laverne's vibrator in an upstairs bedroom. Couples or threesomes were drifting off to the bedrooms. I sighed with contentment. My feelings of estrangement from that morning seemed distant indeed. This was where I belonged; at last after much searching I had found my niche—it was here in Eddie Holzer's arms.

The door flew open and crashed against the wall. Snow swept in. A dozen huge figures in felt boots and dark quilted jumpsuits and visored helmets tramped in. They looked like astronauts on a moon mission, only more sinister and not so clean-cut. The band stopped abruptly. The dancing couples looked up and pulled apart.

The snowmobilers lined up across one end of the room. Their tiny eyes, almost lost in the dark caverns of their helmets, gleamed with lust. They began moving forward as a line, clomping one booted foot slowly in front of the other.

Mindless panic gripped me as they herded us together like sheep for the slaughter. A figure on an outside edge reached out and grabbed the wrist of a bare-breasted woman in low-slung blue jeans who was cowering by the wall. She tried to scratch at his eyes, but her fingernails skittered down his tinted plastic visor. She tried to bite his hand, but got a mouthful of padded leather. She screamed and struggled as he started dragging her to the door. Several women moved to help her, but became immediately aware that they had pressing problems of their own as the line of dark figures closed in.

Apparently what they had in mind was a Sabine women scene. Each would grab one of us and throw her across his snow machine and disappear into the night. I saw no reason why they shouldn't do this, as long as they left me out of it.

Eddie moved away from me and stood directly in their path with her hands resting on her hips. A figure in the line was moving toward me. I couldn't see through his visor very well; what little light there was was reflecting off the plastic rather than penetrating it. But I could have sworn I recognized Ira's alarmed eyes and his flaring nostrils and his full quivering lips. His expression wasn't malicious, though; it was wistful. I looked back somewhat wistfully myself, as Juliet must have gazed at her Romeo among his enemy kinsmen.

"*What* do you think you're doing?" Eddie demanded in a voice that would have caused flowers to wilt in the spring. The row halted abruptly, lead feet extended. Atheliah sauntered up to Eddie's side. She was casually removing the leather case from her ax. She flicked its blade with her thumb and looked serenely at the snowsuited specters as though they were a row of saplings to be felled.

"Get out of our house and off our land," Eddie ordered, in a tone that indicated that "our" implied at least thirty-seven percent of the American people in a recent Harris poll, and not several dozen terrified females.

The line stood still and mute for a full minute, the confrontation being waged in a dimension not involving, for the moment, words and actions.

Finally, the man who had been approaching me, Ira it did turn out to be, raised his visor, knightlike, and said sheepishly, "We just heard the music and thought we'd drop by."

Eddie looked at him with amazement and said, "Well, you're *not* invited, so get your trespassing ass out of here. And take your macho friends with you." She turned her back on them and signaled to Bev Butch to start playing. Shakily, the band swung into an uncoordinated rendition of "Great Balls of Fire."

The snowmobilers skulked toward the door with sulky backward glances. When they were out on the porch, Eddie stalked over and called after them, enjoying her command, "And don't come back until you're invited. Which will be never!"

Glumly, they stepped into the snow. I heard one mumble something about being "pussy whipped." Two, as they stomped past the towering bluish ice sculpture of the female torso, applied their shoulders to it and brought it crashing to the ground, where it broke into a thousand pieces.

The next day as people were leaving, Eddie issued invitations to a carefully selected handful to join our Free Farm Third World Women's Collective. When questioned about the Third World bit, she replied casually, "Oh, my lover is part Cherokee Indian; and of course her parents are Appalachian coal miners."

"Oh wow!" said the woman who had challenged her, as impressed as any suburbanite would be to learn that a neighbor was a Worthley graduate.

I preened shamelessly.

"And of course *my* father was Puerto Rican," Eddie added. I looked at her questioningly.

"Well, he might have been," she replied defensively after the woman left.

We didn't make any converts that afternoon, but we did feel we'd planted the seed in several receptive heads. We had also forged sisterly bonds with other area farms, and we had made plans to get together soon for the countercultural equivalent of afternoon bridge or morning coffee—some consciousness-raising.

After we had tamed the debris in the cabin, Mona, Atheliah, Eddie, and I went skiing. Laverne stayed behind for an assignation with her vibrator.

We skied in silence for several miles, savoring the quiet after the din of the weekend. We skied across meadows and through snow-laden pine forests. We peeked into hemlock trees and found deer hideouts—branches pinned tentlike to the ground by snow, and the snow within packed by tiny hoofs. Winter birds hopped around in the branches. The weak winter sun ducked and darted behind the clouds and the tall treetops. I was pervaded by a great sense of peace and well-being.

"Whew! It's nice to have *that* over with." The others gave me looks of reprimand to indicate that I wasn't displaying the appropriate collective feeling. "Well, it was kind of crowded and noisy, don't you think? And the *mess* of all those bodies trying to eat and sleep and shit at once!"

"Those 'bodies' were our sisters," Mona pointed out.

"Sisters or not, it's nice to have them gone," I insisted with good humor. No one replied.

We skied on, our tips clacking together, and the snow crunching under us, and the sun flashing on our faces. If not God, then Someone equally influential was in heaven, and all seemed right with the world —which sentiment was a considerable relief after my seizure of unutterable loneliness yesterday morning in the midst of my eighty sisters. We herringboned briskly up a hillside.

As we began to descend the opposite side, a deafening boom enveloped the countryside. We looked at each other with concern.

"A sonic boom," Eddie said confidently. At that point, we almost ran head-on into a chain-link fence.

"What the fuck?" Eddie grumbled. With annoyance at having our course disrupted, we turned south and skied alongside the high barbed-wire-capped fence. After fifty yards we came to a sign—white with red lettering saying, "Keep Out! Gun Testing Range."

We looked at each other in astonishment. We were in the middle of a woods in an underpopulated area of a rural state. For several miles we had seen no other person, and only a handful of houses. *What* guns, for God's sake, and who was there to test them?

We skied on, following the fence, intent upon satisfying our curiosity. Meanwhile, shattering blasts kept rocking the small valley. Abruptly, the fence turned a corner. So did we, following it like Dorothy of Oz on the Yellow Brick Road.

Several hundred yards and one right angle later, we found ourselves at a locked gate on which was a large sign reading "Keep Out. Gun Test Range. General Machine, Inc., Ludbury, Vermont." Inside were clutches of men in army fatigues tending large mortar-type guns.

"Christ, they're everywhere," Eddie whispered. "They won't be content until they've killed us all." She began trembling. I'd never seen her frightened of anything. But here she was, clearly having an anxiety attack such as seized all the rest of us on a regular basis. The confrontation with the snowmobilers must have drained her of her weekly allotment of courage.

I took one of her arms, which was rigid with terror, and Atheliah took the other, and between us, we managed to slide her back into the woods, where she regained command enough to yell back toward the firing range, "Goddam butchers!"

However, when we were about halfway back to the cabin, toiling through deeply drifted snow in a broad field, we heard a roar overhead. Stabbing our poles upright in the snow, we clapped our gloved hands over our ears. Three low-flying jets, in perfect formation, came straight at us. They were the flat triangular kind that looked like silver airborne stingrays.

Eddie screamed, "Oh Christ! They've *got* me!" And she threw herself headfirst into a snowdrift, tangling her skis around her in the process.

The planes passed by well above us. The three of us dragged Eddie out of her snowbank. She sat quivering in the snow, her face buried in her hands.

"Are you okay?" I asked finally, disturbed by this display of weakness in my tower of strength.

Wordlessly, she untangled her skis and stood up, and we pressed on.

The next morning everyone left the cabin but me. Eddie and Laverne went down to the clinic. And Atheliah and Mona skied to their old farm to borrow some soybeans.

I was sitting in the kitchen, my feet propped on the stove, savoring my solitude like the counterrevolutionary that I was beginning to think I really was: I was sick to death of sharing with the sisters. Suddenly I heard a snowmobile in our meadow. Reluctantly, I plunked my feet to the floor and looked out. Hopping off his Deluxe Sno Cat 44 and pulling off his helmet was Ira. I felt a fleeting pang of pleasure, which I promptly squelched. After all, but for Eddie, he would have carried me off into the night last Saturday.

"Yes?" I inquired coolly, sauntering out onto the porch. Ira wore a quilted snowsuit; his dark curly hair was a scrambled mess from his helmet, and his smiling white teeth were dazzling against his ruddy complexion.

"Howdy. Ira Bliss," he said, slipping off his huge black leather glove and offering me his hand.

I carefully ignored the hand and asked, "What do you want, Mr. Bliss?"

"Ira," he said, flashing his smile, his nostrils flaring. "May I come in for a minute?" He blew on his hands and rubbed them. He was right. It was cold. I was shivering in my turtleneck.

"I don't see the need for that."

"Look, ma'am, I'm freezing."

"Then don't roar around on your toy sled at sixty miles per hour."

"All right, look," he said, raising his arms as though someone had stuck a pistol in his ribs. "I run with a rowdy bunch. Sometimes they do things I don't care for, and I go along with them because I don't have the strength of character to stand up to them. But that's really why I'm here. To apologize for Saturday night."

Ira had captured my sympathy. I knew what he meant: I ran with rowdy groups, too, and often lacked the gumption to be different when I didn't approve of their activities. I smiled in spite of myself, a faint smile that acknowledged kinship. "All right, Mr. Bliss. Come in and warm up by the stove."

He sat down opposite me and unzipped his jumpsuit to the waist.

He was wearing his tight red shirt, the one from the Vietnam blood drawing that displayed his impressive musculature. I studied those taut sinewy muscles, trying not to be too obvious about it. His body was so different from a woman's, with which I had been mostly occupied for almost three years. Eddie's body was all firm mounds and smooth curves and secret folds. One model probably wasn't any better or worse than the other, but they certainly were different.

I cleared my throat, trying hard to think of some unprovocative topic for discussion. "Well . . ." we said in unison. Then we laughed nervously in unison.

"I have a second reason for being here," Ira admitted. "I sell life insurance. No, wait! Before you tune me out, just listen to what I have to say. Now, I know that you and your friends are pretty independent women. But have you ever thought about what happens if one of you were to die? That sounds pretty morbid, but it's a topic we all have to face sometime or other, right? Okay, so traditionally, people have thought of life insurance as something a man takes out to provide for his wife and children should he die. Well, you don't have children to look out for, I gather, but you *do* have a chance to provide for the people closest to you, should something happen to you. There must be someone who could profit from your death, right? Uh, that's not exactly what I meant. . . ."

I hadn't tuned Ira out. I was listening carefully. This wasn't the first time the topic had occurred to me, of what would happen to Eddie if I suddenly died, which I was bound to entertain as an ever-present possibility, considering who had reared me. There was no way I could alter my trust fund so that Eddie could have my dividend checks. The fund would revert to the Major, who conceivably had gunmen on my trail for that very reason, since I hadn't written home since picketing his factory. What could Eddie do to support herself when I lay six feet under? Things she would hate, things that would destroy her defiant spirit—waitressing, chambermaiding, secretarial work. She was poor, I was rich. It was through no fault of her own, and it was not to my credit. I should share the wealth, should make provisions to continue sharing it once I was gone.

Seemingly surprised at not being put down, Ira continued, his Victor Mature forehead gleaming with sweat from the stove heat. "Now, there are two types you might want to consider—term and whole life. Term requires a relatively small premium in return for which your beneficiary receives the face amount of the policy should

you die within the term period. Whole life is more an investment.
You pay premiums during your lifetime and should you live to ninety-
six, you get the face amount back. Which plan you would choose
would depend on your financial circumstances and your insurance
goals. Do you mind if I ask what you live on?"

Abruptly I snapped out of my calculations. "Yes, I do. I don't see
that it's any of your business."

His eyes became wide and alarmed. "I'm sorry. I was just trying
to help."

"*I'm* sorry, I didn't mean to bark at you. I'm interested in what
you've been saying, and I'm not sure how to proceed."

"Well, first of all, who's living here with you?"

I glared at him suspiciously. "What does *that* have to do with
anything?" Suddenly, I was seeing him as the front man for the Stark's
Bog Marauders.

"Well, I mean, if you're thinking of insuring yourself, it helps to
know how many people you're trying to provide for, right?"

Just then our truck roared up the driveway. I glanced around
guiltily. I had been talking alone with a man, with a Stark's Bog
snowmobiler—and I had been enjoying it. What was Eddie going to
say? "I think you'd better go."

"Wouldn't your friends like to hear about insurance possibilities?"

"No, they wouldn't," I assured him. "I want it to be a surprise,"
I added, to soften the fact that I was kicking him out. I opened the
door and shoved him out. He stepped off the porch, zipping his
Ski-Doo suit. As he waded through the broken bits of the Women's
Weekend ice sculpture, Eddie came stomping over. She shook a fist
at him, in which she clutched a piece of paper, and she yelled, "And
you can tell your friends to go fuck themselves!"

He turned around, startled. "Look—"

"Just *go*," I said grimly, pushing him toward his machine.

As he roared off, Eddie turned on me, trembling with rage. "So
that's what goes on here when I leave, you sneaky bitch! But I *caught*
you."

"Nothing 'went on,' Eddie, I assure you."

"*Shit,*Ginny! I may be poor, but I'm not dumb! I *saw* the way you
two were looking at each other, all guilty and conspiratorial! Goddam
it, I *saw* him putting his clothes on as he left! Stop lying to me, whore!"

I decided to fight fire with fire. "Shut up, you maniac! I *said*
nothing went on and I *meant* it! I don't lie, Eddie, and least of all to

you. But so what if something *were* going on? Where are all your big ideas about sharing the wealth? Or don't those ideas extend beyond sharing my dividend checks? What about all the garbage you're always spouting about mingling with The People? Doesn't that include mingling on terms of warmth and affection? I'll tell you what, Eddie, I've put up with all I'm going to with this jealousy number. You're really fucking me over. I swear to God, I've never been unfaithful to you, but you're driving me right into Ira Bliss's bed!"

"Stop threatening me," she said, shocked to hear me talking back so forcefully.

"I'm not threatening you. I'm just explaining what's happening. I'm outlining for you the dynamics of our relationship so that you won't be too surprised when things turn out the way you're programing them to."

We stood glaring at each other over the mountains of snow from the tumbled statue. I shivered.

"Christ, I'm freezing," I mumbled, depleted of emotional energy. "Come inside and I'll tell you why he was here."

As we sat around the stove with Laverne, Eddie said wearily, "Let *me* tell *you* what happened first. We got to the office and found that a window had been smashed and the lock on the door had been sawed off. Wait. There's more. Inside, red paint was splashed all over the walls and the furniture. The pamphlets had been burned in the metal trash can, and the ashes were dumped all over the floor. And one wall was literally papered with those damn 'Abortion Is Murder' stickers."

"Oh God," I moaned, burying my face in my hands. "Clearly we've gone about this the wrong way."

"*Us?* What can you expect from a bunch of mentally retarded fascists?" I decided not to point out that these "mentally retarded fascists" were The People, the hope of the radical left.

"Read this." She thrust her crumpled paper at me.

A childish, almost illegible handwriting on a piece of pink letter paper decorated with wild flower sketches read: "Dear Pinkos: If you want to raise your families in our town like normal people, and go to our church, and send your children to our school, we welcome you to Stark's Bog. But if you want to destroy the family and defy the will of the Lord, we don't need none of your kind around here corrupting our children. This is just a warning. Sincerely, Some Concerned Citizens."

We three stared at each other with restrained terror.

"I think we're in over our heads," I suggested.

"So you can see why I was upset when I drove up and saw that macho pig here," Eddie said. "I do apologize, Ginny."

"It's all right."

"So why *was* that bastard here?"

"Believe it or not, he was here to apologize for the other night. No kidding, he really was. And he was trying to sell us a life insurance policy."

"Oh *no*," Laverne groaned.

"You didn't *buy* one?" Eddie asked.

"I considered it."

"Oh God, *life* insurance!" she wailed. "How bougie!"

"Fine. Go ahead. Ridicule me. But what's going to happen to the Free Farm, and to you, if I die?"

"If you die, we'll probably all die with you," Eddie said jocularly. "Or maybe I'll throw myself on your funeral pyre."

I was distinctly unamused. "No, *really?*"

"I'm sure we'd figure something out. You're not as irreplaceable as you seem to think."

"I could get all the money back in about seventy years," I pointed out thoughtfully. Laverne and Eddie fell out of their chairs with laughter.

All of a sudden, Eddie stopped laughing and said darkly, "I don't happen to buy that."

I shrugged. "Well, it's the man's profession. I guess he should know."

"No, I mean I don't buy the idea that insurance *is* his profession."

"What are you talking about?"

"Whoever heard of selling life insurance to women?"

"Not even to liberated women like us?"

"What kinds of questions did he ask you?"

I tried to reconstruct the scene. "He asked what we lived on and whom I was living here with."

"Aha! I *knew* it! He's an FBI agent! I'm sure of it!"

Laverne was massaging her left thigh thoughtfully. "Oh, come *on*, Eddie," she said.

"Look, he was a decent friendly man, Eddie. That's all."

"He let *you* believe he was decent. Don't you see, Ginny? He's trying to make you fall for him so that he can use you as an informant." Her eyes were gleaming.

"Crap! You've been watching too many grade B movies."

"Look, I'm not holding it against *you*, Ginny. But he's definitely putting the make on you. I've seen the way he looks at you. Now, I'm not saying that you're responding—even though you *have* been out of the office several times when I've stopped by. . . . But I just want you to be aware of what's going on so that you won't get hurt. And so that you won't hurt us. The man is an FBI agent, Ginny. I'm sure of it."

"You flatter yourself, Eddie. Why would the FBI waste its time on small-time hippies like us?"

Eddie looked injured. "*Well*, for *lots* of reasons—drugs, political protests, the money we've given to countercultural enterprises. Maybe they think we're concealing political fugitives or draft dodgers. Remember, we're citizens of a fascist state. Why, I can think of any *number* of things we've done that might merit attention from the FBI."

"You're crazy!"

"I may be. But I know what I know. And I know that you'd better watch out for that man."

"You're not jealous or anything like that?"

"*Me? Jealous?*" She laughed. "Jealousy is a bourgeois emotion based on property instinct, and I don't believe in private property. You're a grown woman, Ginny. You're free to come and go as you like, to choose friends and lovers as you deem appropriate. I wouldn't *think* of trying to restrict your options in any way whatsoever. I just want you to be cognizant of the possible political repercussions that your indiscriminate balling might have on your sisters, that's all."

"*What* balling? Christ, Eddie, I just met the man formally today! Anyway, I don't ball indiscriminately. You know that. But lay off me, or I might."

"Don't threaten me, Ginny."

"I'm not threatening. I'm just warning."

"And *I'm* warning *you*."

"Well, now that we're both well-warned. . . ."

One night after supper we all sat around the stove chewing peyote buttons that were the consistency of orange peels. I was nibbling at mine, trying to avoid swallowing. Atheliah was sharpening her ax. Mona, in languid bumbling movements, was making a couple of dried arrangements with weeds and seed pods she had gathered through the snow in the meadow that afternoon. Scattered liberally through each arrangement were stalks of dried marijuana, which heretofore had hung in bunches from the kitchen beams. She was trying to conceal them in preparation for the FBI raid that she and Eddie were convinced was about to descend upon us.

Laverne was massaging herself behind her collarbones with both hands, her blond curly head back and her green eyes closed with contentment. Eddie was sitting facing me, holding my head between her hands and tilting it this way and that. "No, really, Ginny," she insisted. "I think I can see the Indian in you. In your forehead and your cheekbones. Well, in your coloring, too, for that matter."

"It's just one thirty-second of me, Eddie. Everyone has sixteen great-great-great-grandmothers, and only one of mine was an Indian. Her contribution is very diluted, I'm sure."

"No, I definitely see it. Don't you, Mona?"

"Far out," Mona muttered, her bruised eyes beginning to glaze over behind her purple lenses, and her straight black hair getting tangled up in her dried weeds.

We heard a roar down by the beaver pond. Eddie jumped up and stalked to the window and looked out. "Come here quick!"

We all raced to the window. It was very dark out, but as we stood watching, headlights appeared all along the hilltops behind the pond. They wound their way down toward the pond, back and forth through the bare trees. More kept coming, rank after rank, over the hills from town.

The pond had frozen by now, and the machines proceeded out onto the ice. The whining roar was deafening, even at our distance and inside the cabin. There must have been a hundred or more. It looked like a coven of witches assembling.

Before we knew it, a bonfire was blazing on our shore. Races were under way across one end of the pond. At the other end, the beavers' frozen mud lodge had been packed with snow and was being used as a jump, as the more daring drivers hurtled off it at top speed, flew through the air, and landed with a jolt many yards in front of it.

We looked at each other hopelessly. The five of us against a hundred Stark's Bog thugs and assorted wives and girl friends. We resumed our seats in the kitchen. Mona passed around more peyote buttons, and we sat chewing them like cows their cud. When we went to bed, the party to which we were not invited was still in progress. We crammed pillows over our ears and finally managed to sleep—very late.

The morning after our fifth sleepless night, Eddie organized our defense. We carried bucket after bucket of water onto the pond surface. The race track was lightly packed with snow. With our buckets we created discreet patches of glare ice, with special attention to the spots at which the machines made turns.

That night, in order not to miss the action, we put on our skis and glided down to the pond edge for ringside seats. There were no bushes to hide behind. But we felt confident that if we sat still, our presence on that moonless night would go unnoticed.

At what had become the usual time, the headlights appeared on the hilltops and wove down to the pond. For a while, the drivers—men, women, and children—loitered on the ice socializing and tossing around empty cans and papers and bottles. Then the races got under way. Like the charioteers in *Ben Hur*, two drivers, on their knees in their seats, would start out even. Scowling and shouting obscenities, they would climb to higher and higher speeds, each straining to pull ahead.

Several races were run without a hitch. Our icy patches appeared to be a bust. Just as we were about to herringbone back to the cabin, a machine suddenly spun sideways out of control. Its driver flipped high in the air. As the machine spun, it crashed into a second machine, causing that one to lurch sideways and dump its driver on the ice. I was watching with dread, waiting to see if the man who had flown through the air was hurt. I hadn't expected such dramatic results from our little stunt. As I sat with my heart in my throat, Eddie started cackling with glee.

"Shut *up*, Eddie," I said, gouging her with my elbow. She was howling louder and louder. Soon the other three joined her, rolling in the snow and screaming with delight.

Some men were squatting examining the icy patch. They looked up and glanced around. "They'll *hear* us," I whispered.

Unfortunately, they had already. The man who had flown through the air was walking shakily on the arm of another man, flexing his knee joints. He had removed his helmet. I could see that it was Rodney. And the man with Rodney was none other than Ira.

Rodney stared toward my friends who lay writhing in the snow with laughter. Someone turned his machine around so that the headlights lit us up as though we were on stage.

Rodney limped over to his machine and hopped on. He headed right at us.

"He's going to run us down!" I yelled to the others. I started waddling ducklike on my skis away from the pond.

Eddie leapt up and poled herself fast out onto the ice right into Rodney's path. His headlights shone directly on her as he bore down at forty-five miles an hour. Eddie stood there calmly on her skis, her hands poised on her poles.

"Get out of the way, Eddie!" I screamed, as the machine bathed her in its flickering headlights.

Just as the machine reached her ski tips, Eddie deftly jumped sideways. As she did so, she raised her arms high over her head and planted her pointed ski poles in Rodney's sides, like a banderillero planting darts in a charging bull. Rodney screamed.

The four of us halted our frantic stumbling up the hill, turned around, and began schussing toward Eddie to drag her away.

In a blind rage, the poles sticking out of his sides and swaying in the wind, Rodney spun around and headed back for Eddie, who was standing placidly, evidently awaiting her death, hypnotized like a deer by car headlights.

Ira ran to his Sno Cat and hopped on and also roared toward Eddie. Oh no, was *he* going to run her down, too? She didn't stand a chance of dodging two of them. She had been right all along: Ira was no friend, he was in league with the others. Mona and Atheliah and Laverne and I poled frantically across the field trying to reach the ice.

I watched in terror as the two hulking machines converged on Eddie, who stood there without flinching. Then I realized that Ira was trying to force Rodney off course, like a police cruiser pulling over a speeder. Their front runners collided, sending up a flurry of sparks. As Ira edged Rodney ever so slightly out of his direct line on Eddie, he screamed to her, "Get *out* of here!"

At last Eddie started stumbling toward us on her skis. Without her poles she was helpless, but if she took off the skis, she'd be in snow to her waist. Atheliah and I each took an arm and dragged her up the meadow.

For good measure, we grabbed sleeping bags and evacuated. "Does that look like the action of a man who's trying to do us in?" I demanded grimly of Eddie, as we poled through the woods to Mona's and Atheliah's former farm.

When we returned a few days later, our cabin was still standing. There were no visible signs of damage, and no one had looted our supply of soybeans. We were quite busy that week. The weather was warming up during the day, and the sap was rising in our sugar maples. Every morning four of us drove our huge work horses in their clanking harnesses up the hill to the sugar bush. The fifth person stayed behind to do the housework and fix the meals. By the end of the week, we had washed out all the buckets and hung about half, drilling holes and inserting metal spouts and hanging the buckets on the spouts.

In spite of the skirmish, our pond was still serving as the town race track and social center. Drivers continued to use the lodge of the poor traumatized beavers as a jump. The participants continued to strew cans and wrappers all across the ice. Exhaust fumes continued to form a ground fog through our valley. The deafening roar continued to make conversation in the cabin without shouting an impossibility.

But we had learned to live with this mechanized Winter Wonderland, since the only alternative appeared to be *not* to live with it by not living at all. We had all learned to live with it except Eddie, who continued to sulk and brood and fill the wood stove with crumpled sketches of diabolical traps based on Vietcong guerrilla techniques. "We *can't* just sit back and take this," she insisted. "Human beings can adapt to almost any level of degradation, that's not the point. Sure, I *could* put up with it. The point is, I don't think we should. If someone hits you, you hit back immediately, or else you end up with numbers tattooed up your forearm."

On her less rational nights, Eddie lay writhing on our bed, clutching a pillow around her head to blot out the din and gnashing her teeth.

"We stretch a single strand of barbed wire tight between those two birches to the left of the pond," she suggested one night. "We attach it to the existing fence so that it looks like an extension of it. We use old wire so that it looks as though someone just forgot to take it down. Then, when those damn machines come hurtling down for an evening of fun on *our* property—crunch! The wire gets all tangled up in their goddam runners!"

"No, I don't want any part of it," I said, and was roundly seconded by the others. "If we can just endure this for another month, the snow will turn to mud. Maybe we can find another farm by next winter."

"Yeah. In the middle of a gun-testing range," Eddie sneered. "What's the matter, Ginny? Afraid your Stark's Bog boy friend will hurt his shiny big machine?"

I glanced at her wearily. "I assure you you're mistaken. And he *did* save your life."

"*Saved* my life! Please—spare me your melodrama. I was handling the situation just fine by myself. Who asked him to interfere?"

I stared at her in disbelief.

"I swear," she went on cheerfully, "you guys are the most timid, unimaginative bunch of gutless females I've ever had the misfortune to cohabit with. If the Klan had knocked at your door, you would have helped them tie the noose, wouldn't you have? And *you* most of all, Ginny. After what your people went through on the Trail of Tears, you can just sit back and take all this?"

"Which people?" I asked, forgetting about the one and a half ounces of dilute Cherokee blood coursing through my veins. "I don't believe in violence."

Eddie snorted incredulously. "That comment doesn't make any *sense*. That's like saying that you don't believe in *rain*. It's all *around* you, baby!"

"That doesn't mean I have to rush out into it."

"Mao says, 'All power comes out of the barrel of a gun,' " Mona mumbled.

"Perhaps there are some more rarefied possibilities with the Stark's Boggers than their doing us in, or our doing them in?" Atheliah suggested in her Julia Child voice.

"Garbage!" Eddie snorted. "Che says, 'In revolution one lives or one dies.' "

I searched my memory for some equally profound remark from someone with credentials impressive enough to counteract Che and Mao. All I could come up with was a line from the Beatles: "All you need is love." It didn't seem to pack much punch.

"The strong survive," Eddie went on, "and the meek perish! If you all won't look out for yourselves, I guess I'll have to look out for *all* of us." She stomped from the room.

Mona glanced around defiantly, stood up and followed.

Laverne, who as usual was wetting her lower lip with her tongue and then caressing her lip with her finger, shrugged and went upstairs. Soon the electric lights began flickering, and gasps of fulfillment drifted down to Atheliah and me. I sat staring at the floor. Atheliah was sharpening her ax, her bushy red head lowered with concentration.

Finally I broke the silence. "Atheliah, you've known Eddie longer than I have. Do you think she's been acting—strange the past month or two?"

Atheliah sighed and looked up. "Well, Eddie has always been very—definite in her opinions. But—I don't know really. You could be right."

"I'm *scared*, Atheliah." Atheliah looked down with embarrassment.

Just then there was a scream and a sizzling sound from upstairs, and all the lights went out.

"What was that?" Atheliah asked.

"I don't know," I whispered.

A door crashed open. "Christ, they've come for us!" Eddie yelled. "*See!* What did I *tell* you? We're sitting ducks!" She sounded as though she were careening around the living room bouncing off the walls like a trapped bird.

"*Who* has?" I yelled.

"Where?" Atheliah shouted.

"What happened?" Mona called, running in.

Finally Mona had the sense to light a match. By its glow, she located a candle. By the candlelight, I could see that Eddie had crammed herself into a living room corner behind a chair. She crouched there, a lamp poised for hurling, her eyes shifting wildly.

I kept expecting the doors to be broken down, or the windows to be bashed in by rampaging snowmobilers. But, as I got a grip on myself, I realized that there was no noise out of the ordinary—only the roar from the pond.

"I think a fuse blew," I suggested.

"Where's Laverne?" Mona asked.

"Someone screamed," Atheliah said. "It wasn't Ginny or I. Was it either of you?"

We ascended the stairs single file, led by Mona carrying the candle.

Halfway up, our heads were enveloped in smoke. "Hell, they've set the fucking cabin on fire!" Eddie yelled, pushing past Mona and grabbing the candle and racing down the hall, leaving the rest of us in blackness.

"Quick! In here!" Eddie yelled from Laverne's room.

My rainbow curtain was in flames, and part of the wall next to it. Eddie was beating out the fire with a pillow. The smoke was thick. We were all choking, tears streaming down our cheeks.

"The window!" Mona yelled.

Atheliah bashed it out with her ax.

Before long, the fire was out, and much of the smoke had dissipated. One whole corner was charred. Finally, it occurred to us to worry about Laverne. Looking around, we finally found her, nude under her army surplus sleeping bag. Her eyes were closed, and her face was the color of her blond hair. She appeared not to be breathing.

"Smoke inhalation," Eddie announced grimly. She began administering mouth-to-mouth resuscitation. "Call the doctor, for Christ's sake!" she gasped, between breaths into Laverne's lungs, as we all milled around.

"We don't have a phone," I pointed out.

"We'll go get him," Mona said, racing out with Atheliah thundering close behind.

Laverne was responding to the Kiss of Life. Before long, her lungs began pumping on their own. A few minutes later, I heard the truck return from town. Looking out, I was distressed not to see the doctor. Instead, Atheliah and Mona hastily strapped on their skis and schussed down to the pond.

Soon a single snow machine emerged from the herd and roared up toward the cabin. Atheliah and Mona herringboned frantically after it, but were soon obscured by swirling clouds of snow and exhaust.

The driver leapt off his machine before it had stopped, threw off his helmet, and tore inside. We heard him flying up the stairs. It was the doctor, looking unprofessional in his quilted ski suit; but we weren't complaining. Nodding soberly at us, he began inspecting Laverne's face, turning it this way and that. He removed the sleeping bag from her chest and listened to her heart with his head on her breast. He timed her pulse. He looked at her gums, lifted her eyelids, thumped her chest. Folding down the sleeping bag another turn, he rolled out one of her knees and discovered raw burned patches on the insides of her thighs. With a frown, he noticed an electrical cord. As he pulled on it, Laverne's vibrator popped out of her. Eddie and I looked at each other with alarm, and swallowed.

The doctor held the phallus-shaped vibrator, turned it over, sniffed it, scratched his head. It had a big crack all the way up it. Laverne had apparently achieved her goal of the Ultimate Orgasm.

The doctor, an elderly gray-haired man, looked up and said fumblingly, "Uh—what exactly—uh." Setting the vibrator down, he returned hastily to his inspection of Laverne.

His diagnosis formed, he stood up, blushing, and said, "Yes, well, your friend here is unconscious. She's had a bad electrical shock from her—uh—yes. Plus smoke inhalation. And her electrical burns need attention. I suggest we go to the hospital in St. Johnsbury right away. If you'll go by way of town, I'll pick up my car. I can come back for my snow machine tomorrow."

The next day I called the stockbroker in New York about the fire damage done to his cabin. He said he would get in touch with his insurance agent, who would be in touch with us.

One evening shortly after this, I was alone in the cabin. Laverne had gone home to Chicago for skin grafts on her thighs. Mona and Atheliah and Eddie had gone to a nearby farm. A woman who had been at the Women's Weekend was in labor at that very moment and had sent a friend over to invite us to watch the delivery and eat the placenta with her. I'd decided I wasn't hungry. Besides, I was by now cherishing, as a starving man does food, my delicious stolen moments of counterrevolutionary solitude. I just sat, doing nothing, listening to the snow machines on the pond.

My precious solitude was short-lived, however. There was a roar in the yard; and with a long-suffering sigh, I stood up. Walking over to the door, I could see that it was Ira. I smiled at him, wondering if all FBI agents were so handsome and sensuous-looking.

"Hello," I said, thoroughly prepared to consort with the enemy.

"Hello. Hear you've had some trouble?"

"A little."

"Do you mind if I come in and look at it? I wrote the fire insurance for this place. I'll have to do a report."

The stockbroker had said his agent would be in touch. I had expected someone from New York, not Ira Bliss IV. Could this be a clever ruse by the FBI to gain entry, to sniff out the marijuana in Mona's dried arrangements? Ira smiled. I let him in.

We went into Laverne's bedroom. The winter wind was howling through the smashed windowpanes. Ira whistled when he saw the charred corner. "Why by God, I'm surprised the whole *place* didn't go up. Lucky for you it didn't, cause the entire fire department was down at the pond that night."

He unzipped his quilted suit to his waist and took a pen and a small notebook out of his shirt pocket. He strolled around making notes. "Have you had a builder in to do an estimate?"

"No. Should we?"

"Make it two. Looks like there was some faulty wiring. Must have started inside the wall. An electrical fire. Were you using some kind of old wornout appliance up here that night—a coffee pot or something?"

"Something like that."

"A-yup. That's what it was, all right. An electrical fire in the wall, by Jesum. The worst darn kind. Hard to put out." He snapped his notebook shut. Tilting his head to one side, he looked at me with curiosity and asked, "Have you always—uh—lived with women?"

Remembering Eddie's warning—that he was putting the make on me so as to use me as an informer—I decided to turn him off forever. "Yes, it's true. I've always found men totally disgusting."

He looked at me with renewed interest. I had misread him. There were some men, some women too, who thought that their charms alone could cause the sap to rise in the swamp maple in midwinter. Ira was apparently such a man.

"You know, I've been thinking about life insurance," I said hastily, to change the subject. Besides, I *had* been thinking about life insurance, since my death was seeming ever more imminent. I wanted to tidy up my affairs, as it were, and leave Eddie and the Free Farm provided for.

Ira looked up, pleased. "It seems like a pretty good idea," I added.

"It *is*." He flipped open his notebook and began scribbling figures. "Now I have a plan here that would give you the kind of coverage . . ." He whirled around to show me what he'd written. As he did so, he accidentally butted me with his shoulder. I lost my balance and fell backwards, landing on my back on Laverne's bed. As I fell, one of my legs became tangled behind one of his knees, causing it to collapse. He fell forward and landed on top of me.

We lay still for several startled moments, trying to figure out what had happened, me with my face buried in his chest of curly hair.

I heard a voice in the doorway hissing, "I knew it!" Footsteps stomped to the stairs.

With all my strength, I shoved Ira off and raced down the hall. Eddie was at the foot of the steps, stalking into the living room.

"Eddie, it's not what you think!"

She stopped and turned to look at me. Her eyes were bloodshot and filled with tears; her face was white, and her mouth was pinched. "I *trusted* you, Ginny," she said in a trembling voice. She whirled around and headed across the living room.

"And I haven't betrayed your trust, Eddie!" I yelled.

I charged down the steps, three at a time. Halfway down, I twisted my ankle and fell the rest of the way. By the time I had picked myself up and limped across the living room, Eddie had leapt onto Ira's Sno Cat 44. I hobbled out the door and screamed, "Wait, Eddie! Listen to me!"

She gave me the finger as she lurched off down the meadow on the crazily careening machine. Opening it up to top speed, she traced a huge circle in the meadow, clinging desperately to the handle bars on the turns. The wind was lashing her braid. Ira by now was leaping through the deep snow under the full moon in pursuit of her.

The throttle wide open, she shot down the far side of the meadow toward the pond. It looked as though she had in mind a kamikaze mission, in which she would mow down as many of the congregated snow machines and drivers as possible, in the process of killing herself. Some of the drivers had seen her coming and were yelling at her and at each other, and were scurrying around mindlessly like ants under an overturned stone.

But just before Eddie reached the pond, Ira's Sno Cat appeared to hesitate slightly. The next instant, Eddie's head flew off her shoulders and bounced and spun across the ice like a crazed basketball. I watched with utter appalled disbelief: What I had just seen couldn't possibly have happened! Ira's Sno Cat coasted to a stop, and Eddie's headless body rolled off the seat and onto the ice with a dull plunk.

Screams and yells blended with the din of motors. I started running toward her, but the snow was to the top of my thighs. I pitched and heaved like a hooked fish but was getting nowhere.

"Lie down and roll!" Ira yelled from where he lay, exhausted, halfway down the meadow.

As instructed, I lay on the snow and rolled like a child down a grassy bank, with my arms stretched over my head. When I was on my stomach, with my face pushed into the snow, I would stick out my tongue and scoop up a taste. When I was on my back, I could see the gorgeous full moon. It wasn't possible that what I had just witnessed had really occurred. It had to be a dream. Relieved by that conclusion, I decided to enjoy my roll through snow down a moonlit meadow.

My head hit hard against the ice. I looked around, dazed. All the machines and their drivers were clustered several dozen yards away. I stood up and walked in that direction. People stepped aside to let me through, as though I were a leper. When I reached the center of the circle, I saw the doctor standing and talking with Ira, who had his hand on his Sno Cat handle bar. And on the ground, completely covered by a blanket, was a nondescript mound. A few inches of braid stuck out from one corner. Over at the shoreline, stretched between two birch trees that shone white in the moonlight, twanged a single strand of barbed wire.

"There's no blood," I said to the man next to me, shaking my head in wonderment. The man looked at me strangely, edging away.

Ira came over and took my arm. I looked up and smiled pleasantly. "It's a funny thing. There's no blood." He led me to a borrowed machine, sat me on the back, and drove me slowly up to the cabin.

Inside, I asked him, "Did you notice? There was no blood."

"How can I help you with this?" he asked in a choked voice.

"I never want to see you again. Please go away."

In the middle of that night, half-asleep, I scooted over to fit myself into the curve of Eddie's body so that we could sleep as we usually did, as two interlocking S's. I scooted some more, fumbling with my hands for her warm smooth flesh. I scooted some more—and fell out of bed.

As I lay dazed on the cold plank floor, the events of the evening returned to me. I couldn't wrap myself around Eddie, she wasn't here. She was in the funeral home in Stark's Bog, finally at peace with The People. I sat up and wrapped my arms around my legs and rocked back and forth, moaning. I dug my teeth into one knee.

Christ, I wanted her so much! I imagined skiing into town, sneaking into the funeral parlor, searching through the coffins, finding her . . . headless. That body that had given me such intense pleasure—how was it possible that it could be cold and inert, unresponsive? That body that had trembled and shuddered under my hands—I could caress it through all eternity and it would never stir again. But if those familiar mounds of flesh weren't "Eddie," what *was?* Where *was* she?

I tasted blood. I had gnawed through the skin on my knee.

Unable to track down Eddie's mother, we made the arrangements. When her ashes were returned from the crematorium in Montreal, the others agreed that I should dispose of them in solitude as I thought most appropriate. One afternoon I took the pot and walked out to our garden. The weeds and crop residues from the previous summer poked up through the snow. With a shovel, I cleared the snow from the tomato patch. One handful at a time, remembering with a faint pained smile lying there while Eddie lectured me on how weeding the tomatoes would weaken them, I scattered the ashes. Then, with the shovel, I replaced the snow.

Mona and Atheliah and I tried to carry on with the Free Farm as we felt Eddie would have wanted us to, rather than shutting down for an extended period of mourning. Sugaring was in full swing, and every day we had to collect the sap, in addition to barn chores and housework and stints at the clinic. But my efforts were lackluster. As far as I was concerned, the dynamic had departed. At various points throughout the day, I would pause at my tasks and stare off into the distance and wonder why I was bothering to do whatever I was doing. The only thing that kept me at it was some obscure notion that my halfhearted activities were a tribute to the memory of Eddie.

Several times a week one of us had to stay up all night in the sugar shack to stoke the fire to boil down the sap. One night I lay on the floor of the shack, drenched in sweat from the heat of the fire. In a detached intellectual fashion I was exploring the topic of Eddie's death: Had she ridden into the barbed wire that night by accident or on purpose? In other words, was it entirely my fault, or only partially so? Had I unwittingly driven her to suicide by feeding her insane jealousy? Or had she merely been caught in her own diabolical trap? There was no way I could ever know. I would carry the question, and the guilt, with me to my own grave. . . .

Suddenly I smashed my fist into the wall in frustration and collapsed on the floor sobbing.

As I wiped my tears with my shirt sleeve and sniffled, a snow machine arrived. The door of the shack opened and there was Ira, his nostrils flaring and his sensitive mouth quivering.

"Look," he said hastily, in answer to my obvious lack of enthusiasm, "I feel terrible about your friend. I haven't been able to sleep. I don't exactly understand what was going on that night, but I feel somehow responsible. Isn't there anything I can do?"

"It's not your fault. But please go away and leave me alone."

"Won't you at least explain what was going on?"

"No." He backed out the door, looking at me pleadingly.

The next few days, there was an unpleasant odor around the cabin, and particularly in the kitchen.

"Death," Mona said darkly. "It's the smell of death."

I shuddered. Then I went into the living room and got sticks of sandalwood incense for us. We lit them and waved them around, and soon the room smelled much better. We repeated this ritual for several nights running.

Then one morning when the three of us were on the hill collecting sap, the cabin below erupted in flames with a great whoosh like a gigantic gas oven lighting.

The cabin had burned to the ground before the volunteer fire department, in their black hats and yellow mackintoshes, could even get up the hill from town. The snow was melted for several hundred yards in every direction.

As Atheliah and Mona and I stood surveying the smoldering and flaring ruin, Ira came over and asked us questions in a very official tone of voice. "Gas leak," he finally concluded as we described our efforts to expel the odor of death with our incense sticks. He looked at us as though we were aborigines. "You smelled gas and you lit *matches?*"

Mona glared at him with hatred for his macho ability to cope with plumbing and wiring. She and Atheliah stalked to the truck, announcing that they were going back to their old commune. I said I'd be over later, I wanted to be alone.

The fire engines roared away with the volunteers clinging to them, disappointed to be done out of an opportunity for heroism. Ira walked toward his red fire chief's car with its flashing roof light. Part way there, he turned and said delicately, "If you need a place to stay, I have a big house with lots of extra rooms."

Gratefully, I walked to the car and climbed in next to him. I felt the need for some order in my life.

10

Friday, June 30

———————————— □ ————————————

On the third morning after her transfusion, Mrs. Babcock discovered a tarry black material in her stool.

"It's melena. From gastric bleeding," Dr. Vogel informed her briskly, not looking at her. "I'm putting you on a bland diet. And a different medication—ACTH." He prodded at her abdomen. "And this afternoon we'll administer another two units of whole blood.

"There's very little doubt in my mind," he added, half-sitting on the end of her bed, "that it's a question of sequestration, presumably in the spleen. We're about to pin it down. We're doing platelet antibody tests at the moment. Purpura haemorrhagiea, you have, Mrs. Babcock. Werlhof's syndrome. Idiopathic thrombocytopenic purpura, Mrs. Babcock. Morbus maculosus werlhofi." He recited these names as though invoking Roman deities to her bedside.

Mrs. Babcock nodded gravely, trying not to show irony. Why, this blond man was young enough to be her son! His pleased expression over his mastery of these complex medical terms amused her. She recognized it so well from when the children were young. Karl would offer grandly to show her his Boy Scout knots. She would watch closely, forcing herself to be interested in sheepshanks and half hitches. She would ask him questions about their uses and virtues, and he would give her lengthy dissertations with that exact same look of self-importance over acquired expertise. Then he would pull a knot tight to demonstrate a point, and the rope would unravel and fall limply to the ground. Karl would blush and stammer. Picking it up, he would clandestinely consult his handbook, while explaining that he had done that on purpose in order to illustrate how *not* to tie a clove hitch.

She wished Dr. Tyler were around. They'd been through so much together—births, deaths, menopause, strep throats, Pap smears, depressions. At least he would level with her. His age and his experience permitted him to admit it when he didn't know what he was doing.

"Young man," she asked Dr. Vogel, who was listening to her heart through his stethoscope, "how sick *am* I?"

He straightened up and averted his eyes. "Hmmm, yes, hmmm, well, obviously you're quite ill or you wouldn't be here, would you?" As she nodded in agreement, he edged toward the door.

"Might I die?" she inquired calmly, hoping to catch him off guard.

He cleared his throat and frowned. "I wouldn't say you could *die* . . . but, on the other hand, no one lives forever."

As she lay there trying to diagnose this answer, he slipped out the door, letting in a burst of words from next door: "You run until you drop, and then you pick yourself up and you run some more! Do you understand what I'm saying, men? You—"

Mrs. Babcock reviewed her situation. Wesley had died of a heart attack on his office floor. Two months later she had had a bloody nose lasting for several hours. A tourniquet test and platelet count had sufficed for Dr. Vogel to prescribe prednisone. It had worked, and she was out of the hospital in a week. Three months later an identical episode had occurred. Three weeks ago, a year to the day after Wesley's death, her nose had begun bleeding again. The drug had not worked this time. The transfusion had worked only briefly. Tests were being done. Other treatments would be tried. But what was *really* going on? Why was she being treated like an idiot child? Whose body *was* it?

The door opened and in slouched her daughter in bib overalls and a dingy T-shirt that read "Boone's Farm Apple Wine." Mrs. Babcock closed her eyes and sighed with exasperation. "Where did you get *that* outfit? At the feed store?"

Ginny glanced at her sullenly. "I'm sorry if it offends you, Mother. These *happen* to be the only clothes I own."

Mrs. Babcock sighed. "Poor dear. I *know* how difficult it must be to make ends meet on only $8,000 in dividend checks a year." She forced herself not to study Ginny's braless breasts. Watching her children develop physically had never ceased to amaze her. True, she and Wesley had set the whole process in motion, but almost immediately it became apparent that genes, and not they themselves, were running the show—laying down the framework and fleshing it out. If *she* could have run things, she'd have arrested their development at around age five. She had adored their compact little bodies at that age. No longer did every object in the house represent a potential calamity. No longer did they require her constant vigilance and assistance. When they'd dance to their records, they were so breathtakingly graceful and unself-conscious that tears would come to her eyes. And yet they had still required her in other ways, had scrambled onto her lap for cuddling and tickling and reassurance.

But there was a descent into a pit before them. They grew up overnight upon starting school and shrugged off caresses and insisted on doing everything for themselves and no longer sought the safety of her lap for recharging. Having finally learned to accept responsibility for them gracefully, she was now suddenly expected to unlearn all that and let go of them. And then the physical transformations—the boys' voices began cracking, they became as awkward and as timid as two-year-olds, but covered it over with an irritating braggadocio. Ginny had begun menstruating, had developed hips and breasts. It was appalling really—because it meant that these creatures weren't a superior species after all. They would lust and hunger and burn, just as their parents had. And out of it all would come children of their own, to whom *they* would look wistfully, hoping for more original things.

Wesley had taken it especially hard, for well-documented psychological reasons, when Ginny began dating, and coming in late with her make-up smeared all over her face. He always said it was like having some scuzzy ground hog take a bite out of a prize eggplant you'd been nurturing to perfection in your garden all summer. And when they'd seen Ginny in the emergency room after she fell off the Cloyd boy's motorcycle—her back red and skinless like a raw roast beef, and her leg purple with a jagged bone poking through the skin—she and Wesley had fallen weeping into each other's arms.

All Ginny's adult life Mrs. Babcock had had to force herself not to think about who was doing what to this young female body that she simultaneously loved and loathed. For the sake of Ginny's mental health, she had struggled to develop a sublime indifference. Besides, it was ridiculous—her feeling of physical possessiveness. And yet after so many years of tending this body—bathing it, dressing it, feeding it, binding up its wounds—how could she be expected to feel otherwise? Now that Ginny had a child of her own, was she aware of these undercurrents? Probably not. Ginny didn't seem to be aware of anyone's feelings except her own—or else she wouldn't be in her mother's sick room in bib overalls and a T-shirt.

Ginny sat down and stared at this shrew who was inhabiting her submissive mother's body and who kept insisting on making unexpected appearances. "I'm sorry you're not feeling well today," she offered, studying the hideous bruises on her mother's arms and reminding herself that the woman was very ill. In truth, Ginny was resentful at the way the whole thing was dragging on and on, and was guilty at being resentful. But after all, she *did* have her own life to lead, such as it was.

"I'm sure," her mother said sardonically, adding as though reading her mind, "I'm sorry I can't just die and get it over with, so that you can get on with your life."

"Mother, for Christ's sake!"

"Ginny, I've *asked* you to spare me your blasphemies. Do you *mind?*" Mrs. Babcock herself was a little startled at these appearances of a personality she didn't recognize as hers. These great bursts of irrational hostility were suddenly surfacing. She had simply been born in the wrong generation: When she had been a child, children were expected to defer to their parents in everything, to wait on them and help around the house and so on; but when she became a parent and was ready to enjoy her turn at being deferred to, the winds of fashion in child rearing had changed, and parents were expected to defer to their children in hopes of not squelching their imagination and creativity. She had missed out all the way around.

But the interesting thing was that since she had begun giving vent to her irritation—in other words, since Ginny had arrived—she hadn't been depressed. Before, if the children's behavior had annoyed her, she had blamed herself for the way she had brought them up. She was a failure at her chosen vocation—parenthood—and she had sunk deeper and deeper into the black pit of self-condemnation, had drugged herself into immobility with the pills that Dr. Tyler had given her, and had lain around the house feeling hopeless and worthless. But no more. Not now, when one would most expect her to be depressed, lying in a hospital bed with her hematopoietic system collapsing.

Forcing herself to be amiable, Mrs. Babcock said, "Well, dear, tell me about yourself. What have you been doing for the last year?"

Ginny grimaced and searched for an answer. "I saw Clem Cloyd the other afternoon."

"*Please*," Mrs. Babcock said, closing her eyes. "Don't talk to me about that boy. I've never forgiven him for nearly killing you."

"He's changed."

" 'Wolf cubs remain wolves, even though they may be reared among the sons of man.' "

"But he *has*, Mother. He's a family man now—a wife and three children."

"So I hear. What of it? Attila the Hun had children, too, you know."

"Apparently Clem has become very responsible, Mother. And he no longer feels the need for his death-defying stunts. Father used to say he was a brilliant farmer."

"So your father said."

"Did you know he preaches?"

"Are we talking about the same Clem Cloyd?"

"I *told* you he's changed."

"I'll believe it when I see it. Which will be never."

"Well, he asks about you. He's very concerned about you."

"And what do you hear from Ira?"

"Oh, not much," Ginny replied blandly. "He's very busy this time of year selling trail bikes." Was there no way to tell her own mother that Ira had kicked her out, that she hadn't heard from him at *all*, that she didn't know how Wendy was? She had spent several days getting up the nerve to phone them last night, but there had been no answer. What she *really* wanted was to ask her mother what to do. After all, what were mothers for? But she already knew what her mother would say: "Extramarital sex is vulgar." And "Children need their mothers." And "You must do your duty." If the story didn't just finish her off within seconds.

They sat in silence, Ginny trying to decide whether or not to mention cerebral hemorrhage. Should her mother be told so that she could be preparing for instant death? *Was* there any preparing for instant death? How would you prepare? No, it was too horrible—knowing that at the next moment your brain might erupt in great geysers of blood, turning the contents of your skull into a gory mush. Panic clutched at her stomach and she grew dizzy. No, it was better for her mother not to know at all.

The two women exchanged strained smiles, the echoing silence starting to turn awkward, symbolic of the years of silence between them.

"I thought I'd call Karl and Jim," Ginny said casually.

"Why?"

"Well, just to tell them that you're sick and in the hospital. I'm sure they'd want to know." In fact, she felt they should be placed on alert for a deathbed scene.

"I don't really see the need for it. It's not as though I'm dying or anything! I mean, I didn't tell you all the other times, did I?"

"No, you didn't. That's what I mean. I wish you had. Why do you have to be such a martyr all the time, suffering in obscurity?"

"I can't see any point in getting everyone all upset over nothing, that's all. Just because I'm indisposed doesn't mean that you can bully me, Virginia Babcock Bliss. So please don't call them. I'll write them about it in my next letter."

"Do you promise?"

"Yes, I promise. But I don't see that it's any concern of yours, frankly."

"It's just that you've always been so resolutely secretive about everything."

"*I* have been? Mata Hari is calling *me* secretive?"

"Well, you're right. As a family, we just don't communicate, do we?"

The term "communicate" amused Mrs. Babcock. It was such a cliché, on the lips of every intense TV talk-show guest in the country. "Yes, I am aware that we don't—communicate," she replied. "But you have to understand that that's one of my few remaining pleasures."

Ginny snorted with laughter. She had to admit that her mother could really be very funny. Not often enough, unfortunately. Or rather, not at the right moments. "All right. Go ahead, Mother. Turn it into a joke. But it's the truth."

Mrs. Babcock nodded tolerantly at her daughter. "Yes, dear, but I think you'll find that really important things eventually get themselves communicated. Not necessarily in so many words."

"If you say so," Ginny said, thinking of her broken marriage, cerebral hemorrhage, all the various topics she was incapable of broaching.

Finally she stood up, saying lamely, "I have to find Dr. Vogel to ask him some stuff about the transfusion this afternoon."

In fact, she had to grill him on the topic of her mother's bleeding stomach. She descended to the basement lab in the elevator. In one corner of the metal box was a small puddle of drying blood.

The elevator came to a stop. Ginny didn't move. She was transfixed by the blood. She felt nauseated, but she couldn't take her eyes off it. Whose was it? What sort of vessel had it sloshed out of? Was it healthy or diseased? What was its clotting time, its platelet lysis time? What type was it? As she stared, the puddle seemed to throb, in obedience to its absent heart. Blood, all the same everywhere— each person's the ionic composition of dilute sea water, containing cells that performed the same functions, governed by the same enzymes and hormones. And yet, in spite of all this sameness, like snowflakes or fingerprints, samples from no two people were identical. So many things to go haywire. . . .

"Miss? *Miss?*" An orderly in white stood impatiently outside the elevator.

"Excuse me," Ginny said, stepping out in a daze.

She walked into the impersonal green-walled lab office. The secretary's desk chair was empty. Ginny peeked around the doorway. Dr. Vogel in a white lab coat was peering through a microscope, continuously readjusting the focus. Next to him sat a centrifuge and a rack of test tubes. He was making hurried notations on a record form.

"Dr. Vogel?"

He looked up. "I'm sorry, Miss Babcock. I'm very busy right now. Could you leave a message with my secretary?"

"She's not here."

He averted his eyes as Ginny walked over to him. "Would you say the transfusion hasn't worked?"

"Well, she's just had one. And it performed the function we intended: It relieved her anemia and cut down her bleeding temporarily while we worked at isolating the cause. But of course her platelet count is back down now—to 25,000/mm^3."

"Compared to what?"

"Compared to right after the transfusion, when it was in the vicinity of 100,000/mm^3."

"May I look?"

"Well, I don't know. . . . This is highly unconventional, Miss Babcock, your coming in here like this."

Ginny looked through the microscope and saw clusters of transparent blobs on a grid of etched squares. So these were the culprits —her mother's languid platelets. They might even be her own, left over from the transfusion.

When she looked up, Dr. Vogel was holding a test tube with some red liquid in it, blood presumably, up to the overhead light. He studied it intently. Flipping on a fluorescent light directly over the counter, he picked up a second test tube and glanced back and forth between the two.

"What are you doing?"

"We're testing your mother's blood for platelet antibodies to determine if her ITP is being triggered by an autoimmune mechanism. We've incubated some of her serum with your blood and a sample of the drug your mother was on prior to admission, and we're checking for clot retraction."

"*What* drug?"

"Amitriptylene. Elavil to the layman."

"For *what?*"

He glanced at her, amazed at the breadth of her ignorance. "For depression, of course."

Of course? Ginny winced. Dr. Tyler had mentioned depression. Now this. What had her mother been depressed *about?* Mr. Zed's death? The Major's death? Guilt swept over Ginny. Her children had been a disappointment. Ginny didn't know precisely what her mother had wanted from them, but she clearly hadn't gotten it. It was evident from the way she spoke of Jim and Karl—tolerantly, but with frowns and sighs. And presumably she spoke to them of her in the same way. Maybe her mother was right after all: Important things *did* eventually get themselves "communicated," one way or another.

"Well, I think we have every reason to believe we're about to get this thing under control, don't you?" he asked.

Ginny struggled in the grip of her need to believe this. Due to having been reared by parents who were incapable of saying "I don't know," she knew that she suffered from what the psychology texts at Worthley had labeled an Authority Neurosis. She had gone through life setting up tin gods who were supposed to restore to her the sense

of certainty she had enjoyed under her parents' rule. Although this
desperate longing for someone who really knew what he or she was
doing remained, common sense told her that Dr. Vogel was just an
ordinary flawed and confused mortal like herself. "I don't see why
not," she replied, not believing it. "But how sick *is* she?"

He blushed and averted his eyes. "Miss Babcock," he finally answered, "you ask that as though I can give you a number on a scale
from one to ten. I *can't*. Besides, I've been trained to save lives. I don't
believe in writing patients off." He bent over his microscope by way
of dismissal. Ginny glared at him. What did *that* mean?

Mr. Solomon and Sister Theresa were in the middle of a discussion
when Ginny arrived at the sun porch to witness her mother's lunch.

". . . and so you see, Sister, there's nothing in man that is *vorth*
extending throughout infinity. I mean *really*, Sister, vould you vish us
on eternity? No, it doesn't make sense. Ve are a flawed species. The
only thing to be said in our favor is that our bodies can rot and be
devoured by grubs and vorms; and the elements that are released can
go into making up the bodies of a different—and ideally not morally
retarded—species."

"My dear Mr. Solomon, my heart goes out to you," Sister Theresa
said, fondling her "Not My Will But Thine" medal. "If that hope is
the only force that sustains you, I don't know why you're still alive.
I really don't. Perhaps it doesn't make *sense* to you that our Lord can
esteem us and provide for us in spite of our many vanities and frailties,
but can't you *feel* it in your heart? Look out there, Mr. Solomon," she
invited, gesturing in the direction of the factory. The electric chimes
were playing "You'll Never Walk Alone." "When you see sunlight
playing on the meadows, don't you feel here"—she patted the site of
her missing breast—"that there are factors even *you* haven't taken into
account, forces you know not of, that God's in His heaven and all's
right with the world? Because, believe me, Mr. Solomon, He *is*."

"Since you put it that way, Sister," he said, patting his emphysema-
tous lung, "no, I don't feel it here. I think—"

"Stop it!" Mrs. Babcock screamed, hurling her bowl of cream
soup on the floor. "Can't you two just *shut up?* You go on and on and
on, saying the same things over and over again. Neither of you is
affected by what the other says, or even listens to it! Why can't you
just be quiet? Mrs. Cabel is the only one in this room with any sense."
She stood shakily, as the others stared with alarm.

She started her agonizing shuffle toward the door. Ginny jumped up and took her arm. They started down the hall, leaving the others to cope with the spilled soup and broken china.

"Mother—" Ginny began, framing a gentle reprimand. True, her mother was sick, but there was no reason to turn into a savage.

"Not *one* word. Not one word."

As Mrs. Babcock struggled up the hall on her aching legs, something happened. It was as though her brain were shifting gears. The hall telescoped—it looked miles long. She shuffled along, holding Ginny's arm. She could have been walking like this for minutes or for months. She didn't know or care.

Back in bed, she lay limp and lethargic. It was as though a plug had been pulled and her vital energies were flowing out of her. But it wasn't the weariness of depression. That she was thoroughly acquainted with. Depression was a very active state really. Even if you appeared to an observer to be immobilized, your mind was in a frenzy of paralysis. You were unable to function, but were actively despising yourself for it. This frame of mind was entirely different. Its only emotion, if it could be called that, was sublime indifference. Nothing mattered anymore. If she was dying, so be it. Languidly, she raised an arm and observed the bruises—dark red and deep purple and green. What did this grotesque arm have to do with her? For heaven's sake, what was all the fuss about?

A haze had settled in over the room. People were rushing around, doing different things to her pathetic body. Their voices as they questioned her urgently hummed and buzzed like angry bees. She wanted to tell them all just to relax and leave her alone.

Dr. Vogel, who had come running, turned to Ginny and said, "She seems all right. All her vital signs are in order. Maybe she's just tired out."

As her mother lay limp with blood from another donor running into her arm, Ginny watched "Westview General" on television. Doctors Turcott and Adrian, the two handsome bachelor main characters, were performing an impossibly intricate operation that was snatching a small boy from the jaws of death, and were at the same time cracking jokes and quoting Shakespeare and making dates with the surgical nurses, who somehow managed to look provocative in low-fashion sterile gowns and caps.

But gradually, as though catching an infection from her mother, Ginny felt herself being flooded with cosmic indifference. She just stopped caring—about the young surgeons on "Westview General," about her ill mother, about Wendy and Ira. It was as though the incredible strain of the past few weeks had mounted to a point beyond which she could not go. Her system was simply shutting down; her emotions were closing up shop. There she and her mother lay, in their separate beds, awash on a healing sea of indifference.

Because it *was* healing, there was no question in Ginny's mind. It was an inexpressible relief just to give up. People came and went, marked charts, plumped pillows, straightened sheets. "Beat the Clock" came on the television, and a frazzle-haired woman in a yellow slicker tried to balance milk cartons full of water on her forehead while flying across the stage on a skate board, as the huge monster clock ticked away relentlessly devouring her prize money.

"Turn it off, would you please?" Ginny asked Mrs. Childress. And the two of them, mother and daughter, floated on through the afternoon as their ancestral clock on the bedside table ticked ever more slowly. Ginny couldn't tell if the clock was running down or if her ears were going haywire. But she didn't really care. Eventually the clock stopped altogether.

Ginny reached the big house in the same languid frame of mind. Her determination to struggle, against anything, had vanished as completely as last winter's snow under the hot spring sun in Vermont. She got the mail from the box. In it was her letter to Miss Head, unopened and marked in Miss Head's pinched handwriting "Return to Sender." Without emotion, Ginny slid it into her overalls pocket. She strolled with indifference past the Southland Realty FOR SALE sign in the front yard.

She went upstairs to her room, which was untouched since she had lived in it nine years ago. A canopied double bed with a cannon-ball frame, a skirted dressing table, a Queen Anne highboy. Her mother had been suggesting gently, ever since she had left home, that she sort out the stuff in her closet. And each time her mother had hinted at this, Ginny had snapped back, "Why? Are you planning to take in roomers or something? What's wrong with it the way it is?" Nevertheless, each trip home she had gone to her closet to clean it out. Each time she had become engrossed in a scrapbook or a diary; each time she had decided that there was nothing she could part with. Her complete set of Hullsport High athletic game programs from 1960–1962; the sales slip from her first Never-Tell bra; the list in Joe Bob's childish scrawl of all the Hullsport High couples in 1962 who had "gone all the way"; her moth-riddled flag swinger jacket and the flag with "To Strive, To Seek, To Find, and Not To Yield" on it; the ribbon from the Persimmon Plains Burly Tobacco Festival; her shoulder pads and face-guarded helmet; four strapless net and chiffon gowns; a stack of Scrooge comic books, which were collector's items by now. Each time she had decided that they all had to stay.

Besides, Ginny had somehow always felt that if she actually cleared her stuff out, her mother might move someone else in. An irrational feeling, since there was no one around the house needing a room, but there it was. She still thought of this house as "home," this room as "her room"; not Ira's stone house in Vermont, not her garret at Worthley, not the Cambridge apartment or the Stark's Bog cabin.

The past had always been more real, more present to her than the present. But this day, without regret and without satisfaction, with total indifference, Ginny cleaned out her entire closet, bundling up all the stuff and toting it out back to the trash cans. She had fantasized that she and Wendy would live in this house, that this would be Wendy's room, that she would continue to hoard all her junk to show Wendy. But she knew now that this would never happen, it was absurd to keep this clutter around any longer. It was time to purge herself of her constipated past.

Back at the cabin, the screeching of baby birds greeted her. Languidly, she got their gooey food from the refrigerator and dropped a few balls of it and some water down their gaping throats, without pleasure and without concern. If they died, so be it. Then she lay down on the big double bed where she had been born. She lay, without guilt over inactivity, without the satisfaction of well-earned leisure, without agony over past failings or apprehension about her uncertain future.

Mrs. Babcock woke up the next morning as though stung awake by bees. All she could think about was the previous afternoon, which she had spent in bed utterly motionless and emotionless. She had been demoralized and had just given up. It reminded her of the descriptions of people in the last stages of consciousness before freezing, when they acquiesced to the idea of death and gave up the struggle to stay alive. Well, she never would get out of this terrible place that way. And here when she had so much to do—notes to write thanking people for flowers, her embroidery stitches to practice, the last volume of the encyclopedia to get through.

She climbed down and headed for the bathroom, glancing out the window and smiling with pleasure at the antics of the red squirrels, who were carefully dropping twigs down onto the people entering the hospital.

Looking in the mirror, she prodded the cotton wads in her nose and noted with satisfaction that they weren't soaked through. Nor was the pad between her legs. And when Miss Sturgill whisked in and performed the bleeding test, her time was six minutes. The transfusion had worked again.

She took the silent clock in her lap and wound it until it wouldn't wind any more. She remembered its running down the previous afternoon—only at the time, she hadn't thought of it as "running down." She had pretended that she was a child and that time was telescoping, as it did for children. She was contrasting what time used to be like when she was a schoolgirl, when summer vacation would stretch out luxuriously before her like an eternity. A day then had been the equivalent of a week now. A day now was nothing more than a sneeze. Time played tricks on people as they aged. She remembered from the encyclopedia that time seemed to expand as metabolic rates increased. The lifetimes of fast-moving unstable particles increased as their speed increased; when motion approached the speed of light, time slowed to such an extent as to appear to be standing still. Children had high metabolic rates; those rates slowed as a person's body reached maturity and began its decline. As the metabolic rate slowed down, time sense speeded up. Easy to explain, painful to experience. Just as you began to feel that you could make good use of time, there was no time left to you.

She realized that the clock she had just wound wasn't ticking. Why not? What had happened to it? Perhaps Mr. Solomon. . . .With remorse, she recalled her scene at the lunch table. How *could* she have screamed at poor Mr. Solomon and Sister Theresa, suffering, and perhaps dying, as they both were? In their conditions they were entitled to talk about whatever they wanted to. It seemed ludicrous to *her* to debate the nature of God, but if it comforted *them,* why shouldn't they? If it upset her, she shouldn't go to the sun porch.

With a great burst of energy, she got out of bed and walked to Mr. Solomon's room and apologized. Then to Sister Theresa's room.

"Please. Don't apologize, Mrs. Babcock. I understand," Sister Theresa assured her. Mrs. Babcock doubted that she did. "I know it's sometimes difficult to accept the workings of our Lord, Mrs. Babcock. For the believer, death is the whole meaning of life. But for those outside the fold, death renders life absurd, full of pain and poignancy."

Mrs. Babcock nodded solemnly, determined not to reply, since any reply she could possibly make would sound glib or cynical in the face of such spiritual ardor. If she had to choose between the two, Mrs. Babcock would pick Mr. Solomon's bitterly jocular nihilism any day. Fortunately, she didn't have to choose. She could suck what was helpful from both attitudes, for use when she too was *in extremis*—as she clearly was *not* now, in spite of Sister Theresa's insinuations to the contrary.

Ginny's eyes snapped open. She lay fully clothed on the bed; sunlight was streaming through the window. With disgust, she realized that she'd squandered the entire previous afternoon and evening, lying around in some sort of neurotic stupor when she had so many urgent responsibilities—kudzu to chop, birds to feed. She had had a definite brush with what the psychology texts at Worthley had referred to as "ego chill."

She leapt up and stalked into the living room, where the baby birds were screeching from their wicker basket. It was a wonder they hadn't starved in the night. She got their food. They squawked angrily, their beady black eyes gazing at her with despair, and their tiny yellow beaks quivering convulsively. Ginny dropped balls of the paste into their mouths and followed it with driblets of water.

Closing the lid, she got down Birdsall's book and searched through it as frantically as she had searched through Dr. Spock when Wendy had been an infant, for some clue as to what she should be doing. Were they screeching with such desperation because they were flourishing, or because they were in their death throes? Professor Birdsall wasn't giving away any secrets. Like the ray of light in Einstein's theory of the universe, she kept circling back and ending up where she had started—at the sentence that read, "It is best to kill such birds should they be found, to avoid prolonging their suffering."

"No!" she growled. Who the fuck was Professor Wilbur J. Birdsall anyhow? There he sat in his laboratory at the University of Chicago, miles away from the wild birdlife that was his life's work.

What did he know? It was conceivable that he was wrong about swifts' digestion. The babies were accepting the gooey mess of flour and tuna and hamburg. They weren't vomiting it back up. What was happening in the face of dire necessity might be very different from what happened in the leisurely laboratory circumstances concocted by Professor Birdsall. She had to beat back her Authority Neurosis and trust her own observations.

According to Birdsall, the babies were nowhere near being ready to fly. Could the same principle apply? Faced with the necessity of flying, would their wing muscles and feathers develop faster than usual? Or would they crash and die? Ginny decided to find out. They were locked in a race against time. Birdsall maintained that wild birds raised in captivity often died quite soon anyway. Ginny had to set her birds free before they either died or developed an unrenounceable dependence on her. But maybe they were already too dependent, since she couldn't, as a bird parent would, show them how to find bugs and seeds, or how to build a nest? Or was all that information encoded in their genes? If so, all the more reason to urge them off on their own, before those instincts were clouded over by artifice.

She opened the basket and unhooked the two fledglings from where they hung and carried them outside into the bright sunlight. They closed their black eyes and began screeching in protest. Setting one down, Ginny stroked the fluffy gray feathers of the other with her finger. It opened its tiny eyes and stared into hers. She held out her hand with the bird perched on it. Nothing happened. She made him perch on her index finger. Still nothing, no cooperative movements from him. He opened his beak and squawked with unhappiness.

Ginny enfolded him in her hand and rubbed his head. Then she tossed him into the air, like throwing confetti. He plummeted down, wings tight to his side, like a fluffy black bullet, and crashed into the kudzu.

Sighing, Ginny picked up the other one and repeated the process. Then she returned to the first one. According to her half-baked theory, development could occur in response to need. She had to convey to the centers in their brains that controlled physical maturation the urgency for wing feathers and muscles. So she tossed both, screeching with misery, a couple of more times before returning them to the basket.

As she collapsed on the sofa next to them, she heard a crackling sound in her pocket. She drew out the letter to Miss Head. Anguish stabbed through her. Miss Head, whom she had loved, whatever that might mean, who had loved her after her fashion, no longer wanted anything to do with her. Apparently seven years wasn't time enough to heal the wounds Ginny had inflicted. Ginny knew that she had behaved badly. Miss Head had shared all the things that were most important to her; and Ginny had repaid her by kicking her in the teeth. If seven years wasn't time enough for Miss Head to forgive her, most likely an eternity wouldn't do. She felt tears poised in her eyes and allowed herself the luxury of letting them overflow. She licked them off her checks. They tasted salty, like sea water, like blood.

Wiping her face with her tie-dyed T-shirt, she stood up and prepared to leave.

When she got to the big house, she jumped out of the Jeep and charged across the weedy front yard to the Southland Realty sign. She gave a great heave and wrenched it out of the ground and tossed it way under the spreading branches of the magnolia tree. Then she lowered her face into smooth creamy magnolia blossoms and breathed deeply of the cloying scent. The petals enveloped her face. The odor summoned up a dizzying succession of summer weddings, high school dances, holiday feasts, at which the gorgeous blossoms had always been featured as centerpieces. She broke off a couple and placed them carefully in the Jeep.

Then she strode around the house and stared with dismay at her formal gowns, which were billowing out of a trash barrel like froth on an overfilled beer mug. Resolutely, she removed from the barrel everything she had dumped into it the previous afternoon. It took several trips to cart it all back up the stairs. She replaced it in her closet and chests exactly as it had been before her neurotic seizure of destructiveness. She could imagine Wendy's delight over the Scrooge comic books. She would pull out all the stuff and tell the fascinated child everything—well, almost everything—that she had done and expected and planned for as a girl. This room could be Wendy's. She removed from her bookcase her favorite tattered book from her own preliterate days. Its chewed torn pages featured pictures of baby farm animals with their mothers, in poses of affection and concern—lamb and ewe, colt and filly, piglet and sow. She put it in a large brown envelope and addressed it to Wendy. . . .

When she got to the hospital, Ginny was pleased to find her mother sitting up writing letters. Her eyes were bright, and her face didn't look quite so puffy. "Hello," her mother said with a pleasant smile.

"Hi!" Ginny took a wide bowl into the bathroom and filled it with water, and floated the two magnolia blossoms. She placed the bowl on her mother's bedside table, proud of her thoughtful initiative in the face of the almost overpowering promptings toward passivity that flooded her whenever her mother was around to arrange, handle, manage, organize.

Her mother stared at the blossoms with surprise. "Why, thank you, dear. They're lovely."

"They are, aren't they?"

"I only wish I could smell them."

"You'll be able to before they've gone by," Ginny assured her. Her mother nodded in serene agreement.

Ginny glanced at her mother's chart, which someone had forgotten to remove from the room—clotting time, six minutes; platelet count, 110,000/mm^3.

"Fantastic!"

"Yes, it is, isn't it? I almost feel as though I could endure the craft program this afternoon."

"Well, don't get *too* carried away. Hey, the clock's working. Did it just run down yesterday, or what?"

"I don't know really. Mr. Solomon did something to the spring mechanism that runs the pendulum, and it's all right again. He's amazing, you know. He could scarcely see the clock because of his cataracts, the poor old thing. But he was able to diagnose it and fix it almost by touch. He said it's really a fine one. German, he says it is. I can't imagine how my family ended up with it. That branch was mostly Scotch-Irish."

"Well, but that kas in the downstairs hall is Dutch, isn't it?"

"Yes. I didn't think you children ever listened when I told you about these things."

"I wouldn't have *had* to listen, Mother. As many times as you ran through your heirloom routine, I'd be bound to have just *absorbed* all the relevant information."

"I wasn't *that* bad."

"That's what *you* think."

"Well, it wasn't all my fault. You children used to clamor around me unmercifully to bring down my pictures"—she gestured to the photos on the wall—"and to tell you about 'the man who got his head knocked off by the truck.' "

"*We* did? *You* were the one who was always trotting out those pictures, Mother, as a didactic exercise about our own mortality."

Mrs. Babcock smiled with exasperation. "I'm sorry, dear, but you're wrong. The three of you, especially you, used to be obsessed with injuries and accidents and fires and theft. It used to worry me terribly. I couldn't figure out how I'd failed you, what I'd done or not done to make you so insecure and frightened all the time. I finally concluded that it was because your father left to go off to war when you were only two months old. The world and its relationships must have seemed very tentative to you at too young an age."

"That's not how *I* remember it. I remember *you* as the fearful one, Mother. 'You can't be too careful,' you'd say all the time. 'If you ride your bicycle in the road, dear, expect to be run over by a truck,' " Ginny mimicked.

"And *death*," her mother continued. "You used to go on and on about it. Why did people die? What happened to their bodies? How could God let people die? Would God die? Did He have a wife and would she die? Did you have to die? When would your father and I die? What would happen to you if we died right then and left you all alone? Could you have the car for your own after we died? It went on and on. It used to get so ridiculous that your father and I would finally collapse in laughter. And then you would start crying and accusing us of not caring if you died. I worried about it for years. You always used to plead with me to dig up the cats and dogs and birds that we buried in the back yard so that you could see what had happened to their bodies."

Ginny was shaking her head no. "But *you* were the one who kept harping on death, Mother. You'd sit around all day, day after day, writing up epitaphs and obituaries and memorial services for yourself. And dragging us around every summer to family cemeteries to do tombstone rubbings and stuff."

Mrs. Babcock looked at her strangely and frowned. "You're exaggerating, dear. True, I *did* at one point do an epitaph and a format for a memorial service. But that's not unusual. It's like making up a will. You do it once to be sure that your wishes are down explicitly in writing. And you may go back and touch it up a time or two as your ideas change. But mostly you do it so that your survivors will have something to go by when they're finally faced with the task of disposing of you and your effects. But I've *never* written an obituary for myself. I wonder where you got that idea?"

"I don't know," Ginny said lamely. "But what about the tombstone rubbings, Mother? You have to admit to dragging us through a hell of a lot of graveyards in pursuit of your forebears."

"I don't know about 'a lot.' I was interested for several years in tombstones as a sort of—you know, folk art form."

Ginny stared at her mother suspiciously. Whose version of their shared past was accurate? And how could their versions be so different?

"Whatever happened to those baby birds you found? Are they still alive?"

"Yeah. I've been feeding them. You know that bird book? The one by a guy named Birdsall? He said you might as well kill baby swifts if you found them because they needed regurgitated food from their parents. Well, I've been feeding them hamburg for a week and they're still alive."

"So much for the experts," Mrs. Babcock said grimly, thinking of her own case. But the second transfusion had worked. Today she was feeling great. Maybe young Dr. Vogel could be trusted after all.

"Yes, so much for the experts. It occurred to me, though, that maybe what happens in a laboratory is different from what happens in real life. I mean, my birds *had* to learn to cope with undigested food. And they appear to have, ahead of schedule. Does that sound possible?"

"Certainly it does. Likely, even. You can force an apple tree to fruit by cutting a strip of bark from around its trunk. I read it in the encyclopedia. But you know these experts."

After lunch Ginny watched "Hidden Heartbeats" from the spare bed.

"What are we *doing* this for?" her mother asked with a tolerant smile. "Think of all the classics I haven't read."

"We're hooked."

"Yes, but I don't even *care* what happens to these people. And I *still* have to know."

"Face it, Mother. We're both shameless gossips at heart."

"We could pretend that we're sociologists, and that we're merely clinically interested in what keeps millions of American women glued to their television sets every afternoon."

"Let's!"

That afternoon's installment was a shocker. Frank had discovered that his cherished little daughter had actually been fathered by his wife's brother-in-law's great-uncle, and that his wife was still seeing the old man and receiving gifts from him on the sly—giant stuffed animals from F.A.O. Schwartz's for the child, for instance. In a heart-wrenching scene, Frank turned Linda out of his house, vowing never to let her see the little girl again. Parts of the ridiculous plot were hitting uncomfortably close to home for Ginny.

During the commercial, as an anthropomorphic white tornado swirled around a startled housewife's toilet bowl, Ginny said, "You know, I'm really shocked. I thought that Frank knew all along that he wasn't Marty's real father."

"You *did?* Why would you think that? No, I never felt that he knew."

"Still, he's reacting somewhat excessively, don't you think?"

"Do you think so?"

"Well, I don't see what all the fuss is about. I mean *really,* is sex, or who people have it with, all that important?"

Mrs. Babcock looked at Ginny thoughtfully, expecting what she was going to say to outrage her. "I think that extramarital sex is vulgar. It makes sex both too important and not important enough."

Just as Ginny was about to reply angrily, the program resumed, and they fell silent, absorbed in the moral dilemmas of modern America. The half hour ended with Frank's trying to explain to the pitiful little girl that her mommy was gone forever. Ginny was pro-foundly moved by the child's incredulous distress, the more so as she recalled from her psychology texts at Worthley how the early loss of a significant love object predisposed someone to incapacitating depressions as an adult.

Gruffly, Ginny said, "I don't really think a child that age knows the difference. As long as there's someone responsible around to care for it."

Her mother studied her, then said quietly but with conviction, "Small children need their mothers."

"Garbage! *Any* warm body will do!" She was close to tears.

That night Ginny climbed the path to the springhouse alongside Clem. Maxine followed. The springhouse from the outside looked just as it always had—built of weathered boards and listing away from the hillside. The door was still chained and locked, but hanging on it was a crude hand-lettered sign that read "Holy Temple of Jesus."

Half a dozen people stood chatting outside. Ginny didn't know any of them, though they were prototypes of people she'd known all her life, or that portion of her life spent in Hullsport—the area farming families. The men wore clean pressed work clothes, dark green or khaki. Their hair was neatly combed and parted and slicked down. Some carried instrument cases. The women wore bargain basement flowered house dresses, and white socks and flats. Their hair was tied back into frizzy pony tails. Although most looked older, they treated Clem and Maxine with a respect bordering on deference, and kept referring to them as Brother and Sister Cloyd. Ginny hadn't heard unrelated people call each other brother and sister since she'd left the Free Farm. She was seized by a bout of culture clash.

This faded quickly when Brother Cloyd began introducing her around as an old friend. She was well aware that Clem was counting on her not to divulge to his brothers and sisters in Christ the fact that he and she had "known" each other in the true biblical sense on the floor of their Holy Temple not ten years earlier. Ginny had cleaned up her act for the evening, had rejected her various inflammatory T-shirts, and was wearing her patchwork peasant dress. She had even wetted her hair down in a feeble effort to subdue it.

Inside, lined up across the stone floor, were several rows of crude benches that faced a raised dais. Ginny noticed that the furniture Clem had made when they were kids remained; the bookshelves where he had kept his pornographic paperbacks now held tattered hymnals. The small table she had perched on the last time she had been here, right before leaving for her freshman year at Worthley, had been converted into an altar. It was covered with a clean white fringed cloth. Hanging on the wall above it was a simple wooden cross. And the stream continued to gurgle along in its stone channel, giving the place a refreshingly damp cool feeling on the hot summer night.

Ginny sat on a bench in back and tried to make herself as inconspicuous as possible, which wasn't very. She was still stunned by the transformation in Clem. Not only that his crippled leg had regenerated itself—she was getting used to that major miracle. Primarily she was amazed by the change in Clem's manner. She remembered him as a sour, antisocial, borderline-pathological boy. And now here he was at the door of his springhouse, greeting his parishioners—transformed into a warm, self-confident man. He had spent his adolescence pursuing death and had escaped it only by divine intervention. But here he was now, running a large and successful farm, raising a family, ministering to his flock. How was it possible? Ginny had known that human beings were flexible organisms, but she hadn't known that they were *this* flexible. Perhaps there was hope for the species after all.

Three men were on the front platform unpacking their instruments—a bass fiddle, a guitar, drums. Another man who had just come in carried a large black box to the altar, set it down reverently, and backed away.

Eventually, there were some twenty people sitting on the benches. Maxine was standing on the podium in front of the men with the instruments, just as she had stood on the platform at the Bloody Bucket all those years ago wailing "When My Pain Turns to Shame." The golden cross wedged between her mammoth mammaries flashed in the light from kerosene lanterns as she led songs Ginny didn't know —gospel songs in close harmony pleading with sweet Jesus to show the Way.

Gradually, the tempo of the songs began to pick up, and soon there was a lot of clapping and dancing in the aisles. Some young girls beat on tambourines up front. People began shouting over the music, "Yes, Lord!" and "Sweet, sweet Jesus!"

The rhythmic clapping was exercising a hypnotic effect on Ginny. From the start she had been clapping and trying to sing along, just to fulfill the requirements of polite guesthood. She had fully expected to find the evening tedious, was in attendance solely in order not to hurt Clem's and Maxine's feelings. What she had *not* expected was to be caught up in the flood of emotion surging through the room. She had not expected to find herself clapping with cheerleader-like enthusiasm. And she had especially not expected to launch into a version of the Hullsport High chicken scratch in front of her bench. Nor had she expected to be watching with sympathetic comprehension when a woman dancing in the aisle next to her fell to the floor and began twitching spasmodically and babbling.

Most of all, she had not expected to see Clem walk up to the dais and light the wick sticking out of a Dr. Pepper bottle filled with kerosene. The hard-driving gospel music continued: "It's God all over the ocean./ It's God all over the sea./ It's God all over creation/ And it's God all over me." Two parishioners were now speaking in tongues, and several more were shouting to Jesus fervently and snapping their bodies at the waist like whips. Clem called out over the din in a calm voice, "Remember, brothers and sisters. Only those anointed by the Spirit. Don't misread the signs, brothers and sisters.

If you do, you'll get hurt. The devil is lurkin here tonight jes waitin for a chance to deceive. So don't misread your state of grace."

Then Clem slowly ran the fingers of one hand through the flame from the Dr. Pepper bottle. He held out the bottle, offering it to the audience. A man in green work clothes, the one who had set the black box on the altar, came forward. He took the bottle and ran his hand back and forth through the flame. A couple more men came forward —and passed the bottle back and forth as though it were a joint at a pot party.

Then Clem walked calmly to the mysterious black box and unlatched it. Reaching in, he pulled out a snake. Ginny gasped. She could see even from the back of the room that the snake, patterned in varying shades of brown, was a copperhead. Every southern child, Ginny and Clem no exceptions, grew up terrorized by copperheads. Their protective coloration allowed them to blend into the leaves of a forest floor. And unlike rattlesnakes, they gave no warning prior to striking. The Major had considered it his personal crusade to instill in his children a healthy horror of copperheads, such that Ginny, even now and in Vermont, where it was too cold for copperheads, spent all her time on woodland walks scouting the ground diligently for color irregularities that might indicate a lurking copperhead. She knew from the Major how to slash X's with a pocket knife over the fang marks in order to suck out the venom.

She stopped clapping, stopped mouthing words to the unfamiliar gospel songs, stopped doing the chicken scratch, and gaped in fascinated horror as Clem took the copperhead gently in his two hands and held it up to his face. With one little finger, he turned the copperhead's head—and its fanged mouth—until he and it were gazing into each other's eyes. There was a faint smile on Clem's dark Melungeon face.

At any moment, Ginny expected the snake to bury its poisonous fangs in Clem's cheek. She clutched the bench in front of her and was mentally reviewing her slashing and sucking techniques. Meanwhile, no one else seemed remotely concerned, or even interested. The singing, the clapping, the dancing continued. Five men up front continued to pass the flame of the Dr. Pepper bottle over various parts of their bodies.

Clem lowered his hands and held out the copperhead to one of the men, who calmly took it in one hand and held it up to his face. Clem reached in the black box—a celestial snake pit apparently—and casually took out another copperhead. This continued until five copperheads and two diamondback rattlesnakes were being passed around, and until Ginny was in a state of nervous collapse in the back row.

Eventually, all the snakes found their way to Clem. He ended up holding two in his hands, with two more wrapped around his arms and one hanging around his neck. A rattlesnake lay on the podium, and he caressed its pale belly with his stockinged foot. The second rattlesnake lay at striking distance just behind him, positioned on an open Bible on the altar, its tongue darting in and out rhythmically.

Clem said something to the men playing the instruments, and the music stopped abruptly. All eyes focused on Clem. He cleared his throat and said quietly, "They says this here can only be done with music. They says the rhythm of the music hypnotizes the snakes. Well, ah don't hear no music now, friends. The Lord does *what* He wants to *when* He wants to. I ain't tamin these here serpents, brothers and sisters. You know that. The Lord is. He's here among us right now. He could kill me any second by turnin one of these devils loose. But He ain't, cause He's usin me as a channel to display to you His power over Satan." Ginny glanced around nervously, prepared for anything now—to see God even.

"These serpents is deadly," Clem continued. "Don't kid yourselves, brothers and sisters. They're powerful. But they ain't as powerful as the Lord! Behold the power and the glow-ry of your Lord!" He raised the snakes in his hands on high. Emotion of some sort—awe? terror?—surged through the the room like a gust of wind. Ginny felt it grip her stomach.

Then Clem dumped all the snakes back into their box and fastened the lid.

Next he turned around and started preaching, quoting the gospel according to St. Mark: " 'And these signs shall follow them that believe; in my name shall they cast out devils; they shall speak with new tongues; they shall take up serpents; and if they drink any deadly thing, it shall not hurt them; they shall lay hands on the sick, and they shall recover.' " In a quiet eloquent voice, Clem simply pointed out that everyone present had either witnessed or participated in all these things, except for their visitor, who was attending services for the first time. He considered this fact—that all the brothers and sisters had witnessed and participated and that no one had been hurt—a sign of God's approval of their undertakings. The state had a law against what they were doing. They might be thrown into prison at any moment because of their faith. But what were the prisons of men compared to the prison of the flesh? The true believers in any era had always been hounded and persecuted abominably. But their souls flourished as their flesh suffered.

As Ginny walked down the hill with Clem, neither said anything for a long time. "What did you think?" Clem finally asked.

"Well—I don't know—I mean, it was amazing, wasn't it? Actually, I don't know what to think, Clem."

"Don't think, then. What did you *feel?*"

"I felt—" Ginny pondered the question. "I felt scared. I'm terrified of copperheads."

"So are we all. So *were* we all, that is. But didn't you feel the presence of our Lord, restrainin the snakes and protectin His believers?"

Ginny searched her memory of the evening for evidence of God's presence. She realized that that search was based on the fallacious assumption that she knew what God's presence would feel like. "I just don't *know,* Clem," she said, anguished. She knew she was ripe for conversion. From Psychology 101 at Worthley, she recognized in herself all the symptoms of Incipient Conversion Syndrome: She was severely demoralized in her personal life; all the various traditional ties and beliefs had failed her, were failing her. She knew that if she didn't watch out, she'd be fashioning copperhead necklaces with the best of them.

"Ginny, I almost killed you ten years ago," Clem was saying fervently. "I'd purely love to make hit up to you by givin you a *new* life in Christ." He gazed at her searchingly with his dark soulful eyes.

"I don't know, Clem." She had without question been dazzled by the evening's performance. She needed to be alone to sort out her array of responses—the primary one appearing to be the recognition that Clem had *not* changed after all; he was still dealing in Death, still trying to subdue it to his command.

"Think about hit," Clem instructed her. "Come see me when you've made your decision."

What decision? she wondered as she drove back to the cabin. It was one thing to acknowledge the existence of a God, of powers and forces beyond your intellectual grasp. After all, *something* had been going on. Clem's leg had regenerated itself, and the copperheads hadn't struck, the flame hadn't singed. But it was quite another thing to play hot potato with copperheads yourself.

II

Wedded Bliss

□

". . . and so there she stood with her packed bags. I just looked at her. I couldn't believe she was leaving. Jesum Crow, she'd given me no warning. I thought everything was fine. I had no idea she was unhappy." Ira frowned and drew deeply on his cigar as he described the breakup of his marriage to a woman from New Jersey whom he had met during his senior year at the University of Vermont.

"What was she so unhappy *about?*" I asked in disbelief, gazing fondly at his sensitive face, which was bronzed from the winter sun.

He looked up. "I asked her that as she stormed out. She screamed, 'I'm unhappy because it's never occurred to you that I might be unhappy! You're so content that you make me sick!' I *still* don't know what she meant. I thought we had a very nice life together."

"So what happened?"

"She left me."

"You mean you didn't yell at her, or drag her back into the house, or beat her up or something?"

"Who, *me?*"

"Well, isn't that what she wanted from you?"

"Did she?" he asked, perplexed. "But I'm not *like* that, Ginny. I just wanted a quiet gentle woman to come home to after a hard day. I'm so *lonely* here in this big empty house all by myself."

There was nothing more appealing to me than a big empty house after the crammed cabin—unless it was the concept of myself as a "quiet gentle woman" after my years as a semiprofessional Valkyrie. I gave Ira a quiet gentle smile.

We were married on the beaver pond a month after my move to his house. He wore his best black quilted jumpsuit. I bought a violet one for the occasion, feeling that white would have been stretching credibility. The minister from the Community Church wore a navy blue Ski-Doo suit, as did Ira's best man, the loathed Rodney Lamoureux. Ira's sister Angela, in a pale green jumpsuit, sang the theme song from *Doctor Zhivago*.

When Ira tried to slip the wedding band on my finger, I wrested it from him and zipped it into my pocket, thinking of the Major's missing finger. Ira looked at me with distress, his sensitive mouth trembling. But the awkward moment was glossed over by the tactful minister, who signaled Ira to kiss me and be done with it.

Mona and Atheliah lurked on the outskirts of the gathering on their skis. They hadn't wanted to come at all, had finally agreed to only as a personal favor to a misguided sister. I saw this ceremony, taking place on our very battleground, as a healing ritual for the community. Perhaps now the Stark's Boggers and the Soybean People could put behind them their mutual enmity and move on into a bright united future. I was the sacrificial virgin, as it were.

This was how *I* saw it. Mona and Atheliah saw it as a sell-out, a betrayal of the memory of Eddie Holzer. Nevertheless, as Ira and I roared off on his Sno Cat, hotly pursued by the wedding guests on their machines, Mona and Atheliah did deign to throw handfuls of long-grained unsprayed brown rice from a knapsack on Mona's back. I was touched. Symbolically speaking, they were signaling their wish that Ira's and my union be fruitful.

On our wedding night, at a motel near the Granby Zoo in Quebec, Ira first made love to me. As he undressed, I discovered with a jolt that his handsome tan ended at his neck. His actual body was pasty white. He was a very proficient lover, though, screwing with an enviable vigor, as though he had a train to catch. His sensual good looks—his quivering nostrils and sweaty forehead and high cheekbones—had suggested that he would be good in bed. Unfortunately, I was not. After many minutes of vigorous activity, Ira looked down, gasping for breath, sweat pouring down his face, and panted, "I'm sorry, but I can't wait for you any longer, Ginny. Jesum Crow, I don't think a woman could expect more than three hundred and ninety-six strokes from *any* man!"

I was readily agreeing as he came into me in a great burst.

"What was I doing wrong?" he asked later.

"Nothing. You're a marvelous lover. But the first time with anyone is always difficult." How could I explain to him that my sexual activities in the past had always taken place under threat of imminent discovery by punitive authority figures? I was conditioned to associate sex with terror. Now that intercourse was allowed—applauded, *required* even—I was incapable of response.

Upon our return from the Granby Zoo, Mom and Dad Bliss flew up from Florida for a belated reception, which was staged by the Women's Friendly Circle of the Community Church. The Friendship Hall was a large bright open room with pine-paneled walls and a linoleum floor. Furnished with folding tables and chairs, it was identical to every parish hall, rod and gun club, Moose lodge, and civic center in the nation.

The Stark's Boggers clustered at one end, as far from me as possible. The minister, however, did come over and request that I call him Uncle Lou. He was a short round man with wispy white hair and pink cheeks and thick rimless glasses.

"I'm sorry not to have called on you yet," he began, tugging at his stiff white collar and stretching his chafed neck. "If you'll pardon my saying so," he whispered with a confidential chuckle, "it was around town that Ira's bride was of the Catholic faith."

I looked at him and said nothing.

"What church did you say you attend?"

I hadn't said. "I don't go to church." His face turned a brighter pink. Instantly I felt sheepish and apologetic, ready to assure him that I was Baptist, Methodist, Dutch Reformed, whatever he liked. "But I was raised in the Episcopal church."

"Oh, that's a *nice* faith."

"Yes."

"Sometimes these interdenominational marriages work out fine. Just fine."

Ira kept dragging friends and relatives over to meet me. He was anxious for me to like them, anxious for them to like me. After he'd introduced us, he'd rush off in search of a new victim, leaving the current one and me staring mutely at each other.

I asked one such woman, Ira's former high school English teacher, who had a jovial smile and frazzled brown hair, "Well, how are you?"

"Good."

"Nice supper tonight."

"It wasn't so bad."

"Well, I certainly do like Stark's Bog."

"I hope you're not like the *last* one."

Just then Ira whisked up with an aunt in tow—a large old woman in an aqua lace suit. "This is Ginny, Aunt Bernice. She used to live back on the Stockwell farm," he explained before racing away.

She said, "So *you're* the one."

"How do you do? I don't think we've met before."

"You don't, huh?" Her steely eyes glinted.

"No, but I've seen you in the store some."

"Could be. Could be." She stared at me, waiting to see what I wanted from her.

"Well!" I said in cheery desperation. "I think I'll just have another piece of this lovely cake, if you'll excuse me." I'd used this excuse four times. I had wedding cake crumbling out my ears.

I stood all alone munching. It wasn't that the Women's Friendly Circle was unfriendly. It was just that we had nothing much in common other than Ira. And unlike southerners, who were reared to chat amiably for hours with total strangers, Vermonters weren't bred for volubility. If Ira hadn't kept dragging people over, I could have stood alone all evening and left without exchanging a word with anyone. Making the best of bad material, I chose to think of this trait as "tolerance."

But then Rodney came sauntering over. He looked almost human in his suit and tie. "Enjoying yourself, *Mrs.* Bliss?" he asked with an evil grin.

"Sure. Why not?"

"Well, live it up while you can." I looked at him questioningly. "Look, let's not play games. Ira's my best friend, and he's made a bad mistake. You treat him good, or you'll have *me* to answer to. He's been hurt enough by women."

"Why don't you mind your own business, Rodney?" I gasped as he slithered away.

Ira rushed over. "Are you having a good time?" he demanded, studying my face for clues.

"Yes, of course. Marvelous!" I said, laughing gaily.

"I know it's difficult for you—an outsider among all my people."

"Yes, but they're wonderful," I assured him, too brightly. Could this marriage be saved?

"These things take time. I just *know* once they get to know you they'll love you as much as I do." He leaned down and kissed my cheek. I smiled bravely, as he wandered off in search of introducible friends.

Uncle Lou came up again and asked, "Now what church did you say you attend?"

"I don't attend *any* church." I sighed.

"Well, then," he said, businesslike, "look me right in the eye, and people will think we're just talking." *Aren't* we, I wondered as I stared into the watery blue behind his thick lenses. "Dear Lord, help this Thy servant who has strayed to recognize her arrogance in casting off Thy church. Bless her union with Ira Bliss, and if it be Thy will, grace it with children. Guide her, Father, in setting up a fine Christian household that will be a haven of peace and goodness in a heathen world. Help her to pursue works that will make her a credit to her community and an aid and comfort to her husband and children. Amen."

"Amen," I said fervently. This was in fact my wish: to win over the Stark's Boggers and become a credit to their community, to provide as much aid and comfort to Ira as he had been supplying to me. "But don't you think it's possible to have a good marriage without going to church?"

"Possible," he conceded, closing his eyes and shaking his head sadly. "But doubtful. Doubtful."

Much more crucial to the health of our marriage than our ensuing record of church attendance was the fact that our next 172 attempts at intercourse were dismal, from Ira's point of view. They were easy to count because we made love every Monday, Wednesday, and Friday night. Ira had read in the *Reader's Digest* that the average American couple had sex twice a week. Hence we would have it three times a week. Tuesday night was his volunteer fire department meeting, at which he drank Genesee beer and played poker into the early morning. Thursday was our square dancing night with the Stark's Bog Wheelers 'n' Reelers. Saturday night we went on his Sno Cat back to the beaver pond with everyone else in town. Sunday night was his Cemetery Commission meeting. That left Monday, Wednesday, and Friday for sex. He wrote it in on the kitchen calendar in red pencil each week so that we would be sure not to forget. I had wanted order in my life, and order was what I was getting.

Each morning we got up at seven. While Ira did fifteen minutes of chin-ups and push-ups and running in place, while he showered and shaved, I cooked his breakfast: two fried eggs over easy, two strips of bacon, two slices of buttered toast with jam, orange juice, and coffee. He proudly remarked that he had eaten the exact same breakfast every morning for fifteen years. At 7:50 he was out the door and into his red fire chief's car on his way to his office on Main Street. Here he spent the morning selling either Sno Cats or Honda trail bikes, depending on the season. He also investigated insurance claims and discussed convertible versus renewable policies. Like a lung surgeon who owns a tobacco farm as a tax write-off, Ira got his customers both coming and going—sold them his machines, then sold them insurance policies covering what could happen on these machines.

As the bell on the steeple of the Community Church chimed twelve, he walked in the door for his lunch of Campbell's tomato-rice soup and a bologna and cheese sandwich on Wonder Bread and coffee. At 12:50 he returned to his office, for more discussions—of participating versus nonparticipating policies, of decreasing term and endowment policies, minimum deposit plans, variable-life plans, double indemnity, waiver of premiums, and guaranteed insurability riders.

While Ira was assisting the males of Stark's Bog with their financial planning, I ironed his shirts. He liked them ironed a certain way, folded just so. I patted them fondly as I folded. I scrubbed his toilet bowl. I waxed his floors. It was a huge house—a great hulking antique stone colonial, built by his forebear Father Bliss, whose brooding portrait hung over the parlor mantel. The family resemblance was appalling: Father Bliss had the same wide alarmed eyes, the same flaring nostrils, the same gleaming cheekbones and high forehead as Ira himself. Only the hair was different. Ira's was dark and curly and hung down over his forehead. Father Bliss's was tied back in a pony tail, a Colonial hippy. Father Bliss had been a Scottish stonemason, had come to Vermont because of the marble and granite quarries being opened up, had built stone houses around the state, including the one of which Ira and I were now custodians. He had also carved gravestones. Some of his remarkable productions stood in the small family plot out back—angels with round faces and hollow haunting eyes, enough to frighten anyone back from the shores of the Styx. Ira had grown up in this house. His father had been a farmer. Upon retirement he and Ira's mother had sold half their acreage to buy a luxury condominium in Boca Raton. The developers of the Bliss farm,

Pots o' Gold, Inc., from Brooklyn, were building an Authentic Vermont Village in a nearby meadow, complete with prefab covered bridges and sugar shacks.

Ira's ancestral manse was so vast and rambling that there was no end to the housework. As soon as I had dusted and polished my way through the antique pine furniture to the end of the ell, it was time to return to the formal parlor and start all over again, under the stern gaze of Father Bliss. In short, my married lot was harsh and tediously predictable. I loved it. I adored knowing exactly what I would be doing for the entire upcoming month. I wallowed in the luxurious knowledge of where Ira was at each moment, whom he was with, what my assignments were. I had tasted freedom at the Free Farm. It had killed Eddie, had nearly killed us all. I preferred my new life in this antique stone cage.

As the church bell chimed five, Ira would stride in. We ate dinner at six on the nose—steak or chops or a roast, potatoes, bread, pie and coffee. After dinner, Ira would take a cigar from a silver box on the sideboard. He would pour a shot glass of brandy. With his penknife, he would carefully cut off the round tip of the cigar. Then he would place the other rounded end in his mouth and suck at it and twirl it for a while. Finally, he would dip this end in the brandy and then fit on a silver cigar holder. Lighting it, he would draw deeply and settle back in his rush-seated armchair. "Are you happy with me, Ginny?" he'd ask anxiously each evening. "*Please* tell me if you're not. How will I know if you don't?"

"Ira, I couldn't be happier," I'd reply. "I *love* our life together." And I did.

"So do I," he'd assure me. "It's so wonderful having you here. I've been so lonely."

At seven thirty Ira left for his meeting for that evening. (I envied him all his meetings, begrudged them to him: He would have so many entries in his obituary, and I would have none.) If it was a night marked on the calendar for sex, Ira and I would watch an hour of television. Then we would march upstairs and get on with it.

"What am I doing wrong?" he would ask, bewildered. "Believe me, Ginny, I've never had this problem before. As unhappy as my first wife must have been, I *know* I satisfied her sexually."

"It's my problem, not yours," I'd comfort him, as he lay with his head on my chest. "But I really don't see why I have to have an orgasm. I mean, I'm perfectly happy just watching you have one." The truth was, I was afraid of having an orgasm. With Eddie, I had lost all track of time on such occasions, had penetrated into a realm in which Eternal Present reigned. All sorts of weird things had gone on. I didn't want anything to do with that stuff anymore. I *loved* knowing exactly what time it was, what minute of what hour. I didn't *want* to make time stand still, or the earth move, or any of the rest of it. I wanted to stay firmly in touch with this world, fully in command of my senses.

"But I feel inadequate just using you to come into. Men want women to experience the same joy they're experiencing."

"I don't see why. They've gotten along just fine for centuries without worrying about their women's joy quota. Why now?" I didn't see how I could explain that I was burnt-out emotionally, that I wanted only peace and quiet and an orderly life from him. After all, he was a modern male, believed in equal orgasm for equal effort. How could I persuade him just to use me and not fret about it?

But Ira was inconsolably distressed that I wasn't scaling the heights. "Ginny, I'm not making you happy," he'd insist after dinner, drawing on his cigar and studying my face anxiously. I decided to try to accommodate him, as a gift for our first anniversary. So one Wednesday night in March, after fifty eight minutes of excessively imaginative foreplay and approximately 212 thrusts, I faked it. I gasped and groaned and shuddered and heaved, like Olivia de Havilland in the last throes of doomed childbirth in *Gone With the Wind*.

For good measure, I whispered fervently in his ear, "Oh Ira, I'm so happy. Thank you."

He rolled over and switched on the light, beaming with delight. Then he leaned down and studied my chest, poking my flesh with his finger. He looked up, no longer beaming, his sensitive lips quivering. "You just *pretended*, Ginny. You *lied* to me."

I opened one eye in the midst of my Academy Award-winning swoon and stared at him. How had he known? "How can you *say* that?" I asked, more as a genuine question than as a protest.

"Your chest. Women have red rashes on their necks and chests after orgasm."

Shit. "Not all of them do, I bet." I would have to speak to my make-up man.

"But you *did* fake it, didn't you?"

I nodded yes guiltily. "I was just trying to please you, Ira."

"Jesum Crow, Ginny, a man doesn't want to be defrauded into his pleasures! *Please* don't do that again."

"I won't. I'm sorry, Ira. And I *will* try harder to have a real orgasm."

"I should hope so."

By now we were well into our second spring of connubial delights. Bulldozers had appeared in the field outside the kitchen window. They were grading roads for the chalet section of the Pots o' Gold Vermont Village. Ira was now playing golf and/or riding his trail bike on Saturdays during the time he had devoted to snowmobiling in the winter. Trout season was also upon us. I spent three days making sixteen apple pies for Ira to take to his family's fishing shack in the nearby mountains. He was going for the first week of the season with eight assorted male relatives. He confessed that he used up all his vacation time each year in this fashion—a week during trout season, a week during bird season, a week during buck season, and a week during ice fishing season. In addition, he went for two weeks each year with his National Guard unit to Camp Drum in upper New York State. If I should want to go on a trip, I'd have to go alone. But if I did, what would his family say? But I was perfectly content in Stark's Bog.

Because of Ira's meetings and sporting events and job, I was finding myself with free time on my hands, even with that mausoleum of a house to clean. Consequently, I made a momentous decision: I would join the surprise shower circuit.

I had tried very hard to switch from high profile to low profile, for Ira's sake. I had packed away my army fatigues, my lumberjack shirt, and my olive air force parka, my Sisterhood Is Powerful T-shirt, my combat boots. I had gone to St. Johnsbury and had bought some polyester pantsuits and jersey tops. I had unbraided my hair and now wore it pulled back and tied with a scarf. But people still crossed to the other side of the street when they saw me coming. At least they couldn't see the butterfly tattooed on my hip that Eddie had loved to nibble and kiss. Even so, only Ira's popularity prevented my being carried out of town on a rail.

At the weekly Wheelers 'n' Reelers square dances in the school gym, I would wander blindly, tripping and stumbling, through the intricate figures in my crinolined skirt and puffy scoop-necked blouse. The other dancers would push and pull me into position. The men in their cowboy boots and western shirts and string ties seemed to me to seize my hands for a promenade with great reluctance. The women, their full skirts swirling as we performed our "Birds in a Cage" maneuvers in mid-circle, eyed me with distaste. And each time Rodney was compelled to do-si-do with me, he would scowl back over his shoulder, his folded arms held high, and would snarl, "Don't forget. I'm onto you, *Mrs.* Bliss." I would fall into Ira's arms with relief when it was time for him to swing me as his corner lady. He would hold me tightly against his chest and would study my face. "Are you having fun, Ginny? Isn't this great stuff?"

"Wonderful!" I'd gasp gaily, twirling off to another do-si-do with Rodney.

But Angela, Ira's younger sister, had befriended me. She had been to secretarial school in Albany before relenting and returning to marry her high school boy friend and live happily ever after. She would always say reassuringly, "Jesum Crow, Ginny, I saw hippies a *lot* worse than you in Albany."

Angela was a big gun on the surprise shower scene and among the Tupperware party set. (Actually, the two groups were one and the same.) She also happened to be refreshment chairman of the Women's Auxiliary of the Stark's Bog Volunteer Fire Department. In short, Angela was my "in."

I started out modestly by attending a Tupperware party at Angela's split-level ranch on the opposite edge of town. Fifteen women of different ages were there. Angela had warned them in advance so that they wouldn't blanch too noticeably as I walked through the door. Several of the less socially hardy had left in a huff. Those who remained behaved admirably, there being an awkward silence of only three and a half minutes upon my arrival. I smiled a lot to indicate my unimpeachable good will, and I talked as little as possible, intent upon mastering the jargon and discerning the sanctioned topics for conversation first. These turned out to be as follows: 1) the weather; 2) one's children; 3) cooking; 4) the weather. I had no children, and clearly none of the assembled were into soybean casseroles. But vis à vis the weather, I snatched the ball and ran with it.

"Gee, mud season is really hanging on this spring, isn't it?" I asked a large gray-haired woman with a wart on her nose.

"Yes, it is," she agreed, startled to be addressed by a reformed Soybeaner on such a harmless topic.

"Some weather for May, huh?"

"A-yup."

"I keep waiting for some sunshine," I confessed.

"Hmmm," she replied noncommittally. Could the same sun that shone on Soybean People possibly be the one that shone on Stark's Boggers? she appeared to be asking herself.

"Do you think it's unusually cool this spring?"

"Well—don't know. Could be." She glanced around the room at her friends, fearful that they might think she was conversing voluntarily with this subversive.

"Maybe we're skipping spring and moving right into summer!" I laughed weakly.

She looked at me with distaste. Undaunted, I said, "Yup, sure looks like we're due for a gorgeous summer after this rotten spring."

Just as I was exhausting my variations on this theme, our area Tupperware representative, a svelte young woman in a navy pantsuit and a blond bouffant such as I hadn't seen since the Bloody Bucket, stood up and welcomed us and began her pitch designed to raise our kitchen consciousness.

"Now, girls," she began urgently, "I *know* you've all been *waiting* to hear about the grr-eat new Tupperware products that have just come out, designed as always to help today's busy homemaker. So I won't waste another minute!" A dizzying succession of plastic bacon keepers, cauliflower crispers, bowls and canisters and molds swirled from hand to hand. Each woman was inspecting them with the eye of an expert jeweler for cut diamonds, turning them this way and that, making remarks to neighbors.

"Yes, girls," the Tupperware lady continued, "this is *exactly* why we sell our kitchen-tested products on the unique home party plan, so that all the outstanding features can be demonstrated right in the comfort of your own living room. Treat your Tupperware as you would your hands, and it will give you a long life of faithful service, and open up whole new worlds of food economy and flavor. . . ."

By the end of the "party," everyone in the room had committed herself to dozens of plastic objects. Except me. I had bought nothing. I was overwhelmed with all the things my kitchen lacked. How had I managed to get meals on the table to date? Angela assured me as I departed in a daze that I hadn't wrecked my chances on the Tupperware circuit simply through failing to buy, that I could make up for this lapse in manners at the next party.

Soon after this Angela got me invited to a surprise shower for one of Ira's cousins, who was about to marry a local boy. Our unfortunate victim, Wanda Bliss, sauntered into our web of deceit (which we had woven in her very own television room) wearing rollers the size of bed springs. She squealed with terror and tried to dash out when she saw three dozen of her closest friends and relatives bobbing up from behind couches and chairs. Her mother forced her to return. Chagrinned, but pretending to smile, she opened the mountain of gifts and passed them around. Mine was a tin serving tray with wooden handles, and with a picture of a covered bridge and "Vermont, The Green Mountain State" painted on it. Everyone passed it on as though it were the meal tray from a plague patient when she read the card saying that it was from me.

I was sitting next to Angela, taking mental notes on proper surprise shower conduct. A box came by. Angela looked in and sighed with envy. She turned around to a middle-aged woman and whispered covetously, "Don't you just *love* it, Aunt Clare? It's *impossible* to find a decent bureau scarf these days. Don't you agree, Ginny?"

Pleased to be included, I replied, "I know what you mean."

A pair of hollow-stemmed champagne glasses etched with frosted bride and groom silhouettes came by, followed closely by plastic place mats with a Kodachrome Vermont landscape and a psalm printed on each. Angela leaned across me and demanded, "Will *your* family eat squash, Jean? I can't get Bill to *touch* it!"

Jean allowed as how Hal would leave her on the spot if she ever dared to serve squash on his dinner plate.

"Ira hates squash, too," I offered companionably.

Several stacks of sheets and towels later, Angela said out of the corner of her mouth, "You should have *seen* Jimmy the other day, Bernice. He got Bill's razor and lathered up his face and shaved himself! At five and a half!"

"Five and a half! Goodness, don't they grow up fast!"

"I know. They act so big, and then they get all tired out and come crawling up on your lap wanting to be babied."

"Isn't it the truth?" confirmed Bernice. "Well, baby them while you can, Angela honey, because it passes so quickly."

By the conclusion of this shower, I had decided that elopement had a lot going for it. Angela told me as we left that she was pretty certain that, after a few more showers, she would be able to get me voted into the Women's Auxiliary, especially since Ira was the president of the fire department. Perhaps she could even get me in in time to work on the fashion show.

"What does the auxiliary do?"

"Oh, we mostly clean up the room after meetings. Pick up the bottles and stuff. Sometimes we make refreshments for the meetings."

"I'd like that," I assured her.

"I've thought about our little problem, Ginny," Ira said one night in bed.

"*What* problem?" I wasn't aware that we had any. For me, everything was peachy. That day I had been voted into the Women's Auxiliary. Unanimously, Angela said. Except for Jean, and what could you expect from a woman like that?

"The fact that I'm not satisfying you sexually."

"Oh but you *are!*"

"Please, Ginny. I've asked you not to lie about it."

"But I don't *want* to be satisfied. Or rather I don't mind not being. In other words, I *am* satisfied by the state of our sex life."

"No, you're not. I've thought about it a lot. And I've figured out what the trouble is." I looked at him expectantly. To have problems solved before you'd even acknowledged their existence was the height of luxury. "You're used to a very exciting life, Ginny—Boston and all your . . . different friends."

"Who? *Me?*"

"Yes, you *are*, Ginny."

"But I'm *not*, Ira. Really. I just got in with the wrong crowd. I'm not really like that at *all*," I insisted, believing it.

"No, living with me must seem very dull after all that."

"I *like* it dull. Uh, I mean I don't think it's dull at *all*. I like our life the way it is, Ira. I wouldn't have married you if I didn't."

"So—" he said, ignoring me, "I've decided to try to make things more exciting. I so much want you to be as happy with me as I am with you, Ginny." He threw off the bedcovers and revealed his gorgeous nude muscled body, pale white below his neckline. But there was some black contraption obscuring his genitals.

"What in the hell?"

"A leather jock strap," he said proudly. "Go ahead. Feel it." I poked it tentatively. "Do much for you?"

"Well, I don't know—"

"Now! For you!" Out from under the bed he pulled a transparent raincoat and held it up for me to put on. "Go ahead! Put it on!"

I did—and felt like a topless traffic cop.

"What do you think?" he asked with boyish delight.

"Neat."

He turned out the light and embraced me. I crackled like a cellophane toilet paper wrapper. "Uh, now what, Ira?"

He sat up and turned on the light and took a book off his bedside table and consulted the index. "Uh, yes, well. I guess we're just supposed to look at each other. It says some women are turned on by the smell and feel of leather."

So Ira and I sat and looked at each other. Then he took off his jock strap, and I slipped out of my transparent raincoat, and he settled his furry head between my tanned legs—a tarantula nestled in a bunch of overripe bananas. As Ira amused himself, I pondered the topic of whether to take pot roast or pork liver out of the freezer for supper the next day.

I didn't come. Ira sat up and marked two X's in the book over the sections entitled "Leather" and "Polyethylene." "Now, don't be discouraged, Ginny. Each time we'll try something different."

On Memorial Day morning, I stood on Main Street and watched as Ira marched by in his olive National Guard uniform, followed closely by Boy Scouts, Cub Scouts, Brownies, and Girl Scouts. The Stark Mountain Regional High School marching band came next, led by prancing majorettes who were nowhere near as good as I remembered being. Then came the fire department float, featuring a uniformed representative from each National Guard unit in the area. They were saluting a bank of flowers tilted against the truck cab. The flowers were white carnations, some dyed red and blue and densely packed in a wire frame to form an American flag. A hand-printed inscription around the truck bed read, "Serving to Keep America Strong and Free." Then came some volunteer firemen, in their swept-back hats and raincoats and rubber boots, hanging from the town's gleaming hook and ladder truck.

After the parade, the men and boys had been invited to the General Machine Gun Testing Range—the one Eddie and Atheliah and Mona and I had discovered—to view a new type of mortar launcher to be used in Vietnam. Half the men in town had been working on the project for over a year. They took as much pride in it as their forebears must have taken in their spikes and staples in the 1800's when General Machine had been a nail factory.

Meanwhile, the women and girls went to the parish hall for the Women's Auxiliary fashion show. The fashion coordinator from Sears, Roebuck in St. Johnsbury had outfitted us auxiliary members and had written the script, which Angela was reading:

"Lovely Ginny Bliss waltzes into summer in her . . ." That was my cue. The thought had flickered through my diabolical brain to whisk out attired in my transparent raincoat and Ira's black leather jock strap. Eddie would have done it. But I was trying hard to forget Eddie. I never allowed myself to think of her. The only time she sneaked up on me was when I was asleep. She would appear in dreams, saying in an accusing voice, "You keep thinking I'm, like, dead or something." Then I'd reach out to embrace her. And I'd wake up and find myself clinging to Ira, who would interpret this as an invitation to roll on top of me for a tryst, while I choked back sobs of longing for Eddie and tried not to fantasize that Ira's hands and mouth and tongue moving across my body were hers. I was grateful to Ira for taking me on. If I couldn't throw myself into sex with him, at least I wouldn't cuckold him spiritually by pretending that he was someone else.

I swept out in my backless pink paisley halter-front harem pants. ". . . in this fetching nylon acetate ensemble. The halter front with its matching fabric tie strings, and the billowing legs of the look-alike pants"—here I turned and paused to display my fabric tie strings— "will make you feel like a pampered slave girl in an opulent harem, when that sultan of yours comes home at night." I took several steps so that my legs would billow. "Accented with a handsome wide copper bracelet"—I held up my shackled wrist—"and glittering gold sandals—just the thing for a Stark's Bog back yard barbecue. Or a Bliss family Memorial Day picnic, Ginny?"

I smiled ingenuously and descended the steps to a thunder of applause. I was pleased. I had finally been accepted, had overcome my Soybean origins. No one knew about my nocturnal lapses.

After the fashion show, we womenfolk split into our rival clans for family picnics. Almost everyone in town was related to one or more of the five main families, the Blisses being one. The Bliss family picnics were always held at the old homestead—Ira's and my house —regardless of which hapless relative happened to inhabit it at the time. And this picnic was no exception. I had been up all night chopping potatoes for potato salad. Ira was back from the firing range by the time I got home and had removed the cover from the swim-

ming pool and had tapped a keg of Genesee. His relatives were
starting to drift in. I couldn't tell them apart—they were all solid,
well-built people with dark or gray curly hair. Old men kept putting
arms around me and whispering, "Ira's a lucky man to have such a
lovely bride." Ira watched with pride and gratitude: His family had
accepted me. I smiled at the old men warmly.

About a dozen times I had the following conversation, spoken
parts interchangeable:

"Hot enough for you?"

"Looks like a nice afternoon for a picnic."

"Yes, we're sure as hang lucky. It's rained all week."

"Do you think it'll rain this afternoon?"

"It might. See those dark clouds in the west?"

"Probably not before time to go home, anyhow."

"Probably not. It was a late mud season, so we've earned a pretty
summer."

"A-yup. Well, excuse me, I'd better go for a swim before it clouds
up."

"It might do it."

"I sure hope not."

"Me, too."

But after all, just because we shared an affection for Ira was no
reason to assume that we had anything else in common—other than
living under identical cloud cover.

It was getting dark, and yes, rain clouds were rolling in from the
west, by the time the last of the Bliss great-uncles departed. Ira and
I sat by the pool among fallen baked beans and guzzled the remaining
quarter keg of flat Genesee.

Then the storm arrived. Huge raindrops splatted on the concrete
where we sat. Trees lashed their branches like whips. We were getting
soaked. Where was my transparent raincoat now when I needed it?
Thunder rolled, and lightning crackled. It was the first storm of the
season, a treat in snow country after endless months of silently drifting
white fluff. There was something so refreshingly candid about an
electrical storm. You knew where you stood. Nature was out to sizzle
you alive. Whereas delicate snowflakes crept up on you stealthily and
smothered you unawares.

Rain swept in in sheets. Water ran off our noses in torrents. We
giggled like children and raced for the house. Once inside, dripping
on the indoor-outdoor carpet in the TV room, Ira turned to me with

his special look that indicated that it was 8:30 on a Friday evening, sanctioned by the calendar for sex. He unbuckled his belt.

"You are *going* to have an orgasm tonight," he informed me.

"But really, Ira, I don't want one."

"I don't care what *you* want. *I* want you to be happy." His dark liquid eyes studied with hunger my breasts and stomach under my clinging wet shirt. "If this doesn't do it, I don't know what will."

"If *what* doesn't?" I asked fearfully.

"Stay here." He charged upstairs and returned with his manual and a paper bag. As he read the instructions for tonight's gymnastics, I observed his cock stirring the leg of his madras Bermuda shorts.

He turned to me, breathing heavily, his nostrils flared. Out of the paper bag he whipped—a pair of handcuffs.

"Oh Jesus," I moaned. I had been here before—bound to the sleeping platform in the bomb shelter by Clem's motorcycle chain.

"Really, Ira, I'd rather just do it in bed without a lot of fuss."

"No, no. I want things to be exciting for you, Ginny. I don't want you to be bored with me."

With a sigh, I removed my clothes as Ira threw off his. "Now what?" I asked sullenly, standing nude, damp and chilled, in the middle of the television room floor.

He led me a few steps by the arm. Then he pulled up two antique ladder-back chairs with rush seats. He climbed up on his, indicating to me to climb up on mine. When I had done so, I found myself eye to eye with the huge oak beam that ran the length of the room. Ira unlocked the handcuffs and snapped one side around his right wrist. Then he reached over the beam and snapped the other side onto my left wrist.

"All right, now hold onto the chain with your chained hand, or you'll hurt yourself." When I was doing this correctly, he continued, "Now lower yourself slowly off your chair."

I did so, and soon we were dangling chest to chest by one arm from the beam, joined by the handcuffs. Ira was very excited. His erection was gouging me in the side like a surgeon's hand prodding an appendicitis victim.

"What do you think?" he gasped, bending his head to French kiss my armpit.

"Very nice," I assured him, feeling that my handcuffed arm was about to pop out of its socket, like the Major's ring finger.

"Will this do the trick, do you think?"

"I'm not sure I get the picture. . . ." Ira wrapped his free arm around my waist and pulled me to him.

"All right, now put it in."

I stared at him for a moment in disbelief. Then I obligingly raised my dangling legs at different angles, but never the appropriate one for achieving insertion. In the process, I kicked my chair over. I felt like a marionette with tangled strings. Finally, I accomplished the feat of coupling with my husband by wrapping my legs around his waist. But in this suspended entanglement neither of us was capable of moving an inch.

"Did the book say exactly how to do this?" I asked, suppressing a grimace as my shoulder began aching unbearably.

"Not really. It just said something like 'Once hanging together in this fashion, you will have no difficulty discovering delicious new ways to tease each other to climax.' "

"Oh."

Shortly I said, "Uh, Ira—I think I'd better get down. My arm's really hurting."

Ira sighed, defeated again, his erection starting to wilt inside me. "Okay." He took the handcuff key, which he'd been holding in his free hand, and reached up to unlock my wrist. As he did so, he dropped the key.

We looked at each other in horror as the full magnitude of our plight dawned on us. The silver key glittered mockingly on the carpet, while the lightning flashed and the rain drove in sheets against the windowpanes. My shoulder no longer hurt—it was completely numb. But now my wrist was sending messages of agony to the pain centers in my brain. I had rubbed a bracelet of raw flesh by my flying mid-air contortions.

"Ira, if you can stand in your chair, that might lower me enough to pick up the key with my toes."

Thinking it worth a try, he searched for his chair with his feet. As he did so, he kicked it over. "Jesum Crow," he groaned. Reaching up to the beam with his free hand, he did a miraculous one-handed chin-up, which lowered me almost to the rug.

But not quite. My pointed toes hung one inch above the glittering silver key.

"Lower," I said softly.

"I can't," he gasped, through gritted teeth. Just then his bicep gave out, and he fell back down, jerking me up to where I'd been before.

We looked at each other with despair.

"I'm sorry," he whispered.

"You meant well."

"I just wanted to make you happy."

"What's going to become of us? We'll starve, won't we? Or will we die of thirst first?"

"Someone will miss me at the office, or at one of my meetings. They'll come out to check on us and ..." We glanced at each other, trying to decide whether we'd rather be living or dead when we were discovered by one of his aunts.

"Your Aunt Betty is coming back for her ice cream freezer on Sunday." He nodded yes, his eyes closed and sweat dripping from his handsome high forehead.

The phone rang. We looked at each other with renewed hope. Mother Bell lived. The phone sat on a table against the wall right under this beam.

"If we throw our arms sideways, Ginny, I think we can scoot toward the wall."

The phone stopped ringing. We tried Ira's plan, and it worked. Each scoot produced an agonized wrenching of my captive shoulder. But, in time, we worked our way to the wall. Ira reached down with his feet and picked up the receiver. He transferred the receiver to his free hand with a movement that even a tree-swinging orangutan would have envied. Then he dialed experimentally with the second toe of his right foot.

He looked at me blankly. "Whom shall we call?" he asked, pressing the button with his toe to clear the line.

"Uncle Lou?" Ira was unamused. "How about the police?"

"There aren't any police in Stark's Bog. You know that."

"The fire department."

"Good idea." He started dialing. Then he realized that the fire department number was our own, he being fire chief.

"*I* know," he said, inspired. "Rodney."

"*No!* I'm not having that macho rapist seeing me naked and at his mercy."

"*Someone's* going to."

"Not Rodney."

"Who then?"

"Angela?"

"Are you kidding? It would be all over town in minutes!"

"I know! Mona."

"*Who?*"

"A woman who lived with me at that cabin."

"Well, all right. I suppose so," he muttered unhappily. "What's her number?"

He dialed with his toe and handed me the receiver. With relief I heard it ringing. The last time I'd called her commune, their line had been disconnected for failure to pay a bill. A male voice answered. There was much laughter and loud music in the background.

Atheliah sounded pleased to hear from me. "Why don't you come on out? We're having a planting festival, a fertility thing."

"It sounds like fun. But I'm afraid I'm—tied up at the moment. Actually, I'm in a bit of a spot, Atheliah. I hate to ask this of you right in the middle of a party. But could you *please* come to Ira's right away and help me out?"

"Now? Tonight?"

"It's incredibly important, Atheliah, or I wouldn't dream of asking you. I can't really explain it to you over the phone. But *please.*"

"Well, all right, yeah, sure. If I can find some wheels ... (Al, can I take your truck to Stark's Bog? Sure, we can all go!) ... I'll be right there, Ginny." She hung up before I had a chance to ask her not to bring her friends.

A few minutes later eight people with pupils in various stages of dilation stumbled through the door. They looked at Ira and me, dangling nude over the telephone, with no more than passing interest.

Mona came over and gazed up through her purple-tinted goggle lenses and said blowsily, "Like, far out, Gin."

Atheliah stood beside Mona and looked up at me with affection and said, "What can I do for you, Ginny?"

I nodded to Ira, dangling beside me, and said, "Do you remember Ira? Ira, this is Mona and Atheliah, whom I lived with in the cabin the winter before last?"

"How do you do?" Ira asked, looking down through his hairy armpit. "I do remember seeing you around. You were at our wedding, weren't you?"

They nodded politely.

"Actually, the reason I called ... Do you see that key on the rug over there? Would you mind handing it to Ira? And putting those chairs under our feet? Thanks so much.''

Ira unlocked us, and we climbed down, rubbing our raw wrists. "Can I give you a beer?'' Ira offered.

"Sure, thanks,'' Atheliah said. "But we really can't stay. It looks as though the road to the farm is washing out, and we want to be on our side of it when it goes.''

Ira passed cold Genesee all around. "Thanks *so* much for coming, guys,'' I called as they trooped out the door. "How about lunch next week?'' I asked Mona and Atheliah. "Monday say?''

"Far out,'' Mona replied.

Two days later Ira left for his two-week army summer camp at Camp Drum, and I was left alone in his cavernous house. His relatives kept appearing to pick up serving dishes from the picnic.

"Where were you Friday night after the picnic?'' his Aunt Betty demanded. "I called to see if I'd left my sweater by the pool, but no one answered. I couldn't imagine where you'd gone.''

"We were tied up right after the picnic,'' I explained, fond of my little pun by now.

"Lovely day we had for the picnic. Weren't we lucky?'' Aunt Betty demanded.

"Weren't we, though. But that was quite a storm that evening.''

"Wasn't that a *storm? Goodness,* what a storm!''

"Yes, that storm was really something.''

"We were just blessed that it held off for the picnic.''

"We sure were blessed. And then it cleared right up for the weekend, too.''

"I noticed,'' Aunt Betty said, as tired of the topic as I was.

On Monday afternoon Atheliah and Mona and I lay nude by the swimming pool next to plates piled with gnawed bones from chicken left over from the picnic. They had just informed me that Laverne had gone into a nunnery near Chicago, having experienced a conversion during her near-electrocution.

Mona trailed the fingers of one hand languidly in the swimming pool. "So you're doing the whole bougie trip again, huh, Gin?''

"Looks like it,'' I said yawning, no longer feeling defensive about my bougieness.

"What do you *do* all day here alone?'' Atheliah asked with concern. I described my typical day—Ira's schedule, the unending housework, the surprise shower circuit, the Wheelers 'n' Reelers, the Women's Auxiliary.

Mona shook her head slowly with admiration. "I've got to hand it to you, Ginny. I thought it would freak you out for sure. But you're really doing the whole number. Far *out.* You've infiltrated Stark's Bog!"

"I *guess* you could call it that. . . ."

"Are you, like, getting through to them?" Atheliah asked.

"With what?" I asked, having totally forgotten the rationale I'd given them for my marriage, about being a hostage in the peace treaty between the Stark's Boggers and the Soybean People.

"Like, are you laying the whole trip on them?" Mona asked, her bruised eyes gleaming with revolutionary fervor.

"Which trip?"

"*Which* trip? About their fueling the war machine, about the death-dealing society they're participating in."

The thing was, by the time I had infiltrated to the heart of Stark's Bog, I had *become* a Stark's Bogger. I now had much more in common with Angela Bliss Blair than I did with Mona and Atheliah. People *became* what they did.

"No," I said quietly.

Atheliah looked at me with disappointment, Mona with scorn.

"You mean you *like* living like this?" Mona asked in disbelief, waving her hand around to include the baby blue swimming pool and the antique stone colonial.

"Sure. It's all right," I said softly, thinking of Eddie, how horrified she'd have been to see me now.

"What would Eddie say?" Atheliah said sadly.

"I never think of Eddie," I said quickly, bathed in pain.

"Your loyalties certainly are short-lived," Mona said. We lay in silence. Soon, they got up and dressed and left.

During the two weeks that I was alone in that echoing house, I came to a decision: I wanted a baby. Father Bliss had been dead for one hundred and fifty years, but he lived on in that stone house. He lived on in the memories of his descendants, who passed on to their children the story of his carving five miniature tombstones in the back-yard burying plot for his five children who died of smallpox in one month. He lived on through his genes. You had only to look at the current-day Bliss clan to see the features that remained constant, even through the onslaught of intermarriage. Looking at them all, I knew what Father Bliss had looked like, would have known even without his brooding portrait in the parlor. Living in his house and among his descendants, I felt his continuing presence.

Well, I, too, wanted to be a continuing presence. That was why I needed a baby. This child would be my hostage against Death.

"Ira, how do you feel about our having a baby?" I asked a couple of days after he returned from his mock war, sore and exhausted.

"You're not . . . ?"

"No, no. I was just thinking about it while you were gone."

He beamed. "Ginny, I'd *love* to have a baby. My first wife never wanted children, so I didn't want to suggest it to you."

"Ira, I want your baby," I said fervently. We made love, even though it was 7:15 on a Tuesday night. Ira missed his fire department meeting, and the phone rang unanswered fifteen times as the firemen tried to locate him. And I had an orgasm, one that outdid even those with Eddie. Ira lay with his head on my rash-covered chest and wept with joy. His warm tears bathed my splotched breasts.

Bird season came, but Ira stayed home to bring me saltines in bed for my morning sickness. The snows began, but Ira's Sno Cat sat untouched in the tool shed while he lay with his head on my belly listening for heartbeats and letting the fetus kick him in the face from its uterine fastness. Rodney came by to take him ice fishing, but Ira lent him his drill and stayed home to massage my swollen ankles. No longer did he demand of me if I was happy. He knew I was, and I knew he was.

Never was a child more eagerly awaited. Or so it seemed to us. I read book after book on childbirth, things like this: "Bach's Fifth Brandenburg Concerto welcomed our daughter into this world! Our daughter! This lofty victorious music provided the background for her first yell, her lusty salutation to her triumphant parents! I glow with delight as I gaze down at our little cherub. She enthralls me! I experience a profoundly reverent serenity in the depths of my soul, as after an assignment successfully completed!" No wonder there was a population crisis, I reflected, if delivery did all that for a woman. I couldn't wait. At last I had found myself; all along I had been destined to be a brood mare. Why had it taken me so long to come around to accepting my fate with grace?

One afternoon I came waddling down the stairs and into the living room in pursuit of a Rolaid. The room erupted with shrieking faces.

I fell to the floor in terror, tripping over a cord and bringing a lamp smashing down on my head. Angela, who had arranged this surprise shower, hovered anxiously over me while Ira's assembled aunts and cousins and I all waited to see if I would miscarry. When it appeared that I would not, I was able to stop spitting and snarling and cursing Angela and get on with opening my gifts.

Freshly armed with stacks of crib sheets and stretch diapers, outfitted with bushels of large safety pins, I was now ready for anything the maternity ward might bring.

Except for the pain. Such pain isn't possible, I told myself as I lay writhing on my labor bed. I had been pleading like a junky for a fix of Demerol. The delivery itself, which I watched in mirrors even more intricately arranged than those Laverne had employed to view her cervix, passed in a blur of vivid colors—green from the baby's first of many bowel movements, the black of her Bliss hair, the red of my own blood. Rather than the sense of triumph my books had promised, I felt mostly relief to have the unendurable pain over with.

Wendy had been born shortly before the opening day of trout season, but Ira's fishing tackle hung unused in the mud room. Instead Ira lay on our bed and watched with fascination as the tiny girl baby kneaded my bulging breasts and nuzzled and suckled them. At last, a profession I could summon some genuine enthusiasm for: wet-nursehood.

Every morning at ten Ira would rush home from his Sno Cat salesroom to help me give Wendy a bath. We would gaze enraptured as she flailed at the water in the small white bowl with her pudgy arms and legs. Had any couple ever before produced such a perfect little body? We thought not. We would encase her, like a baked pigeon in clay, in a gooey white crust; so entranced were we that we'd fail to notice that one was powdering where the other had already oiled.

At night when Ira came home, his first question was always, "Well, and did our little angel have a bowel movement this afternoon?"

"Oh yes."

"Still hard?"

"No, softer this time, thank goodness."

"Like oatmeal, or more like banana?"

"Well, less like thick cream soup than yesterday. More like scrambled eggs. Only brown."

"Not green?"

"No, caramel colored, rather than chocolate."

"Did she have to strain?"

"Some. But not like yesterday."

"Sounds pretty good," said he, aficionado of feces.

Ira and I would lie in our bed at night after she had finished nursing and was spewing white vomit all over our sheets, and we would inspect minutely each tiny, painfully perfect limb and feature, like new-car owners searching for dents and scratches. Never did an infant have less privacy. She would casually kick out a foot, or wrinkle her forehead, or purse her lips, and we would both instantaneously snap to attention, searching for ways in which to satisfy whatever cryptic whim she might be expressing.

One night at supper I said to Ira, "Why don't you take a week off so that we can go to Tennessee to show Wendy to my parents?" Except for rare trips to Montreal and Boston for a hockey or baseball game, Ira had been out of Vermont only during his army years at Fort Dix and during summer camp at Camp Drum. He said resolutely that if New Jersey was what the rest of the world was like, he wanted nothing to do with it. "Guess I already live in just about the nicest place around," he'd say smugly. "Why do I need to go to Schenectady?"

Meanwhile, Ira had choked on his pork chop. "You said your parents were dead," he said with astonishment.

It was true. I had told him my parents couldn't come to our wedding or reception because they were dead. "They *were*, to me, at that time," I explained feebly, incapable of justifying my cutting them out of my life in hopes of minimizing their bourgeois influences on me. In retrospect, what I had done was clearly unjustifiable. I saw going home to them with a husband and a baby as a gesture of apology and reconciliation. "*Please*, Ira. Tennessee is not like New Jersey." I carefully refrained from claiming that Tennessee was *nicer* than New Jersey.

Ira stared at me and then returned sadly to his pork chops. "All right," he finally said. "Then we could go down to Boca Raton to show her to *my* parents. Let's do it in March." I knew that only the prospect of displaying Wendy would ever have budged him out of Stark's Bog.

My parents greeted us at the airport gate as though we were immigrant relatives who had finally made it to the New World. I had never before experienced such rib-smashing embraces from them. Mother's Instamatic devoured yard after yard of film. Clearly, they were savoring their victory: after more than four years of silence, unbroken by so much as a covered-bridge post card asking for bail, their wild-eyed daughter had returned to the fold (as they had assured each other she inevitably would) with a handsome son-in-law and an adorable granddaughter in tow. Their Ginny had finally come around.

They were very discreet, however, about not rubbing it in. Mother immediately assumed complete care of Wendy and allowed her to wreck her house without so much as a concealed grimace. Wendy was by now learning to walk and careened around grabbing hold of things like tablecloths set with heirloom china in order to steady herself.

The Major put his arm around Ira's shoulder—Ira glancing down uneasily to note his missing finger—and led him on a tour of his factory and his farm. He took him to play golf at the country club. He even discussed the possibility of buying a whole-life policy.

One afternoon while Ira and the Major were out golfing and Wendy was napping, Mother and I sat in awkward silence in the living room, listening to the ticking of her steepled family clock.

"We've missed hearing from you, dear," she began with considerable embarrassment.

"Yes, well . . ."

"I hope you've been well and happy." I glanced at her with restrained hatred for her charity. Here she'd been hoping I was well and happy, and I'd been in Vermont wishing they would drop dead so that I could finally escape their all-pervasive influence—having realized some time back that even when I wasn't living the life they had reared me for, I was still reacting *against* them; so that how I'd lived had never yet been a pure decision of what *I* really wanted. It was a most unsettling insight. It shot theories of free will all to hell.

"I *have* been well and happy, Mother. In between being sick and miserable."

"Oh well, that's life," she said glibly, closing the door on the topic.

But wait! everything in me raged. *Why* don't you want to hear the ways in which I've been sick and miserable? Because I knew she didn't.

"Such a delightful child—Wendy."

"Thank you, Mother. I must be doing something right for a change, huh?" Mother chose to ignore my challenge, as usual.

"You mustn't wait too long to have your second," she said in a confiding tone, having welcomed me into the charmed circle of multiparous mothers without consulting me. "It's fun for them to grow up together."

"To tell you the truth, Mother, the thought of a second child has never entered my mind." That was a boldfaced lie. In fact, I knew that motherhood was my chosen profession. I was good at it. It blissed me out, as Eddie used to say. I had finally found myself. And the thought of a second baby had definitely been festering in my mind for the past couple of months. However, I felt Mother's remark was presumptuous. I didn't like her taking my allegiances for granted.

She looked taken aback. "Oh well, excuse me, Ginny. It's just that only children are often so lonely. And having two makes taking care of the first one so much easier."

"If you ask me, that's like saying that we can get out of Vietnam by invading Laos." Why did I have to be so insistently snippy to my poor mother?

Mom and Dad Bliss's luxury condominium rose up like a gray stone asparagus spear on the Boca Raton coastline. "Boca," they called it.

"Kids! Don't you love them? Have lots! Fill Father Bliss's house to the rafters with them!" Mom Bliss instructed me one afternoon on the beach while Ira was off playing golf with Dad Bliss. Mom Bliss was lying in a red-flowered bathing suit in the damp sand, sinking slowly, with water seeping up around her. Wendy was tottering toward the surf as it receded, then squealing and tottering back to me as new waves broke and swept in. It was hard *not* to love kids in that setting—their perfect compact little bodies baked brown under the scorching sun; each shell, each bird, each piece of slimy seaweed a thing of wonder and mystery. Watching Wendy was like drinking a six-pack of Geritol; my senses, jaded by four months of blinding white snow, opened up like starving Venus's flytraps would during black fly season in Vermont.

"There's nothing more rewarding for a woman than watching her children flourish."

"What if they *don't* flourish?" I asked, trying hard to resist this brainwashing by secret agents for the goddess of fertility. Damn it, I wanted this second baby I was about to embark on to be my own pure unbiased decision. But was such a decision possible?

"Yes sir, it's just so everlastingly *interesting* having children around."

"How come you moved to Boca?"

"Well, it's just so *cold* in Vermont as you get older."

"Don't you miss seeing your children and grandchildren?"

"Dad and I have earned a rest," she said, forgetting that she was in the middle of a P.R. job for parenthood. "Angela would come over with her four and say, 'Mom, would you keep them for the day?' It just got to be too much. I've spent my whole *life* looking after kids —eight of them. Did *we* ever have all this fancy birth control stuff you kids today have? *We did not!* No, we had our babies as they came, and were grateful if we lived through it! And I *never* asked *my* mother to keep them, you can bet. So I think I deserve some peace and quiet before I die."

On the plane home, while Wendy was struggling to get down from my lap, in order to lurch down the aisle tripping up stewardesses and snatching magazines from passengers, I said to Ira, "Our mothers think we should have another baby."

Ira looked up in surprise from *Road and Track* and said, "Well, so do our fathers. So do I. Don't you?"

Apparently, people on all levels had already made the decision. I resented being transformed into a baby machine. "I don't know."

"You *don't know?* Well, we can't have just *one* child."

"Why not?"

"But people don't *have* just one child. Jesum Crow, Ginny. Besides, you want a son, don't you?"

We went from perpetual midsummer in Boca to deep-drifted spring in Stark's Bog, with only our tans to remind us that we'd been away. Snow had piled up in our absence to the bottom of our downstairs window sills, and temperatures hadn't been above freezing for ten days.

"There now, wasn't that neat getting away for some sun in the middle of winter?" I asked Ira.

"I don't see why we need to go all the way down there. Vermont gets sun, too, you know."

"Where?"

Two months later Wendy and I rushed back to Tennessee under considerably less gala circumstances: the Major was dead, of a heart attack on his office floor. I saw Jim and Karl for the first time in several years and discovered that we now had very little to say to each other, in spite of our shared past. As the Major's coffin was lowered into the ground, I reflected that it really wasn't enough: The fact that he was leaving behind him these offspring to bear his genes into the future really didn't compensate for the extinction that he had always insisted lay beyond the grave.

Back in Vermont, things were suddenly different. Wendy stubbornly insisted on a cup when I offered my breast. I was destroyed. I had intended to nurse her for at *least* another year, in keeping with my Earth Mother self-image. This was my first hint of the enormity of my folly: Wendy was supposed to be an extension of me, my lifeline to the Future. Was it really possible that she might have things *she* wanted to do?

What she now wanted instead of my milk were foodstuffs she could dump on the floor and hurl around the kitchen. Spinach began flying against the walls like bugs splattering against a car windshield in midsummer. What she wanted was to toddle furiously through the house, her damp diapers sagging behind her. What she wanted was to cling to the living room bookcase five times a day and drag down all the books, which I would foolishly replace each time in preparation for the next.

My schedule had become nothing more than a superimposition of Ira's schedule on Wendy's. Wendy was up at six thirty for her breakfast of mashed fruit and hot cereal and milk. She roared around on her missions of destruction while I mopped up the kitchen, washed down the walls, shampooed the rug, fixed Ira's breakfast. When Ira left, Wendy went back to bed until ten. At ten she had her bath, which Ira no longer rushed home to witness, then her lunch of mashed something or other and milk; then another crawl or toddle through the house to re-create the havoc I had undone during her nap. Then another nap until two, when we watched "Hidden Heartbeats" and "Westview General," a relic of our lost nursing days. Then supper of chopped meat and vegetables and milk, most of which ended up on the floor and on her shirt and on my face. Into her sleep suit to be ready for an hour of attention from Ira when he got home. That meant I had to myself an hour and a half in the morning and two hours in the afternoon, between the hours of six thirty in the morning and ten thirty at night, when I fell into an exhausted sleep—during which time I had to do my housework, iron Ira's shirts, fix dinner, scrape Wendy's food off the walls, wash and fold her diapers. It was too much—even for a glutton for structure like myself.

I began to resent every volume Wendy pulled down, every diaper

I rinsed. I even hated her charming clowning antics designed to amuse me, like when she'd stand with her back to me and bend over and look at me upside down through her legs. Even if I took her outside and tried to pull the weeds in our borders, when I looked around she'd be hanging over the swimming pool staring at her reflection. Or she'd be halfway down the driveway toward the road. My former neat orderly life was chaos. My serene placid Stark's Bog personality was frayed and frazzled. My polyester pantsuits were splattered with apricot. And on top of it all, Wendy was displaying an alarming interest in giving up her morning nap.

I had been too wrapped up in Wendy to bother finding babysitters, so I never went out. I was on leave from the Women's Auxiliary, and I hadn't been to a surprise shower since my own over a year ago. The only people I ever saw were Wendy and Ira. I clung desperately to Ira. When he came in at night, my first words were invariably, "What's the gossip? Whom did you see today? What's new?"

And the hideous thing was that, to hear Ira tell it, *nothing* was ever new. He never brought home juicy tidbits about the latest premarital pregnancies and closet alcoholics. He'd never even reveal who had bought how much insurance naming whom as beneficiary. Ira didn't have a malicious bone in his body; he didn't approve of gossip. That was why it was occurring to me that basically I loathed him. His bland, amiable acceptance of everything and everyone in his narrow little world was driving me bananas. I had originally considered this quality tolerance developed to a lofty degree, a tolerance that had allowed him to marry a Soybeaner in the face of dismay from friends and family. I was coming to suspect that the quality was instead an absence of discernment. Ira had no taste—not *poor* taste, *no* taste. For instance he had married me, who was clearly not what he wanted or needed (in spite of my efforts to convince us both that I was the quiet gentle woman of our dreams). For Ira, nothing was any better or any worse than anything else. His rotten friend Rodney Lamoureux at least snarled and snapped and fought for what he thought was right, like Eddie herself. Never mind that what Rodney and Eddie thought was right was usually wrong.

"What's new?" I'd demand as Ira walked in the door at night.

"Nothing much."

"Whom did you see?" I'd pant.

"Nobody much." He'd shrug off my interrogations to inquire

about teething and toilet training. Wistfully he'd ask about my period, in hopes that an intrepid sperm had skirted my stalwart diaphragm. (I continued to postpone my decision on son production.)

One night in early fall he skulked in guiltily. As I hung on him and searched his face for evidence of tidings from the outside world, he mumbled sheepishly, "Thought I might go up to camp with Rodney this week. Shoot me some birds."

I let my arms fall from around his neck and stared at him, stricken. So! Ira was intent upon breaking up our home. All right. If that was the way he wanted it, let him desert his wife and child. I turned away, swallowing tears. "Fine!" I said brightly. "Great! Just run along and have fun! Wendy and I will be just *fine,* and waiting for Daddy when he gets home! Won't we, Wendy?"

Since my marriage I had resolutely avoided the evening news on the theory that if you don't like something, it's best to insulate yourself from it. Unread magazines and newspapers from the past year sat in piles in the television room. But that Monday night, when Ira and I would have been making love if he weren't off shooting birds, I sat down and watched Howard K. Smith, John Chancellor and Walter Cronkite back to back. Then I stayed up all night reading my way through the stacks of newsprint.

It was incredible! Monster tanks were rolling through rain forests leaving wakes of dead bodies. Nuclear warheads dotted the globe with the frequency of mice turds in my cupboards. Starving children were fighting over undigested grain in cow dung. Busloads of black children were being overturned by white mobs. The oceans were poison soups. Jesus Christ, Eddie was *right* after all! Ours was a death-dealing society. How was it possible that I was still alive? And here I had been fretting over whether or not to conceive another ruling-class consumer. It was obscene.

I leapt up and stalked back and forth through the echoing house. Then I flung myself on the parlor couch and stared up at pony-tailed Father Bliss, thinking about the Major's coffin being lowered into the ground. It's not enough! It's not *enough,* I kept wailing. So what if you *do* have descendants? That still doesn't prevent your suffocating on factory emissions, doesn't prevent your being sizzled in a nuclear holocaust, doesn't prevent your dying an agonized death. If you are *lucky,* the most you can hope for is to be lowered into the ground where you will rot and be eaten by worms. . . .

The world *needed* me, and I was trapped here in the woods rinsing bibs and mashing bananas! For a fucking little vampire bat of a kid who flourished by sucking my strength, leaving me shriveled like a poorly embalmed mummy in the process. . . .

In a moment of clarity, I realized that I had gone crazy overnight. I picked up the phone and called Angela, the only person I could begin to talk to in town. After the usual politeness, I exploded, "Don't you ever get *tired* of it all, Angela—the same thing day after day after day, year after year? Meals to cook, beds to change, laundry to fold, toys to pick up. Baths, naps, diapers. Trout season, bird season, buck season. It just goes on and on. Nothing ever changes. It's like being in prison. And meanwhile, people are dropping like flies, and the world is collapsing, and—"

"Oh sure, I get like that sometimes," Angela interrupted, clearly confused by my call.

"What do you *do?*"

"Oh, Bill and I scream at each other and kick and throw plates. And then Bill drags me off to bed and knocks me up and I have another baby." She laughed merrily.

I stared at the phone in horror. "*Really?*"

"You should have another baby, Ginny. Really you should. Two are so much easier than one."

She *has* to think that, I reminded myself carefully. She has four. She wants to think she's taken the best possible course. She's out looking for converts, like everyone else.

"That's what everyone always says. . . ."

"Oh, but it's true. And it gets easier with each one. Why, I'm so relaxed with four that I'm about to fall apart." It was true. Angela did look unhinged most of the time. Her children were all about two years apart. Most people's were. That meant that Angela's method of fighting the domestic doldrums would last for about fifteen months between the birth of the last child and the conception of the next. Wendy was older than fifteen months. Any day now Ira and I would be dragging each other off to bed to make another baby in an effort to restore my sanity. I preferred to think that conception was a rational decision. But if I wanted my babies to be rational decisions, I had better pull myself together and get busy deciding whether or not I wanted another.

When Ira returned from his great bird hunt, I was lying in a state of nervous collapse on the parlor couch staring at the portrait of Father Bliss. Books from the bookcase lay strewn over the floor.

Spinach was caked all over the kitchen and all through my hair. I had just completed a series of letters—requesting brochures on land purchases in the Klondike, job opportunities in New Zealand, immigration policies in Zambia. This behavior was in keeping with the adage that had ruled my life to date: "When in doubt, cut out."

"Where's my little angel?" Ira asked, flinging half a dozen decaying sparrows at me to clean for supper.

"Damned if I know," I whispered.

"*What?* You *don't know?*"

"The back yard maybe?"

Ira raced into the yard calling, "Wendy, Daddy's home!" The calls got farther and farther from the house, and increasingly panicked.

Ira found Wendy careering down the road to town on her chubby little legs with her damp diapers trailing in the dirt. When he carried her, miraculously unharmed, into the house, he was quivering with rage. I had never seen my assiduously good-natured husband angry before. I watched, fascinated, delighted, as his black eyes flashed sparks of fury.

He went upstairs and put Wendy in her crib. Then he came stomping down and stood looking at me, speechless.

I shrugged indifferently. "I counted up today. I've been at this baby stuff for twenty-seven months. And I'm tired of it."

"*Tired* of it?" he shouted. "So you just thought you'd let her wander down the road and get run over, so that you won't have to be bothered with her anymore?"

"I didn't know she was in the road."

"That's just the point!" he yelled. "*You didn't know where our baby was!*"

"Baby this, baby that. I'm *sick* of fucking babies!" I screamed. "Maybe I want to think about something else for a change, *talk* about something besides bowel movements, *do* something besides rinse diapers!"

"Well, that's *tough* if you're sick of it, Ginny," Ira snarled. "Because you and I have quite a few more years left of Wendy. I know you're used to just packing up and leaving when you get tired of things. That's how you've lived your whole life. You're a spoiled brat! But you *chose* to have this baby, Ginny. It was *your* idea. Just remember that. And you're dang well going to care for her! It's your *duty!*"

"Go fuck yourself," I suggested calmly. I hurled his dead birds at him. "And take your goddam sparrows and shove them up your ass."

"If you use your Soybean language on me *once* more, Ginny Bliss, I'm going to knock the hang out of you!"

"Well, well, Prince Holier Than Thou shows his true colors," I said thoughtfully, extending my bare foot and studying my toenails. "Mr. Bland has come out of his closet to side with his illustrious array of bigoted relatives—the charming and fascinating folk of Stark's Bog, Vermont."

I looked up to discover Ira's rifle aimed at my head.

"I'm going to splatter you all over this room if you don't shut your filthy dyke mouth!" he gasped.

I looked down the barrel without emotion. So this was it? Death had been stalking me all my life and now had the upper hand. It appeared I was to die a homicide victim in a stone colonial in Stark's Bog, Vermont—an unexpected fate for a country girl from Tennessee. Well, so be it. It was my just deserts. I had married a man without "loving" him, whatever that lofty term might mean, which I no longer knew. I was in the process of coming to loathe him, a kind and decent man, for being exactly what I had married him for being—responsible and reliable and disciplined, and predictable and dull and boring. Ira had fulfilled his end of our bargain by providing me with an orderly life, but I was apparently no longer prepared to fulfill my end by being a quiet gentle woman who was a joy to come home to. I closed my eyes and waited for my head to smash to bits, like a dropped pumpkin.

Nothing happened. I heard sobbing. I opened my eyes just as Ira hurled his rifle into the corner and collapsed weeping into Father Bliss's wing chair. We fell asleep and slept there all night. The next morning I woke up with a throbbing headache and the nausea of self-disgust. I opened one eye and discovered Ira gazing at me with despair. We flew on wings of contrition to embrace each other in the middle of the floor and to bathe each other's face in wild kisses. We spent the hour until Ira left for his office vowing to lead a new life of domestic devotion ever afterward.

"I want to make you happy, Ginny," he murmured.

"I *am* happy, Ira," I murmured back, trying to convince us both.

"We'll make a son tonight," Ira promised, as he nibbled my ear lobe just before rushing out to his car.

That night for supper I served up the game birds. I covered their pathetic little heads with lettuce leaves from my salad and poked away loyally, trying to flake the hauntingly meager layer of flesh from the delicate framework of bones.

"Delicious!" Ira informed me, just as Eddie had always done concerning soybean croquettes.

"Delicious," I echoed weakly, acutely conscious of the fact that I was about to have a son implanted in my womb. Mother had always insisted that personal preference was irrelevant, that the doing of one's duty was what counted. It was my duty to provide my husband with an heir, and that was that!

But, as it turned out, that night wasn't an auspicious one for son making. Although the orgasm I had experienced during Wendy's conception hadn't recurred, Ira had given up trying to make our sex life exciting. Hanging from the beam had shaken his confidence in his manual. The project he was now devoting his considerable organizational skills to was producing a son. He had clipped an article from the *Reader's Digest* on determining the sex of a baby at conception, based on the different rates at which male and female sperm traveled under different vaginal conditions. Marked in red pencil on the kitchen calendar now were the days of my menstrual cycle most propitious for the conception of a male. I felt like a medieval walled city about to be besieged. Ira bought me a douche bag and mixed up a solution in a jar. He was resolutely abstaining from sex so as to amass sperm for the big assault.

"But why does it have to be a son?" I asked.

"Why a *son? Everyone* wants a son."

But I wasn't even convinced I wanted another *baby,* never mind its sex. However, if I wasn't going to fill Father Bliss's house to the rafters with descendants, what *was* I going to do? What excuse could I give Ira to delay or call off this procreative blitzkrieg? I had no idea. And there was my duty to be performed.

The first couple of attempts failed. Ira's sperm had undoubtedly drowned in the sea of baking soda solution he had pumped into me with the douche bag, as I lay sprawled in the bathtub pointing out weakly, "But Ira, I'll probably give birth to a batch of cookies, after all this baking soda."

It was late fall by now. I stuck Wendy in a back pack and began taking marathon hikes across fields and through woods and down into valleys. These trips were tainted with a certain wistfulness: If I didn't hike now, I'd soon be pregnant and unable to hike very far with Wendy on my back. Wendy loved her new vantage point and bounced with glee as we walked. Or she would exhaust herself with her bouncings and babblings and would fall asleep with her head on my shoulder. Sometimes I wasn't home to fix Ira's lunch, or got home so late that supper wasn't on the table until seven and Ira was late for his meetings. Much of the time the house was a shambles. I had simply stopped trying to keep up with it all. I did no more than an occasional pickup and a token vacuuming. Sometimes I would put a load of dirty clothes in the washer and leave them there for a week or more, forgetting to switch them to the dryer; they would emerge covered with green mold.

Ira was becoming sullen. He no longer assured me of his concern for my happiness. "It's not that you're asked to do very much," he complained one night after a supper of TV dinners as he drew on his cigar.

"Not *much!*" I itemized the details that went into maintaining the slave labor camp he called his home.

"But Ginny, it's your *job.* I work all day doing lots of things *I* don't like so that we can have money to live on. Adults have to work to live. It's as simple as that. You're *not* doing your duty, Ginny."

"God!" I gasped with outrage. "You and your accountant mentality!"

"If you don't want to live in my house and be my wife and have my babies," Ira notified me, very sure of himself, "you'd better be thinking about what you *do* want to do." He took down the calendar and devoted himself to a calculation of my fertile days for that month.

On one of my walks, I ended up at the beaver pond, having approached it unexpectedly from a new direction. Wendy was asleep. I held my breath, waiting to be socked with a gutful of emotion at the sight of the place. I had been back since, but only at night on the back of Ira's Sno Cat, which wasn't the same as being there alone in late fall during the day.

So far the emotion was mild, bearable, pleasantly nostalgic. I walked around the edge of the pond. The sun was indirect but hot, and the meadow of dried timothy rustled as I walked slowly up through it toward the cabin site. Some black charred rubble remained, not much. The winters' snows had been about their healing work, washing the ashes down into the meadow. A few bold burdocks had fought their way up through the ruins.

I looked down toward the pond, so still and quiet compared to that last insane winter. Occasional water bugs scooted across the surface, sending out patterns of concentric ripples. The dead gray trees, not as ominous as usual under the bright sun, stood like silent brooding sentinels to the human folly that had surrounded them that winter.

I strolled around slowly, testing myself for emotion, like dipping a toe in hot bathwater, heading ultimately for our former garden site. It was completely taken over by a tangled riot of weeds. Growing up from the tomato patch where I had spread Eddie's ashes were some dried goldenrod. I picked one stalk and stuck it through my button-hole.

I walked down the path toward Mona's and Atheliah's farm. The path was overgrown, nearly undetectable. I thought I might stop by and say hello. I hadn't seen them for over a year. The last time had been in the IGA. They raced up with arms outstretched to embrace me. I glanced around nervously. Two of Ira's aunts and several cousins and the owner of the store were watching. Where did my loyalties lie? I knew by now that both sides refused to let them lie in both places. It was a wrenching moment of truth. My arms rose flutteringly from my sides of their own accord. Hastily, I drew them down and greeted Mona and Atheliah coolly, with words alone. I had made my choice. But I was now no longer quite so sure about it.

I stood overlooking the rambling house. A party was in progress. They had probably drummed up some obscure saint's day as an excuse for a festival, or perhaps it was an Indian summer rite. Black pots were being stirred over fires. People lay around in the sun, mostly undressed, playing instruments, smoking dope, laughing. A wild running and leaping game was going on where the corn field had been. I saw no evidence of even a token garden this year. I started down the hill toward the encampment, with a big smile on my face.

Then I stopped abruptly and stared at the scene, while the pain I had been expecting finally swept over me in a great tidal wave. I gritted my teeth and shut my eyes tightly against it. I shook with agony. And I knew that there was no going back. I didn't know how to go forward, but I knew I couldn't go back. I would turn into a pillar of salt, like Lot's wife fleeing Sodom. But I wanted to go back. I wanted to loll in the sun with Eddie again and smoke dope and laugh and forget about baking soda douches and dirty diapers. I wanted to default on my duty. But the flip side of lolling in the sun was the burst of insanity that resulted in my neglect of Wendy, the day Ira found her in the road. The two went hand in hand and had killed Eddie. . . .

Wendy awoke with a start and began whimpering. I slid off the pack and lifted her out. Then I sat against a rock, holding her on my lap facing me. I kissed her chubby face, all flushed and damp and grumpy at being awake. She smiled reluctantly. I bounced her and blew in her ear to cheer her up. She laughed, but angrily, not wanting to.

My little vampire bat grabbed the dried goldenrod out of my buttonhole. I restrained an impulse to grab it back. I forced myself to sit and watch calmly as she slowly dismembered it, leaf by leaf. Then I took the pack in one hand, and Wendy's moist chubby little hand in the other, and we tottered back through the woods toward town.

12

Friday, July 7

□

By now, when Ginny tossed the baby birds into the air, they at least flapped their wings cooperatively as they plummeted to the ground like stones. They were getting the idea. They were exercising their muscles, and perhaps even hastening the development of feathers. She told herself that their learning to fly would happen like Wendy's learning to walk: One moment she was crawling, watching adults towering past, and the next moment, in a burst of inspiration, she too was walking. One morning the birds would suddenly fly away and never be seen again. Ideally.

Twice a day, in the morning when she got up and in the late afternoon when she got back from the hospital, Ginny would take them outside, stroking their heads with her index finger. By now those heads were covered half with the fluffy gray down of infancy and half with sleek black adult feathers. The down stuck out in unruly clumps from the smooth shiny hood that would soon extend to cover their backs as well. They were ugly, she had to admit it. They looked like Australian kiwi birds. They were clumsy and awkward and ugly, like any adolescent form of life. If she hadn't been a compulsive personality, she'd have flushed them down the toilet. She had to force herself not to strangle them. What in hell was she doing saddled with two young birds who screeched mercilessly the minute she set foot in the cabin? Didn't she have enough problems without theirs as well, what with going every day to play Clara Barton to her mother's Camille?

When Ginny reached her mother's door, she paused. Over the past two weeks she had developed a real reluctance to enter this room. She never knew what new horror of physical dysfunction would greet her. The second transfusion had worked for four days. The various membranes had stopped leaking, her mother's platelet count had risen, her bleeding time had fallen. Then everything had broken down again.

Taking a deep breath, she knocked, waited, then pushed in the door. How dreadful to be always available like this, for a woman who cherished her privacy. Her mother looked up from her encyclopedia and smiled faintly.

"Hello, Mother." Her mother nodded.

Ginny sat down and tried to think of something cheerful to say. "Pretty day out," was the best she could do.

"Is it?"

"Remember those birds?"

"Yes. How are they doing?"

"Fine. I'm giving them flying lessons."

Her mother laughed. "That should be entertaining. What do you do—jump off the porch flapping your arms?"

Ginny smiled. "Actually, I just toss them into the air and let them figure it out. I wonder, though. Do you suppose birds know how to fly instinctively, or do they learn by watching their parents?"

"Hmmm. Good question. I don't know. Did you look it up in that book?"

"Birdsall doesn't know either. Or if he does, he's not telling. What I can't figure out is if I can speed things up. I have to get rid of them before they're totally dependent on me. After all, I won't be here much longer."

"Well, *I* could always take over when you go back to Vermont." Mrs. Babcock was surprised at the ease with which this rolled off her tongue. Was Ginny *going* back to Vermont? Mrs. Babcock had reason to think not, adding up several dozen facial expressions and a few veiled remarks. And she herself wouldn't be out of this hospital any time soon, if at all. This morning in the bathroom mirror she had discovered blood blisters on her gums. It appeared that the mucous membranes of her mouth would be the next tissues to let her down. She hadn't yet notified Dr. Vogel or Miss Sturgill. She was feeling very protective toward them, and most of all toward her own worried and unhappy daughter. They were all young people, caught up in the problems of living, blissfully unaware of those of dying.

Ginny winced, both at her mother's belief that she'd be out of the hospital soon, or ever, and also at her mother's assumption that she herself would be returning to Vermont. Although this was what she now thought she wanted. It was agony returning every evening to the empty cabin. When her evenings had been crammed with Wendy's bath and bedtime, with dirty dishes, with eleven o'clock feedings, with lovemaking, she had wished fervently for just *one* long luxurious evening uninterrupted by demands from her insatiable child and husband. Now, after two weeks of such evenings, she couldn't bear it any longer. She would pace the floor, hovering over the phone, struggling with herself not to pick it up and call Ira and beg his forgiveness. A dozen times a night she would open the refrigerator door and stare into it without being hungry. Cups of cold coffee and tea sat undrunk all over the living room. She would devote more time than she ever had to Wendy and Ira to her ridiculous birds—putting fresh grass in their basket, cleaning up fallen bits of food, stroking their ugly heads, when they only wanted to be left alone to sleep. The night noises—bull frogs in the pond, and locusts and lowing cattle—would alarm her into double-locking the doors and shutters and propping a loaded rifle by the front door. She would fling herself down on the couch and snatch a book from the bookcase, but her mind would be in Vermont —picturing Ira settling back in his armchair and drawing on his cigar, while Wendy scrambled onto his lap and intently tried to poke a finger through the smoke rings he'd blow for her. Ginny would crawl miserably into bed and wrap her arms and legs around her pillows, pretending that they were Ira's warm body.

All the comfortable domestic routines she had found so tedious toward the end—she had nothing now to take their place, and familiar patterns didn't fade easily on their own. She wanted them back. She ached for the familiar odors—Ira's cigars, Wendy's baby powder, the lemon oil on the antiques. The familiar sensation of Ira's hands moving over her body, Wendy's chubby fist clutching her index finger as they walked. True, she had had her reasons for placing all this in jeopardy by taking on Hawk. What had they been? They had seemed so crucial at the time, and now she couldn't even remember them. . . .

"I don't know if the birds could adjust to a new mother figure,"

Ginny said weakly. "I'd rather have them on their own before I leave."

As they labored down the hall to lunch, they heard angry voices in Mrs. Cabel's room. On the open door hung a sign saying "No Visitors." The voices were now discernibly Mr. Solomon's and Sister Theresa's. Mrs. Babcock stopped.

"Did I tell you Mrs. Cabel went into a coma yesterday afternoon?" Mrs. Babcock asked, watching her daughter's face closely to learn if this would upset her.

"No, you didn't," Ginny said, guarding herself against revealing any emotion. "I'm sorry."

Inside, Mrs. Cabel's room was identical to Mrs. Babcock's but with no ancestral portraits or clock, fewer flowers and cards. The same wall of windows, the same fake Danish modern furniture, the same twin beds. Mrs. Cabel lay flat in one, her eyes closed. Various tubes ran down her nostrils and into her arms, and a bank of machines with a vast expanse of knobs and dials, like the control panel on a space capsule, sat next to the bed.

Mr. Solomon in a navy wool robe and brown leather slippers was standing at the foot of the bed with his arms outstretched, apparently blocking Sister Theresa. Sister Theresa in her hospital-issue gown and robe towered over little Mr. Solomon, whose thick glasses flashed like a Morse code transmitter as he gesticulated angrily with his head.

He was growling in a low voice, "The *hell* with your 'dignity' and 'self-possession' for her spirit, Sister! Can't you grasp the fact that *this is all there is?* Let the voman have her last few days of biological survival. She'll spend eternity in a cold black void!"

"*No*, Mr. Solomon," Sister Theresa insisted, her face flushed with thwarted conviction. "There is within each of us a spirit that survives the dissolution of the flesh. Life on this earth, in and of itself, is not sufficiently sacred to warrant our reverence. It's the *quality* of that life, Mr. Solomon, that counts. We *must* set Mrs. Cabel free from her pointless misery. She's ready now. She's a caged bird. It is interfering with the will of the Lord to hold her back like this, lashed tightly to her rotting flesh with plastic tubing by well-meaning but godless people!" She tugged emphatically at her "Not My Will But Thine" medal.

"The *fact* of human life is sufficient reason for its inviolability," Mr. Solomon snarled, scooting sideways to block Sister Theresa's renewed efforts to get to Mrs. Cabel. "Each individual life is precious

beyond all question of interference by another. There is no need to
prove someone's right to continue living."

Mr. Solomon, noticing Mrs. Babcock and Ginny, said gruffly, "Go
get Miss Sturgill, please. Sister Theresa is trying to pull the tubes out
of Mrs. Cabel."

"Isn't that decision up to her family?" Mrs. Babcock inquired,
with an uneasy glance at Ginny.

"They're relying on the doctors," Sister Theresa replied. "But I
know Mrs. Cabel, and I know what she'd want."

"And *I* know Mrs. Cabel, and *I* know vat she'd vant," Mr. Solomon growled.

Since Mrs. Cabel hadn't been able to speak since she'd been here,
could only bob her head and drool, everyone tended to interpret her
enigmatic nonreplies as agreement. Mrs. Babcock had seen Mrs. Cabel cornered by both Mr. Solomon and Sister Theresa. Each would
expound to her as though she were a new convert, and she would bob
her head and drool and point to her fluffy red slippers for approval.

That afternoon during its training flight, one of the birds flapped
its wings more enthusiastically than usual and glided for several yards.
As Ginny watched, applauding, it crashed with a sickening crunch into
the trunk of the pine tree—and fell lifeless to the ground. After staring
at it with disbelief for several minutes, Ginny tossed it into the kudzu,
close to tears.

Now there was one.

The next day Ginny found her mother lying supine with her eyes
closed. Something about her face looked odd, other than its now
familiar roundness and yellowness.

As she studied the sleeping face, its eyes opened. Her mother
nodded. "I'm afraid I can't talk very clearly," she mumbled. "My
gums are packed."

"Why?" Ginny asked with alarm.

"They're bleeding."

The two women looked at each other helplessly. Ginny pushed
back her mother's lower lip to reveal cotton rolls, like those a dentist
would use.

"When did this happen?" Ginny asked, sitting down abruptly.

"Yesterday." Mrs. Babcock's various membranes were rupturing
one by one. It was logical to assume that one day soon her brain tissue
would hemorrhage and her cranial cavity would turn to mush. Should

Ginny be told this? No, it was better that she not know, better that they continue to pretend that all would be well. Anticipation was usually far worse than actuality.

Ginny sat thinking of cerebral hemorrhage. For the hundredth time she asked herself if her mother should be told, so that she could be preparing?

"It's good of you to keep me company. I know you must be eager to get home to Wendy and Ira," Mrs. Babcock said casually.

Ginny looked away quickly, unable to withstand her mother's gaze.

"How is Ira managing?" Mrs. Babcock went on relentlessly. She was worried. She didn't want to pry, but she had a right to know if the well-being of her granddaughter was being attended to.

Ginny shrugged. "Ira's sister keeps Wendy during the day and Ira has her at night. Fortunately, I don't regard myself as indispensable to my household, the way you always did."

Mrs. Babcock raised her eyebrows at this unwarranted attack. Yes, she was clearly treading on touchy ground.

"I think it's *good* for Wendy to have close relationships with other adults," Ginny continued belligerently. "It will give her something besides me to reject when she's an adolescent."

Mrs. Babcock laughed. "I wouldn't count on it. I always forbade you children to chew gum on the same principle. I thought maybe then you'd rot your teeth to defy your father and me, rather than smoke and drink and take drugs and—so on. But it didn't work, did it?"

Ginny smiled. "No, I guess not."

"I must say I was always so *surprised* at the degree of defiance I could provoke in you children. I always thought of myself as being too amorphous to butt heads with. It must have been like locking horns with a marshmallow."

"Well, it's true that you didn't seem to understand what was expected of you. I remember one time screaming, 'I hate you!' And you replied calmly, 'Well, that's what parents are *for*, dear.' "

"Oh dear, did I really? I do apologize. It must have been very frustrating."

"Well, the Major made up for it."

They smiled at each other like soldiers who have been through a war together.

Dr. Vogel appeared in the doorway, a huge Good Humor man

in his white lab coat. He marched across the room demanding, "How are we this morning, Mrs. Babcock?" He looked at her chart and frowned. He studied the filter paper from that morning's bleeding time test. He removed the stained cotton rolls from under her lips and poked at her gums. He asked her to open her mouth wide and inspected the insides of her cheeks.

"Well!" he said, trying to sound cheerful in the face of massive evidence to the contrary. "We've been consulting some specialists at Duke Hospital about you, Mrs. Babcock. We've concluded that our next step is to remove your spleen." Mrs. Babcock and Ginny stared at him numbly. "There is evidence to suggest, Mrs. Babcock, that your platelets are being kept out of circulation in your spleen."

"What makes you think so?" Mrs. Babcock asked. She had heard so many definitive diagnoses.

"Hmmm, yes. Well, your platelet count is reduced. That fact is the only positive evidence one has to go on with ITP. Any further diagnosis is based on negative evidence, a process of elimination, so to speak. We've eliminated factor deficiencies, such as cause hemophilia. The smear study of your bone marrow indicates normal numbers of platelet precursors. But something is happening to those platelets upon leaving your bone marrow, Mrs. Babcock. We suspect that some serum factor is rendering them abnormal, hence subject to sequestration and destruction by your spleen."

"Is this operation—standard for ITP?" Mrs. Babcock inquired.

"Yes, certainly. If steroids fail."

"And what is its success rate?"

"Fifty to eighty percent of ITP patients who are operated on are cured by splenectomy. In your case, Mrs. Babcock, I think we have every reason to expect favorable results. We've held off to discover if the steroids wouldn't do the trick. We'd rather not operate on someone with a severe bleeding problem. But we feel that the time has now arrived."

The operation went well. Mrs. Babcock was transfused with fresh platelets to minimize postoperative bleeding. Her platelet count was high, and her bleeding time was low. The hemorrhaging of her various membranes ceased. For five days.

On the fifth day, gastric bleeding resumed. Her platelet count dropped like the altimeter of an aircraft in a nose dive.

When Ginny sought out Dr. Vogel in his lab, he looked gaunt and haggard, in spite of his fifty excess pounds. Averting his eyes, he said defensively, "The histological analysis of her spleen showed all the nonspecific changes characteristic of ITP—hypertrophy of the lymphoid follicles, dilated sinusoids, varying numbers of megakaryocytes, eosinophils, and neutrophils—"

"Dr. Vogel, I don't know what you're talking about," Ginny interrupted.

"All I'm saying is that the splenectomy is a therapeutic failure, but not a result of misdiagnosis."

"Who's accusing you of misdiagnosis?"

"Well, you're accusing me of *something*, Miss Babcock, the way you keep coming down here and glaring at me all the time."

"You're paranoid, Dr. Vogel." But as she thought about it, she realized that she *was* accusing him of something—of failing to live up to the myth that modern medicine was invincible. He couldn't help it if his advance men had been overzealous in their claims.

"Perhaps I am," he said thoughtfully.

"*Now* what?"

"I don't know."

"As far as I can see," Ginny explained to Maxine and Clem as she sat in their cluttered kitchen that afternoon, "the doctors have tried everything they can think of. What she needs now is a miracle." She immediately regretted her choice of words. Since her evening in the springhouse, she had resolutely avoided the topic of religion with Clem and Maxine. The few times they'd met, they had studied her face eagerly, waiting for her to tell them that she was prepared to join them in the springhouse again. Each time she had deftly sidestepped the issue of her spiritual malaise. She wasn't in any condition to decide anything, and was struggling not to succumb, for once in her life, to the nearest sympathetic shoulder.

Clem's eyes gleamed with fanaticism as he pleaded, "Give the Lord a chance, Ginny. He healed my leg. He can heal your mother's blood."

"What would it involve?" Clem's regenerated leg was difficult to dispute. After all, didn't the Lord traditionally work in mysterious ways?

"Could you bring her to the Temple?"

Ginny pondered the topic. "I don't see any way I could get her out undetected. Besides, it would be very difficult for her to climb that hill."

"Never mind. I'll come to *her*. After a service. When I feel the power upon me."

"That would be great, Clem," Ginny said, trying to decide how to present this to her mother. What harm could there be in giving Clem a chance? Wasn't it worth a try? It wasn't as though they had to convert on the spot.

Back at the cabin, she took her one remaining bird outside for his flying lesson. She perched it on her finger. They stared at each other, her blue eyes studying its tiny beady black ones. The bird flung open its beak and craned its gaping pink throat upward and screeched: *Feed me, Mother!* Irritably, Ginny turned her hand around and tilted it, hoping to jar the bird into unexpected flight. It flapped its wings desperately to maintain its balance. It wasn't remotely interested in flying. It was interested in being fed. All day long if possible.

Ginny tossed it mercilessly into the air. It *would* fly, damn it! For a couple of seconds, the bird held its wings tight against its sides and lost altitude like a kamikaze plane. Finally, hurtling toward the ground, it spread them and flapped halfheartedly, soared for several yards and landed gracefully. One day before long, the bird would finally catch on and would swoop away, higher and higher into the sky. Two things worried her, though: If it landed, it probably wouldn't know how to take off again. The other problem was that the bird couldn't eat or drink on its own. She had tried putting a dish of bread crumbs and another of water in its basket. She had held its head in her fingers and had pecked its beak in the crumbs and had helped it scoop water. Then she had stopped feeding it, to see if it would figure things out. It hadn't. It had merely screeched louder and longer, until she'd finally had to feed it to maintain her borderline sanity. What would happen to this pathetic specimen of birdlife if it did simply take off one day? Would it watch the other swifts and learn how to sweep down over the pond and scoop up a beakful of water? Or be ostracized for smelling like humans? Would it starve? Or return in defeat, requiring her to feed it for the rest of its life as her penalty for getting involved in the first place?

That night Ginny found her mother lying staring at the ceiling. She didn't acknowledge Ginny's greeting.

Ginny decided to come right to the point. "Mother, do you remember I told you about Clem Cloyd's leg's being healed? Well, Clem wants to try healing you. What do you think?"

Mrs. Babcock said nothing for a long time. She had grown up in the rural South surrounded by every form of religious perversion. She had been raised in the Southern Baptist church, deserting it for the Episcopal church largely at the insistence of Wesley, who wouldn't hear of subjecting his children to baptism by immersion or to weekly diatribes about hell-fire and eternal damnation. Although she admired the dignified language of the Anglican prayer book, found solace in the antiquity of the rituals, she still nurtured in her heart a fondness for the fervid fundamentalist sects of her homeland—the faith healers and snake handlers, those who saw visions and rolled in aisles and spoke in tongues. She had read repeatedly, when she had woken in the middle of the night and been unable to sleep, from her worn Book of Common Prayer—The Order for the Visitation of the Sick, The Communion of the Sick, The Order for the Burial of the Dead— searching that melodic and dignified language for some clues as to what was happening to her, how to cope with it. She found few. And here she remained in this bed, deteriorating. But she suspected she lacked the one element essential to faith healing—faith in that form of healing. However, if God should choose to use Clem Cloyd as His instrument, she was more than prepared to return to the faith of her fathers.

"Why not? We've tried everything else."

Clem walked in the door the next night dressed in green work pants and a fresh white shirt. He held his hands up, palms inward, like a surgeon in sterile gloves. Or as though his fingers were the prongs of a horseshoe and the good luck would flow out if they pointed groundward. He was glowing with faith and confidence.

After greeting them, he invited them to pray. It was a simple little prayer, which asked that God's will be done, but that that will include healing Mrs. Babcock. Then, his eyes tightly shut like a child making a birthday wish, he placed his supercharged hands on Mrs. Babcock at different spots—her head, her heart, her incision.

He promised to return after the next service, when he would be recharged with the power and the glory. After his departure, they alternated between feeling silly and feeling superstitiously hopeful.

The next day Mrs. Babcock's right retina hemorrhaged.

As she lay in the dark with platelets transfusing into her arm, Mrs. Babcock watched a thunderstorm out her window with her function- ing eye. High winds lashed the branches of the elm. Presumably the chattering squirrel family was snug inside a hollow somewhere along the trunk. Patterns of lightning kept imprinting themselves on the black sky. Try as she would to compare these fluorescent patterns to cracks in dinner plates, or earthquake fault lines, she kept seeing them as luminous circulatory systems.

That afternoon Ginny, lying on the spare bed, had read to her from the last volume of the encyclopedia. The electric chimes at the church circle were playing "Make the World Go Away, Take It All Off My Shoulders."

" 'Yantra,' " Ginny read. " 'Any physical form which can convey a charge of symbolism. Used in several types of yoga as an object for "worship," i.e., an object serving to focus the attention and emotions of the devotee, and to identify for him stages in his progress toward spiritual enlightenment. . . .' " Ginny's voice was quavering. Mrs. Babcock looked at her questioningly. "I—did some Yoga in Vermont. With a friend named Will Hawk. It was quite—an experience." She inhaled deeply in what looked like an attempt to quell warring emotions.

"And did you gain enlightenment?"

"About some things," Ginny replied, with evident pain. "But not about what I was supposed to be, I suspect."

"My conclusion from nine years of encyclopedia reading," Mrs. Babcock offered, "is that all the great world religions have been training systems to instruct adherents in how to die."

"Oh, come *on*. There *has* to be more to life than death!"

"*Why* does there?"

As she watched the lightning, Mrs. Babcock formally acknowledged that she was dying. This last month in the hospital was merely the graduation ceremony. The process itself had been under way for years. A leaf, she knew from the encyclopedia, began dying in midsummer, when the days were long and hot. The vivid green leaves on the elm outside, for instance, had already begun dying. In midsummer, in response to genes and hormones and environmental influences, the delicate balance in a leaf—between growth and decay, between order and chaos, between elaboration and disintegration—tipped in favor of decay. The amount and kinds of proteins being synthesized altered gradually over the weeks and months, carrying the leaf inexorably toward that final moment when a light breeze would suffice to dislodge it and swirl it away.

However, it was one thing to acknowledge intellectually that she wasn't going to leave this hospital alive. It was, as she knew, another thing entirely to accept that fact emotionally. She had no idea how far along that route she might have progressed, if at all. The leaf, before it was allowed to drop off the branch in autumn, was first required to export to the tree proper a goodly portion of the nitrogen and minerals supplied by the tree throughout the summer. In addition, the dying leaf paid its rent for branch space by returning to its woody host an acid formed during the leaf's death throes which granted the tree winter hardiness. Without this acid the tree as a whole would perish in an early freeze. And the tree wouldn't loose its hold on the leaf until it had secured this acid.

More and more over the past several days, she had been swamped by her past. People and incidents that she hadn't thought about in years kept popping into her mind and dragging her down the dim corridors of her memory. For instance, she had recalled vividly the first and only time she'd been back to Sow Gap since leaving for Hullsport with her parents when she was five. When she was ten, her father's father had died, and she and her parents had gone to the funeral.

The trip, a hundred and fifty miles of rugged foothills, had taken two days in the shiny new Ford. The deeply rutted road looked like a hog wallow. Every couple of hours they got bogged down, and her father had to pry the auto out of the mud with logs and boards. Twice he had to go in search of farmers with mules to drag the car out. There were rivers to ford, mountain gaps to cross. Parts snapped on the auto and had to be fabricated out of scrap iron in farmers' junk heaps.

Throughout the trip, her mother, in her flowered hat and white gloves and silk print dress, kept repeating, "Honey, you must never be ashamed of your origins. Your people are hard-working, God-fearing folks. Hardy pioneer stock. A little backward maybe, a little slow. But hard-working and God-fearing."

These sermonettes had first suggested to the little girl that there might be something wrong with her origins. All kinds of questions started assembling themselves in her brain: Apart from this mud-bound marathon of a trip, why had she and her parents never been back? Why had they left in the first place when all their relatives were there? Why hadn't she seen her grandparents since she was five, her aunts and uncles and cousins?

They had arrived just as her grandfather's coffin was being lowered into the ground in a family plot on a hillside. Off into the distance rolled ridge after ridge of mountain, rising up abruptly from deep valleys. And directly below was Sow Gap—consisting of a handsome red brick courthouse on an unpaved street, surrounded by a couple of sandstone churches and several frame stores. There she had stood in a ruffled chiffon dress with ribbon ties, surrounded by cousins she had never met in neat dresses made of flour sacks. They, their clothes, and their town, in spite of evident tidiness, appeared ineradicably smudged from the omnipresent coal dust.

The supper after the funeral was a boisterous affair, held in the sagging gray house of her father's brother, Reuben. Fortified with a jug of clear corn liquor, Reuben asked the little girl and her father to go fishing afterwards. "Fishing" consisted of throwing sticks of dynamite into the creek behind his house and collecting the stunned fish that were thrown up on the bank.

"Reuben, that's illegal," her father complained after the first explosion. "That's against the *law!*"

"Zedediah, *ah* am the law," he replied, swigging from his jug.

The next day Reuben drove them out to the mine where her father had worked before leaving for Hullsport, the mine where Reuben himself still worked. It was basically a dark hole in a hillside with metal tracks running into it. Some tar-paper sheds clustered around outside it. And all around that black hole were heaped great piles of smooth reddish stone. Her father wandered around nervously, peering and looking generally uncomfortable in his suit and starched collar. She sat on a slag heap with Uncle Reuben, who sorted through the chunks for fossils—imprints of prehistoric plants, complete with every vein and stem, imprisoned for all eternity in the soft stone.

"Nothing won't never change them plants now," Reuben said gravely to his fascinated niece. "They done been here for thousands of years. Millions maybe." She picked out a couple of the choicest to take home.

That night at supper, in a room packed with relations, Uncle Reuben demanded of Mr. Zed, "Why ain't you never been back afore, Zed? It like to killed Pa, you runnin off like that without nary no reason."

In indirect answer, Mr. Zed regaled the assembly with the incident that had preceded his removal to the area that eventually became Hullsport. His cousin Zeke Hull had been running for sheriff on the

Democratic ticket. Mr. Zed had been a Republican and hadn't liked
Zeke anyway, and so had refused to work for his election. "If you
can't count on yer kin, who *can* you count on?" Zeke had demanded.
And he had come gunning for Mr. Zed, who had had to gallop off
into the woods on his horse and hide in a stream bed for a couple of
days, with his electioneering cousin hunting him like an animal. Zeke
had been elected anyway and had served as sheriff for many years, just
recently being shot to death in a gun battle with a moonshiner.

"Now's Zeke's dead, I figure it's safe for me to visit," Mr. Zed
explained to his assembled critics.

Mrs. Hull told that night about teaching at the state reform school
for girls in the next town, while Mr. Zed was working the mines. One
afternoon as she was leaving, her students surrounded her buggy,
intent on turning it over. She had fought them off like Cyrano de
Bergerac, with a long hat pin.

Her young daughter sat listening and staring in disbelief at her
dignified parents—her father in a dark suit and starched collar, and
her mother in her silk print dress and costume jewelry and well-
coiffed hair, her mother who now had two maids and spent most of
her time rushing off to meetings of church groups and civic clubs in
a flowered hat and white gloves.

Just before the Hulls were to leave, Uncle Reuben, swigging clear
corn and negotiating the hairpin mountain turns near his house like
a race driver, ran Mr. Zed's new Ford off a steep ridge. Reuben rolled
out unharmed, limber as a rag doll from his home-brew, but the Ford
bounced on its hard rubber tires down the cliff and crashed into a
hundred pieces in the cove below.

On the train home, in a passenger car squeezed between cars piled
high with glistening black coal, the little girl demanded, "How come
we moved away?" She had loved the family dinners, crowded with
her flamboyant aunts and uncles and cousins, in contrast to the lonely
Hullsport dinners in the echoing formal dining room with just the
three of them.

Her parents laughed with embarrassment, as though the answer
should have been self-evident. "For *you,* honey," Mr. Zed replied.
"To give you opportunities we ain't never had."

Opportunities to do what they never really said. Not in so many
words. But they always let her know when she was going astray from
the master plan—for instance, with the scene they had thrown when

Ned Ketchum, her high school swain, a farmer's son, had asked Mr. Zed for permission to marry her, in place of her going north to college. And so she had gone off to Bryn Mawr, her parents beaming approval as the train pulled out. *Their* daughter, with an ex-coal miner for a father, in the Ivy League!

Mrs. Babcock had returned to Hullsport, had married a Harvard graduate, had begun a family. All according to the plan, *improvements* on the plan. Her delighted parents had moved the young family into the huge white house and had watched from the cabin the prospering of their apparently charmed line. Mr. Zed was the most important man in town, ably backed up by his debonair son-in-law. It had been a long hard crawl from Sow Gap to Hullsport, but Mr. Zed had made it, an Appalachian Horatio Alger. And Mrs. Hull had made it. She was an officer in half a dozen clubs and circles, spent every weekday at meetings, and spent most of her time while home on the phone arranging those meetings.

Mrs. Babcock had always felt that that was no way to run a home —with maids and your one lonely child doing all your housework. Which was why she had dedicated herself solely to her house and family, pledged all her energies to their care; she would be a living reprimand to her own mother. Which was why she had eventually ended up on the cabin couch one afternoon during the Tired Years, worn to a frazzle by her selfless devotion, wailing, "I'm just so *tired*, Mother. I can't stand it anymore. What should I do?"

And her mother, seeing this monument to human doggedness that she and Mr. Zed had constucted so patiently through the years about to crumble into divorce or mental collapse, said coldly, "You must do your duty." Meaning her duty to her parents, to her husband and children.

But then Mrs. Hull had died. Wesley had converted the factory to munitions following Mr. Zed's retirement. And Mr. Zed had gone sour on his life and works, and therefore on his daughter's life and works as well. He began referring to Wesley as "that carpetbagger" and "that Episcopalian"; and he began planting kudzu all around the town and factory in hopes that they would be swallowed up. The founding of a town, the establishing of the Hull line, became trivial to him in the face of his mate's death, in the face of his own approaching death. And the life that Mrs. Babcock had lived, largely in obedience to her parents' visions, had begun to seem trivial to her too, as

her own children packed up and moved far away and put an end to
Mr. Zed's Hullsport saga.

The next afternoon Ginny and Mrs. Babcock lay watching "Hidden Heartbeats." Linda was in a frenzy of remorse over having betrayed Frank and having been banished from ever seeing her little
daughter again.

During a commercial in which a young mother was trying to get
her bowels functioning again after childbirth, Mrs. Babcock said, "So
you've left them?"

Ginny froze in the act of maiming her cuticles with her teeth.
"Who?" she asked finally.

"Ira and Wendy."

"I didn't say that," Ginny said, unable to meet the gaze from her
mother's unbandaged eye. "Did I?"

"You've as much as said it several times."

"I have *not*."

"Then how do I know it?" her mother asked with a sad smile.
"Ginny dear, I'm afraid that, underneath it all, you and I are more
alike than either of us would care to admit."

Ginny glared at her with distaste. She simply couldn't see that they
had much of anything in common, other than some specks of DNA.
Why, it was all they could do most of the time to converse in a civil
fashion. Their civil discussions weren't interesting, and their interesting discussions weren't civil.

She had told her mother about Ira and Wendy? She searched her
memory, trying to recall when this revelation had occurred. Then,
unexpectedly, she began shaking with silent sobs. She looked at her
mother in anguish. Then she closed her eyes and asked, "What should
I *do*, Mother?"

After this outburst, Ginny lay silent, wondering why she was even
asking when she knew exactly what her mother would say: Do your
duty, go back to them, make amends, spend the rest of your life in
propitiation for the pain you've caused them. And then she realized
she was asking exactly in order to be told those things, so that when
she did in fact go back, she could blame all ensuing unhappiness on
her unfortunate mother.

Mrs. Babcock lay locked in a silent struggle for a long time. Her
first impulse, successfully squelched, was to reach out and hold Ginny

and tell her that everything would be all right. Her next impulse, under which she now lay writhing, was to issue instructions to do this, do that. Or to be specific: Do your duty. Exactly what her own mother had told her. And after all, what other model did she have to guide her? Besides, you wanted so much to protect your children from mistakes and failure and suffering. Small children were like planets, harnessed to their parents in orderly orbits by the firmly balanced forces of attraction and resistance. But these orbits as children aged became more cometlike; your offspring began swinging in wild ellipses in and out of your own force field—almost breaking away entirely, but then swooping back in to set off a riot of sparks and static with their conflicting charges. One didn't issue instructions to comets. Grown children did what they had to do, and parents could only grit their teeth and watch and pray for them to get through it.

Besides, what if Ginny's duty to Ira and Wendy didn't happen to coincide with her duty to herself, as it was possible that Mrs. Babcock's might not have during the Tired Years? And who was to know that but Ginny herself? Parents expected too much of children; it was unfair to use them, as she now recognized she herself had been used, to fulfill parental ambitions or philosophies.

"I don't know what you should do, Ginny," she replied finally, with enormous difficulty. "You must do as you think best."

Ginny's eyes snapped open, as though she were Sleeping Beauty just kissed by the prince. She stared at her bruised mother. Mrs. Babcock opened her good eye and stared back. Was it possible that the generational spell had actually been broken? They smiled at each other, their delight mixed with distress.

13

The Mandala Tattoo

------------------------------ □ ------------------------------

I was lying by the pool in a red paisley bikini. The late spring sun was hot on my back. In half an hour Wendy would wake up from her nap. Ira had left a few days before for Camp Drum with his National Guard unit. I should have been delighted with my two delicious weeks of being unpressured by strategy sessions on how to nail Ellie Ovum with Sammy Sperm; they had been going on for six months without success. Each time after intercourse now, Ira insisted that I lie on my back with my legs propped against the wall for at least half an hour, to maximize the number of sperm charging up my tubes. And on the key day each month, he had taken to rushing home from the Sno Cat showroom every two hours for a round of baby making. Each month as the day for my period had arrived, we had both held our breath —me with dread, and Ira with anticipation. Each month so far I had been able to send up a silent flag of celebration as the faithful red tide had begun.

But I was now past the point of finding pleasure in brief stolen moments of solitude. I lay aching with misery, my white skin sizzling in the sun. What was bothering me most was knowing that day exactly what I would be doing a year from that day, five years from that day: shopping in the IGA and chatting about the weather with the same people, most of them related to Ira; I would be performing my role with variations on the same schedules now being pursued by Ira and by Wendy and by our as-yet-to-be-conceived son.

I had gone that morning in my red club blazer to a meeting of the Women's Auxiliary. We were setting up the fall schedule for cleaning the fire house. My despair at my manifest destiny must have been showing, although I was trying very hard to discuss with conviction what a beautiful sunny day it was and what a shame it was to be inside.

Angela patted my forearm and whispered sympathetically, like an actress in a laxative commercial, "You look down today, Ginny."

I nodded glumly.

"Take my word for it. Have another baby."

Like a Greek chorus, two women next to her picked up the theme; and soon it had spread around the entire table like athlete's foot at a swimming pool: "You shouldn't wait too long to have your second." "Only children get so lonely." "Aren't kids great?" "You're so much more relaxed after the first one." "Two are so much easier than one." "The more, the merrier!" "Cheaper by the dozen!"

I was definitely in a trap. What made it even worse was that it was a trap of my own making. I had my dividend checks, true. I could take Wendy and leave. But where would I go? What would I do? At this point, I was prepared to seize on anything that promised delivery from the deadening boredom of my routines. As I lay gnashing my teeth in existential despair, I heard a male voice behind the eight-foot plank fence that Ira had put up to keep Wendy out of the pool. "Hello? Hello?"

I threw on a terry cloth robe and went to the gate. A young man was standing by the back door. He was shirtless, dressed in dirty bib overalls hooked on one side, with a fringed leather jacket hanging open over them. He had a Kelty pack on his back. It wasn't an unusual sight. The Long Trail, which joined up with the Appalachian Trail, wasn't far away. Hikers occasionally turned up to make a phone call or something. Also the workmen from the Pots o' Gold condominium site sometimes came over for water or to use the phone.

As I walked toward him, I could see that he wore a sweat-stained red bandanna around his long matted light brown hair, babushka-like. From one ear lobe dangled a silver ring, and from it a small silver jingle bell. Because of his full tangled beard, only his lips and nose and eyes were visible. He looked like a sheepdog.

"Yes?"

He jerked around, his eyes alarmed.

"Can I help you?" I asked, perplexed that I'd triggered such a strong fear reaction.

"Oh. Yes, ma'am. I wondered if I could please have a drink of water?" I gazed at him, intrigued. He had a southern accent, southern manners, a rarity in Stark's Bog.

"Sure. Just a minute."

When I came out with ice water, this Jean Lafitte in his red bandanna was looking through the fence at the pool. He had removed his leather jacket. The back of his overalls was stained dark with sweat, and he was wiping his forehead with his forearm.

He downed the water in one long gulp and handed me the glass, saying, "Thank you, ma'am."

Charmed as I had never been by a southern accent in the South, I asked eagerly, "More?"

"No, thas just fine, thank you."

"Where are you from in the South?"

The same alarmed furtive look as when he had first seen me came over this face—came into his eyes actually, since the rest of his face was well concealed by his beard. I was studying those eyes as intently as Coach used to study the slot machine windows at the Liberty Café in downtown Hullsport. "How did you know I was from the South?"

I laughed. How does a sow know her piglets? "By your accent."

"I thought I'd gotten rid of that by now."

"Sorry," I said, shaking my head. "But then I can pick out a southern accent in a city street at rush hour, because I'm from Tennessee."

"No shit," he said with a comradely smile. "Where in Tennessee?"

"Hullsport. Near the Virginia border."

"I'll be damned! I've driven through there a hundred times heading north. Jesus, what a pit! That's where that fuckin munitions plant is, isn't it?" I nodded coolly. *I* could dump on my home town, but no outsider had better try. "Georgia, I'm from. Atlanta. But I've been away a long time."

"What are you doing up here?"

He glared at me and said curtly, "It's a long story." Then he added, "God, don't you *love* this heat? Jesus, I haven't sweated like this since Georgia in July! I don't know how people live up here in this goddam icebox!"

"I don't either," I agreed grimly. And then, inspired to an un-

characteristic display of southern hospitality by the presence of my
fellow countryman, I added, "Would you like a swim before you
leave?"

He glanced nervously around the yard. "Far out." We went
through the gate. I removed my robe and sat by the pool. He took
off his babushka and shook out his damp hair. He unhooked his
overall straps and let them fall and was suddenly nude.

I was stunned. I suppose I had been expecting him to be wearing
jockey shorts like Ira's, with racing stripes down the sides, which he
could use as trunks. Or maybe I'd planned on his donning his bandanna like a loincloth. In any case, I stared. His body had an intriguing
symmetry that Ira's, because his face was beardless, lacked: This man's
penis, hanging in its mat of pubic hair, was the mirror image of his
hairy face with its prominent nose.

After I had recovered from the aesthetic pleasure of this discovery,
I pondered the ethics of the situation à la Stark's Bog morality: Here
was a man I'd just met, nude next to me by my swimming pool, while
Ira was away serving his country. My moral diagnosis didn't look
good. Screw them all, I thought bravely, as my countryman plunged
into the water. With his hair and beard soaked, and somewhat tamed,
he looked more human, less like a sheepdog. He began doing laps in
an easy freestyle. I sat watching the sun flashing off his shiny brown
shoulders as he churned up and down the pool. Then I noticed with
concern what looked like a huge dark bruise on his upper left arm.
It spread over his bicep and flashed and rippled in the sunlight as he
swam. God only knows what terrible thing he'd done to himself.

Eventually, he jumped out and sat in a spreading puddle next to
me. I handed him a towel, and he scrubbed his hair and beard, and
rubbed his body dry. As he did so, I discovered that the dark blue
patch on his arm wasn't a bruise or a wound after all. It was a huge
tattoo. I stared at it, fixated. It was circular, with an elaborate filigreed
circumference. Immediately inside the filigree were two bands of
what looked like stylized flower petals. And within the bands of petals,
four triangles of graduated sizes, points up, interlocked with four
identical points-down triangles to form dozens of smaller triangles and
tetrahedrons. The effect of the design was to suck my attention in past
the filigree, through the flower petals, across the geometric grid—to
the inner triangle in the exact middle. After the careful, precise styliza-
tions, the figure in this central triangle was startling in its baroque
convolutions. It was skillfully built up by contrasting swirls of dark

blue tattoo ink with the brownish skin tones of the man's arm. Out from this chaos of clashing blobs of color popped the most hideous monster I'd ever encountered, even in the midnight horror features at the Family Drive-In in Hullsport. Its huge eyes bulged with rage. On its head was a crown of tiny skulls, with a sacrificial flaying knife rising up out of the center. Pointed animal ears grew out of the monster's head. Its mouth was contorted in a frightful grimace that revealed pointed fangs. And out from this mouth appeared to spew dark streams of blood, or perhaps vomit. This blood, or whatever it was, as it gushed from the monster's mouth immediately formed swirling patterns and became one with the orderly mesh of surrounding triangles.

"That was fantastic," he said as he pulled on his overalls. "Thank you."

"You're welcome," I replied automatically, unable to remove my eyes from his arm. It made the butterfly tattoo on my hip, which I had thought pretty skillful, look as crude as the skull and crossbones gougings of Clem Cloyd on his forearm with his knife.

The gate handle rattled. I knew it was Wendy, up from her nap, having scrambled over her crib bars and crashed to the floor and come in search of me—the latest trick in her arsenal of infant liberation stunts. L'il Abner, however, didn't know this, and he started at the noise and crouched like a cornered animal.

"My child," I explained. I opened the gate and picked up Wendy and set her on my hip, all damp and squishy and smelly in her dirty diapers.

"Who that?" she asked, jabbing at the man with her fat finger. "Who that, Mommy?"

"That's a man who's just had a swim in our pool."

"Who that?"

"That's a man who came over from the hiking trail to get a drink of water."

"Who that?" she asked again, tilting her head and looking at me with a puzzled expression. I knew that this would go on all afternoon unless I channeled her conversational prowess onto another topic.

"Would you like some juice and a cookie?" I asked her. "Would *you?*" I asked the young man.

"I don't want to put you out, ma'am," he said, his eyes greedy.

"It's no trouble," I assured him, lapsing readily into the folkways of the South, where, as the saying goes, men put women on pedestals and then use the pedestals as footstools. "Will you please watch the baby a minute? Don't let her get too near the edge. She thinks she can swim. She keeps jumping in and plummeting straight to the bottom." He laughed, displaying bright white teeth through his thicket of facial hair.

I returned with lemonade, paper cups, cookies, and a clean diaper. Wendy was playing a game with the man in which she toddled to one side and headed toward the pool; he would scoot sideways to block her, and she would run head on into his legs. She would resolutely careen in the opposite direction and head for the pool again, only to be cut off once more. She was giggling with a mixture of delight and frustration, and was clutching with one hand at her soggy diapers, which were drooping down her pudgy thighs and threatening to trip her. The man was looking down at her with a pleasant grin.

The three of us sat cross-legged on the grass, and I passed out the lemonade. "You seem familiar with the wiles of children. Do you have some?"

"No, I've never been married," he mumbled. "And that's the only way I'd want to get into a baby trip with a woman. I've been around friends' children a lot. But to tell the truth—pardon me, delightful baby—the concept of parenthood never really appealed to me."

"Oh, come on! How could any adult not relish the prospect of a baby of his own—to carry his genes proudly down through the centuries?" I asked this sarcastically, mocking my former romantic notions of what parenthood entailed.

"I never looked at it that way. I always saw the world as a stage —from too much Shakespeare in prep school, I guess. And any child of mine would be a ballsy young actor waiting to run me off stage altogether, watching and waiting to bury me, so that *he* could assume center stage."

"Hmmm," I said thoughtfully, wondering if that line of reasoning could serve to sour Ira on the idea of a son. I noticed that this man had, between sentences, managed to wolf down most of the cookies. "Would you like a sandwich?"

What I could find of his face, behind his beard and underneath his hairdo, blushed. "Forgive me for eating all the cookies. I haven't eaten since yesterday morning."

"Good Lord." Why in the world not? I wondered. "Do you like bologna and cheese?"

He grimaced. "Just plain cheese would be great."

As he finished his third sandwich, I asked casually, trying to figure out his story, "You say you're hiking the Long Trail?"

He gave me his suspicious alarmed look and eventually nodded yes, his mouth crammed with Wonder Bread. "Going home," he mumbled, chewing ravenously. "To Georgia."

"You're hiking the *entire* trail?" He nodded. "How long will it take?"

He shrugged. "A few months, I guess. I don't know. When I get there, I get there. *If* I get there."

It was moving on toward late afternoon. The young man showed no eagerness to get back to the mountains. Sated, he stretched out in the slanting sun, his head on his pack, and fell asleep.

As the sun was setting, he sat up and stretched and yawned. I had fed Wendy and put her to bed. I was about to settle down to Walter Cronkite and some serious nail chewing.

"Look," I said, standing over him, "do you want to stay here tonight? It'll be too dark soon to find the trail."

Without hesitation, he said, "Yes, ma'am, I sure would. Thank you very much."

"My name is Ginny. Ginny Bliss," I offered, wondering what Mother would say. Would Wendy and I be murdered in the night, and the Bliss family silver stolen?

He glanced around nervously and said in a low voice, "You can call me Hawk."

Hawk slept that night in the guest room.

We spent the entire next day by the pool, with me disappearing periodically to fetch food, or to put Wendy down for her nap, or to whisk her inside for abortive attempts at toilet training. Both of us hopped in and out of the water regularly to cool off. As we baked, we talked a great deal, on through the long lazy afternoon.

Hawk said he'd been living in Montreal for a while. "You wouldn't *believe* how cold it gets there in the winter!" He shivered just thinking about it. "Those streets act like conduits. Icy blasts funnel right down them. You're standing at a bus stop and this cyclone of snow sweeps toward you. You can't even see the headlights of your bus. Oh Christ, it's so awful!"

We swapped horror stories about the frozen North—ten-foot drifts, thirty-eight below zero nights, and falling icicles. It was an interesting variation on the weather conversations that dominated the social life of Stark's Bog.

"You know," he said, "when I was growing up, I was always dragged to all these preaching missions and revivals and stuff. I don't know, you probably were too. Tennessee's in the Bible Belt, isn't it? And on Sundays, rodding around in your car, the only radio stations you could get had these Holy Rollers screaming at you about the fiery pits of hell. But you know what? Hell, in my own personal mythology, isn't raging fires and stuff; it's silent snowbanks and long gray afternoons when the thermometer won't budge above minus twenty."

"And those nights when the wind is howling through your house and shaking the windows in their frames and making your tin roof flap," I offered, caught up in the theme.

"And in a city, when a street drain backs up, and the crosswalk is knee deep in frozen mush. And your boots leak and your toes go numb," Hawk added.

"And in April when the snow melts all at once and turns the fields into squishy bogs, and all the dirt roads into vast rutted seas of mud. And swarms of cluster flies crawl out and swirl around sluggishly and get tangled up in your hair!"

We both laughed with delight at finding someone with whom to share our *most secret* thoughts about our adopted home. Our heritage was a relentlessly baking sun.

"Why did we leave?" I asked mournfully.

"Jesus, I hated those summers down there!" Hawk drawled. We both howled with laughter.

"Oh, *God* yes!" I agreed. "Remember lying in bed at night in a pool of sweat praying for even just the faintest breeze through the window?"

"And during the day, downtown, with the heat rising up from the concrete in these great scorching waves, and bouncing back and forth between the glass buildings. And that horrible soft squishy feeling the macadam would take on, so that you expected to be in it up to your knees at any moment," Hawk said.

"And being so exhausted from just trying to breathe that all you could do was lie panting in the shade like a dog."

"But I will say this for it," Hawk said. "These Yankee winters and southern summers do serve a purpose."

"What's that?"

"Well, just imagine if everywhere were perpetual autumn or spring—a mild sun and temperatures in the sixties and seventies, say. You'd really start feeling pretty good about yourself—as though you had things under control, knew what you were doing. As it is, though, at almost every spot on earth you get fried by the sun or blasted by blizzards. You're reminded of what a puny little insect you really are, and of how you're kept alive in *spite* of all your pathetic weaknesses."

"You've been listening to too many Holy Rollers!"

He didn't smile. "No, wait!" he insisted. "This is *very* important. Now! The earth is tilted on its axis, which is what causes the seasons. Right? Okay. Well, in a mathematically perfect universe, one would expect the earth's axis to be exactly vertical to its path around its sun. I mean, it's just more geometrically pleasing that way. But if it *were* vertical, there would be no seasons. Weather at any given spot on earth would be constant. Right? As a result, I bet you *anything* that the people living at any given spot, provided they didn't wander aimlessly around the globe as everyone is doing nowadays, would evolve the physical characteristics to cope with their climate. The Eskimos would grow luxurious fur and would stay deliciously snug without igloos and whale fat. And the Mexicans would sprout cold shower faucets from their skulls. But Montreal and Tennessee would have an endlessly moderate fall-type climate."

"Sounds delightful."

"Yes, of course it does. That was the problem. That's why the axis had to be tilted. People weren't suffering enough. They had no appreciation for their own frailties. They had no incentive to seek out other dimensions of experience that might be more hospitable. Plus, they were locked in. They were born, grew up, and died right in the same locale. Their bodies couldn't cope with the climate changes if they left their own region. Their internal thermostats lacked flexibility, so their brains lacked flexibility. Can you imagine how someone covered with fur would flee in terror from someone with a faucet growing out of his head?"

I laughed. "That's very good, Hawk."

"Thank you. Actually, it's not impromptu. I'm writing a book about it."

"Really? What kind of book?"

"I've created a new category. It's called historical science fiction."

"Oh?"

"I'm tracing in ten or twelve volumes the history of creation, from beginning to end, with emphasis on the recent past, covering such themes as the meaning of life and the nature of truth and beauty."

"I see," I said noncommittally.

"But I can't reveal any more at the moment," he added in a whisper, "for fear of being overheard and drawing down upon your lovely sequestered home greedy droves of clamoring literary agents and editors."

"I quite understand."

Later, as he turned over to toast his hairy chest, he asked, "How come you're up here?"

"Well, to simplify the saga—I went to college in Boston, and then I moved to a farm near here a few years ago with some friends."

"What? You mean an earth trip?" I nodded, smiling tolerantly at my former self. "No shit! I didn't figure you for the freak type."

"That was in my younger years. Before I settled gracefully into middle age."

"Hmmm, yes. Middle age *is* a state of mind rather than a question of years. I'm there myself, now that you mention it. In fact, I've been thinking lately of shaving off this ridiculous beard. I no longer have any protests to make, except to the sadist who constructed me as I am."

"Don't be rash," I suggested. "Just slip into middle age gradually. It's easier that way. In other words, just snip off bits of your beard a little at a time."

"How did you end up in this museum curator's wet dream?" he asked, gesturing to Father Bliss's fortress.

"I married the man who owns it."

"Who has left you, or what?" I was starting to wish that I had detected a note of hope in Hawk's voice as he asked that. But I suspected that I was merely projecting.

"No. He's just away for a few days." Instinctively, because of my upbringing, I cringed, knowing I should have said that Ira would be back this afternoon, in case this man Hawk was considering holding Wendy and me hostage or something.

"Is he a—native, or whatever you'd call long-time residents?" I nodded. "What's it like—living here?"

"Really, I guess it's pretty much like living anywhere else—Hullsport or Cambridge or anywhere."

"What do you do all day?" He rolled over on his stomach and inspected me in my bikini with detached interest, as though I were a laboratory specimen.

"Well, the same thing people do anywhere, I guess. I cook meals and wash dishes and fold laundry. The baby takes a lot of time. She and I go on walks and do the shopping and just mess around. I go to a few meetings and showers and stuff."

"Ah, community!" Hawk sighed. "Do you travel?"

"I've been on one trip in four years—to Tennessee and Florida to show the baby to her grandparents. Oh yes, and I went to a funeral in Tennessee for a weekend."

"What do you and your husband do for fun—like on a Saturday night or something?"

"We watch television, or we go out riding on his Sno Cat. Or we square dance at the elementary school. Or his family—he has this vast network of aunts and uncles and cousins and brothers and sisters— they come out for picnics and holiday dinners."

"What's he like, your husband?"

"Ira? Oh, he's very kind and decent and considerate. He loves to fish and hunt and does them very well. In fact, everything he does, he's accustomed to doing well. He's quite attractive, I suppose—sort of dark and muscled and high-strung-looking. He sells insurance and snow machines and makes a fair amount of money at it. He's very organized and dependable." Until this point, everything I had said about Ira and Stark's Bog had been in a detached tone of voice. But halfway through, Hawk had started grinning. The corners of my mouth were now twitching faintly, too, when I added, "That's why I hate him."

Hawk sighed and nodded sadly and said, "Yes, I know what you mean. Order achieved by exclusion, rather than order achieved through combating and subduing the chaos." I nodded, pleased to have the issue spelled out so succinctly for me by this stranger. "It's too bad, though."

"Yes, it makes me very sad."

"And you're thinking about splitting?"

"I think he'll probably put a bullet through my head first."

"These pleasant orderly types are the ones who do that sort of thing, you know," he cautioned me. "One day the chaos we've so resolutely lopped off unexpectedly rears its ugly head, and we're done for. We've developed no defenses against it." I noted with interest his use of the collective "we" and wondered if it was a gesture of generosity or if he was speaking from personal experience.

"We?"

He closed his eyes and shook his head to indicate that I wasn't to question further. There was an awkward silence.

"Actually, I *have* thought about leaving, off and on," I said, to gloss over the tense moment. "But where would I go? I've lived with different kinds of people. I've lived in a city, in the country, in a small town."

"How about a suburb?"

"Well, I suppose that's a possibility. But I'm beginning to suspect that the problem isn't the place or my partners—but me. I apparently haven't been able to achieve a balance between my need for stability and order and my need for variety and excitement. 'Flexible strength,' it was called in Introductory Psychology in college—like a used Kleenex."

"You're aware," he intoned, "that that's a politically reprehensible attitude, that any personal problems are the fault of a corrupt society, and that that society must be altered—or preferably destroyed?"

"Yes, I'm aware that I'm being reactionary."

"Good. Then we can still be friends," he said, his teeth white through his tangled beard. "Because you've just painted yourself into my corner. We can huddle together and hold hands while waiting for the New Left lynch mob to arrive." Then he added in a voice tinged with desperation, "But there *has* to be a way to change."

"Do you really think so?"

"Yes. There *has* to be."

Just then a car horn tooted, and a booming male voice called out, "Anybody home?"

Hawk leapt up and crouched against the fence. He hissed at me, his eyes wide with alarm, "No one must know I'm here!"

I thought his reaction excessive for the crime of sunning nude next to a married woman while her husband was away. But I nodded to him as I headed for the gate. "*No one!*" he whispered urgently.

Ira's Uncle Dean, a short man with a huge pot belly, was in the garage looking around.

"Hello, Uncle Dean!"

"Whybygod, Ginny! Decided nobody was around, so I was going to borrow Ira's chain saw and leave him a note."

"Ira's not here, but help yourself to his saw."

"Where is he?"

"At Camp Drum with the National Guard."

"Jesum Crow, I'd forgotten. Don't get too lonely now, will you?"
I promised him that I'd try not to.

"Pretty day, huh?" I pointed out.

"Beautiful. Just beautiful. Going to be a beautiful week."

"Is that what they say?"

"A-yup. But these weather men, they're never right."

"It's only their life's work."

"What? Oh yes, life's work. Right." He put his arm around me
as I walked him to his car. He carried Ira's yellow chain saw in his
other hand. He leaned over and whispered in my ear, "You got any
exciting news for us yet?"

I looked at him indignantly. "What do you mean?" I asked, knowing perfectly well what he meant.

"Hang, you don't want to wait too long now to start on your
second."

Feeling ornery, I said, "Uncle Dean, people don't always get what
they want."

"Oh, I'm sorry. I didn't *know*. Forgive me, Ginny."

"It's all right," I assured him with sad dignity.

When I got back to the pool, Hawk was still crouched against the
fence like a cornered animal. "He's gone," I notified him.

He collapsed in a heap. "Did you tell them you'd never heard of
me?"

"What are you talking about?"

"The FBI."

"That was my husband's uncle. Now what's this all about? What
horrible thing have you done, that you should be such a nervous
wreck?"

He stood up slowly, his face haggard; he walked back to the pool
and lay face down in the grass. "I should have told you right from the
start," he said miserably. "Now I've implicated you, and you can get
in a lot of trouble."

"For what?"

"For harboring an army deserter."

It was my turn to look at him with alarm. The term "deserter"
resounded with such sinister associations in my mind. A deserter: a
coward who had abandoned his post at a battlefront to roam through
the surrounding countryside raping and looting and murdering. Men
without consciences who would flee to save their own necks, leaving

their braver comrades weakened and more vulnerable to attack. I glanced at him uneasily.

He was studying my reaction. Finding what he expected, he shut his eyes and nodded his head knowingly and said softly, "Yes, but it wasn't like that at all."

And, in fact, I still trusted him, my flash of conditioned panic notwithstanding. After all, although to the Stark's Boggers Hawk was all the heinous things I had already thought of, to Eddie he would have been a war hero. I had an obligation at least to hear him out before kicking him into the road.

"Well, as long as I'm already implicated, why don't you tell me exactly what I'm implicated *in?*" I suggested.

He sighed wearily. "It's a vast saga of grief and misery."

"We've got several days before my husband gets back from the National Guard."

"Your husband's off with the *National Guard?*"

Indignantly, feeling penitent for having talked so candidly with this deserter about the failings of my kind and loyal Ira, I said, "He views his obligation to his country differently from you. I don't see why that's any reason to ridicule him."

He stopped laughing. "I'm sorry if it sounded as though I were, because I wasn't. I was just struck by the irony of it all—him off serving his nation, and his wife back home entertaining a deserter."

I flinched. I too had been struck by the irony, which I felt cast me in a not altogether flattering light. In short, I felt guilty. It was marital infidelity at its most pure. "Go on," I commanded unpleasantly.

Hawk's father, a retired army colonel and an American Legion Post Commander, had been in Belgium in World War II and in Korea —silver star, bronze star, purple heart. Dinner table conversation frequently included his story about being shot down over occupied France and having to parachute out and find his way to the border without food or a compass. Hawk's grandfather, a general in World War I, had fought at the Somme. His great-great-grandfather, a Confederate officer, was killed in a charge at Lookout Mountain. And so Hawk had grown up surrounded by plastic howitzers and model armored support vehicles. He had jumped out of trees with a parachute of silk scarves tied to his shoulders.

After military academy in Atlanta, he was turned down by West Point. In a funk, he went to Alabama Tech and studied electrical engineering, the first Hawk male in three generations not to be a career officer. One morning after graduation he found himself standing with a raised hand under a touched-up photo of President Nixon. And the next thing he knew, he was marching back and forth at Fort Maynard chanting, "I wanna go to Vietnam! I wanna kill the Vietcong!" A huge billboard of a handsome GI bayoneting a sinister little yellow man in black pajamas towered over him everywhere he went.

"It was a conditioning thing," Hawk explained, as I changed Wendy's diapers on the grass and scowled at her for failing to give me a cryptic signal to spirit her into the toilet as Dr. Spock had assured me babies much younger than she did effortlessly. "The point was to get us so scared and so exhausted that we did exactly as we were told. My mind shut down completely, and I became a highly trained instrument that responded instantly to outside commands. Once during a bayonet drill, though, my mind began stirring and yawning and peering out at the activities of this body under its supposed control. It was jabbing at a sandbag and shouting, 'Kill, kill, kill!' This four-foot drill sergeant who'd done two tours in Nam was all purple in the face from yelling, 'Stab low and pull up, you mother fuckers! Rip those gook guts right out!' My brain freaked out! I started giggling, then guffawing. Soon I was doubled over in paroxysms of glee. And here came this Napoleon bellowing about how he was gonna bust my ass and knock the shit outa me and kick my fucking teeth in. But I couldn't stop. He stood over me and growled, 'Well, you ain't gonna be laughin where you're goin, boy! You lie round laughin over at *Nam* and you get your fuckin head blown off!'

"To show us how the semiautomatic on the M-16 worked, this guy blew the head off an alley cat in a garbage can. And one afternoon he invited me to his quarters and showed me the skull of a Vietcong, which he'd scooped out and dried like a Halloween pumpkin. Then he hauled out this album of photos of mutilated bodies. I said, 'Hey man, I don't wanna look at these. This little hobby of yours is weird.' And he said, 'Well, son, you'd better get used to lookin at them, cause where you're goin you're gonna see plenty.' "

Hawk went to Vietnam in the grip of the basic male thing: Here was this rite that would either make a man of you or destroy you. If you returned alive, you'd somehow conquered Death. Naturally he assumed that he would be one of those to return—loaded down with medals just like his father. But once there, his only concerns became enduring the incredible boredom and staying alive and getting home, which required doing as he was told. Out on a patrol he and four others abducted a Vietnamese girl from a field near a village. Hawk protested faintly and was told to shut up. He speculated on pulling a John Wayne and rescuing her. Then he pictured himself in a jungle grave with a bullet through his head. Or returned to Atlanta in a body bag—a war hero. It was one of those jarring moments when a person realizes that he's stepped out of the familiar everyday world into a realm of primal lawlessness in which anything goes. The girl panicked and started kicking and scratching. The others slapped her around. Finally Hawk joined them in raping her.

I looked at him with alarm: I was alone and defenseless with a rapist. What should I do?

"You have to understand that I was almost a virgin," Hawk explained grimly, as I stared at him with horror. "I'd done the usual back-seat grapplings when I was at military school. At Tech I went once to a black whore—and came all over her before we were even undressed. Once I wrangled a date with a townie who'd reportedly 'do it for anyone.' I got her drunk so that she wouldn't notice my ineptitude, and she passed out. So I screwed her anyway, and then cleaned her up. She never knew. Junior year I fell hopelessly in love. But my girl's education was very important to her, and we didn't want to risk wrecking it by getting her pregnant. So we had this beautiful chaste relationship for over a year. I went off to war knowing that she'd be through school when I got back, and all would be well. I'd have saved myself for her, and she for me, and we could spend the rest of our lives making up for lost time.

"While I was raping the girl, I looked down at her face. She was staring at the sky with resigned hatred. One eye was swollen shut, and she'd bit through her lower lip. I lost my erection. I pretended to come. One of the guys dragged her to her feet. She spat in his face. He started shouting things about 'gooks and yellow cunts and slant-eyed sluts,' and then threw her down and shoved a grenade up her. We heaved what was left of her body off a cliff." He was talking mechanically, gazing off into space. "I had thought I was hero material. That day I learned I wasn't."

Wendy toddled over and squatted down and tried to fondle his penis. He pushed her away gently. I continued to stare at him, alarm and disgust vying with compassion.

What he mostly felt, he said, was relief. Poof! She was blown away, and he didn't have to think about her anymore. After all, if it hadn't been for all those scrawny pathetic gooks who couldn't take care of themselves, he wouldn't have had to be stranded in some God-forsaken rain forest in the first place.

By the time they got back to camp, the relief had worn off. He expected a bolt of lightning with their names engraved on it to arrive from Uncle Sam. But nothing happened. To his dismay. He expected to be punished, he *wanted* to be punished—to be dismembered with the assembled troops looking on and jeering. But no punishment arrived.

So he punished himself. He stopped eating and sleeping. He lay in his tent crying and reviewing obsessively the various points at which he could have taken a stand and saved the girl. When he did sleep, he dreamed that his cock was being chopped off in wafer-thin slices. He fought with his friends. In the field it was all he could do not to turn his rifle on himself. The post psychiatrist gave him some pills and suggested that he relax. The chaplain recommended that he sit in the chapel and lay his sorrows on Jesus. His lieutenant said, "This is *war*, soldier, not a Sunday school picnic." When Hawk wept all over him, he got upset and counseled him to fake a physical ailment.

Hawk was past faking anything, so he reenlisted to get leave. He went to Atlanta and told his family he was deserting, that the beaches of Los Angeles weren't in immediate danger but that his mortal soul was. His father nearly had a coronary. He went to his girl's college and asked her to come with him. She said she never wanted to see him again if he was such a coward.

"I drove due north. Went through Hullsport in fact. Went through Washington and drove slowly round and round those convoluted cloverleafs near the Pentagon staring at the place. I reflected on how my life was turning out so different from the mold it had been cast in. And for a little while, my crime assumed a place in a meaningful pattern, as though its function had been to jar me irretrievably out of that mold.

"I drove up through Vermont. It was autumn, and the trees were dazzling. I crossed the border at Highgate Springs. The border guard asked me my name and place of birth. 'Your reason for visiting Canada?' 'Pleasure,' I said with my first grin in months, and I drove away—free! It was as though this great weight had been lifted off my shoulders: I didn't have to do what *anyone* said, I had only myself to account to. The sun was shining, and the sky was that brilliant Kodachrome blue you get on a crisp fall day up here. I laughed out loud. I was on a real high, burning pure adrenaline. And when I came down, I crashed but good. Anyhow, Ginny, that's my fugitive story.''

I stared at him. I had recovered from my alarm. I was now trying to digest the fact that here was a whole range of experience I'd had no contact with. The Vietnam war had been a symbol to me for years, an abstraction signifying various things. I'd never known anyone who'd been in it, much less anyone who'd left it. It occurred to me that deciding what to do about it constituted the real rite of passage for the males of my generation. How they conducted themselves would determine the course of their futures. And like the puberty rites of a primitive tribe, only the males were privy to the secret joys and terrors of the ordeal. A woman could only watch with awe from the sidelines at the grim and terrible struggle. Just as males couldn't really participate in a woman's equivalent ordeal of what to do about an unwanted pregnancy. The issues of life vs. death, an individual's duties vs. his rights, seemed to get grappled with quite early by a great many people.

"So why in the world have you come back? What happens if you're caught?''

"Five years in prison getting fucked up the ass. But to explain why I'm back, I'd have to continue my saga.''

"Please do.''

"Well, I applied for landed immigrant status and got it. I rented a room in a decaying townhouse on a dingy side street in the French section of Montreal. And I took a job cleaning up the operating rooms at the hospital next door.

"Then the Montreal winter set in. Day after day with no sun. Snow piling up and turning to gray mush. Wind blasting down the streets. I was afraid to make friends because then I'd have to own up to being a deserter. I was in continuous fear of being tracked down and shanghaied back to the States. I would freeze at footsteps behind me; I'd shrink up against buildings to let people pass. Every time my landlady knocked at my door I'd panic.

"Plus the double culture shock. I was out of the military. After fourteen months of knowing exactly what to wear, and having my meals set before me, being told when to get up and how to spend my entire day, my every movement was suddenly no longer planned for me. I was in a daze for weeks—getting to work late, forgetting to eat, ending up with all my clothes dirty at once.

"And then the culture shock from no longer being in America. I hadn't thought much about this in advance. I knew Canadians spoke English. Why, Canada was like the fifty-first state, I thought. Well, that attitude was exactly the problem. I felt Canada's resentment of America very strongly. And here I was in the French section with storekeepers glaring at me when they had to switch to English. Or at least I *felt* they were glaring, from the depths of my paranoia. I felt hated on every hand—by Canadians for being American, by the French for being English, and by the whole world for being a deserter.

"And at work I was mopping up the operating rooms and carting out stained linens and collecting soiled instruments. Blood and pain and unhappiness all around me. I might just as well have stayed in Vietnam.

"I had written my family and my girl begging for their understanding and had gotten no reply. I was cut off from my old life, but I hadn't been able to set up a new one. I read one morning in the paper about a deserter's crossing the border into the States; he'd been caught, had panicked and pulled a gun, and was shot to death by the guards. The reality of my situation was getting home to me. I began not sleeping and having gory nightmares. It was all I could do to drag through the dreary days.

"One day as I was leaving a bookstore, the clerk said in an American accent, 'Hey man, you a deserter?' My paranoia from all those weeks alone and terrified just swept over me. I crouched and started backing toward the door. 'Hey man,' he said, 'stay cool. I'm a deserter, too.' Later I asked him how he could tell and he laughed. I was apparently as identifiable as a Girl Scout in full regalia, with my short hair and green canvas jungle booths and army-issue field jacket.

"Well, the next thing I knew, my life was like a college reunion. This guy was taking me to all these meetings of deserters and draft dodgers. Every night was like a party. I would tell all about all the hideous things I'd seen and done, and they'd tell me all the hideous things *they'd* seen and done. And, like, I wasn't alone with my crime anymore. It was such an incredible relief. I went around the operating rooms smiling all day. These new friends dispersed a lot of my paranoia by telling me that the FBI wasn't allowed into Canada. In short, I was safe.

"Spring had arrived. The trees in the parks were leafing out. The snow and ice had melted and washed out to the St. Lawrence. I got very involved in resister politics, went to meetings, discussed policy decisions, organized demonstrations, printed pamphlets, arranged housing. I worked like a fiend for six months, every spare moment devoted to war resistance. What had seemed an isolated leap, undertaken in desperation, had been taken by thousands of other men at the same time! It was a heady discovery.

"But over the months, I discovered that this moral force that I had thought was united behind the great and glorious cause of war resistance was in fact fragmented into dozens of small interest groups that regarded each other with contempt. The resistance was a Tower of Babel. The dodgers were condemning the deserters for having gone into the army in the first place. The resisters still in the service were condemning the deserters for not having stuck it out to subvert from within. For that matter, the resisters in the service were criticizing us *all* for requiring men less educated and less monied to be killed in our places. Resisters in America—those in jail and in the service and underground—were criticizing us exiles, saying we'd done just what the American government wanted us to do by leaving. Joan Baez did a concert and ended it by reprimanding us for not being back home in jail with her David. The exiled draft dodgers were criticizing the jailed dodgers for being on a martyr trip. The deserters were accusing the dodgers of head tripping, of not *really* knowing what they were talking about. And of course, everyone was down on the CO's. Almost everyone I knew up there had applied for CO status at one time or another and had been turned down. They used CO applications as a stalling device, but they never actually performed alternate service, because that was still cooperating with the war machine.

"In Canada it was the American exile types versus the Canadian immigrant types: The exile set wanted to use Canada as a base for a United States government in exile; whereas the immigrant types wanted to go native, become citizens, take Canadian wives, and raise lots of little Canadians. The exiles charged that the immigrants just wanted to vanish into the Canadian middle class without having made any impact on the American government; and the immigrants accused the exiles of using Canada in as politically predatory a fashion as the American corporations were using her economically. Even the immigrant group was fractionated into those who really did want just to blend into Canadian life, those who wanted to organize against American colonialism, and those who wanted to organize the French against the English. And the exiles were fragmented into those who were just against the Vietnamese war, and those who were opposed to capitalism in any of its manifestations. Then there were the earth trippers, who insisted that we forget about America *and* Canada and the French and the English and move to the countryside and dig in for the Apocalypse.

"Well, it was just exhausting really. I had been so happy that day in the bookstore when I'd found another deserter. And now I was miserable.

"I began staying in my room all the time. I'd never done drugs before, even in Nam with them all around—just some beer, and grass a few times. But I really went at it now. Soon I had eaten or injected or smoked or sniffed everything I could get my hands on—psilocybin and peyote and LSD and hash and cocaine, aspirin, glue, nitrous oxide, pemoline, yohimbine, ritalin, reserpine, chlorpromazine, codeine, atropine, kava-kava. I had a deserter friend who was as disillusioned as I. He'd come over and we'd drop a tab of acid; and when we got tired of tripping, we'd take some thorazine to bring us down. And when we were so far down that we felt like shit, we'd take some dexedrine to level us off. And then we'd start in on something else. Or we'd get out our speed collections and trade pills like two little kids swapping marbles: 'I'll give you six greenies and twelve black beauties, for eight purple hearts and eight dexies.' After one of those weekends, a junky could have lived off our vomit for weeks."

"What was it like, all that stuff?" I asked, as fascinated as a child at a candy counter.

He looked up at me, surprised. "Didn't you play around with this garbage when you were out on the farm?"

"No, I never got into it. Some grass, half a peyote button. Frankly, I was scared."

"You were right to be. I was crazy then. The fact that I survived more or less intact is a tribute to the indestructibility of the human body. Artificial interference with states of consciousness is a mistake."

"Yes, but what was it *like?*"

"Oh," he said yawning, "the usual. I ascended into heaven and met God, who put His hand on my shoulder and called me 'son.' He conveyed me to the abode of Infinite Truth, where my sharpened powers of perception commanded instant insight into the nature of pure existence."

"*Really?*"

"*No. Not* really. The whole thing was a ghastly mistake. I thought

I'd throw down a few pills and—zap!—instant answers. I ended up this phase of my journey to your back yard yearning to kill myself, but in a frenzy of terror that if I did, I'd go straight to hell for my hideous crimes. It was awful. I'd sit there for hours in my room with a razor blade poised over my wrist, trembling with fear as I imagined what the afterlife had in store for me—too many southern revivals in my boyhood. I could *feel* my flesh roasting on those spits, man! God bless the Southern Baptists! They're the only reason I'm still alive today. If that's a boon."

"To me it is," I told him, gazing with admiration. I'd never known a war hero before. I knew I'd never have had the gumption to do as he'd done. I was dazzled. "Would you like to sleep with me tonight?"

He said with wounded dignity, "No, thank you."

I did a double take. Was it possible that he had refused me? After all, various people had been vying for a decade for the privilege I'd extended to him as a reward for his bravery. And he had *turned me down?*

"I don't 'sleep around,' or whatever that phrase is," he explained. "I haven't really been able to stomach the idea of sex since—my war crime." I looked at him, my eyes gleaming—a mission! I could restore him to sexual health thereby contributing to the war effort without leaving my back yard—and perhaps I could relieve my unutterable boredom at the same time! I conveniently put out of my mind the fact that my tutoring anyone in lovemaking would be like Helen Keller's conducting bird watches. I also put out of my mind the fact that I had a functioning husband whose moral stomach would find adultery indigestible. "I'm not interested in casual sex," he continued. "I'm interested in deadly serious sex. I'm interested in using disgusting animal lust in controlled doses, like a poison administered for thera- peutic purposes, to get beyond sex and out of my wretched body. Kularnava Tantra says, 'As one falls on the ground, one must lift oneself by aid of the ground.' Are you interested?"

"I don't know if I'm interested or not. I don't know what you're asking." The earth was quaking. This discussion felt momentous.

"Ginny, I've been looking for you for months. I thought I'd have to go south to find a woman tuned to my frequency, but here you are. Will you be my shakti?"

"Pardon me?" I was immensely flattered that he thought we were "tuned to the same frequency."

"Are you interested in uniting with me in the holy sacrament of Maithuna?"

"I'm sorry?"

"Maithuna. Ritual coition."

"I thought you didn't *want* to sleep with me?"

"I *don't* want to 'sleep with you,' " he said with distaste. His switch had clearly been flipped, just as Miss Head's switch was flipped by questions about Descartes, or Eddie's by remarks about the ruling class. I had arrived with Hawk at that jarring moment when you finally discover after hours, days, years of talking, what obsession it is that gets a person through the night. "I want us to use carnal desire, Ginny, as a vehicle for achieving spiritual illumination, as a means of effecting reintegration of our opposing polarities. The generative forces that fetter our souls to samsara can instead be used to fuel our escape into the ineffable bliss of divine union."

"Far out," I said, grinning. I'd never been propositioned in such an exotic fashion.

"Look," he said sharply, "this is my last chance. I've tried everything else I can think of. I've been training myself for this for a year now. If you can't be serious about it, Ginny, if you can't open yourself up to the possibility of transcendence, if you just want someone to roll around the yard with—please say so now, and I'll head south."

Well, I had no objection to union with my polar opposite. "Forgive me. I didn't mean to sound frivolous. I'm very interested, but what would it entail?"

"I think it would take me about four weeks to train you for the Maithuna."

I whistled, unable to restrain my standard reaction of burlesque to any unfamiliar concept. "Wow! That's what I call foreplay!"

He glared at me and began to stand up. "All right. Forget it. I'll push on."

"Okay, Hawk. Don't rush off. It won't happen again, I promise."

He sat back down. "Are you prepared, then, to place yourself in my hands?" Was I ever! But I didn't express my readiness in that fashion. I nodded meekly. "You must accept the fact that I am more spiritually evolved than you and that I can 'see' what you need. You must repose complete trust in me and adopt an attitude of obedience, both inward and outward, at all times. Is that clear?"

I nodded doubtfully, my fingers mentally crossed. But after all, I'd entrusted myself to the far more shaky hands of, say, Clem Cloyd in the past.

"All right. When does your husband get home?"

"In a little more than a week."

"How would he feel about my staying in your house and training you?"

I collapsed in helpless laughter.

"I could train him, too."

"I'm sure he wouldn't hear of it," I gasped between giggles.

Then I stopped and thought. Considering Ira's approach to our sex life, maybe he *would* be interested in a rigorous disciplined training period, leading up to the Ultimate Orgasm. I pondered the topic, as I calmed myself. Then I remembered Hawk's deserter status, the need to maintain secrecy about his presence and therefore the need to explain it to Mr. National Guard. "No, I can't see it working. He'd turn you in to the Feds in a minute."

"Hmmm. Well, you must expect to sacrifice anything you hold dear—for the sake of spiritual fulfillment. Will you leave your husband and child and come with me to Montreal for your training?"

Panic seized me. Hawk had sacrificed all his ties and prospects, the good opinion of all the people close to him, when he had deserted. He was now asking me to perform a woman's equivalent sacrifice— to leave my house, my husband and baby, to leave my reputation in shambles, to drop everything and follow him. And here I didn't even know his parents. It was out of the question. As often as I had chafed under the whole boring setup in Stark's Bog, when it came right down to it, something in me wanted and needed what it represented. My struggle must have been mirrored in my face.

Hawk said quietly, "No, it's no good now. When you're ready, you'll *know*. One day the knowledge that this is what you have to do, to free yourself from the trammels of the flesh, will descend upon you with such clarity and conviction that you won't give it a second thought. Or even a first one. But you're clearly not ready for the path of renunciation yet."

I heaved a sigh of relief. There were certain advantages to being spiritually retarded after all. Never in my life had I experienced clarity and conviction in a decision. Usually I drifted blindly into irremediable situations, or had a decision wrenched from me with much pain and struggle, like an impacted wisdom tooth. The prospect of clarity and conviction was tantalizing indeed.

"But how can we work this out then? If I can't stay here, and you aren't ready to come with me, I don't see how we can swing it."

In a burst of undoubtedly divinely sanctioned clarity, I said, "*I* know! We have this secret room in the cellar. It was built for hiding runaway slaves on their way to Canada."

"Oh God! Perfect!"

We rushed down into the dim dank earthen cellar. The room was disguised as a cistern, and you entered through an arched brick wine cellar, one wall of which was a rack of barrels that swung out to uncover the narrow passageway into the room. The room itself was six by nine feet with brick walls and floor. A small transom let in a little light from outside. It was absolutely empty except for some fallen chunks of mortar.

"Fantastic!" Hawk announced. I thought it was creepy myself. But I swept it out and brought in a cot and a folding television tray and a camp stool. Hawk set his knapsack in a corner. He was enchanted. I was wondering how Father Bliss, whose wraith undoubtedly inhabited the wine cellar, was feeling about all this. Did he consider me to be upholding family tradition by hiding the unjustly hounded and hunted, or did he think me a deceitful bitch who was betraying his six or seven times great-grandson?

"We'll begin tonight," Hawk informed me, as I left to fix Wendy's supper and put her to bed. A shiver of desire shot up my spine, such as I couldn't recall feeling for many months—not since Wendy's conception, to be specific.

That night I descended to Hawk in a nightgown/peignoir set with my well-jellied diaphragm in place, expecting God-only-knows-what transports of ecstasy after a long dry season.

Hawk hardly even glanced up as I wafted into his room. He sat cross-legged on the brick floor laying out tarot cards. He'd hooked up a battery lantern overhead and had boarded up the transom.

He pointed for me to sit down opposite him, which I did, arranging my flowing peignoir to cover my knees. He gave me the cards to shuffle and cut. Then he laid them out in silence. He pointed to me what to do, drawing so many, turning over certain ones. He studied the groupings and made notes in a small notebook. Then he studied his notes. I felt very nervous. What cards should I have been picking to indicate sexual prowess and spiritual gifts? What previously well-concealed character flaws was he uncovering from my card configuration?

Finally he looked up and nodded with satisfaction. He pointed to a card of a skeleton in black armor on a horse, under whose advancing hoofs people were falling. He murmured, "Hmmm. Death. Excellent. It looks good."

"*Death?*" I shrieked. Good God, I'd done it again! Gotten involved with a necrophiliac! Why did I always pick psychopaths for boon companions, or they me?

"Shhh. Just relax. The Death card is beneficent. It represents the sloughing off of carnal desire, the conquest of physical death through the regeneration of the soul; destruction followed by transformation. Hippies in Montreal do readings over and over again trying to turn up Death in exactly this spot. But it's happened for you the first time, and effortlessly, just as it did for me. The signs look very good for us, Ginny."

Pleased with my spiritual potential, I swept back up the stairs in my swirling chiffon, having been dismissed by Hawk, who was now referring to me as his shishya. I was content to have him call me whatever he wanted as long as he got down to business pretty soon.

The next morning when I reported for instruction, Hawk said, "Today and tomorrow are exceptions, but from now on, I expect to be left alone in the morning so that I can work on my book."

"Certainly. Shall I bring you breakfast?" I asked, eager to serve.

"Yes, thank you. Yogurt and whole wheat toast and mint tea; please." I reviewed our cupboards, stuffed with Wonder Bread, and tried to figure out how to fulfill his commands.

"Today and tomorrow, however, we will be doing a special exercise. I will need your uninterrupted presence. Can you take your child elsewhere?"

I seized on the idea of Angela and said I'd see what I could do. "I'll need you down here all night, too," he added. "Try to send her somewhere overnight."

I floated up the stairs on billowing clouds of passion and performed the unprecedented step of asking Angela to take Wendy for two days and the night while I "went to St. Johnsbury to shop and visit friends." She was so stunned that I would have the gall to ask this of her with her four kids and new baby that she agreed to it.

I had never been separated from Wendy overnight before. I knew as I left her off at Angela's with her overnight case that this should have been a traumatic moment for us both. Angela stood cradling her new baby and waiting for me to exhibit the appropriate emotions. She kept making leading remarks like, "Oh, I know how hard it is leaving them for the first time. . . ."

I split as soon as I could, without a twinge of remorse, as Wendy stood forlornly folding and unfolding her sticky little hand in a farewell wave. I turned on the siren of Ira's fire chief's car and flew home on wings of treaded synthetic rubber. Once again I jellied my diaphragm and inserted it and descended to my shiva, as Hawk had told me to refer to him.

My shiva wasn't in his subterranean chamber. I dashed out back and found him by the swimming pool. He was nude, crouched with one leg extended straight out behind him, its foot braced. His other leg, bent at the knee, was bearing the weight of his trunk, his chest being propped up on its thigh. His hands were clasped behind his back, and his nose was touching the big toe on the foot of his bent leg. His wild scramble of light brown hair hid his eyes.

Eventually he stood up and, switching legs, resumed the posture.

"Verya stambhanasana," he notified me when he finally stood up.

"I beg your pardon?"

"Semen retention posture," he explained, resuming his crouch with switched legs.

"Why would you want to do a thing like that?" I asked in the injured voice of a prostitute whose client is wearing a condom to prevent venereal disease.

Hawk ignored me. When he stood up again, he motioned for me to follow him. He asked for sandwiches, which I made in the kitchen, and a pitcher of water. Then we descended to the basement, my nipples tingling with excitement.

As I sat expectantly on his cot, he plugged the cracks around the transom with socks from his pack. As the room grew progressively darker, I became intrigued by the extent of his modesty. He didn't want us to see each other's body, or what?

When the room was thoroughly black, Hawk felt his way to the door and said, "I want you to stay in here as long as you can. Lie on the cot as motionless as possible. If you have to take a leak, use this jar in the corner. And you can eat the sandwiches and drink the water when you're hungry or thirsty. I'll be upstairs. You're on your honor to follow my instructions. If you don't, you'll miss the point and we'll merely have to repeat the exercise."

"What am I supposed to *do?*"

"Concentrate on doing nothing. Okay?"

"Okay," I said, dismayed at not being ravaged, ritualistically or otherwise. "But what *is* the point?"

He looked at me with disgust. "You don't learn anything by being told. You learn by being in situations that compel you to experience certain things."

"I see. . . ."

I settled back on the cot and waited for spiritual illumination. Would I recognize it when it arrived, I wondered. I had thought as my eyes grew accustomed to the dark that I'd be able to see more— the bricks in the wall or something. This didn't happen. I continued to see nothing. I held my hand in front of my face and wiggled my fingers, but I couldn't see them. I could hear nothing, not even the the birds that must have been warbling outside the boarded transom.

After a while, as I lay perfectly still, I lost all feeling in my arms and legs. They ceased to exist. Thanks to Descartes, I had the reassurance of knowing that, since I was still thinking, I was still in existence. I moved one index finger and noted with relief the scratchiness of the wool blanket under me. Then, slowly, tentatively, I laid one hand against the cool rough bricks of the wall. I was cheating; Hawk had instructed me to do nothing, to move as little as possible. I jerked away my palm and returned my arm to my side.

I fell asleep. When I woke up, I was very hungry. I grabbed the wrapped bologna and cheese sandwiches off the television tray and ate one. I couldn't believe how good it tasted; normally I choked down bologna almost as unenthusiastically as I had soybean croquettes at the Free Farm. Still hungry, I gobbled a second sandwich. Then I drank two glasses of water.

I lay back down. I drifted in a state of semisleep, passing freely in and out of dreams and waking fantasies, none of particular profundity. Twice I got up and urinated in the jar in the corner. Hawk had said I could emerge whenever I wanted, but to try to stay there as long as I could. It appeared to me that I could easily stay all day if it would make Hawk happy. But I wasn't noting any particular increase in clarity and conviction, in intuitive knowledge. Was I failing some test? Was I supposed to be developing stigmata or something? In despair at the thought that I was blowing my chances for the Maithuna, I reached out for another sandwich and devoured it.

As I chewed, it occurred to me, in passing and without alarm, that perhaps Hawk was carting off the Bliss family antiques in a U-Haul truck at that very moment. Maybe he would vanish from my life as

I lay here in the dark. Maybe he had mortared over the doorway, as in Poe's "The Cask of Amontillado," and I'd never see daylight again. These fantasies left me sublimely unperturbed. I had been buried alive by a psychopath; I had been expecting a similar fate all my life. It was no big deal. I fell asleep again. When I awoke, I guzzled more water.

Suddenly the door opened. "How'd it go?" Hawk asked, pulling his socks out of the cracks.

"Fine. But nothing much happened, I'm afraid."

We went up into the kitchen. I glanced around the familiar room with delight. It seemed so unexpectedly fresh and clean and attractive. The yellow print wallpaper was unusually vivid, and its pattern of rust and green geometrical designs leapt out at me. The bottoms of the copper pans hanging on the wall gleamed like bright eyes.

"What have *you* been doing all day?" I asked Hawk. "It looks as though you've been cleaning my kitchen."

"No," he assured me with a faint smile. We walked outside. The birds seemed to be screaming in the trees. And the grass shone in the sun with a green more vivid than I'd ever seen. I blinked my eyes several times, dazzled.

"You'd better go pick up your child."

"It's okay. I arranged to leave her overnight. I can get her tomorrow morning."

Hawk looked at me with a faint smile and said, "It *is* tomorrow morning."

"What are you talking about?"

"How long do you think you were down there?"

I considered the question, trying to pinpoint some frame of reference. I'd gone down at 8:30 in the morning. I'd eaten three sandwiches and drunk some water. . . . According to my calculations, it would have to be early evening. But then why was the sun in the east, not even to the midday point overhead? I looked at Hawk with alarm.

"It's eight in the morning."

"How can that *be?*" I gasped, outraged. I felt like the Parisians in the Middle Ages who rioted when Pope Gregory XIII subtracted ten days from the calendar to synchronize it with the solar year: They thought they'd lost ten days of their lives. I had lost one entire night of my undoubtedly foreshortened life!

Hawk was studying me with detached interest. Apparently he enjoyed driving people to insanity.

I turned on him, sputtering. He shrugged. "Do you or don't you want me to train you? I never said it would be fun or painless. And I never said you'd come out of it with all your most cherished notions intact."

"I don't like being used as a guinea pig."

"I'm *not* using you as a guinea pig. I already *know* what I'm teaching you. I'm just trying to get you to entertain in your conscious mind the things you already know unconsciously."

"Hmph!" I had enough trouble with my conscious mind, without its being swamped by inane information from my unconscious. But if this was what it was going to take to get laid by a war hero, I supposed I'd have to put up with it.

When I got to Angela's, Wendy raced to me and threw her arms around my knees shrieking, "Mommy! Mommy!" I swept her up and hugged her, feeling odd because according to *my* version of reality, I'd hardly more than left her. But clocks everywhere insisted on pointing out my error. The whole idea, according to Hawk, was that it *wasn't* "my error," that my version was valid. But how was one to, say, bake a presentable pie for Ira's hunting trips on inner space time?

Angela was cuddling her new baby, who wore a pink stretch suit and flailed her little arms as though at an invisible punching bag. Her tiny head was covered with tufts of fair brown hair. Her soft spot throbbed. Longing gripped me. I craved a new baby to hold. Sensing this, Angela reluctantly handed hers to me. I held her gingerly, having already forgotten, after so little time, how to position a baby to keep its head from snapping off its wobbly neck. I leaned down and sniffed, always having loved the odor of baby powder and the generally fresh new scent of an infant. I fondled her firm flesh through the stretch fabric of the suit. Today, as a result of my sensory deprivation in the cellar, the scent, the feel of the flesh, were almost overpowering. My dormant maternal longings were rekindled. I stared at the baby with adoring desperation and shook under the strain of wanting one so badly. Babies were my bailiwick, what did I want with transcendence?

Angela smiled, taking it all in with approval. "Ira tells me you have your hearts set on a son this time."

"I wouldn't drown either kind in the bathtub," I admitted. Wendy was scaling my legs in a frenzy of jealousy. I handed the sweet-smelling bundle back to Angela, reminding myself firmly that all the world adores a kitten, but who needs another cat?

While Wendy played, Hawk lectured me by the pool on nostrils

—which, it turned out, were not nostrils at all to the cognescenti but were rather extensions of astral ducts that conveyed cosmic energy to the body.

"You breathe moon breath for twenty-four minutes through the left nostril; then you switch and breathe sun breath through the right nostril for twenty-four minutes."

"*No,*" I said, scandalized not to understand the workings of my own nose. "Even with my adenoids out?"

"Only when you're breathing through the right nostril should you undertake actions requiring physical exertion and emotional commitment. And only when you're breathing through the left should you begin calm steady activities."

"That sort of limits you, doesn't it?" I could just picture myself waiting around all morning for my breathing to switch to my right nostril so that I could start vacuuming.

"No, it doesn't, because you can change back and forth at will once you develop the skill. For the commencement of the Maithuna, for instance, we both have to be breathing through our right nostrils."

I shot him an ironical look. I could see us lying there all night trying to synchronize our nostrils and forever being out of phase, like Scarlett O'Hara and Rhett Butler in *Gone With the Wind,* each wanting the other only when the other had decided to leave.

"Ginny," Hawk said sharply, "I think your attitude toward this whole thing sucks, frankly. I've been putting up with it, thinking that you'd outgrow your juvenile need to ridicule unfamiliar concepts. But if you can't cultivate some reverence, we might as well call the whole thing off."

"Please don't, Hawk. I'll work on my attitude, really I will, Hawk."

"All right. But if I have to mention this again, that's it."

Looking at me sternly, he lay on his side and showed me how to switch from one nostril to the other, with his thumb under his ear and his fingers on his forehead. Then he demonstrated another method, massaging his big toe on the opposite side from the nostril he wanted to activate. I practiced these until I had discovered that they really did work; then I sat pondering the unfathomed mysteries of my neglected flesh.

That afternoon while Wendy was napping and Hawk was meditating, I went to the cellar to retrieve Hawk's breakfast tray. On his cot were some stacks of paper. Unable to restrain myself, I poked through them. They were sections of his historical science fiction novel. Glancing nervously toward the doorway, I read a dozen pages, in which a Vermont farmer and his wife by accident shot down a ski jump one night on a snow machine. As they sprawled unconscious on the slope, the Management Outpost in charge of the Milky Way galaxy zeroed in on them in response to vibrations from the crash. Interpreting the curious pattern of ski trails as fumbling Earthling requests for divine assistance, the Management Representative, with uncharacteristic benevolence, materialized an Earth-style executive suite at the Outpost and whisked the Vermonters into it. As they stood in their snowsuits dripping and blinking, he tried to recall the formula for transforming himself from a blinding patch of light into a form discernible to limited Earthling sense organs. Finally he managed to materialize in a quilted ski-mobile suit, discovering to his chagrin that he had given himself a long tail by mistake. He decided to leave the tail and hope that his guests, and especially the Home Office, wouldn't notice.

" 'Interesting place, Earth,' the Rep said charitably, actually regarding it as the most hideous hell hole in the entire universe." Then he described his stint there as a Trainee several millennia ago, just as Earth was coming down with its disease. He had been an Aymara Indian stonecutter near Lake Titicaca in Bolivia. The force field of a passing comet had conflicted with that of Earth, resulting in continuous lightning for days, which set off forest fires all across the globe and drove wild beasts down into the towns. Earth's axis had shifted and its rotation had slowed and its crust had heaved and buckled in great booming earthquakes. Volcanoes had spewed; tidal waves had uprooted huge trees and tossed boulders as though they were pebbles. Then Earth's poles had switched, and the Rep was no longer able to communicate telepathically with the other Trainees or with Management. This altered force field also jammed his materialization mechanism, and he was trapped in his Earthling body.

The ensuing decades were a grim struggle for physical survival. Rain, evaporated from the seas by the heat of the fires and volcanoes, fell endlessly, and everything rotted and mildewed. Crops couldn't grow. Daylight was a perpetual twilight due to volcanic dust. Scavenging hordes of starving Earthlings plundered the countryside. The Rep hid his family in a cave and they lived like savages, while friends and relatives died all around them from epidemics and malnutrition and demoralization. Those who survived were those who were able to develop ferocity and greed and cunning—the opposite of the qualities valued in pre-catastrophe society. Their chests expanded like those of asthma victims from the strain of having to breathe more air to absorb the same amount of oxygen. New babies were stunted and sickly.

The Rep retained no memory of his original mission. Management sent a Supervisor to Earth to report on which Trainees could be rehabilitated and which would have to be abandoned. The Rep, responding to the timbre of the Supervisor's voice as he stood at the cave mouth asking for shelter, fell to the floor among gnawed bones, clutching his bloodied stone ax, and wept. Management was eventually able to rewire his scrambled neural networks and recontact him. And when he died, he was given his current desk job on the frontiers, which he regarded as a steppingstone to more important posts closer to the Home Office.

" 'So you see, I know what it's like to be an Earthling, incarcerated on your burnt-out cinder of a planet with no way out that you can see,' the Rep said sympathetically, smoothing the distinguished full head of gray hair he'd indulged in during this materialization. 'I know you loot and murder with positive pleasure. But your moral retardation isn't really your fault. It was just one of those unfortunate accidents that go on somewhere in the universe all the time. But it does provide the more promising Earthlings like yourselves with the opportunity to understand the full horror of being cut off from Management.'

" 'Jesum Crow, where the hang *am* I?' muttered the farmer, blinking.

"The Rep looked at him with dismay. He hadn't succeeded in making his guests feel at home, in spite of the executive suite. What had he overlooked? He definitely needed to brush up on his knowledge of rural American folkways. He'd ask his Assistant for a report right away. But his guests weren't exactly Mr. and Mrs. Sociability. Sighing, he hung up an X-ray and showed them Earth—a black pinprick afloat in a dark gray patch, surrounded by trillions of blindingly bright patches and pinpricks. He explained to the uncomprehending couple that the gray area was quarantined in hopes of containing the infection. Management was administering radiation and antibodies in hopes of effecting a cure; otherwise, the area would have to be plowed under and reseeded."

The Rep then ushered the bemused Vermonters into the lab where new planets were being created. In micro-climate cages plants and animals and insects to suit the unique physical conditions of each prospective planet were being materialized. One planet with high gravity, for instance, was stocked with short squat creatures. Once the general pattern was established, the different species had to be balanced in terms of reproduction and predation. The Rep described the difficulties he had getting technicians even to look at Earth, since the way Earthlings were hogging Earth's Life Force Allotment (LFA) from the other species was so aesthetically appalling.

" 'And, of course, our scientists have their personal tastes to consider in designing their planets—colors, shapes. It's rather a game.' He sighed plaintively. 'I always did want to be in on the creative side of the business. . . .' "

"I couldn't help but glance at your book just now," I confessed to Hawk when I returned to the pool. "I hope you don't mind. I found it very entertaining."

"It's not intended to entertain. It's intended to develop in readers the mental set that will allow them to regard my 'fiction' as a possibility."

"I see. You mean you really think that's what's happening?" I was beginning to suspect that I might have erred in my selection of an instructor in transcendence.

"I didn't say that! I just don't want you regarding it strictly as entertainment." He tugged irritably at the jingle bell hanging from his ear lobe.

The next day we cleansed the astral ducts that led from my etheric double, whatever that might have been, into my "gross physical organism."

"You respire approximately 21,666 times a day," Hawk informed me. "Most of these breaths are a rapid shallow panting that fills about one-sixth of your lungs and serves only to keep your physical body functioning at a level of minimal competence. You must learn to breath in such a way as to send a potent charge of prana to your root chakra, to arouse your dormant kundalini and fan its spark into an all-consuming flame. Which will leap up your spinal channel toward the crown of your head and unite with the mahakundali of shiva in residence there, polarizing each of your cells."

"Pardon me?" Once again, I was wandering blindly in a sphere with its own jargon, every bit as specialized as Joe Bob's football terminology or Miss Head's pronouncements on Descartes. I had some vocabulary work to do, if my relationship with Hawk was to flourish. But did I want it to flourish? I was no longer so sure, after my encounter with his book. Was he insane, or was he a prophet without honor in his own country?

"You will understand," he replied, waving my questions away like so many gnats.

We sat by the pool with our legs crossed and emptied our minds of trivia. I was trying to decide whether concern over the possibility of Wendy's falling into the pool constituted a triviality in the realm in which we were dealing. Then we emptied our lungs by drawing in our abdomens. We inhaled seven times, paused, and exhaled seven times. This we repeated ad nauseam, mentally intoning "om." I waited for my kundalini to leap into flames, but nothing happened.

"Nothing happened."

"Would you know if something happened if something *did* happen?" he asked, gazing at me with an irritating serenity. "In your current crude state, the subtle ranges of impact aren't available to you. You're expecting immediate and dramatic results, but it doesn't work that way. That was how I approached drugs in Montreal—for on-the-spot enlightenment. You're so fucking goal-oriented. If you have sex, you want an instant orgasm."

"Not necessarily," I protested, injured by his mistaken estimate of my character. How many Monday, Wednesday, and Thursday nights had I spent pleading with Ira *not* to force me to have an orgasm? "Maybe you're just projecting your personality quirks onto me."

"*I* do not project. I have subdued my personal desires to such an extent that I no longer *have* desires. If one is empty of desire, one has no need to project it onto other people."

"How do you know when you're empty of desire?" I asked, genuinely perplexed.

"You *know*," he promised me, crossing his eyes and closing them, and rotating his stomach muscles like twiddling his thumbs.

He stood up and assumed the semen retention posture, motioning for me to copy him. I did so, confused, since I had no semen to retain. Wendy wandered over, her wet diapers drooping, and tried to imitate us, sticking one chubby leg behind her and reaching intently for her big toe with her nose. She tumbled over and hit her head on the concrete and began howling. Hawk looked up at her angrily, while I cradled her and rubbed her bump. His expression said clearly: You must make the break with these distracting worldly ties. I turned my back on him.

During Wendy's nap, Hawk led me to a spot in the back yard near the Bliss family graveyard. He thrust four sticks into the ground to form a square. On them he placed a stiff straw place mat from my kitchen table. Then he scooped up some topsoil and carefully picked out all the clods and sticks and stones. He placed a mound of this sifted topsoil on the mat. Using a smooth stone, he leveled off the mound into a plate-sized disk.

We sat on the grass a couple of yards away and stared at this mudpie through half-opened eyes. Hawk said we were trying to summon up within ourselves its spiritual image. He mumbled lover's endearments to it like, "Vast Expansive One, Fruit Nurturer, Concealer of Subterranean Secrets." And I contemplated the phrase "dust to dust" as he had instructed. I was trying to decide through how many human and animal and plant bodies the material in the mudpie had been recycled since its creation.

Eventually Hawk and I began opening and closing our eyes, like camera shutters, trying to imprint its spiritual image on our retinas. Finally, Hawk grabbed my arm. At last, I thought, as he dragged me across the lawn toward the pool. This is it!

He pushed me down by the pool and threw himself down beside me and closed his eyes. "Do you see it?" he demanded urgently.

I closed my eyes expectantly. But I saw the usual uninspired black. In desperation I searched the black for even the faintest flicker of illumination. I saw nothing. Should I lie? Would Hawk be likely to perform ritual coition with a devotional dunce?

"See what?" I asked noncommittally.

"The luminous disk, purified from all its gross material imperfections."

"Uh—"

Just then Wendy, bless her heart, tottered through the gate, saving me from having to reveal to Hawk that he'd chosen a spiritual pygmy as his celestial sex partner.

That night after Wendy was in bed, I hunted out our Christmas tree lights in the attic, at Hawk's request. We fixed up two strings, one all red and the other all blue. With an elaborate series of extension cords, we managed to hang the red one around Hawk's basement room. Then we both sat in the lotus position on his cot. He was wearing my twenty-one jewel Lady Bulova. He instructed me to concentrate on the topic of the passage of time, with my eyes open, and to notify him when I thought that half an hour had gone by.

It seemed a simple enough assignment. I slouched over in my lotus position and braced myself to counts to sixty thirty times. This time I would not fail Hawk.

After counting to thirty ten times, I became bored and decided to drop it. I let my thoughts wander randomly.

Finally, deciding that half an hour had to be up, I signaled to Hawk. He glanced at my watch and made a notation on a piece of paper. Then he took down the red lights and strung up the blue ones, and I repeated the tedious exercise.

Then the blue lights came down, and the red ones went back up. And then vice versa. I was finding the whole thing pretty dumb. There had to be easier ways to find extramarital sex.

After the fourth round, Hawk said, "All right. That's enough." I sighed with relief.

"Under the red lights you called twenty-four and a half minutes and twenty-seven minutes half an hour," he informed me. "And under the blue lights you called thirty-two and thirty-three minutes half an hour."

Oh dear, I had flunked again. I couldn't even judge time accurately. What hope did I have of ascending into heaven? I looked at him and shrugged apologetically. I *had* tried.

"If this doesn't suggest any conclusions," he said testily, combing his fingers through his matted beard, "then I'm afraid I can't help you."

I skulked upstairs to my lonely king-sized bed.

The next morning, after breathing exercises, the veerya stambhanasana, and mudpie contemplation, Hawk said wearily, "I was hoping that this wouldn't be necessary, but I'm afraid it is. Can you send the baby out for the day?"

Off Wendy went to Angela's, and back I raced with Ira's siren whooping to insert my diaphragm. I found Hawk waiting for me on the cot. A glass and a pitcher of water sat on the tray. I cleared my throat alluringly in the doorway.

Hawk looked up, his bell jingling in his ear lobe. He gestured to me to lie on the cot beside him. Demurely, I did so. He looked down at me. I closed my eyes, waiting to be kissed.

He got up and started rifling his pack. "It's okay," I whispered. "I have my diaphragm in."

"Pardon me?" he said, extracting a small plastic vial from the pack. He poured liquid from it into the glass and filled the glass with water and handed it to me.

I drank in little uninterested sips. "What is it?" I asked, hoping it was an exotic aphrodisiac from the French section of Montreal.

"LSD-25."

"*LSD?*" I shrieked, sloshing the liquid onto the cot.

"Just relax and finish drinking it."

"But I don't *want* LSD."

"Do you or don't you want to participate in the Maithuna?" he inquired coolly.

"Yes, of course. But I don't see what LSD has to do with screwing."

His face behind his shaggy beard flushed bright red. "God*dam* it! How many times do I have to tell you that it's not *screwing?* It has nothing whatsoever to do with the filthy disgusting bumping and grinding you're accustomed to!"

"How do *you* know what I'm accustomed to?" I shot back, furious at allowing myself to be drugged and sold into white slavery so trustingly.

"I *don't* know, and I'm not remotely interested. What I've invited you to undertake with me has no relation to your past seizures of lust, whatever form they've taken. I am *trying* to teach you to think of yourself as other than a physical body to be 'satisfied.' You are the eternal feminine principle. I am the eternal masculine principle. As we mate, we will balance opposing forces and requite our longing for wholeness."

In a fit of fury at his pomposity, I tossed down the rest of the liquid. Where did blue balls fit into all this, if orgasm wasn't our goal? Had I sacrificed my virginity to a myth?

"And besides, the fact that you are unable to entertain the notion that there *might* be some connection between LSD and what you so repulsively refer to as 'screwing' is exactly why we're having to go through all this tedious preparation. *I've* been ready for the Maithuna for weeks. *I* certainly don't need this. I'm doing it for you. So that you can experience transcendence, too."

I glared at him. I had by now decided that he hadn't really given me LSD, that this was one of his fucking little tests designed to reveal my true character, in all its outstanding flaws. I leaned against the brick wall and folded my arms and sneered.

"It's starting to take effect, isn't it?"

"*No.* Absolutely *not.*"

"You're thinking that I've tricked you, that it wasn't really LSD, that I'm trying to make a fool of you." I looked at him in stunned surprise. *Did* the creep have uncanny powers of perception from his idiot training after all?

"I've had enough LSD to float a battleship," he informed me, appraising my reactions from my shifting facial expressions. "The general pattern is usually pretty predictable, allowing for variations introduced by personality differences. So please spare me the boring details of your miraculous visions in the upcoming hours. Other people's drug trips, like other people's dreams and other people's romances, are unremittingly tedious for nonparticipants."

"The thing I hate most about you," I replied calmly, "is that you're such a goddam hypocrite. You *said* you no longer approved of artificial means for altering states of consciousness." The bricks of the arched ceiling were starting to rearrange themselves. I decided to pretend not to notice their antics, preferring not to expose myself to Hawk's ridicule by claiming to be experiencing hallucinations. I could picture him returning to his deserter friends and regaling them with the story of my hallucinating after drinking plain water. I could see the entire radical world snickering.

"I *don't* believe in it just for kicks." Never before had I noticed how his mouth pursed in slow motion as he talked, like a landed fish gasping for air. "This isn't for kicks. This is for a specific purpose, administered by someone who can guide you through it and indicate significant aspects." His eyes were two ice-blue mentholated throat lozenges. His tangled beard was thousands of matted spiders flailing their snarled legs.

The arched bricks had turned to streams of rainbow colors.

"Are you feeling anything yet?" boomed a hollow voice like the surf crashing in an ocean cave.

"No."

In fact, I *wasn't* feeling anything. How could I be? I no longer possessed any sense organs. That unattractive husk of flesh I had formerly been so pleased to refer to as "me" lay limp and flabby beneath me. What possible contact could that stinking chunk of decaying meat ever have had with wonderful me? Why, I had no more relation to it than I did to that other disgusting mound of tissue and cartilage that lay propped against the wall watching "my" body out of ice-blue lozenges.

I started giggling. It was so ludicrous. Here I had spent a lifetime feeding and clothing and adoring that hunk of flesh—and all along, it had been dead! What a joke! I screamed with laughter. The blob of adipose against the wall smiled tolerantly, not knowing that it was dead, too. I knew that it was true—that that other blob had drugged me in order to ship me to Morocco—but the joke was on him. He'd be selling a twitching corpse! I howled with glee.

Hawk was slowly removing his blue work shirt. This operation required several hours. I scrutinized it, absorbing every detail—his fingers fumbling with the buttons, his arms moving up and out of the sleeves; the fur on his flexing chest muscles waved like prairie grasses in the wind. He stood up. And up and up and up, like Jack's beanstalk. The tiny cubicle was a hundred yards deep. Hawk strutted across this expanse like a minstrel in a cakewalk.

Eventually, he was sitting next to me. *Who* was? What was he sitting next *to?* What was this? He was trying to show me something? *Me,* who already saw all? How could he be bothering me with such a petty topic as his tattoo.

Hawk kept thrusting his arm into my face, flexing and unflexing his bicep so that the tattoo swam and trembled and quivered. Soon my eyes fixed on its outer borders. I stared at the filigreed circumference with wonder. Hawk was right to insist. It merited my attention after all. It was alive. The elegant etched pattern breathed and shuddered and throbbed and swirled. All the colors of the spectrum, one after another, wound their way through the maze of filigree, like visible electricity through electrical circuits.

My attention hopped abruptly to the bands of stylized flower petals just inside the filigree. The variegated colors were still with me; but in this context of soft unfolding petals, the colors didn't snake, they swept—in dizzying waves, one color after another illuminating the undulating petals.

Suddenly I found myself enmeshed in the grid of interlocked triangles. Here, the geometric shapes popped out at me, ablaze with constantly shifting colors.

This was neat, but suddenly I felt wary. It was all a trap. I was being led, like Hansel and Gretel by the witch's candy cottage, into the center, toward the fetid jaws of the grotesque monster who lived there. I understood in a flash of insight that that hideous ghoul had spewed out of his bloody craw these charming patterns of shifting colors, solely in order to lure me into his lair.

". . . be aware of the different levels of organization," Hawk was saying. His voice boomed as though from a vast underground cavern.

And Hawk was in league with that monster! After all, the monster lived on Hawk's bicep, didn't he? I snarled at Hawk and turned my head away from his repulsive arm. Safe! I hadn't looked!

I felt a hand on my face, and found myself once again staring at the quivering tattoo, being sucked in past the cunning filigree and petals and triangles to the monster at the center. "No!" I screamed. Or thought I screamed.

"You must look at it!" a voice boomed, bouncing off the walls like shock waves in the Major's blast chamber.

"But I don't *want* to."

"You *must!*" the voice commanded, with the intonations of a Wagnerian deity.

I closed my eyes obstinately. A chaos of color swirled across the black behind my lids. I felt nauseated. Watching the riot of colors with no framework to organize them was making me dizzy and unspeakably anxious. I tried to stack the colors as though they were Wendy's blocks, but I couldn't hold them still, couldn't control their wild dance.

Just as I felt I was about to start retching, my eyes popped open wide. My attention was dragged rapidly past the snaking filigree, past the freshly opened petals, past the disciplined but playfully throbbing geometric grid—right into the gaping jaws of the monster. I screamed with terror. The soft moist black of its cavernous mouth was flooded rhythmically with molten streams of blood that spewed up from its craw. In the pulsing red glow, I could see sharp white fangs, poised to crunch down on me. From this perspective I could see that the elaborate outer patterns of the tattoo were nothing more than congealing swirls of gore.

"Shift your focus," a hollow voice was roaring urgently. "Make the blue-black the background. Look for the pattern formed by the flesh tones."

I could feel my eyes, of their own accord, squinting and opening wide; my head was thrashing from side to side. I couldn't *see* any flesh tones; all I could see were constantly changing swirls of color.

All of a sudden the monster was gone. In its place was a pale grinning death's-head, similar to those on Father Bliss's tombstones. It had a round face and wide surprised eyes. Where the monster's skull crown and flaying knife had been were a pair of graceful, fanciful, dappled wings.

I studied the grinning death's-head with delight. How could I ever have been afraid of this kindly creature, I wondered. Its eyes blinked at me in sympathy. Under its gaze, I found I could step back and look at the tattoo as a whole—the way the bands of design set each other off to advantage by contrast.

". . . the upended and right-side-up triangles suggesting yin and yang, active and passive, masculine and feminine . . ." the annoying voice was booming didactically.

"Shut up, Hawk," I suggested gaily, and returned to my private study of the patterns of organization, patterns too profound and complicated to sully with those absurd jabberings known as words. I contemplated the subtle ways in which the variegated bands drew attention ever inward toward the center.

". . . the three corners of the triangles representing the intellect, the emotions, and the physical function . . ."

"Fuck you, Hawk!" I shrieked, laughing wildly. I felt I really owed it to him to discuss the topic of his overweening ignorance. But to cross such a vast quagmire, where did one begin? Besides, I was too caught up in the impressions that were cascading down on me as though from a towering waterfall. I smiled at the friendly death's-head, acknowledging its clever device of disguising itself as a monster in order to frighten off the unworthy, of which I was clearly not one.

Just then the amiable death's-head receded and was swamped by the returning monster. I screamed and shuddered and cowered under its gleaming fangs.

I remembered the trick. It had worked before. Maybe it would work again. I opened and squinted my eyes, and moved my head side to side. After several years of effort, the monster vanished and the death's-head reappeared, and with it the atmosphere of giddy joy. But this time, the giddy joy was no longer comforting, even in contrast to the monster. It grated and jangled. It made me want to leap up and dance crazily like a puppet with high-voltage power lines for strings. I no longer knew which was worse—to cower with terror, or to twitch with undirected glee. I swung crazily back and forth between the two for at least a millennium, dreading to stay with the monster, but dreading equally the jangling death's-head. The dread being equal, which, I wondered, was "real"?

Then I understood what had happened. Neither was "real." Both were real. I had finally cracked up. I was now diagnosably schizophrenic. And as a schiz, I was for the first time gaining insight into the nature of ultimate reality.

Then it occurred to me that maybe I could run the entire show. Maybe I could find some measure of relief in at least being in control of this bedlam. And eventually I discovered that I could manipulate the monster and the death's-head at will. All that was required was a shift in focus. When I made the flesh tones serve as a backdrop, the monster appeared, and I collapsed in quivering terror. When I made the blue-black tattoo ink the backdrop, the smirking death's-head appeared, and I twitched and jangled with giddy exuberance.

After several dozen journeys back and forth, I made an interesting discovery: The appearance of these two had ceased to trigger the accompanying emotions. This was the next phase in the etiology of my schizophrenia: Part of me had become a spectator, an overseer of the pathetic mound of tissue that was witnessing monsters and death's-heads. "I" was now of an altogether higher order of existence, where emotional reactions were regarded with the same measured concern as a child's queasy stomach, upset from gobbling too much ice cream.

In several staggered flashes of insight, like flashbulbs popping around a celebrity, I understood the Cartesian mind/body split. I also understood Beauty and Truth and Ultimate Reality. Unfortunately, I lacked the words to explain it all to poor Hawk, who sat huddled in woeful ignorance beside me. In fact, I concluded that there was nothing that I *didn't* now understand. My thoughts raced and swirled like darting birds, linking up in ever more intricate patterns and tying all existence into one neat bundle of interchangeable subatomic particles, all activated into the appearance of a cosmos by . . . *me!* In short, I was God. I could create and destroy this world by nothing more taxing than a simple act of will. I laughed munificently, as befits a resident deity.

Then I stopped laughing. Yes, it was true: I had transcended even laughter. With serene clarity, I surveyed all that I had created, and I found it good. Never mind trivia like wars and poverty and injustice. They were merely chimera. Bishop Berkeley in Philosophy 108 had been right all along. I had conjured up the entire world for my private entertainment. Rape and murder were merely my divine stag films. Only I existed. Neat and marvelous me! Oblivious to piddling human emotions, able to regard the multiple miseries of existence with detached amusement, I had clearly arrived at the pinnacle of spiritual evolution, and was in imminent danger of becoming the world's leading citizen.

After several centuries, spent basking in the glow of my moral perfection, I happened to glance up and see Mr. Army Deserter himself, hiding his shame behind his bushy beard, swaying above me and holding a gleaming syringe the size of a Nike missile. He reached down and unzipped my jeans. I shrieked with laughter at the idea that he thought he could screw God. He had had his chance when I was a mere mortal, and he had turned me down. Now that I had become a deity it was out of the question. I pushed his hands away.

"I'm going to inject this in your hip to bring you down," he thundered, jabbing me through my jeans.

Down it did bring me. Down and down and down. Spiraling down from heaven and into the murky twilight depths of hell. A fashion show was in progress, featuring the Seven Deadly Sins—Miss Malice, Miss Greed. They were all actually me. Coal miners were being crushed in roof falls, runaway slaves were cowering in subterranean chambers, soldiers in army fatigues were lined up to rape young Oriental girls. I was right in the thick of it all, unprotected by my celestial mask which had enabled me to see it as constructs of my mind. I was trapped in my sodden body. Each thought felt as though my brain were wearing Joe Bob's wrist weights. I fell asleep.

When I woke up, Hawk handed me two pills and a glass of water and said, "Take these. They'll make you feel better." The only thing that would have made me feel better, I was convinced, was a cyanide capsule. Hoping that in fact Hawk was murdering me so that he could loot the house, I washed them down.

Within a few minutes, I had returned to "normal."

I sat up abruptly and said, "Oh God! I forgot all about Wendy! Poor Angela!" I glanced around frantically and leapt to my feet. I had told Angela Wendy would be there only for the day, not for supper and the night as well.

"Relax," Hawk drawled, glancing at my Lady Bulova. "You've got all afternoon."

I sat back down on the cot, bewildered. As far as I was concerned, at least a decade had elapsed. I had a throbbing headache.

"God, it was amazing. . . ."

"Please," he said, closing his eyes and shaking his head, so that his bell jingled. "I'd really rather not hear about it."

"Yes, but—."

"Don't marvel, damn it! The mechanism is really quite simple, as you must know from college courses. The reticular formation at the base of the brain is a kind of filter that governs the number and nature of sensory stimuli allowed to enter the brain proper. Hallucinogens dismantle that filter, and your consciousness is swamped in sensation. Perceived duration of time is directly proportional to the number of sensory impressions being received in the brain. If you're being flooded with sensations, more time will seem to have elapsed than if you're deprived of sensations. Big deal."

"But if it's no big deal," I growled, unhappy to have my mystical experience reduced to the level of physiological filters, "why did you bother slipping me the LSD cocktail?"

"Because if I'd just explained the arbitrary nature of time to you without your having experienced it, it would have been meaningless." I decided not to confess that it *still* wasn't particularly fraught with meaning. I was sulking. If I couldn't be God, then I wouldn't be *anyone*.

"The thing is," Hawk explained, rolling over on his stomach by the pool later that afternoon, "I can't decide whether to have my novel be a comedy or a tragedy."

I looked at him blankly, not remotely interested in the agonies of artistic creation. "Does it make any difference?"

"Of course it does. It determines the whole structure. The essence of comedy is that life goes on; the main characters are survivors. They keep popping back up whenever they're knocked down. In tragedy, though, the heroes usually die and drag kingdoms down with them."

"I'm afraid you've lost me," I said yawning. "I mean, it sounds as though you've got it all figured out, even if I don't understand you. So what's the problem? Aren't those categories irrelevant to science fiction?"

"Oh, not at all. I've barely begun. I can see it being at *least* ten volumes. I still have to trace the origin of man, of life, of the earth, of the sun, of the elements, of the atom. I've got billions of years still to cover. And the comedy/tragedy question is crucial. Picture the universe contracted into one solid mass, which is a possible scenario for its end. Two things can happen: The fusion reactions can produce a gigantic explosion that would spew all the particles outward again, reversing time. That would be a comic ending. Survival would be the keynote. The end of one universe would signal the beginning of another. Or else all the particles could collapse in on themselves to form a body with such immense gravity that not even light rays could escape. Any residual matter in the universe would be slurped into it. This Black Hole scenario would be the tragic ending—destruction of Matter as we know it.

"I've already rejected a second tragic ending—the Entropy one. It would have required the universe not to have contracted but to have continued expanding. In order for movement—change of any kind—to occur, an energy process must take place. But any energy process forfeits a tiny portion of the energy produced, in the form of heat which dissipates at large. Heat flow is a one-way thing—from a warmer body to a cooler one, never the reverse. So picture a universe in which nothing is hotter or colder than anything else. The stars would have radiated all their heat and warmed the black void between them by the most minute fraction of a degree. Planets would have fallen into their suns. Eventually suns would fall into the centers of their galaxies, and galaxies into the centers of their galaxy groups and so on, until we would be left with one big burnt-out cinder in a vast cold black void."

"That one's kind of catchy."

"Yes, but 10,000 billion billion years is a lot to ask one author to cover."

Ira came marching home as scheduled. It seemed that at least a couple of centuries had passed—due no doubt to the enormous amount of sensory material I had absorbed through my reticular formation in his absence.

The afternoon of his return, he checked the kitchen calendar and informed me with a gleam in his eye, "Tonight's the night, Ginny! If we don't get a son tonight, we never will! I've been storing my sperm for two weeks!"

"Neat."

After Wendy was in bed and the supper dishes were done and Walter Cronkite had spread his messages of good cheer, Ira took my hand and led me up the stairs. I felt like Marie Antoinette en route to the guillotine. A new personality had had life breathed into it by Hawk. It was as yet frail and tentative and would be smothered under the least adverse pressure. I didn't see how I could possibly give birth to this new personality for Hawk, and to a baby son for Ira at the same time. The moment for a choice had arrived, I knew, as I douched with baking soda solution.

I walked resolutely into our bedroom. Ira was lurking under the sheets. I started taking my underwear out of my drawers. I loaded it under my arms and walked out. I had decided: My heart was in the cellar.

"What are you *doing?*" Ira called.

"I'm moving to the guest room."

"You're *what?*"

"Moving to the guest room."

"*Where?*"

"The guest room."

"The *guest* room?"

"The guest room."

"Tonight?"

"Right now."

"Then I'll come in the guest room with you."

"That won't be necessary," I replied coolly.

"It will be if we're going to have a son," he said grinning lecherously.

"But we're not."

"Not what?"

"Not going to have a son."

He stared at me, stricken. "What do you mean?"

"I don't want any more babies," I blurted out.

" 'Don't want any more babies,' " he repeated slowly to himself.

"Ira," I said, turning to him sadly, "let's not beat a dead horse."

My days once again became structured. Now, however, I was working around three people's schedules—Ira's, Wendy's, and Hawk's. I was getting up and feeding Ira and tending Wendy in the morning while Hawk worked on his novel. I stir-fried vegetables in a wok for Hawk's lunch, hiding the wok just as Ira appeared in the doorway for his Campbell's tomato-rice soup. After Ira had left, I'd feed Wendy and put her down for her nap. Then I'd race to the basement for my exercises, which now included mudpie staring, the semen retention posture, and various breathing exercises. We intoned "om" 108 times daily. We listened with our right ears for the Inner Sounds, which were to take the form of humming bees or tiny chinging bells or an ocean roar or a flute, according to our degree of spiritual evolution. I heard only my heart, masquerading as a bass drum; that put me at the bottom of the heap, evolutionarily speaking. We visualized floods of colors bathing different parts of our bodies. We contracted our anal sphincters while envisioning a current of serpent fire wafting up our spinal channels to the crown of our heads.

We shut off one nostril and inhaled and exhaled through the other in various intricate patterns understood only by Hawk. We forced air against our cheeks until they bulged. We imagined the life force flowing into our lungs with every breath. We placed clasped hands over the transformation centers of our solar plexi and pictured brilliant spiraling tongues of flame being fanned to incandescence by our breath. We drew our abdominal walls back and forth spasmodically, causing our breath to take the form of staccato gasps. We placed our right palms, middle and index fingers outstretched, over our hearts and repeated "om" and "hum" forty-two times in alternation with our heartbeats, while visualizing our hearts as arched black caverns dimly illuminated with a throbbing red glow.

It beat the hell out of housework. "I just don't understand you, Ginny," Ira would complain at night when he came home to find wet shirts mildewing in the washing machine. "If you're not going to be my wife, if you're not going to cook my meals and clean my house, if you're not going to share my bed and raise my children—what *are* you going to do?"

I'd smile serenely as I shoved TV dinners into the crusted oven. It was quite simple really: I was going to ascend into heaven. On my back.

Hawk was in high spirits. He had finished his first volume on the creation of the universe. The farmer and his wife had returned to Vermont as prophets for the Management Rep. In payment, the Rep had materialized for them a brand-new Sno Cat with leopard skin seats, to replace the one they'd busted up on the ski jump.

Hawk had also come to a decision on the structure for the remaining nine volumes. It would be a comedy with the Big Bang ending.

Hawk was also delighted at the way our training sessions were going. He felt that my attitude toward the Maithuna was finally assuming the appropriate reverence, now that I was becoming accustomed to the paradoxical concept of using lust to transcend itself. The Maithuna had to be performed on the fifth day after the cessation of my menstrual period, so that Hawk had been charting my periods as carefully as Ira had in his pursuit of a son. Hawk had announced that the Maithuna would take place in two more days, following one further exercise.

This exercise occurred while Ira was at his volunteer fire department meeting. I descended to the runaway slave room all atremble in anticipation of the Maithuna. Hawk was sitting on the floor in the lotus position with his tongue protruding from his lips, drawing in a breath with a loud hiss. I knew better than to interrupt him when he was soliciting prana, so I sat quietly on the cot and surveyed the room to discover what spiritual treat was in store for me tonight. On the television tray sat a lighted white candle. Next to it was a mirror, lifted from the upstairs bathroom. Otherwise the room was dark. In front of the tray sat the camp stool.

Hawk motioned for me to sit on the stool facing the mirror. "Now!" he said briskly, combing his beard with his fingers. "Pick some one part of your anatomy to focus on—your chin or your nose, say. Not your eyes." I rejected my pert little ski jump of a nose, although I had always regarded it with affection, because it was too close to my eyes and I kept glancing into them. I settled on my lips instead.

"After we do the standard 7:1:7 breathing," Hawk said, "I want you to concentrate on the chosen feature without blinking and with your eyes half-closed. Try not to think at all. And remember: no blinking. And when your eyes start to unfocus, allow them to. Don't refocus."

We breathed rhythmically for a while. Then Hawk said softly, "All right. Begin now."

I was relaxed from the breathing, and I regarded my lips with detachment, trying not to enumerate the various ways in which those two curious flaps had gotten me in trouble in the past.

As I stared, inhibiting my impulse to blink, I could feel my eyes shifting out of focus, as Hawk had said they would. I didn't fight it. I allowed them to unfocus, as I continued to stare at the mid-point of my upper lip without blinking.

I found my other features, on the periphery of my vision, becoming blurred and unidentifiable. As I watched, they seemed to alter subtly. Gradually, my face took on the appearance of someone else's —no one I knew. Before I could examine the topic of whose it might be, it had again shifted slightly; and it continued shifting in a slow, steady kaleidoscope of human physiognomy. I was somewhat alarmed: I didn't care for some of the faces mine was mutating into. Some seemed kind and warm, others hard and malevolent.

As this germ of alarm began to sprout, clouds of fog began rolling in from the sides of the mirror. Soon, the features reflected there, whomever they belonged to, were almost entirely obscured. The only indication that an image was present was a faint glow outlining the head. I was dissolving in creeping clouds of mist!

I panicked at the prospect of imminent annihilation. I opened my eyes wide and blinked them several times, as Hawk had instructed me not to. The fog and the glow vanished instantly—and there I was, staring at myself in a mirror. I was breathing fast with fear.

"What's wrong?" Hawk asked innocently.

"I was vanishing!"

"Good."

"*Good?* It was awful. I was being annihilated."

"Relax. You were *supposed* to vanish. That was the whole point of the exercise."

"Very cute!"

"For Christ's sake, where's your scientific detachment?" Hawk drawled. "Why do you have to turn everything into some sort of cosmic melodrama? The explanation is very simple, and I'm sure you could think of it yourself if you weren't so insistently agog. Your eyes function on movement, change. Normally, when you're looking at something, your eyes are in constant motion, taking in the object in quick little glances at component parts. When you inhibit this foveal shift, by staring steadily without blinking, you can produce a kind of temporary blindness. The point is, all our senses are instruments for detecting change. They function through registering movement— your eardrum vibrates with sound waves, and you hear; a stimulus moves across your skin, and you feel. But tonight you reduced your input of visual movement to a minimum and were able to shut down one of your senses very briefly. Now, what if you were in a situation in which there were no change at all, in which all your senses shut down—would you yourself cease to exist?"

I looked at him blankly, blinking, still shaken from my confrontation with annihilation.

"Did you cease to exist when you intentionally shut down just one of your senses?"

"I'm not sure."

Hawk sighed. I was apparently missing yet another vital point. "What if you were in a realm of existence where there was no matter, and therefore no change? Your sense organs wouldn't function, true, but you wouldn't *need* them to function either, would you, since their *raison d'être* is to assure physical survival by detecting and warning of change?"

I frowned. He cast his eyes to the ceiling with disgust.

"All right. Let's try a different approach. Time is measured by movement of objects through space, by change of position, right? By the movement of the earth on its axis; once around is called a day. By the movement of the earth around its sun, once around being called a year. By the vibrations of a tuning fork, or a quartz crystal. By the rotations of cesium 133; 9,192,631,770 cycles of the frequency involved in the transition between two energy levels is called a second. By the movement of a pair of hands around a clock face. By the movement of a shadow on a sundial. Fifteen degrees of longitude on a globe equals one hour. Wendy asks you, 'How long is an hour, Mommy?' And you reply, 'As long as it takes to get from here to St. Johnsbury and back.' In other words, as someone once said, time is an illusion perpetrated by the manufacturers of space. Time is nothing more than a succession of objects in space.

"Likewise, movement through space, distance, is measured by *time*. Someone says, 'How far is it to Montreal from here?' And you say, 'Two hours.' The ancient Persians had as a basic unit of measurement the parasang, which was the amount of level ground covered in one hour by a man on foot. And interstellar distances are stated in terms of light-years—the distance light travels in one year. But it is possible, likely even, that there are forces moving faster than the speed of light; we just wouldn't be able to detect them with our sensory equipment in its current form."

"I know all that," I said smugly. "I took physics, too, you know."

"Maybe you already know it, but have you used it to draw any conclusions relevant to your own existence?"

"Maybe."

"I'll state my point in so many words. You can say you already know that, too, but *I* don't think you do. The day I shut you in here in the dark you experienced the way time speeds up when sensory stimuli are reduced. Well, here is my final question before the Maithuna, which will occur tomorrow night." My heart leapt, my breathing quickened. I almost didn't hear his final question, which was: "Just because we can't conceive of an existence apart from time and space doesn't prove that such existence is impossible. What happens to time when *all* sensory input is cut out?"

I couldn't see the point. Not caring, I raced upstairs somehow to get through the long hours until time for the act for which I'd been training for four weeks.

Ira went off the next night to a special session of the Cemetery Commission. I kissed him guiltily as he left. Wendy was already in bed.

I took a bath, as I had been instructed, in order to allow free flow of my bio-electric current. I anointed myself with Chanel No. 5, which Ira had given me for Christmas. Then I put on my rose negligee and tied a green silk scarf around my neck, Dale Evans style. I had asked Hawk if I should insert my diaphragm, it being a possible fertile day. He had said not, since its presence would interfere with my bio-electric current. Anyway, he assured me, since he now had complete control over ejaculation, there was no need for it. Our union wouldn't involve a standard orgasm; therefore, pregnancy wasn't a possibility.

I glided out to the Bliss family cemetery. Hawk was already there, in a brown terry cloth robe belonging to Ira. He was setting up the ultraviolet mosquito lamp from the terrace. The ultraviolet wave lengths were supposed to stimulate my muladhara region, whatever that might mean.

Hawk had fashioned a low table with a board and bricks. It was covered with a white linen cloth. On it sat two candles, a platter with some food, a bottle of Southern Comfort and two liqueur glasses, a pitcher of water and two Welch's grape jelly glasses. Next to the table was stretched Hawk's sleeping bag.

And behind the sleeping bag hovered the gaunt hollow-eyed angels carved by Father Bliss on his children's tombstones. Next to these tombstones was Father Bliss's own stone, carved by him in advance, featuring a skeleton holding a scythe in one hand and an hourglass whose sand had run out in the other. At the top of the slate stone were two trees, one of which lay fallen on the ground. They symbolized the two huge black locusts that now towered over the stone house in the front yard; one had been planted by Father Bliss and the other by his wife, when they had moved into their new house right after their wedding.

The hill on which the cemetery sat dropped off into the valley where the Pots o' Gold vacation homes were pushing up through the soil like sprouting seeds. A ground mist was swirling in around them. The June sun had just dipped behind the far hills.

I was feeling uneasy. "Does it really have to be out here? Couldn't we do it in the cellar?"

"The symbolism of the site is very important."

"Uh, Hawk," I asked, considering the topic for the first time, "what exactly is going to *happen?*"

He shrugged. "How should *I* know? I've never done this before. I was trying to suggest aspects of what I think *might* happen with some of the exercises."

I began trembling with an emotion that could only be diagnosed as acute fear. "Is it possible," I whispered, "that we could really screw ourselves up? Isn't this just as artificial a means for altering states of consciousness as LSD?"

He glared at me. "So you're chickening out, Ginny? I just wish you'd told me before I wasted four weeks training you."

"I'm not chickening out. I was just curious."

"Look," he said, running his hand through his beard, "this is an ancient technique. The Ratnasara says, 'He who realizes the truth of the body can then come to know the truth of the universe.' We've been giving all this attention to our bodies, not as an end in itself but in order to use them as instruments for the attainment of moksha—liberation."

I looked at him doubtfully, stretching my neck to loosen the uncomfortably tight ritual scarf. That may have been what Hawk had been doing, but I reflected that my motives were considerably less lofty. It occurred to me that I might have to be punished for my sacrilege by the guardian of moksha.

"People have been doing this for centuries," Hawk added.

"But not *me.*"

"*Please* don't back out now. I've been preparing for tonight for over a year. It's all that's kept me going, Ginny. It's really my last chance. Do you have any idea how difficult it is to live with yourself once you're aware of the hideous things you, and most of your fellow humans, are capable of? I *have* to find a more hospitable dimension or I'm done for."

Put that way, his face contorted with agony, how could I refuse? I nodded my go-ahead.

Hawk lit the candles. We sat in the lotus position in front of the low table and did 7:1:7 breathing for twelve cycles. Then we held our breath and concentrated on our muladhara centers, between the anus and the genitals, which we stimulated by contracting our anal sphincters and visualizing ourselves uniting, in our respective roles as cosmic consciousness and cosmic energy.

After we had repeated this a dozen times, Hawk tapped the bottle of Southern Comfort with his finger and said, "Phat." Then he waved his hand around it as though he were a magician trying to make it disappear and intoned, "Hung." He joined his thumb and ring fingers and gestured toward the bottle saying, "Namah." My only hope was that Hawk knew more about what was going on than I did.

Unscrewing the cap of the Southern Comfort, Hawk brought the bottle to his face and closed off his right nostril and inhaled. Then he closed his left nostril and exhaled. Filling the liqueur glasses, he handed me one, and we tossed down the sweet burning liquid in one swallow. He refilled our glasses. We each took a piece of bologna from the china platter and repeated together, "Shiva, Shakti. I purify my lustful flesh." Then we ate the bologna, which signified animal life and bodily development, washing it down with Southern Comfort.

Hawk refilled our glasses. We took a chunk of Chicken of the Sea tuna, which represented generative powers and aquatic life forms, intoned "om" six times, and ate it, again washing it down with Southern Comfort.

Then we took a saltine apiece, which represented grain and earth elements; after chewing it slowly, we tossed down another shot of Southern Comfort.

We repeated this procedure. The quart bottle of Southern Comfort was now half empty. I had the uneasy feeling that at other times, in different places, this ritual had been meaningful. But tonight, in Stark's Bog, its significance was escaping me.

We sat with closed eyes meditating on our upcoming union. Then we tossed off another glass of Southern Comfort saying, "Kulakundalini."

We drank jelly glasses of water. Hawk handed me a cardamon. We studied the coarse outer husk. Then we broke through the husk to the grain and contemplated the two symmetrical halves, joined to form a whole. We chewed them slowly.

Removing my rose negligee, I crawled over to the sleeping bag and arranged myself, while Hawk adjusted the bug lamp so that its rays fell upon my body, which was now bare except for the ritual neck scarf.

Hawk sat down next to me, the bell in his ear lobe jingling. He gazed upon my body with admiration and was supposed to be seeing in it the mystery of creation, the bejeweled vault of all riches, the begetter of the cosmos. It was this megalomaniacal attitude that Hawk had to achieve in order to distinguish our upcoming coition from ordinary vulgar human intercourse. The burden of the evening was riding on him. It was a lot to ask of him, to see all those superlatives in my somewhat flabby flesh, which was etched with silver stretch marks from Wendy's birth. I could see in his hairy face the strain of this leap of the imagination. He'd invested his all in the outcome of the next hour. What if we failed to attain whatever it was we were supposed to attain? If we did attain it, would we know that we had? I clutched the sleeping bag spasmodically, and my breathing became jerky from the mounting tension. A casual roll in the hay with a war hero was all I'd had in mind all those weeks ago. How had I been foolish enough to get involved in transcendence?

I tried to calm myself and think only about the energizing union of polar opposites, the harnessing of the blind life force, as represented by me, to material creation, as represented by Hawk. I breathed deeply, following the 7:1:7 plan.

Hawk placed his hand over his heart and muttered, "I am Shiva. I am She." He knelt over me and gingerly placed his index and middle fingers over my heart, on the top of my head, on my eyelids, on the center of my forehead. He mumbled words I couldn't make out as he progressed to my throat, my ear lobes, my breasts and upper arms, my navel, thighs, knees, feet. And finally my yoni, as he chose to refer to my cunt.

Then he removed Ira's robe. His erection pointed to the heavens like a Gothic spire. He lay down on my right and waited for his breathing to switch. Mine had already switched.

We assumed the tangled ritual position by my raising my legs and his moving his upper body away from me and inserting his right leg between my legs. The result of these contortions was that his lingam, which was the Maithuna term for cock, entered me slightly. We both trembled violently as it did so, and my yoni contracted with excitement. We gritted our teeth and forced our hips not to move reflexively.

Initial impulses successfully overcome, we began the wait. We were to lie joined like this for thirty-two minutes, meditating upon the ineffable bliss of divine union, and visualizing the currents flowing across our bridge of flesh, at the end of which time something profound, unlike any previous experience, would occur. Samarasa. Nirvana. Transcendence of time and death. Participation in infinity and eternity. God knows what.

I lay still and pondered cosmic currents in the relaxed detached fashion Hawk had recommended. This was not difficult because I was very drunk from the Southern Comfort. Hawk's assignment, however, was more difficult. It was his show, and if he allowed himself to ejaculate, our act would become commonplace fucking. Perish the thought. His lingam was alternately wilting and then swelling like a tampon in a toilet bowl.

I opened one glazed eye and glanced at him. Beads of sweat were popping out on his forehead. He was red-faced from trying to swallow his tongue in order to forestall orgasm. My heart went out to him, but I didn't know how to help, other than to lie very still. I stroked his damp forehead soothingly. His grimacing face began to go slack, and he started the 7:1:7 breathing. I withdrew my hand and closed my eyes and floated on a seductive sea of Southern Comfort, visualizing the languid healing heat of a southern summer. I descended into a deep drunken sleep.

I awoke to sounds of sobbing. Squinting through a throbbing headache, I glanced around. Far more than thirty-two minutes had passed, I was sure. The purple glow from the mosquito lamp bathed the immediate scene—me, Hawk asleep beside me wrapped in my legs, the littered board table. We were covered with dead mosquitoes. Then I noticed that Hawk's and my joined genitals were bathed in a *white* light as well. I followed the beam to its source, a flashlight. The holder of the flashlight was also the source of the wracking sobs that mixed with the pulsing croaks of frogs in the Pots o' Gold valley.

I strained my eyes through the dark. It was Ira.

"Back from your meeting so soon, dear?" I gasped.

He sobbed in reply. I gingerly removed Hawk's wilted lingam from my yoni and sat up and grabbed my rose negligee, which I had worn on Ira's and my wedding night. I was covered with goose bumps. The night air had turned chilly.

"It's not what you think, Ira," I told him, wincing as he turned the flashlight beam on my face.

"What *is* it then?" he rasped.

"We weren't having sex," I explained reasonably.

Ira kicked over the board table, and the china platter smashed on a brick. "Jesum Crow, Ginny! I've been standing right here *looking* at you!"

"Yes, I know it *looks* like sex, Ira. But it *wasn't*. You'll just have to believe me," I pleaded.

"*No!*" he shouted. "I will *not* believe you, Ginny! You and your hippy friends—you think you can rip off us honest hard-working sincere suckers! You've been *using* me, Ginny! No *wonder* you won't fulfill your wifely obligations. I bet this has been going on the whole time we've been married. How could I be so thick as not to have *seen* it? You live off me—your straight idiot of a husband—and you carry on the way you always have with your weird friends!"

"That's not *true*, Ira! I've *never* been unfaithful to you. And I'm not being now. This man and I, we were—uh—trying to transcend the bondage of our flesh."

"Oh *sure!* Call it anything you want, Ginny, but I've had *enough!* Do you understand? You've done nothing but hurt me and make fun of me from the first day we met. I want you to leave *now*. And take your freaky friend with you."

"Now?"

"Now. This minute. Go to your friends at their commune. Go sleep with this hairy creep in the woods like the animals that you both are. Go anywhere. I don't care anymore. Just get out of my life!" He began sobbing again.

Hawk yawned and sat up and glanced around, blinking vacantly with his bell jingling. Gradually his memory started functioning. As it did, his face clouded over with anguish.

"Oh *Christ!*" he wailed. "I fell *asleep!* Jesus, I *blew* it! A whole *year* and I fucked up! Oh *God!*" He looked around wildly, saw me, and moaned, "Ginny, we *blew* it! We fell *asleep!* Oh God!"

I nodded toward Ira. Hawk realized that we weren't alone, and looked up at Ira, who stood shaking with sobs. "Ira, this is Hawk. Hawk, my husband, Ira."

Ira snarled. Hawk gazed up at him uncomprehendingly. Finally he jumped up and extended his hand, his southern manners rising to the occasion. Ira drew back his fist and slugged him in the face, knocking him down.

"Now get out of my yard, both of you."

"What about Wendy? Children need their mothers, Ira."

"*No* child needs a slut for a mother."

Hawk and I skulked into the house, followed by Ira. As we entered the kitchen, Hawk, dressed in Ira's robe, his eye swelling shut, said sensibly, "Now look, Ira—"

"Get dressed and get out of here," Ira said calmly, taking a .22 down from the wall.

I dressed in a pantsuit and stuffed a few toilet articles in my pocketbook. I couldn't believe I was being kicked out, couldn't believe how few rights I had that would allow me to stay. After all, it was Ira's ancestral home, his town, his relatives, his furniture . . . his daughter? I had been merely a temporary fixture. Since I had failed to meet specifications, I was being disposed of. Until now, I had been swamped with remorse over hurting Ira, however unintentionally. But now I began getting angry. He felt *I* had used *him*. How about all the meals I'd cooked, the mountains of shirts I'd laundered and ironed just so, the bizarre sexual perversions I'd had to endure? Did they count for nothing?

I tiptoed into Wendy's room. She lay sleeping, all damp and flushed, her tiny hands folded into fists, breathing heavily. She was his, like everything else in sight. But unlike everything else, she was also mine. I would get her back. I leaned down and kissed her cheek. She sighed in her sleep and turned over.

At the door, Ira was clearing his throat, his gun resting on his hip. As we walked down the hall, he said plaintively, "Everyone in town always told me not to get mixed up with the Soybean People. I thought I knew what I was doing. I thought I could change you into a decent God-fearing woman."

"Well, I guess everyone in town was right, and you were wrong, huh?"

"I guess so."

"Don't take it so hard, Ira. A snake will always be a snake, even if you put a chain around its neck and try to make it walk upright."

It was past midnight. Hawk and I had slept for over four hours during the Maithuna. As Ira stood in the doorway with his rifle on his hip, we trudged away from the huge stone fortress and down the dirt road toward the Canadian border. We slept that night in a field. Hawk didn't speak. His face was a mask of mute suffering.

The next morning when I woke up I found Hawk lying staring at the sunny summer sky, his hands folded under his head.

"Well! Where to now, Hawk?"

He didn't reply, didn't even appear to have heard me. I ran my hand in front of his eyes. He didn't blink. Slowly, he turned his head and stared at me without recognition. Unnerved, I repeated, "Where shall we go? The world is ours!"

He stared at me without answering. Then he resumed staring at the sky.

"Hawk?" I asked anxiously. No glimmer of a response.

"*Hawk!*" He remained motionless, expressionless.

I tugged insistently at the ring in his ear lobe, like a farmer grabbing a recalcitrant bull by the ring in its nose. "Look, Hawk, it's not the end of the world. Really it isn't. We're all trained now. We can try the Maithuna again on the fifth day after my next period. It's no big deal. We just have to switch from Southern Comfort to wine."

He continued staring at the sky.

"Hawk, I mean, *really*. This is ridiculous, sulking like this."

He said nothing, stared fixedly at the blue summer sky. I grabbed his arm in the vicinity of his mandala tattoo and shook it fiercely; it was like shaking a corpse.

I lay back down and stared at the sky with him. I enumerated the possibilities for me and my zombie. We could return to Ira's. I could turn Hawk over to the FBI, and plead temporary insanity and beg Ira to take me back. I could take Hawk and hike over the hill to our left and join Mona's and Atheliah's commune. I could leave Hawk here, lying in this field, and fend for myself, returning to Hullsport or something. I could take Hawk back to Montreal, braving the border guards, maybe locate some of his friends, live with him if he wanted, or strike out on my own.

I rolled up the sleeping bag and attached it to the pack frame. Then I shook Hawk and pointed to the pack. Obediently, he allowed me to hoist it onto his back. Then I took his hand and led him like a pack horse. We climbed a hill and walked along a ridge until Mona's and Atheliah's rambling house was directly below us. Then we tacked down the hillside through the woods toward it. I felt as though I was perhaps finally coming home, after a long and painful exile among strangers.

When we reached the house, it was empty, deserted. The front door had popped open and swayed in the breeze. We walked inside. Most of the debris had been shoveled off the living room floor. The caravan had moved on. Panic gripped me. I had been counting on them for advice, or at least for moral support.

I searched through all the rooms, but could find no trace of con-

tinuing human habitation. I stuffed a few discarded T-shirts in the pack
and removed it from Hawk's shoulders and led him to the couch and
sat him down. He stared intently at his dirty fingernails. Then I sat
down, too, and stared at Hawk. He had been such a dictator while
he was training me, had known exactly what to do when. Where had
that personality vanished to now, when we really needed it?

"Now what, maharishi?" He continued studying his fingernails as
though he hadn't heard.

I walked into the kitchen. There were some large jars of brown
rice and soybeans, dried fruits and nuts, sesame seeds and sunflower
seeds. Moths swooped around in them like flying reptiles. I took two
handfuls of dried fruit and gave one to Hawk. We sat and munched
gravely on the leathery apricots and pears.

Were FBI agents really lurking around waiting to descend on
Hawk? If so, would Ira be likely to hear about it and draw the
appropriate conclusions? This farm would be the first place he'd send
them, in a seizure of National Guard-ly wrath. I was aiding and
abetting a fugitive. I was in this up to my ears. What was I to do?

I studied Hawk. In his fringed leather jacket and bib overalls and
beard and tangled hair, he looked like the quintessence of army
deserterhood. I got some scissors out of a kitchen drawer. Then I
sheared Hawk like a sheep, cutting his beard down to stubble and
hacking away at his hair. He didn't appear to notice. Then I got
the razor I used on my legs out of my pocketbook. Lathering him up,
I shaved him. I removed the silver ring and jingle bell from his ear
lobe. Then I helped him, unprotesting, out of his leather jacket and
overalls. The pin-striped pants to an extra suit I had brought were
cuffed and fashionably loose. They fit him well and looked like men's
slacks. The jacket, however, was ridiculously tight, and the sleeves
came halfway up his forearms. I let him wear his work shirt instead
and sandals. Even so, he looked remarkably clean-cut and fresh and
innocent without his mangy beard. I was startled to see his chin after
all these weeks. No wonder he had hidden it. It was weak and reced-
ing.

I plopped down on the sofa. Clearing my throat, I said, "Do you
think we should go to Montreal, Hawk?"

He didn't look up from his fingernails.

"How difficult will it be for you to get past the border guards?"

Sighing, I pulled him up from the couch. I loaded the pack on his
uncomplaining back, and we struck off northward through the woods.

When we hit the road to the border crossing, we hitched a ride with some young kids in a Volkswagen bus. The border guards were so busy searching for drugs that they didn't pay any attention to us middle-aged straights. I had remembered by then that Hawk had landed immigrant status anyway. He was already on Canadian soil and so was home free.

In Montreal I decided we might as well live it up for a night on Ira's credit cards while we (read: I) decided on our next move. We swept into the Bonaventure Hotel. A Chinese coolie relieved Hawk of his pack and led us down endless interconnected carpeted corridors to a vast chamber, outfitted with fold upon fold of thick drapery and two king-sized beds. The windows across one wall looked down many stories to a scenic parking lot.

Hawk sat in one upholstered armchair, and I sat in the other. "Look, Hawk, I think you're overreacting. Yes, we blew it. We drank too much Southern Comfort and passed out. But so what? We can restage it using grape juice or Seven-Up or something. That can't be what's really bothering you. What's wrong?" In fact, I was awash with guilt. Perhaps my rotten attitude toward the Maithuna, regarding it largely as an opportunity to get laid, had played a major role in wrecking it.

For the first time all day, Hawk responded. He looked up out of bloodshot blue eyes and croaked, "Entropy."

"Entropy?"

He rubbed his clean-shaven face furiously with both hands, like Samson discovering his shorn head. "They've finally got me," he whispered.

"*Who* has?"

"Don't you see?" he asked with an incredulous smile. "They're going to suck all the heat from my body before I have a chance to get out of it. I'll be trapped in it and will die."

"*Who* is?"

"I have to get south," he muttered.

"You *can't* go south. You'll be thrown in prison."

"I *am* in prison," he croaked.

"Hawk, I've really had enough of this nonsense," I snapped, like a spinster schoolteacher. "Now, you just pull yourself together."

He glared at me sullenly. "If you weren't already dead, you'd feel it, too. Entropy—sucking all the warmth from your body." He started shivering spasmodically, and his teeth chattered.

"It's actually very comfortable in here," I notified him. "Seventy-four degrees. Fingertip control in every room." His shuddering increased, and he wrapped his arms around himself.

I studied him hopelessly. I figured that if I continued to treat him normally, didn't go along with his game, maybe he'd snap out of it as abruptly as he'd snapped into it.

"Come on," I barked like an army sergeant. "We're going out for dinner. Please try to behave."

I turned in at a trendy-looking spot on a quiet side street, dragging Hawk behind me. Smart couples were sitting at tables under an outside awning. A large neon sign of an American Gothic-type farmer read "Old MacDonald's."

Inside, the bar was a feed trough with a cover. The bar stools were old tractor seats mounted so as to swivel on milk cans. On the wall behind the bar were pictures of stylized domestic animals, silos and tractors, made by gluing exotic beer labels into patterns. The chrome shot spouts on all the lined-up liquor bottles were in the shape of cows' udders.

I directed Hawk to a tractor seat and sat in one next to him. I ordered us Bloody Marys, feeling extravagant, backed as I was by Ira's credit cards. The waitress, dressed in tattered Daisy Mae cutoffs and a bandanna halter and a huge straw hat, inquired with a French accent, "Two Red Roosters?"

"Whatever," I said with a shrug. The drinks when they arrived had miniature pitchforks for swizzle sticks.

After a few minutes, I went in search of the ladies' room, which was decorated to look like an outhouse.

When I returned, Hawk was no longer there. I assumed he was in the men's room and sat down to wait. A man sitting next to me in suede overalls and brogan platform shoes started humming "Red River Valley" under his breath.

Finally he turned to me and asked, "What ya reading?"

I was holding a Montreal guidebook in one hand. "*The Autobiography of Alice B. Toklas.*"

"Yeah? Is it good?"

"If you're into that kind of thing," I replied, glancing around uneasily for Hawk.

"Do you like Red Roosters?" my friend in the neighboring tractor seat asked, his eyes fixed on my tits.

"What? Oh, Red *Roosters.* Yes. Yes, I do."

"Want another?"

I stared at him with surprise. It invariably amazed me when some-one tried to pick me up. I would *never* be able to assume that someone would rather talk to me than to stare off vacantly into space. The male ego was truly an object of wonder.

"No, thank you. I'm waiting for my date."

"Yeah? Well, he went out the door about ten minutes ago."

I looked at him quickly. "Are you *sure?*"

He nodded. I scrambled down and raced from the restaurant. I charged around all the adjacent blocks searching for him. Then I decided he'd gotten tired and had returned to the Bonaventure.

When I got back to our room, Hawk wasn't there. Only his pack remained.

I collapsed on the vast bed and fell asleep.

The next morning I went to the offices of the various war resister groups and inquired about Hawk. After getting absolutely nowhere and finding the men behind the desks reluctant even to talk with me, I realized that my image was at fault. In my Sally Suburban pantsuit with my hair tied back with a scarf, I looked like a wronged wife. I went and had my hair cut in an Afro, and I bought a patchwork peasant dress and some hand-tooled leather clogs on Ira's charge cards.

In my new disguise, I returned to the offices and inquired anew about Hawk. This time a couple of men confessed to having known him but not having seen him for several months. One gave me his old address. I checked it out. It was a dingy crumbling townhouse well away from the downtown area. The dumpy woman behind the desk remembered Hawk, but hadn't seen him lately. I entered a Missing Persons report with the police.

For a couple more days I prowled around following various dead-end leads, trying to find people who had known him. I had concluded that eventually he would surface and return to his old friends and old haunts. I planned to be there to take care of him when he did. It would be my life's work: I would take a room somewhere, find a waitress job, and spend my free time scouring Montreal in search of my war hero. What else did I have to build a life around?

I returned to Stark's Bog to gather up my sparse belongings. I was dumped from the bus right next door to Ira's office. I was toting Hawk's nearly empty pack, having checked his belongings in a locker at the Montreal bus station until I should return to claim them.

Ira blanched when he saw me. He drove me to the house in his fire chief's car. Among my waiting mail was a letter from Mrs. Yancy asking me to come to Hullsport and be with Mother, who was hospitalized with a clotting disorder. On the way to the St. Johnsbury airport, with Hawk's pack filled with all my worldly possessions in the trunk, Ira notified me that he intended for Wendy never to see me again. She had had a few difficult days but was now happily absorbed into Angela's brood. I owed it to her to stay out of her life.

14

Saturday, July 22

□

Ginny stood looking down at her sleeping mother. Cotton plugs in her nostrils and gums, a pad between her legs, new bruises on her arms and calves. Her right eye bandaged. She had developed a slight temperature.

Any day now her mother's brain might hemorrhage. There was no longer any way to avoid acknowledging it. Her mother hadn't been out of bed in almost a week. She lay all day without talking. The nurses whisked in and out, doing this or that to make the bruised flesh more comfortable. Ginny had lately been thinking of her mother's body·as an apple, formerly firm, now fallen and rotting. It was an appalling image, but she couldn't seem to banish it. Like an apple, its entire purpose for existence had been to transport, protect, and nurture the seeds of new life. Now that these once new lives—Karl, Jim, and Ginny herself—were ripe apples themselves, her mother's function had ceased. She was being disposed of. She was lying in a hospital bed rotting. She had been used. It wasn't fair. But then, as she had always insisted, *life* wasn't fair.

Ginny strolled into the hall. Coming from Coach's room were droning commands: "Get me out of here *right now*. Do you hear me? I want out of here right now. No ifs, ands or buts, *now!*" Ginny was incapable of saying whether Coach was living in the past or the present at this point. He knew he was in the hospital and really wanted out, or he was wrapped up in some drama out of his past?

Stationed in Mrs. Cabel's doorway was Sister Theresa in her hospital robe and gown. A hand clutched either side of the door frame. In front of her, his nose at her chest level, stood Mr. Solomon, quivering with rage in his blue wool robe.

"The voman is *suffering*, Sister Theresa!"

"How can you *know*, Mr. Solomon? A human being is more than just a biological mechanism. Mrs. Cabel's spirit may be *thriving* in her impaired body, for all we know."

"Acts of omission are no less morally reprehensible than acts of commission," Mr. Solomon insisted. "Compassion requires that I not lie in the next room listening to her moan if it is vithin my power to alleviate her pain. Let her *rest*, Sister, in that great black void on the other side."

"That is *not* compassion, Mr. Solomon. You are not thinking of Mrs. Cabel's suffering. You are thinking of how to relieve your *own* suffering at having to listen to her. If you were truly compassionate, Mr. Solomon, you wouldn't exhibit such overweening impatience as Mrs. Cabel works out her role in the cosmic scheme."

"Cosmic scheme! You and your celestial vet dreams! There *is* no cosmic scheme, Sister! This life is *it*. Rendering this life as painless as possible is the only virtue man is capable of. Ven pointless misery can be averted, the ends justify the means. Step aside and let me by, Sister!" He snatched futilely at her beefy arms.

"Such means as you are referring to, Mr. Solomon, can *never* be justified by any circumstances. You seem to regard man as master of his fate. But man is much more than just his intentional side. Your proposed system of ethics makes human rationality the basis of morality and puts man at the center of the universe, determining its purpose—"

"*Someone's* got to determine its purpose, Sister," Mr. Solomon interrupted, "and your God is out to lunch. Your attitude, Sister, is the most profoundly *irreligious* one I've ever heard; you attribute everything to divine purpose and leave no scope for human responsibility. You are incapable of going beyond your sense of dependency on your God to become an active agent in the universe."

"In *fact*, Mr. Solomon, whether you know it or not, this universe is being administered quite handsomely without our assistance. So say those with eyes to see. You might do well to concentrate on developing such vision. Man's assignment is to live morally by discovering the meaning of the universe and conforming himself to it, rather than trying to fashion the universe to *his* purposes. You want complete control over life and death, Mr. Solomon, but you don't—and can't —have it. . . ."

Ginny's head was spinning as she returned to her mother's room. Eddie had been right: People should be prohibited from ever beginning a sentence with "Man is . . ." And more important, hadn't Sister Theresa and Mr. Solomon done complete turn-arounds in their stands on the advisability of snatching the tubes out of Mrs. Cabel? How had this changeover occurred? Ginny pondered their lines of reasoning. Mr. Solomon had switched from insisting that the prolongation of human life under any circumstances was the greatest good, to insisting that physical comfort and relief from pain was the greatest good. And Sister Theresa had switched from maintaining that God's plan included releasing Mrs. Cabel's spirit from her body on the spot, to maintaining that God's plan included confining Mrs. Cabel's spirit to her body until He in His infinite wisdom felt she was ready to leave it. Intriguing. But what intrigued her most was their regarding themselves privy to knowledge of the highest good and of God's plan, respectively. How had they arrived at this enviable state of clarity and conviction?

Her mother was awake. Her unbandaged eye was staring out the window at a red squirrel in the elm tree. As they watched, the squirrel took a running jump and landed on the tip of a neighboring branch. The branch sagged under the squirrel's weight. Ginny and her mother smiled at each other, charmed by the squirrel's casual grace.

"Mr. Solomon and Sister Theresa are at it again," Ginny said.

"Oh?"

"Now *Mr. Solomon* wants to unplug Mrs. Cabel, and Sister Theresa won't let him. Each has a whole new set of equally convincing arguments."

Her mother smiled faintly. "They're playing word games. It's a waste of time. You don't figure these things out by talking about them."

"I've noticed." The confrontation had reminded Ginny of Wendy. Not surprisingly, since Wendy was now springing into her mind at the least excuse. As she drove down the road, each child she passed required a second look to be sure it wasn't Wendy. In a store, almost unconsciously, she would gather armloads of the foods Wendy favored; she would sit at the cabin absently munching animal crackers by the hour. The few times the phone had rung, she'd raced to it, certain that it was Ira and Wendy. She was obsessed and she knew it. And she couldn't stop herself.

Anyhow, Mr. Solomon's and Sister Theresa's debate had recalled Wendy's preverbal days. Ginny and Ira would sit talking to each other after dinner. Unable to stand being left out any longer, Wendy would interrupt, babbling incoherently at a furious rate, and gesturing with her hands for emphasis, and staring intently from her mother to her father, convinced that her sounds were as meaningful and as worthy of attention as those of her parents. And she was probably right.

"But what *do* you think about euthanasia?" Ginny asked. Perhaps her mother's detached intellectual observations on the topic would give Ginny insight into her mother's situation.

"I *don't* think about it as a topic with a capital E—Euthanasia. I think everything depends on the circumstances in which it is embedded."

"And in Mrs. Cabel's circumstances?"

"I think she should have expressed her wishes in writing a long time ago."

"But since she apparently didn't?"

Her mother shrugged. "It's not my concern."

"Mother, one time you asked me not to let you die a lingering death," Ginny blurted out. "Do you want a gun or something?" There. For better or for worse, it was out in the open.

Her mother smiled again and for a long time said nothing. Ginny blushed scarlet, as she had years ago when her mother had told her about menstruation. The two topics—death and sex—were surrounded with equivalent taboos, required equal delicacy. She'd probably blown it by being so blunt.

"I remember saying that," her mother finally replied. "That was when I was younger, and infinitely more romantic about death. Thank you for asking. But no, I don't want a gun. I'm not in much pain, just enough to prod me into doing what I know I have to do—close out my accounts. I'm realizing that, like everything else, even death requires elaborate preparations."

They sat in silence for several minutes, listening to the ticking of the steepled clock.

"There *is* a point to suffering, you know," her mother added offhandedly.

"What *is* it?" Maybe there was actually a reason that her life to date had resembled the Stations of the Cross?

"To make you glad to give up life, ready to embrace death."

"Oh, *neat.*"

Ever since her mother's retina had ruptured, Ginny had been reading to her extensively from the last volume of the encyclopedia. This day she read the final entry, concluding her mother's nine-year project: " 'Zwitterion (Dipolar Ion)—A molecule containing both acidic and basic groups may be expected to neutralize itself with the production of an internal salt or, as it is commonly called, a zwitterion.' "

Her mother nodded with satisfaction and lay silent with her eye closed. Then she asked Ginny to collect some papers from her desk at the house, and to arrange for her lawyer to come.

For two days she busily consulted with her lawyer and sat up in bed writing on a pad propped against her knees. On the third day she handed Ginny a sheaf of papers. Ginny flipped through them—the format for her funeral, a list of pallbearers, the outfit she wanted to be buried in, her epitaph, a list of furniture to be kept in the family, various financial data. Distressed, Ginny stared at the neat lists.

Matter-of-factly, her mother said, "I've just sold the house and farm."

Ginny looked at her with alarm. "*Mother!*"

"Yes?"

"But you can't just *sell our house.*"

"*Why* can't I? It's mine, isn't it?"

"But what if *I* wanted it?" Ginny wailed.

"Ginny dear, the biggest favor I can do you is to sell that house. It's my parting gift to you. Every house should be sold before it's allowed to become a monument. The past, doted over, distorts the present," she said firmly, with the conviction of personal experience.

Ginny stared at her, her eyes filling with tears. It was worse than being pushed out of the nest; the nest was being sold out from under her.

"But I *would* like you to have my clock, to take with you wherever you decide to go."

"Thank you," Ginny mumbled, unable to look at her.

" 'To you from failing hands we throw the torch,' " her mother quoted with a wry smile, as she picked up the clock and handed it to her.

It seemed to Ginny that she was like a runner in an endless relay race, being passed the baton. Just so, she would one day hand the family clock to Wendy. "Yes, but it's not enough," Ginny muttered. What the hell difference did it make if life went on, if the Hull/Babcock/Bliss line flourished, when you yourself would most likely die a horrible death full of pain?

"No, it's not enough."

Ginny knew her mother had faith, whatever that meant. Not Sister Theresa's faith that Our Father Which Art in Heaven would answer to cries of "Daddy." Nor Mr. Solomon's faith in an endless black void of rest and oblivion. Like the veins of coal through the mountains where she'd been born, her mother's faith laced her entire being. But faith in *what*, Ginny hadn't figured out, intended to find out very soon.

As she turned to leave, she set the clock back on the table, feeling that her mother should have it beside her now more than ever.

"No," her mother said. "Take it away please. And the pictures, too."

That night Ginny phoned Jim at the last number he'd given their mother. A young man said, "Jim's, like, split."

"Where to?"

"Don't know, man."

"It's important. His mother is very sick."

The young man covered the phone and yelled something unintelligible. When he came back on, he said, "He's, like, back-packing in the High Sierras."

Ginny called the Park Service, who felt it was unlikely that he could be located any time soon without more specific information.

Karl in Germany said he'd be home as soon as he could. Apparently the army, though dealing in mass death, reverenced individual death enough to grant leave at times like this.

The next day, as she entered her mother's room, Ginny noticed how bare it looked without the clock and pictures and encyclopedias. It could have been any room in the hospital. Except for some vases of flowers, Ginny had carted off all external traces of her mother's personality.

Her mother lay looking out at the squirrels. Ginny sat down. They didn't speak. Ginny couldn't think of anything to say. No more encyclopedias to read from. To turn on "Hidden Heartbeats" now seemed distinctly inappropriate. Ginny sat in silence, watching the squirrels. Her mother lay in silence, watching the squirrels. Ginny was longing for some sort of neat statement from her mother, like the closing passage of a novel, that would deftly sum up the meaning of life, that would grant Ginny the gumption to go on with it. A dissertation on "What I Believe and Why." No such statement was forthcoming, and it was impossible to ask.

They floated suspended in silence for several days. Without the ticking of the clock to cue them in, time ceased to exist in its usual sense of being a relentless continuum leading from some past moment toward some future moment. Time now just existed as a whole, with Ginny and her mother encased snugly inside it, as though in a cocoon. Time lost its power to command. They took to judging segments of time by their quality, not by their duration. A nurse would arrive with an injection of an experimental drug. The pain of the injection and the pointlessness of further drugs made that particular bundle of time unpleasant, made the nurse's removal from the room pleasant. Flowers and a card from a friend would arrive. The scent would fill the room, for Ginny to sniff and report on; the colors would dazzle; a note on the card would touch them. That chunk of time would be of outstandingly high quality. Meals would arrive, bland and boring and repetitive, and those parcels of time were so mediocre as not to merit their awareness. They floated through time as though it were a sea of pudding filled with raisins they nibbled with delight, and pebbles they spat out with irritation.

Except for brief visits to the cabin to feed the young chimney swift and send it on its training flights and to check the mailbox for notes from Ira and Wendy which never arrived, Ginny was now spending most of her time in her mother's room. She slept in the spare bed. It wasn't that her mother needed her. Her mother appeared to need no one. They never spoke. An observer would have said her mother was severely depressed. But on the whole, Ginny thought that she probably wasn't. She was silent, unresponsive, it was true, but more because she seemed wrapped up in an interior dialogue that required all her concentration. This was why Ginny spent most of her time now at the hospital. She needed her mother, or rather needed to go through this vigil with her in hopes of being tossed some crumbs of the wisdom her mother was acquiring in her solitary confrontation with Death.

One morning Ginny woke up to find her mother already awake,

sitting up watching the squirrels with her good eye. The one they had concluded was the father was sitting on a branch on his haunches munching seeds. A streak of early morning sunlight fell across his glistening red back. His fluffy tail twitched rhythmically as he stuffed seeds into his tiny mouth with his delicate paws. The elm tree swayed in a light breeze, and its leaves shimmied.

Ginny glanced at her mother. Tears were flowing down her cheek from her good eye. Ginny was bathed in pain. She clambered down and snatched up a Kleenex and careened to her mother's side and started blotting.

"It's all right, Mother," she blurted out, on the verge of tears herself.

Her mother closed her eye and shook her head slowly. Her mouth was contorted in pain. "No. No, it *isn't* all right at all."

Ginny stopped blotting and backed over to her own bed. She couldn't recall ever having seen her mother cry. Her mother had always gallantly put a good face on things—to the point of foolishness perhaps. It seemed to Ginny that she was witnessing a lapse of faith.

Tears continued to squeeze out from under her mother's eyelid and dribble down her face. Ginny certainly didn't want to require now, as she and her brothers and her father had always done in the past, that her mother "put a good face on things." So she sat quietly and watched her cry.

Mrs. Childress lumbered in, normally a raisin in their pudding. Today, though, she was definitely a pebble: She carried a lancet for a bleeding test. When she saw Mrs. Babcock's tears, she raced to the Kleenex box and started blotting, just as Ginny had done, muttering, "There, there, Mrs. Babcock honey. It's gonna be *all right*."

Mrs. Babcock scowled.

Mrs. Childress crammed a thermometer in her mouth and sliced her ear lobe. When she had left, shaking her head in dismay at the result of the bleeding test, Mrs. Babcock snapped at Ginny, "Pull the shades down please. And get rid of those flowers."

That afternoon, Mrs. Babcock's other eye was bandaged to relieve eyestrain and a headache. She now lay in a darkened, soundless, scentless room with bandages over both eyes. It was impossible to tell if she was awake or asleep most of the time. It occurred to Ginny that her mother might be terrified, thinking she was alone in a black void.

"Mother?" Ginny asked urgently. "Shall I get a book and read to you?"

Her mother didn't answer. Ginny decided that she was asleep. But eventually her mother replied quietly, "I'd like to be alone now please."

It was like a slap in the face. Ginny was being dismissed, and at a time when she had thought she was being useful. "Yes, of course," she replied in a startled voice, scrambling to her feet. She reminded herself that during childbirth, she had wanted at certain points to be alone with her pain. Also, she felt she understood from her sessions with Hawk something of what her mother was doing, consciously or not: weaning herself from her senses, trying to prepare for a dimension in which a space-time limitation didn't exist. She was undoing all the ties that bound her here, including her affection and concern for her own daughter. But the dismissal was still hard to take.

"But, Mother," she cried, like an abandoned child, "what about all the junk in the closets at the house? What should I do with it?"

Her mother turned away without answering.

Back at the cabin, Ginny took the young bird out of its basket. It squawked with delight when it saw her. She fed it little balls of the disgusting meat paste in between its screeches.

Then she carried it outside on her finger. As they reached a part of the yard that she had cleared of kudzu for use as a landing strip, the bird plummeted from her finger of its own accord. Flapping furiously, it managed to swoop across the yard before gliding in and touching down. Ginny applauded. Any day now the bird would fly off and leave her here alone. This thought filled her with dismay. Startled that it should, she examined her dismay. After her initial fascination with the birds had worn off, she had resented them, had yearned for them to leave, had had to restrain herself from strangling them. But now as the day for the last one's departure approached, she was seized with anxiety. How could it possibly cope without her? It would starve, crash, be devoured by predators or rejected by its peers. It *needed* her.

More to the point, she realized with surprise, she needed it. If *its* well-being during these weeks had been her foremost concern, she wouldn't have kept it in the basket. She'd have perched it on a branch outside. She had needed it, had needed something to fret over and fuss with, something to stand in for Wendy. Maternal behavior couldn't be turned on and off at will, like a faucet. Once triggered, it remained—and it inevitably sought an object. What was she to do with these infernal instincts of hers when the bird had gone?

Reluctantly, Ginny perched it on the window sill inside. The window needed washing badly, but since the cabin was already sold, why bother? Through the murky haze, the bird could see the yard and the pine tree and the kudzu-covered field down to the pond. And occasionally it could see adult chimney swifts, its rotten parents among them perhaps, with their sleek forked wings and velvety wheat-colored chests. They would dive-bomb the pond, darting in from nowhere and swooping in a breathtaking arc to barely skim the pond surface. The bird's head turned alertly as it followed the activities of its elders. The little creep actually looked eager to join them. That was the thanks she got for her weeks of devotion.

The next day her mother's room was dark with the shades still drawn. Her mother lay very still, breathing heavily, her eyes bandaged and her face round and yellow.

"Mother, it's me—Ginny." Her mother didn't stir. She was either asleep or uninterested.

Ginny lay on the spare bed and brooded. Her mother had a hell of a nerve—bringing her into this life in the first place, and now ducking out without having provided her with essential information about its conduct. And after all these weeks Ginny had spent hovering by her bedside gratifying her every whim. Since when had her own mother ever refused her time and attention? Goddam it, her mother *owed* her some explanations! About life and death, about love and marriage and motherhood! She was furious. Sitting up, she said loudly, "*Mother!*"

The round yellow bandaged face showed no sign of response. As Ginny glared at it, her rage began transmuting itself into misery. The misery of a child lost in busy city streets. She threw herself back down. Christ, her mother was abandoning her! She'd die, and Ginny would be left behind all alone. Panic seized her. Tending her mother had filled the void for a time, but the void was still there, waiting. Where would she go? What would she do? Was it even possible to live once you'd tasted the imminence—and eminence—of Death? Death was easy for the dead. But how were the living to cope with it? "Mother!" she wailed.

No answer.

After several hours of studying her unresponsive mother in silence, Ginny returned to the cabin. It was mid-afternoon. The sun was bright and hot. Bees bumbled languidly.

She picked the small bird out of the basket and placed it on her finger. It blinked its beady black eyes and opened its pink mouth for food. As Ginny walked toward the door, the bird suddenly plunged from her finger and darted crazily around the room. This was the moment Ginny had thought she'd been waiting for. Like a child learning to ride a bike, all of a sudden, in a flash of inspiration, the young bird had grasped the concept of flying! Unfortunately, this moment was supposed to have occurred outside.

The bird flapped madly around the living room, bouncing off the walls. Ginny decided to do nothing, for fear of frightening it even more. She would wait for it to alight, when she would grab it and carry it outside.

Eventually the bird did alight, on the mantel. Ginny crept over to it. Just as she lunged, the bird took off in a panic. Apparently it had already forgotten Ginny and her weeks of care and concern? That was gratitude for you.

The living room was dark and cool. The bird headed for the light —the window where it had sat looking out. It crashed into the glass and dropped dazed to the sill. Before Ginny could get to it, it took off again. It circled near the ceiling, screeching.

Then the bird spotted more light, an exit perhaps. It swooped down toward a large mirror in an ornate frame that hung over a low chest. Just as it reached the gleaming mirror, the bird did a crazy convoluted half-turn in mid-air and darted away. It had thought its own reflection was an enemy?

Ginny raced over and propped open the screen door with the decorative quartz rock on the front porch. Maybe she could herd it out to freedom. She crept to the far side of the room to await her opportunity.

The bird was now flying frantically back and forth between the murky window and the flashing mirror.

Ginny finally saw her chance. The bird had fluttered into the mirror, turned around, and was heading for the window. If she leapt out at the proper angle, she could frighten it out the door. She jumped toward the bird, waving her arms. The bird darted sideways in a panic. And crashed into the window, its wings outstretched, cracking the glass with its head.

It dropped to the floor, fluttered spasmodically, and lay still. Ginny ran over, tears streaming down her face. She picked it up. It was warm and twitching. Its creamy velvet breast throbbed crazily, and its forked wings flapped weakly. The filmy inner eyelids were drawing down over its black eyes. It shuddered, stiffened, and died in her hands.

The next day Ginny's mother didn't answer her greeting. Ginny couldn't tell if she was asleep or just making herself unavailable. She sat and waited for a sign from her. Nothing happened. After a while, she walked to her mother's bedside. She regretted interfering in her mother's efforts to sever her earthly connections, but she felt she had something significant to offer.

She began talking quietly as though her mother was awake and listening. "The last bird died yesterday. I was taking it outside. All of a sudden it just hopped off my finger and started darting around, trying to get out. Finally it crashed into the window and fell on the floor dead. *Mother*," she said with emphasis, "the bird beat itself to death on a closed window. But the door next to it was *wide open*."

Ginny ceased abruptly. Her mother didn't so much as stir. She was asleep. She hadn't even heard.

After a couple of minutes, though, her mother smiled her familiar wry smile and nodded her head slowly and said with amused detachment at Ginny's earnest metaphorical efforts, "Maybe."

A few moments later she added, "Look after yourself, Ginny dear."

"You, too, Mother," Ginny replied in a choked voice.

Ginny got a phone call after midnight. She raced to the hospital in the Jeep. Her mother had had a major motor seizure beginning in her right hand and spreading through the right side of her body. She was in a coma. Ginny could scarcely see her round yellow face, now paralyzed on the right side, for the team of white starched technicians who hovered over her, making a pincushion of her hip with injections —anticonvulsants and corticosteroids. A bottle of fresh platelets hung dripping into her arm. Dr. Vogel was lifting her eyelids and studying her pupils with a small flashlight, pounding her patellae with a rubber hammer, rubbing the soles of her feet for Babinski reflexes. With huge syringes laboratory workers were withdrawing blood samples, bone marrow smears.

Ginny elbowed through these battalions to Dr. Vogel and tugged at his lab coat. "Let her go," she said quietly.

"Please!" he hissed. "Can't you see I'm busy?"

"She's ready. Let her go."

He seated Ginny in a chair and demanded rhetorically, "Do you or don't you want your mother to live?" She sat watching and listening to the low hum of consulting technicians.

"We've done everything possible," Dr. Vogel informed her wearily, five hours of injections and extractions later.

"I know you have, Dr. Vogel. And we appreciate it," Ginny assured him, trying to keep him from crying, which he looked as though he might begin to do at any moment.

An hour later her mother died, quietly, without regaining consciousness.

Ginny went back to the cabin and lay down on the bed in which she had been born and wept—because the people she had loved had all grown up and moved away and changed; because mountains corroded and rivers carved new courses and nothing stayed the same forever; because every living creature, herself included, had to die, and die alone.

Then she dried her eyes and straightened the bed and followed her mother's very complete instructions on how to organize a funeral. Karl showed up in time, straight and tall and handsome in his uniform, the bearer of the Major's baton in the relay race of life. Then he and she grimly sorted through the contents of the two houses, filled the trash barrels with memorabilia, put the heirlooms in indefinite storage and sold the rest of the furniture, completed the sale of the two houses and farm to the Major's successor at the plant, signed endless papers, deposited chunks of cash in bank accounts for themselves and Jim, wrote large checks to the government, kissed and parted, conceivably for forever. Because their mother had always drummed into them the knowledge that each time they said farewell to someone, they might never see that person again, or at least not alive and well.

Ira answered the phone.

"Ira, this is Ginny. My mother is dead."

There was a long pause. "I'm sorry, Ginny. She was a fine woman."

"Thanks," she said, wondering why she did so. What did she have to do with her mother's being a fine woman? "How's Wendy?" She could hear her crying in the background. Pangs of maternal longing swept through her.

"She's fine, just fine. She goes to Angela's when I'm at work."

She forced herself not to ask if Wendy missed her, the way she missed Wendy. "Poor Angela. Doesn't she mind?"

"What's one more when you already have five? The more the

merrier," said he, who had never spent an entire day alone with a young child in his life.

"Ira, I—" She almost asked if she could come back. The poor dear man. She had hurt him terribly, had callously offended his standards, however stifling she might find them. There had to be some way to make amends, to go back to him—but on terms different from their previous neurotic symbiosis.

"Yes?" Ira asked eagerly.

"I—I—"

"Ginny, when are you coming home? Wendy and I need you."

Ginny's staunch resolve to redefine their relationship turned instantly to mush. She needed them, too. Now more than ever, when she had no one else. "Well, Ira, I—"

"Please come back, Ginny. We can have another baby and everything will be fine. The house is a wreck. I haven't had a hot meal in weeks. Wendy cries herself to sleep at night. She needs a full-time mother, Ginny. And I need a wife. A *real* wife."

Ginny froze, thinking of her bruised mother, who had been a real wife, a real mother—for as long as she was needed. How would her mother advise her? To profit from her example and behave differently, or to copy her martyrdom and thus validate it? Ginny studied the question. Then she remembered that what her *mother* wanted or didn't want of her was no longer to be the determining factor in her life. The leading lady had magnanimously removed herself from Ginny's script. Ginny was on her own. And there was too little time left to condemn herself to a living death at age twenty-seven. "No," she said faintly.

"No?"

"I'm filing for divorce, Ira. And I want Wendy."

"To marry that hippy creep?"

"No."

"Where are you going?"

She paused, trying to decide. "I don't know."

"Of *course* you can't have Wendy. I'm not having my child raised by a lunatic."

"A lunatic who *happens* to be her mother," she pointed out, warming to the fray.

"Hasn't the poor child suffered enough from you? You run off with another man without so much as saying good-by to her—"

"You chased me out with a rifle in the middle of the night."

"—and now when *you* need *her*, for sick reasons of your own, you crawl back trying to weasel your way into her affections. But it won't work, Ginny. She doesn't want you anymore. She already calls Angela 'Mommy.' Give the child a break. Leave her alone."

Ginny was breathless with pain at the thought of Wendy's calling Angela Mommy. "But I thought she cried herself to sleep?" she gasped.

"Hardly."

"But that's what you *said*."

"You flatter yourself. You know, marrying you was the biggest mistake of my life."

"I wouldn't class it among my finest hours either." Wendy, her infant Isaac, lay on the altar. Was she prepared to sacrifice her to the god of selfhood? Or would she crawl back to Ira on his terms, which appeared to be the only ones he was capable of considering?

"I'm sorry about your mother," Ira said, softening. "She was a fine devoted family woman. You could do worse than to model yourself after her." In the course of their conversation, they had been through the sentic cycles of longing and anger. Ginny could tell from the tone of Ira's voice that they could now proceed to regret and reconciliation if she would cooperate. She could do worse than to model herself after her mother, he had just said. And yet even her hyperdevoted mother, in the end, had had to dismiss Ginny for the sake of her own development.

Quietly, she hung up. Then she collapsed, shivering, on the bed next to the phone. She had phoned Ira with every intention of effecting a reconciliation on renegotiated terms. She had accomplished the exact opposite. If she was no longer Ira's wife, Wendy's mother, her mother's daughter, who *was* she?

In a panic, she called Georgia information and got the number for Hawk's home. It was a shot in the dark.

A deep authoritative male voice with a thick southern accent answered.

"Hello. I'm a friend of Will's. I wonder if you could tell me how to get in touch with him?"

The man on the other end paused and cleared his throat. "May I ask who's callin, please?"

"Sure. My name is Ginny Babcock. I knew Will—uh—at college."

"That so? Well, this is William's father."

"How do you do, Colonel Hawk? Will used to speak of you." She was deliberately increasing her southern accent, hoping to capture his trust: She was his fellow countryman—countryperson, as Eddie would say.

"I'll be quite honest with you, Miss Babcock. William is in the VA hospital at Athens right now."

Ginny gasped.

"William has had some trouble the past few years. His mother and I knew something was wrong when he deserted from the army a couple of years ago. He'd been in Vietnam and he came home talkin about 'war crimes' and imperialism and hippy nonsense like that. And then he ran away to Canada. We thought he must have been drugged by SDS or somethin.

"Well, he came crawlin in one night several weeks ago. Literally crawlin, Miss Babcock. Through the grass in the front yard on his belly. Talkin about somebody's bein after him. He looked as though he hadn't eaten in days, and he hadn't shaved in a week. He kept insistin that 'They' were tryin to suck the heat from his body. We'd say, '*Who* is, William?' And he'd mutter, 'Management.' Damned if *I* knew what he was talkin about. The doctors have diagnosed him as a paranoid schizophrenic."

Ginny felt ill. Hawk's father sounded faintly pleased: His son was not an army deserter, he was sick. His son was not rejecting his father's way of life—his son was a crazy.

"I see," she said weakly. "I'm so very sorry."

"Well, at least he finally came home and faced up to his responsibilities like a *man*," his father said cheerfully.

She hung up. Every cell in her cried out in requiem for Hawk, her heroic nonwarrior. But she didn't feel up to mourning him properly. She was all mourned out.

As she lay on her bed, she reflected on her mother's death. She had learned at least one thing. Dying was apparently a weaning process; all the attachments to familiar people and objects had to be undone. There her mother had lain, her body decaying and in constant pain, her eyes bandaged, her surroundings sterile, nurses and doctors rushed and overworked, food bland and repetitive—what was there that could possibly have held her? There was a family clock. There was a huge white house, built by her megalomaniacal father. There were cherished photos of ancestors. There was a red squirrel in an elm tree. There was her anguished daughter, demanding as her right to be told things that could be learned only by going through them. All these had had to go. Her mother had had to work on doing without them because she must have suspected that she was about to leap into a realm where she would have none of these familiar comforts to orient her, where unresolved earthly attachments would only have flayed her to bits. Like a squid, she had carefully drawn in her tentacles. And presumably, when she had done so, she ended it all, of her own accord, springing away free at last from the bruised body that had served her well and then had failed her abysmally. Having been preceded by this deliberate diminishment of self, by this scaling down of earthly existence to a recurring series of unpleasant or uninteresting routines, her death had been like the dislodging of a dried brown leaf from a tree branch in a soft breeze. Rather than like the violent uprooting of a healthy sapling in a hurricane, as had been the case with Eddie, who had had so much still to do and so much still to learn.

Or at least that was how Ginny chose to think of the process that her mother had undergone. How was she to know? But if that view was correct and one ended it by choice when the weaning was accomplished, then Ginny felt that her time had come too. She had died several small deaths already, to ways of life and people loved. The Big One didn't seem very imposing anymore. Everyone who had been important to her was now dead, or as good as dead for her purposes. She had nothing that she dreaded being severed from. Her tapes had been erased. What was there to hold her here? Why should she go through forming new attachments, only to have to renounce them later when Death finally brought her to her knees? Why not end it now? As she saw it, the only way to outwit Death was to kill herself.

As she had lain trying to nap the afternoon after her mother's death, Ginny had fantasized that she was standing at the bottom of a down escalator in a huge department store. Bells were bonging in the background summoning clerks. Joe Bob in his Gant shirt and chinos grabbed her hand and made her run with him up this down escalator. After decades of effort, with sweat pouring down their faces, they reached the top, where the Major was waiting. But just as Ginny reached out to embrace the Major, Clem, in his studded jeans and red silk windbreaker, grabbed her hand and dragged her down the up escalator. They ran and they ran, like chipmunks on an exercise wheel, Clem lurching and hobbling on his bad leg. Her mother was waiting at the bottom. But just as Ginny stumbled toward her, Miss Head in her gray bun and Ben Franklin glasses pulled Ginny back onto the down escalator. Then, at the top as Ginny reached out for the Major, Eddie dragged her off to charge down the up escalator. After Ira had made her run with him up the down escalator, she finally collapsed in exhaustion while going down the up escalator with Hawk. As she was being carried under the moving steps, down into the guts of the department store, she reflected that, after all that effort, she hadn't made any progress, as Hegel had promised that she would. And as she imagined the escalator mechanism chewing her to bits, she sighed with relief.

Ginny changed into her best bathing suit, for the same reason that her mother used to recommend wearing good underwear when leaving the house. Except her best bathing suit wasn't for the benefit of the emergency room staff—it was for the Hullsport mortuary trade. She wanted to look her best when she arrived at the Slumber Room to be powdered by the waxen yellow hands of Mr. Renfrew.

She grabbed a rope and the oars to the rowboat. Down by the pond she dumped a modest boulder into the boat. Then she rowed to the canvas-covered dock, unloaded the boulder, and climbed out.

She wrapped the rope around the rock and tied it tightly. Then she tied the other end around her ankle. Glancing around, she made her peace with the kudzu-covered hills and the log cabin where, on different occasions, she had been very happy. But really, enough was enough. All around her frogs were devouring grasshoppers, snakes were swallowing frogs whole, Floyd Cloyd's sons were slicing snakes like salamis, and Death lurked around waiting to consume little boys. It was all too much. She didn't think even Management could expect her to endure it for much more than twenty-seven years. Like a snake swallowing its tail, she had come full circle: She had returned to her birthplace to die.

She picked up the boulder. Closing her eyes, she dropped it off the edge. She heard it splash and waited to be tugged down to a murky scum-covered grave.

Nothing happened. She opened her eyes and glanced down. A couple of coils of rope still lay on the dock. Disgruntled, she hauled the boulder back up. This time she wrapped the rope many times around the rock and around her ankle to take up all the slack.

Again, she took her leave of the green hills, which writhed with rustling kudzu and the struggles of dying creatures. Again, she tossed the boulder into the water with a big splash. With satisfaction at a job well done, she felt her leg being jerked out from under her. Her eyes closed, she lost her balance and tumbled toward the water.

And landed in the rowboat, which had shifted and drifted in front of the dock as she had been retying the stone.

Her leg hung out of the boat and was being wrenched out of its pelvic socket by the heavy stone. The entire right side of her body was badly bruised by the fall. As she lay there becoming slightly seasick, she considered the unappetizing nature of what she was about to do. Either the rope would rot and she'd float to the surface for some poor trespassing fisherman to find, or she'd decay among the seaweed and be nibbled to bits by scavenging bluegills. She'd befoul the water, which supplied the cabin sinks. Weaning themselves from material concerns or not, housewives, however inept, are constitutionally incapable of total indifference to the messes they leave behind them.

She untied the rope and rowed back to shore. She took a rifle and a handful of bullets from the gun rack by the fireplace. She hiked up the kudzu-covered hill behind the pond. She recalled with delight how Clem and she as kids had hollowed out tunnels through a kudzu field near his house, matting down areas to form interconnected chambers, like an anthill. She hollowed out such a chamber for herself, a crypt of greenery. She would never be found. The voracious vines would devour her, just as they had devoured Mr. Zed's headstone. No one would face the gruesome task of disposing of her remains. They would think when she couldn't be located, "How like her mother she was. Thoughtful to the end."

She sat down in her kudzu chamber with her knees propped up. With the rifle barrel in her mouth, she found she could pull the trigger with her big toe. She gazed through the leaves at the scum-covered pond and at the log cabin where she had first entered this inadequate life. The cabin now belonged to strangers. The past was dead and gone. It was all finished. She had no place to go and no one to love and all her underwear needed washing.

She took a bullet and rolled it thoughtfully between her thumb and index finger. Abruptly, she picked up the rifle and opened the bullet chamber. She took the bullet and inserted it. . . .

. . . Tried to insert it. The bullet wouldn't go in. It was too big for this type of rifle. She had brought the wrong kind of bullet for the fucking gun!

In despair at having her plans for the afternoon thwarted, she jumped up and raced down the hill, the rifle waving in one hand like a Comanche's in a raid. Tripping and stumbling on the vines, she sprinted to the cabin and searched the gun rack frantically. No bullets to fit her .22, no rifles to fit the bullets in her hand. Karl had taken them all for himself when she wasn't looking, the grasping bastard.

She seized a hunting knife down from the wall. Sitting on the stone steps she made a small experimental cut in her left wrist. Laying the knife aside, she watched as a drop of blood popped up and grew and grew, into a large red globule. If she smeared this blood onto a slide and placed it under Dr. Vogel's microscope, she'd witness a universe in miniature. She'd see teeming swarms of dots floating around mindlessly in plasma. It would look almost like the photo in her college astronomy text—taken by a high-powered telescope in toward the center of the Milky Way galaxy—of the amassed suns of billions of invisible planets.

If she stained the slide properly and increased magnification, she would view the red oxygen-carrying cells, the less populous but more varied white cells and—the platelets. The platelets, those tiny cells that, malfunctioning, had killed both her mother and the Major, being too sparse and inactive in her case and overly so in his. And here Ginny sat with her platelets poised briefly between the two. In time, genes being what they were, her platelets would probably have let her down too.

But her platelets being functional for the moment, the blob of blood on her wrist was now viscous with fibrin. Miss Sturgill would have admired her clotting time. She hadn't kept track of it, but it was negligible compared to her mother's.

If she could have shrunk herself down to microbe size and insinuated herself into the area of the knife cut, she'd have been able to witness a high drama. Shock troops of phagocytes would be arriving via the area capillaries. They'd be sticking to the capillary walls until they could extend artificial feet through the overlapping cells of the vessel walls. They'd drag themselves along after their "feet," out of the blood vessels and into the fray. Sniffing like bloodhounds, they would track down the thousands of bacteria that had invaded via the knife point. Antibodies and various other chemical solutions would already have arrived to bathe these invading bacteria so as to render them appetizing. The encircling phagocytes would then proceed to embrace like Russian politicos these newly delectable bacteria, devouring them whole and alive. Various proteins were also arriving to mend the sliced tissues. The healing process was undertaken instantly and automatically by the bloodstream. In a matter of days, the cut would be healed, and healed so perfectly that no one would be able to locate it.

Unless the knife point had introduced an especially belligerent germ, one with an outer wall that could shed the libations from the antibodies. Such a germ would be able to repel the hungry phago-cytes, gain a foothold, reproduce, and perhaps destroy her with its wastes, as had happened to Dixie Lee Hull with her recipe card.

And yet, as far as Ginny with her crude senses was concerned, nothing much was going on. She'd sliced her wrist, and the cut had already clotted. And now came the last series of questions that she intended to allow herself in this life. Was she a cell in some infinitely larger organism, an organism that couldn't be bothered with her activities any more than she could be with those of the 60 trillion cells in her own body, as long as they performed their assigned functions? And were there, say, white blood cells that—not being able to see themselves as Ginny could, as a group, under magnification, stained to highlight determining characteristics—had not been able to figure out what their "assigned function" was, whether they were supposed to perform as macrophages or neutrophils or eosinophils or lym-phocytes? And did those perplexed blood cells then take it upon themselves to self-destruct in a huff at not receiving enough individual attention and guidance from her personally? Autophagy, it was called, when cells unleashed on their own cytoplasm their suicide bags of digestive enzymes. Autophagy, which literally meant "self-eating."

Ginny was reminded of Clem's description of a revolting incident during his adolescence in which he and his hoodlum friends had hunched over their own laps, vainly trying to eat themselves. Onan-ism, autophagy, suicide, it was all the same—a component part trying to run the whole show. She smiled reluctantly and returned the knife to its sheath.

Like most of her undertakings, her proposed suicide had degene-rated into burlesque. Apparently she was condemned to survival. At least for the time being.

She went into the bedroom. She wrapped her mother's clock in her faded Sisterhood Is Powerful T-shirt and packed it in Hawk's knapsack with her other scant belongings. She left the cabin, to go where she had no idea.